Cloudsplitter

Also by Russell Banks

Cloudsplitter

A NOVEL

Russell Banks

HarperFlamingo
An Imprint of HarperCollins*Publishers*

HarperCollins books may be purchased for educational, business, or sales
promotional use. For information please write: Special Markets Department,
HarperCollins Publishers, Inc., 10 East 53rd Street, New York, NY 10022.

FIRST EDITION

Designed by Joseph Rutt

Library of Congress Cataloging-in-Publication Data
Banks, Russell, 1940–
    Cloudsplitter : a novel / Russell Banks.
        p.   cm.
    ISBN 0-06-016860-9
    I. Title.
PS3552.A49C57 1998
813'.54—dc21   97-22163

98 99 00 01 02 ❖/RRD 10 9 8 7 6 5 4 3 2 1

Author's Note

This is a work of the imagination. While some of the characters and incidents portrayed here can be found in accounts of the life and times of John Brown, the famous abolitionist, they have been altered and rearranged by the author to suit the strict purposes of storytelling. These characters and incidents, despite their resemblance to actual persons and known events, are therefore the products of the author's imagination. Accordingly, the book should be read solely as a work of fiction, not as a version or interpretation of history.

Nevertheless, the author wishes to acknowledge with gratitude the help and inspiration that he has received from Oswald Garrison Villard's magisterial *John Brown: A Biography Fifty Years After* (Boston, 1910), Richard Boyer's *The Legend of John Brown* (New York, 1973), and Stephen Oates's *To Purge This Land with Blood*, second edition (Amherst, Mass., 1984). They are excellent, deep works of biographical history. This, it bears repeating, is a work of fiction.

The author also wishes to acknowledge and thank the many people who so generously provided information, aid, and encouragement, among them: Edwin Cotter, superintendent of the John Brown Farm and Grave, in North Elba, N.Y.; Michael S. Harper; Thomas Hughes; Paul Matthews; Chuck Wachtel; Cornel West; C. K. Williams; friends and colleagues in the Creative Writing Program and African American Studies at Princeton University; Ellen Levine of the Ellen Levine Literary Agency; and, most emphatically, Robert Jones of HarperCollins Publishers.

for C.T., the beloved,
and in memory of William Matthews (1942–1997)

... and I only am escaped alone to tell thee.

JOB 1:16

I

I

Upon waking this cold, gray morning from a troubled sleep, I realized for the hundredth time, but this time with deep conviction, that my words and behavior towards you were disrespectful, and rude and self-ish as well. Prompting me now, however belatedly, to apologize and beg your forgiveness.

You were merely doing your duty, as assistant to your Professor Villard, who in turn is engaged in a mighty and important task, which is intended, when it has been completed, not only to benefit all mankind but also to cast a favorable light upon the family of John Brown. And since I myself am both—both a man and a member of the family of John Brown—then I myself stand to benefit twice over from your and Professor Villard's honest labors.

Self-defeating, then, as well as cruel and foolish of me, to thwart you. Especially when you are so clearly an open-minded, sincere, and intelligent seeker of the truth, the whole truth—so help me, Miss Mayo, I am sorry.

I ask you to understand, however: I have remained silent for so many years on all matters touching on Father and our family that by the time you arrived at my cabin door I had long since ceased even to question my silence. I greeted your polite arrival and inquiries with a policy made nearly half a century ago, a policy neither questioned nor revised in all the years between. Policy had frozen into habit, and habit character.

Also, in the years since the events you are investigating, my life has been that of an *isolato*, a shepherd on a mountaintop, situated as far from so-called civilization as possible, and it has made me unnaturally brusque and awkward. Nor am I used, especially, to speaking with a young woman.

I remind you of all this, of my *character*, I guess you could call it, so that you can place my remarks, memories, and revelations—even the documents that you requested and which I will soon sort out and provide for you—into their proper context. Without continuous consideration of context, no truth told of my father's life and work can be the whole truth. If I have learned nothing else in the forty years since his execution, I have learned at least that. It is one of the main reasons for my having kept so long so silent. I have sat out here tending my sheep on my mountaintop, and the books and newspaper articles and the many thick volumes of memoirs have come floating down upon my head like autumn leaves year after year, and I have read them all, the scurrilous attacks on Father and me and my brothers in blood and in arms, as well as the foolish, dreamy, sentimental celebrations of our "heroism" and "manly courage" in defense of the Negro—oh, I have read them all! Those who made Father out to be mad, I have read them. Those who called him a common horse thief and murderer hiding beneath the blanket of abolitionism, I read them, too. Those who met Father and me and my brothers but once, on a cloudy, cold December afternoon in Kansas, and later wrote of us as if they had ridden with us for months all across the territory—yes, those, too. And those who, on hearing of Father's execution, wept with righteousness in their pious Concord parlors, comparing him to the very Christ on His very cross— I read them, too, although it was hard not to smile at the thought of how Father himself would have viewed the comparison. Father believed in the incomparable *reality* of Christ, after all, not the incorporeal idea. Father's cross was a neatly carpentered scaffold in Virginia, not a spiked pair of rough timbers in Jerusalem.

Forgive me, I am wandering. I want to tell you everything—now that I have decided to tell a little. It's as if I have opened a floodgate, and a vast inland sea of words held back for half a lifetime has commenced to pour through. I knew it would be like this. And that's yet another reason for my prolonged silence—made worse, made more emphatic and burdensome and, let me say, made confusing, by the irony that the longer I remained silent, the more I had to tell. My truth has been held in silence for so long that it has given the field over entirely to those who have lied and risks having become a lie itself, or at least it risks being heard as such. Perhaps even by you. Thus, although I have begun at last to speak, and to speak the truth, it feels oddly and at the edges as if I am lying.

I say again that I am sorry that I rebuffed you the other day. You are young and may not know, but solitude, extended for a sufficiently long time, becomes its own reward and nourishment. And an old man's voice aloud can become repugnant to his own ears, which is perhaps why I have chosen to write to you, and to write at as great a length as will prove necessary, instead of merely speaking with you and politely answering your questions in person as you wished. The anxious bleat of my sheep, the bark of my dog, and the gurgle and crack of my fire—these, for decades, are practically the only voices that I have heard and spoken back to, until they have become my own voice. It is not a voice suitable for a lengthy interview with a young, educated woman like yourself come all the way out here from the city of New York to my hill in Altadena, California.

What sense could you have made, anyhow, of an old, bearded man

bleating, barking, and cracking all day and night long? I picture you—
had I actually granted the interview that you so kindly requested—
becoming embarrassed, confused, finally angry and resigned; and
you, closing your notebook and taking polite leave of me, reporting
back to your eminent Professor Oswald Garrison Villard at Columbia
University that you arrived too late. Poor old Owen Brown, third son of
John Brown, the last living witness and party to the Pottawatomie massacre and the victories and tragedies of Bleeding Kansas and the long,
terrible series of battles in the War Against Slavery that culminated in
the disastrous raid on Harpers Ferry—that pathetic, aged, solitary man,
Owen Brown, is now quite mad himself, and so we shall never know
the truth of whether his father, too, was mad. We shall never know if
John Brown was in his right mind when he butchered those men and
boys down on the Pottawatomie that awful night in '57. Or whether,
when he terrorized the pro-slavers in Kansas, he was in fact the old-
time, Puritan hero and military genius that so many made him out to
be. Or if, when he took Harpers Ferry and refused to flee into the
mountains, he had by then lost his mind altogether. The son himself,
the hermit-shepherd Owen Brown, is mad, you would say to your professor (and perhaps are saying to him even now), and we shall never
know conclusively if the father was mad also. Thus, given what we
already know of John Brown, you will say, and in the absence of significant evidence to the contrary, we must concur with our century's
received opinion and, before the next century begins, adjudge him a
madman.

　　I hope, therefore, that your quick receipt of this first of what shall
be several, perhaps many, such letters will slow that judgement and
eventually reverse it.

Was my father mad? I realize it is the only question that can matter to
you. Since they first heard his name, men and women have been asking

it. They asked it continuously during his lifetime, even before he became famous. Strangers, loyal followers, enemies, friends, and family alike. It was then and is now no merely academic question. And how you and the professor answer it will determine to a considerable degree how you and whoever reads your book will come to view the long, savage war between the white race and the black race on this continent. If the book that your good professor is presently composing, though it contain all the known and previously unrecorded facts of my father's life, cannot show and declare once and for all that Old Brown either was or was not mad, then it will be a useless addition to the head-high pile of useless books already written about him. More than the *facts* of my father's hectic life, people do need to know if he was sane or not. For if he was sane, then terrible things about race and human nature, especially here in North America, are true. If he was insane, then other, quite different, and perhaps not so terrible things about race and human nature are true.

And, yes, just as you said, I am probably the only person remaining alive who has the knowledge and information that will enable you and your professor to answer the question. But you must understand. The three-hundred-year-long War Between the Races, from before the Revolution up to and including Harpers Ferry, was being fought mainly as the War Against Slavery. Then, briefly, in '61, it became the War Between the States. And from then until now, there has been such a grieving, angry clamor that I knew I would not be heard, except as one of the sons of John Brown trying to justify his father's and his own bloody deeds—a puny, crippled man who fled the carnage he helped create and for the rest of his long life hid alone in the West.

The truth is, for us, the so-called Civil War was merely an aftermath. Or, rather, it was part of a continuum. Just another protracted battle. Ours was very much a minority view, however. It still is. But from the day it began, to Northerner and Southerner alike, the Civil

War was a concussive trauma that erased all memory of what life had been like before it. On both sides, white Americans woke to war and forgot altogether the preceding nightmare, which had wakened them in the first place. Or they made it a pastoral dream. Even the abolitionists forgot. But for those few of us whose lives had been most thrillingly lived in the decade preceding the War, one thing has led obviously and with sad predictability to another, with no break or permanent ending point between the early years of the slave uprisings in Haiti and Virginia and the Underground Railroad in Ohio and New York and the Kansas battles and Harpers Ferry and the firing on Fort Sumter and Shiloh and Gettysburg and Vicksburg and Appomattox Courthouse and the killing of Abraham Lincoln and the savage, dark, murderous days that have followed, even to today, at century's end. They are like beads on a string to us, bubbles of blood on a barbed steel strand that stretches from the day the first enslaved African was brought ashore in Virginia to today, and we have not reached the end of it yet.

Thus, when the Civil War ended, I found myself feeling towards the rest of my white countrymen, both Northern and Southern, the way Negroes in America, and Indians, too, must always have felt towards white Americans generally—as if the white man's history were separate from ours and did not honor or even recognize ours. That is yet another reason why I have remained silent for so long. I did not want my testimony captured and used in the manufacture of an American history that at bottom is alien to me. I did not want to help tell a story that, when it does not ignore mine altogether, effectively contradicts it. That would be treasonous. It would aid and abet our common enemy, who wants nothing more than to declare the war between the races non-existent. Or if not non-existent, then short-lived and well over.

So now perhaps you understand somewhat why I drove you off, and why I have come in this way to call you back again.

❏

There is yet a further reason, I suddenly realize, for my having called you back, and I must attempt to confess it, painful as it is to admit, even to myself.

I am dying. Or I am already dead and have been dead these forty years, with nothing left of me, who once was Owen Brown, except a shadow cast on the near wall by my lamplight and these words tumbling from me like a death rattle, a last, prolonged exhalation. Absurd as it may sound to you who read these words, it is to me the literal truth. I am more the ghost of Owen Brown than I am the man himself.

Although I was but thirty-five years old in '59 and escaped from Harpers Ferry like a rabbit through the corn and ended up safe here on my western mountaintop, my life since that day has been an after-life. In recent years, as I have grown into an old man, there have been dozens, perhaps hundreds, of mornings when I have wakened in my cold cabin with my lungs flooded and, before the sun has dried the dew off the window pane, have concluded that sometime during the night I finally died. But then hunger or some other bodily need or the animals—my dog scratching at the door, the sheep bleating, the cry of a hawk—bring me back to the sad awareness that, no, I have not died, not yet, and thus am obliged once more to grope through the gray veils that wrap me and come to full wakefulness and begin again the daily rounds of a man alive.

Until the night that followed your arrival at my door, however, when I must indeed have gone deeper into the embrace of death than ever before. So that when in the morning I finally woke, if waking it truly was, I knew beyond all doubt that I am now he who was Owen Brown. Not he who *is* Owen Brown. Not that crotchety old man you met growling at you like a bear in its cave, but his past, his childhood and youth and his young manhood, that's who I am. It was as if your visit had sounded a final knell that drove me into a purgatory which I had been longing for all these years but had neither the courage nor the wisdom to seek on my own. As if, now that I am here, there is no going forward or back, no possible ascent to heaven or descent to hell, until I have told my story.

Thus these words, these letters, and the packets of materials which in time I will turn over to you. All my worldly effects, as it were, I bequeath to thee. Make of them, you and your professor, whatever you will. In the long, ongoing War Between the Races, this, I suppose, must be my final act, and I pray only that, before I am in error judged good, if cowardly, and my father mad, if courageous, I be given the time to complete it.

It is all very strange. Now that I have opened communications with you, I find myself unable to keep my inner voice silent. I have given off all work—my sheep and the spring lambs wander the grassy hills unaccompanied in search of water and pasturage, protected only by my faithful little dog, Flossie, who returns from the herd every few hours to the cabin door and scratches and whines outside, as if angered by my protracted absence and intent on rousing me from an inexplicable sleep.

But I am not asleep. I do now and then drift towards a dozing state, but I am driven back from it each time by the rising sound of my voice, as if it, too, has a will of its own and, like Flossie, does not want me to sleep. Whether I am seated at my table, as now, writing the words down, or in my chair in the darkness by the window with the silvery moonlight falling across my lap, or lying in my cot by the back wall staring at the low ceiling all night long and into the next day, my ears are filled always with my own voice. The words are like water in a brook that bubbles from an underground spring and spills downhill across rocks and fallen trees to where it gathers in eddies and builds a dark, still pool, moving me finally to rise from my cot and sit down at my table and begin again to write them down, my purpose being merely to break the little dam or jam and release the pressure against it and let the flow of words resume.

It is more than passing strange. And joyous, somehow. I see where I am, and yet it is as if I who was Owen Brown have flown from my mountaintop. I have today been recalling an earlier, my first, departure from this place and its similarity to this day's dying—although that was literal and this, of course, is merely figurative. Then, just as now, what a strange joy I felt! It was a full decade ago, in the spring of '89, and I had been lingering alone on this high, treeless hill for close to thirty years, waiting for the moment of my death to finish its last flash through my weary body, biding my time, helpless and silent as smoke and with all the patience of the long-dead. I was waiting, silently waiting, not so much for my actual death, which meant little to me, one way or the other, as for the pine box that contained my bones to be carried three thousand miles from the hills of California back along the railroad lines to my family's house and farm in the Adirondack mountain village of North Elba, New York. To the place that, because of the Negroes living there, we called Timbuctoo.

A letter from a distinguished woman in the East who had long honored Father's deeds had arrived at my door, just as you arrived in person last week. It informed me, not of the needs of an illustrious biographer, as you did, but of the coming re-interment of the last of the bodies of those who had fallen with Father at Harpers Ferry. The letter invited me to attend the ceremonies, which were to be held on the upcoming ninth of May, Father's birthday, at his gravesite, where my brothers' and companions' old bones, gathered from shallow graves in Virginia and elsewhere across the country, were at last to join his.

Until that cold morning, for the thirty long years since the end came at Harpers Ferry, I had hoped for no other event, for no additional particularity of circumstance, than that *my* poor bones, too, *my* remains, at last be interred there. With or without some slight cere-mony, it did not matter a whit to me—so long as they were deposited in my family's yard in the plot of hard, dark, and stony ground that sur-rounded the huge, gray boulder in the meadow before the house. For those many years, I had been waiting for nothing but the fit and proper burial of my crumbling, shrouded old corpse in that precious dirt alongside the bodies of my father, John Brown, and my brothers Watson and Oliver, and my companions in arms who had fought beside me in the Kansas wars or were cut to pieces in the raid on Harpers Ferry or were executed on the scaffold afterwards.

All those moldering bodies! All those yellowed, long bones and gri-macing skulls carted in boxes unearthed from shallow graves and buried there alongside one another! And now mine also!

But, no, not yet. I wrote back at once, saying only that I would not come, giving no excuse and explaining nothing. I was still very much alive, and silence and solitude had to remain my penance and my solace. I would not, I could not, give them up.

But then, one morning shortly after my curt note had been posted, I woke in my cot and, as I have said, believed that, finally, I, too, had died. Soon, of course, and as afterwards became usual, I saw that sadly I was not dead yet. I was still he who *is* Owen Brown, he whose dog wakes him and brings him shuffling to the door, he who releases his herd of merinos from the fold into the sloping meadow below, then returns to his cabin and washes his face in cold water and commences living another silent, solitary day.

Was it, in hopes that I was wrong, an attempt to test my reluctantly drawn conclusion that I had not died yet—as perhaps I do here now, writing these words to you ten years later? Was it an attempt to accom-plish in life some new arrangement for my death? I cannot say why now and could not then, but that very day I decided to depart from this mountain for a while and return finally to our old family home in the

Adirondacks, where my only proper grave lies even today. I arranged for the care of my sheep and my dog with a neighbor in the valley and departed straightway for the East.

I had long believed, or, to be accurate, had long wished, that I would arrive at North Elba from the east somehow, not the west. That I would emerge from the broad shade of Mounts Tahawus and McIntyre. At my back, long streaks of early morning sunlight would slide through familiar notches in the mighty Adirondack Range and splash down the valleys and spread out at my feet before me like a golden sea washing across the tableland. I had imagined that the spirit of Owen Brown, third son of Osawatomie John Brown, like a spot off the morning sun itself, would come rapidly up along the broad meadows we named the Plains of Abraham, for that is what they first brought to our minds, with the snow-covered peak of Whiteface beyond the house and a crisp Canada wind striking out of the northwest.

I pictured it early in the day, still close to sunrise or shortly after it, when at last the beloved house stood in front of me. The house would be pink and gold in first light and stout and square as the day we first came here from Springfield, the way Father described it at the supper table in our house down there and drew its plan in his notebook to show us. I had imagined the plank door closed tight and latched against the nightfrost—it was to be early spring or fall, a string of silver smoke curling from the kitchen chimney, and no smoke at all from the parlor chimney opposite, where last night's fire would have long gone out, the log turned to ashes, powdery and cold, bricks chilled like ingots.

These anticipations were left-over memories, however. Rags and tatters fluttering brightly across my darkened thoughts. From my haunt in the San Gabriel Mountains in the far West, I could not know who lived in the old house nowadays. My stepmother, Mary, and my sisters and remaining brothers had all fled the place decades before to Ohio, Iowa, Oregon, and Washington State, scattered across the country by the winds of war and its callous aftermath. Did anyone live there at all? The window glass was to have been iced over, etched with florid designs, I thought.

No, I came instead, not from Tahawus and McIntyre in the east with dreamily imagined, celestial hoo-rahs and fanfare to announce me, but almost casually, as if out for a stroll along the road that led from the settlement, where the new train from Albany had let me off. I came walking alone out of the northwest, with Lake Placid and scarred old Whiteface Mountain at my back. And I came not as a disembodied spot of first sunlight, for I was no spirit and there was no sun that day—it was a cold, gray mid-morning, with a low sky that threatened snow. I arrived instead as an actual and embodied old man with a long, white beard, dressed in my plain wool suit and cloth cap, picking my way along the dirt road with my hazelwood stick. All the old familiar aches and pains came with me, too—the arthritis in the hips and the cold throb of my crippled left arm, uselessly bent against my waist, my permanent banner to boyhood carelessness and deceit.

My return to Timbuctoo in '89 was closer to dream, however, than to a lived thing, or even than to memory. At least, that is how I am remembering it now. There was a rhythmical, purposeful continuity of sensation and perception, and no mere disorganized intermingling of fact, emotion, and idea, such as memory provides. A snowflake passed by my face, and then several more, and the breeze abruptly shifted from my back to my front, bringing with it a light, gauzy wash of snow. The large, wet flakes struck my beard and body, and, amazed, I watched them melt away as fast as they fell against my warm clothing and hands. Whatever world I was presently inhabiting, a dreamer's, a ghost's, a madman's, I was surely an integrated part of it, subject to the same physical laws as were all its other parts. No mere invisible witness to nature, as I had hoped, I was in sad fact one of its functioning components. Or else we were both, the entire natural world and I, merely the imaginings of a larger, third Being.

The snow shower blew over, and then, suddenly, I realized that I was not alone on the road. A short ways ahead of me, a group of perhaps a dozen children and a pair of young women walked steadily along in the same direction as I, marching, it seemed, in loose formation, with one woman at the front and the other at the rear. No doubt for the very same reasons as I, they were headed from the village in the direction of the farm.

They were white people. I note that because, when I turned and glanced behind me, I saw an elderly Negro couple—a man in a dark woolen suit not unlike mine and a proper wool fedora and a woman in a long black dress, bonnet, and cape—coming slowly along. They each carried what appeared to be a Bible, as if marching off to church or coming straightway from it. Then, behind them, where the road emerged from an overhanging thatch of tall white pines, came a second group, six or seven Negro people of various ages, at least three generations. And these Negroes, too, were dressed as if for a formal occasion. There was a dark-faced man among them who for a second I thought was Father's dear friend and mine, a man whom you may well have heard of by now, Mr. Lyman Epps. I was somewhat disoriented, however, due to fear and excitement, and could not be sure. Hadn't he died long ago? I, of all people, should know that. Was this his son, perhaps?

But, in spite of my confusion, I knew where I was. Not a great deal had changed in the thirty years that I had been away. I instantly recognized the land and the rise and fall of the narrow road, which, owing to the springtime ruts and mud, obliged me to keep to the high center as I walked. On either side, under shade in amongst the trees and in the protected glens and dales, slubs of old, crusted snow still lingered.

There was a light wind soughing in the high branches of the pines, and I heard in the distance the mountain run-off in the West Branch of the Au Sable River, where it gushed under the bridge on the Cascade Road and from there tumbled down these rocky heights northeast all the way to Lake Champlain and on to the St. Lawrence and the great North Atlantic Ocean beyond.

On my right, set up in the sugar maples, was the Thompson farm, gone to ruin now, with the barn half-fallen and the fields on either side shifting back to chokecherry and scrub pine, but still recognizably the same four-square, cleanly constructed dwelling place of the family I loved second only to my own. Beyond the house, sheds, and barn, and beyond the lilacs gone all wild and tangled and still a month from blooming, a grove of paper-white birch trees mingled with aspens on an uphill meadow. Their spindly limbs floated in silhouette inside pale green clouds of new buds, like the delicate, blackened skeletons of birds. On the further slopes, dark maples and oak switches twitched leafless in the breeze.

I was situated at that moment in the turning of the northern year, when the end of winter and the start of spring overlap like shingles on a roof and the natural world seems doubled in thickness and density. A slight shift in the direction of the wind cools the air a single degree, and suddenly a puddle of standing water is covered with a skin of ice that, seconds later, as the same wind parts the clouds and opens the sky, melts in the sunlight. At this moment, all is change. Transformation seems permanent. I was trembling with a type of excitement that I had never felt before, a powerful mixture of anticipation and regret, as if I somehow knew that eternal gain and irretrievable loss were about to be parceled out equally—as if the idea of justice were about to be made a material thing.

I briefly looked back and saw that there were still more people of various ages and stations filing along, some white and some black, and

I recognized that we were a procession. There was a horse-drawn carriage just entering the clearing before the Thompson farm, driven by a bearded white man of middle age, with his stout wife seated beside him. Following the carriage came a large, canopied wagon pulled by two matched teams of rugged Vermont Morgans, with a white man in a black ministerial suit at the reins and a young Negro man similarly clothed situated next to him. There seemed to be hundreds of people coming along, and though the impulse to stand aside and watch everyone pass by was stronger than mere curiosity, the impulse to fall in and keep step with the others was stronger still, and I turned away and continued forward along the road.

In a moment, I had passed the turning and entered a section of the road that led through a stretch of tall white pines, where it was dark as night, almost, and more patches of old snow remained, radiating light and cold. A sudden, strong gust of wind blew through the pines and swirled the branches overhead, filling my ears with a sound that made my heart leap with pleasure, for it had been a lifetime and more, it seemed, since I had last walked beneath pine trees that sang and danced furiously in the wind like that. Briefly, I was an innocent, wonderstruck youth again, newly arrived in the Adirondack wilderness. The road was covered with a blanket of soft, rust-colored needles, and I inhaled deeply, losing all my thoughts in the vinegary smell, stumbling backwards in the flow of time.

When I passed out of the pine forest, the road dwindled to a track and entered a broad, overgrown meadow, yellow and sere with the old, winter-killed grass and saturated with run-off from the slopes above. We cleared this meadow ourselves the first summer we came to this place, my younger brothers Watson, Salmon, Oliver, and I, and grazed Father's Devon cattle on it, leaving the stingier, rock-strewn, upper fields for the Old Man's blooded merino sheep. But now the whole expanse of cleared land was drifting back to forest, with only a patch of it remaining in grass and that spotted all over with new sumac and masses of tangled brush.

The first time that I walked this path to our farm was back in '49, when I came over from Lake Champlain on the Cascade Road with the family and Lyman Epps and saw the house here on the southern end of the promontory that we were told was called the Tableland but which Father insisted would be called the Plains of Abraham. In his usual way, he had imagined everything for us beforehand—the house was as he had said, and the barn would be exactly where he drove his stakes, facing due southeast across the Plains of Abraham into the mighty Tahawus, as the Iroquois had named it, the Cloudsplitter, so that year-round, from the barn and from our front door, we could watch the sunrise inch north in spring and then south in fall, passing like a clock hand between it and Father's second-favorite mountain, McIntyre, marking the slow, seasonal turn of the heavens—for Father had wanted us to mark God's perfect logic as much by the motion and movement of the planets and sun above as by the symmetries that surrounded us here on earth.

Seven years later, I walked up to this place from the Indian Pass accompanied by a dead man's body and two fugitive slaves and came to the house and delivered all three over to my family and fled this house and valley for Ohio and then for Kansas. Of this, you know nothing, of course, but you shall know, I promise. Three years after that, the Old Man and I came home for the even more portentous departure for Harpers Ferry. They were hard arrivals and departures. But in between and before and after, there were the thousands of easy, domestic comings and goings that a farming family is obliged to make—daily we walked and sometimes rode this line back through the woods that linked our home to the larger world, beating a footpath into a track and a track into a road which connected eventually to all the other roads that we would travel together and alone.

Considered in all the tossed and turbulent terms of my life, this fading path through the woods—for the trail crossing the meadow had diminished now to little more than that—was like the central nerve of my body, its very spinal cord. Everything of moment branched off that nerve, everything in a sense originated there, and ultimately everything must loop back and end there. And so, apparently, it had, for here I was, walking it again.

The great, broad plain and our farm just beyond the crest of the meadow were still hidden from my view. Up ahead, the children and their female teachers had nearly reached the crest, and beyond that line were the snow-covered mountain peaks—pale wedges rising from the near horizon like the sails of approaching galleons. Then, one by one, the children followed their teachers over the top and disappeared, as if jumping off a precipice. Dutifully, I trudged up the slope behind them and in my turn came to the top. And when I gazed down, I saw that I had arrived finally at my home.

A vast crowd of people had assembled below in the front yard of the house and all about the front and sides of the barn. There were many wagons, four-in-hands, buggies, and fancy carriages with men and women seated on them, and quite a few men up on horseback, and large standing groups of people of all ages. A significant number of these appeared by their dress and bearing to be personages of no slight importance in the world, reverends and top-hatted bankers and the such. I saw a lot of Negro people there, too, poorer folks than the whites, most of them elderly. They kept mainly to the side and to themselves, although here and there a richly dressed black man mingled informally with the whites, and there were even a few white individuals standing amongst the blacks. At the further edges of the crowd, back by the barn and along the far side of the house, boys and dogs chased one another in the usual way, while in amongst the adults, numerous small children sat perched upon their fathers' shoulders.

The huge throng was assembled in a vast semi-circle, as if in an ancient amphitheater, between the old house and barn and the great, gray stone in the center. It was a grand scene! With affection and a kind of gratitude, with feelings beyond speech, I gazed down on the poor, bare buildings that we had lived and worked in all those years, that had sheltered and shielded not just us Browns but also the hundreds of fugitives who had come to our door seeking succor and protection from the wilderness and the snows and cold winds and all the terrors of the flight from slavery.

At the center of the arc of the crowd was the huge, gray rock— intimidating, mysterious. Like a chamber it was, a room filled with solid granite. Next to it stood the old, Puritan-style slate gravestone that memorialized the death of Great-Grandfather John Brown, Father's namesake, which Father had lugged up from Connecticut so as to memorialize on its other side the death of brother Fred in Kansas as well. The worn slab marked Father's own grave now. A short ways beyond the rock was a mast-high flagpole with no flag a-flying, and at its base three lines of soldiers in dress uniform had assembled formally in drill order, standing at parade rest.

Then came the abrupt further edge of the clearing, where the wide swale of forest began, copses of fresh-budding hardwoods and great stretches of evergreens, as the land gradually rose towards the snow-covered peaks of the mountains, and above the mountains, glowering, dark gray sheets of sky stretched overhead front to back and covered us all like a canopy. It was to me a wonderful sight!

I glanced back, and sure enough, here came hundreds more people along behind—the same elderly couple and the family of Negroes and the loaded wagon and carriage I had seen back by the Thompson place, and many more behind them, afoot and on horseback and in wagons and coaches. What a marvelous celebration! I thought, and hurried on, nearly tumbling in my eagerness to descend from the high overlook to the plain below.

When I reached the crowd there, I passed around the back of it and made my way towards the near side of the house and there slipped along the edge of the crowd, around and between carriages and tethered horses. They were all strangers to me, and I to them. Thirty years had passed since I had been in a public gathering of any sort, and I was a young man then, standing in Father's shadow. Who would recognize me now? Whom would I recognize? No one living.

Most of the people stood idly by, talking lightly and taking their ease, as if awaiting the arrival of a master of ceremonies. Their attention seemed to be directed with intermittent watchfulness towards Father's rock at the front, and I moved in that same direction myself. Barely the top of it was visible to me as I passed through the multitude, but I was drawn straight and swiftly to it, as if the rock had been magnetized and I were a pin on a leaf afloat in water.

And suddenly there I was, clear of the crowd and standing alone before the rock, with Great-Grandfather Brown's old slate marker posted beside me on the right, and Father's bones buried deep beneath it. In front of me, looming like some high altar from pagan times, was the great, gray stone. It seemed to shine in the milky morning light, and its surface was coldly clarified and dry, like the skin of a statue of a mythological beast. As I neared the rock, everything else blurred—the crowd of people, the house and barn, the mountains around—and faded altogether from my view. All was silent.

Before me, incised into the skin of the granite, were words, letters, numerals as familiar to me as the lineaments of my own face, yet a rune. A stonecarver, sometime in the years since I had seen it last, had cut into the rock the letters and numerals that spelled out Father's name and the year of his execution. I looked upon them now, and I fairly heard, instead of read, the name and year spoken aloud in Father's own unmistakeable voice and pronunciation, *John Brown 1859*, as if he himself had been miraculously transformed into that rock and I into the quaking, white-bearded old man standing here before him, and the rock had spoken his riddle.

Then, feeling directed to its presence by Father himself, I looked down to my left and saw the hole in the ground. The hole was pure black, like carbon, and neatly cut, about six feet across and six wide. It was freshly dug and deep. From where I stood I could not see the bottom. The soil was dark, wet, having only recently thawed, and was heaped in a neat cone at the further side. I turned away from the huge boulder and moved slowly towards the blackness—for that is what it was, a six-foot square of blackness, a door to another world than this— and felt an almost irresistible tug, a pull beyond yearning, to go forward and enter it, to step off this too solid earth into blackness, as if taking that final step were as simple as walking through the portal of one room into the next.

I stopped, but could not say what stopped me. Gradually, though, I began to hear noises again, and the crowd and yard and buildings around me drifted back into my ken, and I found that I had left Father's presence and had rejoined the multitude. Dogs barked, children cried and laughed, men and women chattered with one another. Horses creaked in their harnesses, and wagon wheels crunched across the ground. A crow called out. The breeze blew, and clouds shifted overhead. I smelled tobacco smoke and oiled leather, horse manure, woolen clothing, and winter-soaked old grass and leaves.

I cannot say if it was cause or effect. But when I found myself once again in the midst of the spectacle and not cast outside it, I was able to back quickly away from the black hole in the ground, to turn and move off from Father's rock, there to take up an obscure position more or less in the middle of the crowd, to stand and wait with them for the rest of the people to arrive and for the ceremonies to begin. I was waiting now, like the others, for the speeches, the prayers, and the singing of the hymns, for the ornate box of the crumbling remains of eleven murdered men to be lowered into the ground:

Watson Brown

Oliver Brown

Albert Hazlett

John Henry Kagi

Lewis Leary

William Leeman

Dangerfield Newby

Aaron Stevens

Stewart Taylor

Dauphin Thompson

William Thompson

and also the body of this man—Owen Brown—who had lived for so many years longer than the others, brought back at last from Altadena, California, to join the bodies of his martyred brothers and compatriots in the grave beside his father's grave.

But, instead, I who am Owen Brown stood aside and watched, as the remains of those eleven men—separately shrouded and then placed together tenderly in a single huge box with their names engraved on a silver plate—disappeared into the black hole that had been cut into the hard ground next to Father.

There were songs, prayers, and speeches. And then the flag went up, and the soldiers fired their guns into the air in full military salute.

The Negro man who so resembled Father's dearest friend, Lyman Epps—or, truly, was it Lyman's son?—stepped forward and in a trembling, sweet tenor voice sang the Old Man's hymn, "Blow, Ye Trumpets, Blow."

And, finally, the crowd dispersed.

And I remained there at our old farm alone—alone to face these somber graves at the foot of the great, granite stone with Father's name and death date carved upon it. Alone before the cold spring wind blowing across the plain from Tahawus. The Cloudsplitter.

Alone—all, all alone!

I hesitate to tell you this, but I must, or you will not understand what I did and why. You will not even understand what I am doing now.

Though the burial ceremonies had long since ended, and the crowds had gone, I remained, as if forbidden to leave. If I had believed in the God of my fathers, I would have thanked Him for bringing me here at last. But I did not believe in God, then or now. So, instead, I thanked my fellow man, the living men and women whom I imagined digging a hole in the dirt way out west and pulling from it the box with my body in it and bringing it here and setting it down into the ground before me. For though the carcass is riddled, broken, and finally devoured by worms, the spirit survives it, like its very own child. The spirits whose bodies lie buried in mountains of Arctic ice or beneath shifting desert sands or in unmapped potters' fields paved over by modern city streets—graves where no one pauses, where no one stands and says the name of the dead and goes silent and listens for a moment to hear the dead man or woman speak—those spirits are just as I have been, far away on a mountain in California all these years, speaking only to the sky, the sun, the moon, the cold stars above. And where there are no ears to listen, there is no story to tell. There is only a ghost bawling into the empty night.

Thus, at Timbuctoo, standing in the doorway of my family's house, believing that my body lay crumbling in a box alongside the bodies of my father and brothers and all those who were with us at Harpers Ferry, I felt assured at last of a listening ear. There I could imagine a curious and affectionate man or woman or child, a white person or a black, an ordinary American citizen come to this place to tender his respects and to wonder about the life of my father, Old John Brown, Captain Brown, Osawatomie Brown, and his sons and followers who were martyred far away in Virginia for their violent opposition to the enslavement of three million of their fellow Americans. And because I could imagine such a person being at that place—I had *seen* such a person, seen hundreds of them, that very morning!—then I could imagine myself, for the first time since the end came, coming forward coherently into speech. And so I spoke, and much of what I am telling you now I said then, too.

Take that as an analogy, Miss Mayo. And if my words sometimes seem scattered to you or if I appear confused by the events in my life or by the actions and natures of others, if I wander and ruminate distractedly at times, then, please, forbear, for at such times I have for a moment or two merely lost my ability to imagine you reading these words, and my story therefore has briefly come undone or has regressed to a moan or a childish, half-forgotten, incantatory chant invoked to ward off my loneliness. It will pass, it will leave off—as soon as I picture you wandering down the lane that leads to our old farmhouse, where you stop and stand thoughtfully for a while before the graves by yonder huge, gray boulder. Do not worry, for, even though you cannot see me, I will look out and see you and will come quickly forward to speak to you.

I stand at the door in the evening light and gaze out upon the greening valley beyond Father's somber rock and the graves that surround it, and my thoughts spread into the past like fingers groping in the dark, touching and then seizing familiar objects that lie situated in oddly unfamiliar relations to one another. In such a way am I obliged to reconstruct my past, rather than to recall it. Or perhaps simply to construct it for the first time, for it was never so clear and coherent back when I was living my life as it seems now.

These words are my thoughts given shapely proportions and relations to one another. My story is my only remaining possibility for an
ongoing life, which is how it must be for everyone, living or dead.

In the distant, dusky light of a fading day in May, I peered across the
fresh, wet meadow grass to the sooty Adirondack mountains. It was the
eighty-ninth anniversary of my father's birth; I was alone; it was late in
the day; and a garrulous apparition is what I had become, lingering at
his own, at his father's, his brothers', and his fallen comrades' gravesites,
speaking into the fast-approaching night and then talking still, talking
even, when it came, in darkness.

Let it darken down. It mattered not a whit to me. Let the earth turn
and the moon wax and wane and the tides rise and fall. Light or dark,
warm or cold, early or late—I require no lamp, no fire, no sleep. Let the
rain fall, the cold winds blow; let the snow come tumbling from the
skies and the clouds scatter and the skies turn bright with sunlight on
the morrow and the hills glisten in the dew.

I no longer know physical discomfort, nor even fatigue. I have
been freed of all that. The world, simply by virtue of its continuing
presence, directly pleasures me, as would any dream of life delight a
man dropped permanently into sleep. This may be purgatory, but I take
it as a long-desired and wholly unexpected gift. The dream of a dream
come true. And it's as if at the end of the dream there waits, not an
awakening, but . . . what? A further, deeper dream? Silence, perhaps.

Yes, the silence of the-truth-be-told.

My thoughts and memories and even my feelings spin and spiral
upwards like silk ribbons, where they float vividly amongst old, nearly
forgotten memories of Kansas and the wars we fought then and afterwards. But the ribbons keep losing their momentum and tumble back
down again, as if, due to the cold of a particular altitude or by having

entered some atmospheric level where the elements differ from those here below, they are converted from silk to iron and are drawn back to this hard Adirondack earth by the punishing force of gravity.

Again and again, I move through the abandoned, darkened house and attempt to leave this place and find that I cannot. The door lies open before me; I came in through it as easily as a summer breeze. Yet, still, I cannot go back outside, cross the deserted yard before the large rock and the graves, and pass back along the road I came by and head out across the valley towards Mount Tahawus, retracing my morning steps and disappearing into the mists that hover tonight over its broad flanks.

What seemed at first a blessing—my finding myself located here amongst the crowd of mourners and celebrants at the ceremonial burial of the bones of my brothers and the other raiders from the Virginia attack—seems now almost a curse. I left this farm to all intents and purposes permanently way back in the autumn of '54, when I went out to fetch poor brother Fred from Ohio and instead disobeyed Father and went down into Kansas with Fred and joined up with our older brothers, John and Jason, and thus an account of the events that took place during the years that I spent in North Elba is a story of no great significance in history. But those few years seem now like the large wheel in a clockwork, the wheel that drives all the other wheels, which are smaller than it and advance more rapidly on their axes and at differing speeds. They measure out the individual seconds, minutes, and hours of my entire life, of Father's entire life and the life of my family. Driven by that great, slowly turning wheel, the smaller wheels tell littler stories, which are like tales or essays measured against a long romance. They are the stories of Bleeding Kansas, of the abolitionist movement, of the Underground Railroad, of Harpers Ferry, and so on. None of them, however, is *my* story, the one I am compelled to set down here, as if it were a confession of a great crime that, amidst all the fury and in the noise and smoke and carnage of great events, somehow went unnoticed when it occurred, unpunished afterwards, and unrecorded by you historians and biographers. Mine is the one account that explains all the others, so it is no great vanity for me to tell it.

Even so, after a lifetime of keeping silent and allowing you historians and biographers to establish and make permanent your received truth regarding John Brown and his men, to correct your record is not really why I tell it now. I tell it now because I cannot cease speaking until I have finally told the truth and can lie down in the grave alongside the others, dead, properly dead and buried and silent, and forgiven by them at last. I have begun to see that *they* are the ones to whom I speak. Those who died. No one else. Not you, Miss Mayo, and not your professor. And I do not haunt them; they haunt me. And their haunting will not end until I have revealed, not to you, but to *them*, my terrible secret.

A man can keep a betrayal like mine shut inside himself and unacknowledged all the way down the years of his life to his grave. But the dead whom he betrayed will not let him rest until he has finally revealed it to himself and confessed it to them. The world need not know it; only those whose deaths he caused must hear him. The world at large can go on making up, revising, and believing its received truth. (It will do so anyway—history little notices last-minute or even deathbed confessions.) The received truth of history is shot through and falsified by unknown secrets carried to the grave.

The burden of carrying a terrible and incriminating secret for a lifetime, of dying with it untold, is not great. It's done all the time. For long periods of one's life—especially if one goes off, as I did, and lives alone on a mountaintop—one doesn't even have to think about it. As the years go by, it grows encrusted with rationalizations and elaborate, self-serving explanations and gets distorted by the pliability of living memory, one's own and others'. And so long as one remains silent, other people will inevitably construct a believable narrative that makes the inexplicable plausible.

What really happened at the Pottawatomie massacre? Why did Old Brown go down into Harpers Ferry and stay there long after he could have come out alive? Why did he take his sons and his sons-in-law and all those other fine young men to certain death with him? How did his third son, Owen Brown, come to be the one son who escaped? All these inexplicable events have been explained hundreds of times, hundreds of ways, some of them ingenious, some foolish, all of them plausible. But all without the backing of truth.

No matter. So long as I remained silent, so long as I myself did not try to explain the inexplicable, my secret went unnoticed and proved thus to be no great burden for me to keep untold, to keep unrevealed, even to myself.

I had believed, when I first agreed to write to you, that it was my task to tell Father's untold story, to fill out the historical record with my eyewitness account so as to revise once and for all the received truth about John Brown and his sons and followers. All my life I had resisted doing that, and it seemed wonderful to me that, as it then appeared, I had been given a final chance to set it down. But now it seems that I am not so much revising history as making a confession of a crime, a terrible, secret crime which—if I had been able to keep to my original intentions and long-nurtured desires and had not been obliged to pass beyond them, there to discover strange, unexpected new intentions and desires—would have remained safely hidden. A crime still known by me alone.

This, then, is not simply a report to you or Professor Villard. A dead man confesses to other dead men so that he may join them. And to dead women, too, all of them gone before me now—stepmother Mary, sister Ruth, my younger sisters, Annie, Sarah, and even the lastborn, Ellen—the women who lost and for the rest of their lives grieved over father, brother, husband; the women who, though their bodies were not buried here alongside Father's and the others', nevertheless are out there with them, waiting to hear me. I confess to mere acquaintances and strangers, too. I confess to all the men and women, Negro and white, who believed in Father and his mission, who gave him their life's trust and treasure and even gave him their sons and brothers.

I peer from the window and now and again step forward into the doorframe and look away into the darkness. There they are. All of them are out there; a vast multitude silently awaits me, as if I were on a brightly illumined stage and the broad, grassy valley were a darkened amphitheater. In dim, reflected moonlight I see their sober faces uplifted, expectant, as free of judgement of me as I am of them, for they cannot know their own true stories until they have heard mine.

They knew me, and they hear me now neither with particular sympathy nor without it, for, while no one of them may have committed any such crime as I, they all surely were tempted and at times were as confused as I and as enfeebled, conflicted, and angry. Certainly my brothers were, and my sisters and stepmother and the young men who sacrificed their lives in the long war against slavery. I knew them, too, and in those terrible, fierce years leading up to Harpers Ferry there was not a one of them who was at all times clearer of motive and understanding than I. They will not judge me. They will merely hear me out. My account is a gift. Permanent rest, for them as much as for me, is impossible without it.

2

You may not know this, but I have been remembering what follows here below and don't know what else to do with the memory than to convey it by this means to you. Somehow, my words seem more a proper indictment written down like this; they cannot be so easily ignored or forgotten or denied by me as when I merely mouth them.

In the spring of '31, when he was four months old, my brother Fred's birth-name got replaced by the name of an earlier Frederick, a boy who was born between me and Ruth, a five-year-old boy who had died in March that year of the ague. I cannot recall even the face of that first Frederick. And, to my regret, I long ago forgot the birth-name of the second, the infant who eventually became the true Frederick, our Fred, and there is no one else left who would remember it.

Then, a year and a half after the re-naming, in the autumn of '32, when my sister Ruth was three years old and little more than a baby herself, we lost our mother. We were living in the wilds of New Richmond in western Pennsylvania, having recently removed there from Hudson, in Ohio. The new Frederick was by then nearly two. There was another baby, unnamed, who was born and died a few days before my mother herself died. John and Jason were eleven and ten and were out of school and regularly employed in the tannery with Father. I was eight and thus still a schoolboy.

But until Mother died, we Browns had been to all appearances a normal family of our time and place, if a bit overly strict in matters of religion. After that, we became like some ancient Hebrew tribe of wanderers and sufferers, burdened by the death of women and children and by our endless obligations to our father's restless, yet implacable, God. Isolated from our neighbors and tangled in tribulation and increasingly dire financial circumstances, we were weighed down further by complicated vows and covenants that made sense only after Father had explained them to us. And even though his explanations made our life briefly comprehensible, since there was always a reason for everything that we did, over the long run they made things worse, for he likened our life, not to the lives of the modern American people who surrounded us, but to those of his Biblical heroes. It was as if, after Mother died, we moved outside of conventional time and wandered with our herds and puny belongings through some distant land and epoch, so that we were not living in Ohio, but in Canaan, not in Pennsylvania, but among the Philistines, not in Massachusetts, but in Pharaoh's Egypt.

Probably, Father had viewed himself and others in that peculiarly vivid, Biblical light from early in his life, for he had been a devout and an unusually imaginative Christian since boyhood, when he had practically memorized the entire Bible. But, for me, it began when Mother died. It seems strange to me now, strange that I didn't know it earlier, when I was still a believer, but as my Christian faith secretly began to fade, a fading surely occasioned and probably even caused by the sudden death of my mother, I came gradually, at the same time and pace as the fading, to an awareness of the unusual degree to which our lives as a family and as individuals were described, prescribed, and subscribed by the Bible. The Word of God. His Holy Writ. As understood, interpreted, and applied by our father, John Brown. It was almost as if we were characters in the Good Book and had no other lives or destinies than what Father said had been given to us there.

Let me tell you how it was then. Because after Mother died, everything changed, and I want you to know us in the ways we were not generally known, for better or worse. I don't know if somehow Father himself became a different man, a man more forcefully committed to the liberation of the Negro, and more religious, even, than he had been before, or if instead everything and everyone merely remained the same, and it was I alone who had changed, a small boy who suddenly saw things about his life and circumstances that until then had been invisible to him. But whichever it was, for me, at least, everything changed.

I have been remembering this morning how it was when I entered the darkened room, the small front parlor of our log house, and learned that Mother had died. It was still a rough and wild section of the country there in New Richmond, and I came home from the simple, one-room log schoolhouse that Father had built when we first settled in the region, where the young fellow from Connecticut taught the children of the settlement. Mr. Twichell was his name, Joseph Twichell. Him you may not know of yet. He was a fine young fellow, hardly more than a boy himself, freshly graduated from Yale College. Father, on one of his early trips east to sell cattle, had met him at an abolitionists' meeting and had convinced him to come all the way out to the Western Reserve, so that he could serve the Presbyterian God and His Son, not in New Haven amongst the wealthy, educated class of people that he sprang from, but away in the wilderness, teaching rudimentary reading, writing, and figuring skills to the children of lowly shepherds, farmers, and tanners.

Mr. Twichell was a slender, almost delicate fellow with a pointed Yankee face, all narrow nose, chin, and forehead—a face made of small, delicate bones. And I remember him with pleasure and ease, for he bore immense good will towards children, as if he thought the ways in which we were treated by adults would shape our minds and morals for the remainder of our lives. This was an unusual perspective in those days, especially way out there in the Western Reserve amongst families with no time for coddling the young, no use for it whatsoever. Teach them merely what they need to know for doing their basic business and for keeping them from being cheated by strangers, then send them home to clear the forest and work the farm—that was the prevailing viewpoint.

I returned from school one autumn afternoon along towards dusk, hopping like a red squirrel through fallen leaves. I can hear the rustling sound of the leaves, ash, hickory, and oak, and can smell their dry, cinnamon smell in the clean, cool autumn air cut through with woodsmoke as I passed the cabins of my schoolmates in the settlement and moved further down the narrow, rutted road towards Father's tannery and our isolated house just beyond. Too young to join my brothers at the tannery and too old to stay at home with the babies, I went alone to school in those days. But—and here is something else that you cannot have learned elsewhere—I had a constant companion then, an imaginary boy who was as real to me as a twin brother and whom I had named Frederick, no doubt because of some half-buried worry about the recent transfer of the name from the dead brother to the living one.

I had revealed his existence to no one but Mother, for I knew that she and only she would look kindly on him. My companion was, in a strange, prescient way, very much like my brother Fred would soon become, when in a few years we in the family would begin to understand that, in certain, crucial ways, Fred was different than the rest of us children, especially we boys—or, to put a finer point on it, that Fred did not *feel* things the same as we did, as if he were more sensitive to cold than we or less sensitive to heat—and, as a consequence, Fred would have to be treated more carefully than we were. Already Father had begun to arrange a special set of rules for Fred, which did not deny him the rights and privileges enjoyed by the rest of us at the same age but did not require him to take on the same responsibilities, either.

Even then I saw that Father was a genius at legislating rules and regulations for the governance of the numerous members of his family, adjudicating over everything domestic, from the most trivial quarrel and difference of opinion and desire to the most complex and lofty difference of principle. Notwithstanding his claim that he was, at bottom, even amongst his family, a democrat, Father exercised all the authority of a monarch, and got away with it, perhaps because he was never arbitrary or whimsical and never compromised merely in order to obtain some vaguely dissatisfying middle ground. At our supper table, Father's seat was the seat of government, all three houses of it, executive, legislative, and judiciary. His constitution was, of course, the Bible, in particular the Old Testament. His Declaration of Independence and Preamble were the Books of Genesis and Deuteronomy. His Bill of Rights was taken straight from the New Testament: love the Lord thy God above all else, and treat thy neighbor as thou wouldst have him treat thee. Christ's first Commandment and His Golden Rule—these were the scales upon which Father weighed all our needs, decided all our disagreements, and meted out to us our punishments and rewards.

Fred's was a difficult case to rule on, however. From the time he first began to speak, it was evident that he was an innocent, that he was a boy incapable of lying. He was not like the rest of us. He always told the truth with perfect, natural, unthinking ease, and as a result—not for any lack of intelligence, but due to his primitive honesty—he was incapable of understanding that others often lied to him. Even after he became a man. Thus, unlike the rest of us, unlike me in particular, Fred could not protect himself against liars by lying to them first. He was not simple—his understanding in many areas was as good as the next fellow's—but to most people he must have seemed mentally slow. And because they treated him that way and consequently were wont to cheat and mislead him, we were obliged to protect him as if indeed he were. At home amongst his three older brothers and sister Ruth and the younger ones when they came along, our stepmother Mary's children, his innocence, as he grew older, reflected only badly on the rest of us—especially on me, for I was as a boy an incorrigible and incompetent liar. It was an early habit, and I do not know how it came to be that, but once begun, it could be stopped only with extreme diligence and discipline, neither of which could I properly muster myself, and so, frequently, I found myself corrected and chastized by others, especially by Father and his fierce belt.

When, with my imaginary Frederick at my side, I turned in at the tannery yard, I saw at once that something strange and ominous was going on. The blindfolded horse on the bark-grinder had come to a stop and stood unwatched in the center of the yard, with the long wooden arm of the grinder still attached. There was no smoke coming from the chimneys of the tannery, none of the usual signs of activity— of hides being hung to dry, of John, Jason, or the other workers hefting baskets of wet bark from the vats or lugging freshly scraped skins in and out of the low storage sheds, of customers going over accounts with Father, and so on. And before the house, three saddle horses stood hitched.

With my Frederick close behind, I began to run towards the house, as if I had already divined what had occurred. But I did not know, I could not have known, for Mother had seemed perfectly well that morning, although once again she had not come to the door and waved us off when in the gray dawn light my Frederick and I had set out for the schoolhouse. But somehow, suddenly, on this day I knew—perhaps because I feared so powerfully the loss of my mother that no other eventuality mattered to me and on this day was finally no longer able to suppress that fear: I knew that her continuing inability to rise from her bed was not what Father had said, the consequence of fatigue and a result of the sadness of having recently lost her newborn infant. Those things passed, not easily but naturally; they were part of the seasonal round of our and our neighbors' daily lives: the dark fatigue of women and the death of infants. But this, I suddenly believed, was different.

So strong was my fear of losing Mother that, as long as nothing had happened to her, no matter what other disaster befell us, it would be as if nothing bad had happened at all. Her essential goodness and her love of me compensated for everything that was not good. And in an unpredictable, unstable world, where babies died before children and children died before adults, where without warning twisters and droughts and hard freezes descended on us like Biblical plagues and ruined a year's and sometimes a lifetime's careful husbandry of crops and livestock, a world in which the God to whom everyone prayed for mercy and justice seemed not to care one way or the other, in such a precarious, incomprehensible world, my mother's love was the only kindly constant, her gentle smile my sole comfort, her soft, shy voice the music that pacified my turbulent mind.

I dropped Frederick's hand and ran full speed towards the house. Frederick laughed, as if I had invented a game, and gave chase, trying to tag me. At the door, he finally tagged me on the shoulder and said, "Ha! Got you! Now get me!"

I shook his hand away and tugged frantically on the door and banged on it, crying, "Mother! Mother! Let me in!"

It would not give, try as I might to open it. I was sobbing, hammering against the door with my fists now, enraged and terrified. Whether it was barred from the inside against me or in my panic I simply could not work the latch, I do not know; I hurled my weight against it and kept crying, "Mother! Mother!"

Then suddenly the door swung wide, opening into the small, darkened room. I found myself facing Father's broad chest. His arms reached around me and held me tightly to him. I remember his stifling smell of leather and blood and wool. I glimpsed behind him the shadowy forms of my older brothers, John and Jason, and several men and a woman, people I knew from their outlines but did not at that moment recognize—they were merely adults, large people, shades blocking out my mother's light. Foremost amongst them, and darkest, was Father. He wrapped me in his iron arms, holding me face-first against his woolen shirt, and said, "Owen, come on outside for a moment. Come, son, and let me speak calmly with you. Come outside, Owen," he said, and he moved me backwards out to the stoop, where my Frederick was standing, bewildered.

Frederick said, "Don't cry, Owen. I only meant to tag you. I didn't mean to hurt you."

Father held me firmly by the wrist, and as he drew me across the stoop, I squirmed and tried in vain to break free of his grasp. "Come here, son," he said to me in a low voice. "Come on now, let's sit down and talk. I must talk a moment with you."

He sat on the step and finally released his hold on me, and when he did, I shoved him aside and ran back through the slowly closing door into the house. "Owen!" he called, but too late.

The room was dim, cold, and damp, like a sepulchre, and although it was crowded with people, I saw no one in the room now, except Mother, who lay on her and Father's day bed near the window, fully dressed, her eyes closed, as if she were asleep. Father's brother, Uncle Frederick, he for whom my dead brother had originally been named, was there, up from Ohio, and he quickly moved towards me and grabbed me by the shoulders and tried to move me back outside, away from Mother.

I wrenched myself free of his grasp and ran straight to her and clutched both her hands in mine. They were as cold as clay and as inert, and at first I was afraid of them, as if they were small, dead animals, skinned and dried. But they were my mother's hands, as familiar to me as my own, and they were all I had left of her, so I pulled on them, as if to lift her up from her bed or to yank her back from the abyss into which she was falling. I drew her into a half-seated position on the day-bed. But her head flopped to one side like a doll's, and her weight became too much for me, and her body began to tilt towards the wall. Her face was turned entirely away from me then, and suddenly it was as if she were pulling against my grasp, shoving me from her.

I unclasped my hands from hers and watched her slip away from me. Her body fell back onto the day-bed and then slid over the lip of the abyss into the darkness. She was gone. Gone. And in that instant, although I was still a child, I understood to the bottom of my soul that I was now alone. I knew, too, that I would remain so for the rest of my life.

Slowly, I turned and left the darkened room. Father waited outside, still seated on the doorstoop. I sat down beside him, taking the same position there as he, head down, hands on knees, back straight. Father and son. We did not speak.

I never saw my mother again. I never saw my imaginary companion, my poor lost Frederick, again, either. My father would soon remarry, as you know, a good woman whom I called only Mary, never Mother, and she would provide him with eight more children. But nothing would be the same for me, ever again. I mark the end of my childhood from that day.

I'm sorry. I can write no more today. I will resume, however, as soon as my hand is steady again and my mind cleared of this embarrassing self-pity.

Following yesterday's letter, I've been recalling this morning those early days in New Richmond and the peaceful prior years of my boyhood in Hudson—both wildernesses of the old Western Reserve when we resided there, as fraught with difficulty and danger on our first arrival and settlement as was our Adirondack mountain farm later. We lived in our villages then amongst wolves and bears and mountain lions in deep forests that blocked out all light in the lost ravines. We lived close to Indians, Iroquois, mostly, suspicious and withdrawn and silent, who sometimes left their forest enclaves and visited our villages to trade, but mainly kept a safe distance from us. And there was the occasional fugitive slave, coming up from Kentucky or the mountains of western Virginia by way of the Underground Railroad, run generally by the Quakers back then, and passing through to Canada—a quiet, frightened, day-long visitor hidden in the attic of our house and spirited on under hay in Father's wagon as soon as night fell to the farm of a Quaker or some fellow radical abolitionist twenty or thirty miles to the north.

But recalling those days of long ago, after having seen all of the civilized world that an ordinary man needs to see in order to know the true nature of people in society, I am struck by nothing so much as our sustained virtue and orderliness. Wherever we lived in those days, wherever we set up our house and farm and commenced doing business with our neighbors, we were like an island in a sea of chicanery, godlessness, disorder, and willful ignorance. For we Browns were distinct; we were different from most of those who surrounded us. We were surrounded not just by wilderness but by reckless sinners.

As individuals and as a family, we were sinners, too, of course, like all men and women, but ours was the fastidious sin of pride, for we were proud of our difference and took pleasure in enumerating the ways in which it got daily manifested. We even prided ourselves on the number of occasions and the ways in which our friends and neighbors were affronted by our virtue and orderliness or found it strange or eccentric and as a result held themselves off from us, choosing to view us, as did the Iroquois, from what must have felt to them a safe distance.

Our pride, that subtlest and most insidious of sins, got manifested in a variety of ways, but, all reports to the contrary, I do not believe that we were arrogant. Certainly Mother, and later my stepmother, Mary, and my sister Ruth were not arrogant. And the younger children were all naturally modest and shy, boys and girls alike, and were constantly encouraged to remain so when they ventured out into the wider world than home provided, and for the most part they did. My older brothers and I, too, strove not to lord it over others less fortunate than we, less disciplined, less inclined to sacrifice their force and time on earth for the greater good, what Father called "the commonweal." And even Father himself was not arrogant—although he was indeed commanding and headstrong—and made only those demands on us that he made on himself as well, and made no demands on others, but wholly accepted people as he found them. To Father, other people chose to live our way—and there were a few here and there who did—or they chose not to. It was the same to him, either way.

On the other hand, though there was never a man so detached from the sinner who so loathed sin, when it came to the sin of owning slaves, which Father labeled not sin but evil, all his loathing came down at once and in a very personal way upon the head of the evil-doer. He brooked no fine distinctions: the man who pleaded for the kindly treatment of human chattel or, as if it could occur naturally, like a shift in the seasons, argued for the gradual elimination of slavery was just as evil as the man who whipped, branded, raped, and slew his slaves; and he who did not loudly oppose the extension of slavery into the western territories was as despicable as he who hounded escaped slaves all the way to Canada and branded them on the spot to punish them and to make pursuit and capture easier next time. But with the notable exception of where a man or woman stood on the question of slavery, when Father considered the difference between our way of life and the ways

of others, he did not judge them or lord it over them. He did not condemn or set himself off from our neighbors. He merely observed their
ways and passed silently by.

And he knew all the ways of men and women extremely well. He
was no naif, no bumpkin. My father was not the sort of man who
stopped up his ears at the sound of foul language or shut his eyes to the
lasciviousness and sensuality that passed daily before him. He never
warned another man or woman off from speech or act because he was
too delicate of sensibility or too pious or virtuous to hear of it or witness the thing. He knew what went on between men and women,
between men and men, between men and animals even, in the small,
crowded cabins of the settlements and out in the sheds and barns of
our neighbors. And he knew what was nightly bought and sold on the
streets and alleys and in the taverns of the towns and cities he visited.
The man had read every word of his Bible hundreds of times: nothing
human beings did with or to one another or themselves shocked him.
Only slavery shocked him.

Father was a countryman, after all, a farmer and stockman much
admired by other farmers and stockmen, a workingman who could roll
up his sleeves and cut timber, tan hides, or build a stone wall alongside
the roughest men in the region. And although he was a failure at it, he
was a businessman, too, a man who traveled widely, to Boston and New
York and once even to England and the European continent, and
stayed in hotels and taverns where prostitutes plied their trade in the
lobbies and drinking rooms below and visited the men he traveled
with in their rooms next to his, with only a thin partition between.
Father knew the ways of most men and women, and he did not loudly
condemn them. He merely elected to behave differently, to go his own
way, to keep himself pure, and to marry young.

Our virtues as a family were, of course, guided and enforced from
our earliest childhood years well into adult life by Father's own exam-

ple and by his steady instruction. Although, when we did become adults, after about the age of sixteen or so, his manner of dealing with our lapses changed, in that he no longer chastized us or enforced his will and the wisdom of his ways with the rod and belt or punished us for our disobedience. Instead, he merely withdrew from the offender the shining light of his trust. And no punishment was so powerful a corrective as that. He did not require that we share with him his deep, unquestioning Christian faith, as long as our every act was a reflection of our belief in the rightness of the Golden Rule and our love of the Truth. "If you cannot be a believing Christian but will nonetheless do unto others as you would have them do unto you, and if you will obey the first commandment of Jesus Christ and only substitute the word 'Truth' for God, then I swear that I shall not disavow you." That was his pledge to us.

My brothers, John and especially Jason, took him at his word, and by the time they turned twenty, they had already long abandoned the Christian faith and had become rigorous but upright freethinkers in matters of divinity. When I, a few years behind, saw that this did not cause a significant rift between them and Father, I secretly followed suit. Our loss of faith did not please Father, naturally, and he never ceased to speak of it, but he nonetheless knew that there was no way he could command us to maintain our faith, any more than God could command him to maintain his. And so, instead, he grieved over it and constantly upbraided, not us, but himself, for having failed us as a teacher and father.

There was no way we could disabuse him of this notion. Nor did we especially want to, for it was one of his virtues, after all, and we held all his virtues in the highest esteem. And because our close adherence to his example was what gave to the family as a whole its character, its defining nature and difference from other families, we could not reject the worth of a single one of his virtues without rejecting an essential aspect of the family as well. Which would have been like choosing the life of the outcast. So that if Father grieved over his failure as a teacher and father, then John, Jason, and I were obliged to grieve over our failure as pupils and sons.

Nevertheless, despite the differences in degree of our faith in Father's Lord and his Saviour Jesus Christ, we were a pious little clan, we Browns. The daily round of prayers and hymn-singing, Father's morning Bible lessons, and his insistence on interpreting all events in Biblical terms were of great value. They disciplined and ordered our attention together as individuals and as a group. They woke us from our self-absorbed slumber, connecting us one to the other and all to the larger world outside, and linked that world to the great, overarching sphere of Truth, or God, which we loved before all other truths, or gods.

I remember Father's surprisingly lovely singing voice—surprising because his speaking voice was somewhat reedy and thin, a consequence less of his language and attitude than of his physical nature. When he sang, however, his voice was strong and melodic and pitched high, like a young boy's. He sang sweetly, yet with sufficient force to redden his face, which, when we were children, invariably brought smiles to our faces. He would notice, before we could cover our mouths, and would smile also and sing all the more loudly. In making a joyful noise unto the Lord, smiles and even laughter were permitted, and our favorite hymns were the joyous, loud ones, like "Blow, Ye Trumpets, Blow." At prayer, however, or during the daily lesson, we knew to keep our heads lowered, our brows knitted as if in sober thought, our hands clasped together, and no catching one another's amused eyes when Father, as he occasionally did, due to the fervency of his feelings, lost the train of his thought and fell to stammering or repetition.

In those days, to anyone who saw us, we were naturally regarded as pious. But not in the strict Methodist or old German Lutheran manner, as we have sometimes been portrayed. No, piety in us Browns was an attitude of respect which we held towards the Truth and our fellow man and which we strove to maintain daily in all our small as well as our large affairs. Our rituals and forms of worship, which were mainly the basic, old, New England Presbyterian forms, functioned, at least for me and my brothers and, perhaps to a lesser degree, Ruth and the other, younger children, merely to remind us of that respectful attitude and, every morning and evening and over every meal, to renew it in our hearts and to place that attitude of respect, of reverence even, in the forefront of our minds.

And if respect for the truth and our fellow man was the basis of our piety, then there was probably no more consistent and singular expression of our piety than our adherence to the principle of honesty in all our dealings, as much with strangers as with each other, as much with enemies as with friends. It sometimes made us appear odd to folks who were not so insistent on honest dealings, and it made Father, in the end, an incompetent businessman. But for us, that oddity, as I said, was a point of pride. And although we were often obliged to forgo an easy advantage, especially when it came to matters of money, our honest dealings frequently obliged decent people in turn to deal the same way with us, and we were thus sometimes able to prosper by it.

But it is well-known that from earliest childhood we Browns were taught not to lie. We were chastized severely when caught doing it. It was Father's first corollary to his first commandment. If ye love the Truth, then ye cannot lie. Less well-known, perhaps, is the fact that I was the worst offender amongst us, as a child, that is; and in the early days, when he was a young man and Mother was alive, Father was more severe in his punishment and in his means of correcting us children than later, and we sometimes did not understand why he beat us so energetically and for so long. (There was the danger, perhaps especially with me, of his bending the branch too far and breaking it off, instead of correcting it to straightness; or of having it snap back defiantly against him and end up bent the other way, permanently misshapen. But I knew nothing of that then.)

By the time I was five or six years old, well before Mother had died, I had already begun to manifest the habit of lying to an exceeding degree, even for a child. I seemed to take sensual pleasure in it and almost sought out occasions for lying, making up tales, entire adventures, elaborate encounters, and so on, which had never taken place. I went beyond mere exaggeration, and although I oftentimes partially believed in the truth of my accounts, just as I believed in the corporeal reality of my imagined companion, Frederick, there nonetheless was a side of me that was wholly aware of their falsehood and was pleased by it. It gave me momentarily a sense of importance to say that I had seen a bear when I had not, to report on the visit of an Indian when no such person had appeared, to claim that I had been complimented by the schoolmaster, Mr. Twichell, when he had for days ignored me altogether and in fact seemed to think me rather a dull child.

I remember vividly a significant alteration of this wretched habit, so that in later years, when I lied, it was no longer out of blind compulsion but rather as the product of a conscious, calculated decision. Once, in New Richmond, Grandfather Brown, whose namesake I was, came over from Akron to visit us for a few days. It was during the dark months not long after Mother died, when Father had fallen into one of his periods of silence and withdrawal and passivity, and it had gone on dangerously long, so that family members and neighbors, too, were concerned for the welfare of his five children and for his own physical and mental health. Father was prone to such periods anyhow, especially following a spate of trouble, but this time he seemed unable to end it, unable to pass through his grief and loss and get on with the everyday business of his life.

Grandfather Brown stayed for a week, I remember, and as the end of it approached, Father was returning to his old, custodial self. When he roused us at dawn, the downstairs fires were now lit, and when the workers arrived at the tannery, Father was there to greet them and lay out the day's work. In the evenings, he had resumed his reading aloud from the Bible to the younger children, and before we went to bed he totted up the day's accomplishments and failures of each child and listed tomorrow's obligations—to wash down the kitchen floor, sweep the yard, bring in the early peas, repair the sheepfold, separate the pullets from the hens, and so on—from each child, according to age and ability, an accounting of his or her allotted task, and to each child the next day's charge.

I myself greeted this return to the old routines with mixed feelings, as if I almost missed the gloom and silence and inactivity that had followed Mother's death. But the others all seemed relieved and for the first time in months happy and playful again, so I tried to join in. But then, on the final morning of Grandfather's visit, when I passed alone through the parlor on my way out to school, I espied on the mantelpiece, where he had placed it the night before, Grandfather's large gold watch and chain. It was a particular treasure to him, engraved with his initials, a bit ostentatious, the one vanity that that otherwise simple and utterly unpretentious man indulged in. I picked up the watch and held it for a moment, then slipped the watch, which he in his antique way called a chronometer, into my trouser pocket and dashed away to school with it, while the old man slept peacefully in the next room.

What were my motives? I did not know then, nor do I today. Except to say that the timepiece drew me like a talisman, a magical amulet. Since Grandfather's arrival, I had been studying it at every opportunity, aware constantly of its location, whether in Grandfather's vest pocket or on the sideboard or mantelpiece or in his tough, leathery hand. And once I had it in my possession, I felt wonderfully, magically empowered by it, as if it were the legendary sword, Excalibur, instead of a mere man-made timepiece. As if, with the watch in my pocket, I were a grown man in charge of my own life, not a boy anymore.

At school, in the clearing by the woodshed, where we children loaded the day's stovewood to carry inside, I showed the watch to my friends, claiming that my grandfather—a man born before the Revolutionary War, I proudly pointed out—had given it to me, because our names were the same, Owen Brown, which was why the initials engraved on its case were the same as mine. The initials were mine in actual fact, I said. See? *O.J.B.*

My friends, the boys especially, were impressed and crowded round me to see it the better, imagining the watch and heavy chain, as I did, worn in a Colonial soldier's waistcoat pocket by me, or someone sharply resembling me, as he marched heroically into the smoke and fury of Revolutionary battle.

At once, however, I realized that I had gone too far and now would have to swear the other children to secrecy. "Don't say nothing to Mister Twichell about it," I said. "My father was supposed to be the one who got Grandfather's watch, and he don't know yet that it's gone to me, instead. Grandfather said he'd tell him today, while I'm off the place."

I was betrayed, of course. Not by one of the children, though. By Mr. Twichell himself, who had stood at the doorway and had observed my little performance from across the schoolyard. When I passed by the schoolmaster and entered the building with my armload of fire-wood, he tapped me lightly on the shoulder, smiled down, and said, "Owen, when you have put the wood in the box, come and show me what you were showing the children."

I did as instructed, and he took the timepiece and turned it over, examining the initials and the fine face with the Roman numerals. "How did you come by this?" he gently asked.

I looked around and saw that all the children were watching, wait-ing for me to reveal my lie, for at bottom they had known the truth, or at least had known that I was lying, and now I was about to be exposed in public, not just as a liar, but as a thief as well. I hesitated a second, and Mr. Twichell said again, "How did you come by such a marvelous instrument, Owen?"

I sucked in my breath and quickly repeated the lie that I had told the children outside.

He gazed at the watch for a few seconds, admiring it, and when he handed it back to me, asked if I could read the time from the markings on its face. I nodded yes, and he asked me how I knew which was which, for they weren't numbers, were they? They were X's and V's and I's.

"They're in the same place as the regular numbers," I said.

He said that was so, and then told us to take out our slates and begin the day's lesson, which turned out to be—fortuitously, he said, winking broadly at me—upon the difference between Roman and Arabic numerals. In a surprisingly short time, every child in the room could write in Roman any date the teacher called out to us and any hour, the number of the states in 1776 and the number today in 1833, the white population of the United States, the Negro population of the United States, the total of the two, and the difference between.

At day's end, when I passed out of the schoolhouse, Mr. Twichell stopped me at the doorway and handed me a small, folded sheet of paper. "I'm sorry, Owen," he said, in a voice so soft that only I could hear it. "This is for your father. Please, don't fail to deliver it to him." I took the note with trembling hand, for I knew what it said, and slipped it into my trouser pocket, next to Grandfather's watch. "You may read it if you wish," Mr. Twichell added. He seemed sad and guilty, almost, and I knew why. But he had done the right thing. I was the sinner, not he.

I did not read the note; I could not. I did not deserve to. Dutifully, when I arrived home, I went straight to Father, who was at work inside the tannery, and passed the note to him. He slowly unfolded the paper and read it. Finally, without a word, he held out his hand before me, and

I drew the watch from my pocket and laid it flat in his huge, callused, outstretched hand. He thanked me, turned to Grandfather, who had been seated on a stool next to the fire, watching, and gave it over to him. Carefully, Grandfather examined the watch, as if checking it for damage, and placed it into his vest pocket. Then he took up his walking stick, rose creakily, and walked from the room to the yard, where my brothers were at work.

Father said, "Is there anything you can say in your defense, Owen?" His face was very sad and downcast, like Mr. Twichell's.

"No."

He sighed. "I thought not. Come with me," he said.

We went to the barn, where it was dark. Motes of hay drifted slowly from the lofts through beams of light shining through the cracks and openings above. He told me to remove my shirt, which I did, while behind me and out of sight he took from its nail on the main post of the barn the hated piece of cowhide which, years ago, long before my birth, he had tanned and cut into a long strip strictly for the purpose of chastizing his children. I bowed my head and waited, shivering, for the first blow against the cold skin of my bare back.

And when the blow came, the force of it sent my breath from my body, and before I could inhale, the second blow came, harder than the first. Twelve times he lashed my back, one for each hour on the face of the watch, he told me, as he swung the leather strap again and again, each stroke shoving me nearly off my feet. Twelve strokes, he said, so that I would forever associate this particular punishment with my lie. "Twelve strokes for telling people that you owned what was owned by another. For lying." Each stroke drove me a step forward—twelve steps in a circle in the dirt floor of the barn.

Finally, he stopped. I had not wept and was surprised by that and wondered if somehow, due to my sinful nature, I had lost the capacity for it. Father said, "There are also sixty minutes on the face of a watch,

Owen. And not only did you lie, you stole. You coveted your grandfather's property and stole it from him." To my amazement, then, Father turned me around to face him and handed me the leather strap and stripped off his own shirt. "As much as you've failed me as a son, I've failed you as a father," he said, and he got down on his knees before me. "We're connected, our sins are connected, in the same way as the sixty minutes and the twelve hours on the face of Grandfather's watch are connected. Therefore, you must place sixty lashes on my back. Then you'll never forget how we, you and I, and Grandfather, too, all of us, are connected in all our thoughts and deeds."

Bewildered at first and frightened by his command, I nonetheless did as I was told and struck him across his naked back with the leather, his own whip of chastizement. It was a feeble blow, but it was all I could muster. "Harder!" he instructed, and I obeyed. "Harder still!" he commanded, and so I did, again and again, growing stronger with each blow, until I had lashed him all sixty times. And then, at the sixtieth and final blow, at last I began weeping copious tears.

"Now, Owen, now you see how it is between God and man," Father said to me. "Now you're weeping. And when the Bible says, 'Jesus wept,' you know why He wept. Don't you?"

I could not answer.

"Don't you?"

"Yes," I said. "I understand now." And I put my shirt back on and left him there alone in the dim light of the barn, praying quietly to God for forgiveness.

I will tell you another story of our life then and of early deceit and punishment, one that, like the other, will bear significantly on later events. More so than any of our neighbors, wherever we lived, we Browns kept the Sabbath holy. Defined precisely, in the way of Father's literal ancestors, the old New England Puritans, and of his spiritual forebears, the ancient Hebrews, our Sabbath began on Saturday night at sundown and ended at sundown the following day. Father brooked no variations or exceptions to this rule. Sometimes we children argued with him as to whether the Saturday sun had actually set yet, for there was still light filtering through the trees from the west, and John or Jason might contend that if the trees behind the house had been cut, then there would be at least another half-hour of daylight, so it was not truly sunset. But Father would have none of that, answering, "Yes, John, and I suppose if the western hills were not there, we'd have fully an hour of daylight left. Come in now, boys, and honor the Lord with your silence."

And after a few more minutes of broody grousing around outside, we'd give up and come trooping into the house, latching the door behind, to commence our twenty-four hours of confinement, of silence, prayer, and contemplation of the Lord. It was an imprisonment, broken only by the need the next morning early to tend to the animals and later to join in the few hours of worship at church that, when we were young and living in Hudson and New Richmond, Father was still able to insist on. Of course, after he broke with the Hudson Congregationalists over the slavery question back in '37, an event you have no doubt already uncovered in your researches, after that, we no longer had even the diversion of church services when the Sabbath came around. Instead, we prayed and sang together at home, and Father preached.

It was difficult for us children, though, especially when we were very young. We moped and drifted somberly about the house, not free even to work or whittle some little tool or toy, no spinning or weaving for the females, no cooking, no household projects, for any of us. Silence, prayer, contemplation, and—except for the Bible—no reading. From our rooms upstairs we peered dreamily out the windows, as ordinary Christians passed down the road on their way to town or cut through the yard into the woods beyond with their muskets on their shoulders, gone deer hunting or out for grouse or partridge, and how we envied them. The girls as much as we boys. We were all fairly high-strung, active children used to constant physical exertion, and to put a twenty-four-hour halt suddenly once a week on our wild spirits, which usually got exercised harmlessly in work and outdoor play and sports, was an extreme imposition, often too extreme for us to place upon ourselves without heavy enforcement from Father.

Sometimes, usually by early afternoon on Sunday, by which time we had become explosive from the confinement and silence, we older boys would contrive to escape from the house for a few hours and return before sundown without being missed. Father's habit was to retire to the parlor and sit in his chair by the window with his Bible on his lap and read silently, now and then dozing off. It was usually one of the younger children who saw the Old Man's chin finally fall to his chest and heard him start to snore, and who, on our orders, would tiptoe up the narrow stairs to the rooms above with this welcome intelligence, and, John in the lead, we older boys, sometimes with Ruth tagging along behind, slid open a window and crept along the ridge of the shed roof to where we swung out onto the branch of a maple tree and quickly scrambled to the ground. Then for a few hours we were free to race through the woods like buckskins, shrieking and hollering to one another, making all the wild noises that for fifteen or twenty long hours we had kept bottled up inside our chests.

I remember, for powerful reasons, one Sabbath in particular, which I will describe, for it has a meaning that extends into the later part of my story. It was late in the fall of '33, when I was but nine years old, the year after Mother died, and our stepmother, Mary, had been living with us for only a few months. A nearby neighbor and not much more than a girl herself, Mary had first been hired by Father to keep house and care for his younger children during the days, while he ran the tannery, but soon he married her. She was then pregnant with her first child,

Sarah, born the following spring. I remember little else of that sad whirl of a year, except what happened to me on one crisp, sunshiny day, when John, Jason, and I, as we had done a hundred or more times, made our escape from our father's and new stepmother's dark, silent house to the large, bright world outside.

I was then a cold, withdrawn child, hopelessly saddened by the death of my mother. The pain of my days and nights was such that I thought of little else and thus was to all appearances a permanently distracted child, one of those children who seem neither to know nor to care where they are or who is with them. I was a boy whose gaze was always inward and fixed there, not on himself, but on some imagined closed door. I have seen dogs whose beloved masters have gone into the house, leaving the animals to wait outside, there to sit on the cold stoop, staring at the door with unbroken gaze. I was like that poor animal, and the door was the death of my mother.

John went first out the window and crept along the ridge of the steeply pitched roof of the shed, followed by Jason. Then me. At the end of the roofline, there was a two-storey drop to the ground, which had been dug away for the entry to our root cellar below. A sturdy, full-grown maple tree stood at the back of the shed, with several branches close enough to the structure that a medium-sized boy could in a single move slide down from the ridge of the roof to the eave, where he could leap out and catch onto the tree and from there make his way easily to the ground. Without hesitating, John reached the end of the ridge, turned, squatted, and duck-walked quickly down the wood-shingled slope, sprang into the air, grabbed the branch of the tree, and like a squirrel hurried down its length. Jason, grinning, was right behind him.

Then came I, walking in a kind of haze. I made my way to the end of the roof. But instead of stopping there and lowering myself to a sliding position, like the others, I simply continued straight on, as if the ridge of the roof extended below me. I remember stepping off the roof into open space and falling for a very long time through sunlight and bright green leaves and blue sky in a dreamy downward flight, pulled, not by gravity, but by some force even more powerful than gravity. I was like the boy Icarus, who flew too near the sun on unnatural wings and was hurled back to earth as punishment for his pride and vanity. Down, down I fell, crashing at last against the stone steps to the root cellar.

I must have reached out at the last second with my left arm, as if to push the ground away, for the arm lay beneath me, crushed by my own weight and the force of my fall. I was fully conscious and at first felt no particular pain, but when John and Jason reached me and rolled me over, I saw that my arm had been snapped almost in two by the cut edge of the stone steps. Jason began to howl at the sight of it, for one of the bones above the wrist had torn through the flesh and sleeve, and the arm was gushing blood.

I was in terrible pain then. I could not say anything; I could not even cry. Everything was yellow and red, as if the earth had caught fire. Jason was bawling in terror. John whispered hoarsely, "Shut up, Jason! Just shut up! You'll bring the Old Man!" But then he saw my arm and realized that it was all up with us. "Run and get Father!" he said. "But go back up the tree way. Go through the house, tell him Owen fell from the roof and we saw him from inside. He won't lick Owen now anyhow, and maybe he'll let us off, too."

Jason did as he was told, and a moment later Father appeared, towering over me and John, his huge, dark shape blocking out the yellow sky. John stood and stepped quickly away. "He fell off the roof, Father," he said. "We saw him from inside."

"Yes. So it seems," Father said. His hands were chunked in fists on his hips, and he surveyed the scene, looking first up at the ridge of the roof, then along our route to the eave, to the maple tree and the ground.

To John, Father said, "You and Jason came out the window and climbed down the tree to help him, did you?"

"Yes, Father."

Swiftly, he descended the steps to where I lay all crumpled and broken. Crouching over me and examining my arm, he said to me, "You appear to have been sufficiently punished, Owen. I'll not add to it. Your brothers, however, will have to wait for theirs."

I remember Father tearing the sleeve off my shirt and tying the scrap of cloth tightly around my arm above the elbow to stop the bleeding, talking calmly all the while to the other boys, saying to them that, because they were my elders, he held them responsible for this injury, and they were only making it worse for themselves by lying about it now. He instructed Jason to bring him some kindling sticks for a splint from the woodbox inside and a sheet from one of the beds, and then he grasped my broken arm with both his powerful hands, and when he wrenched the bones back into alignment, the pain was too much for me to bear, and I lost consciousness.

I am recalling this event now with difficulty and almost as if it happened to another person, for it was so many years ago, and the crippled arm of the man I later became completely displaced the pain endured by the nine-year-old boy I was then. My arm did not heal straight and remained locked in a bent position, as you may have observed when we met, and all my life my left hand has worked more like a clever claw than as a proper match to its twin. It was indeed, just as Father said, my punishment. It was a permanent mark, an emblem, placed upon my body like the mark of Cain, which all could see and I myself would never be able to forget. So that, all my life, every time I reached out with both arms to pick up a lamb or shear a sheep, every time I laid a book on my lap and opened it, every time I sat down to eat or prepared to dress myself or tie my shoes or undertook some simple household task, I would remember not the pain of my fall and the long recovery and healing afterwards, but the fact of my having disobeyed and deceived Father.

It was the last time any of us sneaked out of the house on the Sabbath, although I suspect that years later, when the event had faded into family lore, some of the younger children, Salmon, Watson, and Oliver, took their Sabbath-day turn at chancing Father's wrath. We never spoke of it, but no doubt John and Jason were chastized severely with Father's leather strip. Although nearly as tall as Father, especially John, who turned thirteen that year, they were boys still and slender, and Father had no compunctions then about laying on the rod. I do know that for many weeks, while I carried my arm like a dead thing in a sling, they were made to do my chores, and long years later, whenever we worked alongside one another, they were still somewhat solicitous of me, as if they had retained a measure of guilt for my being crippled. I, of course, as I have done here, blamed only myself.

That was in New Richmond, but today I am reminded of an episode from those days in Hudson, Ohio, before we went to the Pennsylvania settlement. It was one of the few occasions when we boys managed to get the best of Father. John, Jason, and I stole some early cherries from the orchard of our Uncle Frederick, who lived nearby. It was done at John's instigation, of course—Jason, even as a boy, was unnaturally scrupulous about such things, and I, who was then about seven (Mother was still alive, I remember that, so I must have been seven), was always the follower of my elder brothers. One of the hired girls who lived and worked at Uncle Frederick's saw us stealing the cherries and reported it to her older sister, and together they marched straight to their employer and told him of our crime, exaggerating by tenfold the small quantity of cherries we had made off with.

After Uncle Frederick had taken the girls' information to Father, we received from Father a quick licking, which was appropriately perfunctory, considering the smallness of our crime, but it left us, especially John, feeling vengeful against the hired girls, whose names were

Sally and Annie Mulcahy, poor, orphaned Irish girls brought out west from the city of Pittsburgh. They were near our age, and I suppose we believed that they had betrayed us to the adults out of no more decent impulse than to advantage themselves at our expense.

Within hours of our licking, John had filched from the barn a small tin of cow-itch. You, a city woman, may never have heard of it, but "cow-itch" is the common name for a salve infused with the hairs of the cowhage plant, which hairs, applied to human skin, burrow into the skin at once, causing great pain for a long time, as if barbed needles had been thrust into the sufferer's nerves. It is excruciatingly painful against human skin and sears it for hours afterwards and cannot be washed or wiped off. We used it as a vermifuge against certain diseases of the skin of cattle and sheep. Father always kept a supply with him, for even when he traveled, he brought along a medicine kit for animals; if not for his own livestock, then for demonstration purposes, as Father was forever educating the farmers and cattlemen and sheepmen he met along the way.

That evening after supper, we sneaked over to Uncle Frederick's house and smeared the stuff liberally over the seats of the outhouse, which we knew was used strictly by the Mulcahy girls. They lived in an attic above the kitchen wing and had a separate entrance and staircase to their quarters. We had often noticed them coming and going early and late, and we knew that they usually visited the outhouse together, especially after dark. In fact, their practice, strange to us, had become something of a joke to Uncle Frederick and the rest of the family (not to Father, naturally, nor to Mother, both of whom disapproved of coarse humor). But Uncle Frederick liked to say that Sally Mulcahy couldn't do her business without Sister Annie along, and Annie couldn't do hers without Sister Sally. So far from home and living on the frontier among strangers, the girls were, of course, merely afraid and naturally shy.

None of that mattered to us, however. When we had finished our devious work, we hid in the bushes near the outhouse and waited for the results. Shortly before dark, the two girls came tripping down the outside stairs from their attic, crossed the back yard to the outhouse, and went inside. In less than a minute, one of the girls began to shriek. Then the other. "Something's bit me! Ow-w-w! Something's bit me!" cried Annie. "I'm afire!" her sister answered. "Me bottom's afire! Ow-w-w!" We, of course, thought the whole thing hilarious and could barely keep still or silent, while the girls howled in terrible pain. They ran from the outhouse, their skirts up and knickers down and their bright red fannies aflame. Laughing and clapping one another on the back, we three bad boys crept off through the underbrush to home, properly avenged.

It did not take long, however, for Uncle Frederick and Aunt Martha to conclude that their Irish girls had been victimized by none other than the Brown boys, who, in their view, were allowed by Father to run wild as Indians anyhow. Frederick, who was Father's younger brother and a deacon in the Congregational Church, was a shopkeeper in the town of Hudson. He was less rural and pious than Father, less withdrawn from the larger community, and despite his sometimes bawdy humor, he was a stern, demanding man. He and his wife, Martha, were childless and perhaps envied Father's much admired fruitfulness and thus thought him not as properly rigorous a parent as they themselves would have been, had the Lord blessed them in a similar way.

When Martha and Frederick brought their accusations of our "vicious, bad behavior" to Father, he agreed to punish us severely, but only if we were proven guilty by objective evidence or confession. To his credit, Father never simply sided with adults against children. And there being no objective evidence, no eye-witnesses, he needed a confession. Thus we were interrogated by him for several long hours that night. But we did not crack. We simply denied that we had been over at Uncle Frederick's house and claimed that we'd been hunting up a lost lamb at the time of the incident, and no amount of verbal rebuke or recrimination from Father made us back down. Secretly, we believed that we had been in the right and our lie was justifiable. Our earlier punishment for stealing the cherries had not fit the crime. Finally, Father seemed to give up and told us that we'd have to sleep in the haymow in the barn tonight. Not as punishment, he said, but as an opportunity to discuss amongst ourselves the wrongfulness of our act and the nasty work we were doing to our souls by refusing to confess it.

This was a ruse. The haymow, where we sometimes slept by choice on hot summer nights or for occasional mild punishment on cold nights, had a scuttle that led directly to the cattle stanchions below. We knew from past experience that a person could stand below the scuttle and hear every whispered word above: we had stood there ourselves and overheard conversations above that were presumed to be private, and Father had done it to us as well, repeating our overheard words back to us later as a joke.

We vowed, therefore, to be silent, and no sooner had we settled ourselves for sleep in the haymow than we heard the barn door below creak open and a few seconds later heard Father's breathing and now and then heard him shifting his weight at the lower end of the scuttle. For a long time, we listened to him, alert as deer. Suddenly, John got up from the hay where we lay and loudly announced, "I'll tell you, boys, if someone's standing down there at the bottom of the scuttle, he's going to get clubbed with this!" Whereupon, in a fury, he picked up a large chunk of wood, a heavy piece of a joist four or five feet long, and strode to the scuttle and without hesitation simply tossed it down the chute.

It was a startling thing to do! If it had hit Father, it might have killed him. But the Old Man must have jumped aside at the last second, for we heard the timber bang resoundingly against the floor below and, an instant later, heard the barn door open and then close, as Father tiptoed away. I remember lying up there in the hay for a long time afterwards, shaking with fear and biting off a sudden, inexplicable impulse to laugh aloud.

John was altogether silent and lay a ways apart from me and Jason, and, when Jason said, "What if you had hit him?" did not answer. Turning to me, Jason said, "You know, we're lucky it didn't hit him," and to my astonishment I found myself laughing loudly, wildly, almost crying. I rolled back in the hay and turned myself over and around, squirming like a snake, all the while laughing hilariously, as if a great joke had just been told me. And when at last the laughter stopped, and I lay still, I realized that I had wet myself. My trousers were soaked. Ashamed and miserable then, I crawled as far from my brothers in the haymow as I could get and curled up like a little animal in the far corner and lay awake for most of the rest of the night.

We had defeated Father, yes, indeed, but the event had terrified us. Or at least it had terrified me. As for my brothers, I cannot say. It was one of those things we never spoke about afterwards, even years later, when there was a second humorous event involving cow-itch, which with surprising pointedness, involved Father as well.

I wonder if I should tell it here, for it seems, except in my memory of the event, unrelated. Yet there is no more compelling principle of organization in this long telling than that of memory, and no other principle of selection than that of revealing to you what you cannot otherwise know. So, yes, I'll tell it here, and you can decide for yourself if you can take from it further understanding of my father and of me.

One night many years later than the event described above, when we were living in Springfield—in the fall of '47, it must have been, the year before Father made his first journey to North Elba—after several nights of listening to John preach the virtues of some of the newer sciences and health therapies, such as phrenology and Mesmerism, which he was then studying in a mail-order course from New York City, Father, who had been airily dismissive of all such notions, agreed to attend a demonstration by a well-known hypnotist, a Professor La Roy Sunderland. Coming from Father, this was a considerable and unexpected concession, and John was delighted by it.

Together, the three of us, Father, John, and I, marched off immediately after supper to the Palace Theater, where we took our seats as near to the front as possible. The Professor was an imposing figure of a man, with a flowing blond beard and a scarlet face and a grand, oratorical voice and manner. Most if not all of the people in the audience that night were true believers in the powers of hypnotism, so the Professor had the pleasure of speaking to the already converted, and his demonstration was laced with sarcastic, condescending references to those ignorant folks who, like Father, "preferred superstition to science." This did not sit well with Father, naturally, and he squirmed and muttered throughout, as the florid Professor, with charts of the brain and diagrams of nervous impulses and connectors, explained how hypnotism successfully blocked off pain and could be used wonderfully, if only people were sufficiently enlightened, in surgery and in the treatment of fractures and injuries.

He had many anecdotes to bolster his reasoning, and after a while, when he felt that his audience had been adequately instructed and prepared, he called for some volunteers, so as to demonstrate before our very eyes the power of this marvelous new science. Immediately, a halfdozen men and women, mostly young, left their seats in various sections of the auditorium and made their way to the stage.

"The man's a charlatan," Father grumbled in a low voice. "His 'volunteers' are no more genuine than play-actors."

"So why don't *you* volunteer, Father?" John suggested.

"I think I'll enjoy the show more from here, thank you."

"What about you, Owen?" John said.

"No," I said. "I'll just watch, and make up my mind later." I was shy about being seen up on a stage like that. Because of my arm, perhaps, but mainly because of an innate desire to blend in with the crowd and not seem showy or self-advertising. Besides, I did not particularly want to play a role in this ongoing quarrel between John and Father. It was their fight, not mine. For some years now, John had seemed intent on converting Father to his belief in "science" and "objectivity," which Father well knew was merely a covert way of arguing with him about the truth of the Bible and religion. I had long since decided to keep my apostasy as private as possible and never tried to defend it against Father's faith.

From his group of volunteers, Professor Sunderland selected the most attractive person, a buxom, fair-skinned young woman with brown hair wound neatly around her head, and drew her to the center of the stage. He asked her if she had ever been hypnotized before. She responded in the negative, and he said, "Excellent, excellent," and invited her to sit down on a stool that his assistant had placed there. When she was seated, he proceeded to wave his fingers lightly before her face and then asked her to count aloud backwards from ten. Before she reached five, she had ceased counting altogether and was gazing insensibly out at the audience.

"This lovely young lady," the Professor announced, "has not left us. She hears and understands my every word. She has, however, been rendered insensible to pain."

"Nonsense," Father muttered.

The Professor informed the young woman that she would not remember any of what was about to occur, that he would do nothing to harm her or anyone else, and he would not ask her to do or say anything that was morally repugnant to her. She gave no indication that she had heard or understood him but merely sat there on the stool with a small smile on her lips, as if she were remembering a pleasant incident from earlier in the day. She seemed quite peaceful and at rest.

At a gesture from the Professor, his assistant suddenly appeared beside him with a lit candle. "Extend your left hand, palm to the floor, please," the hypnotist said, and the woman instantly complied. When he brought the flame of the candle to within an inch of her palm, she showed no evidence of having felt its heat. For a long time, he held it there, before taking it away and handing it back to his assistant, retrieving this time a bit of ice. He told the woman to turn her hand over, which she did, and he placed the ice into her hand and closed her fingers over it. Her pleasantly calm expression and relaxed physical manner did not change; the cold bothered her no more than had the heat.

At this point, the Professor's assistant brought out a medium-sized anvil, an object he carried with obvious difficulty, due to its great weight, probably some seventy-five pounds. The hypnotist hefted the anvil, then passed it to one of the sturdy young men amongst the volunteers still on the stage, and noted that the young man had difficulty hefting it. "Is it genuine?" he asked the fellow, who grinned and said yes. "Our frail young woman," he said, "will handle this anvil as if it were made of paper. It will seem to her as light as a sack of feathers."

Suddenly, Father stood up and was calling out to the Professor. "Hold on there, mister! Just hold on a minute!"

"Sir?" The hypnotist was clearly startled and perhaps a little alarmed. Father's manner was severe, and he seemed, even to me, in a fume.

"The woman is insensible to pain, you say!"

"I do, indeed."

"Well, sir, I do not believe you or her! You have not sufficiently tested her, as far as I am concerned. I believe that I can make her *instantly* sensible to pain, if given the opportunity."

Professor Sunderland hesitated a moment, as if taking the measure of his opponent. Then he smiled politely and said, "Sir, you may yourself test the subject. But only if you yourself are willing to undergo the same test." The man had met this sort of challenge before.

Father, who had already moved from his seat to the aisle, stopped in his tracks. "Well, sir, *I* am not the one claiming to be insensible to pain. No one has waved his fingers before *me* and said abra-ca-dabra."

"To be sure. But to protect my subject from injury, I must insist that you yourself endure whatever pain you wish to test her with. How do you propose to test her, may I ask?" He smiled broadly at the audience.

Father would not back down. His face reddening noticeably, he made his way down to the front and mounted to the stage, where, to my surprise, he produced from his coat pocket two small vials. Then, turning to us, he announced that one of the vials contained ammonia, which he was sure would cause the girl to flinch and weep. In the other, he said, was a strong medicine known as cow-itch, which he was sure many in the audience were familiar with, although I suspected he was wrong on that. The ammonia alone, he said, would do the trick, and he uncorked the bottle and held it under the nose of the girl. He held it there for nearly a full minute, to be sure that she inhaled it. She made no response at all.

The crowd was delighted and applauded cheerfully.

"Ah, but now, sir," said the Professor, "*you* must undergo the same test."

Father said, "She may have held her breath."

"Try it again, if you wish. And hold it there as long as you like."

Again, Father held the ammonia below the girl's nostrils, this time for perhaps three minutes, while we all watched her face carefully for the slightest sign of discomfort. But it was as if the bottle were filled with fresh spring water.

Professor Sunderland finally reached forward and took the bottle from Father and gently turned Father to face the audience. "Now, my friend, let us see if you do indeed have ammonia here."

Father closed his eyes and faced squarely ahead. And when the Professor waved the vial under his nose, Father jerked his head back and visibly winced. The audience broke into loud laughter and applause.

"The woman has some ability to hide her reactions to strong smell," Father said. "Let me try her with the cow-itch."

"As you wish, sir," said the hypnotist.

With the corner of his handkerchief, Father applied a swab of the stuff to the girl's bare neck. She did not flinch or change her expression in the slightest. Father's shoulders sank.

"Well, my friend, may we test you the same way?" said the hypnotist. "You have the advantage of her, I notice, as a man apparently used to working outdoors in the sun." He crooked a finger over Father's collar and drew down his leather tie, exposing to the audience Father's dark red neck. "May I?" he politely asked, and took the handkerchief from Father's hand and rubbed it vigorously across the back of Father's neck.

The Old Man winced, but he did not otherwise reveal the awful pain that I knew he was experiencing and which was growing worse by the instant. Poor man. Along with everyone else in the audience, John was laughing loudly now, as Father struggled to maintain his composure and depart from the stage as swiftly as possible. Practically at a run, he came back up the aisle and, ignoring us as he passed, kept going, straight out the door.

"Should we go with him?" I whispered to John.

"Naw, he'll be fine," he said, grinning. "In a few days."

I departed from my seat then and followed the Old Man, feeling too much sympathy to leave him alone. I found him outside on the street, clawing in a frenzy at his collar, struggling to rub the stuff out, but only succeeding in driving it deeper into his flesh. I decided to say nothing and accompanied him all the way home in silence, hanging back a few steps while he stopped at nearly every light pole to rub the back of his neck violently against the cold metal like a poor, stricken beast. It was a pathetic and oddly moving sight, and I was as much fascinated and compelled to stare as I was embarrassed by Father's antics. I felt ashamed for looking at him. But how I enjoyed seeing Father suffer in public! And how, at the same time, I wished it had not happened at all.

These small stories which I have lately written out for you have drawn me back to the origins of our larger story, to the unknown parts of it, at least. And there is a particular, important book in our life as a family which you may not yet have come upon in your research. Half a century ago, it was very popular amongst the abolitionists. I have this morning retrieved it from the box of Father's books, which, as you know, remain, along with many of his letters, in my custody, and have been recalling the first time I read in it. The book is called *American Slavery as It Is: Testimony of a Thousand Witnesses*. I urge you to read aloud the portions of the book which I will copy out here below, so that you will have a more exact idea of how it was for us. We were seated around the fire in the kitchen fireplace of the old Haymaker Place in Hudson, Ohio, where we then lived. Father opened it to the first page and, with his voice very loud, commenced to read from it. After he had read for several moments, he passed the book to us and bade each in turn to read from it.

First, my stepmother Mary read, haltingly and sometimes stumbling over unfamiliar words, for she was not a skillful reader. Then my brother John, who was eighteen years of age that winter, rapidly read a page or two. And after him, Jason, who was seventeen, in a voice that was almost a whisper, took his place. Finally, the book came to me, and I began to read.

> We will, in the first place, prove by a cloud of witnesses that the
> slaves are whipped with such inhuman severity as to lacerate and
> mangle their flesh in the most shocking manner, leaving permanent

scars and ridges. After establishing this, we will present a mass of
testimony confirming a great variety of other tortures. The testimony, for
the most part, will be that of the slaveholders themselves, and in their
own chosen words. A large portion of it will be taken from the
advertisements, which they have published in their own newspapers,
describing their runaway slaves by the scars on their bodies made by the
whip. To copy these advertisements entire would require a great amount
of space and flood the reader with a vast mass of matter irrelevant to the
point before us; we shall therefore insert only so much of each as will
intelligibly set forth the precise point under consideration. In the column
following the word "WITNESS" will be found the name of the
individual, his place of residence, and the name and date of the paper in
which it appeared, and generally the place where it was published.
Following the identification of each witness will be an extract from the
advertisement containing his or her TESTIMONY. . . .

I stopped and looked up at Father, expecting him to reach forward
for the book. But he merely nodded for me to go on, and so I obeyed.

WITNESS: Mr. D. Judd, jailor, Davidson Co., Tenn., in the
"Nashville Banner," Dec. 10, 1838. TESTIMONY: "Committed to jail as
a runaway, a negro woman named Martha, 17 or 18 years of age, has
numerous scars of the whip on her back."

WITNESS: Mr. Robert Nicoll, Dauphin St., between Emmanuel
and Conception Sts., Mobile, Ala., in the "Mobile Commercial
Advertiser," Oct. 30, 1838. TESTIMONY: "Ten dollars reward for my
woman Siby, very much scarred about the neck and ears by whipping."

WITNESS: Mr. Bryant Johnson, Fort Valley, Houston Co., Ga., in
the "Standard of Union," Milledgeville, Ga., Oct. 2, 1838. TESTIMONY:
"Ranaway, a negro woman named Maria, some scars on her back
occasioned by the whip."

WITNESS: Mr. James T. De Jarnett, Vernon, Autauga Co., Ala., in the "Pensacola Gazette," July 14, 1838. TESTIMONY: "Stolen, a negro woman named Celia. On examining her back you will find marks caused by the whip."

WITNESS: Maurice Y. Garcia, sheriff of the County of Jefferson, La., in the "New Orleans Bee," Aug. 14, 1838. TESTIMONY: "Lodged in jail, a mulatto boy having large marks of the whip on his shoulders and other parts of his body."

WITNESS: R. J. Bland, sheriff of Claiborne Co., Miss., in the "Charleston (S.C.) Courier," Aug. 28, 1838. TESTIMONY: "Was committed to jail, a negro boy named Tom; is much marked with the whip."

WITNESS: Mr. James Noe, Red River Landing, La., in the "Sentinel," Vicksburg, Miss., Aug. 22, 1838. TESTIMONY: "Ranaway, a negro fellow named Dick—has many scars on his back from being whipped."

WITNESS: William Craze, jailor, Alexandria, La., in the "Planter's Intelligencer," Sept. 21, 1838. TESTIMONY: "Committed to jail, a negro slave—his back is very badly scarred."

WITNESS: James A. Rowland, jailor, Lumberton, N.C., in the "Fayetteville (N.C.) Observer," June 20, 1838. TESTIMONY: "Committed, a mulatto fellow—his back shows lasting impressions of the whip and leaves no doubt of his being a slave."

WITNESS: J. K. Roberts, sheriff, Blount Co., Ala., in the "Huntsville Democrat," Dec. 9, 1838. TESTIMONY: "Committed to jail, a negro man—his back much marked by the whip."

WITNESS: Mr. H. Varillat, No. 23 Girod St., New Orleans, La., in the "Commercial Bulletin," Aug. 27, 1838. TESTIMONY: "Ranaway, the

negro slave named Jupiter—has a fresh mark of a cowskin on one of his
cheeks."

WITNESS: Mr. Cornelius D. Tolin, Augusta, Ga., in the "Chronicle
Sentinel," Oct. 18, 1838. TESTIMONY: "Ranaway, a negro man named
Johnson—has a great many marks of the whip on his back."

Here, with trembling hand, I delivered the book across to Father,
who throughout had sat peering somberly into the fire that blazed in
the great open fireplace. He brought the book near to his face, as he customarily did, and in his reedy voice continued where I had left off.

The slaves are often branded with hot irons, pursued with firearms
and shot, hunted with dogs and torn by them, shockingly maimed with
knives, dirks, &c.; have their ears cut off, their eyes knocked out, their
bones dislocated and broken with bludgeons, their fingers and toes cut off,
their faces and other parts of their persons disfigured with scars and
gashes, besides those made with the lash.

We shall adopt, under this head, the same course as that pursued
under previous ones—first give the TESTIMONY of the slaveholders
themselves to the mutilations &c., by copying their own graphic
descriptions of them in advertisements published under their own names
and in newspapers published in the slave states and, generally, in their
own immediate vicinity. We shall, as heretofore, insert only so much of
each advertisement as will be necessary to make the point intelligible.

Father ceased to read, and we five sat for a moment in silence. All
the younger children were long asleep in the rooms above. Then Father
passed the book, still open at the page where he had left off, over to me,
and falling into the antique manner of speech that he sometimes used,
especially when overcome by emotion, he said, "Owen, thou hast still at
times the voice of a child. Read these words, so that we may better hear
in thy innocent voice their terrible, indicting evil."

Not fully understanding, I nonetheless obeyed, and read on.

WITNESS: *Mr. Micajah Ricks, Nash Co., N.C., in the Raleigh "Standard," July 18, 1838.* TESTIMONY: *"Ranaway, a negro woman and two children; a few days before she went off, I burnt her with a hot iron on the left side of her face; I tried to make the letter M."*

WITNESS: *Mr. Asa B. Metcalf, Adams Co., Miss., in the "Natchez Courier," June 15, 1832.* TESTIMONY: *"Ranaway, Mary, a black woman; has a scar on her back and right arm near the shoulder, caused by a rifle ball."*

WITNESS: *Mr. William Overstreet, Benton, Yazoo Co., Miss., in the "Lexington (Kentucky) Observer," July 22, 1838.* TESTIMONY: *"Ranaway, a negro man named Henry, his left eye out, some scars from a dirk on and under his left arm, and much scarred with the whip."*

WITNESS: *Mr. R. P. Carney, Clark Co., Ala., in the "Mobile Register," Dec. 22, 1832.* TESTIMONY: *"One hundred dollars reward for a negro fellow, Pompey, 40 years old; he is branded on the left jaw."*

WITNESS: *Mr. J. Guyler, Savannah, Ga., in the "Republican," April 12, 1837.* TESTIMONY: *"Ranaway, Laman, an old negro, grey, has only one eye."*

WITNESS: *J. A. Brown, jailor, Charleston, S.C., in the "Mercury," Jan. 12, 1837.* TESTIMONY: *"Committed to jail a negro man, has no toes on left foot."*

WITNESS: *Mr. J. Scrivener, Herring Bay, Anne Arundel Co., Md., in the "Annapolis Republican," April 18, 1837.* TESTIMONY: *"Ranaway, a negro man, Elijah; has a scar on his left cheek, apparently occasioned by a shot."*

WITNESS: *Madame Burvant, corner of Chartres and Toulouse Sts., New Orleans, in the "New Orleans Bee," Dec. 21, 1838.* TESTIMONY:

"Ranaway, a negro woman named Rachel; has lost all her toes except the large one."

WITNESS: Mr. O. W. Lains, in the "Helena (Ark.) Journal," June 1, 1833. TESTIMONY: *"Ranaway, Sam; he was shot a short time since through the hand and has several shots in his left arm and side."*

WITNESS: Mr. R. W. Sizer, in the "Grand Gulf (Miss.)," June 1, 1833. TESTIMONY: *"Ranaway, my negro man, Dennis; said negro has been shot in the left arm between the shoulder and elbow, which has paralyzed the hand."*

WITNESS: Mr. Nicholas Edmunds, in the "Petersburgh (Va.) Intelligencer," May 22, 1838. TESTIMONY: *"Ranaway, my negro man named Simon; he has been shot badly in the back and right arm."*

Long into the winter night I read, my voice breaking like glass at times, as it did then naturally, due to my youth, but more particularly because of the horrors that loomed before my eyes. My breath caught in my throat, my eyes watered over, my hands trembled, and it seemed that I could not go on saying the words that described such incredible cruelties. Yet I continued. It was as if I were merely the voice for all five of us seated together in that candlelit room before the fire, and we were together very like a single person—Father, Mary, John, Jason, and I, bound together by a vision of the charnel house of Negro slavery.

I said the words on the page before me, but I felt situated outside myself, huddled with the others, listening with them to the broken voice of a white boy reading from a terrible book in a farmhouse kitchen in the old Western Reserve of Ohio. Those cold, calm accounts from newspapers, those mild and dispassionate descriptions of floggings, torture, and maimings, of families torn asunder, of husbands sold off from wives, of children yanked from their mother's arms, of human beings treated as no rational man would treat his beasts of burden—they dissolved the differences of age and sex and temperament that separated the five of us into our individual selves and then welded us together as nothing before ever had. Not the deaths of infant children, not the long years of debt and poverty, not our religion, not our labor in the fields, not even the death of my mother, had so united us as our hushed reading, hour after hour, of that litany of suffering.

In my lifetime up to that point and for many years before, despite our earnest desires, especially Father's, all that we had shared as a family—birth, death, poverty, religion, and work—had proved incapable of making our blood ties mystical and transcendent. It took the sudden, unexpected sharing of a vision of the fate of our Negro brethren to do it. And though many times prior to that winter night we had obtained glimpses of their fate, through pamphlets and publications of the various anti-slavery societies and from the personal testimonies given at abolitionist meetings by Negro men and women who had themselves been slaves or by white people who had traveled into the stronghold of slavery and had witnessed firsthand the nature of the beast, we had never before seen it with such long clarity ourselves, stared at it as if the beast itself were here in our kitchen, writhing before us.

We saw it at once, and we saw it together, and we saw it for a long time. The vision was like a flame that melted us, and afterwards, when it finally cooled, we had been hardened into a new and unexpected shape. We had been re-cast as a single entity, and each one of us had been forged and hammered into an inseparable part of the whole.

At last, after I had recited the irrefutable and terrifyingly detailed rebuttals to the slavers' objections to the abolition of slavery—with Objection III, "Slaveholders Are Proverbial for Their Kindness, Hospitality, Benevolence, and Generosity"—I saw that I had come to the end of *Testimony of a Thousand Witnesses*. I closed the book on my lap. I remember that for a long time we remained silent.

Then slowly Father got up from his chair and placed a fresh log on the dying fire and stayed there, his back to us, his hands hanging loosely at his sides, and watched the flames blaze up. Without turning, he began to speak. He was at first calm and deliberate in speech, as was his habit, but gradually he warmed to the subject and began to sputter loudly, as he often did when excited by the meaning and implications of his words.

He reminded us of an event some two years past, when, in this same month of November, on learning of the assassination, in Alton, Illinois, of that holy man Elijah Lovejoy, Father had publically pledged his life to the overthrow of slavery. We all knew this. He had done it in church, and we and our neighbors had witnessed his pledge, and so had the Lord, who sees everything, Father declared. And we and the Lord had also seen that, since then, just as he had done all the long years of his life before making that pledge, Father had continued to be a weak and despicable man.

We said no, but he said yes and waved us off. The truth was that he had not made himself into the implacable foe of this crime against God and man which he had sworn publically to oppose. Then he said, "My children, the years of my life are passing swiftly." He fisted his hands and placed them before his eyes like a child about to weep. He said that while he had been idling selfishly and in sinful distraction, lured by his vanity and by pathetic dreams of wealth and fame, the slavers had dug in deeper all across the Southern states. They had spread out like foetid waters, flooding over the plains into Texas and the territories. They had steadily entrenched themselves in positions of power in Washington, until now the poor slaves could no longer even raise their voices to cry for help without being slain for it or being swiftly sold off into Alabama and Mississippi. Black heroes, and now and again a white man like Lovejoy, had risen in our midst and were everywhere being persecuted and even executed for their heroism, legally, by the people of these United States.

"My children," he said, "it's mobs that rule us now. And all the while Mister Garrison and his anti-slavery socialites bray and pray and keep their soft, pink hands clean. Politicians keep on politicking. For the businessmen it's business as usual: 'Sell us your cheap cotton, we'll sell you back iron chains for binding the slaves who pick it.'"

Father then cursed them; he cursed them all. And he cursed himself. For his weakness and his vanity, he said, "I curse myself."

He turned to us and now crossed his arms over his chest. His face was like a mask carved of wood by an Indian sachem. His eyes gazed sadly down at us through holes in the mask. It was the face of a man who had been gazing at fires, who had roused the attendants of the fires, serpents and demons hissing back at the man who had dared to swing open the iron door and peer inside. We all knew what Father had seen there. We had seen it, too. But he, due to his nature and characteristic desire, had gazed overlong and with too great a directness, and his gray eyes had been scorched by the sight.

I was a boy; I was frightened by my father's face. I remember recoiling from him, as if he himself were one of the guardian serpents. I remember Father looking straight into our eyes, burning us with his gaze, as he told us to hear him now. He had determined that he would henceforth put his sins of pride and vanity behind him. And he would go out from here and wage war on slavery. The time has come, he declared, and he wished to join the time in full cry. "And I mean to make war by force and arms!" he said. "Not such weak-kneed war as Mister Garrison is determined to make, he and that crowd of Boston, parlor-polite abolitionists. I mean to make the sort of war that was waged by the great Negroes, Cinque, Nat Turner, and L'Ouverture, and by the Roman slave Spartacus. I mean to make war in which the enemy is known and strictly named as such and is slain for his enmity to our cause."

He called us his children, even Mary, and said that the time for talk was past. The time for seeking the abolition of slavery by means of negotiations with Satan had always been long past. There never was such a time. Therefore, before us, his beloved family, before his wife and sons, and before God, he was making tonight his sacred pledge.

Here Father explained what we already knew, that he had long entertained such a purpose anyhow, despite his slackness and distraction, but that he now believed it was his duty, the utmost duty of his life, to devote himself to this purpose, and he wished us fully to understand this duty and its implications. Then, after spending considerable time in setting forth in most impressive language the hopeless and hideous condition of the slave, much of the details borrowed from our just-completed reading of Mr. Weld's *American Slavery as It Is*, Father seemed to have finished his declaration, when suddenly he asked us, "Which of you is willing to make common cause with me?" He looked from one face to the next. "Which of you, I want to know, is willing to do everything in your power to break the jaws of the wicked and pluck the spoil from Satan's teeth?" He put the question to us one by one. "Are you, Mary? John? Jason? Owen?"

My stepmother, my elder brothers, and I, we each of us in turn softly answered yes.

Whereupon Father kneeled down in prayer and bade us to do likewise. This position in prayer impressed me greatly, I remember, as it was the first time I had ever known him to assume it, for normally he remained standing in prayer, with his hands grasping a chair-back and his head merely lowered.

When he had finished the prayer, which was for guidance and protection in our new task, he stood, as did we, and he asked us to raise our right hands to him. He then administered to us an oath, which bound us to secrecy and total devotion to the purpose of fighting slavery by force and arms to the extent of our ability.

"We have thus now begun to wage *war!*" he declared. Although it seemed to me then, as it does now, so many years later, that he had already begun his war against slavery numerous times before this, here he was, in a sense beginning it again. And although I did not know it on that particular night, he would find himself obliged to bind himself to this sacred purpose many more times in the future as well. Father's repeated declarations of war against slavery, and his asking us to witness them, were his ongoing pronouncement of his lifelong intention and desire. It was how he renewed and created his future.

Tonight, however, was significantly different. This was the first time that he had determined forthrightly to take up arms and wage war by force. Also, and more importantly, perhaps, it was the first time that I myself was a part of his pledge, that we all were sworn together, bound by our war on slavery to see the end of it, or of us. The overthrow of slavery was no longer Father's private obsession. I had allowed him to make it mine as well.

3

There is something that I have always wanted to explain, because in the various considerations of Father's lifelong commitment to the overthrow of slavery, it has been much misunderstood. A great but little noted problem faced by Father throughout his life was his constantly divided mind. This division arose because, as much as he wished to be a warrior against slavery, he also wished to be, like most Americans, a man of means.

To be fair, it was a more basic and praiseworthy need than that. He had a large family, after all, and merely to house and feed and clothe them required enormous, sustained effort, especially if his only sources of income were his farm and his tannery. And by the time he had reached his mid-thirties, he was beginning to fear that, because of this requirement, he would always be a poor man with no time to wage war against slavery. His poverty, therefore, sabotaged his moral life. That is how it seemed to him. And that is what eventually led him down a path that very nearly did indeed sabotage his moral life.

Despite his having been poor and struggling since childhood, the Old Man himself dated the onset of his true financial woes to his thirty-ninth year, to the period of what he called his "extreme calamity." Father always believed that there were three ways to make money in America: manufacturing or growing things; buying things low; and selling things high. A man who did only one of these would forever remain poor. He had to do at least two of them: best if he did all three, but without capital to invest in large-scale manufacture, impossible. A farmer made things, as it were, and sold them; a tanner did the same. Father had tried making and selling for nearly two decades, but he was still poor and exhausted: the process of manufacturing food, livestock, or leather goods took too long and consumed all a man's days and nights, and thus he would never in his lifetime accumulate sufficient capital to manufacture steel, for instance, or some other item of great cost where the margins of profit were large enough to enrich him in his own time. He might turn to buying low and selling high, then. And what could be easily bought and rapidly sold by a man with little or no capital? Land. Hundreds of thousands, millions, of acres of loamy land rolling west from the Alleghenies all the way to the Mississippi and beyond. There was no greater or cheaper material resource available to an Ohio man in those days.

Inexpensive, arable land—it lay for miles all around him, and every month new immigrants from the crowded New England states and the eastern seaboard cities and even parts of Europe were pouring into the Western Reserve, bringing with them an insatiable hunger for farmland. They would also need new roads and canals to ship their produce east, new settlements and villages to reside and do business in, new schools and churches and public buildings to accommodate their expanding society. But before all else, they needed land, for they were mostly small farmers and young, and they brought with them or could easily borrow the necessary cash to buy it with. And in those years the bankers were eager to loan money with little or no collateral to secure it, for they well understood that a man who did not need that land for his own use, if he borrowed enough money to buy it first, could turn around and sell it for a higher price tomorrow, could pocket the difference, borrow more and buy more and sell that, too.

❏

Basically, that was how Father fell into debt—by following the advice of bankers—and afterwards no amount of time and energy spent at war against the slavers, no amount of preaching to his neighbors, and no amount of training and conditioning his large family to become an army for the Lord could keep his mind free of his terrible indebtedness. Thus his divided mind.

It was very complicated, how Father first got himself into debt and then proceeded to worsen his situation permanently, and as I was but a boy in my early and middle teens then, I did not much understand it. Besides, it was not then or ever Father's way to provide people with the details of his business matters, so that most of what I know I learned years later and gleaned from others. He could not keep everything from us, of course. Especially since we, his family, had so often to cover for him and over time were called upon to make so many material sacrifices that were a direct result of the Old Man's schemes. But I do not think that anyone—family member, friend, or business associate, or even Father's own lawyers, when later he was suing and being sued—knew all the facts of his financial dealings. He tended to give out partial or contradictory information and sometimes even false information, all designed, or so it seemed, to keep his interrogator from asking further questions, as if somewhere at the bottom there were a secret fraud, when in fact there was none—it was only Father who was being fooled, and for the most part fooled by himself. He was deceived by his desires, actually, which is why, when it all came crashing down on his head, he blamed his own greed and vanity.

Early on, his secrecy had sprung from an ingrained sense of decorum and desire for privacy. Then for many years, when he was in flight from bankruptcy and, later, from the consequences of bankruptcy itself, he probably felt that secrecy was necessary to protect his family and business associates. "A man who is wholly candid about his finances, who opens his ledgers to anyone who asks, such a man abandons his responsibility to others," Father insisted, although he had arrived at this philosophy by a somewhat circuitous route. It served him well in the end, however, and others also. After Kansas and Harpers Ferry—when what had originally been Yankee manners, and then self-interested necessity, had become military policy—these habits of secrecy and occasional dissembling protected many of the people who were his chief supporters, and they may well have even saved the lives of some good men, like Frederick Douglass and Dr. Howe and Frank Sanborn.

It started back in the middle '30s, after Father had closed down his tannery in New Richmond and returned to Hudson, Ohio, where, like so many other men of small money and big ideas, he got drawn into buying land and farms on easy credit and unsecured loans. Of course, with hindsight one can say that it was inevitable and hardly inexplicable, and having found himself dangerously overextended, he should simply have cut his losses and gotten out. But the Old Man, once he had determined that optimism was realism, could not be shaken from his course. After all, just take a look around, he would say in those early days of the land boom. All over the Western Reserve, men clearly less intelligent and hard-working than he were getting fabulously rich. Why not jump in himself? And why not bring in friends and family, too? Share the coming harvest.

At first, however, and for a long time, he successfully resisted the temptation to join the general run to speculate on land with borrowed money. That was when optimism was *not* realism; it was fantasy, or worse. He saw it then as a sickness, the mentality of a stampeding herd. And he justified his resistance, typically, on moral grounds, on principle, fortified by the Bible. As in Deuteronomy 15:6: *Thou shalt lend unto many nations, but thou shalt not borrow.* As in Proverbs 22:7: *The rich ruleth over the poor, and the borrower is servant to the lender.*

Later, when he began to borrow, it was on principle then, too. He borrowed everywhere from everyone—from his father and brothers in Akron, from rich men and poor, banks, friends, and strangers. He had a well-deserved reputation for probity and honesty, and so great was his belief in his ability to take the measure of land (a not altogether unfounded belief: though self-taught, he was a skillful surveyor and possessed a sensitive, knowing eye for good farmland) and so attractive a talker was he that, once he set his mind to make a purchase, it was not difficult for him to convince others to become his partners and to loan him the money for his share of the partnership as well. From this side of the fence, however, he took to citing Luke 14: 28–30—the story of the man who tried to build a tower and did not have sufficient material to finish it and was mocked by his neighbors. And 2 Kings 6:4–6—the story of the borrowed iron axe-head that fell into the water and was made to float and was not lost. And also, from 2 Kings 4:1–7—the story of Elisha's widowed daughter-in-law, whose sons were taken in bond by her creditors, so she borrowed many vessels from her neighbors, and the vessels were made to fill with oil, which were then sold to pay all her debts, even that for the borrowed vessels, freeing her sons and leaving the rest for her and her sons to live luxuriously on afterwards.

Sadly, Father's Bible failed to warn him that the newly elected President, Martin Van Buren, would abruptly establish the National Bank and change the lending rules, causing the famous Panic of '37. Thanks to Van Buren's National Bank, soon all the small-monied borrowing men like Father were left holding packets of worthless paper— piles of currency issued by the various states and high mountains of mortgaged titles to vast tracts of western land and farms that could be neither sold for one-tenth their costs nor rented for the interest due on the unsecured loans that had purchased them barely a year before. The lucky fellows and the bankers and politicians who understood the system and thus had been able to anticipate the sudden deflation of value that inevitably follows hard upon a speculative boom, those men sold off their properties early and high and walked away counting their profits. Within weeks, they were doing the President's bidding, calling in their neighbors' loans and hiring sheriffs to seize land, houses, livestock, and even the personal property of the foolishly stubborn men who persisted in believing that the decline was only a temporary aberration. For those men, men like John Brown, surveyor, tanner, and small-time stockman, the collapse of the land boom was catastrophic.

Thus, by the summer of '39, Father—who two years earlier had thought himself practically an Ohio land baron, who in his mind had laid out an entire town on five thousand mortgaged acres overlooking the Cuyahoga River, where he expected soon to see a government-financed canal that would be as enriching to him as the Erie had been to developers in western New York; a penniless man who owned title to two mortgaged farms he did not live on and one, the Haymaker Place, that he loved and hoped to make his family estate one day; a one-time tanner of hides raising thoroughbred horses and blooded Saxony sheep, who rode about like a squire in a carriage behind a matched pair of gray Narragansetts, all this on borrowed money—that man suddenly, inexplicably, found himself hounded by bondsmen, banks, process-servers, and sheriffs.

Bound as much by principle and Biblical text as when he had stayed out, Father with foolish consistency covered his borrowings with more borrowing and dropped deeper and deeper into debt. In '37 and '38, with everyone else rushing to sell short and salvage what little property he could, Father, almost alone, refused to get out. "This too shall pass, children, this too shall pass," he would say. "We must be patient." But all his promissory notes, which had been piled on top of one another even higher than any of us had imagined, were coming due. One by one, his titles began to be seized, titles that he had used to guarantee second loans, which afterwards he had used for the purchase of still other properties, until finally it began to look as though he would lose all his plots of land, his canal-side properties, also his carriage and Narragansetts and the blooded stock. Even the house we lived in, the Haymaker Place, was under siege, the sweet little farmstead that we older boys and Mary, sister Ruth, and the younger children had been managing well enough to keep the family adequately fed and clothed, while Father raced around the countryside frantically trying to keep his paper empire from being blown utterly away.

He was in those days more frightened than I had ever seen him before or afterwards. The growing violence of his words alarmed all who heard him, especially Mary and us children. The more frantic and frightened he became, the more reliant on his Bible for guidance and on his moral force for instruction he became, but now his discourse was a tangle of contradictory quotations and maxims that even he could not unravel. "This prolonged tribulation, if it be the will of Providence, must be endured with cheerfulness and true resignation," he instructed us. "We must try to trust in Him who is very gracious and full of compassion and of almighty power, for those that do not will be made ashamed. We must not be ashamed, children! Remember that Ezra, the prophet, when himself and the capitivity were in a strait, prayed and afflicted himself before God. So must we go and do likewise."

Thus, though we had come to dread the announcement of any new scheme or plan to make money and at last turn things around, it was with barely concealed relief that we greeted his decision to round up a herd of miscellaneous cattle from all over the county and drive it east to Connecticut, where there was a ready, cash-paying market operated by the agency of Wadsworth & Wells, a company that Father had dealt with successfully in the past. In short order, he managed to put together a sizeable herd of cows owned mostly by Grandfather and several of Father's friends, with seventeen head of our own, all but our last two milch cows. He drove his cattle aboard the barge at Ashtabula, and we waved him off and, when he was out of sight, happily embraced one another, glad to see him gone from us for a while, so that we could re-gather our wits and reclaim a shared sense of reality.

When he went east in '39, Father's real plan, which he did not reveal to those who had entrusted him with their cattle, was not merely to raise cash by selling livestock to Wadsworth & Wells, but also while there to negotiate still further loans in New York or, if necessary, up in Boston, to cover his growing losses back in Ohio. It took him only a few days to fail in New York; bankers there had already withdrawn all spec-ulative loans from the Western Reserve and were not about to risk more. Directly, he went on to tap the more deeply rooted money trees in Boston, and when he returned to complete his cattle-dealing in Hartford, although lugging an empty bucket, he was once again brightly optimistic. He never said who, but someone up there had allowed Father to believe that within a few days, a week at the most, of his return to Hartford, he would receive an unsecured loan of five thou-sand dollars. I suspect his supposed benefactor was a wealthy aboli-tionist like Mr. Stearns or even Dr. Howe, whose wife, the poet, was rumored to be an heiress, but it might have been a Yankee banker still looking to extract titles to western lands from a bumpkin in need, a rich man only temporarily deluded as to his own best interests by Father's enthusiasm, naïveté, and evident honesty.

Five thousand dollars. The figure is important. This was the amount for which Father had recently been sued by the Western Reserve Bank of Warren, Ohio, for having defaulted on several loans. Judgement had been found against him, and unable to pay even a por-tion of the debt, he was being threatened with outright bankruptcy or jail. At the last minute, an old friend from Akron, Mr. Amos Chamberlain, had kindly taken over the note for him. To guarantee *that* loan, the Old Man had written Mr. Chamberlain a note against the

Haymaker farm. What he did not tell Mr. Chamberlain or the Western Reserve Bank was that the Haymaker title had earlier been used to guarantee any number of additional loans of money for the purchase of other large plots of land along the Cuyahoga River. It had been done pursuant to the digging of the proposed Ohio-to-Pittsburgh canal, which, unfortunately, had ended up going in further west, near Cleveland. It was another of his schemes gone bad, still unpaid, and one of the bottom cards in Father's shaky house of cards.

A few days passed, and no money arrived from Boston. A week. Then another. Every few hours, Father walked from the office of Wadsworth & Wells, which he was using as his headquarters, to the post office, only to return empty-handed, puzzled, increasingly angered, and very frightened. At best, he would lose everything: the farm and livestock, the house and all its furnishings—everything! How would he feed his poor babies? How could he face his family and friends? Then sometime during the afternoon of June 14, 1839, Mr. Wadsworth went into the office of his company and discovered that the sum of five thousand dollars had been removed from the cash box. As the box was undamaged and still locked, he knew at once who had taken it. Besides Mr. Wadsworth and Mr. Wells, only Father, their trusted agent, who might now and then need a few dollars in order to help conduct their business, had a key.

I do not know what my father was thinking while he stood that day in the empty office, counting out the money. He could not possibly have gotten away with it. And the betrayal! He was almost a partner, a trusted confidant of Messrs. Wadsworth and Wells, their reliable procurer of western cattle, one of the most knowledgeable and honest stockmen they had ever worked with. He must have felt like a child who has long protected one lie with another and has woven an entire fabric of lies, laying one strand atop and under the other, and has come eventually to long for the truth to stand revealed, not because he loves the truth, but because exposure will bring an end to the agonizing labor of weaving a world of falsehoods. To get it over with, simply to make sense of his daily life, the child finally tells an utterly outrageous lie, one that cannot be believed. With a single lie, he overthrows the entire false world and reinstates the true. The theft from Wadsworth & Wells was like that, for nothing Father could say to explain it would be believed by them, and for a single moment, as he reached into the cash box and counted out the five thousand dollars, Father must have been that child. He closed the box and placed it back inside the cabinet and locked both.

At once, he sent the money off to his friend Mr. Chamberlain in Ohio, who would on receipt of it relinquish back to Father the title of the Haymaker Place. All was well again. Until, of course, later that evening, when Messrs. Wadsworth and Wells both presented themselves at the door of Father's room at his Lawrence Street boarding house. When they knocked, Father, in what he regarded as a remarkable coincidence, as if the Lord were introducing him back to himself, happened to be reading in his Bible, John, Chapter 10: *He that entereth not by the door into the sheepfold, but climbeth up some other way, the same is a thief and a robber.*

Mr. Wadsworth and Mr. Wells said that they had come to his chamber, not to accuse Mr. Brown of theft, but simply to ask into his use of the five thousand dollars. They thought that he must have needed it to make a large purchase for them, and they wished to know what it was.

He did not lie; he could not; he told them straight out: he had taken it for his own use. But it was only a temporary removal, he insisted, for he fully expected to receive the same amount in hours or, at the most, days, from a party up in Boston. This was true enough. And had he not at the same time believed that he was owed that much and more by Wadsworth & Wells, he said, money owed for the eventual sale of the cattle he had delivered to them from the west, he would have felt considerable anguish and remorse for having removed the money prematurely. But while he was truly ashamed of having gotten himself into a situation whereby he needed the money desperately and at once, he felt on the other hand no shame for having actually taken the money, no guilt.

Now, though he no longer owed five thousand dollars to his old friend Amos Chamberlain, he owed it instead to Wadsworth & Wells, who, with some justification, felt that while they may not have been exactly robbed of it, neither had they willingly loaned it. At that awful moment of his discovery, seated before his stern, skeptical discoverers, the Old Man had no choice but to comply with their demand that he sign over to them, contingent upon his return of their five thousand dollars, the one remaining property in his name, his beloved Haymaker Place, which sheltered his wife and children.

Meanwhile, the expected money from the mystery loaner in Boston did not materialize. I suspect that it had never been more than a mild promise merely to consider his request, but the Old Man, when he wanted, could make a polite rejection seem its opposite. They waited a week more, and finally Mr. Wadsworth declared that he and Mr. Wells would hold whatever monies they got for selling the herd of cattle against his eventual repayment of the money he owed them or until the sale of the Haymaker property. They had no way of knowing the true value of the farm, of course, or whether it had any prior liens on it, so they simply used the cattle as collateral. And they told him that, regretfully, they would no longer be able to rely on him as their western agent.

At that point, Father had no choice but to leave Hartford and make his somber way homeward. Thus he returned to us a humiliated man and poorer by far than when he had left to put his affairs at last in good order. Poorer, more desperate, and deeper in debt than ever, this time to men who, unlike Mr. Chamberlain, unlike Grandfather and our other relatives, friends, and neighbors back in Ohio, had no particular interest in protecting John Brown and his family. There was nothing for it then but a steady worsening of his affairs. Like Napoleon in Russia, he had advanced too far beyond his meager resources, so that he could no longer retreat back to a safe base, there to wait out the winter storms. Instead, he would have to slog and thrash his way forward, a blind man in a blizzard. And so he did for the rest of his life, dragging us along behind.

Back in Hudson, like a man switching a single pea beneath three shells, the Old Man managed to forestall disaster and hold on to the Haymaker Place a while longer, until the following year, the summer of '40. After much legal wrangling and suits and counter-suits leading all the way to the Ohio Supreme Court, a final judgement had been found. Bankruptcy was unavoidable. This time, all Father's debts were being called in, and his beloved old Haymaker Place had at last to be abandoned.

To his further horror, the original lien against the place had been called in by the bank and sold at auction, with Mr. Amos Chamberlain the eventual buyer, and the proceeds from the sale, once Father's loans from the bank were covered, were to be paid against the sum owed Wadsworth & Wells. Mr. Chamberlain, in what Father saw as an unforgiveable betrayal, had managed to find the cash to offer the bank eight thousand five hundred dollars for the place. "If the man had that sort of money," Father fumed, "he might've loaned it to me and let me keep the farm, so that I might feed my family!"

Blinded by his anger, Father was unable to accept the reality of the situation. He refused to turn the farm over to Mr. Chamberlain, and as a consequence, one warm day the county sheriff and his deputies came out to the farm to put us off it. The Old Man viewed the Haymaker Place as his last stand. "I *need* this farm! I must hold it and work here, if

I'm ever going to provide my creditors with their just due," he insisted. In recent months, he had abandoned all vain fantasies of spinning gold from straw and had wisely resumed tanning hides on the property, his most reliable means of support over the years, where his labor and skills and those of his sons were sufficient to turn a small profit. Thus he had come to imagine for the first time in years a realistic way of slowly working himself out of debt, one hard-earned dollar at a time. But he needed the house and its outbuildings and the stands of shag-bark hickory that surrounded the farm in order to accomplish it.

The prospect of losing the place put him into a mindless frenzy. "Boys, we will fight them to the death! A man must defend his property!" he declared to us that June morning. "It's an old story. If it can be made merely to *appear* that Naboth the Jezreelite has blasphemed God and the King, then it will be perfectly right and good for Ahab to possess his vineyard! So reasoned wicked men against Naboth thousands of years ago, boys, and so they reason against me today!"

We were all at midday dinner in the house, Oliver but a baby then, the kitchen full of babies, it seemed—Charles, who would die in the terrible winter of '43, and Salmon and Watson, and little Sarah, who was six and who would also die in that winter of '43. Fred, then a sweetly meditative child with none of his later turbulence, was nine; Ruth was but eleven and already performing the labors of a grown woman; and there was I, at sixteen, like a large, housebound dog, simple-mindedly excited by the loud, rough noise of Father's voice; and Jason, two years older, silently observing, placid, skeptical but loyal; and John, the eldest, eager to display his superior understanding of the situation and his willingness to stand fast with the Old Man.

Father's voice cracked and split in the fire of his feelings. "I warned them, I told them this morning at the bank, warned them straight out. I told them that I would shoot down their agents, if they came to take my home and land from me, and I swear, that's exactly what I will do! I wanted peace, but this . . . this A*hab*," he spat, "will not let me have it!"

Mary—I think of her now, but I did not think of her then—poor, distressed Mary, with all her small children to tend to, while her husband raged and his elder sons urged him on, must have desired then, as so many times before and later, all the way to the terrifying end days in Virginia, just to be rid of men altogether. She knew better than any of us that there was no way for our family to survive these difficult times except by means of patient, quiet application of our daily labors, and while the Old Man appeared often to agree, when he became frustrated or frightened he could not keep his anger or his fantasies leashed. And we older boys took our lessons from him.

Father loaded his musket and instructed John, Jason, and me to do the same. Then we four marched from the house down to the town road, where there was at the edge of the property an old, low log cabin built by the original Haymaker, which we used now as a storage shed for hickory bark and lumber. "Here we shall make our stand," he pronounced, and commanded us to spend our time fortifying the structure with whatever boards and timbers there were lying around. He had work at the tannery and at the house yet to finish, he said, and would protect the property from there. He ordered us to stay at the cabin night and day. Ruth or he himself would bring us food and fresh clothing. "And if the rascals show their faces, boys, fire once into the air to signal me, and I'll come a-running. They'll see then that we are serious about this!" he declared, and he was off, loping back up the slope to the house, leaving us alone in our outpost.

"Well, if the sheriff does show," Jason soberly said, "let's just be damned sure he knows we're only firing in the air."

John agreed. "That's all the Old Man wants anyhow." His voice had a quaver to it. "He knows that when they see we're serious about defending our home, they'll likely back off."

"Yeah, well, I'd like to make it count," I said. "I'd like to take one of them Ahabs down." I aimed my musket out the window of the cabin. "Just like that. Boom! Take down the chief. One shot, and the fight's over. That's how you do it, y' know."

"Don't be an idiot," John said. "Come on, give us a hand. We've got to turn this cabin into Father's idea of Ticonderoga."

"Or Zion," Jason added.

The afternoon of the first day passed quickly, and then Ruth brought us our supper, and darkness fell. We kept watch throughout the night and slept in four-hour shifts. The next day, we busied ourselves building a sort of palisado of old boards and odd-sized timbers around the front of the cabin, a peculiar-looking wall that seemed to have no military or domestic function, for it was incapable of keeping anyone out or in. It was more imagined than real, but the entire episode was more imagined than real.

Which made it perfect for me. I kept my musket close by while I worked, and every now and then dropped my work, grabbed up the gun, and, crouching low to the ground, aimed into the nearby bushes. "Boom! Got 'im! Victory for the Browns! Death to the invaders!"

By the end of the second day, we had grown bored and restless; even I. Father came down from the tannery, where he was hard at work filling orders for hides, and bucked us up, or at least me, with talk of bloody defiance, and then strode back to the house again. We were not altogether unhappy to be freed of our usual tasks at the tannery, but we were growing impatient for action.

Early the following morning, we were up and about the cabin, grumbling over the uselessness of our charge. "This whole affair is just another of the Old Man's damned fantasies," Jason said. He was lumped up in a corner of the cabin, sulking in his blanket. "I'll be glad when he gives it up. Even if it means we have to go back to scraping hides."

John, who was then a sometime student of business accounting and commerce in a school over in Akron, sat on the dirt floor by the window with a book in his lap, studying his lessons. "There's nothing to be done anyhow. The law's the law," John said without looking up. "The Old Man just takes a while to realize it. He'll come around eventually. He always does."

I stood at the open doorway, where, looking right, I could see along the broad road from Hudson, and, on the left, Father trudging down the lane from the house with our breakfast in a sack, hot corn bread, I hoped, and plum jam and boiled eggs. Father apparently had already been hard at work in the tannery, for, despite the morning coolness, he was not wearing his usual coat and shirt, only his red undershirt, with his trousers held up by wide suspenders.

He was fifty or sixty yards from the cabin, when I heard horses coming along the road and turned and saw a group of men approaching, three or four on horseback and several more in a light trap drawn by a pair of roans. One of the riders I recognized as the county sheriff, another as Mr. Chamberlain, the newly despised new owner of our farm. I also recognized several of the riders as Mr. Chamberlain's sons. The men in the trap I assumed were deputies. It was an impressive force, and they appeared well-armed.

Still some distance uphill from us, Father saw them, too. "Shoot them if they come off the road and step a single foot onto our land, boys!" he hollered, and I ducked into the cabin, where John was already scrambling for his musket.

Jason peered out the window that faced the road and said, "Oh, no. They've come." John and I swiftly stood side by side at the door and made our guns visible to the riders, who were now pulling up before the cabin and our rickety wall, although they were not yet on our land, so we were not obliged to shoot. Father, in his undershirt and galluses, was a ways off but coming on with purposeful stride and a steadily reddening face. He had no gun in hand, only our poor breakfast.

"Shoot that traitor Amos Chamberlain, shoot him first, boys!" he shouted. "He's the villainous one! Spare the others—they're just doing their legal duty!"

I took dead aim at the forehead of the bearded, bulky Mr. Chamberlain atop his chestnut stallion. Then I heard a rustling behind me and turned and saw Jason clambering out the rear window of the cabin. He had left his musket leaning against the wall. In a second, he was gone, disappeared into the heavy brush. "Jason's fled!" I whispered to John.

"He's not stupid," John said in a low voice, and I saw that my brother had lowered his musket and was standing forward in the portal. Then, with his gun pointed peacefully at the ground, he stepped outside the cabin and walked slowly towards the intruders.

Unsure of what to do now, I kept my gun trained on Mr. Chamberlain and looked to my left towards Father, as if for instructions. Up the sloping lane behind him, I could see my stepmother with the infant Peter in her arms and the seven younger children beside her on the wide porch of the white, two-storey house. Salmon and Watson were holding on to the dogs, and Ruth had in her hands a large wooden bowl. The unpainted barn and tannery shed and the sheep pens were off to the right of the house, with the vegetable garden on the left and then the apple orchard and Father's mulberry trees and the corn field further on. Rising slowly behind the house were wide rolling green meadows bordered by leafy oak and chestnut trees and our two remaining milch cows and the mares grazing in the shade by the stone wall at the near edge of the hickory forest. It truly was a lovely farm, the prettiest place we had ever lived in, Father's last remaining tie to an orderly life.

Slowly, I lowered my gun and stepped forward beside John, as Father came up, still holding the sack with our breakfast. I remember smelling the corn bread, stronger even than the smell of the sweating horses and men grouped before us.

"H'lo, Brown," the sheriff said, and he cleared his throat and spat a stream of tobacco. He was a tall, mustachioed man with a paunch the size of a wicker basket. "I guess you know why we're here. We don't need to have no trouble. This can all go peacefully."

"There'll be no peace in this place, so long as that man insists on taking my house and land!" Father said, pointing fiercely at Mr. Chamberlain, who puffed his considerable size up and chewed his thick lips in fury.

The sheriff went on calmly, as if Father had said nothing. "You got to give it over, Brown. Otherwise, I'm going to have to place you under arrest. The law is clear here, Brown. Any further quarrels about deeds or title you got with Mister Chamberlain here you can settle in court on your own later. Right now, though, the place and its contents is legally his. You and your family, you got to clear out."

"We will not leave our land!"

"It's not your land anymore, Brown!" Mr. Chamberlain shouted down.

"You won't pack up your family and personal household articles and go peacefully?" the sheriff said.

"He can't take no household articles!" Mr. Chamberlain cried. "They're all going to be auctioned off, soon's he clears out. He knows all this! He's just stalling till he can sneak off with property that isn't legally his no more."

"Be quiet, Amos," the sheriff said. "One more time, Brown. Make it easy on yourself and your family."

"In order to take my land," Father declared, lapsing, as he often did when his feelings were high, into Quaker speech, "thou must first squash me and mine beneath thy foot! I will not help thee in this heinous act!"

"Oh, dammit, then. You're under arrest, Mister Brown," the sheriff said, and he ordered Father to step up peacefully into the trap. "Don't make me put irons on you, Brown. This is a tough enough business as it is, putting folks off their land, without you making it any tougher."

Then, to my shock and sharp disappointment, Father's shoulders sagged. He meekly asked if he could first retrieve his shirt and coat and his Bible from the house.

"You let him back inside that house," Mr. Chamberlain warned, "he might decide to make a stand. There's no telling what he'll do to it. You've got him now, so take him in."

Father looked plaintive and hurt. "But I must have my coat and shirt. I am not properly dressed, sir. And my Bible. I need it."

The sheriff hesitated a few seconds, but then said, "No, c'mon, Brown. One of your boys here can bring your coat and so on, they can bring it to you later. I got to lock you up."

"A-hab." Father said the word slowly and gave it the shading of a curse. But all the force seemed to have gone out of him. He handed me the sack with our breakfast and slowly stepped up into the trap and took a seat behind the driver.

We stood there by our ramshackle wall, John and I, and watched the men ride off with their sad, slumped prisoner. He sat in the wagon in his red undershirt, miserable, humiliated, gazing back at us. I waved goodbye to him, but he made no sign.

Finally, when they had gone from sight, Jason stepped cautiously around the side of the cabin and came and joined us.

"Jason, you're a bloody coward!" I shouted at him.

"Sure. You bet I am."

John said, "Let it go, Owen. Jason did right. The Old Man had to lose this one. And he knew it. He was just blustering. He lost it way back. No sense making a fight over it now. They'll let him out by tomorrow morning, if not before."

"What's in the bag? Breakfast, I hope. I'm hungry as a hog," Jason said, and reached for the sack in my hand.

I jerked it away and then swung it at him, smacking him on the forehead.

"Hey, hey, hey!" John said. He took the bag from me, and the two of them walked slowly away, up the lane towards the house, dividing the johnnycake and boiled eggs between them, while I hung back, standing alone by the side of the road, fighting off a boy's angry tears.

But by the same afternoon, Father was back. He walked down the road and up the lane to the house, where, with as much dignity as he could muster in his undershirt, he somberly greeted us all around. Then he marched straight to the tannery, where he had hung his shirt and coat on a peg, and when he had decorously dressed himself in his accustomed clothing, as if preparing to go to church, he told us, in a somber, measured way, what had happened. The sheriff had delivered Father to the Akron jail, had even locked him inside a cell, but then had released him at once on his own recognizance, pledged to appear at trial later in the month. Mr. Chamberlain had agreed not to prosecute, so there would be no trial, as long as by that time we had departed from the farm with no more personal property than we were permitted under the bankruptcy proceedings. "We must obey the law, children. Hard as it is," he said.

"But we were supposed to take a stand!" I declared. "You said we'd stand and fight. I was willing to shoot the man down, Father. I was! I was all ready and had the man in my sights. Jason, he took off like a coward, but John and I—"

"Enough!" Father said. "I am a fool. That's all. It's *my* fault that we've come to this terrible a pass. If you want to shoot someone, Owen, shoot me." He placed a heavy hand on my shoulder, then removed it and walked ahead of us to the house, to sort and separate and inventory all our farm and household goods for the auction.

❑

Even today, so many years later, more than a whole lifetime later, I can recall every one of the items exempted from public auction. They were the articles that we carefully separated from the house and barn and put out onto the porch and yard and then packed into our wagon one by one, and later unpacked and packed again, over and over, hauling them through the next nine years by cart, canal boat, and on our own backs, from one temporary domicile to another, all the way to Springfield, Massachusetts, and eventually to the cold, hard hills of North Elba, where, at last, we set them down and they stayed put.

There at the Haymaker farm, I followed Father like a scribe from one end of the crowded porch to the other and across the front yard, writing in a tablet, while he strictly enumerated each of the articles and goods that the law permitted us to own and carry off. I made two copies of the list, one to be delivered to Mr. Chamberlain, signed by John Brown and notarized, and one for ourselves, which, for a long time, wherever we lived, Father kept posted on the kitchen wall, as if it were a reminder of his wealth, instead of his poverty.

For years, every morning, afternoon, and evening, we passed by this list, until it was engraved in our memories, like the books of the Bible or the names of the English kings. We older boys, especially Jason, could recite them like an alphabet, and often did, to the amusement of Mary and the younger children and to Father's slight consternation—although he surely saw the joke, for he could have removed the list from the wall at once, if he'd wanted.

10 Dining Plates
1 set of Cups & Saucers
1 set Teaspoons
2 Earthen Crocks
1 Pepper Mill
1 Cider Barrel

4 Wooden Pails
6 Bedsteads
1 Writing Desk
4 Blankets
1 Wash Tub
1 pr. Flat Irons

Also, these provisions:

1 bushel Dried Apples
20 bushels Corn
15 gals. Vinegar
8 bushels Potatoes
1 bushel Beans
20 gals. Soap
150 lbs. Pork
10 lbs. Sugar

These books:

11 Bibles & Testaments
1 vol. Beauties of the Bible
1 vol. Flint's Surveying
1 vol. Rush
1 vol. Church Members' Guide
36 Miscellaneous Works

These "articles and necessaries":

2 Mares
2 Halters

2 Hogs

19 Hens

1 Mattock

1 Pitchfork

1 Branding Iron

1 Handsaw

4 Old Axes

2 Beaming Knives

2 Roping Knives

2 Ink Stands

4 Slates

4 cords of Bark

2 Saddles

1 ton of Hay

19 Sheep pledged to S. Perkins

1 Shovel

1 Harrow

1 Plane

1 Log Chain

1 Crow Bar

2 Milch Cows

2 Hoes

1 Iron Wedge

1 pr. Sheep Shears

3 Pocket Knives

4 Muskets with Powder, Caps & Balls

And this clothing:

2 Overcoats

5 Coats

10 Vests

12 prs. Pantaloons

26 Shirts

10 Women's and Girls' Dresses

3 Skirts

2 Cloaks

4 Shawls

8 Women's and Children's Aprons

5 prs. Boots

3 prs. Shoes

13 prs. Socks & Stockings

7 Stocks & Handkerchiefs

4 Bonnets

1 Hat

5 Palmleaf Hats

8 Men's and Boys' Cloth Caps

1 Fur Cap

1 Leather Cap

Such were all the worldly goods of a farming family of thirteen people, and over the following years our inventory did not vary much, for we did not add to our property: that was quite impossible, except here and there, with the addition of a revolver, for instance, or a few more cows or hogs. We simply replaced what wore out or got eaten.

4

Certain things said and described in my last missive have prompted in me fresh thoughts and memories of how we as a family loved Father, and how I in particular loved him. But from the tender shape of your inquiry when we met, I deduce that you and Professor Villard believe my father to have been a great man. I'm not so sure I agree.

Perhaps my opinion on this question is of no account here, for I was never in a position to take his measure, except as his son. And maybe we mean different things by greatness. I wonder if you mean something more like fame. For me, Father could have been great without having been famous. Nonetheless, I can understand your position. You have a historian's perspective.

To you, it matters not that during his lifetime, like all abolitionists, Father was a much despised man, and that not just slaveholders hated him, but Whigs as much as Democrats; that he was hated by white people generally; and then, after Kansas and Harpers Ferry and during the Civil War years and beyond, even to today, that he was reviled by Southerners and Copperheads and even by many who had long supported the abolitionist cause, Republicans and the such. Nor, very probably, does it matter to you that he was also widely admired and even loved, loved passionately and almost universally by Negroes and by the more radical white abolitionists, and that he was celebrated and sung by all the most famous poets, writers, and philosophers here and abroad. What matters to you is that between those two extreme poles of opinion concerning John Brown, since December 12, 1859, every American man, woman, and child has held an opinion of his own. So, yes, Miss Mayo, if greatness is merely great fame and is defined by an ability to arouse strong feelings of an entire people for many generations, then Father, like Caesar, like Napoleon and Lincoln, was indeed a great man.

But who amongst your new, young historians and biographers, even amongst those who loathe him or think him mad, has considered the price paid for that sort of greatness by those of us who were his family? Those of us who neither examined him from a safe distance, as you do, nor stood demurely in his protective shadow, as we have so often been portrayed, but who lived every single day in the full glare of his light?

We were, after all, none of us dullards or witless. Every one of us Browns was of the energetic, sanguinary type, stubborn in thought and garrulous in speech. Why, even poor Fred, for all his innocent simplicity, when grown was a formidable figure of a man, independent and capable of astonishing acts: witness his bravery at the Battle of Black Jack in Kansas; witness his shocking self-mutilation. And both of Father's wives, my mother, Dianthe, and my stepmother, Mary, were willful, extremely capable women of considerable intelligence and sound judgement. How else could they have managed the hard life that Father imposed upon them?

We were not easily cowed or led. We rose early, worked hard, and talked constantly. We reacted intensely and elaborately to every person, idea, and opinion that passed into our ken, to everything that occurred in the private life of each member of the family and that we heard about in the larger world as well. Whatever passed for news in those days, especially if it in the slightest way concerned the slavery question, went discussed at our table and afterwards around the fire and while we rode into town for supplies and worked in the fields and tannery. We talked and talked and talked, and we argued with one another; even the smaller children, though they could barely form sentences yet, were encouraged to speak out on great topics and small. And at night in our beds, lying in the darkness of the loft, we continued talking, arguing, explaining, with lowered voices now, slower, rumbling towards sleep, one by one breaking off from the discussion of right and wrong, true and false, until one voice only remained, speculative, exploratory, tentative, and then, at long last, silence.

Only to be broken at first light, usually by Father at the bottom of the stairs, calling to begin the day: *Rise and shine, children! Rise and shine!* He'd already be up and dressed, with his Bible open on the table where he'd had his few moments of solitary study. And the round of the day would begin again, like a great wheel spinning, and its prime mover was not the sun—it only seemed so—but Father and his words and his bright, gray-eyed face. For, compared to the rest of us, no matter how hotly burned our individual flame, Father's was a conflagration. He burned and burned, ceaselessly, it seemed, and though we were sometimes scorched by his flame, we were seldom warmed by it.

True, I loved the man beyond measure. He shaped me and gave me a life that took on great meaning. Many was the time, however, when I grew angry and wished to flee from him and his harsh, demanding God. Yet I stayed. It's strange, but regardless of the pain and self-recrimination that my inability to worship Father's God caused me, during all those years when other young men were separating themselves off from their fathers and mothers and establishing their own households, often far away in the West, more than any other single thing, it may well have been my discomfiting apostasy itself that kept me at his side. I was not as intelligent or skilled as some of my brothers and sisters—as

Jason, for instance, who, besides being saintly in his moral sensitivity, was an almost preternaturally clever mechanic and agronomist. And compared to Ruth, whose emotions were consistently of an even and balanced nature, I was turbulent and changeable and sometimes truculent. Unlike the eldest of us, John, who had a deep, philosophical cast of mind, I seemed often shallow and merely pragmatic. Thus I was an ordinary fellow struggling with a tangled, profoundly conflicted set of views and feelings, and I came late, slowly, and only partially, and in fits and starts, to a clear understanding of the true nature of my relation to Father and to the family as a whole, and I just as often lost my grasp on the subject as I discovered it. I was like Jonah, it sometimes seemed, fleeing not God's wrath but His will and His fierce, irrefutable logic. I cannot speak for the others, of course, but we often had to console one another to keep ourselves from falling into despair because of having temporarily lost Father's approval. To a surprising degree, we who fell away from belief in Father's God were able to do so, perhaps were invited to do so, because we were stuck with Father himself for a God, and try as we might, we could no more escape our god than he could his. Especially I.

It is ironic, then, that Father regarded as his supreme failure his inability to bring all of us children to share his belief. We were godly enough in our comportment; we were pious. But we would not believe. Even some of his daughters, as they became adults, would not believe. Although, unlike us boys, they did not think they should tell him of it. Perhaps because they were women and had more faith than we males in the usefulness of secrecy and decorum, perhaps because they were kinder than we—regardless, for all of us, it was as if Father's own light burned so brightly that it eclipsed the Sun that shone on him. Thus it came to seem to us that it shone on him alone. And because from him we received only reflected light, as from the moon, we were not always so much warmed by it as merely illuminated.

❏

There did come a time, however, when I arrived at an understanding and got a glimpse of the cost of the only path through life that was not revealed to us solely by Father's light. It was in the fall of '46, I remember, and Father was out east alone, in Springfield, establishing his warehousing scheme for Mr. Simon Perkins, of whom you have no doubt already heard. We were then living on Mr. Perkins's farm in Akron, not as servants, exactly, but at his sufferance, which Father preferred to think of as a partnership.

Ruth was seventeen years old that fall, a blooming young woman whose sprightly company was much sought after by the young fellows in the neighborhood, for her good sense, her good humor, and her broad-faced good looks. Not including Fred, who was sixteen years old and more or less looked after himself, there were six young children then at home—the youngest being Amelia, or Kitty, as we called her, who was barely one year old. Consequently, Ruth was obliged to be constantly at work with Mary, caring for the younger children and managing the house. Oliver was only six years old, but the other boys, Salmon, Watson, and Fred, were, like me, tending Mr. Perkins's—and, as Father would have it, John Brown's—large flock of sheep and running the farm. Mutton Hill was our affectionate name for the place, and an appropriate one, for Mr. Perkins's flock numbered close to two hundred at that time.

All told, it was not a difficult operation, but there was no leisure time for any of us, a lack that was probably felt more by poor Ruth than by anyone else, due to her oncoming young womanhood and the presence there in Akron of a lively community of young men and women her age, all of them scouting and reconnoitering each other with the intensity and restlessness typical of rural youth in the throes of first rut. Despite her high spirits, Ruth was, as always, singularly pious and virtuous, but that did not mean she was not as moody and distracted as the other boys and girls of her acquaintance. Perhaps, because of her piety and virtue, she was even more agitated than the others. But who can say? I'm probably thinking of how I myself was at that age; I know next to nothing of what females experience.

Even so, I remember her seeming sometimes to smile absently and day-dream her way through those long, darkening fall afternoons and in the evenings to sigh a lot, letting loose with plaintive exhalations, as if pining for a lover far away. She had no lover, of course; and no one special was courting her then. But she was on occasion uncharacteristically withdrawn and thoughtful that summer and fall and was noticeably awkward at times, which was unusual enough for us to comment on, and when she bumped her head or stumbled over a doorstoop, we teased her for it.

I have been unfortunately blessed by having been placed in my life so as to witness firsthand most of the tragic and painful events that have afflicted my family, and thus have been too often obliged to carry the sad news to the others. This is no complaint, but there was a peculiar loneliness to the task, for neither was I the victim nor was I permitted to fall down in the dust and grieve: I had to speak as if I had no pain. For most of my life, it seems, that is how I was forced to speak. Perhaps that is why, when I grew older and the great events that marked our family were in the past, I withdrew to my mountain in California and remained silent altogether; and why now, when I know that I will never again have to witness the suffering of my loved ones, for they have all died or grown old themselves, I am compelled to tell so much.

On the occasion of which I speak here, I was obliged to write Father a terrible letter. I cannot now say exactly why I was chosen, but John and Jason were living apart from us for the first time, and there was no other adult at home then, except for Mary, whose letter-writing skills were not so developed as mine, and Ruth, who, as a principal in the awful news I was obliged to transmit, had been rendered incapable of speaking for herself, either in a letter or in person. *Dear Father,* I wrote with trembling hand. *I do not know how to begin, for I must write to you of a dreadful event which occurred here the evening before last.* Mary was upstairs in the girls' bedroom with three-year-old Annie, who had been feeling poorly all day and appeared to be coming down with the croup, which had almost taken her off the previous spring, so it was an occasion for some alarm. I heard Mary's footsteps overhead as she walked back and forth in the bedroom, from Annie's small bed to the nightstand and dresser, easing the child into bed and towards sleep. Oliver and Salmon were in the second bedroom, the loft where we boys slept, practicing the wrestling holds that I had taught them earlier that summer, making their usual grunting sounds, as if they were ancient Greeks in an arena instead of little American boys grappling on the floor and colliding with the homemade furniture of a farmhouse bedroom. Watson was up there with them, seated on one of the beds, no doubt, instructing his younger brothers and criticizing their lack of wrestling skills. Fred and I were in the parlor, off the kitchen, where he sat by the front window, talking through the glass to the two little collies outside, who leapt about and barked at the sight of his friendly face, hoping to be let in where it was warm and where all their people had gone.

Having just set and lit the evening fire, I was seated next to it and, as I had made a trip that afternoon into town for feed and some nails, was preparing to enter into the account book the day's expenses. Mr. Perkins was responsible for all costs associated with the keeping of the flock, and thus we kept scrupulous track of our expenses. *I would have written to you at once, but there has been no time for it until now. Our little Kitty has died, a painful & tragic death with much suffering that thankfully she did not have to long endure.* From where I sat, I could see around the corner the tin bathtub on the floor of the kitchen. The kitchen stove, however, was out of my line of sight, as were Ruth and the baby, Kitty, whom I could hear gurgling and burbling over one of the house cats. Ruth was silent. Perhaps she, like Fred in the parlor, was looking out her window in the kitchen, looking not at the dogs begging Fred to let them come inside but at some imagined young man strolling down the pathway from the road from town, a beau come to call, a sweetheart of her own venturing forth to meet her large, boisterous, somewhat notorious family in the absence of the stern, demanding father, hoping to befriend the brothers and talk politely and deferentially to the woman of the house, so that when the father returned they would all speak well of the young man, and the father would then allow his eldest daughter to go walking with him. *Kitty's untimely death was the result of a simple, blameless accident. It was in the evening about 7 o'clock & Ruth was heating water, so that the little children could bathe; and due to some business about the house, what with the usual commotion of the children & cooking supper, the water heated to a boil, and when Ruth ran to fetch the pot from the stove, she did not realize it was so hot & as a result she dropped it; & the boiling water splashed all over little Kitty, who was standing naked next to her waiting for her bath, and who evidently swallowed a great gulp of it when it spilled over her body, which was a mercy, for otherwise she would not have died so swiftly and would have lingered in terrible pain.* I heard a horrible yowl, the cry of a wild animal, not that of a human being, and not so much a cry of pain as an enraged, savage shriek. That was the last utterance made by our baby sister Kitty, who had just begun to walk and say our names in ways that made us laugh and re-name ourselves, a blond, pink-skinned, robust child, made suddenly monstrous by her wild, final howl.

And then, just as suddenly, there was silence in the whole house. *It was a terrible scene, Father, as you can no doubt imagine, horrible to us all; & especially to poor Ruth, who is suffering from unspeakable guilt & remorse. She has shut herself away from the rest of us, & weeps constantly, & when she does speak, it is to beg for forgiveness, especially of Mary, who is seriously shaken from the incident but asks me to say to you that she trusts in God and knows that Kitty is in heaven with Him.* The silence may have lasted no more than a second, but it seemed to go on for a long while, before Ruth began to moan, "Oh-h-h, oh-h-h . . . ," a moan that, in contrast to Kitty's howl, was purely, uniquely, pathetically human, a noise that is made by no creature but one who has been the direct cause of the death of a child.

Without having observed anything of the accident, except for the steaming skin of water that spread slowly across the floor towards the empty tin bathtub, I knew at once what had happened. And I believe that Fred knew, too, for we looked at one another for an instant, and his eyes were filled with unutterable sorrow. *Ruth begged me at first not to write to you, so that she could be the one to bear this burden; but then said that she could not do it. So I have done it.* By the time I reached the kitchen, Mary had come down the stairs, her face white with knowledge of what had already happened, and we saw Ruth standing in the far corner of the room with the scarlet body of the baby in her arms. The large black kettle, like a head with a gaping mouth, lay on its side on the floor next to the stove, the spilled, translucent water a carpet of snakes spreading around table legs and chairs.

Ruth's eyes had rolled back, and she was making a guttural noise now, as if she were choking. The baby had already died. Its scalded, bright red body was emptied of spirit. It was a thing, a tiny, shriveled sack, and its small soul was bouncing wildly around the room near the ceiling, like a maddened, dying moth, a bit of quickly diminishing light. I held Mary by her shoulders, and together we approached Ruth, and very gently Mary reached out and took the body of her baby from her stepdaughter, turned, and walked away from us into the parlor, past poor Fred, who stood at the door with his hands over his ears, as if he still heard the baby's howl. Silently, I came and stood before Ruth and held her in my arms, but she was insensible of my presence and went on making a choking noise, her head tilted back, eyes whitened and unseeing, as if she had fallen into a deep trance. *She needs to hear from you, Father, the same as she has heard from Mary & me (& from John & Jason as well, for they have come down from Ashtabula). She needs to hear that you do not blame her for the death of Kitty. She blames herself more than enough for any of us to add a word. I tell you, it was not Ruth's fault. She will never see it that way herself, however. It was a simple accident, & any one of us could have been the agency for it to happen as easily as was poor Ruth.* Mary dressed the body of the child in a tiny flannel nightgown, wrapped it in a blanket, as if preparing it for sleep, and that same night I went into the barn, and as Father himself had done only a few years before, in that terrible winter of '43, when four of his children sickened one by one and died, I built for the first time in my life a small pine coffin.

The boys, not knowing what else to do, followed me out to the barn and in the dim lantern light watched me in silence, as I had watched Father, the four of them standing there like somber acolytes, learning how to cut the boards to the correct size for the body of a child, so that the coffin would hold the child snugly, without confining it or bending it out of its natural shape, watching me carefully plane and fit the boards neatly together and drive the nails without damaging the wood and hinge the cover and latch it. *We have buried little Kitty out behind the house, near where you planted the crab-apple trees last spring, & I am making a proper marker for her that will say her dates and name, & any little motto, if you wish one for her. Mr. and Mrs. Perkins have been a great comfort to Mary & to the rest of us, & Mrs. Perkins has taken Annie & Oliver over to the big house for the time being, to make things easier for Mary; & many other local folks have come to the house with condolences & sympathy.* At the burial, I touched Ruth on the cheek with the fingertips of my right hand and put my claw of a left hand around her back and drew my sister close to me, as if to take into myself her grief and to share with her the shame she felt. The others at the graveside, our friends and neighbors, looked at us, and I was glad of that, for I wished them to see that all of us Browns were equally to blame for the death of our Kitty and that, therefore, no single one of us was to blame. *I am sorry, Father, to be bringing you such terrible news. I hope that the business is going well. No particular problems with the flocks or the farm here. Your loving son,*

Owen Brown

It was not until nearly a fortnight had passed that we heard from Father at last. Due to the inescapable daily requirements of our livestock and the farm, which honor no human tragedy, the life of the family had resumed its old patterns and routines and had connected back to its various larger cycles by then; and even Ruth had made a few tentative steps back into the fold, as it were, although she was a much altered young woman. She had become the sober, even melancholy woman that she would remain for most of her life thereafter, even during her happiest years, when she and Henry Thompson were courting up in North Elba and in the first year of their marriage, before Henry rode off with us to Kansas.

Father's letter, arriving as it did after we had already commenced to accommodate our lives and feelings as best we could to the death of Kitty, was painful to read aloud, as was our custom with all his letters, and, later on, difficult for me to copy, as per his instructions, for Father had long since told us to be sure that all his letters were copied and saved, and as I had the best handwriting of any in the family at that time, the task usually fell to me. *My dear afflicted Wife & Children,* he wrote, and I wrote after him. *I yesterday at night returned after an absence of several days from this place & am utterly unable to give any expression of my feelings on hearing of the dreadful news contained in Owen's letter of the 30th and Mr. Perkins's of the 31st Oct. I seem to be struck almost dumb.* Not likely, I thought. For I was angry at Father, not so much for his letter, which was about all he could have said under the circumstances and which was very much in his usual voice. I suppose I was angry at his not being present when we all, and especially Ruth, suffered from the death of little Kitty, so that not only did we have to endure the horror and pain of that event alone but we had to report it to him as well—for his judgement, his huge perspective, his words of beneficence or condemnation, as if he were some lord high sheriff and we were his serfs who had to account for the loss of one of our number—without mentioning in our account that she whom we had lost was an especially beloved child, without mentioning that the awful conditions of her death had inflicted lifelong pain and shame in the heart of one of us in particular.

None of this, of course, was Father's fault; yet that did not hinder my anger, as I copied his letter into the green school notebook used for the purpose. *One more dear, feeble child am I to meet no more till the dead, small & great, shall stand before God. This is a bitter cup, children, but a cup blessed by God: a brighter day shall dawn; & let us not sorrow, like those who have no hope. Oh, if only we who remain had wisdom wisely to consider & to keep in view our latter end.* This, I knew, was a pointed reference to me and to John and Jason, for surely we were the ones who were obliged to "sorrow like those who have no hope" of ever being amongst the small and great standing before God. Our sorrow, mine and my brothers', was the greater, Father implied, because as unbelievers we believed that we would not see poor Kitty again, and that was too bad, just too bad, and nobody's fault but our own. According to Father, the brighter day was not ours to believe in, and thus we had no wisdom wisely to consider.

In normal circumstances, this difference between us and Father did not create any painful conflict; but when we, too, were suffering, when we ourselves were grieving, it only angered us that he regarded the ragged edge of our pain as merely a consequence of our moral failings. There was no telling him of this, however.

Oh, we could tell him of it, yes; but he could not hear us, his own belief was so powerful, so constantly clanging in his ears: with all those hosannas, halleluiahs, and simple hoo-rahs he was hearing, it was to his large, hairy ears as if nothing but a serpent's hiss were coming from our mouths. *Divine Providence seems to lay a heavy burden & responsibility on you in particular, my dear Mary; but I trust that you will be enabled to bear it in some measure, as you ought. I exceedingly regret that I am unable to return & be present to share your trials with you; but anxious as I am to be once more at home, I do not feel at liberty to return to Akron yet. I hope to be able to get away before very long; but cannot say when.* These words I could barely transcribe without breaking off the point of my pen, and the tension in my hand caused me to spatter the paper with several ugly blots of ink. But he was not through. *I trust that none of you will feel disposed to cast an unreasonable blame on my dear Ruth on account of the dreadful trial we are called to suffer; for if the want of proper care in each & all of us has not been attended with fatal consequences, it is no thanks to us.* With a cold fury in my heart, though I said nothing of it to anyone, I saw that Father could forgive Ruth only by including the rest of us in her blame, which, of course, allowed him to forgive no one. As he saw it, not just Ruth, but we, all of us, were guilty of wanting proper care, so that it was only the Lord's will that had kept the rest of us from the fatal consequences of our sloth and inattention.

If I had a right sense of my habitual neglect of my family's Eternal inter-ests, I should probably go crazy from shame, he said, and I transcribed. And as he had apparently not gone crazy, were we to assume then that he did *not* have a right sense of his habitual neglect of his family's Eternal interests? Was that his point? Or was he merely changing the subject, at which he was so skilled, in order to invite us to reassure *him*, to praise him, to be thankful that he was out there in Springfield looking after his family's temporal, rather than Eternal, interests? *I humbly hope that this dreadful, afflictive Providence will lead us all more properly to appreciate the amazing, unforeseen, untold consequences that hang upon the right or*

wrong doing of things seemingly of trifling account. Who can tell or compre-
hend the vast results for good or evil that are to follow the saying of one little
word? Everything worthy of being done at all is worthy of being done in good
earnest & in the best possible manner. Not that again, I said to myself and
dutifully wrote his words into the tablet as if they were my own. Not
more platitudes and maxims, not more of Ben Franklin's rules for living. *We are in middling health, & expect to write to some of you again soon.*
Our warmest thanks to Mr. & Mrs. Perkins & family. From your affectionate
husband, & father,

John Brown

When I had finished transcribing the letter, I put the tablet away in
the folder where we kept his papers, and we none of us read or spoke of
the letter again. It was odd, for we had suffered numerous deaths in the
family by then, and each of them had drawn us closer together; but the
death of little Kitty caused me, and I think the rest of us as well, to withdraw ourselves from Father to a greater degree than any previous event
or circumstance. Of course, here and there, now and again, one or the
other of us had gone through a period of withdrawal from intimacy
with Father, but it was almost always a solitary act, a brief and lonely
rebellion. But on the occasion of Kitty's death, we all as a group
rebelled, even including Mary, and shut Father away from our feelings
and conversations with one another for many weeks afterwards.

I believe that I learned then for the first time that it was possible to
oppose Father, to swell with anger against him and to walk away from
his sputterings and recriminations, without any terrible cost to my
own sense of worth as a man and without the crippling loneliness that
I usually associated with opposing him. But I could not do it until the
rest of the family marched with me. The awful irony is that we could
never march against him unless one of us was capable of sacrificing
another of us beforehand—as Ruth had sacrificed the baby Amelia, lit-

tle Kitty. Only then could we stand against him and say to him, "Father, you do not understand."

Yesterday, while searching through my cache of Father's papers for the letters concerning the death of poor Kitty, I happened onto another long-forgotten transcription, which I am sure you have not read and which will show you an aspect of Father's character that may surprise and even amuse you. It may also give you some further insight into the true nature of my relationship with Father, so that later, when I have told everything, you will believe me.

The document of which I speak, when it came to my hand, caused me unexpectedly to think back to the time when Father corked his face, as it were, and actually tried to pass himself off as a Negro. It was an audacious thing, but he was fully aware of that and did it anyhow. His ostensible purpose was to instruct and warn. He had carefully composed an essay entitled "Sambo's Mistakes," which he read many times over to any of us who would listen and after much hesitation finally submitted anonymously to the Negro editors of the *Ram's Horn*, in Brooklyn, New York. It was not published, probably because it was seen for what it was—a white man in blackface telling Negroes how to behave. The rejection of his little essay infuriated Father, for he believed that he was saying things to Negroes that they ought to hear and rarely did, except when he himself told them in meetings or when invited to speak to the congregations of Negro churches. He explained that he had chosen to speak as Sambo because when he said these things to Negroes in whiteface, he was perceived strictly as a white man and thus was not truly heard. "Racialism infects everybody's ears," he said. "Negro ears as much as white."

This was in the winter of '48, after we had left Akron and were newly settled in Springfield, and I found the whole thing somewhat embarrassing then, although later on I came to see that in a sense, perhaps subconsciously, Father was advising and correcting himself as much as his Negro brethren. He was speaking his little narrative, in spite of his intentions to disguise himself, with his own genuine voice quite as much as when he wrote letters home and advised and corrected us. This may be of interest to you, for you were born long after Father's death and can have no idea of how he sounded in actual conversation. Father's voice, including his grammar and choice of words and his pacing, was more or less the same whether spoken aloud or written down on paper. It was uniquely his own—although I was often told that I myself spoke very much like him.

Earlier today, I carried Father's original manuscript of "Sambo's Mistakes," from which I had made the "official" copy that he submitted to the *Ram's Horn*, outside my cabin and read it in the dying light of day. It is perhaps the nearness of our voices, his and mine, that enabled me to recall his voice exactly when I read through this composition, for I could hear him speaking to me quite as if he were seated next to me on the stoop, the ink on the paper barely dry.

"Tell me truthfully, Owen," he said, "if you think I have left anything of use and importance out. And note any particular infelicities of language, son, if you will." And then he began to read "Sambo's Mistakes" aloud, very slowly, savoring all the words as if they were great poetry.

> Notwithstanding that I have committed a few mistakes in the course of a long life like others of my colored brethren, you will perceive at a glance that I have always been remarkable for a seasonable discovery of my errors and my quick perception of the true course. I propose to give you a few illustrations in this and the following paragraphs.
>
> For instance, when I was a boy I learned to read, but instead of giving my attention to sacred and profane history, by which I might have become acquainted with the true character of God and man, learned the

best course for individuals, societies, and nations to pursue, stored my mind with an endless variety of rational and practical ideas, profited by the experience of millions of others of all ages, fitted myself for the most important stations in life, and fortified my mind with the best and wisest resolutions and noblest sentiments and motives, I have instead spent my whole life devouring silly novels and other miserable trash such as most newspapers of the day and other popular writings are filled with, thereby unfitting myself for the realities of life and acquiring a taste for nonsense and low wit, so that I have no relish for sober truth, useful knowledge, or practical wisdom. By this means I have passed through life without profit to myself or others, a mere blank on which nothing worth perusing is written.

But I can see in a twink where I missed it.

Another error into which I fell early in life was the notion that chewing and smoking tobacco would make a man of me but little inferior to some of the whites. The money I spent in this way, with the interest of it, would have enabled me to have relieved a great many sufferers, supplied me with a well-selected interesting library, and paid for a good farm for the support and comfort of my old age; whereas I now have neither books, clothing, the satisfaction of having benefited others, nor a place to lay my hoary head.

However, I can see in a moment where I missed it.

One of the further errors of my life is that I have imitated frivolous whites by joining the Free Masons, Odd Fellows, Sons of Temperance, and a score of other secret societies and chapters established by and for men of color, instead of seeking the company of intelligent, wise, and good men of both races, from whom I might have learned much that would be interesting, instructive, and useful, and I have in that way squandered a great amount of most precious time and money, enough sometimes in a single year which, if I had put the same out on interest and kept it so, would have kept me always above board, given me character and influence amongst men, or have enabled me to pursue some respectable calling, so that I might employ others to their benefit and improvement; but as it is, I have always been poor, in debt, and am now obliged to travel about in search of employment as a hostler, shoeblack, and fiddler.

But I retain all my quickness of perception and see readily where I missed it.

An error of my riper years has been that, when any meeting of colored people has been called in order to consider an important matter of general interest, I have been so eager to display my spouting talents and so tenacious of some trifling theory or other which I have adopted, that I have generally lost all sight of the business at hand, consumed the time disputing about things of no moment, and thereby defeated entirely many important measures calculated to promote the general welfare.

But I am happy to say that I know in a flash where I missed it.

Another small error of my life (for I have never committed great blunders) has been that, for the sake of union in the furtherance of the most vital interests of our race, I would never yield any minor point of difference. In this way I have always had to act with but a few men and frequently alone, and could accomplish nothing worth living for.

But I have one comfort, I can see with a passing glance where I missed it.

A little but nonetheless telling fault which I have committed is that, if in anything another man has failed of coming up to my standard, notwithstanding he might possess many of the most valuable traits and be most admirably suited to fill some one important post, I would reject him entirely, injure his influence, oppose his measures, and even glory in his defeat, though his intentions all the while were good and his plans well laid.

But I have the great satisfaction of being able to say without fear of contradiction that I can see very quick where I missed it.

Another small mistake which I have made is that I could never bring myself to practice any present self-denial, although my theories have been excellent. For instance, I have bought expensive gay clothing, nice canes, watches, gold safety-chains, finger-rings, breast pins, and other things of a like nature, thinking I might by that means distinguish myself from the vulgar, as some of the better class of whites do. I have always been of the foremost in getting up expensive parties and running after fashionable amusements and have indulged my appetites freely whenever I had the means (and even with borrowed money) and have patronized the dealers in nuts, candy, cakes, etc., have sometimes bought good suppers, and was always a regular customer at livery stables. By these and many other means I have been unable to benefit my suffering brethren and am now but poorly able to keep my own soul and body together.

But do not think me thoughtless or dull of apprehension, for I can see at once where I missed it.

A not-so-trifling error of my life has been that I am always expected to secure the favor of the whites by tamely submitting to every species of indignity, contempt, and wrong, instead of nobly resisting their brutal aggressions from principle and taking my place as a man and assuming the responsibilities of a man, a citizen, a husband, a father, a brother, a neighbor, a friend, as God requires of every one (and if his neighbor will not allow him to do it, he must stand up and protest continually and also appeal to God for aid!). But I find that, for all my submission, I get about the same reward that the Southern Slavocrats render to the dough-faced statesmen of the North for being bribed and browbeat and fooled and cheated, as the Whigs and Democrats love to be, thinking themselves highly honored if they be allowed to lick up the spittle of a Southerner. I say I get the same reward!

But I am uncommonly quick-sighted, and I can see in a twinkling where I missed it.

Another little blunder which I have made is that, while I have

always been a most zealous abolitionist, I have been constantly at war
with my friends about certain religious tenets. I was first a Presbyterian,
but I could never think of acting with my Quaker friends, for they were
the rankest heretics, and the Baptists would be in the water, and the
Methodists denied the doctrine of Election, etc., and in later years, since
becoming enlightened by Garrison, Abby Kelley, and other really
benevolent persons, I have been spending all my force against friends
who love the Sabbath and feel that all is at stake on that point.

Now, I cannot doubt, notwithstanding I have been unsuccessful, that
you will allow me full credit for my peculiar quick-sightedness. As fast as
I say il, I can see where 1 missed it!

Father lowered the sheaf of lined pale blue paper, looked to me, and
awaited my admiration. "Well? What do you think, son?" he asked.

"Yes . . . well," said I. "Yes, it's . . . it's very good. And you seem to have
touched on everything that concerns you. Though it does end rather
abruptly, don't you think? I mean, is it enough simply to keep saying
that you see in a twink where you have missed it?"

"No!" he said. "Of course not! That's my point. Or will be, when I
have made it. It's what my second chapter will propose: what to do
when you have seen the error of your ways. You see, American Negroes
don't have a figure like Benjamin Franklin, and that's what I'm trying to
establish here. A friendly, wise scold. Franklin spoke only to white people, wisely and well, to be sure, but what he said is of little use to a people despised and downtrodden because of their race. Franklin's book
never addresses the whole race question. But Negroes—I'm talking
about the rank and file here, you understand, not the leaders—they
need a book of practical wisdom which is as accessible and amusing to
them as Franklin's is to us white folks, and as down-to-earth. Sambo is
my Poor Richard, son.

"When this is published in the *Ram's Horn*, I'll ask my colored friends what they think of it—innocently, you understand, as if I knew nothing of the authorship, testing their responses, getting suggestions as to what's been left out. And then I'll write my second chapter. A third and fourth chapter will follow, and so on, until I'll have written an entire book, a book that can serve as a new primer for Negroes in the fight against slavery."

"Fine, but why not let a Negro man write such a book?" I asked him, pointing out that there were plenty who were more than capable of it: Mr. Douglass, for instance, or the Reverends Garnet and Loguen. "They could do it without a disguise," I added.

"Please!" He laughed, as if he thought the idea ridiculous. "Owen, we're after a black Ben Franklin here, and none of those fine men is especially humorous or down-to-earth. And even if he were, he'd have to disguise himself just as much as I have. For different reasons, of course. Not because of race, but because he'd be so well-known amongst the Negro readership. Mister Douglass would have to call himself Sambo, too, just as I have, or else he'd sound like the famous Frederick Douglass, and who would believe these were *his* mistakes?"

"Who will believe, Father, that they are yours?"

"No one knows who I am," he said with a wink.

No, indeed. Back in '48 in Springfield, Massachusetts, black or white, they did not know who John Brown was. Not even I knew. There was a day coming, however, and not far off, when the whole world would know his name—from the literary salons of Paris, France, to the humblest white farmer's cabin of Kentucky, from the Scottish castles of the English queen to the daub-and-wattle slave-quarters of Alabama. So go ahead, write your story now, Old Man. Be for black folks a friendly, ordinary Negro scold, and do it while you can. Soon enough the man who is Sambo will be Old John Brown, Captain John Brown, Osawatomie Brown, a man who cannot hide who he is, even behind a beard and a dozen false names, and who can never again claim to be other than white, who can no longer even cultivate a fantasy that he is other than white. Though it will be rarely said so baldly, his race—that he is a white man and in the interests of Negroes has coldly killed other white men—will become the most important thing about him.

The image of Father reading beside me has faded. The light that accompanied my memory of him is gone, and although I cannot see him, I can still hear his voice. He says to me, "It's very dark here. You don't mind the darkness, Owen? And the cold? It's grown very cold since the sun set. Why not go inside and light a fire?"

"I do mind the darkness. It's making me feel too much the pain of being alone. But the cold, no. I don't feel the cold."

"Then go inside your cabin, my boy, and light a candle."

That was the winter and spring when we lived in Springfield in the house on Franklin Street, a wood-frame row house no wider than a single room, somewhat dilapidated, barely furnished, in a neighborhood of mostly Negro freedmen, people who were even poorer than we. We were content, however, because for the first time in several years we were residing together, a regular family, and Father was not working someplace far off, careening about the skies like a wandering star or a comet due to return home sometime in the distant future. Even John, with his new wife, Wealthy, was with us that year, helping Father run Mr. Perkins's wool warehouse.

John was easier to deal with than Father, or so it appeared, for as soon as John arrived from Ohio, the buyers of our wool began asking to see him, instead of the Old Man. This left Father free to pursue his several projects concerning the welfare and future of the Negroes in Springfield, who that year were particularly alarmed by the growing number of slave-catchers prowling through Northern cities. Father's abolitionist work had taken on a new intensity there and a freshened singleness of purpose, probably because of the presence in Springfield of a large number of freedmen who were agreeable to him for their intelligence and for the ferocity of their opposition to slavery. It no doubt helped that he, in his fervor and clarity of purpose, was agreeable to them as well.

I myself was attached to the warehouse, where I was responsible for cleaning and sorting the wool that came in from the west, mostly from Father's and Mr. Perkins's associates in Ohio and Pennsylvania, and attending to its proper storage and, when the occasional sale was made to one of the woolen manufacturers, packing and shipping it on to the huge new factory looms of eastern Massachusetts. It was boring work, but not particularly arduous, and left me perhaps too much solitary time for dreaming about a future that in my heart I suspected would never be mine.

My dreams were for the most part the foolish fancies of a very naive and unusually immature young man—a shepherd boy's idea of sophisticated Eastern society. I was twenty-four years old that winter, and Springfield was the largest town I had ever seen. The regular proximity of exotic (or so they seemed to me) young women kept me in an agitated state of mind and body, and I spent many an evening and early morning hour walking the streets alone, not so much to look at the young women, for they were not so much to be found on the streets during those hours anyhow, as to be alone with my tangled thoughts and feelings, struggling to control and organize them.

Most of my thoughts and feelings were surely driven by simple, natural male curiosity, unnaturally heightened by my lifelong fear of women and my shyness when among them and the rural isolation of my life so far, but they disturbed and confused me. I hesitate to make this confession, especially to someone I do not know and a woman, and very possibly I will write this down and then burn it, as I have certain other pages already written. In fact, I cannot say for certain if I have sent you some of these pages, all of them, or none. They are scattered and strewn about my table and cabin, and much of the time, when I am not seated here with pencil in hand, I am confused and lose myself and can't distinguish what I have done from what I have not done.

I will tell everything. During the daylight hours, whenever I noticed an attractive woman, whether a pious young woman at church or a neighborhood friend of Ruth's or one of the daughters of a Negro cohort of Father's at an abolitionist meeting, I quickly averted my gaze and made every attempt to remove myself from her presence. But later, in the nighttime—while alone and walking the gaslit streets of the city, down along muddy, trash-strewn lanes and alleys by the river and past the taverns and brothels there, where I lingered outside and peered through fogged-over windows and glanced furtively through doors as whiskeyed patrons entered and left, and along tree-lined boulevards up on the heights where the large mansions were located and I stopped and gazed across lawns to darkened verandas—I imagined all sorts of encounters with all types of women, and little plays took place on the stage of my mind, in which I spoke all the parts.

"How do you do, miss? Are you out for an evening stroll? May I accompany you a ways?"

"Why, thank you, sir, I would appreciate your company and protection. Are you a native of these parts, sir? For I do not think I know you."

They were pathetic little dramas, which enflamed my passions and sent me reeling back to our house on Franklin Street, where the rest of the family slept peacefully and virtuously. There I would toss and writhe in my cot in the room that I shared with my younger brothers, miserable, guilty, self-abusing.

Thus I little noticed the continued and worsening illness of another of the children, the baby, Ellen, born in Ohio the previous autumn, and I did not realize that my stepmother, Mary, had not fully recovered from her lying-in period following the birth. I lived in a household whose rhythms and concerns were being shaped once again by illness, and I did not notice. Here I was, this large, healthy young fellow lumbering out to work at the warehouse every morning, returning in the evening for supper and then slipping out again, stumbling through his days and nights with his mind filled only by the turbulence of lustful fantasies at war with private shames, while the rest of the family worried over another frail and failing babe and a mother unable to recover from the rigors of giving birth. In such a way did my preoccupation with trivial sins, with my sensual indulgence and guilt, cause me to commit a graver sin and to feel no guilt for it. No wonder Father seemed short with me that winter and spring: in my self-absorption, I thought that he and Mary and the rest of the family, John and Wealthy, Ruth, even the younger children, were casting me out, were not including me in their circle of intimate relations—when in fact it was I who had cast them out.

Then one night late in April, a few weeks before we planned to depart for our new home in the Adirondacks, I left the house in an unusually heightened state of alarm. I felt I had reached a fork in my road, and if I did not take a turning now I would be forever bound to follow the track I was on. A foolish desperation, I know, but the oncoming move to the wilderness of North Elba frightened me. We had begun dismantling and packing up our life in Springfield, almost without having yet settled there, and the house was filling with crates and cartons, and Father was making lists of goods and tools and was negotiating for a large wagon to carry everything north. That very evening he had informed me over our supper that my job would be to take the boys Salmon and Watson out to Litchfield, Connecticut, where he had been boarding his merino sheep and small herd of Devon cattle at the farm of a cousin, there to gather the livestock and move them north separately from the rest of the family, to meet up in the town of Westport, New York, on Lake Champlain.

I nodded and, on getting up from the table, sullenly announced that I would be going out to say goodbye to a few friends, since I did not expect to see them again. Father showed no interest in my stated intentions: I did not know, of course, thanks to my inane self-absorption, that his mind and the minds of everyone else in the family were very much distracted by the worsening condition of the sick baby, Ellen. It appeared to me that, but for our preparations to move, life was going on as usual. Except, as I saw it, no one particularly cared about me. So deluded was I that I had grown angry at them, at Father especially, for not having asked me pointedly where I was going, who were my friends, why did I need to tell them goodbye with two weeks yet to go before we left town? For not having caught my lie.

In a huff, then, and puffed up with self-righteous relief, I left the crowded little house on Franklin Street and made my way downtown towards the dark, broad Connecticut River, where barges and sloops and Long Island coasters tied up at the docks, and their crews and the stevedores gathered in dim, smoky taverns. In and around these taverns and boarding houses there were women—women waiting for the company and pay of lonely men and boys who came ashore for a night or two, women waiting for the drovers and woodcutters from the hills of Vermont and New Hampshire to come in from the marketplaces of the town with fresh money in their pockets and reckless intentions in their hearts.

Women, women, women! The mere *idea* of femaleness made me mad with desire, although I knew not what it was exactly that I desired. Sex? Copulation? Simple, carnal love? All that, I suppose. All that. The very fact of it. But something else, too. I craved knowledge, knowledge of a sort that up to then I'd had no access to, and here I speak of the certain and unmistakeable smell of a woman, the touch of her soft skin, the flow of her hair across my hand, the sound of a woman's whispered voice in my ear, even the sight of her naked body. What were these smells, touches, sounds, and sights *like*? I had never experienced these aspects of femaleness. But I knew they existed, and that small knowledge made me wildly desirous of the further, larger, and much more dangerous knowledge beyond.

It was a warm night, the April air thick with the smell of lilacs and new, wet grass. I strode along, determined tonight not to leave this river town without learning at least something of what I was sure I would miss afterwards—for the remainder of my life, as it seemed. For I still believed the Old Man then, believed him when he said that our move up into the Adirondack wilderness of northern New York would be permanent. And had accepted that, because of the blacks settled there, Timbuctoo would be our base for all future operations in the war against slavery. I was sure that my permanent, lifelong job would be to run the farm and tend the flocks, so that Father could preach and organize and fight, activities to which his character and temperament were so much more neatly adapted than mine. I felt that I had reached the end of a conscripted childhood and was about to begin a similarly conscripted adult life. But on this April night, for a few hours, at least, I meant to be a free man.

I saw several women and avoided passing each one by crossing the street to the other side. But then came one I could not avoid, and after I had passed her by with my habitually averted gaze, she called out, "Hullo, Red! Would y' be needin' company tonight?"

She was a girl, practically, I had glimpsed that much, and red-haired herself, perhaps fourteen or fifteen years old, with bright white powder all over her face and a broad slash of painted lips and smudge-blackened eyes. She wore erratic scraps of cloth elaborately draped across her shoulders, wrapped, sashed, and pinned so as to suggest an exotic gown, although it was more a child's motley costume than a woman's dress.

I stopped and turned back to her, and she said, with a curl to her voice and a pronunciation that was noticeably Irish, "You're a big feller, ain't you, now."

Because I could see that she was a child, she did not frighten me as a full-grown woman would, and I took a step towards her. "I'm . . . I'm only out for a walk," I said. She was small and thin. Her head, covered with a crumpled black lace bonnet, came barely to my chest, the thickness of her wrist seemed not much greater than that of my thumb, and her waist was smaller than the circumference of my right arm.

When I approached her, she stopped smiling and stepped back from me into a bank of shadows that fell from a cut-stone retaining wall. We were down by the canal tow path, with the river passing in the darkness below and a cobbled street out of view above. I heard a horse clop past and the iron-sheathed wheels of a wagon. It was a lonely, dark, and dangerous place for a girl, even a girl such as she—perhaps especially for one such as she, whose purpose for being there was to solicit the attentions of men likely to be drunk or angry, men likely to regard her as disposable. More particularly, of course, she was there to solicit men like me—timid, passionately curious bumpkins, who would pay to use her, yes, but would not otherwise harm her.

I was useless to her, however, a waste of her time, for I had no more than a few loose coins in my pocket. Father, I thought, with more coins in his pocket than I, would try to save such a woman. He would lecture her on the evils of her ways and give her his last money and instruct her to go home and feed herself and her babes, if she had any. John and Jason were both recently married and, even if they had been as unattached as I, would have done likewise. I knew that I, however, had I the means, would only try to use her. I am confident that Father never in his life performed the sexual act outside the matrimonial bed (where, to be sure, he performed it frequently); the same for my brothers; but I, by contrast, even at the young age of twenty-four, still and perhaps forever too much the son and brother, could not imagine myself as husband, as father, as regular visitor to the marriage bed. And so here I was, where my father and brothers would never be, soliciting a prostitute.

Though I was a full-grown man, I wore my manhood like an ill-fitting costume—not unlike the way the girl before me wore her make-up and rags, her woman's costume. We had met in the shadows of a high stone wall, two children ineptly disguised as adults. But where she had costumed herself as a grown woman in order to keep from starving or freezing to death, I was a child got up merely to accommodate the size and appearance and the startling impulses of a man's body. But I was probably no more successful at disguising my childishness than she, and in a diminished sense, I, too, was in danger out here—a cull, easy prey to robbers, tricksters, confidence men and women, cutpurses and cutthroats of every stripe.

"I . . . I have no money," I said to her.

"Aw, come on, now, a nicely dressed feller like yourself?"

"Yes. I live not far from here. I'm just walking, out for a walk . . . as I said. I . . . I like to be by the river."

"Then what d' you want with me?" She took a further, backwards step into the deeper shadows, and I could not make out her powdered and painted face any longer.

"Nothing. Nothing. Just . . . I'm sorry, miss. I didn't mean to scare you."

"You didn't scare me."

"No?" I moved towards her, and she jumped awkwardly away, like a broken-winged bird, her parti-colored feathers all dusty and awry. I reached out with my right hand and placed it on her bony shoulder. Instantly, she ducked out from under it and turned her back to me, pressing herself against the cold stone wall.

"I won't hurt you," I whispered.

"You can't touch me 'less'n you pay."

I reached into my pocket and drew out the few coins that remained, a gratuity I had received the day before from a Lowell merchant who'd had me haul five hundred weight bales of wool to his cart— copper pennies, enough for a single loaf of bread, no more. "Here, this is all I've got." Looking warily at me, she half turned and opened her tiny hand; I passed her the coins, and they disappeared into her rags at once.

I peered down at my feet, embarrassed and unsure of what to do next, and when I looked up again, the girl had slid down along the wall and was about to bolt. "Hey, where're you off to!"

"No place!" she said, alarmed, and stood stock-still, half hidden in the darkness.

"But you took my money!"

"Y' don't get much for coppers, y' know."

"But you were running off."

"I was only movin' out of the walkway some. C'm'ere, an' be nice, mister. Don't fret none, I'll give you some of what y' want, darlin'. C'm'ere, now," she said to me in a lulling tone, as if she were trying to calm a large, frightened animal.

I moved abruptly to her but did not dare touch her this time. I was not afraid of her so much as afraid of myself. If I touched her, I did not know what would follow. Then, suddenly, it was she who had touched me. Her hand stroked me between my thighs, and a second later she was unbuttoning me, using both her hands. Before I could fully register what was happening, it was over: she was standing and wiping her mouth with the back of her hand, a distant look on her face, as if she were calculating the few measly items that she might purchase with the pennies I had given her.

I turned away and quickly buttoned my trousers. "I . . . I'm sorry," I said, without looking around at her.

"What for?"

I turned and faced her. She drew her shawl over her scrawny shoulders and seemed about to leave. "Well . . . that, I guess."

"You got what y' paid for. No more."

"Yes, I know. You're right. I just . . . well, it's terribly wrong, that's all. And I'm sorry for that."

She shrugged and started off. "G'bye, dearie. Come back when you get your wages."

"Wait!" I called. The girl stopped a few paces off, and I ran up to her. "Don't go yet."

She studied my face carefully, uncertain, a little curious, perhaps, but somewhat frightened as well.

I spoke softly. "I wonder . . . I was wondering if I might . . . look at you. I'm sorry . . . I thought, I wonder if you might let me see you."

She cast a look at me aslant, then glanced up and down the walkway, as if seeking an escape route. "No. No looks. Y' got what y' paid for, mister."

Without touching her, I placed my right hand and left forearm against the wall on either side of her, trapping her in front of me. "I want only to look at you," I said. "Just for a moment."

"*Look* at me? What do y' mean? My bubbies y' want to see?"

"Yes. And the other."

"The other? Naw, you're daft, mister. You're makin' me scared." She had drawn down and in close to herself and had wrapped her thin arms tightly around her chest, making her seem even more like a child than before. Her large, smudged eyes looked plaintively up at me. "Please . . . just let me go now, mister."

"First let me look at you. Then you can go. I won't hurt you."

"Just my bubbies?"

"Yes."

"Not the other?"

"No."

Slowly, she unwrapped her arms, reached under her shawl and fumbled momentarily with the buttons of her frock, and then she drew the clothing aside and showed me herself—a bony pink chest with tiny breasts. The fragile, innocent body of a child. For a second only, I stared, wishing suddenly that I were as able as she to open my own shirt and bare my breast and have it be the breast of a boy and not my thick, heavy-haired chest. So that, even as I humiliated her, I frankly envied her—when at last I realized what I was doing and was shot through with shame and looked away.

I waved my hands at her. "I'm sorry! Please forgive me," I said. "Please, cover yourself. I'm so sorry . . . to have done this to you," I said. Then suddenly, not knowing what else to do, I got down on my knees before her and in silence hung my head.

"Well, you are some crack-brained cull, mister," the girl said. She stepped around my prostrate form, and I heard her footsteps clack against the stone as she made her escape. When I looked up, she was gone. I was alone in the darkness. I heard the slosh of the river down below and the creak and groan of boats and barges bumping against the piers. On the street above, a pair of drunken men walked past. One laughed, the other sang a bit of a bawdy song.

He who once a good name gets
May piss a-bed and say he sweats . . .

They both laughed and passed by. Alone in the night once again, I walked for hours after that, aimless, confused, frightened by the appalling knowledge I had obtained—not knowledge of women in general or of the particular poor, nameless Irish girl whom, for a few pennies, I had used as a common whore, but knowledge of myself. I knew myself now to be vile, a beast. On my own like this, away from Father and the rest of the family, cut loose from their moral and intellectual clarity, from the virtue generated, sustained, and perfected among them, I was but a sack of contradictions and unpredictable impulses: I was a boy locked inside a man's body, my childish innocence contaminated now, not merely by longing and self-abuse, but by sexual contact of the most disgusting sort. I had inflicted myself upon a poor, pathetic street urchin, a whore, yes, but a person who, compared to me, was honest, was virtuous—was innocent. Once again, I envied her, and at that moment would have happily exchanged places with her, if for no other reason than properly to punish myself for my transgressions and my hypocrisy and to reward her for her virtue and suffering.

It should be she, not I, who could freely return to a warm household filled with a loving and upright family; she, not I, who was able to stand alongside her father and mother and brothers and sisters in church and public meetings and to walk freely about the town in the daylight glow of respect and admiration from the citizenry; she, not I, who performed honest labor and received for it shelter, food, clothing; she, not I, whose father, guide, and protector was the good man John Brown. Let *me* be the harlot, the hired property of drunken, brutal strangers. Let *me* go hungry and cold through the nighttime alleyways and dark corners of the town, exchanging brief, obscene gratifications for a few pennies. Let *me* be the victim.

Burdened with thoughts such as these, I slowly made my sorrowful way home to Franklin Street, arriving there sometime in the middle of the night. The house was not darkened, as I had expected, and when I entered I was greeted by Ruth and John and Wealthy, all in their night-clothes, gathered together in the kitchen comforting our stepmother, Mary, who sat downcast at the table with a bowl of warm milk before her. She had been weeping, I saw at once, and when I asked what had happened, John turned to me and swiftly took me aside and informed me that the baby Ellen had died just minutes before. It was a mercy, he said, for the poor little thing had not drawn a proper breath for hours. Father was still with her upstairs, and he could not be separated from the infant. "It's as if he cannot believe her dead," John said. Mother—for he, unlike me, called her that—Mother was all right now. She had accepted the death of the child as an inevitable thing the previous evening, although Father had not, and she had prayed for her to go as quickly and painlessly as possible. But Father had stayed up two whole nights with the babe in his arms, believing that he could somehow save her, even, at the end, trying to breathe into her mouth. But she had died in his arms, and he had refused to lay her down and now was walking up and down in the rooms above, still praying for her recovery.

I remember John saying, "The Old Man can't seem to let this one go." And I remember that he did not ask me where I had been until this late hour. No one asked. Clearly, and rightly, my private adventures and torment were of no account here.

Suddenly, there was Father at the bottom of the back stairs, entering the kitchen, his arms hanging down at his sides, his head lowered, with tears streaming down his face. I had never seen Father weep before, and the sight astonished and frightened me. He sat himself down next to his wife with a groping hesitancy, as if he had lost his sight, and he placed his hands against his face and wept openly as a child. No one said a word. This was beyond our understanding. I do not think that Father loved any one of his children more than the others, and he had lost at that time fully half a dozen of his babes, and he had not wept over any of them, although, to be sure, he had grieved deeply over them all, even to despair. His belief in the Life Hereafter had always been sufficiently strong that he could view their early going as a gift from God for the children and a trial from God for him. But somehow this was different. It was as if this time he believed that he, the father of the child, was being punished, not tried, by her death. "The Lord is filled with wrath against me!" he cried. "The Lord despiseth me!"

"No, no, Father," we all said, and each in his own way tried to console him. We reached out to him and placed our hands on him, and several of us wept with him. Although I did not. I could not. I backed off a ways and watched in shame, for I knew the true cause of Father's suffering, over and above his grief for the lost child. I was the cause. I knew that Father was blaming himself for my sins, condemning himself for not having interceded with me in my frequent lustful wanderings, which surely he had observed and marked. And now he believed that he was being punished by an angry God for his inattention. I did not need to hear Father say any of this; I knew it in my bones.

Slowly, I came forward, and the others, as if they knew what I intended, parted for me and made room for me to go down on my knees beside Father's chair. "I'm sorry, Father, for what I've done. I have sinned, and I am sorry. Please, Father, please forgive me."

At that, he ceased weeping and looked straight into my face. His great gray eyes penetrated my face to my very soul, and he did not flinch at what he saw there, and I did not squirm away from his gaze, much as I wanted to. "Owen, my son. You are a good boy, Owen. I forgive thee," he said in a low voice, and he placed his hands on my shoulders and drew me to him. "The Lord hath taken one child from me and returned to me another, who was lost," he said. "I welcome thee, Owen," he said, and it was as if his words had cleansed me, for at once I felt uplifted and strong again. Whatever Father wished me now to do, I would do without argument, without hesitancy, without fear. I remember, on the night that the baby Ellen died, thinking that.

II

5

I don't know how much time has passed since I began this account—days, weeks, a fortnight—for it is as if I have been elsewhere, a place where time is measured differently and space is not bounded as it is usually. The only thing that grounds me, that stills and locks me into some deliberate measure of time and place, is my intermittent awareness of you, holding these sheets of paper in your hands, reading my words, learning my story and applying it to Father's larger story, the one that truly matters.

I know that in passing, due to my self-absorption and to the vividness of my recollections, I have mentioned many people and events that you know little of, that you may in fact know nothing of, for they have not come down in the historical record. They are not a part of the received truth. It is important that you hear of them, however, for they, like me, are figures in the context of Father's story, which, if he is to be known at all, must be known as well. Let me speak, for instance, of Lyman Epps, the Negro man whom I mentioned earlier, and let me say how we came to know Lyman, how I first came to know him, for he will figure in the larger context of known people and events in a significant way. And his story, unlike the story of the men buried beneath Father's stone in the shade of Mount Tahawus, has not been told before by anyone.

It was in the spring of '50, almost a half century ago, that I met Lyman Epps, when we all first came to North Elba, a few weeks later in the season than now, and I can bring it back to my mind today as if I were dreaming it—I can see the lilacs blooming and the bloodroot, which I had not seen before, at least not to name.

It might have been earlier than now—the first of May, perhaps. For the lilacs that I am gazing at were located in the trim yards of the houses down in Westport, New York, alongside the broad verandas that faced the glittering waters of Lake Champlain and the Green Mountains of Vermont on the further side; and when Father pointed out the little, low blossom of the bloodroot, we were still down in that prosperous village, gathering the family and our livestock to begin our trek up into the mountains, where it would not be warm enough for the bloodroot and the lilacs to bloom until many weeks later.

Father and I had moved his horse, Dan, and the seven head of Devon cattle away from where we had camped, on a hillside clearing at the edge of town, intending to water the animals at a stream nearby. The boys Watson, Salmon, and Oliver, setting out the sheep to graze, had located the stream earlier. The Old Man halted suddenly, and I peered over the bony red rumps and heads of our thirsty beasts to see what was the matter.

"Owen, come, look here," he commanded.

I passed by the cattle to where he stood staring intently down the embankment into a glade beside the rock-strewn stream, which was narrow here and tumbled fast downhill towards the lake. I looked where he had indicated and, as was so often the case, saw nothing. Black flies swarmed about my face, and the cattle bunched up impatiently behind us. Father held old Dan, his chestnut gelding, by the halter and peered into the glade.

"Yes, well, if we needed a sign," he said, with a certain resignation in his voice, "here is one." In profile, Father's unsmiling, clean-shaven face was like a fist. He had a tight mouth with thin lips, a square chin and forehead, and a hooked, short nose, a hawk's beak. You may be unaware that the long beard, with which he was later so often and so famously pictured, he wore only after Kansas, as a disguise, and, indeed, it did disguise him, even to his family, who fondly remembered his daily morning shave, mirrorless by the stove. It was an occasion for us to tease him into almost nicking himself with the razor. "You missed a bit," one of us, usually Ruth, would calmly observe.

A second child, Oliver or Salmon, would add, "Over here, Father, near your big left ear." His ears were unusually large, and to our amusement, their size slightly embarrassed him; although he denied it, of course.

"Where?" he would ask, groping over his heavy jaw with his fingertips.

"The other side! On the other side!"

"The right side, just below your enormous right ear!"

"No, it's the left. His right, Oliver, is your left."

Father would himself grow amused and join the game by feigning frantic confusion and flashing his long razor recklessly like a saber from one side of his face to the other. "Here? Here? Here?" Until Ruth or I or Mary would seriously fear that he was about to cut himself and would say, "Enough. Let the poor man shave his face in peace," and the children would disperse, and Father, smiling lightly, would finish and wipe his face dry.

"It's the May flower," he said to me that morning in Westport. "The bloodroot, we called it, when I was a boy." Following his extended finger, I looked down by the stream and saw in amongst the ferns and mossy stones a cluster of small white flowers near the ground. "The root is red as fresh blood," he said, and told me that the Iroquois used it as pigmentation for their war paint. "The petals, though, they come pure white, like those yonder. Innocent above ground, and bloody below," he mused. He had known it to grow and even blossom under a layer of late snow. It was the first flower of spring, and he was truly glad to see it.

One of the cows smelled the water and started over the embankment, and the rest pulled over behind her, and quickly I stepped around in front of the leader and shoved her back.

"After such tribulation, we may well require a hopeful sign," Father said, meaning the past winter's long, lingering death of the infant Ellen, I supposed, and all his financial woes, which had continued to mount so relentlessly in the last few years.

It was strange to feel sorry for Father, and I rarely did and was almost ashamed of the feeling, as if he had forbidden it. Regardless, I placed my hand on his shoulder and said to him, "The Lord will provide, Father." But the words felt like gravel in my mouth.

"Owen, don't say words that you don't believe. Not even in comfort," he added, and he scowled and turned away and led old Dan and the cattle further up the hill to where the stream ran slowly and there was a shallow pool that the animals could drink from.

Yet, all in all, it was a very pleasant few days, that first stop in Westport, and I almost wished that we could settle there, instead of trekking on to a place that everyone other than Father had described as a howling wilderness. During the last year-and-a-half in Springfield, helping Father and John run Father's and Mr. Simon Perkins's wool business, I had grown somewhat used to the easy sociability and abundant distractions of a town. I somewhat envied John for having been left behind, even though he was burdened with looking after Father's affairs at the warehouse, and I envied Jason, too, and even Fred, who was a full six years younger than I, for having been charged with the care of Mr. Perkins's flocks back at Mutton Hill in Akron.

But there was no arguing with Father on this matter of our settling amongst the Negroes in North Elba. He was dead set on it. They were freedmen, a few were doubtless fugitives, and the wealthy New York abolitionist Mr. Gerrit Smith, out of simple compassion and generosity, but perhaps with a useful moral point to make as well, had deeded them forty acres per family from his vast holdings in the Adirondacks. But in a few short years the rigors of northcountry farming had for the most part defeated them, and the little colony was coming rapidly undone. Father's agreement with Mr. Smith was that in exchange for a sizeable piece of land with an abandoned house on it, to be paid for later at one dollar per acre, we would move there and teach the Negroes, many of whom had been Philadelphia barbers and Long Island shoemakers and the such, how to organize and work their land.

Father did not think he could accomplish this without at least one adult son beside him and had carefully explained why I was the one so designated: John was more capable than I when it came to business; Jason and his new wife were settled permanently, it seemed, in Ohio; and Fred, although twenty years old then, was a person who needed close supervision, which Jason was good at providing. As usual, the Old Man was right, and I had to comply.

The first thing we needed to do was survey and validate their claims, he told me: to keep the Negroes from being cheated by the whites, who had been squatting up there for several generations—ever since the terrible, year-long winter of '06 had driven most of the original settlers out—and had come to think of the whole place as theirs alone. Father's motives were moral and idealistic, the same as had always prompted his political actions, and he described this move as essentially political—for he had visited North Elba alone the previous fall and had come away newly inspired by a vision of Negro and white farmers working peacefully together. His hope now, he explained to us, was to build a true American city on a hill that would give the lie to every skeptic in the land. There were many such utopian schemes and projects afoot in those years, a hundred little cities on a hundred little hills, but Timbuctoo may have been the only one that aimed at setting an example of racial harmony. This would be our errand into the wilderness, he said.

But there was more to it than that. The wild Adirondack landscape had moved the Old Man wonderfully. All that winter and spring, despite the worry and grief he bore over the sickness and long dying of the baby Ellen, whenever he spoke of settling down on the broad table-land between the mountains, his face would soften and flush, and he would sail off in reveries and fantasies more likely to have been generated by a short stay at Valhalla than by a quick visit to a tract of hard-scrabble highlands with a ninety-day growing season and a grinding, six-months-long winter. "Ah, Owen," he would exclaim, "just wait until you see the beauty of this place! It makes you think that during the Creation the good Lord lingered there awhile. There is truly no place I have seen whose aspect has so pleased me as those Adirondack mountains."

On reflection, I believe, also, that there was for Father yet another deeply pleasing aspect of the North Elba project, one that he hid from us then but which I understood later. Its force was stronger than the moral point that he and Mr. Gerrit Smith wished to make and more substantive than the poetic effect of the landscape on his soul. For many years, the Old Man's life had been cruelly divided between his anti-slavery actions and his responsibilities as a husband and father, and despite his unrelenting, sometimes wild and chaotic attempts to unite them, it was often as if he was trying to live the lives of two separate men: one an abolitionist firebrand, a public figure whose most satisfying and important acts, out of necessity, were done in secret; the other a good Christian husband and father, a private man whose most satisfying and important acts were manifested in the visible security and comfort of his family. He was a man who had pledged his life to bring about the permanent and complete liberation of the Negro slaves; and he was the head of a large household with no easy sources of income.

Never having married, I did not experience this sort of division in my life, which is perhaps why it took me until I was practically middle-aged before I was led to these particular sympathies for Father. And I certainly had no inkling of his conflicted state back then, when I reluctantly agreed to join him in his removal of the family from Springfield to North Elba, the tenth move in nearly as many years. Now, however, I can see that, for the first time in his life, Father expected to live as what he regarded as a whole man. In the Adirondacks, amongst the Negroes, he had at last imagined a life that was capable of containing all his contraries. Or so he believed then.

Father turned fifty that spring; Mary was thirty-seven. I am sure that, despite all, Father's errand into the wilderness pleased her, especially after the death of the baby Ellen. It was a fresh start, and Father's reveries and fantasies about the place had convinced her that our life would finally be calm and organized. Mary was a profound and prayerful person, more meditative and inward than the Old Man and most of the rest of us, and the idea of making a sanctuary in the mountains pleased her, especially if it met the Old Man's standards for his and our participation in the struggle to free the slaves. And as far as she and we knew then, the removal to North Elba would accomplish that.

I remember him reassuring her that in a year or even less he would tie up his tangled affairs with Mr. Perkins in Springfield and Ohio and have all his debts at last paid off. Then he would be free to build his racially harmonious city on the hill, raise his prize-winning cattle and sheep on the slopes of the Adirondacks, and live out his years in the comfort of his family and neighbors. He would be a preacher, a teacher, and a farmer, he said. It was all he had ever wanted in life. He did not want to be a great man.

He told her that, told it to all of us, and we believed it, and I'm sure that, sometimes, he believed it, too. I soon learned, of course, that months before, when he had gone to North Elba alone, he had had other things in mind—the scattered, dimly formed, but powerful beginnings of ideas and plans that would develop and coalesce up there in the mountains and that would eventually prove irresistible to him. And, I confess it, ideas and plans that would prove irresistible to me and to my brothers as well.

To get to Westport, the boys Watson and Salmon, who were but fourteen and thirteen years old that spring, and I had traveled separately from the others, for we had brought Father's Devon cattle and his five Spanish merino sheep up along the Connecticut River from Litchfield, Connecticut, where Father had been boarding them, crossed overland to Rutland, Vermont, and passed around the bottom of Lake Champlain to the New York side by the Fort Ticonderoga route. The Old Man, Mary, sister Ruth, and the younger children, Oliver, Annie, and little Sarah, at three years old the second to bear that name, had come north from Springfield in the wagon with all our tools and domestic goods, a pig, some fowl, and our dogs. They had crossed the lake on the ferry from Vermont, arrived in Westport, New York, and set up camp a few days before we got there.

By the time we showed up with the cattle and sheep, Father had already purchased the supplies we would need to see us through to our first harvest, but as soon as I saw the size of the load, I knew that Father's old horse, an animal for whom he had typically developed an intense affection, would prove too feeble to haul it on the flats, let alone over high mountains. The Old Man and I argued a bit over that one, but he relented, for he knew the difficulties of getting up from Lake Champlain to North Elba even better than I.

With regret, then, he decided to sell his precious old horse, Dan, and use his last remaining cash money to buy a team from the shipping agent in Westport, a Mr. Thurston Clarke. As it turned out, Mr. Clarke offered Father a chance to hold on to his money, or most of it, which would have made a useful difference to him later on, but the Old Man gave it over. The red-coated Devon cattle had aroused considerable admiration among the local people there, and Father was briefly tempted by Mr. Clarke to swap a pair straight across for a team of Narragansetts. At the last minute, Father declined the offer.

The reason was the presence of a black man from North Elba—Lyman Epps. *Mister* Epps, as Father always addressed him, to the frequent consternation of any white people who were present. The man wandered into our camp south of Westport the evening of the day after the boys and I had arrived from Connecticut with the cattle and the sheep, and he swiftly proved to be an intelligent, charming man, although I confess that I did not warm to him as quickly as did the others. A wiry, coal-black fellow of medium height and quick movements, he was one of Gerrit Smith's settled freedmen, a well-spoken man in his early thirties, I guessed, who had been a blacksmith in Maryland and knew horses. Many men know horses, but only from the outside; Mr. Epps claimed to understand them from the inside, as if they were people.

He told us that he had come down to Westport from North Elba in search of work: he needed cash to buy seed, because his crops from the previous year had failed, and all his reserves were gone, and he had no more credit at the feed stores or suppliers in the area. But he had been turned away by every blacksmith and harrier in the village, due to his race. In the process, however, he had learned of Father's presence in town—the abolitionist fool from Ohio bent on teaching Gerrit Smith's niggers to farm in the mountains. Father, as usual, had made no secret of our intentions, and we, like the Negroes, had quickly become something of a local joke.

On the subject of horses, the man was positively brilliant, or I should say he *talked* brilliantly on the subject. Such talk pleased the Old Man immensely and probably caused him to disregard the man's occasional gaps in knowledge and experience, for soon he was inviting Mr. Epps to advise him on the purchase of a new team.

While Father's own knowledge of horses was not nearly as extensive and deep as with cattle and sheep, where he truly was an expert, he nonetheless, unsurprisingly, held strong and frequently voiced opinions as to the relative merits of the more popular breeds. Also, he rarely exhibited any particular reluctance to lecture folks on how to raise, train, work, and ride horses. He took advice badly but gave it without stint. Back in Ohio, when we were still living on the old Haymaker farm and Father was first slipping deeply into land speculation, he had expanded his livestock operation beyond sheep and cattle and had even raised racehorses for a few years and sold off the colts and yearlings at the nearby Warren racetrack.

I remember his lectures to us, for we older boys were obliged to care for the colts and break them to the saddle and so on, before they could be sold off. "Remember, a colt should never be frightened," he insisted. "Never. Horses are sensitive beings, very intelligent, easily spooked, so they must be treated with gentleness." Later on, he explained, when you want to bring them under your control, they will trust your intentions completely and will defer to you in all things.

This was not, of course, his philosophy with regard to raising children. Children, the Old Man believed, were innately sinful, and thus they could be broken to the saddle, as it were, only if regularly disciplined and controlled by the rod, and could be saved only by the mysterious dispensation of the Lord's grace. *For whom the Lord loveth he chasteneth, and scourgeth every son whom He receiveth,* he said. *The blueness of a wound cleanseth away evil; so do stripes the inward part of the belly.* And, *Chasten thy son while there is hope, and let not thy soul spare for his crying.*

Horses were evidently already saved, or were at least free of sin, and who could argue with that?

I did sometimes wish, however, that he had applied his views on raising animals to his methods of raising children. Foals, Father told us, should learn the use of a halter very early, with nothing but a gentle touch and voice, and you must break them in to reins slowly and much later, after they have grown easy with the halter. His lectures on the use of the bit and the importance of a soft mouth were impressive, and in demonstrating the process of introducing the bit, he handled the animal with such delicacy and affection that you almost wished that you yourself were the foal.

With all livestock, Father was a gentle man who clearly loved to touch and stroke the flesh of the animal, to examine and, if the animal was healthy and well-formed, admire it and express almost motherly concern over any sign of illness or deformity. He would walk a yearling racehorse out of the barn and run his hands over the withers and back, across the barrel of the animal and its gaskins, fetlocks, and pasterns, ending with an examination of the hooves, making sure that we had been listening when he last lectured us on the proper care of a horse's hoof.

Like most men with a developed affection for animals, Father was an excellent rider, and not surprisingly, he enjoyed instructing us boys and anyone else who would listen on the best methods of bringing your horse to jump over fences or ditches in the fields of the neighborhood and how to bring your horse quickly down a steep slope without risking injury to the animal. And although, at the time, my elder brothers and I were not especially eager to be taught yet again how to do what we thought we already knew well enough, in later years, when we were running for our lives in Kansas, leaping streams and gullies in the dark and crashing through dense copses of cottonwoods, obliging the slavers to stop, back off, muzzle around, and finally give up the chase, I remembered Father's lectures and theories, his endless repetitions of what then seemed but practice for a steeplechase we never intended to enter, and I was glad for having endured them.

That evening at the camp in Westport, Mr. Epps flicked his nervy attention from one of us to the next with no apparent purpose, as if he were sorting out our family's internal relations, trying to discern which of us bore influence over the others, so as to learn whose good opinion would permit him to gain the favor of all.

Was it the children? He first tried chatting up baby Sarah and strange little Annie, whose bluntness seemed to delight him. "You're a very black man, aren't you? Not all Negroes are as black as you," she said straight out, and when no one in the family scolded her, for she had merely uttered a simple truth and had done so without racial prejudice, Mr. Epps laughed heartily at her words.

Or was it one of the young boys in the camp, ten-year-old Oliver, or Salmon or Watson, who seemed to be in charge of the livestock, sturdy, young, high-spirited fellows eager to talk with the stranger and show him the virtues of their herd of handsome red cattle and the purebred ram and ewes? He made much of the animals, shoving his hand deep into the fleeces and exclaiming loudly over their weight and density, but the rest of us merely watched and let the boys take his compliments.

Or maybe it was Ruth, the shy, calmly competent young woman who busied herself with the evening meal and kept her back to the man as much as possible, in spite of his pushing his animated face at her, first at one side, then the other, interrupting her work with over-elaborated questions. "Now, tell me, Miss Brown," he said to her, "who taught you so you come to possess such a knowledge, that you can cook this here panbread and pease porridge and so on, all by yourself out here on a big, open fire for such a large family of people?"

Without looking up, Ruth answered, "My mother," and resumed her silence, which caused Mr. Epps to pay ornate compliments to

Mary—knowing nothing, of course, of our true mother's death eighteen years earlier, for it was she who had taught Ruth to cook, not Mary. He rattled on just the same, as if our mother were still alive.

Or perhaps the person to ingratiate himself with was me, the red-headed young man whose left arm stayed bent as if permanently fixed that way, the tall fellow who stood slightly off from the others, guarded and watchful, which I am sure is how he viewed me that first time. But he did not seem to know how to address me, perhaps because I was closest to his age and a man and therefore would know more easily than the others when he was playing the cheerful darkie and when he was sincere, although I could not.

There was the young woman whom the elder Mr. Brown had introduced as his wife, Mary, a pleasant, open-faced woman who looked twenty or more years younger than her husband, eager to make the visitor comfortable. He tried her, but saw in a moment that she intended to deflect his every inquiry and observation by referring him straight to her husband, the hatchet-faced man from whom the tall young fellow had evidently got his red hair and gray eyes.

All right, then, he would chat up the Old Man himself, jabber with him awhile about horseflesh, for that was what he was concerned about this evening, and it was a subject on which Mr. Epps considered himself capable of sounding like an expert. And, at least to Father, he did so.

He was not especially religious, I noted, for he, as did I, kept one eye open and on the food while Father prayed over it. He loudly exclaimed "A-men!" when Father finished, and ate like a man who had not sat down to a proper meal in a week, which was probably the case. The difficulties he had faced in these last few days in Westport, importuning white strangers who scorned and spurned him, came to my mind, and I began to feel sorry for the man and somewhat regretted my earlier disapproval. I continued, however, to retain a degree of skepticism as to his character.

By the time he left the camp that first night, Mr. Epps had arranged with Father to work as a teamster for us. "Ain't no way to get a team pull that wagon over to North Elba without an experienced driver to discuss the subject with them," he said. "Them mountains scares animals all the way to sick and lazy."

I'm sure the Old Man believed that I, or he himself, was quite capable of driving a team to North Elba, but he admired Mr. Epps's pluck and self-confidence and agreed to exchange some seed and other supplies for his services. No doubt he wanted simply to help the man out.

Early the next morning, Father, Mr. Epps, and I, with the horse Dan in tow, showed up at Mr. Clarke's dockside stone warehouse, a barn-sized storage building with a large stable attached, where he kept six or eight teams of horses and as many wagons, for he hauled freight all up and down the western shore of the lake, from Port Henry to Port Kent and inland to Elizabethtown and even to North Elba.

Father and Mr. Clarke, who was a bespectacled New Englander with a thin face and white chin-whiskers, quickly agreed on a price for old Dan. Then Mr. Clarke tried to sell Father a handsome matched pair of Narragansetts, grays that seemed to be, as he claimed, healthy seven-year-olds. The price was reasonable, but even with what he was being offered for Dan, it was more than Father had in his possession.

I could see the Old Man running down his inventory of possessions, wondering what he could sell to make up the difference. But then Mr. Epps stepped forward and in a clear voice said, "That 'Gansett yonder spavined in both hocks and be done in less than a year. The other one, Mister Brown, he ain't got no heart at all. Narrow chest on him. You take them old Morgans in the back," he advised.

"The bays?" Mr. Clarke said, and he laughed. "Come on, Brown. They're barely worth shoe-leather. Your nigger's off his nut," he said to Father.

The price for the Morgans, because of their age, was less than that for the Narragansetts, but still more than Father had in his pocket. Father said, "I believe I will take my friend's advice," and held out the money, all his money in the world, I knew. "But you'll have to take a few dollars less than what you're asking, especially if, as you say, they're not worth shoe-leather."

Mr. Clarke did not want that. He shook his head and said, "Tell you what, Mister Brown. You keep your money. And you can keep that old broken-down gelding of yours, too. Me, I don't like to see a white man made a fool of by a nigger. So I'll swap you even, the team of 'Gansetts for any one pair of those fancy cows you got. You can choose the cattle yourself."

Father hesitated a moment. Morgans were not so famous then as they are now, especially outside the state of Vermont, and neither Father nor I knew much about the breed. And, whatever his reasons, Mr. Clarke's eagerness to sell us the others did seem to our advantage. But Father said, "No. I will sell you the gelding, sir, as we agreed, and if you'll accept it, I will add to it what remaining cash I have for those bays, the Morgans. As my friend here has advised me. And I will keep all my cattle."

I was not sure he was doing the wise thing, but knew better than to offer my opinion. The Old Man had made up his mind. To my eye, the Narragansetts were definitely the superior team and well worth the weakest pair of cattle from our herd. The transaction Mr. Clarke had proposed would have left us with five cattle, an excellent team of horses, old Dan, and sufficient cash to protect us against a weak harvest.

Father said, "The bays, sir."

Mr. Clarke gave Father a thin-lipped smile, took his money, and wrote out a bill of sale. Then he made Father sign a receipt for the horses. "Just so you don't change your mind, or tell folks I cheated you," he said, and with no more words, he retreated abruptly to his office.

"Well, Mister Brown, you catched the man out," Mr. Epps said, as we unhitched the small, weary-looking pair of Morgans and led them from the darkness of the stable into the bright light of the yard outside, where their looks did not improve. "Believe me, these bays going to carry you where you want to go, and they still be drawing your plow across your field long after you gone. Make you a good saddle horse, too."

The Old Man's eyes flashed with pleasure, and he clapped Mr. Epps on the back. "You know, Mister Epps, I love it when one of these racist Yankees hoists himself like that!" he exclaimed, and laughed.

"Yassuh," Mr. Epps quietly answered, and we drove the horses back to camp.

Shortly after dawn the next day, we departed Westport for North Elba. The sky, I remember, was cloudless and bright blue—one of those cool, dry northcountry mornings that let you see sharply all the way to the far horizon. Our teamster, Mr. Epps, sat up on the box with Mary, who was feeling poorly. Little Sarah, who was four that spring, settled herself happily between her mother and Mr. Epps. The rest of us walked, with Father and me out at the front of the team, while a short ways behind the wagon, Ruth walked hand-in-hand with seven-year-old Annie, and the boys Watson, Salmon, and Oliver herded the sheep, cattle, and swine along at the rear. The horses, to my surprise, seemed untroubled by the loaded wagon, and they responded quickly and smoothly to Mr. Epps's commands. Of course, we were still on a relatively flat, dry road and would be for half the day, at least until we got to Elizabethtown, where the steep ascent supposedly began.

Father wanted us to leave Westport with dignity and evident seriousness of purpose—so as not to comfort any of the locals who might think us foolish or pitiable, he explained. Consequently, we moved briskly, heads held high and eyes squarely on the road before us, and kept the separate parts of our caravan distinct from one another, as if we were a military parade passing in review. We wore jackets and waistcoats and hats, as usual, and the little girls and Ruth and Mary wore mob hats and shawls over their shoulders, and their dark outer skirts were appropriately long. Farmers leaned on their hoes, and women and children came to their kitchen doors, to watch us as we passed out of the town and headed northwest towards the first gentle hills of the interior.

A few miles beyond the settlement, we came to a tilted, unpainted shanty that served as a tollbooth and signaled the start of the new Northwest Road to Elizabethtown, more cart track than road. A bar blocked our way. The Northwest Road had been cut through the forest by a private company that had purchased the narrow band of land on which it ran, so as to profit from the traffic. Evidently, Father had not anticipated this, for when he had made his only previous journey to North Elba last fall, he'd come in from the lake at Port Kent by a some-what more northerly route—through Ausable Forks and Wilmington Notch—with no toll road.

An old, grizzled fellow in floppy trousers and patchwork shirt emerged from the shanty, hobbling on a badly constructed crutch—a veteran, to judge from his U.S. Army braces. He scrutinized our wagon and animals for a few seconds, spat a brown stream of tobacco juice, and said to Father, "Cost you forty cents for the wagon and team. Cost you seventy cents for them there cows. The sheeps and pigs can pass free."

Father drew himself up and said, "My friend, I have no money. We're not hauling freight to sell at a profit. We're a poor family on our way to settle a piece of land in North Elba."

"Don't matter to me where you're headed, mister. Or why. I charges by the axle and the hoof. Far's I can see, you got two axles and at least nine sets of hoofs. I'm ignoring them sheeps and the pigs. You want to use this road, it's going to cost you one dollar and ten cents, total."

"I'll have to pay you on my return," Father said.

"Can't do that."

"And if I refuse to pay you now?"

This puzzled the old fellow. He gnashed his wad of tobacco and spat again. "Say what?"

Father turned to me. "Remove the bar, Owen."

I walked over to the barked pole, which was laid into a pair of notched posts, lifted one end, and swung it away, clearing the road. The toll-taker, with Father blocking his approach to the bar, stared in disbelief. Immediately, Mr. Epps chucked to the horses and drove the wagon through, with Ruth and Annie following somberly behind, and then came the cattle, driven by Watson and Salmon, and the sheep, driven by Oliver and the pair of dogs. Oliver wore a mischievous grin on his freckled face and waved at the toll-taker as he passed by.

Father said to the old man, "I apologize for my son's rudeness. He's nine years old and should know better. And I give you my word, friend, on my next return to Westport, I'll pay the toll." Then he and I replaced the bar and hurried to catch up to the others.

As Father strode past Oliver, he reached out and with the back of his hand struck the boy a hard blow across his unsuspecting smile. "*Never* mock a man for doing his duty," he said, and without breaking his stride moved rapidly alongside me to our former position at the front.

After a few moments, I glanced back over my shoulder and saw that Oliver's face was bright red from the blow. He had turned his head to the side in an attempt to hide his tears, while the other boys stared straight on down the road, politely averting their gaze.

Back in Springfield, Father and I had fitted out the box of our wagon with a white canvas canopy stretched over a bent willow frame, for the purpose of protecting the contents and shielding Mary and Ruth and the smaller children when it rained. Also, we intended the wagon to provide a little privacy and serve as sleeping quarters for the females.

Until Westport, this had worked out fine, but now, with so many supplies added to our household goods and tools, passengers were obliged to stay out on the open seat at the front with the driver, for there was no room for anyone to sit or lie down under the canopy.

We had brought all of Father's surveying tools with us, and his old tanning knives, spuds, and chisels, a small bark mill and various other implements and basins retained from his tanning years, for, during his previous journey to the Adirondacks, the Old Man had observed plenty of hickory trees, both shagbarks and butternut, and he planned to set up a small tannery in North Elba and perhaps teach the trade to some of the Negro settlers. We had also packed into the wagon our broadaxes, hatchets, adzes, hammers, wedges, and froes—tools that we would need for clearing the overgrown land that Mr. Smith had deeded to Father. We carried a pair of grass scythes, a bull rake, hay forks, and reaping forks; we had a small hornhead anvil, various types of nails, jack hooks, and a fine oak tumbril sledge that Father himself had built one winter years ago back in Pennsylvania; we had braces and augers and a good pit saw, a bucksaw, and a half-dozen chisels and planes: we carried all the tools, or most of them anyway, that the Old Man, in spite of bankruptcy and lawsuits, had accumulated and held on to in his various homesteading ventures and numerous business operations in Pennsylvania, Ohio, and Massachusetts.

We also carried our mattresses, bedding, and clothing, and the furniture that Father and Mary had brought out from the house in Ohio to Springfield the year before—a pair of small chests, Father's writing table, Great-Grandfather Brown's mantel clock, Mary's spinning wheel, and Ruth's loom; and all the cooking implements and pots, the bowls, plates, mugs, and tableware; and, of course, Father's big chest of books, which had traveled everywhere with us, from Ohio to Pennsylvania, back to Ohio and on to Springfield, and now to North Elba. To these things, in Westport, we had added kegs of salt, flour, dried beef, corn,

crackers, seed, and feed for the animals, buckets for collecting and boiling down maple sap, a washtub, extra harness, and a plow.

As a result of the great weight of these goods, the wagon creaked
and groaned on its axles. The spring mud had gone out early that year,
fortunately, and the big, iron-sheathed wheels ground down the stone
and gravel of the track, as the team of Morgans drew it slowly from the
broad, greening valley of Lake Champlain to the upland, leafless forests
and the freshly plowed fields and gardens of Elizabethtown.

The bays surprised me with their steadiness and strength, and my
opinion of Mr. Epps rose somewhat, as he eased the animals along in a
calm and confident way, turning to his side now and then to chat with
Sarah or inquiring into Mary's comfort or periodically informing us as
to the names of the streams we passed and occasionally forded and the
names of the snow-capped mountains that slowly hove into view in the
distance. "We coming along the Boquet River here," Mr. Epps told us.
"All the rivers up here flows north to Canada, Mister Brown. Them
rivers and streams just like colored folks, you know, following the
drinking-gourd star. When folks running from slavery see the rivers
start to flow north, they know they almost free," he said. "And that
snowy mountain in the west called Giant of the Valley, and over there
you can see the tip of Whiteface. Can't see none of the truly high ones
yet," he cheerfully informed us, although to my flatlander's eye Giant of
the Valley and Whiteface seemed like towering Alps.

When we entered the village of Elizabethtown—which was the seat
of government for Essex County and where, facing the commons, an
imposing, white-columned brick courthouse was located—I observed
that, off to the northwest, the sky was filling with dark clouds, and
although the sun still shone on us, I feared that it would soon rain.

We stopped on the commons for a rest and food and to water the
animals at a long wooden trough at the side of the road there. While
Mr. Epps and the boys tended to the livestock and Ruth prepared our

lunch of corn bread and molasses, Father and I rigged a cover over the driver's seat of the wagon, so that Mary, who was coughing and appeared to be suffering from the beginnings of ague, would be protected from the weather.

After we had eaten, Father strode off to the courthouse for a brief visit to the office of the registrar of deeds, where, from a cursory examination of the public rolls, he determined, just as he had been told the previous fall by the folks in Timbuctoo, that longtime landholders and squatters in North Elba, white men, were indeed claiming significant portions of the grants that Mr. Gerrit Smith had made to the Negroes. Announcing summarily to the registrar that he intended very soon to survey and to register the deeds for every one of Mr. Smith's grants of land, the Old Man warned the fellow outright not to list any new lands on the Essex County tax rolls without a surveyor's map and proper bill of sale and deed attached.

"Judging from all the fancy brick houses I've seen hereabouts, I believe that there are in this town more than a few lawyers who would be pleased to defend in a court of law the property rights of a free Negro, if they knew they were defending as well the property rights of Mister Gerrit Smith," he warned the registrar. "Mister Smith, as you of all people must know, is the single largest taxpayer in this county," he added.

Delighted, Father reported back to us that the man had received his announcement with an open-mouthed, astonished gape that had made him look extremely foolish, even simple. He imitated the fellow, and we all—except Mr. Epps, I noticed—laughed uproariously, for Father rarely made faces, and he looked quite comical when he did. Even Oliver laughed—although to himself he might have observed that the fellow mocked by Father was no less of a man doing his duty than had been the toll-taker. Inconsistency in small matters was not something that any of us held against the Old Man however. In fact, we almost welcomed it, for in the larger matters, where we, like most everyone else, turned weak and wobbly, he was like purified iron, of a piece and entirely consistent, through and through.

It was close to an hour after noon when we departed from Elizabethtown, heading northwest through a thick forest of pines and balsam trees, and almost at once we moved steeply uphill, with a roaring brook crashing past us over huge rocks from the heights to the village and farms spread out in the valley below. The sky had nearly filled with dark clouds now, and as we ascended, the temperature steadily fell, and soon there was a distinct chill in the air, causing me and the boys to button our waistcoats and jackets around us and Father to haul his greatcoat from the wagon. Ruth and Annie drew their shawls over their heads, and up on the wagon, Mary got out blankets, wrapped one around her and Sarah, passed another to Mr. Epps and a third to Ruth and Annie.

A stiff breeze had come up behind us, and the knowledge that we would soon be wet and cold silenced us. The horses plodded steadily on, slower now but still with a powerful rhythm, despite the unbroken uphill climb and the great weight of the load. Mr. Epps had grown somber. No one spoke as we climbed into the weather. Even the birds had gone silent.

The trail wound slowly ahead between great, tall trees, with the rocky stream still beside us. We had not passed a dwelling place or cleared patch of land for a long while, when suddenly we were over the top, and the trail was passing through a broad intervale between two high distant ridges. We passed alongside a beaver pond spiked with the dark standing trunks of drowned trees, when finally, a little ways further, the Old Man gave a signal, and we stopped.

Here we rested the animals for a while and stood in the shelter of the wagon, our backs to the wind and collars up, hands holding on to the brims of our hats and head coverings. We must have resembled one of the Lost Tribes, wrapped in blankets and old-fashioned woolen garments, clustered around our wagon and livestock on a wilderness trail in the mountains, unsure of whether to push on or go back.

The Old Man studied the glowering sky and said, "Mister Epps, I believe it will soon snow."

"Probably no more than some rain will fall down in the valleys," Mr. Epps said. "But you are right, Mister Brown; going to snow up here. Might amount to nothing, might turn out a real blizzard. Never can tell this time of year. You want to wait it out?" he asked Father. "Can hole up in them trees yonder," he said, pointing out a nearby grove of tall pines backed and partially sheltered by a high, rocky outcropping. The dark cliffs were close enough to the trail so that we could reach their protection easily with the wagon and make a safe overnight camp there.

Several large, wet flakes of snow brushed past my face. Father asked Mary how she felt. "I'm fine," she said. "Don't do anything strictly on my account." But she did not look well: her face was gray and pinched with discomfort, if not pain, and she was shivering.

"I'm concerned somewhat for the livestock," Father said to Mr. Epps. "If we're out here all night in a snowstorm, we'll do fine, but we might lose a few of the sheep. The animals are pureblood and aren't yet bred for winter exposure, and they have been kept inside since November." He asked if there was a farm between this spot and the valley ahead, where the tiny village of Keene was located.

Mr. Epps answered that we would not see a house or barn until we got down off these heights, but we were closer to the Keene valley now than to Elizabethtown, so we should not go back. He remembered that there was a large farm located down in the valley a mile or so this side of the village. We might be able to put up there if this turned into a real storm.

Father removed his hat, and with his hands against his thighs, he lowered his head and prayed silently for a moment, while we stood by and watched. Then he turned to us and said, "Let us keep on, children. Our heavenly Father will protect us."

"Well, yes, but we better cut us a brake while we got good trees for it," Mr. Epps said. "A few miles yonder, them big wheels going to need a spoke pole for getting this load downhill." I quickly pulled the axes from the wagon and took Watson into the trees a ways, and in short order we had cut and trimmed a spruce pole that was long enough to pass through the rear wheels of the wagon.

By the time we resumed our journey, the snow was falling heavily. The mountain ridges on either side had disappeared from view, and as we plodded ahead we could see only a few feet in front of us and to the sides. We were all now shrouded in blankets, except for the Old Man in his greatcoat. The snow was wet and stuck to us, turning us white, even Mr. Epps. Father and I stumbled along in front, searching out the trail a few feet at a time, waving Mr. Epps and the team on as we found it. Hours passed like this, until finally the ground under our feet began to tip and fall away, and we realized that we had reached the beginning of the descent to the valley.

Mary and Sarah got down from the wagon to walk behind it, and Mr. Epps drove the animals now by walking beside them at their heads, talking to them in a quiet, calm voice. Father instructed Ruth to carry Sarah on her back and told Oliver not to let go of Annie's hand. Watson and Salmon were to hold the livestock back from the wagon a good ways, but keep them moving, he said, don't let them huddle up and stall, especially the sheep. Then he and I attached a length of rope to each end of the brake pole. I walked on one side of the wagon, and Father walked at the other, ready for me to shove the pole across to him, under the wagon bed and through the spokes, whenever the wagon threatened to rush the horses.

It was a slow, nasty business, coming down that long, rocky trail ten and fifteen feet at a time all the way to the valley. At first, the slope was a gentle incline, and Father and I were able to hold the wagon off the horses by tying the driver's brake back and pushing uphill against the box from the front, our feet skidding and slipping clumsily in the snow. But soon the descent quickened, and the wagon started to break loose. I grabbed the spruce pole out of the wagon box and slung it across to Father, and we each raced to a tree beside the trail and lashed the rope around it, locking the wheels. Then we let the lines out slowly and inched the wagon down the rough trail, skidding it like a sledge, until the ropes had run nearly all the way out, when we each tied the end to the tree and scrambled down to the wagon and chocked the wheels with rocks. Then we stumbled back uphill to the trees, untied the slack ropes, and walked them forward a ways, where we wound them around a nearer pair of trees. We drew them taut again, reached down with our free hand and removed the chocks, and let the wagon slide another few feet. Over and over, endlessly, it seemed, we followed in the blinding snow the same elaborate, painful procedure, and somewhere out there in front Mr. Epps calmed the snow-covered horses and kept them moving together on the nearly invisible trail. My face froze, and the rope burned my hands raw, and the rocks tore at the tender, exposed skin of my palms and fingers, while slowly, bit by bit, we lowered the wagon through the storm to the valley floor—where, as we descended, the clouds seemed to rise, and the snow gradually turned to sleet, then to cold rain.

By the time we got to level ground, it was almost dark, but we could see again. There were maple trees with fresh buds glistening on wet limbs, a meandering river, cleared, flat meadows covered with new grass, and steep mountains rising swiftly from the plain and disappearing in low, dark gray clouds.

In spite of our ordeal, we appeared to be in good shape. The team of Morgans that Mr. Epps had advised the Old Man to buy looked positively heroic to me now. Mr. Epps seemed as shrewd to me as he did to himself. I grinned at him, and to my surprise he smiled modestly, almost shyly, back.

My hands and Father's were raw and blistered, and our clothes were soaked through. Poor Mary and Ruth and the children came trudging along behind us, looking miserable, wet, and cold, but immensely relieved to be down from the mountain. And further back came the red Devon cattle and Father's precious long-faced merino sheep and the pigs, with Salmon and Oliver, using the collies, dutifully keeping them together, hollering and chasing after the stragglers, beating them back into line with their sticks. A short ways ahead, I saw a white, two-storey farmhouse with a long porch facing the road and a large, unpainted barn and several ramshackle outbuildings behind it, and when I pointed the place out to the Old Man, he merely nodded, as if he had known it would be there and did not need me to show it to him.

Finally, when we had all come up and were gathered together beside the wagon, Father removed his hat and prepared again to pray. This time, however, he ordered us to do likewise. "Let us give thanks, children," he said, and we each uncovered our heads, every one of us, even Mr. Epps.

In his clear, thin voice, Father said, "Heavenly Father, we humbly thank thee for bringing thy children one more time safely through the storm. We thank thee, O Lord, for protecting us and our worldly goods against the travails and terrors of the mountain fastness and the fury of the storm. We who are wholly undeserving of thy boundless care and protection, O Lord, we humbly thank thee. Amen."

Mr. Epps said his "A-men!" and quickly snapped his hat back on. I followed, and the others did also, except for Father, who remained bareheaded, face screwed up and eyes tightly shut. Uneasily, because of Mr. Epps's presence, perhaps, we all walked a few steps away and did not look at the Old Man, and a moment later, as if wakened abruptly from sleep, he re-joined us, seeming somewhat distracted, if not downright dazed. This was his usual manner following prayer, however, and we were all quite used to it and never remarked on it, even amongst ourselves. From our viewpoint, simply, the Old Man prayed with greater intensity than the rest of us. From our viewpoint, the Old Man did everything with greater intensity than the rest of us.

By the time we reached the roadside farm, the rain had ceased, and the clouds had drifted back up the snow-whitened slopes to cover only the mountaintops above, revealing a broad, grassy floodplain here below. A mile or so further, Mr. Epps informed us, was the village of Keene, where eight or ten additional families resided. "Mostly, they just scratches out a living. Not much different from us folks up there beyond the notch in Timbuctoo," he said, pointing to a sharp cut in the distant high ridge to the west.

Father said, "That, Mister Epps, will soon change."

"Yassuh, Mister Brown," he said, and our eyes met for an instant, and I saw that he did not believe that the Old Man would be able to change anything, anywhere.

As we approached the white house and barn, we noticed that the place, clearly a once-prosperous dairy farm, was showing distinct signs of inattention—broken fences and tumbled walls, windblown shingles on the ground, a two- or three-year-old pile of dung collected behind the barn, and none of the abundant cleared land tilled yet.

The place was owned by a man in his mid-twenties, a Mr. Caleb Partridge—whose youth, when he opened the door to Father's knock, surprised me—and his middle-aged wife, Martha. The couple welcomed us in, evidently pleased by the unexpected prospect of extending food and shelter to such a bedraggled party of travelers. Mr. Partridge, a tall, gaunt man with a thick black beard and heavy teeth, had a brutish handsomeness about him. His wife was pink-faced and plain as oats and seemed almost simple in her shyness, for she giggled nervously whenever one of the adults spoke, even when I was the speaker, and listened with great seriousness to whatever the children, Annie and Sarah, offered by way of conversation, as if only they did not frighten her.

The couple, apparently childless, resided there alone with an aged woman, whom the man introduced as his wife's mother. She sat in a corner of the large kitchen, mumbling and nodding agreeably to herself, while we warmed our faces and hands and dried our clothing before the huge fireplace and while Mrs. Partridge fussed over Ruth and Mary and the little girls, bringing cloths to help them dry their hair and serving up bowls of hot cider and ample portions of freshly baked corn bread.

Later, when the boys and Mr. Epps and I had fed and bedded down the animals and returned to the house, we all seated ourselves at the Partridges' long trestle table before a steaming pot of venison stew. Mr. Epps, however, hung back by the corner of the fireplace, where he stood with his dark face held deliberately away from us. Finally, Father noticed him there and said, "Ah, Mister Epps! Come quickly, or your bowl will be snatched by one of these greedy children!"

The Partridges, all three, even the old lady, looked up at Father with expressions of mild surprise on their bland faces. But Mrs. Partridge quickly fetched another plate and spoon, and Mr. Epps crossed to the table and joined us, seating himself with serious mien between me and Watson and directly across from Father, who then took the liberty, as he put it, of blessing the meal—whereupon with great appetite we all did eat.

We stabled our animals in the barn that night and—except for Mary, Ruth, Sarah, and Annie, who were given pallets inside the house by the fire—slept in the loft above. It had once been a fine, tight structure, but now the roof leaked, floorboards were rotting, and the hay was several years old and filled with dust and debris. Two scrawny milch cows were all the Partridges seemed to own for livestock, and they looked like aged, weak milkers ready to quit.

Apparently, most of the Partridges' cattle had died off in recent years or had been butchered for beef or sold. For income during the long winters, Mr. Partridge had taken to killing large numbers of deer and shipping the venison by sledge south to Albany. He complained that the place was too large for him and his wife to work alone, and there were no men in the area who hired out. The woman had inherited the property from her father, a veteran of the Ticonderoga campaigns in the Revolution, who had taken a land grant here as payment for his military services and thus had been one of the first settlers in the region. Mr. Partridge, the landless third son of a New Hampshire grower of flax, had himself been a farmer for hire, had wandered here from New England, and had come to ownership of the farm nearly six years ago by marrying his employer's only child and heir a few months before his employer's death.

I learned all this the next morning, following our departure from the farm, from Father, who had stayed up late talking with Mr. Partridge, after the rest of us had staggered off to the barn to sleep. The Old Man had a way of eliciting personal information from strangers when he got them alone. His questions were disarmingly direct, and his inquiry seemed almost scientific in its detachment, which in a sense it was, for he was not so much interested in a man's personal life as he was in learning about his character and about human nature generally. Usually, when Father interrogated a person new to him, his immediate aim was to move the inquiry, by way of questions about family and background, to the question of slavery and race, so as to distinguish friend from foe, certainly, but also because, according to Father, it was on this question more than any other that a white man revealed the true nature of his character.

"Our benefactor and new neighbor, Mister Partridge," he said to me as we walked along at the head of our little caravan, "is one of those men who says he finds slavery and Negroes equally repugnant. But I believe that he would happily accept both, if it saved his wife's farm from ruin and left him free to hunt and fish." He added, "I doubt he'll be of much use to us."

We had left just at sunrise, under a cloudless deep blue sky with the morning star and a half-moon floating high beside us in the south like a diamond and a silver bowl. The road was somewhat mudded from yesterday's rain, but Mr. Epps expected it to be dried out by the time we got up into the mountains again, where, he explained, the road crossed mostly stone anyhow. After passing through the tiny settlement of Keene—a post office, general store, log church, tavern, and a half-dozen log houses huddled together and guarded by mangy, long-haired dogs that all seemed to be related—we crossed the East Branch of the Au Sable River and made our way easefully uphill past freshly plowed fields, switch-backing towards the notch that cut through the range of mountains which lay between us and North Elba.

I had not liked Mr. Partridge, and I told Father that.

"No," he said, "nor did I. I suspect he beats the woman and secretly mistreats the old lady. The man bears watching, though. Somewhere along the line," he said, "I fear we'll have to cut him down."

This, of course, I could not then imagine, for no one seemed less likely to oppose us and our work with the Negroes of Timbuctoo in any focused way than the lazy young man in whose house we had just stayed. But when it came to knowing ahead of time who would oppose him, the Old Man could be downright prescient. On a dozen or more occasions, I had seen him accurately predict which man from a congregation or town, to keep us Browns from fulfilling our pledge to rid this nation of slavery, would threaten our very lives, which man would simply turn away and let us continue, and which man would join us in the work. The Lord's Work, as Father called it.

"Well," said I, "at least the fellow was hospitable to travelers."

"I would not call it that."

"We're ten people. Nine of us and Mister Epps, and he fed and housed us all, and he let us enjoy his fire and shelter our animals. I'd call that hospitable, Father." Though I did not like Mr. Partridge, in those days I sometimes found myself feeling sorry for individuals that the Old Man harshly condemned.

"You don't know him as well as I."

"Tell me, then. Tell me what you know about Mister Partridge that I don't. Beyond his marrying a homely woman for her property."

"Trust me, Owen."

"Father, I'm trying to!"

We walked in silence for a while, and then Father said, "You remember when he came out to help me hitch the team to the wagon, while the rest of you were tending the beeves and sheep, and Ruth and Mary and the girls were inside the house?"

"I saw him out there, yes."

"Well, the man came up to me and asked for payment for our food and lodging. He presented me with an itemized bill, written out." It was an embarrassment to Father. Not because he had no money to give Mr. Partridge, he said, but because he had not expected it. If he had anticipated Mr. Partridge's charges, he would have negotiated an acceptable arrangement beforehand, and failing that, we would have camped someplace alongside the river. Mr. Partridge had surprised Father, and he found himself painfully embarrassed by it.

We resumed walking uphill in silence, with the wagon and team of Morgans, in Mr. Epps's capable hands, clambering along behind us, Mary and Ruth and the girls all together now on foot and cheerfully admiring the spectacular vistas opening up on either side of the track, and, at the rear, the boys and our small herd of livestock. The road made its circuitous, slowly ascending way along the back of a buttressing ridge. The morning sun was shining full upon our backs now, and it was as if yesterday's brief snowstorm had never occurred.

"I must make a confession, Owen," the Old Man went on. I said nothing, and he continued. "It concerns Mister Partridge. The man's request for payment confused me. I told him that I could not pay him with money, because I had none. I'm ashamed to say that I gave him instead the clock."

"The clock? Your grandfather's clock?"

"Yes."

I was astonished. Except for his chest of books, Great-Grandfather Brown's mantel clock was Father's most valued household possession. Made of cherrywood, it was a treasure that had been entrusted to Father's care years earlier by his own father; it was perhaps his only family heirloom. It made no sense to me. How could he have handed it over to Mr. Partridge so easily? And in exchange for so little—a single night's lodging.

"I simply retrieved the clock from the wagon, unwrapped it, and passed it over to him, and he accepted it as payment quite happily and at once carried it into his house. Where I hope Mary and Ruth did not see it."

I looked back at the women. Ruth held her half-sister Sarah's hand, and beside her Mary held Annie's; the two women were themselves holding hands and chatting lightly to one another. "No, I'm sure they didn't see Mister Partridge carrying off Great-Grandfather's clock. They seem very happy," I added uselessly.

"They will know it soon enough. Oh, I am a fool!" he pronounced. "A fool!"

I did not know what to say, so, as usual, said nothing. Most times, when I did not understand something that Father had done or said, it was because he had acted or spoken more wisely than I. At such times, for obvious reasons, my best course was to remain silent and await the arrival of understanding. In this case, however, the Old Man had indeed been foolish, and by comparison I was the wise one.

Still, I remained silent. I loved my father, and respected him, even when he did a foolish or wrong thing.

By mid-morning, we were well out of the valley, and for a while the track turned steeply uphill. Mr. Epps, or Lyman, as I had begun calling him, got down from the box and walked beside the struggling horses, coaxing them on, and Father and I fell back and got behind the wagon and put our shoulders to it. The dense, impenetrable forests up here had never been cut, even those trees that closed like a pale against the road, and the towering pines and spruces had begun to block off the sky from our view, covering us with thick, cooling day-long shadows.

Although we were now far above the greening valley, the air was still sufficiently warm that most of yesterday's snowfall had melted early and had run off the sides into small rivulets and brooks that dropped away from the ridge, disappearing into the forest, where we could see dark gray remnants of the winter snows, which looked permanent, practically, and glacial. The only birds we saw up here were curious little chickadees and siskins and the occasional screaming blue jay—winter birds. None of the hardwood trees or low bushes had put out their buds yet, and the scattered thatches of grasses we saw lay in yellowed mats, still dead from last year's frost.

Nothing in the natural world appeared ready for the resurrection of spring. Worse, it was as if we were steadily slipping backwards in time, with May and then April disappearing behind us and darkest winter rising into view just ahead. Soon we were struggling through yesterday's unmelted, ankle-deep snow. It was cold and nearly dark here below the tall trees, as if earlier this morning, before crossing overhead, the sun, unbeknownst to us, had reversed its path and had descended and set behind us. Except for Father, we had shrouded ourselves with blankets again. A steady, high wind blew through the upper branches of the trees, raising a distant unbroken chorus of grieving voices to accompany our slow pilgrimage.

After a while, almost without my noticing it, the ground leveled off somewhat, and Father and I no longer had to stay close to the wagon to be ready to push it. Our little group had strung itself out practically in single file, as if we each of us wished to be alone with our morbid thoughts, with Father in his greatcoat up at the head of the column, and then the team and wagon driven by Lyman, and me trudging along in its tracks. Behind me came Mary, Ruth, Sarah, and Annie, picking their way through the snow in a ragged line, while stretching back for many rods walked the livestock, singly or sometimes two animals abreast, with Salmon and Oliver positioned among them to keep them moving, and back somewhere out of sight, Watson and the collie dogs brought up the rear.

The road by now had dwindled to a narrow, palisadoed trail barely the width of our wagon. It no longer switch-backed across the side of the mountain, and there were no longer the occasional breaks in the trees with views of the forested slopes and ridges below. Instead, plunging across slabs of rock and over snarls of thick roots, the trail ran straight into the still-darkening forest, as if down a tunnel, and had we met a wagon or coach coming out of the tunnel towards us, we could not have turned aside to let it rush past. It seemed that there was nothing ahead of us but slowly encroaching snow and darkness.

When, suddenly, as if struck by a blow, I realized that we had emerged from the forest. Light poured down from the skies, and the towering trees seemed to bow and back away. Dazzled by the abrupt abundance of light and space, I saw that we were passing along the shore of a long, narrow lake that lay like a steel scimitar below high, rocky escarpments and cliffs, beyond which there loomed still higher mountains, which curved away and disappeared in the distance. The enormous scale of open space, snow-covered mountains, precipices, and black, sheer cliffs diminished our size to that of tiny insects, as we made our slow way along the edge of the glistening lake. Wonderstruck, gaping, we traced the hilt of the sword-shaped body of water and crossed the long slant of its cutting edge to the point, where we exited from the gorge as if through an ancient stone gate.

We had passed through Cascade Notch, and below us lay the beautiful wide valley of North Elba. Off to our left, mighty Tahawus and McIntyre rose from the plain, splitting the southeastern cloudbank. To our right, in the northwest, we could see Whiteface Mountain, aged and dignified by its wide scars and pale gray in the fading afternoon sun. And between the mountains, spreading out at our feet for miles, lay undulating forests scratched by the dark lines of rivers and the rich, dark tablelands, grassy meadows, and marshes that we would call the Plains of Abraham.

Lyman drew the wagon to a halt, and the family came and gathered around it and admired the wonderful sight together. We removed the damp blankets from our shoulders, folded them and placed them back into the wagon. Then Father took himself off from us a ways and lowered his head and silently prayed, while the rest of us continued simply to admire the generosity and beauty of the land.

For a long time, no one spoke, and then, when Father had rejoined us, Lyman said, "We better keep moving, Browns, if we wants to get home by nightfall." He slapped the reins, and the wagon jerked forward along the rocky, narrow road, and we all moved back into line behind it, walking easily downhill into the valley, as the sun descended towards the hills and mountains beyond.

6

On our arrival at North Elba, after Lyman Epps had departed for his own home, we passed nearly a full week at the long-abandoned farm on the Keene Road, before any of us ventured forth again—time spent unpacking the wagon and cleaning, re-organizing, and repairing the tumble-down cabin and shed, which were too small to be properly called a house and barn. In various ways we were stretching the structures so as to fit our many belongings and our numerous selves. Then, on the morning that I came to breakfast ready to commence plowing the one sizeable, cleared field on the place, Father instructed me not to plow.

This surprised me. With the shortness of the growing season, there was a clear need to get the ground turned over and the seed sown as quickly as possible. It was a clear, dry day, and Watson and Salmon were already waiting for me in the shed. I stood at the door to the cabin on my way outside, while Father perched on a three-legged stool next to the stove, finishing his morning shave.

"You don't want me to plow today," I said to him, making it a statement, not a question. Repeating his words was one of my ways of getting the Old Man to explain his purpose without seeming to question his authority.

"No. Saddle the lead horse, Adelphi, for me. I've developed a real fondness for the animal. And hitch the off-horse to the wagon and load up my transit and lines," he said. "It's time for you and me to call on our African neighbors. Time for us to go to Timbuctoo."

Although I wasn't particularly glad of the chance to put off the plowing, I was eager to see Timbuctoo, for I had never visited a Negro farming community before. As far as I knew, this was the only one in the Northeast, although Father said there were a few just across the border, in Canada. I remember wishing that it had a different name, however. I knew from Lyman that, while the acreage that Gerrit Smith had given them to farm was located in the valley in various spots, the Negroes had clustered their cabins together on a narrow, rising section of the tableland southeast of the village of North Elba. They might have called their settlement the Heights, I thought, or South Elba. But, no, they had named it Timbuctoo.

"Same as Timbuctoo in Guinea," Lyman had explained to me. "You know, like the way white folks call their towns New London and New York and Manchester and such, so as to bring back to their minds the place they came from." They had even made a flag to fly above the settlement, he told me. "Red, like the blood of the slaves, with one star on it. The freedom star."

I could see that from their perspective, although they had no more memory of Africa than I had of England, Timbuctoo was an affectionate and respectful name, which I am sure is how Father took it. No doubt their need went beyond that, for while I was connected to my English forefathers by means of the language I spoke, the Negroes' links to their ancestors had been cut away by slavery, which gave the word "Timbuctoo" a greater resonance in their ears than did words like "Manchester" and "New London" in mine. But I could also hear the whites in the region saying the Negroes' name for their settlement in a derisive and derogatory way.

"Wouldn't it be better, this first time, for us just to walk over there?" I asked the Old Man. "In a neighborly way, as equals among equals?" I didn't want to make our first appearance there with Father up on horseback and me driving a wagon. The picture put me out somewhat, made me feel slightly uncomfortable, for it placed us on a height in our first meetings with these people, who, according to Lyman, owned no horses or oxen, had but a few swine and dunghill fowl, and drew their plows themselves or chopped their soil by hand with hoes and spades. Our elevated position might suggest that we regarded ourselves as Mr. Gerrit Smith's newly hired overseers riding out to examine the number and condition of the plantation darkies.

Father wiped his razor clean and stood and buttoned his waistcoat. Mary, who was again feeling poorly, lay abed where she and Father had slept on the mattress placed next to the stove. The rest of us had slept in the attic above. With just two rooms downstairs, the cabin, though cozy and clean, was crowded as a small boat. "No," Father said. "I can understand your discomfort, but it's necessary for us to make a proper show for them. They are a downtrodden people, Owen. And we need them to see that Mister Smith has taken them seriously enough to send out a significant sort of man to deal with them." When you offer your services to men who consider themselves mighty, he explained, it's good to go modestly and small. An honest man approaches Herod's tent with dust on his sandals. But when you come to help people who for generations have been made to regard themselves as lowly and undeserving, you come as grandly as you can and with fanfare. The first gift we offer them, he said, will be a sense of their great value as human beings. They are not simply the despised ex-property of men, they are the blessed children of God, and until they possess that high a view of themselves, they will not be able to utilize our further gifts. "So wear your coat and hat, son," he said, with a hint of a smile on his thin lips. "And button your shirt to your throat. Today you must look like the son of an important man. A surveyor. You can wear your plowman's smock tomorrow."

Father rode ahead of me, seated like a preacher, erect and reflective-seeming, as if he were not admiring or even conscious of the splendid scenery that surrounded us. He was fully as aware of the landscape as I, however. More so, probably. He no longer surprised me when, after a journey during which I had believed him throughout to have been lost in thought, he gave to Mary or the others who had remained at home a vividly detailed report of everything that we had passed, even including the flowers in the glades, the birds in the trees, and the trees and shrubs, all of which he had carefully noted to himself and had named in passing and had remembered.

"When we have named a thing, we have begun to *see* it," he often said. "And in so doing we praise and give continual thanks to our heavenly Father. Thus it is to God's greater glory that we name the most obscure flower in His field." He had made a game of it when we were children, testing our abilities to identify by name, not the hawkweed or purple vetch or red trillium, which everyone knew and admired, but the tiny heal-all, the spotted knapweed, and the lowly squawroot. Salmon was the best of us. Even as a small boy of seven or eight, he knew the names and uses of hundreds of flowers and plants that the rest of us, including Father, barely noticed. He knew that the burnet weed will staunch a wound, that coltsfoot will cure a cough, and that a sick deer will eat pickerelweed, and he knew where in forest and field to find them all.

Father's and my arrival at the settlement was not quite the grand occasion that I had expected. But it was more the fault of my high expectations than the somewhat dismal reality I encountered, and my expectations, I felt, were more the fault of Lyman than of Father. Earlier, as our journey into the mountains from Westport had progressed, Lyman had spoken to me with increasing friendliness and sincerity. Then, lying side by side in the stale hay of the Partridge barn, he and I had talked long after the others had fallen to sleep. That was when he told me to call him Lyman, since we were close in age, and I agreed, but with reluctance, for somehow my calling him by his given name seemed, in my eyes, at least, to demean him.

"You'll have to call me Owen, then," I told him, and after he had done it several times, it no longer seemed so strange for me not to be addressing him in Father's way, as Mr. Epps.

He was eager to hear about the famous Negro abolitionist and orator Frederick Douglass, the escaped slave who had visited Father several times in Springfield the previous year. Lyman was mightily impressed that Father was sufficiently connected to Mr. Douglass that the great man had actually visited our home and had even stayed overnight with us. I may have been a little over-impressed with it myself and thus doubtless exaggerated somewhat the firmness of the connection, for Father and Mr. Douglass had not yet formed the close association that would mark their later relations. And that in turn might account for Lyman's exaggerated report of the Negro settlement in North Elba, in terms both of their number and of their achievements as settlers. He may have been trying to impress the son of a close friend of the famous Frederick Douglass.

There were, he said, close to a hundred Negroes living in North Elba, most of them freedmen, with a small number of fugitives secreted among them, individuals who could not be named. "Could be, Owen, that I myself am running from a slavemaster," he said, "and the next man be the freedman. You can't know which is which, can't tell one from the other, freedman or slave, unless I name him for you—and even then, how you going to be sure? So long as you know that *one* of us is free, then the next man is safe. Leastways up there in the mountains he's safe, because the slave-catchers, they don't dare show their faces in Timbuctoo."

The Negroes were armed, he said, and would kill any man who came sneaking around looking to haul a single one of them, man, woman, or child, back to slavery. I lay there in the darkness next to him, rapt with pleasure, as he described a remnant people settled in the wilderness and living off the land, an industrious people, secure and vigilant, setting lookouts on the peaks, with elaborate signaling systems, rams' horns and drums, to give the warning whenever a stranger entered their wild domain. I pictured valiant Negroes ambushing their enemies at the mountain passes.

For years, Father had told us stories about the Maroons of Jamaica, whom he so admired—those escaped slaves who had fled into the mountainous interior of their island and who for half a century fought off the mighty British army, until finally the King of England gave up the fight and let them stay in their highland villages, where they raised their families and ruled their territory unimpeded. I saw the Negroes of Timbuctoo as a modern American version of those old Jamaicans, and of the rebellious slaves who had followed Toussaint L'Ouverture into the mountain fastness of Hispaniola, waiting for the moment when they would have the numbers and the occasion to sweep down upon the sugarcane plantations along the coastal plain and strike a death blow against their French owners, freeing themselves from servitude forever. I imagined the Negroes of Timbuctoo to be warriors of that high order.

Lyman told me that they had built their cabins close together all in one place to make them easy to defend, and when they worked their fields, which were often located far from their cabins, they went armed with swords and guns. Even the women and children, he said. I asked who was their general or leader. Was there one among them who functioned as a chieftain, and how had they elected him? I remember peering through a broken window in Mr. Partridge's loft to the shrubby field behind the barn, where fireflies lit up the spring night like the silent firing of the guns of a hundred scattered, hidden warriors—here, here, here; gone, gone, gone—harassing their huge, clumsy enemy, maddening him with the accumulated pain of many small blows struck by an army of black-skinned warriors made invisible by the darkness.

"No one chief rules us," Lyman said. "What we do, Owen, is reason together. We sit and talk things out, mostly amongst the men who knows a thing or two. Men such as myself. And then we comes to an agreement together about how we going to do this and that. Course, there's some folks who gets listened to more closely than the others, there's some who don't get no never mind at all, and there's some who're in between. Me, I'm one of the in-between fellows. On account of my still being a young man and all. But with me working for Mister Brown now, that could change some. Folks up there thinks highly of Mister Brown," he said, wistfully, as if he had forgotten that I was the son of Mr. Brown, almost as if he had forgotten for a moment that I was white, which pleased me. More than that, it comforted me.

It never happened that when in the presence of a Negro I did not feel perceived as white and then at once begin to think of myself in those terms also. No matter how used to the presence of Negroes I became—and since my early childhood, Father, whenever possible, had brought all types of Negroes into our household, providing us with daily, respectful proximity to them—a black person made me constantly conscious of my whiteness. I could not forget it. It angered me in a way that left me secretly ashamed. And on those occasions, in a childish way, I sometimes actually wished that Negroes did not exist— as if their very presence in our country were pestilential and the disease of race-consciousness were their fault and not ours.

I didn't know how to inoculate myself against this disease, except to associate strictly with whites, which I could never do and call myself a man. Because of our history together, I didn't know how to see around or through a black person's race, and thus I could not see around or through my own. And whenever I became aware of my whiteness, I was ashamed. Not just because of the horrors of slavery, although that surely provided plenty of reason for any white American to feel ashamed of his race, but because, in the eyes of the God of my father and, most importantly, in the eyes of my father himself, race-consciousness was wrong. Just as wrong as not being able to forget, whenever I found myself in the presence of a woman, that I was a man and not just a fellow human being. It was as if race-consciousness, like sex-consciousness, were some kind of uncontrollable lust that left a white man with no regard for the deep, personal relations of friendship and family.

Pride, lust, envy—these are the certain consequences of race-consciousness, whether you are black or white, just as they are the consequences of thinking constantly of your maleness or femaleness when in the presence of the other sex. It affects you in such a way that you either feel proud of your race or sex, mere accidents of birth, or envy the other's; proud, you think of the other person as available for your base and sensual use, or else, ashamed, you wish to have the other person make use of you. You do not view yourself or the other person simply as a *person*. Perhaps only the old New England Puritans or certain of their latter-day descendants, like Father, were properly equipped, morally and intellectually, to recognize and defeat such serpentine failings. I, however, despite Father's best intentions and teaching, was not so equipped, and as a result, I frequently added a fourth sin to the list—wrath. For on those occasions when I had become enraged by my inability to overcome my weakness, I directed my anger, not at myself, as I should have, but against the person whose race had made me conscious of my own race or the person whose sex had enflamed me. The latter I might defeat by living like an anchorite and withholding myself from the company of women other than those related to me by

blood, which, of course, is precisely what I have done. The former, however, I could defeat only by abandoning my pledge to dedicate my life
to the destruction of slavery and arranging my life so as to associate
only with white people. But waging war against slavery was my sworn
duty, as marriage was not, and by the time I had reached my young
manhood, thanks to the imprint made upon my mind and spirit by
Father, abdication of it was no longer imagineable.

It was for such complicated and barely understood reasons as
these, then, that I found myself strangely and powerfully soothed by
Lyman's presence that night in the barn in Keene. It was the idea of an
oppressed people's flight to sanctuary in the impenetrable mountains
that seduced me—that and the brief relief from the burden of race-consciousness that came over me as I lay in the dark beside Lyman Epps, a
black man my own age who spoke to me as if I were not white, as if, in
fact, I were black or he were white—as if we two were of the same race.

I lay there in the hay, astonished and full of wonder and delight.
My usual high agitation, which I had come to think of as a permanent
aspect of my mind, had ceased altogether. And for a few precious
moments that night, I did not feel like a stranger to myself. A peculiar
restfulness had come over me like a warm breeze—and I thought that
all the years of my life so far, since the death of my mother long before,
I had been traveling far from home, a child moving through the world
disguised as an adult; and now, unexpectedly, on this May night in a
barn in the Adirondack mountains, I had been allowed to remove my
disguise and settle into my childhood bed, a boy again. I reached out in
the dark and took Lyman's hand in mine, and held it for a long time,
with neither of us moving or saying anything, until, still holding his
hand, I fell peacefully asleep.

The next day, on returning to my usual agitated state, I realized
with horror that, for all its innocence, my simple, affectionate gesture
might well have been regarded by Lyman as brazen or even wanton,

and therefore despicable. To my immense relief, Lyman showed no sign of having misunderstood me, and we continued to engage one another for the rest of our journey to North Elba with the same easy familiarity of the evening before. When our little caravan finally arrived at our new home, Father paid him for his services with the sack of seed and supplies that he had promised, and Lyman waved a simple goodbye and walked on down the road. And I did not see him again until Father and I rode into the place called Timbuctoo.

A few miles south of the village of North Elba, we passed off the old Military Road onto a rutted, rocky lane and into the woods, with Father in the lead on Adelphi and me in the wagon behind him, driving the horse we had named Poke. From the condition of the trail, it was clear that not many wagons had passed this way before, and several times Father had to dismount and clear away fallen branches before I could proceed. Then suddenly we entered a cleared space marred by the charred stumps of trees, and before us were some eight or ten cabins, which were more like shanties than proper log cabins, little huts made of sticks and old cast-off boards and patches of canvas.

It was a camp, not a village, with no sign of the palisade and neat log houses set around a protected square as I had imagined. There was indeed a flagpole set in the middle of the clearing, just as Lyman had said, but the pole, stuck into a pile of rocks, was tilted at a pathetic angle, and dangling from the top was a tattered banner made from an old piece of red wool, a shirt or piece of a blanket, upon which I could make out a roughly cut five-pointed yellow star.

Except for a few undersized pigs rooting about in heaps of garbage and a half-dozen scrawny fowl picking at the wet, smelly ground that lay behind the privies, the place looked abandoned. Then I saw several small children with somber brown and black faces peering out from the doorways, and I noticed that here and there an adult's dark hand had drawn back a rag from a window so that the owner of the hand could observe our approach unseen from the gloom of the cabin.

After a moment, a bearded Negro man of middle-age appeared at the door of one of the shacks and for a second regarded us with caution, when, apparently recognizing Father from his earlier visit, he smiled broadly and said, "Mis-ter Brown!" and stepped forward to greet us. Then several others, men and women with children trailing behind, emerged from their homes—which I must call hovels, for I do not know what else to call them, they were so poorly constructed and maintained. I could not imagine enduring the bitterly cold winter winds and snow with no more protection than those sad bits of shelter provided. I myself would have fled long since, I thought. Or else I would have built me a proper log cabin and fireplace. The lassitude and disarray of these people amazed and bewildered me. They seemed exhausted and demoralized.

Stepping from one of the huts came a man who, after a few seconds of thinking he was a stranger, I realized was my friend Lyman Epps. He looked oddly unlike himself here, smaller, thinner, flat-faced, as if all the force had gone out of him. Even his skin, which previously had been the color of anthracite, had lost its depth and glow and had turned flint gray. Father had commenced to speak with several of the men, in particular to the middle-aged fellow with the beard who had come forward before the others and appeared to be their spokesman. Ignoring me, or so it seemed, Lyman edged past the wagon and attempted to position himself at the front of the group of men speaking with Father—a nervous little colored man he was, uneasy and, as I had first regarded him down in Westport, not to be trusted.

He, of course, had not changed in the few days since I had last seen him. Sitting up on my wagon, the son of the great John Brown, a prosperous white man come with his father to assist and uplift these poor, benighted souls, I was the one who had changed. The other men did not defer to or even acknowledge Lyman's attempts to gain Father's attention; they shouldered him aside and blocked him out entirely, as Father spoke to the group of his intention to survey and stake their property lines and register them with the county clerk's office over in Elizabethtown.

This would entail certain changes in how they did business, he explained, because it meant that they would now be liable for taxes on their land. "But you will own your land, my friends. No man, white or black, can encroach upon it, and you will therefore be free to use it as you please, even to sell it, if you wish, or to pass it on to your children." But in order to pay taxes, he went on, they would have to raise more than just enough to survive on; they would have to raise a cash crop or produce a product which they could then sell in the nearby towns for cash money.

I didn't believe Father was telling these people anything they didn't already know. They weren't European peasants or field hands straight off an Alabama cotton plantation. That was the problem, perhaps. Except for the fugitive slaves amongst them, who could not make themselves known and, of course, could not own land in the United States anyhow and probably would soon disappear into Canada, where they could freely settle, the residents of Timbuctoo were men and women with city skills—blacksmiths like Lyman, waiters, barbers, harnessmakers—people who had made pennies at a trade and had saved them and bought their freedom or, thanks to the kindness of their owners or because they were of no particular use as chattel, had been granted it.

At last, Lyman noticed my presence. Due to my innate shyness, but also because of the complexity and turbulence of my feelings, I hadn't put myself forward and instead had waited for him to make the first gesture. Which he did, but only after finding himself unable to gain Father's attention. He held the ears of the horse Poke and touched the animal's forehead with his own, then looked up at me and smiled and asked, "How's the Morgan horses holding up, Mister Brown?"

"Owen," I said, more a rebuke than a correction.

"They seems rested up," he said. "Fine pair of animals, ain't they? Got some age on 'em, but they gonna give you plenty of service. They be plowing your fields long after you gone from here," he said, repeating what he had said to Father back in Westport—an empty remark now, where before it had been a fresh recommendation and a promise. A slender young woman, round-faced and with slitted eyes, wearing a tattered yellow shift, a knitted shawl over her shoulders, had approached us and now stood behind Lyman, watching him. I raised my hat to acknowledge her, which caused her to look down at her bare feet. She was a pretty, tea-brown woman, with glistening, wiry hair cut short and worn like a tight black skullcap, and she stood with her hands at her sides, as if waiting for instructions.

Lyman put one hand on her shoulder and drew her forward. "Come meet young Mister Brown. This here's my wife, Susan," he announced to me.

"How . . . how do," I stammered, for I was surprised by this information, that Lyman had a wife; in all our conversations, he hadn't mentioned her, not even in passing. I hadn't inquired into his marital state, but nevertheless it's difficult to spend several days and nights with a person, as he had with me, and not mention a wife, if you have one, and consequently I had simply assumed that his silence on the subject, like mine, meant that he was unmarried. Now I found myself angry at him, as if he had deliberately deceived me.

"You never mentioned you were married," I said to him.

Father, having heard me speak, turned and saw Lyman. "Ah, Mister Epps, there you are!" he said, and at once Lyman left me and, with his hand still on his wife's shoulder, moved towards the Old Man, who swung down from his horse and shook hands with him and made a pleasant fuss over the woman—as I should have done.

I did follow the Old Man's example of getting down from the

wagon, though, and joined him as he spoke with Lyman and his wife. Father was gracious with her, as he always was with women; regardless of their race or station, he pointedly treated them as equal to himself. I myself was too shy to speak with any woman directly—except, of course, for my sisters and my stepmother, Mary. It was Mary whom Father was speaking of when I drew up to him. He was explaining that she was ill and needed more help with the household chores than could be provided by Ruth and the younger children.

"Since the birth of our infant who died this April past, my wife has been poorly," he said. "But not so poorly that she could not stand and work, until now. I believe, however, that if she is allowed to keep to her bed for a spell, she will recover."

This was news to me, but Mary naturally did not confide in me, and I confess that I did not make a habit of observing her condition. I bore great good will towards the woman but could not help feeling some-what distant from her, through no fault of her own, certainly. Unlike Ruth, Fred, Jason, and John, I had remained unable to shift my affec-tions for our true mother over to my father's wife.

"Would you be willing to work for me in the fields?" Father asked Lyman. "Susan I would also like to hire, to keep house and care for the smaller children. You could both put up at our place until the fall, eat at our table, and take a quarter-share in the harvest, so that you could then get your own farm off to a proper start next year."

I touched Father's sleeve with my hand. "We have barely enough room for ourselves, Father," I said in a low voice. "The boys and I can handle the planting and haying and the livestock ourselves. Ruth is capable of the rest, with the little ones to help her."

Father gave me a hard look. "Owen," was all he said. He resumed talking to Lyman and Susan, and I stalked off. I knew that Lyman and his wife would agree at once to come over and live with us. However crowded it was at our place, there would be more room for the couple there than in their shack here in Timbuctoo, and a quarter-share of our crop would probably be twice what the man could raise alone on his own land. At our table they would eat a full meal every day, which they surely never did at their own. Also, Lyman's standing in the Negro community, which seemed to me on the low side, would rise considerably from his and his wife's association with our family.

But I also knew what the Old Man was up to: if he was going to be of any use to these people, he needed to bring at least one of them into close affiliation with our family, a trusted and trusting person who would help him penetrate the community, to speak for him to the others and to inform him as to their thoughts and needs. It was how he always worked. Beyond surveying their land grants, beyond teaching the Negroes how to farm in this climate and on this stingy soil, Father wanted to set up an Underground Railroad station in North Elba, where there was none, at least no station with any known connections to the lines that ran to Canada along the New York side of the Champlain Valley. He intended to carry escaped slaves out of the South by way of the Adirondack mountain passes, a route that until now had been used only in isolated cases, when some poor soul somehow got off the main route by accident and slipped through the iron-mining camps on the south side of Tahawus and followed rumor north through Indian Pass to Timbuctoo and then, traveling alone and at great risk, worked his lonely way north and east to connect finally with the Lake Champlain line by means of the Quaker stationmasters in Port Kent and Plattsburgh.

In Father's mind, the passes and ridges of the Adirondacks were the northernmost extension of the entire Appalachian Range, which ran all the way back through New York State to the Pennsylvania Alleghenies down into Virginia and on into the very center of the slaveholding region. His map of the Railroad was unlike anyone else's—unlike Harriet Tubman's, unlike Frederick Douglass's, unlike the

Quakers'. On Father's map, the southernmost lines fed like taproots from the cotton plantations of Alabama, Mississippi, and Georgia up into the mountains of Tennessee, North Carolina, and Virginia, where the main trunk line flowed north and east. It did not split one way towards Niagara and the other towards the Hudson Valley and Lake Champlain, as the other maps had it, but ran in a single line between the two into the rocky heart of the Adirondacks, straight to North Elba, where a long night's ride could get you over the border into Canada.

Father spoke often and elaborately of this map, and to implement it, he needed Lyman Epps and his wife, Susan—because the Old Man worked his Railroad alone. He had always done it that way. Whether in Ohio or Pennsylvania or Springfield, Massachusetts, John Brown ran his own Underground Railroad line, and that obliged him to forge his own connections to the Negroes. Except for the members of his immediate family, Father did not trust white people, not even the lifelong radical abolitionists like himself, as much as he trusted black people. "In this work, it's their lives that are at stake," he often said. "Not ours. When it comes to a showdown, white people can always go home and pretend to read their Bibles, if they want. A black man will have to fire his gun. Who would you rather have at your side, a well-meaning white fellow who can cut and run if he wants, or a Negro man whose freedom is on the line?"

Later in the day, after Father had assured the community that they were the legal landholders in Timbuctoo and that he would return and commence his survey on the following day, we took our leave of the gloomy place. In order to prepare his next day's work, he carried with him all such bills of sale and contracts and deeds as the landholders had in their possession—so greatly did the Negroes trust the Old Man that they willingly delivered up to him their only evidence of their rights to their land. Not that Father would ever betray them; they were right to trust him. But the effect Father had on Negroes was difficult to understand. Mostly I attributed it to the rage against slavery that he never ceased to express; although sometimes, when I was down on Father myself, I attributed it to the gullibility of the Negroes. The fact is, more than any other white man, Father consistently managed to make Negro people believe that their struggle against the evils of slavery and the daily pain and suffering imposed on them by racial prejudice were his as well, despite the fact that he was so often a white man in a preacher's suit sitting up on a very tall horse.

Lyman and Susan, with a single sack of belongings and some shabby bedding and a corn mattress tied in a roll, accompanied us as passengers in the wagon. They sat in the box behind me, and I drove, silent and somber, and as before, the Old Man rode ahead on Adelphi. Every now and then he called back to Lyman and asked the name of a mountain or inquired as to the ownership of a particular stretch of roadside land, and Lyman always had a ready answer—whether it was the correct answer, I could not then say, but I did suspect that he was making them up to please and impress the Old Man. Later, to my ongoing chagrin, I learned, of course, that he had been accurate in every case. He knew the names of all the peaks in our sight, and he knew whose land was whose and the history and use of every landmark. I was behaving like a spurned lover, I knew, but could not help myself.

When we arrived back at the farm, Father presented Lyman and his wife to Mary, who still lay abed next to the stove, looking very ill, I finally realized. Her appearance frightened me—her skin was slack and chalky, her small, plain face was almost expressionless, and she moved and spoke slowly and with precision, as if she were in pain. Expressing pleasure to have Susan as a helpmate to Ruth, she welcomed the couple to the house. "There is not much room here, as you see, but the place is bright and airy," she said to them in a weak voice.

"We will have to get along like Shakers," Father declared. "Which means that Mister Epps will make his bed on the male side of the attic, and Missus Epps will sleep opposite with Ruth and the girls. I trust that won't prove a difficult arrangement," he said to Lyman, who glanced overhead towards the attic and smiled and said that it would be just fine. I do not know what his wife thought. They had given over their privacy, perhaps, but in exchange had received superior shelter. It was, as Father's joke implied, more than a little like the exchange many people made in those days, when they gave up their houses and neighbors and moved in with the Shakers, whose roofs, like ours, did not leak and whose tables provided plenty of simple fare.

I touched Ruth's arm and drew her with a signal to follow me outside. We passed around the corner of the house and made our way up the brushy slope in back, where we both sat on a broad, rough rock embedded in the hillside and looked out over the shake roof of the house to the forested plain and mountains beyond. It was mid-afternoon, and the sun was sliding off to our right a ways, casting over us and the house and small barn long shadows from the pine trees that grew on the hillside behind us. In the meadow, in dappled sunlight, the Devon cattle were grazing, and the sheep were scattered up on the scrub-covered hillside beyond. In front of the house, where the boys were stacking firewood, Father's horse and the other horse stood waiting to be watered and set loose to graze alongside the cattle.

It was a lovely scene, actually—a peaceful, orderly domicile and farm set down in the midst of splendid scenery, a kind of ideal farmstead. Yet, for all that, I saw it as a thrashing and violently upset scene, with its warring elements held in place almost against their nature, constrained and barely kept in check by a trembling willfulness. Father's, I suppose, but, to a lesser degree, mine also.

Ruth seemed to sense the high degree of my agitation, and she stroked the back of my hand, as if to calm me. "What's the trouble, Owen?" she asked. "Did something untoward happen today?"

"No, no, nothing. Although the place, Timbuctoo, was a disappointment to me," I said and briefly described the sad state of the encampment.

She tried to comfort me by saying what I knew myself, that it could not be otherwise, for the poor folks who lived there owned few tools and no livestock to speak of, and, as Father had told us many times, they knew nothing of how to farm in this climate. I had always admired Ruth's character and in some ways envied her, for she seemed to have no difficulty in making herself behave exactly as she should—the good daughter to Father, the loyal and loving stepdaughter to Mary, and, to me and all the others in our family, the perfect sister.

I, however, since earliest childhood, had struggled constantly with a rebellious spirit, my mind in a continuous state of disarray and brooding resentment, and so it seemed that I was forever being placed under the lash of self-chastizement and correction. Alone among my brothers and sisters, Ruth understood this about me and did not condemn me for it. I could never have confessed to John or Jason or even to poor Fred what I then confessed to her. "Oh, Ruth," I blurted, "I want very much just to leave this place!"

"That's a *terrible* wish," she said in a hushed voice, as if I had blasphemed.

"It shouldn't be."

"But Father needs you, and Mother needs you."

"She's not our mother."

"Yes, Owen, she is."

"Not to me."

"We have no other mother. And she's ill and weak, and there's so much to do here before we can call it a proper farm. And Father can't do what he came here to do, unless he has your help."

"I know all that. But I want to leave this place. I want to get away, that's all. From everything. This farm, the Negroes, these mountains!" I said, waving my hand at the peaks in the distance, as if they were ugly to me. They weren't ugly to me, but I was angry and confused—wrathful was what I was, for, uncertain as to the object of my anger, I was smearing it over everything in sight. "How can you *do* it, Ruth? Don't you wish our life were different? Don't you wish we could live normally someplace, like other people, in a town or even on a farm close to other farms? I want to live like the white people in Springfield, or even down there in Westport. This place is a wilderness," I said. "And there's no one here for us to be with, except the Negroes. You should see their place, over in Timbuctoo!" I said, fairly spitting the name. "We're not like them. And we're not like the dumb, ignorant white farmers around here, either. We're different than that fellow Mister Partridge back in Keene, or the squatters living around here trying to steal the land off the Negroes. We're different. And alone."

Ruth put her arm around me, and we were both silent, and after a moment, I managed to clear my mind somewhat and said to her, "I'm sorry, Ruth. I shouldn't be like this with you." She patted my hand sweetly, and we were silent for a moment more. "Tell me what's wrong with Mary," I said. "Is it something serious? She won't die, will she?"

Ruth did not answer for a long time. Then she said, "No, I don't think it's serious. She has female problems, Owen. That's all. From her lying-in last fall with the birth of Ellen, which hasn't healed. She will heal, though, and be well again, but only if she keeps to her bed and rests. Father knows how she is and what's wrong. He understands what she needs. By bringing in the colored woman, he's protecting Mother against her own good nature and her need to be always at work. And with the woman to help, I'll be able to do the rest. And with Mister Epps helping the boys run the farm, you'll be free to work alongside Father and the Negroes. It's only for a few months, Owen, and then our life will settle down again, I'm sure of it."

"It'll *never* settle down again!" I declared. "It's never been settled! Not since our mother died have we been at peace in this family!"

"That's not true, Owen."

"Don't you remember how it was before our mother died?"

"No," she declared, and then abruptly she stood and said, "Come, I must get back to the house. I've got churning—"

"Wait a moment. Just let me tell you how it was then. Because it changed, Ruth, after she died. Believe me, it changed," I said.

"Owen, I know the story. You must settle your mind. You should pray, Owen, that's what. You should pray for forgiveness, and to obtain peace of mind. You're too much alone, the way you've fallen from belief. I can't talk to you," she said firmly, and moved off from the rock where I sat. "Only the Lord can give you what you need. I have to get back to the house," she said, and she turned and left me.

I sat in the shade alone awhile then, remembering how it was when I entered the room and learned that my mother had died. I remembered the darkness that swirled like black smoke about my mother's head as she disappeared into it and was gone. I recalled myself staring at the darkness. It had hardened into a flat black circle that was located in the exact center of my vision, as if a hole had been burned into the lenses of my eyes, and no matter where I looked, it was there, a wafer of darkness, with people and objects disappearing behind it as I turned my head from side to side. I carried that circle before me for many years, and when the hole in my lenses finally healed, there remained scars, opaque and whitened, which every now and then swam into my field of vision and again blocked out the world before me.

As on this late spring afternoon in North Elba, when I stumbled half-blind down from the meadow and entered the cabin, where Father and Lyman Epps and his wife, Susan, stood talking quietly with Mary, who lay abed on a pallet near the stove, while Ruth sat on a stool nearby, calmly churning butter.

I could not see Father at all, although I stared directly at his location and spoke directly to the spot where he stood. Father was in a circle of light, actually, situated somewhere behind it, as if occluded by a sun floating in the space between me and him, so that he was eclipsed by it. On the peripheries I saw Lyman, looking alarmed, and his wife, Susan, frightened also, by my wild visage, no doubt, and the words that splashed from my mouth.

"Father, I have to tell you something!" I began, and then I glimpsed Ruth looking up at me, dismayed, and Mary seeming bewildered and pained by the force of my entry, by the loud interruption of my ill-coordinated and off-balance body lurching through the portal as I broke into the placidity of the room, my voice loud and cracking as I spoke the words. "Father, you must let me leave! Father, I'm sorry . . . ," I began, and then I stopped myself. Struggling to make my desire to flee these mountains known to him in a coherent way, wanting merely his simple permission to go and live as I wished, I felt more like a child overwhelmed by a tantrum than a twenty-five-year-old man expressing his regret that he must disappoint his father in order to satisfy himself.

"You want to leave us?" Father said, pronouncing the words slowly, as if he barely understood them. "You want to fall away from your family and abandon the work we have come here to do? Just as you have fallen away from the Lord and His work?" He paused and drew his breath in through his teeth. "I love thee, Owen, and for just this reason I have prayed for thee ever since I first saw that you had moved so far from the Lord and His word and will. I knew that it would lead here, and that there would come a time when your duty would seem meaningless to you. So where do you wish to go, Owen?" His face, reddened and tight with anger, belied his calm words. His gray eyes had gone cold on me, and I felt an actual chill in my bones, as if a damp breeze had suddenly blown through the room.

"Am I not a man, Father? Am I not free to go where I wish and live as I wish?"

"I wouldn't have you beside me or in my house, if you did not your-self choose to be there. Where do you wish to go, Owen?"

"Well, I want only to leave here. I . . . I'm not sure where I want to go to. Back to Springfield, I guess. To join John there, maybe. To help him, or find work on my own. I don't know."

"So it's not that you've learned of someplace else, then, where you can do your duty to God and your fellow man more effectively than you can here. It's merely that you're loath to do it here. I say that you are behaving in a cowardly manner, Owen. Think like a slave, and you are one. A free man doesn't flee his duty, unless he's able to do it better someplace else. You disappoint me greatly, Owen," he pronounced. "*Springfield!* What can you do in Springfield with regard to your duty, whether it's your duty to your family or to your fellow man, that you can't better do here? We have all pledged, every one of us, to bend our lives to overcoming the scourge of slavery. Some of us do it in order to do God's work, and some others simply because they are human beings who are themselves diminished by the existence of slavery. But for all of us, it is our duty! We've all taken a pledge that, not kept, will betray, not only God and our fellow man and not only our family members, but ourselves! I can't let you do that, Owen. Not without opposing you. I cannot—"

"Oh, stop! Father, stop, please!" I shouted, silencing him, sending him back behind the light of the sun. At the edges, I saw Lyman and Susan step away, as if about to flee. Mary had brought her hand to her mouth, and Ruth was rising from her stool, both of them looking at me as if my face were covered with blood. Which is indeed how I felt at that moment, as if my face were sheeted with a spill of blood. "I can't go, Father! And I can't stay! I can't give myself over to the slaves, and I can't leave them! I can't pray, and yet I can't cease trying to pray. I cannot believe in God, Father. But I can't abandon my belief, either. What am I to do? Please, tell me. What am I to do?"

He reached out of the light then and placed both hands sweetly onto my shoulders and drew me to him in an embrace. "My poor boy," he said in a voice almost a whisper. "My poor boy."

My thoughts and feelings were a tangled mass of contradictions, but his embrace settled them at once and straightened them and laid them down side by side in my mind, like logs of different sizes and kinds placed parallel to one another. An unexpected, powerful wave of gratitude washed over me, when, suddenly, I became aware of a clattering noise, the sound of boots against the floor, the noise of several large people entering the dim room. I heard voices, Oliver's and Salmon's, and the voices of several men—strangers.

Quickly, I stepped back from Father and turned to see three men, accompanied eagerly by Oliver, Salmon, and Watson behind, all six of them making their way into the small room, the men with pack-baskets, their clothes mudded and swatched with briars and leaves, their dirty faces red and swollen from numerous insect bites. They looked embarrassed to have come in upon us so abruptly and made awkward moves to get back outside, bumping one another and the boys behind, so there was for a moment a burly congestion at the door.

Finally, one of the men, a tall, blond, bearded fellow, turned back to Father and smiled sheepishly and said, "I'm sorry, sir, but the lads said for us to come straight inside. Forgive our rudeness for not first announcing ourselves."

Father moved straight to the man, and I found myself standing next to Lyman, who gently touched my arm with his fingertips in a gesture of affection. In a formal and dry tone, Father said to the blond man, "I am John Brown. This is my farm. How can I help you?"

The boys had removed themselves from the cabin, and the two other strangers had followed and now stood in the yard, while the one who had spoken faced Father from the portal. He was of middle-age, tall and athletic-looking, but clearly not a hunter or woodsman or farmer: his clothing, although filthy and matted with leaves and forest debris, was of too fine a cut, and his pack was a sportsman's, not a hunter's. I saw then that, despite his bright and polite manner, the man was sick with insect bites—his face, neck, and hands were puffed up like an adder. He and his companions appeared to have been stung a thousand times by mosquitoes and by the wretched clouds of black flies that populate the forests here. They swarm like a pestilence and are so numerous as to madden and blind a deer and drive it into the water and cause it to drown. If you don't cover your skin with grease or carry a smutch, they can cloud out the light of day, fill your nostrils and ears, and swell up the flesh of your face until your eyes are forced shut.

The man then introduced himself as Mr. Richard Henry Dana, Esquire, of Boston. His companions, who had slouched to the ground next to the house in apparent exhaustion, were a Mr. Metcalf and a Mr. Aikens, also of Boston, and all three, he said, were lawyers out on a wilderness holiday. They had come up from Westport, had passed several days visiting the mining village of Tahawus, on the further side of Indian Pass, had ascended Mount Tahawus with a guide from the village, and then had struck out for North Elba on their own, anticipating a hike of some six or eight hours. But they had lost the blazes of the trail, he explained, and had wandered through the thick, tangled forests for two days with nothing for nourishment but a single trout caught with a bent pin and piece of red flannel by Mr. Aikens. "He thinks of himself as something of a woodsman," Mr. Dana said with a winning smile. Their one fire had been doused by rain, and the black flies had plagued them throughout their ordeal.

"We ask you to spare us a little food, if you can," Mr. Dana said to Father. "And allow us to sleep overnight here on the ground. And perhaps you'll direct us on to North Elba and Osgood's Tavern in the morning, where we've been expected for two days now."

Calmly, Father directed Ruth to bring the men water and a pitcher of milk and some corn bread and to feed them slowly, so they wouldn't vomit it up. "We'll give you a proper meal later, when we all sit down for supper, but that should ease you somewhat now," he said, and he escorted the men outside, led the three of them around to the shaded side of the house, and bade them lie down there, while Ruth brought them nourishment and a salve for their insect bites. He told Watson to bring the men a smutch against the flies and instructed the rest of us to attend to our labors—it was time to bring in the cattle and sheep. There was work to be done, putting up the livestock and milking the cows and building the cookfire in the stove, hauling water from the spring, bringing up a string of trout from the river below, brushing down the horses for the night—the daily round of work that we all fell to without a thought, as natural a part of our lives as breathing in and out.

The storm in my breast and mind had passed. But I knew that it would return. I knew also that it had weakened me so greatly that when it did return, I would be even more dangerously tossed about than I had been today. I did not know what would bring it on—a cross word from Lyman, a disappointment concerning the work with the Negroes, a further decline in Mary's health, or an incomprehensible command from Father—but any one of these alone might be sufficient to set me off again. I was, during those first few weeks at North Elba, precariously balanced between opposing commitments which were set to create the shape of the rest of my life, and I knew that not to choose between them would lead me inescapably to a resolution that expressed, not my will, but Father's.

Mr. Dana was, of course, the world-famous author, who, many years later, after Father's execution had made him world-famous as well, published a detailed account of his fortunate meeting with us that day at the edge of the wilderness. He described Ruth very nicely as "a bonny, buxom young woman of some twenty summers, with fair skin and red hair," and he praised her "good humor, hearty kindness, good sense, and helpfulness." He was complimentary also to Mary. And even to me, whom he remembered as "a full-sized red-haired son, who seemed to be foreman of the farm." Father he got right, and he even mentioned Lyman and his wife, Susan, exclaiming over the fact that they sat with us at table that night and were introduced by Father to Mr. Dana and his companions properly and formally, with the prefixes Mr. and Mrs.

Naturally, at the time of his visit we did not know who he was. Nor did he know who we were. To us, he and his companions were merely a set of pathetic city folks lost three days in the woods. To him, we were a farm family settled in the wilderness, wholly admirable, exemplary even—an ideal American family of Christian yeomen. In his innocent eyes, we were bred to duty and principle, and held to them, he wrote, by a power recognized by all as coming directly from above.

7

Here, Miss Mayo, let me tell you a story, a true story, one of the very few ever told of the Underground Railroad, for, as you must know by now, as soon as the Civil War began, the Underground Railroad was seen strictly as a preamble, and a secret one at that. Its history, its true story, got lost, forgotten, dismissed, even by those whose lives were shaped by it, saved by it, sacrificed for it.

But that's not what I'm intent on setting down here today, a lament or complaint. I merely want to tell you a small story, but one that will flower and grow large with meaning later on, when you see it in the context of the larger story, Father's, not mine. Anyhow, let me commence. In the weeks that followed upon the events which I recently described to you, we Browns did indeed settle into a life at the farm that corresponded to the author Mr. Dana's somewhat fantastical view of us as exemplary American yeomen.

Father and I divided the large attic into two chambers with sawn boards, and with rocks taken from the brooks below the house, we constructed a second fireplace, so that in short order we had a proper farmhouse with a kitchen and eating room, where Father and Mary slept, and a proper parlor downstairs, and two sleeping chambers upstairs for the rest of us. We rebuilt the old privy and repaired and enlarged the crumbling barn and sheds so that we could adequately shelter our animals and store the hay and corn when they came in and firewood for the winter. The boys spent most of their time clearing trees and extending our fields on both sides of the narrow road that passed by the house, cutting and burning the stumps and then planting vegetables in the burned-over ground, like Indians fertilizing the corn, potatoes, turnips, and other root crops with fish that they pulled in great numbers from the streams that churned in those early days with thick schools of silvery trout. Lyman, who was not especially skilled as a woodcutter or farmer, but who had clever hands nonetheless, took to manufacturing and repairing tools and harness for the farm: he constructed a fine chestnut harrow to follow the plow and an iron-railed sledge for hauling logs out of the deep woods, and he and the Old Man set up a small tannery in one of the sheds and commenced to tan the hides of the deer we shot and salted, and soon the women, Mary, Ruth, and Susan, were at work manufacturing shoes and leather aprons and other items of clothing to protect us against the elements.

Every morning, before beginning our day's labor, we gathered together in the parlor for prayers and Father's brief sermon, and even though I had grown long used to these solemn services, they nevertheless uplifted me, as I believe they did the others, and made the day's work easier, for despite my unbelief, the services connected our labor to something larger than ourselves and our petty daily needs. Father's intention, I am sure, was precisely that—to lead us to understand our woodcutting and plowing and constant care of animals, the day-long manufacture of our meals and the permanent ongoing repair of our tools and equipment, and our endless preparation for the long winter, such that we would believe that we were participating in a great cycle of life, as if we were tiny arcs of an enormous curve, a universal template that began with birth and ended with death and which, if participated in fully and without shirking, would lead us to a second and still larger cycle of rebirth and regeneration, to an infinite spiral, as it were. Thus, as the fields were prepared and sown, so too were our inner lives being prepared and sown, and as our land and our livestock grew fruitful and multiplied, so did our spirits blossom and bear fruit, and as we dried and salted and stored our food and supplies in sawdust and hay for winter, so would our spirits and minds be prepared to endure the inescapable suffering and deaths of our loved ones, which would come to us as inevitably as the freezing winds and the deep, drifting snows of winter.

But in those warm days of spring and early summer, as we settled into our farm, the tumult that habitually inhabited my own mind was eased somewhat, and my earlier turbulence and confusion seemed almost to have occurred in the mind of another man than myself, some fellow younger than I, whose wrathfulness and turmoil had kept him from appreciating the singular beauty of the place and the pleasures of hard work well done and the company of a large, skilled, and cheerfully employed family. Towards Lyman I felt a renewed sense of comradeship, as if he were a brother, kin, and despite his having a wife, a woman whom I grew quickly fond of, for her sober wit and decorum. My squallish feelings of before appeared to wane and then to blow away like clouds off the mountains that daily stood before us in their forested summer majesty—great, green pillars holding up the sky— cloudsplitters, indeed.

As he had promised, the Old Man right away took himself off from the farm and began his survey of the lands granted by Mr. Gerrit Smith to the Negroes, assisted sometimes by me or Lyman, but increasingly accompanied by the sturdy, bearded fellow we had met on our first visit to Timbuctoo, a man who, as it turned out, was their unofficial chieftain and an altogether admirable gentleman. Elden Fleete was a freedman from Brooklyn, New York, a self-educated, somewhat bookish man whose mouth, like Father's, was full of quotations from the Bible, but also from the plays of Shakespeare and authors of antiquity. He had been a printer and for many years had edited and published an abolitionist newspaper called *The Gileadite*, which circulated mainly among Negroes in Brooklyn and New York City and was little known elsewhere. Although to my mind it compared favorably to the better-known newspapers, such as *The Liberator*, published by William Lloyd Garrison—who, as I am well aware, is your Professor Oswald Garrison Villard's distinguished, and no doubt much admired, late grandfather. In my praise of Mr. Fleete's little paper, I mean no criticism of your colleague's ancestor.

Mr. Fleete, despite his bookishness, was a humorous, energetic man of high ideals who had come to Timbuctoo not so much to own land and farm it as to help in the creation of an autonomous African community in the mountains of North America. He had come here strictly in order to establish a precedent and model for what he hoped would someday be a separate nation of Negro freedmen on the North American continent. In those early days before the Fugitive Slave Act and the Kansas-Nebraska Act, before it had become inescapably clear to everyone that the slavers had taken over every branch of the government of the United States, abolitionists black and white were much divided over how to deal with the fact that there were more than three million people of African descent living in the United States. Regardless of how, or even whether, slavery was banished from the land, so long as most whites regarded them as inferior, these millions would remain here a despised, abject race incapable of rising to the level of white people. Certain Negroes, like Frederick Douglass, for example, and a few whites, like Father, persisted in believing that white people could eventually learn to regard Negroes as their equals; others thought that the only solution to the problem was to force all three million American Negroes to return to Africa; and there were numerous positions between these two extremes. Mr. Fleete was among a small minority of black abolitionists who hoped that the United States government would establish in the western territories a separate state for Negro freedmen, and he had been calling for this in the pages of The Gileadite. The state would be named Gilead and would be ruled by a legislature and a governor elected by its citizenry. Its people would be no more answerable to the government of the United States than were the citizens of France or England. He had even written a constitution for his nation of Gileadites, which was modeled closely on the Constitution of the United States, except, of course, for the provisions therein designed to advance and support chattel slavery.

Father thought the notion of Gilead the height of absurdity and said so, frequently and loud, but he had high regard for Mr. Fleete's general intelligence and character, and as he was a man much admired by the other Negroes of Timbuctoo, the Old Man befriended him and worked easily with him in the several areas where they found agreement. They both recognized the need to make a proper survey of the freedmen's lands, they both felt the urgency of teaching the residents of Timbuctoo how best to survive as independent farmers and stockmen in this climate, and they agreed on the usefulness of establishing Timbuctoo as an actively operating station on the Underground Railroad.

They knew that the routes in the east along the Hudson and Champlain Valleys and in the west into Ontario by way of Niagara and Detroit were becoming increasingly dangerous in those years and subject to betrayal and savage attack by pro-slavery people residing along the lines and by kidnappers hired by Southern slaveholders. "The fact is, we've got to head up into the hills and move across the ridges and peaks where we cannot be pursued," the Old Man had decided way back in Springfield. Also, he had long wished anyhow to establish an escape route for the slaves which would be protected, not by well-meaning whites, but by heavily armed black men: he believed that only when the Negroes themselves were able to threaten the slavers with deadly force would the cost of the "peculiar institution" become so great as to crumble of its own weight. It was from these residents of Timbuctoo that he believed he would draw his initial cadre of armed black men.

Thus, with Mr. Fleete at his side, as soon as his surveys were finished and the deeds registered at the county courthouse in Elizabethtown, Father at the first opportunity hiked the long way south to Indian Pass, crossing through the tangled forests where Mr. Dana, the author, and his Boston companions had gotten lost, on to the tiny village of Tahawus, which had been settled some years earlier for the purposes of mining iron ore from the red cliffs there. In that isolated place, living amongst a population of mostly Irish miners and their Yankee supervisors, was a family named Wilkinson, people known to Father and Mr. Fleete as dedicated and trustworthy abolitionists, who in the recent past had hidden an occasional escaped slave in their storage cellar or barn until such time as he or, as was sometimes the case, she could be passed along or directed northward through the forests to North Elba and thence on to Canada.

The head of the household, Mr. Jonas Wilkinson, in his capacity of engineer and geologist, had previously worked for Gerrit Smith on certain of his enterprises in the western section of the state of New York, having to do with the construction of canals, and it was through Mr. Smith that Father had first come to know of him. Mr. Fleete, of course, knew him strictly through his benevolence towards the occasional escaped slave who passed through Tahawus and on to Timbuctoo.

The two, Mr. Fleete and Father, arranged to have Mr. Wilkinson notify them whenever "cargo" sent from the South for trans-shipment north arrived at his home. He was to send one of his sons through the forest to our place, and then Father and I, Mr. Fleete and Lyman Epps, carrying rifles as if on a hunt, would go back with the boy, retrieve the cargo, and under cover of darkness transport it back to North Elba, where, as soon as possible, we would move it north by wagon to the next trans-shipping point, which at that time was Port Kent on Lake Champlain, a mere forty miles south of the Canadian border.

By means of carefully worded letters to Mr. Smith at his home in Walpole, New York, and to Frederick Douglass over in Rochester, the Old Man alerted many of the agents, conductors, and stationmasters in downstate New York and Pennsylvania and even as far south as Maryland that there was now an effectively manned link in the Underground Railroad that ran right up the center of New York State straight into the mountainous wilderness of the north. *If we utilize this route,* he wrote to Messrs. Smith and Douglass in a pair of letters which he asked me one evening to transcribe for him, *there is unlikely to be any interference with our shipments from those parties who remain hostile to our interests. It is my fond hope that in time this route can be extended southward through the Allegheny and Appalachian Mountains and that we will have reliable trans-shipping agents and conductors posted all the way to New Orleans.* In a postscript, Father had me add, *I myself must first interview all who wish to join this enterprise, for, as you know, the strength of any chain is determined by its weakest link.*

Cautiously, I pointed out to him that it might prove impossible to interview the agents and conductors, except for Mr. Wilkinson in Tahawus and the fellow in Port Kent, known to us only by name and reputation: Mr. Solomon Keifer was a Quaker shipwright originally from Rhode Island, who for several years had been moving fugitive slaves north by boat. Father's insistence on controlling every aspect of the operation, I feared, would doom it, as it had doomed similar ventures before.

But he would hear none of it. "If a thing can't be done right, then it's not worth doing," he said. "It's the Lord whose work this is, Owen, not

Mister Douglass's or Mister Smith's. I trust only in the Lord. And in myself, who serves Him."

If this venture failed, it would not be because Father hadn't done his utmost to get the job done right. No, he declared, he would interview and appoint every man who wished to act as an agent or conductor for us. No exceptions. And if that meant we could not extend our line and station now to those already in existence among the slaves in the Southern states, well, then, so be it. We would find another way to siphon off the human chattel from the plantations, another way to bring about the collapse of that satanic institution. "We will triumph in the end," he insisted. "But the end may be much further off than we realize, and when it comes, it may appear in terms that we cannot now imagine. In the meantime, Owen, we must trust our principles large and small, for the end is always and forever the Lord's, and thus will take care of itself, with or without us."

Who could argue with him? Certainly not I—who at that age had too little experience of the world, of the Lord's will, and of slavery to know that he was wrong, and too little command of language and the forms of reasoning to name and rebut his fallacies. I was not altogether a passive or unquestioningly obedient son, but I was aware of my own limitations and so allowed him to rule me, in spite of our frequent disagreements and disputes.

Late one bright afternoon in early June, Mr. Wilkinson's young son, Daniel, a boy about the age of Watson, fourteen or fifteen, appeared at our farm bearing the information that cargo had arrived in Tahawus, trans-shipped from the town of New Trenton in Oneida County. Mary, who was beginning by then to recover from her malady, although she was not yet able to take on any of the heavy household duties, welcomed the boy in and gave him something to eat. Meanwhile, Oliver chased down Father, who was off in Timbuctoo helping to raise a barn, and Salmon came for me, who that afternoon had gone with Watson to build an Indian-style fishing weir on the tableland below, where the west branch of the Au Sable passed through a rocky gorge on a corner of our land. Lyman remained waiting at the farm, where he had been constructing a small forge for smithing next to the tannery that he and Father had built.

It was nearly dusk before we all—Father, me, Lyman, and Mr. Fleete—forgathered at the house and then with considerable excitement struck out with the Wilkinson lad for Tahawus, a good eight hours' hike away. The boy was intelligent and articulate and proud to have been given such a heavy responsibility, and as we walked rapidly along, he conveyed his father's message to us in bits, barely restraining his pleasure. He told us that a Negro man and his wife, both in a somewhat debilitated condition, had arrived the previous night. They had been forwarded by Mr. Frederick Douglass himself and had come mostly under cover of night alone from Utica, along cart tracks and footpaths through the woods all the way to the Wilkinsons' house. They were from Richmond, Virginia, and had run off a fancy James River estate, had nearly been caught twice and were terrified of being returned to their owner, who they believed would separate them by selling the man off as a field hand to Alabama, where their owner had interests in a cotton plantation. They were a well-spoken couple, he said, and claimed they could read and write. And there was a considerable reward for their return, he added as a warning, for he knew that this fact increased the danger of transporting them.

I believe that this was the first time that young Daniel had been personally involved with helping slaves to escape, and the thing was for him a considerable adventure. For Father and me, of course, it was a welcome resumption of the activity that had given us so much extreme satisfaction back in Ohio and Pennsylvania, when we used to take off into the hills of Virginia and Maryland or drive down along the Ohio

River with John and Jason and be gone from home for days transporting whole wagonloads of escaped slaves north to Canada, traveling at
night and hiding out in the barns of Quakers and other sympathizers
or camping in the deep woods during the daylight hours. We had not
been able to participate in this activity since Father's removal east to
Springfield, partially because there was in Springfield an already functioning network of abolitionist transporters who were white and with
whom Father would not cooperate, and also because, with all the
demands of the woolen business there, he simply could not take off
and turn day into night carrying Negroes under tarpaulins in the back
of a wagon racing down country roads. Also, in Springfield, there had
been other venues available to his activism.

For Mr. Fleete, this was a great opportunity; without the material
support and protection of the Old Man, he had up to now been limited
to only the most passive of roles in aiding the escapes of his enslaved
brethren. Lyman Epps, like almost every freedman in those days,
wished to work on the Underground Railroad, but he also had a young
man's natural desire to test himself under fire. As it was highly unlikely
that we would meet up with a bounty-hunting slave-catcher and be
obliged to defend our cargo against seizure or that we would be seriously opposed by any local people up here in the mountains, this was a
perfect opportunity for Lyman to do both without risking much. In
those years, most of the settlers in the Adirondacks were New
Englanders, people who, even if not wholly sympathetic with the work
being done by the radical abolitionists, were nonetheless unwilling to
obstruct it, so long as they themselves were not put in physical or legal
danger. They did not like Negroes, but they did not especially want to
help those who enslaved them. If others wished to move them through
to Canada, fine, they would not interfere. Even so, we had to be prepared for any emergency, and thus we marched on to Tahawus under
cover of darkness, and armed.

In the weeks since we first arrived and took up residence there, we had grown increasingly familiar with the forest pathways that linked the various Adirondack settlements, so that now, even at night, we were in no great danger of getting lost, especially since there was a bright, nearly full moon floating overhead. Most of the footpaths we used had been deer tracks laid down in ancient times in the narrow valleys and defiles and along the connecting ridges, followed later by the Algonquin and Iroquois Indians, who never settled here but for hundreds of years had fought each other for control of the region as a hunting preserve. Once you had in your mind a map of the land and understood the logic of its topography, you could pretty well predict where the path from one place to another would be found. In our first weeks in North Elba, Watson, Salmon, Oliver, and I had explored all the woods for several miles around the farm and Timbuctoo and felt as much at home there now as we had back in the neat villages and cultivated fields of Ohio. We'd even taken to racing one another after work up several of the nearby mountains and back to the house before supper, vying amongst us to find the quickest route up and down Pitch-off or Sentinel. Mr. Fleete and Lyman, of course, knew the woods intimately, for they had resided there for nearly three years by then, and Father's recent tramping over thousands of acres of field and forest with his surveying instruments had given him a refined intelligence concerning the neighborhood. When a place enters your daily life, you quickly lose your fear of it, and I almost had to laugh at my first awestruck, fearful impressions of these forested mountains and valleys barely a month earlier, when we came up from Elizabethtown and Keene.

It was nearly dawn, and the moon had long since set behind us, when we finally exited from the woods south of Indian Pass and approached the mines and furnaces of Tahawus and the settlement that surrounded them. We were making our way down a long, rock-strewn slope that appeared to have been burned clear in recent years.

Hovering over the marshes and stream below us, a pale haze reflected back the morning light, with the dark, pointed tips of tall pines poking through. The village was an encampment, made up mostly of shanties for the Irish miners which, in their sad disarray and impoverishment, reminded me of the shanties of Timbuctoo, and as we passed by, we could see the miners emerging from their cold, damp hovels—gaunt, grim, gray-faced men and boys rising to begin their long day's work in the darkness of the earth. Behind them, standing at the door or hauling water or building an outdoor cookfire, were their brittle-looking women, downtrodden creatures in shabby sack frocks who looked too old to have given birth to the babies they carried on their bony hips.

They barely looked up at us as we passed, so borne down by their labors were they. We fell silent, as if out of respect—two white men and two black men carrying rifles come from the woods, led by the son of the company superintendent. As we passed close to the open door of one of the shacks, Father touched the brim of his palm-leaf hat and nodded to a woman who stood there and seemed to be watching us, her round Irish face impassive, expressionless, all but dead to us. "Good morning, m'am," Father said in a soft voice. She made no response. Her eyes were pale green and glowed coldly in the dim light of the dawn but seemed to see nothing. She looked like a woman who had been cast off and left like trash by an invading army.

The haze from the stream below had risen along the slope to the village, slowly enveloping it, erasing from our sight one by one the shanties and the poor, sullen souls who lived there, following us like a pale beast as we made our way along the muddy track that ran through the encampment. When we reached the further edge, we saw ahead of us, situated on a pleasant rise of land, a proper house with a porch and an attached barn, the home of the supervisor of the mines, Mr. Jonas Wilkinson. There I turned and, for an instant, looked back, and the miners' camp was gone, swallowed by the fog.

❏

Mr. Wilkinson told us, "They run off to a surprising degree, the Irish. Though they've got nothing to run to, except back to the wharfs of Boston or New York. A lot of them are sickly by the time they get here and end up buried in the field yonder. They're a sad lot." Mr. Wilkinson was a round, blotch-faced man with thinning black hair and a porous-looking red nose that suggested a long-indulged affection for alcohol. "Ignorant and quarrelsome and addicted to drink," he said. "The females as much as the men. And you can't do much to improve them. Although my wife and I have certainly given it a try, she by schooling the little ones and me by preaching every Sunday to them that will listen. But they breed faster than you can teach them, and when it comes to proper religion, Mister Brown, they're practically pagans. Superstitious papists without a priest is what they are. I've about given up on 'em and just try now to get as much work out of 'em with as little expense as possible before they run off, or die.

"Sorry for sounding so harsh," he said to Father, who sat on a straight chair and grimly regarded the floor. "But what you've got with these Irish is the dead ends of European peasantry. There's little for them in this country. Little enough for them back there in their own country, I suppose," he added, pulling on his chin. "Which, of course, is why they come over in the first place. For them, poor souls, I suppose it's an improvement. They get to start their lives over."

Father stood then and said to Mrs. Wilkinson, who was putting a substantial breakfast on the table for us, "M'am, if you don't mind, I believe we'll eat with the Negroes in the barn and then rest there until nightfall."

"I sense that I've offended you, Mister Brown," Mr. Wilkinson said.

"No, sir. No, you haven't," the Old Man answered. "I am curious, though, as to your reasons for agreeing to aid us in our efforts to carry Negro slaves off to Canada, when you appear to have so little fellow-feeling for the poor indentured men and women in your charge here."

"Ah!" Mr. Wilkinson said brightly—he'd heard this argument before and was prepared, even eager, to answer it. "Slavery is evil! That alone is reason enough for a Christian man to want to aid and abet you. But beyond that, slavery provides the Southerners with an unfair advantage in the labor market. No, sir, for the economic health of our nation, we all must do what we can to bring about the end of slave labor. And this is simply my small part, aiding you and your son and your Negro friends here, and your friend the famous Mister Douglass."

He pointed out that every one of his Irish miners had freely contracted to work here, just as he himself had, and when their terms were over and they had met the requirements of their contracts, they were free to go. Indeed, many of them, he said, chose not to leave and continued on here in the mines. This was not slavery, he said, smiling broadly. "Your Negroes know the difference, I'm sure, if you and your son do not. Ask the Negroes which they would prefer. Slavery in the South, or working as a free man here in the iron mines of Tahawus?" He looked to Mr. Fleete and Lyman, as if for an answer, but they remained expressionless.

Father simply said, "I see. Well, I am grateful to you for your help and for your kindness to us. But I do think, all the same, that we'll take ourselves to the barn now, for I wish to speak with our poor passengers out there, who are no doubt feeling anxious about their situation and require from us a bit of reassurance. They are, after all, in the hands of strangers and in a strange land."

Eagerly, and evidently pleased that he had made himself understood if not admired, Mr. Wilkinson escorted us from the room, leading us through a narrow woodshed that connected to the barn. He said that he would send his wife along with our breakfast and pointed us towards the hayloft above, where we saw looking nervously down at us the faces of the man and woman who had been hidden there the previous night.

As soon as Mr. Wilkinson had left us, Mr. Fleete stepped forward in the dark room, smiled up at the young man and woman, and said his own name, then introduced Lyman Epps, Father, and me, in that order. "It's safe to come down," Mr. Fleete assured the fugitives. "Help them down," he said to Lyman, who scrambled up the ladder and assisted first the woman and then the man in descending to the floor of the barn, where we all somberly shook hands. After weeks of running from the hounds of slavery, of trusting white and Negro strangers not to betray them, of hiding out in ditches and under bridges and trestles, of going days and nights without food or sleep, they were almost too tired to be frightened—but, nonetheless, their eyes darted warily from one of us to the other, for who knew, this could be no more than a white man's clever trap.

Then suddenly, before anyone had a chance to speak and reassure them, Mrs. Wilkinson entered from the house, carrying a tray of corn bread and eggs and smoked pork and a pitcher of fresh milk. "I'll be sure that no one disturbs you," she said cheerfully, and headed back into the house.

Father looked at me, clear irritation on his face. "*Disturb* us?" he said in a low voice. "These Wilkinsons have it all wrong. They can't be trusted."

I knew that, as soon as we got back to North Elba, the Old Man would cut their link from the chain. And with no stationmaster to replace them, the line from the Deep South to here to Timbuctoo would be broken. Better, I thought, to let the Wilkinsons continue to have it all wrong and keep the Railroad running than to try to teach them what's right by putting them off it.

We fell to devouring the food, all six of us—not, of course, until Father had said an eloquent, if somewhat lengthy, blessing. The fugitives, we quickly learned, were named Emma and James Cannon, and they could not have been older than twenty-one, which was unusual: most of the escaped slaves whom we had aided in the past had been closer to middle-age or else were small children in the company of one or both parents. Occasionally, a young man came through unattached— angry, scarred with old wounds, and still bleeding from new—a man defiant from youth, with a runaway cast of mind and a hundred lashes on his back to show for it. These two, however, were almost genteel in their ways, shy and decorous, the least likely type of slave to risk flight: one could say, if one did not regard the condition of slavery itself as pain beyond all sorrow, that they had not yet suffered enough to justify the hardship and chanciness of flight.

But the degradation and humiliation and the invasion and theft of a person's soul made possible by the legal ownership of that person's body can occur without leaving any visible scars on the body, and that is frequently what happened to the youngest and most delicate of enslaved women and men. As was, no doubt, the case with the man and woman before us, whose owner, they told us, had been powerful in the Virginia state legislature, a wealthy exporter of tobacco, and a partner in several vast Alabama cotton plantations. Emma Cannon had served as maid to her owner's wife and had resided in their mansion; James Cannon had been a clerk in the tobacco warehouse.

This was briefly and indirectly the story they told, or, rather, it was what I deciphered of their hushed account, as they answered Mr. Fleete's and Lyman's polite questions, while Father and I sat back a ways and listened in silence. They had been married without their owner's consent or knowledge, and when the slavemaster had begun to express carnal desires towards the young woman, she and her new husband had decided to flee, for she would have had no alternative but to accede to her owner's quickening advances. The reward for their capture was sufficiently large, one thousand five hundred dollars for the woman and one thousand for the man, that they had no choice but to flee straight through to Canada, avoiding wherever possible the more popular and well-known routes.

I thought, The woes of women always exceed those of the men who love them and are sworn to protect them and fail. I could not take my eyes from the tired, placid face of this gold-colored woman. With her head wrapped in a white bandana, she seemed to me wholly accepting of the chaos and danger that surrounded her here and that had pursued her and would follow her from here, and she seemed strangely beautiful for that. Especially when I compared her face to the darker face of her husband, who appeared more frightened than she, nervous and twitchy, a young man who was probably suffering serious regret for having fled the known world, even a precinct in hell, for these unknown forests of the far north.

Later, when Father entered the conversation and began interrogating the young man and woman with regard to the character and abilities of the numerous stationmasters and conductors who had brought them this far, I found myself a comfortable corner of the barn, spread some straw, and lay down. Soon I found myself falling into a sort of reverie. The images of women—white women and black, sick and dying or aged beyond their years—began to haunt me like ghosts, or more like furies, all of them enraged at me for having abandoned them to their terrible fates. It was not exactly dream, not exactly fantasy, either, and I might have dispelled it by simply standing up and crossing the large, dark room to where Father and the others sat. But instead I fairly well invited the figures straight into my mind: the sullen, pale face of the Irish woman with the morning mist rising around her—abandoned by me, who had barely looked behind when we passed; and the scared, bewildered face of the girl humiliated by me in the Springfield alley; and the vulnerable, exhausted, yet profoundly willful face of the woman here in the barn across from me—a man who could not save her, any more than her poor husband could, from the memories of enslavement and the brutal lust of the man who had owned her; and the face of my stepmother, Mary, who had married at the age of nineteen, inherited five of another woman's children, then borne eleven more and seen six of those eleven die, four going in that terrible winter of '43, the last dying in infancy only two months ago—and neither I nor their father could save a one of them. Then the faces of the women swirled and merged and became the face of my own mother, whom I would never see again, not on this earth and not in heaven, either, who was gone, simply that—gone from me and located nowhere else in this perversely cruel universe, which first gives us life amongst others and then takes the others off, one by one, until we are left alone, all of us, alone.

I lay on my side with my coat drawn over my head and squeezed my eyes shut. It has been this way for women and men and their children, I thought, for thousands of years, from tribal times till this modern age, and it will be this way forever. Was this, then, that great cycle of birth, life, and death which my father spoke of with such admiration and belief? The cycle of women, strange creatures, so like us men and yet so different from us, giving birth and watching helplessly as their children die, or dying themselves on the birthing bed, or, if not, then growing old too soon, while the sons who survive grow up to become the husbands, fathers, and brothers who exhaust themselves failing in the attempt to save them, and who then, having failed, spin the wheel again and impregnate them in the dark of night or on the back stairs or in the low attics of the servant quarters—was this Father's great cycle of life?

The fugitives' story had set my mind to working in this morbid way, despite my best attempts to think of other things, to think even of the mild adventure that we men of North Elba were set on. I knew the likely story, the tale of rape that the young woman across from me was not telling us, that she was perhaps not even telling her poor husband. I had heard that tale in many of its lurid forms over the years, and there was no reason to think that she, uniquely, had not been used by her owner to satisfy his sexual desires and that, risking death, she had not fled her owner more to save her husband than her own violated self. Her *owner*! After all these years of hearing it spoken, the word still had the power to shock and repel me. A human being actually *owned* another, he could use her in any way he wished, and he could sell her if he wished, as if she were an unwanted article of clothing. And he owned her husband as well—a fact that made of their pledge of themselves in marriage, one to the other, a dark joke, a sickening, cruel fancy.

I slept and woke and slept again, and when I woke a second time, seated on the floor next to me was Mr. Fleete, leaning against a post and smoking his pipe in a meditative way. I asked him, "Do you have a wife or children, Mister Fleete?"

"No. My wife is dead, Mister Brown. She died young. At about the age of that woman yonder. Died without children."

"And you never thought to marry again?"

He sighed and studied the pipe in his brown hand. A silver strand of smoke curled upwards in the dim light towards the one small window high overhead. "Well, y' know, I thought of it now and again, yes. Especially as regards children."

"Do you think you will marry, then?"

"No, Mister Brown. The world does not need more children. And no woman needs me for a husband. The one who did," he said, "is dead. But I'll be seeing her again in the sweet bye an' bye. Won't I?" he added, and smiled lightly, as if he did not quite believe his own words.

"Yes," I said, and turned away to sleep again, to dream the childhood faces of my sisters, Ruth and Annie and Sarah, each one exchanging her place with the others in my dream, as if the three were one and as if present were mingled with past. In the dream, I was their father, not their brother, yet I was myself and not Father. They were all, first one, then two, then three female children wailing in sorrow, and I was pacing hectically around them, like the blindfolded horse tied to the bark-crusher, marching in a fixed circle, while the three little girls stood crying in the center, lashed to the pole like witches condemned to be burned. I could not tell if I myself had tied them there or instead was marching in a circle around them to protect them from those who would place sticks at their feet and set them afire.

When I woke again, it was closer to midday, and a pillar of light fell straight down from the high window onto the board floor of the barn. I stood and walked across to where Lyman lay on his back atop a saddle blanket, staring at the distant ceiling, lost in thought. The others appeared to be asleep—except for Father, who sat on guard by the door, with his rifle across his knees. His eyes followed me, but his head did not move as I came and sat next to my friend.

"Lyman," I said in a voice almost a whisper.

"Hello, Owen," he said without looking at me.

"I want to ask you about your wife, Susan. Did you come out of slavery with her?"

"Susan?"

"I'm sorry. I know that I haven't inquired much about her," I said awkwardly. "She's somewhat . . . shy."

"So she is. But mainly amongst white folks."

"I'm sorry for that."

"Not your fault, Owen."

"Well, did you?"

"What?"

"Come out of slavery together."

"No. She come north alone. Come out from Charleston, stowed away on a timber boat and sneaked ashore in New Jersey. Down in Carolina, Susan was owned by a crazy man, and she'd a killed him if she hadn't run off first."

"You don't have any children," I said.

"No. No, we don't. Susan has children, though. Three of them. They got sold off south, sent to Georgia someplace, she don't know where."

We were silent for a moment. Finally, I asked, "What about their father?"

"What about him?"

"Well, who was he?"

Lyman turned and looked at me, said nothing, and returned his gaze to the ceiling.

I stood then and went back to my corner, where I lay down on the floor and wrapped my coat around my head again as if to shut out the world and drifted back into a lurid sleep.

Later, to Father, I said, "Tell me about my grandmother. Your mother. Grandfather's first wife. I know little more than her name, Ruth. And that she died young, when you were a boy."

"Yes," he said, and looked away from me. "And I loved my mother beyond measure. Her kindness and piety were great . . . greater than that of any person, man or woman, I have since known."

"When she died, were you as bereft as I when my mother died?"

"Yes, Owen. I surely was. Which is why I took such pity on you then, and why I feel that in many ways I understand you now somewhat better than I understand your older brothers, who suffered less. I was like you, I was barely eight years old, when my mother died. And when Father remarried, I found it difficult to make a place in my heart for my stepmother."

"I've long since come to love Mary as my own mother," I said to him.

He turned to me. "No, Owen," he said. "You have not. Although I know you do love her. But it is your own true mother whom you still hold yourself for, as if awaiting her return. She won't return, Owen. You'll have to go to her. And if you believe you're bound to be with her again in heaven, then you'll be free to leave off this painful waiting and longing that keeps you from opening your heart to your stepmother, and to all other women as well." He knew this, he said, because it had been a danger to him also, and if it had not been for his Christian faith, he would feel today as he had over forty years before, when his own mother died. "I cannot help you, son. Only the Lord can help you."

I stood and walked away from him without saying anything more and returned to my place in the room.

Of the young man, James Cannon, I asked, "Do you have family in Canada who will help you settle there?"

He did not look at me when he spoke, but kept his large, wet eyes fixed before him, as if contemplating something that he could not share with me, a memory, a childhood fear or sorrow. "Family? No, not exactly, Mister Brown. But I 'spect folks will be there to help settle us. Leastways, so I hear. Mister Douglass done made the arrangements."

"Everything will be different now, won't it? Escaping from slavery is like a resurrection, isn't it? A new life."

Slowly, he turned his head and gazed wide-eyed at me, as if puzzled by my words. "More like birth, I'd say, Mister Brown. Resurrection is where you gets to be born *again*."

"What is the name of the man who was your master?"

"His name? Name Samuel," he said. "Mister Samuel Cannon."

"The same as yours."

"Yes, Mister Brown, same as mine. Same as his father, too. Same as my mother."

"So you were born a slave to Mister Samuel Cannon, and your mother was born his father's slave?"

"Yes, Mister Brown. She surely wasn't Mas' Cannon's wife."

"Who was your father, then? What happened to him?"

He looked away from me again. "Don't know. Long gone."

Lyman watched me from a few feet away, listening. Mr. Fleete was asleep; across the room, still seated by the door with his rifle across his knees, Father lightly dozed. The woman, Emma Cannon, lay on her side next to her husband, with her back to us, and I could not see if she was asleep.

"Forgive me for asking," I said in a low voice. "But your wife, Emma. Was her name also Cannon? I mean, before you married her?"

He was a young man, several years younger than I, but at that moment, when he turned his large, dark face towards me and for a few seconds studied my face, he appeared decades, epochs, whole long eons, older than I, and weary, endlessly weary, of my innocence. And when I saw his expression, it was as if in a single stroke I'd finally lost that punishing innocence, and I felt ashamed of my inquiry. I said, "I'm sorry. I shouldn't have asked into your personal affairs. Forgive me, please."

He must have despised me that afternoon, despised all us whites, the Wilkinsons and even Father and every one of the other, more or less well-intentioned, white conductors and stationmasters whose extended hands he and his wife had been obliged to grasp—hating us not in spite of our helping them to escape from slavery but because of it. In ways that were not true for Mr. Fleete and Lyman, we were unworthy of helping him and his young wife. And the terrible irony which trapped us all was that our very unworthiness was precisely the thing that obliged us to help them in the first place.

At nightfall, Mrs. Wilkinson brought food to us a second time, potatoes and a substantial leg of mutton, and when we had eaten, Mr. Wilkinson came and cheerfully bade us farewell and let us out of the barn by a back door, into the dark, adjacent woods. Making our way down towards the valley below the house, we kept to the birch trees, as Mr. Wilkinson had urged, so as not to be seen by the men returning to their hovels from the mines. For both good and bad reasons, although he did not detail them to us, Mr. Wilkinson did not want his Irish workers to know of his involvement with the Underground Railroad.

Hidden by the darkness, as we passed among the thick white trunks of the birch trees, we saw the miners. They were illuminated by the flickering light of the whale oil lanterns they carried—shadowy, slumped figures moving silently uphill. It was like a march of dead souls that we observed, and the image troubled me, and I found myself lingering behind the others, hanging back, fighting a strange impulse to leave the darkness and join them, to fall into line with the returning miners and merge my life with theirs.

Father grabbed at my sleeve. "Come, Owen," he said. "I know what you feel, son. Come away. We cannot help them," he said, and I turned reluctantly from them and followed my father and the four Negroes into the forest.

Shortly before dawn, we emerged from the deep pine woods on the road just below our farm, where Mr. Fleete parted from us to return to his cabin in Timbuctoo. He would not be joining us for the next stage of our journey, from North Elba to Port Kent, nor would Lyman, for our route would carry us through several villages and a generally more settled region than the wilderness of the pass between North Elba and Tahawus, and we did not want to attract undue attention to our wagon, as would surely occur if we were in the company of even one of "Gerrit Smith's North Elba niggers," as the settlers of Timbuctoo were called by the local whites. While there were indeed a number of white abolitionists residing in the region, the Thompson family foremost among them, also the Nashes, the Edmondses, and some others, anti-Negro feeling was starting to run high here, amongst the small farmers in particular, who believed that, thanks to Mr. Smith's land grants and now Father's survey, the Negroes had obtained unfair access to the better part of the tablelands. This resentment fed on the usual racial prejudices of poor and ignorant white farmers and was fattened by the oily words of land speculators and politicians working to please the moneylenders. Father's association with the Negroes was, of course, well known, and the several Sunday sermons that he had given at the invitation of Mr. Everett Thompson, who was a much-respected deacon in the North Elba Presbyterian Church, had enflamed many of the local people against us, and consequently we had begun appearing in public with Negroes whenever possible. "We must not act in the presence of our neighbors as men who are ashamed of doing the Lord's work," the Old Man had insisted, when I counseled caution. "We must force them to confront us, and from that they will in time confront their own consciences, so that when the spirit of the Lord enters them, they will know what is right and will act accordingly."

But Father was no fool, and he knew that it would be dangerous all around to invite any such confrontation while transporting escaped slaves in our wagon, and thus he was obliged to dissuade both Mr. Fleete and Lyman from traveling on with us. Mr. Fleete seemed almost grateful to be let off from it, but Lyman was not. "You might wish I was along, Mister Brown, if some slave-catcher come upon you," he said, as we walked along the road to our farm. The sun was rising full in our face, cracking the horizon just south of the notch. Father and Lyman marched in front, and Mr. and Mrs. Cannon and I came wearily along behind. The long hike through Indian Pass from Tahawus had taken several hours longer than the walk over the night before, as the fugitives were not shod as well as we and, despite the rigors of their flight, were not used to tramping at such length through rough terrain.

"You may be sure that Owen and I can ably defend our cargo, if need be," Father said to Lyman. I myself was not so sure. At that time I had not yet fired my gun at another human being, and to my knowledge the Old Man hadn't, either.

As we rounded the bend before our house, Father suddenly halted and drew back and hurried us all into the chokecherry bushes by the side of the road. He bade us get down out of sight and silenced us with the flat of his hand. "We have visitors," he whispered. "Two horses at the front of the house."

There was a narrow gully that ran back from the road into a dense thicket of silver birch, and Father instructed the fugitives to hide there. "Do not move until one of us comes for you," he instructed them, and at once the man and woman slipped away from us into the gully and out of sight. Then he, Lyman, and I approached the house.

There were two men lounging at the door, one of them known to us—Caleb Partridge from Keene. The other was a long, leathery fellow with a patchwork gray and black beard on his face and the squint and facial color of a man who spent most of his time outdoors, although the clothes he wore belied that—a brown suit and waistcoat and a tall black felt hat. He wore strapped to his waist, in stark contrast to his clothing, a holstered Colt Paterson, a five-shot revolver, the sort of sidearm one usually associated with a police officer or Pinkerton agent. He was a manhunter. The other fellow, Partridge, although unarmed, looked to be his assistant today, or perhaps his guide.

As we approached them, Partridge smiled. Watson and Salmon were just setting out the cattle and sheep to graze in the near meadow, and I saw Oliver in the distance behind the barn, carrying water and grain to the pigs and feed to the fowl. Annie and Sarah were at play with their husk dolls on a stump in the yard beside the house. Ruth and Mary and Lyman's wife, Susan, were nowhere to be seen, probably inside preparing breakfast.

Father stopped a few feet before the visitors, who had gotten slowly to their feet. He cradled his old Pennsylvania rifle, the one with the maplewood stock, loosely in his arm and said, "Mister Partridge."

"Good morning, Mister Brown. How d' ye do? You've been off in Tahawus, your wife tells us."

"Yes, we have. You will introduce your companion to me."

"Been hunting, Mister Brown?" the man said. His teeth were rotted and stained with tobacco. "Looks like you come up empty."

"I do not know you, sir," Father said. At the sound of his voice, Ruth and Mary had come to the window and peered out at us. The boys had stopped their work and were watching us from a distance. Only the little girls went on as before, as if there were nothing out of the ordinary happening.

"Billingsly," the man said. "Abraham Billingsly. Of Albany."

"I take you to be a bounty-hunter, Mister Billingsly. A slave-catcher."

"I am an agent. I am an agent hired to return lost or stolen property to its legal and rightful owner. I have a contract," he added, patting his breast pocket.

"I do not permit slave-catchers to stand on my land, sir. Nor do I permit those who associate with slave-catchers to stand on my land," Father said to Partridge. "You will both have to vacate these premises. Immediately."

The tall stranger took a step forward and smiled and stopped, as Lyman and I moved to either side of Father and let our muskets be seen. In a sleepy drawl, the slave-catcher said, "I merely wanted to make some inquiries of you, Mister Brown. That's all. Your niggers is safe enough. I already seen the wench inside. Her and this one with you, neither of them is lost or stolen, leastways not so far as I know. Matter of fact, your good neighbor here, Mister Partridge, he vouched for them himself. I don't give no trouble to what you call 'free' niggers."

"I'm running you off my property, sir!" Father declared. "Leave now, or we will shoot you dead!"

"No need to get upset!" Partridge said. "This here fellow come by my house yesterday and requested me to take him over here to North Elba. That's all! He's after some nigger couple from Virginia that's killed a man down there and took off for Canada, pretending they was escaped slaves. They got a arrest warrant out for them."

"He has a contract, not a warrant," Father said.

The slave-catcher said, "I heard there was escaped slaves passing through here, Mister Brown, and that you might have something to do with handing them along. You and your family are well-known, Mister Brown. And I heard there was a nigger couple staying in your house. Seemed unusual, so I thought I'd just have me a look at them. I see now that they ain't but field-niggers, though. The ones I'm looking for is a little yellow gal and dark-skinned boy about twenty years old. House niggers, Brown. Not flatfoot darkies like yours."

Father then moved in close to both men, who were considerably taller than he and younger but who backed off from him, for he bore forward with singular purpose and barely contained fury. "I do not want to kill you in front of my wife and children," Father said. "But by God, I will! Leave here at once!"

Partridge stepped quickly away and made for his horse. The slave-catcher followed behind with as much leisure as he dared show, and the two mounted their horses and backed them off towards the road.

"Aim your muskets, boys," the Old Man said, and we raised our guns. I looked down the barrel at the head of the slave-catcher. It felt wonderfully clarifying.

"We're leaving, Brown!" Partridge cried, and he put his horse on the road and kicked it into a gallop and disappeared around the bend.

For a few seconds, the other man remained and stared hard at Father, as if memorizing his face. "Brown," he said, "if you try to move the two niggers I'm looking for, I'll have to take them from you." Then he turned his horse's head and rode it slowly from the yard and down the road towards North Elba, passing within twenty feet of the man and woman he wished to capture and return to slavery.

We lowered our guns, and the family, including Susan, came and surrounded us, fearful, but relieved, and also proud of us. My ears were buzzing, and my heart pounded heavily, and I barely knew where I was or who was with me. Mary was telling Father that the men had arrived the previous evening and had interrogated Susan and had poked through all the outbuildings and rooms of the house. Mary had expected them to leave then, which was her reason for allowing them to examine the place so thoroughly. She said, "I'd have turned them away at once, but they insisted on waiting for your return and asked to sleep in the barn. We felt like prisoners, but I couldn't very well refuse them. I'd have sent one of the boys to warn you if we'd known where you were likeliest to come out of the forest to the road. I'm sure they believed you'd come walking in all unawares with the very couple they were seeking," she said.

"And we would have," said Father. "But for their horses, which I spotted in time."

"That was my doing!" Watson piped. "They had their horses in the barn, so's to hide them from you. But when we went out at sunup to put out the stock, we first brought their horses out, as if doing them a kindness, which they couldn't very well object to."

Father complimented Watson for his cleverness, and then he declared that we must give thanks to the Lord. Following his example, we all lowered our heads there in the bright, sun-filled yard before the open door of our house, and Father commenced to pray with more than his usual fervor. I felt a noticeable relief and, momentarily, a genuine uplifting of my spirit from the experience—not so much from Father's address to the Lord, however, as from standing in the sunlight in a closed circle with my beloved family and our friends Lyman and Susan. There were yellow butterflies all around, a cloud of them in the sunlight, swirling in a spiral, like a beneficent whirlwind.

A few moments later, Watson and I walked back down the road, past the gully where we had hidden Mr. and Mrs. Cannon, to examine the tracks of Partridge and the slave-catcher Billingsly, so as to be certain they had indeed gone. Then we returned and went into the thicket and retrieved the frightened young couple from their hiding place and brought them to the house, where they were fed and hidden for the day in our attic, and as soon as the morning chores were finished, Father, Lyman, and I planned on joining them there, to sleep until dark.

Thanks to our encounter with Mr. Billingsly and his threats, Father had changed his mind and had decided to allow Lyman to accompany us to Port Kent. "I was glad to have him standing with us this morning," he said to me, as we moved through the flock of sheep, separating the first of our pregnant ewes from the others. "At times, I admit, the man seems light-headed, but when it counts, he's firm. I believe he has the courage to shoot a man."

I asked Father, "What do you think about what Mister Partridge said? About the Virginia couple. That they killed a man. He meant their owner, I suppose."

"Perhaps they did kill the man. Their owner. I certainly hope so," he said, his mouth like a crack in a rock. Gently holding one of the pregnant ewes, he examined it for disease, poking through the fleece, comforting the animal while he expertly parted the fleece with his fingertips. "Billingsly is a bounty-hunter, not a marshal. And as soon as Partridge shows him the way to Timbuctoo, he'll be cut loose, so as not to get any share in the reward. And I don't think Billingsly will dare go up against us alone," he said. Then he added, "Even so, just in case, we'll be better armed with Lyman along than we would without him."

When I awoke, it was not yet dark, but then, peering out the small attic window, I saw that Father and Lyman were outside, hitching the team to the wagon. Even in his fifties, the Old Man had physical energy exceeding mine and that of most young men; he required little more than four or five hours' sleep for a long day's or night's work, and when he worked, day or night, he seldom stopped to rest. To my surprise, Lyman, from his first arrival at our house, seemed naturally to keep pace with the Old Man, which I admired and somewhat envied, for it made me feel lazy by contrast and ashamed, although neither of them was thoughtless enough to comment on my need for a normal portion of sleep or to upbraid me for slothfulness, except as a light, affectionate tease.

I hurried down the ladder to the kitchen, where our cargo, Mr. and Mrs. Cannon, freshly washed and for the first time looking unfrightened, were seated at the table with Mary, Ruth, Susan, and several of the children, cheerfully at play with a string game apparently taught them by Mrs. Cannon. I cut myself a large slice of bread and ate and silently watched, until Father came inside and gave us the order to depart. We escorted Mr. and Mrs. Cannon outside and placed them and their bundles and a basket of food for our journey into the back of the wagon, where the couple arranged themselves atop the several fleeces and tanned deerhides and pelts that Father had packed there. These he planned to sell in Port Kent, our ostensible reason for traveling to the town. Then, rifle in hand, Lyman climbed into the box, and Father covered the box and all its contents with a canvas sheet, which he drew tight and tied with the children's cord. I climbed up and took the reins. Father, holding both our rifles, joined me there, and with a somber wave goodbye to the family gathered by the doorway, we departed.

We saw no one along the road to North Elba until we reached the Thompson farm, where Mr. Thompson and several of his sons were crossing the road with their cows, bringing them into the barn for milking, and we were forced to stop. Mr. Thompson hailed us and walked over, while his boys moved the cattle. Of all the white people in the region, he was probably our closest friend and associate. A fervent anti-slavery man, father of a brood of sons more numerous than our own, and a skilled farmer and carpenter, he was the only local man towards whom Father's admiration went without serious provisos attached. He was tall and bulky, built like a cider barrel, and, although red-faced and high-spirited, was deeply religious and, like Father, a temperance man. I liked him for his humorous ways and the ease with which he commanded his phalanx of sons, whose ages corresponded fairly closely to ours. Although the eldest, Henry, was nearly my age, there were still babies being born annually in the Thompson house, one male child after another, numbering now sixteen. Mr. Thompson's wife, the woman who had produced this brood, was large and cheerful, not unlike her husband, and it was perhaps only in hopes of at last bearing a daughter that she continued to allow herself to become pregnant, for she was nearing middle-age and the natural end of her child-bearing years.

Father raised his hand in greeting and touched the rim of his right ear, the common signal for conductors. Mr. Thompson gave the countersign and touched his ear also. "I saw that fellow Partridge from Keene this morning," he said to us.

"Yes," Father answered. "He and his friend, a man named Billingsly, they paid us a visit as well."

Mr. Thompson took a long look at the wagon box. "Do you need help?"

"No."

"Partridge and the bounty-hunter went on to the Negro settlement. You know, John, there's plenty of folks hereabouts, folks like Partridge, who'd happily give aid and comfort to a slave-catcher for the beauty of a dollar or two."

"Where might he light?" Father asked.

"Anybody local would tell the man to wait out to Wilmington Notch. So if I was you, I'd keep moving and moving fast when I got to the notch. It'll be dark by then."

"Thank you kindly," Father said.

Mr. Thompson nodded and stepped aside. His cows had crossed the road and were making their slow way towards his barn. The sun had nearly set over the wooded hills west of Whiteface, and wide plum-colored streaks were spreading across the pale yellow sky. I snapped the reins, and we moved on towards the road that led out of North Elba and passed along the West Branch of the Au Sable, across the flat, marshy grasslands to where the river turned northeast.

Soon it was dark, with the nearly full moon flashing intermittently on our right behind the black silhouettes of the trees. Whiteface towered on our left, its long, pale scars brightly illuminated by the moonlight, and below us the glittering river, making a great noise, narrowed and passed over rocks and cascades as the mountains on either side converged at the notch. For several miles here the road was barely wide enough for a single wagon. On one side the land fell off precipitously to the river, while on the other a sheer rock face where not even shrubs grew rose towards high ledges and outcroppings that nearly blocked the sky.

We had just entered the notch, when Father ordered me to halt the wagon, and after I had done it, he got down and loosened the tarpaulin at the back and folded it over so that Lyman could see out. In a low voice, he said to Lyman, "If someone gives chase, Mister Epps, just fire away." Then he climbed back up beside me, and we continued as before.

The darkened road turned and twisted, and I was obliged to hold the team to a walking pace. The track was narrow and sometimes sloped abruptly down to the edge of the water, then ascended a ways to cross above an overhanging cliff, until, forced by a wall of huge boulders from an ancient landslide, it switch-backed towards the river and descended to the rushing waters again. Day or night, this was a mighty dangerous place. Highwayman, slave-catcher, bounty-hunter—one man alone could stop a wagon from passing here and could keep it from turning back as well, simply by felling a tree or rolling a boulder down from the embankment above. At every turning I was sure we would suddenly be brought up short by an obstacle in the road and would be fired upon from the darkness. Father kept his rifle at the ready and said nothing. The sounds of the horses' hooves were muffled by the roar of the water below, and I felt as if we were passing through a long, dark cave, when gradually I saw that we had emerged from the notch, for the road had straightened somewhat and the hills seemed to have parted and backed away. The light of the moon splashed across the tan backs of the horses; the noise of the river had diminished, and I could hear the comforting clop of the horses' hooves again. It was then that I heard the rapid pounding of my heart, for I had grown considerably more alarmed by our passage through the notch, now that we were safely beyond, than when we were actually doing it. For a long time no one spoke, but after a while, when we were well clear of the notch and passing through the relatively flat valley of the Au Sable where it's joined by the East Branch coming north from Keene, Father said, "I didn't think Billingsly would want to go up against us alone. But the truth is, he could have done us some damage back there."

We were safe now, on the high, more or less straight, northeasterly road to the village of Keesville and on to Port Kent. This was the other of the two roads into the Adirondack wilderness from Lake Champlain. The first was the toll road that we'd taken on our arrival from Westport, through Elizabethtown and Keene and the pass at Edmonds Lakes near our farm. This more northerly route, the old Military Road dating back to the days of the French and Indian wars, once you got through the Wilmington Notch, was wide enough in places for two wagons to pass and took you across the rolling hills and fertile farmlands alongside the now meandering Au Sable and Boquet Rivers directly to the shore of the vast lake. Our journey from here on was uneventful and sped by, as we passed darkened farms and settlements, sighting an occasional herd of deer grazing at the edge of a meadow or a fox darting into the brush beside the road, while the moon slowly ascended from behind us to its high point overhead and then began its descent towards the lake.

After crossing the swaying bridge over the falls at Keesville, we began to get glimpses of the lake now and then through the trees, until finally we came to the high, grassy head of land that forms the protective cove where Port Kent is located, and it was as if we had come to the edge of the sea. Father bade me to stop the wagon, and he got down and helped Lyman and our fugitives climb out of the wagon and stretch their limbs and enjoy the cool, fresh air off the lake. For a few moments, we stood about and rested and ate a portion of the food that Mary had packed for us. We did not speak much one to the other, but instead simply gazed at the beauty of the land and sky and water that lay before us.

The moon had streaked the dark waters with skeins of molten silver. Way in the east at the horizon, the velvety night sky was lit by the pale light of a false dawn, and from our place on the height of land overlooking the broad expanse of the lake, morning seemed imminent. The lake, one hundred four miles long from north to south, was at its widest here, more than twenty miles across to the state of Vermont. A cool breeze blew sharply over the choppy waters to land, and on the far side of the lake a starry sky hovered above the Vermont horizon like a deep blue curtain lit from below.

When it was time to move on, Lyman Epps and Mr. and Mrs. Cannon of Richmond, Virginia, climbed back into the wagon, and Father once again tied down the tarpaulin and came and joined me up front. We followed the road down from the headland to the shore and soon entered the village of Port Kent. We were headed for the boatyard owned and operated by the Quaker Solomon Keifer, whom we expected to show up at dawn to commence his day's work there. The village was still mostly asleep, although here and there we saw a window lit by candles or an oil lamp inside. We passed the main dock and several stone warehouses, after which came a row of small boathouses, until we arrived at the last in the row, where we saw a small sign, *Capt. S. I. Keifer*, above the closed door facing the lane. Here I drew the wagon to a halt and jumped down and tied the horses to a hitching post. A narrow pier ran out a ways into the lake, where a wide-bottomed schooner was tied up—the last leg of our fugitives' journey, their final means of transport to freedom.

A narrow wooden stairway led up from the shore to a crest of land above, where there were a number of houses and a church and meeting house, and Father immediately went that way, in search of Captain Keifer, while Lyman and I stayed with the wagon and our cargo. Feeling we were finally safe, I put my rifle down and untied the tarpaulin, and when I had done so, Lyman came and stood with me in the darkness, stretching his legs and rubbing his aching joints, which signs of discomfort caused me to beckon to Mr. and Mrs. Cannon to come out of the wagon. Slowly, first the man and then the woman emerged from the box and brought their bundles with them and regarded the unlikely scene with curiosity and some natural trepidation, for it must have looked to them that they were about to set off on an ocean-going voyage.

Lyman laid his rifle in the box of the wagon and stepped behind the boathouse a ways to relieve himself, and I began to explain to our fugitives that we were located on the shore of a lake barely forty miles south of Canada. This was the last stop on the Underground Railroad, I was saying, when I heard a man's voice from the darkness behind me.

"Just stand where you are, Brown, and put your hands on your head," he said calmly, and when I turned, I saw him with his revolver on Lyman. It was Mr. Billingsly, the slave-catcher. I slowly lifted my hands and placed them on my head as instructed and as Lyman had already done.

"You niggers, you move over here by me," the slave-catcher said to Mr. and Mrs. Cannon. "And you," he said to Lyman, "you stand by the wagon there with Brown." I saw then that the man was carrying in his other hand a pair of manacles. Extending them to me, he said, "Clamp these onto my prisoners, Brown."

"No," I said. "I will not do that."

He stared at me hard. "You people are crazy, is what."

He turned to Lyman. "Here. You do it, then. Put these irons on them." He held the instruments out to him.

Lyman regarded the manacles coldly. He said, "You the slave-catcher, not me."

At that instant, I saw Father step out of the darkness behind Billingsly. He held his musket at waist level with both hands and had it aimed straight at the small of the man's back. "Put down your gun, Mister Billingsly," he said in a cold, almost expressionless voice.

The slave-catcher's eyes went dead, and he inhaled deeply and did as he was told.

"Lie on the ground, face-down," Father said. Behind Father stood a man whom I took to be Captain Keifer, a short, black-haired fellow with a fringe of beard on his chin. There was a note in Father's voice that frightened me, and it surely must have terrified Billingsly, if he had any sense at all: it was the note of a man whose mind was made up, who would not be stopped from completing the terrible action that he had already decided upon, no matter how the circumstances changed. I knew that he had decided to kill the man. And in spite of being frightened by the tone in Father's voice, I was excited by it.

Mr. Billingsly got down on his knees and then lay on his stomach, his face pressed against the rocky ground, and when he had done so, Father stepped forward and, straddling the man's body, aimed his gun down at his head.

Lyman said, "You ain't goin' to *kill* the man, Mister Brown."

"I am," Father said.

Captain Keifer moved forward then and said to Father, "I pray thee, Brown, do not kill him. It is not for thee to execute the man."

Lyman looked at me with disbelief, and I caught a glimpse of Mr. and Mrs. Cannon as they backed away from the scene to the front of the wagon and stood by the horses, as if preparing for flight.

Shoving the stock against his shoulder, Father looked coldly down the barrel at the man's head. I could see that Billingsly's teeth were clenched and his eyes were closed tightly, as if he expected nothing less than to hear the irritating explosion of gunfire. It was very strange—he did not look like a man who believed he would die of it. He did not seem to believe that he was inside his own body and that his brain was about to be blown to bits.

"Slave-catcher," Father said, "I am sending thee straight to hell."

I did not dare to rush Father and try to seize his weapon—the gun might go off and kill the slave-catcher beneath it, or our struggle with one another might give the man the opportunity to escape, and I did not want that, either—so I stood as if rooted to the ground. But when Captain Keifer stepped firmly forward with his hands extended as if to grab Father from behind, I spoke out at last. "Wait, Father!" I cried. "Back off, and put the man in his own manacles! Let him wear the manacles he planned to use on the Negroes. And let Lyman do it!" I said.

Slowly, Father lowered his rifle and backed away from the slave-catcher. "Put your hands behind your back," he ordered, and the slave-catcher obeyed. "All right, Lyman. Place the chains on him, and lock them tight."

Lyman reached down and grabbed up one of the two sets of manacles and clamped them onto the white man.

Father rolled Billingsly over onto his back, groped through the man's waistcoat pockets until he found the keys, and tossed the keys far out into the cove. He grabbed the second pair of manacles and heaved them into the darkness also, and when they fell into the water, there was a loud splash, and then silence.

A moment passed, and Father said, "Put him into the wagon, Owen." Lyman and I retrieved our guns and together hefted the slave-catcher onto his feet and shoved him into the box of the wagon. While

Lyman stood guard over him, I quickly set about removing the hides and pelts, which Captain Keifer would be selling for us, and placed them inside the boathouse. Father escorted our poor, forlorn, very frightened fugitives directly to the boat, and the captain prepared to set sail at once, for the sun would soon rise and there would be many people coming and going along the shore here.

"Cast off!" the captain called to Father, who promptly untied the lines from the pilings and tossed them onto the deck. The captain loosed and unfurled a small triangle of sail at the bow, which caught the breeze at once, and the schooner moved abruptly away from the dock. The captain was standing at the wheel in the bow, and the couple from Virginia were up on the foredeck, standing together and watching, not us, but the dark northern sky, where there was a star, clear and bold, a diamond. Over in the east, the sky had turned a pale blond color, with the tops of the mountains beyond the lake just visible at the horizon. The captain scrambled forward and let out more sail, then returned to the wheel, and in a few moments the boat had crossed the cove and was rounding the point at the far end, heading for open water.

We left Port Kent at once, carrying the slave-catcher out of town to the point on the headlands above the lake where we had rested earlier, and here Father bade me to pull up. He and I climbed down from the wagon and came around to the rear, where Lyman and I got the fellow out.

When we climbed into the wagon again, with Lyman stretched out in the back and Father and I seated up front, and prepared to leave him, the slave-catcher shot us a puzzled expression—it was the look of a man who did not understand why we had not killed him. Not because he thought we were murderers, but because the logic of the situation had demanded it. It seemed to make no sense to him that he was still alive, and he stared after us with an almost plaintive expression, as if he wanted us to come back and properly execute him.

Father said to me, "Drive on quickly, Owen. I cannot stand the sight of the man." I slapped the reins, and we left him there, standing in the moonlight in the middle of the track, his hands clamped behind him in irons.

We said nothing to one another for a long while, and then, finally, a few miles west of Keesville, Father sighed heavily and said, "I am grateful to thee, Owen."

"You are? For what?"

"For interfering with me. Back there at the lake."

"I feared you would be angry with me."

"No, son. I'm in no way angry. I'm grateful to you. I am. In saving Billingsly's life, you probably saved my soul from hell. Fact is, I'm not ready to kill a man, Owen."

"Not in cold blood," I said.

"Yes, and that's the problem. My killing him would have been murder, pure and simple. I have no cold blood, Owen. Not a drop. I must acquire it."

I did not know what to say to that; I could not begin to grasp his meaning then; so I said nothing and, for the remainder of our journey, drove mostly in silence. There would come a time, however, and not many years later—in the smoke and blood of Kansas, with the bodies of men and boys yanked from their warm winter beds and hacked to death with machetes and lying now in chunks steaming like fresh meat all around us in the frozen grass—when I would remember this small conversation, and I would understand it then, just as I am sure you do now.

8

Our involvement with the Underground Railroad aside, our concern for the welfare of the Negroes of Timbuctoo, and our private virtues, along with the ways in which those virtues organized our behavior—all that aside, Miss Mayo, we were to every casual appearance very much like our North Elba neighbors. Country people. A stranger passing through the broad valley that lay between Whiteface and Tahawus would have had little reason to remark upon us (unless, like Mr. Dana and his party of lost hikers, he sat at table with us and stayed the night). He would likely merely have thought that we Browns were nothing unusual for our time and place. Except, perhaps, for our way of speaking, which a stranger would perceive at once and which was, I believe, regarded by some as downright peculiar. And here, in the matter of the manner of our speaking, we get to a thing that was both striking and readily apparent to all who met us, even for a moment, a thing that, to my knowledge, has never been described before, certainly not in print.

It is perhaps inevitable that the speech mannerisms of a family will be significantly influenced by the single strongest member of that family, and so it was with us. Thus, to a one, even to the littlest child, we sounded very like Father. Elaborately plainspoken, you might say—a manner or style of speech that originated, so far as I know, with

241

Grandfather Owen Brown, who, having had a profound effect on Father's way of speaking, is indirectly an influence on my way, too, even here and now, and on that of the rest of the family as well. So let me speak first of him.

Grandfather, who was born and raised in Connecticut back before the Revolution, chose and spoke his words in that old, now-forgotten, New England Puritan manner—deliberately, carefully, with a few thees and thous for leavening, almost as if he were writing his words down on paper, instead of speaking them aloud. He went beyond even the old New Englanders, however, for Grandfather was a stammerer and as a child had trained himself to speak with a formal, dry precision, slowly and in complete sentences, so as not to be controlled or confounded by his affliction. The man cultivated silences and used them as exclamations. He seemed to rehearse his statements in his mind before making any utterance, which gave to him a stately manner overall and provided others with the impression that he was an unusually reflective man— as, indeed, he was. By thinking his words first, by silently phrasing and parsing them in his mind, and only afterwards, when he was satisfied with their rightness, speaking them aloud, Grandfather cultivated his thought more thoroughly than ordinary folk, and as a result his words not only seemed, by virtue of the way they were presented, to be wise; they in fact, more often than not, were wise. "You think as you speak, not *vice versa*," Father often said, and a man forced by an affliction such as stammering to control his speech will in turn soon learn to control his thoughts. So it was with Grandfather.

Father, with no such handicap as stammering to straiten his way, was obliged to impose one upon himself. When he was a young man, he curbed his reckless speech, and hence his thoughts, by placing into his mouth a stone that was sufficiently large to forbid easy and casual talk, and he carried the stone all day long in silence, except when he deliberately plucked it out and unplugged his mouth, as it were. He used the trick of Demosthenes, but in reverse, and not to overcome a handicap, but to simulate one, so as to obtain its compensatory advantages, which he had observed and admired in his own father.

"The inner man and the outer are one, unless ye be a hypocrite and dissembler. Control one of the two, and soon ye will control both," the Old Man often said, applying his prescription as much to himself as to us children, whom he was instructing. All his instructions, admonitions, and rules were as much for him to follow, honor, and obey as for us. Never did I feel that Father had not himself contended with passions or desires fully as strong as my own, or that he had not, on numerous occasions, felt himself as weak, afraid, lonely, despondent, or frustrated as I and my brothers were, and my sisters, too. Quite the opposite. And from our point of view, all the more virtue accrued to him for his not having given himself over to those feelings. Thus his authority over us resided to a considerable degree in our awareness of his, and not our, struggle with vice, and his, not our, triumph over it.

Similarly, whatever self-imposed deprivation, whatever forms of abstinence, he requested of us, he demanded of himself also, despite what he confessed were his larger-than-normal desires to indulge in them. We none of us drank tea or coffee. We used no tobacco. We drank no whiskey, brandy, beer, or fermented cider, and kept none in the house. A visitor or houseguest unable to endure a meal without these stimulants and intoxicants would have to provide his own and then would find himself in the uncomfortable position of being observed by all the children and even those of us who were adults with curiosity and slight condescension, as if he were a Chinaman sucking on an opium pipe. If one of us secretly indulged in the use of tobacco, tea, or coffee, or accepted a sip of whiskey from a friend or an acquaintance, as each of us, especially we boys, did from time to time, his physical and mental reactions to it were all out of proportion to his expectations, and he backed off quickly and in fear. The high degree of excitation provided by these stimulants and intoxicants, due perhaps to our lack of experience with their use and to our shame, was almost always sufficient to keep us from returning for a second try. In addition, there was the threat of exile, of feeling cast out from the family, to keep us from disobeying Father's rules of abstinence. No one of us wanted to be the only one unable to keep his rules. Whether the rest of the family knew of it hardly mattered: *we* knew of it, and that was enough to guarantee an intolerable loneliness. An occasional taste of that loneliness, like the single sip of whiskey or puff of tobacco smoke, was all any of us needed to renew his commitment to purity, abstinence, self-discipline, and to the orderly comportment of his mind, language, and private acts.

With regard to sexual matters, we all, except possibly poor Fred, were normal enough boys and then young men. Little as I know of what is normal for girls and women in such matters, I assume the same was true for the females in the family. And in this as in all things, Father's advice bore the weight of a proscription and sometimes even that of a command: he advised us boys, offered as if in passing, with no room for discussion or further inquiry, to keep ourselves pure and to marry young and to study St. Paul's letters.

Forgive me for speaking of the subject—I wish above all to be as frank as I have been truthful—but did Father believe that I, at least, was unable to forbear from self-abuse? It's a question that has long worried me. I suspect he thought I was, just as I was sure that my brothers, both older and younger, must occasionally have abandoned themselves to this vice, although none of us ever confessed it. All of us—except Fred, whose sensitivity to sin and whose measure of guilt was so much greater than ours—possessed large animal spirits. John and Jason married young; Fred did not marry. Nor did I. Ruth and Annie married young, as did Watson and Oliver, who, along with Fred, died young. But I lived on for many long years, struggling even into old age to maintain my purity as diligently and with the same meager degree of success and heaped-up unhappiness over failure as when I was a boy. In later years, naturally, my animal spirits diminished to a great degree, and my struggle to control them abated at last. But without the struggle, there was no virtue; I take no particular pride, therefore, in the relative purity of my old age.

All our virtues—of piety, honesty, abstinence, and so on, of cleanliness and orderliness, of devotion to work and industry, of love of learning and of neighborliness—were the products and expressions of struggle. This was not much understood by those who observed us and later wrote about our life and character. Remember, Father, first and perhaps foremost among us, and every other member of the family as well, even including the women, pious Mary, sweet Ruth, and my younger sisters, Annie and Sarah—all of us were *normal* people. Which is to say, there was not a one of us who was not tempted by impiety. And we were intelligently skeptical about so much—Father, after all, encouraged it in us practically from infancy—that it was difficult not to apply that same skepticism to our entire way of life. Many was the time when we wanted to give ourselves over to another way. What *was* this crack-brained obsession with slavery and Negroes anyhow? one might well ask, and sometimes we did ask it as, exhausted and exasperated by another of Father's plans to move us to a new place or to start a school for Negro children or to drop everything and ride off in search of escaped slaves who, without us, would have made their own way to Canada safely just the same, we would look at one another and roll our eyes upward and trudge out to the barn in the dark of night and harness up the horses yet again.

At bottom, then, we were ordinary people and were tempted, not just by impiety, but by typical American dishonesty as well—and not so much to lie or cheat or steal, but simply to push an advantage on occasion, to charge for a service or good whatever the buyer was willing to pay, for instance, instead of charging only what was fair. That is, instead of asking no more than the cost of that same service or good to us. Which was Father's monetary policy's ethical base. We were all obliged to stand upon it firmly, yet here we were, always in deep debt, scrambling for ways to avoid foreclosure, bankruptcy, imprisonment. Honesty in these matters, especially considering our dire circumstances, was thus always the result of struggle, and was all the more virtuous therefore—even as our financial circumstances worsened, and Father tumbled towards out-and-out bankruptcy, and all around us others prospered.

Likewise, our abstinence was achieved only through struggle against constant temptation, for we did not remove ourselves, as Shakers and Mennonites do, from ordinary, daily contact with people who rationalized the indulgence of every sensual appetite. On the contrary, we befriended and moved freely amongst them all—drunkards, boisterers, brawlers, and sensualists of every stripe and type. They were everywhere in those days, especially out at the edges of civilized society, which is, after all, where we most often resided ourselves, and many of them were our strongest allies in the work. We associated with such folks as much on principle as convenience and as a consequence of our natural sociability. We thought it necessary and right and believed that it helped in the work, for there were many radical abolitionists whose genteel fastidiousness rendered them wholly ineffective, and Father enjoyed pointing them out to us. "Boston ladies," he called them, although most of them were men.

No, we Browns maintained our virtue in the face of daily temptation, willfully, elaborately contriving it, as if the virtue were not worth much without it. And though it may have sometimes encouraged in us a feeling of superiority to other "normal" people, that, too, was a temptation to be met, struggled with, and overcome, in public and in private, just as I am doing here, even now. Just as Father himself did throughout his life.

Always, Father taught by example and instruction: the two were deliberately interwoven; he made of our childhood understandings a fabric that could not be unraveled or torn. For instance, with regard to our well-known love of learning, had we not watched since earliest childhood the Old Man every evening turn to his bookcase and draw out from it a treasured, much-thumbed tome and commence to read from it and comment on what he read there, we would not have believed, due to our lack of formal education, that there was anything of great value to be obtained from books, especially such books as Father, no matter how unsettled or hectic the circumstances, loved and studied all his life. Like most of our neighbors and friends, we would normally have thought that books of philosophy and history and natural science were better left to the learned and were not proper fields of study for such rough country types as we. Father's sustained example, however, led us to the experience itself. And by imitating his hard-earned love of learning, we were gradually filled with a love of learning ourselves, and thus we came to possess it as if it were a gift to be treasured for life and not a dour, burdensome consequence of blind obedience, cast off as soon as darkness fell.

We all saw our father, Mary saw her husband, struggle with temptation—he made us see it, he spoke of it constantly: his sensuality, his slothfulness, his vain desire for wealth and fame, his pridefulness—and we saw him daily overcome each and every one of those temptations. How could we not go forward, then, and do likewise? We who were no more and no less sensual, slothful, vain, and proud than he? It was his weakness as much as his strength that guided and instructed us; his pitiful, simple, common humanity that inspired us. Those who later wrote that Father was like an infallible god to us were wrong.

We were much misunderstood always. That, I suppose, is yet another of the many ways in which we Browns paid for our virtues. Poverty is one, too. We were hard-working, a large and highly skilled family of workers, and yet, because of our devotion to our Negro neighbors and their cause, all our enterprises failed. Father was regarded by some, rightly, as a genius when it came to livestock. And he was a self-taught surveyor of great skill and understood all the ways in which a piece of land was valuable or poor. He was a tanner capable at the age of twenty of organizing and operating a large tannery on his own. He was a businessman who understood the subtle connections between the producer of wool, the wholesale purveyor of wool, the manipulation by the purveyor of the market price for wool, and the consequent exploitation of the producer, and he was able to conceive and put into place a complex scheme to block that exploitation. And yet we ourselves remained poor, in permanent debt, living on the kindness and philanthropy of men like Mr. Gerrit Smith and Mr. Simon Perkins. For while in many ways we may well have been self-sufficient, growing all our own food and manufacturing all our clothing and tools, we were obliged to do it on land that, in the end, belonged to others.

Even in North Elba, where Mr. Smith had deeded Father two hundred forty acres of first-rate tableland at one dollar per acre. Father died owing for most of it. The Old Man raised money, many thousands of dollars, for the Negroes from white strangers all over the United States, but when he died, his widow had not a dollar to her name. I remember hunger; I remember cold; I remember public humiliation—these were the hard prices we paid for our much-admired devotion to principle. And I did not think it would ever end, despite Father's schemes and his permanent willingness to launch every year a new enterprise for raising money: gathering wool all over Ohio and Pennsylvania and warehousing it for Mr. Perkins in Springfield until the prices rose; buying and selling purebred cattle; speculating on land where canals were rumored to be going in any day now; and on and on, his face bright with the vision of all his debts at last being paid off, of finally owning his own farm outright, of being able to provide for his large, ever-growing family against the rigors that he believed would characterize the long years ahead. For he was sure that Mary would survive him—she was so much younger than he—and believed that she would be left with young children to care for. He did not want to die without having provided for his widow and children.

To all appearances, though, and compared with our neighbors, especially our Negro neighbors in North Elba, we did prosper. Our farm was a thriving operation. This was mainly due to hard work and Father's great organizational skills. Although I was, in a sense, the foreman, Father was the executive and every day laid out the tasks that we each would attend to. Much of farm life, of course, is a round, and the work is organized merely by the turning of the year and by the slow, regular rhythms of animal life, and it needs no executive, but we were a large family with diverse skills and abilities, children at different stages of growth, from the youngest, who was then Sarah, to the eldest in residence, me, a full-grown adult. And there were the other adults as well— Mary, our mother and stepmother, and sister Ruth, and Lyman and Susan Epps, who had come to seem like permanent members of the household, like in-laws.

We were close, interlocked, like the gears and wheels, cogs and belts, of an elaborate machine. Whatever one of us thought, said, or did had an immediate, felt effect on everyone else. It may be that our family in its closeness was sometimes thought by us to be suffocating and too much controlling of our daily lives, and it must have seemed that way often to outsiders; but we were never lonely, never without a sense of being useful and even necessary to the rest, and never without support and encouragement, even in our moments of greatest despair. For we each took strength, not from Father alone, but from the family as a whole. Father, of course, was the family's mainstay; he provided us with example, instruction, understanding, and strength. As a result, when he himself weakened or fell into despair, it was very difficult for the rest of us not to do likewise. And whenever Father's belief in the rightness and necessity of his path wavered, as from time to time it did, or when his faith in his God was threatened, as happened at least twice that I know of, his forward motion would instantly stop. And when he stopped, the rest of us would slow and wobble on our respective pivots and would soon find ourselves stopped and lying on our sides as well.

In the terrible winter of '43, I remember, when the four children died—the first Sarah, Charles, Peter, and the baby, Austin—Father fell into such a prolonged numbness that, before he recovered his feelings, we ourselves had descended into deepest despond, and he was obliged to nurse us, every one, back to health again. It was as if the sickness that took the children one after the other that bleak winter first invaded his spirit and from him spread like a pestilence to Mary and thence to John and Jason and me and on to Ruth and the younger children, even to poor Salmon, who was only a small boy at the time, seven years old, the youngest child not to be taken from us. It was an unsupportable burden. The fires dwindled and flickered out, and the ashes grew cold, and we walked about the house with our arms wrapped around ourselves and silently cursed the day of our birth. No one of us could rouse the other from his despair.

Father took to his Bible, and for the first time he did not read aloud or instruct us from it. He sat on a stool in the corner, muttering the words to himself, as if seeking, but not finding there, some explanation of why God had done this to us. Poverty he could endure with good spirits, and every setback and disappointment he regarded as temporary. And he had lost a child before, the first Frederick, who had died at the age of five and for whom he had grieved, and after a normal period of mourning he had resumed his life—he even named his next male child Frederick, as I have already described. But this disaster, this terrible loss, was beyond all his worst expectations, beyond all his understanding. His faith was sorely tested by it—that fact alone humiliated him and beat him down. To have four of his beloved children taken from him, each of them in its pitiful turn dying in his arms, this defeated him utterly. There was no one amongst us who could console or uplift him, for all of us, even Mary, had grown so accustomed to relying on him for consolation and uplift that if he was emptied of force, then we were, too.

This was the other, the darker side of our family's strength. When the Old Man went down, we all went down. Happily, almost nothing ever discouraged or defeated Father, except the death of children, which, by the time of his own death, he had endured so many times that his heart must have been nearly covered over with a skein of thick gray scars.

Knowing his terrible, long suffering, one can forgive him anything, I suppose. It rarely happened, he was so strong and so right, but there were times, certainly, when I felt called to forgive Father. Not by him— he seldom asked for my forgiveness, and when he did ask, it was for some trivial transgression, some slight oversight—but called upon by myself alone. In order to save me from him.

Forgive the Old Man, I would say to myself. Come on, now, grow large, Owen, and be generous with understanding and compassion. Yes, understanding, especially that—for when one understands a human being, no matter how oppressive he has been, compassion inevitably follows. Yet there was so much that I could not understand about this man, my father, and the life we led because of him—my thoughts, my questions, were blocked, occluded: by the absolute rightness of his cause, which none of us could question, ever; and by the sheer power of Father's personality, the relentlessness of it, how it wore us down, until we seemed to have no personalities of our own, even to each other. Certainly we spoke like him, but we could not hear it ourselves. We had to be told of it first by strangers.

The Old Man seemed to burn us out: whenever he rode off on one of his journeys to raise money for the work or on business of his own, he left us behind him, glad to have him gone. Yes, thrilled to have him gone—but dry and cold and light, like pieces of char or bits of cinder, like ash. When the Old Man left, we did not speak much, not to one another, not to strangers.

I meant here to write about how we spoke and why our speech was so strangely mannered. I see that I have done something else. I close now, as ash, again . . . or still: I do not know which.

9

It's as if I'm actually living there, in North Elba, and in those olden times when I was young. As if, weeks ago, when I first began speaking of it, I went tumbling down some twisting, narrow shaft that emerged there. And now, still clambering along a descending maze of tunnels and caves, I am unable to find my way back again to the surface of the earth, to my cabin in Altadena and daylight. The only light down inside these cold, rock-walled chambers is the light of memory flaring up, illuminating rough pictures and writings overhead, like those the Indians drew in ages past to invoke and placate their pagan gods. I stand below, gazing in wonder at the pictures, and the figures begin to move and speak, and my wonder, as you have seen so many times in these pages, turns first to warmth of recognition, then to gladness, and then, as the story told by the figures grows violent or somber, turns fearful and sad, I stumble backwards away from the pictures and into the darkness of the cave again. Soon I am falling, scrambling, clawing my way along yet another shaft in this warren, until the floor beneath my feet finally levels out, and once more I stop and stand, and when the light of memory spreads from my face, I see in its glow that I have arrived in a new chamber . . . and there, up on the walls—a mingling of shadow and light—it moves and dances . . .

and another, different event in my long-ago, half-forgotten life commences to unfold before me!

Today as I write I find myself still situated in the chamber of that first summer in North Elba, the summer of '50, when I was twenty-six, and I am recalling that it was for me an especially instructive time, perhaps because of the absence at the farm of my recently married elder brothers, John and Jason, who were ranked above me at that time in Father's little army and who, therefore, normally would have superseded me in the work. Father's work. The Lord's work, as he constantly reminded us, of freeing the slaves. For until the slaves were free—as he told us over and over again—none of us were free.

To Father, white and black Americans alike were bound by slavery: the physical condition of the enslaved, he insisted, was the moral condition of the free. This was not some vague, safely abstract principle, such as propounded by the New England philosophers. No, for Father, quite literally, we Americans, white as much as black, Northern as much as Southern, anti-slave as much as pro-, we were, all of us, presently living under the rule of Satan. It was an inarguable truth to Father that man's essential task while on this earth was to bring both his personal and his civic life into total accord with the will and overarching law of God. And since a republic is a type of state that by definition is governed by laws created and enforced by its citizens, whenever in a republic those laws do not conform to the laws of God, because those laws *can* be changed by men, they *must* be changed by men. And not to change them placed the mortal soul of every one of its citizens in terrible jeopardy. Not to struggle constantly to overthrow the system of slavery was to abandon our Republic, was to surrender our civic freedoms and responsibilities, was to give our mortal souls over to the rule of Satan. We were obliged to oppose slavery, then, not merely to preserve and perfect the Republic, although that alone was a worthy enough task, but to defeat Satan. It was our holy, our peculiarly American, obligation.

Simple. Or so it seemed. For even though I understood Father's logic well enough, I didn't always understand his applications of that logic to the specific circumstances, contingencies, and conditions that arose daily in our lives. Which meant that, on a day-to-day basis, I sometimes did not know right from wrong.

For instance, there was the time—after we had passed the young Negro couple, Emma and James Cannon, on to safety, as we assumed— when we discovered that, in fact, there was considerable evidence that they had murdered their master and that there was indeed a warrant from the Commonwealth of Virginia for their arrest and return. When this came out, many of the whites in North Elba grew fearful and angry. These were the same, good people who, before this episode, as I have shown, had been quietly aiding Father and me and various of the Negroes of Timbuctoo in our attempts to spirit escaped slaves north-ward. Now, however, they wished us to cease this activity. And I found myself in partial agreement with them.

One day several weeks after our misadventure with Billingsly, the bounty-hunter, there appeared up at our farm a United States marshal from Albany—accompanied by the ever-helpful Mr. Partridge of Keene. Bearing a warrant for the immediate arrest and return of Emma and James Cannon for the murder of their owner, one Mr. Samuel Cannon of Richmond, Virginia, the marshal put to Father, as he had to numer-ous others in the village, a set of pointed questions regarding the whereabouts of the couple. Though his interrogation of Father was clearly based on detailed information that had been provided by his guide, Mr. Partridge, the marshal appeared to know nothing of our burly encounter in Port Kent with Mr. Billingsly. Which was natural: it was not, after all, in the bounty-hunter's interest to aid and abet the cap-ture of his prey by a salaried officer of the law, and thus it was unlikely that he would have reported, even to his helper, Mr. Partridge, our having briefly kidnapped him, an incident he probably regarded with a certain degree of embarrassment anyhow.

When Father simply answered that he knew nothing of the Negro couple, there was little the marshal could do but pass north to the next known stop on the Railroad, there to interrogate the Quaker Captain Keifer. Up there, most officers of the law in those days had a pretty good idea of who was working on the Underground Railroad and who was not and, unless prodded by warrants and writs, did little to obstruct them.

It was our white neighbors, the Brewsters, the Nashes, and even Mr. Thompson, who, when they learned of the warrant for the arrest of the Cannons, grew frightened and came to Father and spoke angrily against our having escorted murderers north. Father sat on his stool and, while the men stood around him, heard them out. They were a delegation of three, apparently chosen to represent to Father the views and desires of the entire community. As known abolitionists themselves and friends of John Brown, they were no doubt thought to be more likely to get a hearing from him than if others, less sympathetic to the cause, had come.

Mr. Thompson was their spokesman. "Helping slaves to escape from slavery is a good thing to do," he said. "A good thing. Upright. But, really, John, helping to spirit known murderers out of the country— that's a different matter altogether." He told Father that, as we Browns could not assure the community that the people we were escorting to freedom were decent Christians and not criminals or moral reprobates, it was our neighbors' wish that we cease our activities at once. It was partly a consequence, he said, of our insistence on working outside and separate from the churches and other white institutions and individuals who could provide our cargo with *bona fides* to certify that the fugitives were not criminals. But it was also a consequence, he pointed out, of Father's determination to work with the Negroes of Timbuctoo, especially with men like Elden Fleete and Lyman Epps, men who, Mr. Thompson and the others believed, had no particular interest in farming here. All the whites but Father, Mr. Thompson pointed out, had come here to North Elba solely to farm and raise their families in peace and security. Even many of the Negroes had come here for that purpose. Now, however, everyone, white and black alike, was being interrogated by a United States marshal, and bounty-hunters like Billingsly and lazy rascals like Partridge had taken to skulking around the place. "Let the abolitionist Negroes themselves, Fleete and Epps, conduct escaping slaves, or people who claim to be escaping slaves, on to Canada on their own, if that's what they want to do with their time," Mr. Thompson told Father. "But we whites, John, we should stay clear of it. Completely."

He took a long while to make his case, and when he had finished, Father stood and drew himself up to his full height, which was not exceptional, but because of his large face, he often appeared quite tall. He said, "Gentlemen, you are all my friends. And I would like to put you at your ease, but I cannot just now. I will make my complete answer to your charges and concerns, but I prefer to make it to the entire community, and not just you three. I'll do it come Sunday morning in the church, where I have grown accustomed to speaking now and then. I would be pleased if you gave this out to the others, so that all who have an interest in the matter may hear me."

Then, with no further ceremony or words, he let them out of the house and, by abruptly turning his back and shutting fast the door, dismissed them.

That Sunday morning, a cold, rainy day, I remember, we all, including Lyman and Susan Epps, rode in the wagon into the village of North Elba and marched into the little white Presbyterian church there and took our accustomed seats in our usual pew towards the front. We sat in a single row, with Father on the aisle. There was an unusually large turnout, for this matter had generated considerable heat and feeling in the town. The small chapel was packed with red-faced farmers and their families and smelled of their boots and wet wool clothing. The entire Thompson clan was present, taking up two pews to our one, and I noted Ruth and young Henry Thompson exchange a significantly friendly glance, and I remember saying to myself, A-ha! What have we here?

The preacher, the Reverend Spofford Hall from Vermont, a scrawny, somewhat insipid fellow whom Father abhorred for his lax liberalism in religion, gave out with his usual, mechanical invocation, after which the small choir stood and sang the opening hymn. Sang it with unaccustomed force, I thought, due perhaps to four of the eight being Negroes from the settlement, who must have known that there was scheduled in today's ceremonies a thing of particular significance to them. They sounded like a choir three times their size, and Father's knees joggled up and down in close time to the music, and his eyes glistened happily as they sang.

At last, the Reverend Hall stepped to the lectern set before the spare, New England–style altar and announced in his high, watery voice, "Today our neighbor Mister Brown will address us." Then he stood down and turned the meeting over to Father.

It was a sermon that I had heard by then numerous times and listened to often enough afterwards, and I can hear the Old Man's voice today, these many years later, as clearly as I did that cold, gray morning in North Elba. I see him standing there, straight as a tree, screw-faced and tense, his wet, fox-red hair sticking up, and I listen to him begin his first sentence, and as I write, my mouth seems to open, as if I am to speak his entire sermon for him, word for word.

"Good morning, neighbors," the Old Man said.

"Though outside these walls the rain falls, and the mountains be all hid in clouds, and though the chilled wind today blows out of the northwest, we here inside our small sanctuary are dry and warm together, are we not?

"We are comfortable, friends and neighbors, and we are safe, and we sing praises to the Lord, our heavenly Father, and we offer Him our prayers of thanksgiving, so as to signify our pleasure and our heartfelt gratitude to Him who, at His pleasure, hath granted that comfort and that safety to us. Do we not?

"Comfort and safety which has been granted to *us*—we who clear the forests, we who till the fields, we who raise our livestock. Little people of the valley between the mountains, that is what we are, friends. Men, women, and children struggling merely to survive and if possible to prosper in a hard place in a hard time. Are we not?

"Comfort and safety granted to us—who *deserve* nothing. Who deserve neither comfort nor safety, certainly, but who deserve neither discomfort nor danger, either. Understand me—granted to us, who deserve *nothing*! Not even to exist. Is this not the case, friends?

"I speak of everyone in the community, all of us—the blackest and the poorest among us, and the whitest and the richest. The most innocent, and the most foully corrupted. The most pious, and the least pious. The young, and the old. For we do not, not a one of us, *deserve* to live. It is not something the Lord *owes* us! Can you argue with that, friends?

"So that, if there is a debt, neighbors, if there is something that is owed someone, then it runs the other way, does it not?

"For who among us asked to be born? Who among us made such a request? No, white or black, rich or poor, not a one of us had such a right or even the means to make that request. And now, having been born, having been granted air to breathe and a place to stand upon, having been shown a firmament set between the firmaments, having been wakened from the dreamless sleep of nothingness, now, who among us can say, *This was owed me, this was long owed me*? Or even, *This, Lord, did* I request *of Thee*?

"The Lord giveth, neighbors, and the Lord taketh away. And does He not do so at His pleasure, friends? Not ours! No, it is only at the Lord's own pleasure that we exist, is it not?

"We cannot cajole Him, we cannot argue our case, as if He were an Elizabethtown judge and we a plaintiff's attorney. We cannot even beg. No, all we poor people can do, having come to an awareness of our lives, is give thanks. Give thanks, and then live out our lives according to that high, holy purpose, the purpose of continuing to give thanks, over and over again, amen.

"Contemplate the alternative, neighbors. Briefly, just briefly, is all— for to contemplate that alternative is truly painful. *Nothingness* is the alternative! A blasted absence! Contemplate nothingness for a few short seconds, neighbors, and you will turn away in horror, and *then* you will give thanks unto the Lord. Then you will sing His praises. And you will leap and dance with joy! Not for the pleasure of being alive, for life is all too often no pleasure whatsoever, but you will leap and dance with joy and thanksgiving for having had the opportunity to exist at all!

"I am thinking, this rainy, cold morning, neighbors, of old Job. A farmer and stockman, like many of us here. I am thinking of a pious man with a large, loving family who, like us, lived in a broad valley sur-rounded by mountains, where there were wolves and lions and bears, where the cold winds blew in winter, and where, beyond the moun-tains, there were enemies lurking who coveted his fields and crops and envied the peacefulness and the fruitfulness of his life. Can you imag-ine Job as a man very like us? Can you?

"Against these enemies, and against the wolves and lions and bears, against the cold winds of winter and the drought of summer, against sickness and plague, old Job and his loving family and neighbors nonetheless prospered and thrived, and they and their livestock multiplied in their numbers, until they had become a community in that ancient wilderness, a community much like ours here in our modern, American wilderness.

"And these good folks, old Job and his family and friends, they did everything right. They did it just so. In this they were perhaps superior even to us here in North Elba. For we are sometimes slack and slothful, are we not? And some of us keep not the usual observances in religion, and from time to time we mistreat one another in our families, or we fall to quarreling with each other, do we not? But Job and his family and friends, they were, one and all, a consistently upright people. Especially Job, the Bible tells us. Especially Job. He was a man who, even in that fine a community, was outstanding and much admired. Admired for his piety, his judgement, and his decorum, admired for his kindness and generosity, for his integrity, and for his willingness to keep all God's commandments. Do you remember the story?

"If we ourselves here today could be like any man in the Holy Bible, neighbors, we would be like Job. Am I right? Not for his wealth, naturally—although he had plenty of that, and we wouldn't turn it away. And not simply for the respect and admiration that he obtained from his family and neighbors, although none of us would scorn those. And not for his wisdom and clarity of mind, either.

"No, we would want to be like Job because of his simple goodness, his straightforward decency, and his charitableness. Recall the story. Job was a man who rested easy with himself, the Bible says. We have all known one or two men like that, and we might have envied them, but for the fact that in envying them we would have become less like them than before, for one of their main virtues was that they envied no man. And so we have tried strictly to love such men and to emulate them, have we not?

"Well, old Job was an easy man to love. Even God, who loves all men equally, regarded Job as especially admirable, and thus, when Satan sat down on a rock to criticize these poor, forked creatures that were so beloved of God, the Lord singled out Job for special praise. In this story, friends, the key to Satan's motives is that he did not comprehend God's love of mankind, not even of Job, the best of mankind, the champion human being of us all back in those ancient Biblical days. And so Satan spoke to God of mankind as if we were not worthy of God's love, and he said that, therefore, God should withdraw His love. 'Take it off from them,' Satan said.

"You remember the story, neighbors. Satan argued with the Lord that the only reason we humans were in the slightest obedient to the Lord's commandments was because we expected and often received large rewards for it. For it was true, and it remaineth so, that we are far more likely to prosper when we keep His commandments than when we do not keep them.

"But Satan insinuated that we were a shrewdly calculating lot. That we were hypocrites. And thus we were not worthy of God's love. And if we were not worthy of God's love, Satan reasoned, then we were not worthy of the existence that He had granted us even without our asking.

"A gift unimagined is the gift of God's love. Our very existence is that unimagined gift. That, neighbors and friends, that is why there is *something* and, for us, not merely *nothing*! God's love is the universe's first and only cause, neighbors.

"Well, no one ever called Satan a fool, did they? Throughout the Bible he is called many things, but never foolish. No, sir. He took a long look at this man called Job, this fine man living out there in the land of Uz with his seven sons and three daughters, his seven thousand sheep and his three thousand camels and his five hundred yoke of oxen— quite a plantation was Job's place out there in Uz. And Satan said to the

Lord, 'You know that fellow Job, the one you're always bragging about, the man you're so high on? Well, he's a hypocrite, too. Even he!'

"The Lord saith, 'Ah, yes, my servant Job! But you're wrong. Job is a perfect man. He's the most upright of them all, and he fears me, and he eschews evil.' Thus saith the Lord, neighbors.

"Satan said, 'Sure, of *course*, he fears you and eschews evil and makes all the proper observances and so on. But it's not for nothing. Look at the hedge you've built around the man. Look how he's rewarded for it. But just put forth thine hand against him, Lord, and the man will curse thee to thine face,' said Satan. 'Believe me, that fellow Job, he's a hypocrite,' declared Satan. 'The same as the rest. He may be the best amongst men, but even he is a hypocrite.'

"And so the Lord gave Satan permission to do with Job as he wished, so long as he did not slay him. 'All that old Job hath is in thy power,' saith the Lord to Satan. 'Go ahead, take away everything, and you'll see what sort of man we have here.'

"You remember the story, neighbors. First came the Sabeans, who slew Job's oxen and his asses and even put the servants attending them to the sword. And just as Job was absorbing the news of this loss, another messenger came in and told him that fire had fallen from the sky and burned up all his sheep. And then three bands of Chaldeans fell upon Job's camels, slew the servants attending them, and stole the camels away to Chaldea. And then came the worst thing, friends. Remember? While Job's sons and daughters were eating and drinking wine together in the house of the eldest son, a great wind howled out of the wilderness and smote the four corners of the house, and it fell upon them and killed them all!

"And what did poor Job do in the face of these terrible events? Did he charge the Lord foolishly? Did he rail against God, as you or I might have done? No, Job rent his mantle and shaved his head, and he made a public showing of his sorrow by returning himself as if to his infancy, bald and naked as a babe. And then he fell down upon the ground, and, friends, he *worshipped* the Lord! 'Naked came I out of my mother's womb', he said, 'and naked shall I return thither. The Lord gave, and the Lord hath taken away. Blessed be the name of the Lord!'

"This, neighbors, was no hypocrite!

"But Satan wasn't satisfied yet. 'He hath his life still', Satan pointed out to the Lord. 'But just put forth thy hand now, and touch his bone, and touch his flesh, and Job will curse thee to thy face.'

"The Lord said, 'Go on, try him.' So Satan went forth, and he smote old Job with sore boils from his foot to his crown. He smote him so badly that the poor man could only sit in agony among ashes, scraping his enflamed flesh with a potsherd. Such a figure of pathos and ruination was he that even his wife came out and said to him, 'So, Job, dost thou still retain thine integrity? Curse God, and die', she said to him. 'Husband, curse God and die.' Harsh words, neighbors, are they not?

"But wise old Job, he said to his wife, 'Shall we receive good at the hand of God and not evil also? Foolish woman', he said to her, but she understood him not and left him alone there in the ashes.

"You remember the story, neighbors. Then from the town came Job's three friends to comfort and grieve with him. Eliphaz and Bildad and Zophar were their names, and for seven days and seven nights they listened to Job recount his sorrows and curse, not God, never God, but his birth, his very birth.

"Old Eliphaz the Temanite—a sensible man, we would say, if he came among us today in North Elba—Eliphaz argued that Job must have somehow offended God. 'For who ever perished', he said to Job, 'who was also innocent? Tell me, where were the righteous cut off? Happy is the man', reasoned the Temanite, 'whom God correcteth. Cheer up', he told Job. 'You are being chastized by the Father for your failings.'

"Have you not also been consoled like this, friends, in times of great suffering?

"'Oh, if only that were the case!' was Job's answer. 'Oh, that my grief and my calamity were so evenly weighed in the balance together!'

"And so Bildad the Shuhite spoke unto Job. 'Surely, friend Job, surely God would not cast away a perfect man,' he said. 'And neither will he keep an evil-doer. You cannot be one,' said Bildad to Job, 'so you must perforce be the other.'

"But Job cried, 'No, no, no, a thousand times no! If I justify myself to the Lord, mine own mouth shall condemn me. If I say I am perfect, He shall prove me perverse. The Lord destroyeth the perfect and the wicked *alike*! Even if I were righteous,' Job said to his friend and neighbor Bildad, 'I would not answer with that. Instead, I would make supplication only to my Judge. For look ye, He breaketh me without cause! And you, Bildad, you do not understand any of this.'

"But we understand, do we not, neighbors?

"Then Job's friend Zophar the Naamathite gave it a try. 'You must be lying,' he said as kindly as he could. 'You say to us that thy doctrine is clean, and thou art clean in the Lord's eyes. Well, Job, old friend, that cannot be, else you would not be in such a catastrophic condition. So confess, my brother. Prepare thine heart, and stretch out thy hands before thee towards Him. And then the Lord will reward thee!'

"And Job said to Zophar, 'No, no, no, no! Look around you, fool! Everywhere the tabernacles are full of robbers, and they prosper. Everywhere those who provoke God are secure. Therefore, you, my friends and neighbors,' saith Job to Zophar, Bildad, and Eliphaz, 'you are all physicians of no value.'

"Hear me, friends and neighbors of this village of North Elba. Hear me. Job said, 'You speak wickedly for God and talk deceitfully for Him. You speak in your own interests only. Does not His excellency make you *afraid*? Does it not make you *tremble*?

"'As for me,' Job said to his friends and neighbors—and here I come to the point of my preachment to you—Job said, 'As for me, though the

Lord slay me, yet will I trust in Him and will maintain mine own ways before Him. Miserable comforters are ye all!' Job said to them. 'Ye believe that one might plead with God as a man pleadeth with his neighbor. I cannot find one wise man among you.'

"Have ye not known such miserable comforters as these, friends? They are all around us, are they not? Why, we might even be them ourselves, might we not?

"Where, then, neighbors, shall wisdom be found? And where lieth the place of understanding?

"Behold. I, John Brown, I say to you that it is just as the Bible shows us. The fear of the Lord, that is wisdom. And to depart from evil, that is understanding.

"And you will remember, neighbors, from the old story, there came a whirlwind, and out of the whirlwind the Lord answered Job's cry. 'Of Job's friends and neighbors,' the Lord saith, 'who is this that darkeneth counsel by words without knowledge? And where wast thou,' the Lord saith to Eliphaz, Bildad, and Zophar, 'where wast thou when I laid the foundations of the earth? Where wast thou when I placed the firmament between the firmaments?'

"To them the Lord saith, 'My wrath is kindled against thee! For you have not spoken of me the thing that is right, as my servant Job hath.' And the Lord took from them seven bullocks and seven rams each and gave them unto Job. And He blessed the latter end of Job's life even more than at the beginning with sheep and camels and oxen and asses, and He gave him seven sons more and three daughters.

"Well, neighbors, there you have it. My answer to your charges against me! Now, shall I tell thee the meaning of the story of Job? Shall I again compare us here in this sanctuary today to old Job out there in Uz, a man of principle?

"Or shall I instead compare us to his friends and neighbors, to Eliphaz, Bildad, and Zophar, whose hypocrisy kindled the wrath of the

Lord against them? Which of these ancients resembles us more?

"For, look, ye have counseled me exactly as Job's wife counseled him. Ye have told me to forsake my integrity and curse God.

"Ye hath brayed at me like Eliphaz. Ye hath spoken out against me as if wisdom were thine and thy feet were set in the place of under-standing.

"Remember, neighbors, in the fear of the Lord, that is where wis-dom lies. And to depart from evil, that is understanding. And that is all ye need to know.

"I say to you, miserable comforters! physicians of no value! I tell thee here and now that I and my family shall continue as before—to fear the Lord and to depart from evil. We seek wisdom and under-standing. Those are our principles. We shall live by our principles. You, my good neighbors, you may do as you wish."

Here the Old Man completed his remarks and stepped down and re-joined the congregation. When he had taken his seat, he lowered his head in prayer, and first Mary, next to him, and then the rest of us alongside in the pew did likewise, and as I myself, the last in our group to do so, lowered my head, I noticed that there were a good many other people amongst the congregation who were also following Father's example, as if in this argument with Job they wished pointedly to sepa-rate themselves from the side of Eliphaz, Bildad, and Zophar.

A moment later, the Reverend Hall walked up to the lectern, and although the service resumed in its usual manner, I was not aware of it, for my thoughts were turning around the meaning of Father's talk. I felt myself surrounded by a buzzing light, as if by a swarm of golden bees, and I had to struggle to hear my thoughts. A terrible understand-ing had come over me in the midst of Father's talk, and I did not want to lose it, in spite of its being fearsome and threatening to me.

In Father's words, the figure of Job was, of course, like no one so much as Father himself. As Job stood to God, Father did also. My terrible understanding was that I, too, was like no one so much as Job. Not, however, in my relation to God; but in my relation to Father.

Who was Satan to me, then? Who would test my faithfulness to Father by afflicting me as Satan had afflicted Job? Would I, too, come to curse the day I was born? Would I beg for my own death, as Job had cried out for his and, as I knew, Father, in his periods of greatest despondency, had also? Would I, like Job, like Father, be able to resist the blandishments and sophistries of the hypocrites?

In the Bible, Job is rewarded at the end for his faithfulness to the Lord, he receives from Him new cattle and new children, and Satan is sent packing, along with Eliphaz, Bildad, and Zophar. But, as Father showed, Job's reward is given as evidence of God's power, not His justice. This is what the hypocrites found beyond their understanding. The moral of the story would be the same even if God had not rewarded Job at the end, for it was done merely to punish the hypocrites and confound Satan, not to comfort Job.

Who, then, in Father's story of my life, plays the role of Satan? Who wishes to prove me a hypocrite?

The terrible answer, the only possible answer, was that anyone who opposes Father as Satan opposes God, could, if I merely questioned Father, prove me a hypocrite. That answer turned me into a trapped animal, a fox with a paw clamped in an iron-toothed jaw. To escape it, I would be obliged to gnaw at my own flesh and separate my body from itself. Freed, I would be a crippled little beast unable to care for himself, unable even to flee. I would have obtained freedom, yes, but freedom for what? To huddle alone in the bushes nearby, there to die slowly of my self-inflicted wounds. No, I thought. Better the intimacy of iron against my wrist. Better the familiarity of my own teeth closed inside my mouth. Better boils, a potsherd, ashes. Better to curse ever having been born.

❏

Predictably, with a few changes made—none of them, however, designed to placate the wishes of our white neighbors—Father went straight back to work on the Underground Railroad. In his mind, all our white neighbors were now cowards and hypocrites, every one of them, and periodically he denounced them to any of us in the family who would listen. He denounced even his good friend Mr. Thompson, for, although the Old Man at first thought that he had successfully shamed our neighbors with his sermon, his message evidently hadn't taken hold: no one in the village was willing anymore to aid him in his efforts to spirit fugitive slaves out of the country—except, of course, for the Negroes themselves. And except for the rest of us Browns. Meaning me, I suppose, although there was considerable sacrifice required as well of the others in the family, who had to accommodate themselves to Father's and my and Lyman's frequent and protracted absences from the farm.

The most significant change in our *modus operandi*, however, was in cutting Mr. Wilkinson of the Tahawus mining camp out of the operation. In a flurry of letters to Mr. Frederick Douglass in Rochester, Father made it clear that he would not work with the man. Thenceforth, cargo from the South would have to be shipped to Father in North Elba via an agent named Reuben Shiloh, in care of a Mrs. Ebenezer Rankin, resident of the town of Long Lake, New York, a small, rough lumbering community in the southern Adirondack wilderness about forty miles from North Elba. Reuben Shiloh was in fact Father himself, a pseudonym. Mrs. Rankin, his point of contact in Long Lake, was the elderly widow of a veteran of the War of the Revolution. She lived alone in a cabin on the land her husband had homesteaded after the war, was regarded in the village as mildly eccentric and harmless, and, due to her deep religious feeling and independence of spirit, was sympathetic to the cause. Father first met her after a sermon he had made on the subject of abolitionism at the Congregational church there in Long Lake and, as was his wont, had trusted her instantly. Generally, the Old Man made decisions as to a person's trustworthiness at once and without consulting others. When it had to do with business matters, of course, he was usually wrong, well off the mark, absurdly so; but when it concerned the question of slavery, he was almost always right.

"It's a thing you can tell in an instant. You know it from a person's speech or the cast of his eyes, as soon as you begin to speak with him on the subject of race," he said, trying to explain his procedure. "Early on, Owen, I conceived the idea of placing myself, when speaking of such matters with white people, in the position of a Negro." Which is to say that he listened to whites and watched them as if his self-respect, his well-being, his very life, were always at stake, and consequently, as he claimed, he quickly saw things that most whites ignore or blind themselves to. For example, if he spoke of the horrors of slavery to a stranger and the man's face went all slack and sad over it, as if he wished to be admired for the tenderness of his feelings, then Father knew not to trust him. But if the man reacted, not with sadness and regret, but with righteous wrathfulness, then he would brighten and feel secure in confiding in that person. Father said he loved seeing that old-time righteous anger fill up a white man's face. It happened rarely, however. "No, Owen," he said, "when it comes to race and slavery, white people, try as they may, cannot hide their true feelings. Not to their fellow Americans who happen to be born black, that is. And not to me, either. Only to themselves."

Mr. Wilkinson of Tahawus had not hidden his true feelings, not even from me, and I believe that he somewhat resented being cut away from the operation, not out of any love for the Negro or some deep desire to help destroy slavery, but because his work on the Railroad made it significantly easier for him to view himself as a man who acted kindly towards people he regarded as his inferiors. Perhaps he believed that by working for the Underground Railroad and alongside Father, whose motives were pure, he might be able to strike a balance against his hard treatment of the indentured Irish miners and their families. At any rate, soon after he was dropped by the wayside, he joined, unbeknownst to us, with our known enemies, with the slave-catchers and bounty-hunters, with the folks in the region who regarded us as fanatical trouble-makers, and with the marshal from Albany, whose pursuit of the Virginia couple accused of murdering their master had continued throughout the summer.

The marshal, whose name was Saunders, had gotten himself caught in a squeeze between the Canadian and American authorities and also between the states of Virginia and New York, as the Canadians, after conducting an extensive investigation, had asserted unequivocably that the Cannons had never crossed the border at all. The authorities in Virginia insisted that the couple had been last located over in New-Trenton, New York, where they had been detained briefly by a local deputy whom they had somehow bribed to leave their cell door unlocked—the money for the bribe possibly originating with Mr. Douglass, who had visited the couple during their brief confinement. The New-Trenton deputy was himself now awaiting trial, and in order to save his own skin was telling Marshal Saunders everything he knew or thought he knew about the Cannons and their confederates.

Meanwhile, we were moving regular shipments of human cargo over Father's, or Reuben Shiloh's, new link between Long Lake and North Elba, and due to the rising vigilance of the authorities and the greater presence of slave-catchers west of us in Buffalo and east of us in Troy, our cargo was increasing significantly in volume and degree of risk, so that three or four times a week we were obliged to make a run down along the old Military Road from North Elba through the pine forests and across the swamps and muskegs to the cabin of Mrs.

Rankin, where we loaded up and then raced back through the night to Timbuctoo, and the next night moved our cargo on to Port Kemp, where Captain Keifer carried it aboard his boat and sailed it north to Canada.

It was a wild and exciting time. We were like a gang of outlaws, Lyman and I and Mr. Fleete and Father, armed and reckless, and several times we narrowly escaped capture. Lyman seemed to have found his proper vocation. He grew stern and brave and was no longer so garrulous and puffed up as he had sometimes been earlier. Our days on the farm now seemed merely to be resting periods, interludes that we impatiently waited out, until we again received word from Mrs. Rankin that a new shipment for Reuben Shiloh had arrived in Long Lake, and we would be off, Father and Mr. Fleete on horseback, Lyman and I in the wagon, with our guns close at hand and supplies and tarpaulins and blankets stashed in the bed of the wagon. At Mrs. Rankin's cabin we'd hole up for the daylight hours in the shed she had out back, beneath which we had early on dug a secret cellar hiding-place where the escaped slaves could await our arrival undetected. And then at sundown we'd load the fugitives into the wagon—men, women, and children in various combinations. We'd cover them with the tarpaulin and race back northeast to Timbuctoo, and if we made good time, we'd keep right on towards Port Kent, arriving there just before sunrise, and Captain Keifer would transfer the cargo from our wagon to his boat. Later that same day, usually in the afternoon, we would pull into the yard in front of the house in North Elba, men and animals alike exhausted and hungry, and we'd eat and fall into bed and sleep like corpses for ten or twelve hours.

Twice, I remember, we were accosted by law officers—a sheriff in Long Lake and a deputy U.S. marshal in Ausable Forks—but on both occasions our wagon was empty, and after suffering a brief and surly interrogation, we were allowed to continue unimpeded. Nonetheless, we were ready for the worst. Although we weren't actually pursued at any time and thus weren't obliged to fire our weapons, there was always the danger of betrayal and discovery. People would look up from their work in the fields and woodlots and stare at us as we passed by or peer out the windows of their bedrooms late in the night when the sound of our horses' hooves and the loud rattle and clack of the wagon disturbed their sleep. Those people must have known who we were and what we were up to.

Our operation, however, was narrow, secretive, and private, cut off from any communications with the communities that surrounded us, cut off, even, from the rest of the anti-slavery movement and its committees and churches and the old mainlines of the Underground Railroad. We worked in a kind of darkness and solitude, as if no one else on the planet were engaged in the same or similar activities. As if there were no one who was not utterly opposed to our activities. And, as had happened in the past, back in Ohio and Pennsylvania, where for an extended period we shuttled fugitive slaves successfully out of the South into Canada, we got caught up in the day-to-day rhythms and excitement of the work, and this put us off the larger rhythms of the movement as a whole. It was as if our little four-man operation, our overnight link between Long Lake and Port Kent, New York, were the entire anti-slavery program for America. It wasn't arrogance or pride that did it, although it did sometimes seem that Father honestly believed that under his leadership our work was more crucial to the movement than any other and that it was more rigorous and disciplined, morally clearer, better planned, and more efficiently executed than the work of everyone else—beliefs dangerously close to arrogance and pride. No, we lost sight of the larger picture because we were obliged to respond constantly and quickly day in and out to the immediate needs of desperate people who had entrusted their lives to us. And just as we forgot about the helpful existence of our distant or indirect allies, we forgot about the conniving actions of our distant and indirect enemies. We operated without reconnoiter and in the absence of intelligence.

Thus we were not prepared for the re-appearance, one hot August afternoon, of Marshal Saunders at the farm in North Elba. He arrived on horseback in the company of a pair of sober-visaged deputies, bearing testimony from Mr. Wilkinson of the Tahawus mining camp, who the marshal claimed had accused Father and me and two unnamed Negroes presently residing in the vicinity of North Elba of having aided and abetted the escape of the indicted murderers James and Emma Cannon, of Richmond, Virginia.

The officers came up on us shortly after we had returned from a two-night run to Port Kent with four Maryland Negroes—an elderly man, his daughter, and her two nearly grown sons. Our wagon was empty, and Father and I, fortunately, were alone, as Lyman had accompanied Mr. Fleete back to Timbuctoo, there to rest and afterwards to do some much needed blacksmithing among the Negro farmers.

We were standing outside the house by the water trough, stripped to our waists, washing ourselves. The boys and the women, including Lyman's wife, Susan, were cutting the first crop of hay in the front field. Father looked up at the three men, who sat relaxed and open-faced on their horses as if they meant us no harm. Introductions were not necessary, and Marshal Saunders got straight to the point of this his second visit to our farm. When he had told us of Mr. Wilkinson's betrayal, he said, "Mister Brown, I've not come here to charge you and your son with anything. I'm here peaceable. But I do need to know the names of the two colored men who helped you carry the Cannons through here. It wasn't but a month ago," he said, with a slow smile. "You no doubt recall their names."

Father dried himself deliberately and said nothing. He looked at me, and I saw his boiling rage. Then he passed the drying cloth to me.

"If we helped anyone named Cannon, and I don't recall that we did, but *if* we did, then my son and I did it alone," Father said. "Wilkinson is a liar."

Marshal Saunders said that he was looking for a slim, dark Negro man in his twenties and a heavy-set mulatto man in his fifties with a full beard. "I'm going to assume, Mister Brown, that you and your son here didn't have no notion that the coloreds from Virginia was murderers, all right? And you thought you was only helping a couple of escaped slaves scoot through to Canada, that's all. Just as was the case with Mister Wilkinson down there at Tahawus. And I don't consider him a liar, sir. I realize that you all were only doing what you thought was your Christian duty. Your Negro associates, however, probably knew better. They have their little secrets that they keep from us," he said sourly. He believed that they probably knew where the Cannons were hiding. His aim was to cut a deal with our friends. The same deal, he said, that he was cutting with us. If they could give him some small help in locating the Cannons, then he wouldn't press charges against anyone up here in North Elba. "They're free niggers, far as I'm concerned, and that's how I'll treat them, so long's they do the same as you and give me a bit of help in performing my duties as a federal officer of the law. You understand what I'm telling you, Mister Brown?"

Father stared up at the man in silence. The horses shifted their weight, sweating under the sun. "Certainly I understand," he finally said. "But I will not help you, sir. My son and I, if indeed we did help some poor Negro slaves escape from the evil clutches of some Southern slavemaster—a man who may well have deserved to die anyhow, since well-treated slaves rarely risk the rigors of flight—then we did so on our own." The burden of proof lay with the marshal, Father pointed out, and he believed that giving a stranger in a strange land a ride in your wagon was not yet illegal in the state of New York.

Well, yes, the marshal agreed. It was a gray area of the law, a person might say. Father would benefit everyone concerned, however, himself included, if he saw fit to aid the law. The marshal rolled his head slowly on his shoulders, as if his neck were stiff and this were a casual conversation. The two deputies kept their right hands open and close to the handles of their revolvers.

Father said, "You don't know who you're looking for, except on Mister Wilkinson's perjured say-so. And I can't help you, and if I could, I'll tell you frankly, sir, I wouldn't. Find your Negroes on your own," he snapped, and he turned and walked towards the house.

"It could all unravel on you, Brown!" the marshal called after. "I might bring Wilkinson himself up here, so's he can identify the two niggers for me, and when it comes to saving their own dusky skins, who knows what them fellows'll say then?"

Father wheeled and glared at him. "Do as you wish! Bring Satan up from hell, if you like, and have him pick a pair of Negroes from the crowd for you. I'll not help with work like this!"

The three turned their horses abruptly then and rode out of the yard, and without looking back, they galloped down the road towards the settlement. A moment later, when I went inside the house, I found Father already seated, still shirtless, at his writing table, furiously scratching out a letter.

"Who are you writing to?" I asked him.

"John and Jason."

"In Springfield? And Ohio?"

"Yes, of course!"

"They may not be there now," I said. "They might've already left for here." Barely a week before, a letter from John had arrived, saying, among other cheering things, that he and Jason intended soon to come up to North Elba for a short visit, to see the place and the family and to settle a few business matters with Father that could best be discussed in person.

"All the better. But in case they haven't, this will bring them promptly." He blotted the letter and passed it over to me to read.

> *Come hither at once, boys, and come armed, for we need to snatch a few poor creatures from out of the mouth of Satan before he devours them! A proper show of Christian force and clear intent to rain fire down upon the heads of these local malefactors and hypocrites ought to clarify matters here, leastways enough so that we can continue doing the Lord's work and help bring about the downfall of slavery by making it too costly to maintain against the combined wills of white Christians and of the desperate, courageous slaves themselves. Come hither to North Elba now, my sons! Come and stand with us as true, courageous, righteous Soldiers of the Lord! Your loving father,*
>
> John Brown

I pointed out that it might be ten days or two weeks before they received his summons, and the whole affair could well have blown over by then. "And besides," I said, "they might've already left Springfield to come here anyhow. Why bother writing this at all?"

Father looked up at me with an expression that flowed from puzzlement to slight disgust. "Owen, sometimes I think . . . ," he said, then began again. "Owen, I sometimes believe that you must become a *hotter* man than you are." And with a little wave of dismissal, he returned to his letter, signed it, and placed it into an envelope and sealed it for mailing.

I stood by the window for a moment and, peering out at the mountains, saw that it was clouding up in the west to rain. I felt weary, almost dizzy, from two sleepless nights and ached in my bones for rest and wanted nothing more than to sleep for a day and a night. But I knew I could not do that yet. I pulled on a shirt and trudged from the house, across the yard towards the field, to help the family bring in the hay.

Scythe in hand, I crossed the road, and as I neared the others, I heard rapid hoofbeats behind me and, turning, saw Father ride out. He was headed towards the village to get his letter into the afternoon post to Westport, whence it would make its slow way south to Massachusetts, and the sight of the man, wrapped in haste and single-mindedness and rage, fatigued me now beyond all imagining. It nearly repelled me.

A short ways beyond, bent over in the field, was the rest of my family—my stepmother and sisters in starched bonnets like white flower-tops and my brothers under the shade of their straw hats working with their backs to me and against the wind that riffled across the field of yellow hay, flattening and silvering it in the fading afternoon light. They seemed at such peace with the world, so at ease with themselves, that I envied them and, momentarily weak and guilty, my conscience enflamed by Father's example and his cruel remark, felt cut off from them, as if I were a member of a completely different family.

There followed then a rapid succession of events, one leading swiftly to the next, and it seemed at the time that there was nothing we or anyone else could do to stop or deflect them. First, that same evening, when Father returned from posting his letter, he came all boiling with unusual rage. The family, me included, was at the table, eating supper, when he galloped into the yard on his poor old tired Morgan horse, strode into the house, and poured out his story in a torrent of words, shocking us with the ferocity of his anger and frightening the younger children. Sputtering and spitting, he bore us the news that when Marshal Saunders had earlier interrogated us, he had lied. It was a lie of omission, but a heinous lie nonetheless, Father declared, for the marshal had not told us that he had brought Mr. Wilkinson along with him and that he had kept the man hidden down the road a ways from the farm. Loud talk of murder and lying federal law officers and hypocrisy, of revenge and bloody rebellion, of laying about with the jawbone of an ass and chopping off the heads of serpents—we were used to that from Father. But here, tonight, in our farmhouse kitchen, our domestic sanctuary seemed to have been invaded for the first time, and the calls to violence were no longer made with regard to some distant or even imaginary place and time. They were more than metaphorical. Father wanted blood, real blood, and he wanted it now.

The Old Man had learned from the folks in Timbuctoo that after having been rebuked and rebuffed by Father, the marshal and his deputies had gathered up Mr. Wilkinson from his hiding-place, and the four had ridden over to the Negro settlement, where the traitorous villain Wilkinson had identified Lyman Epps and Mr. Fleete as our cohorts. Then, despite Lyman's and Mr. Fleete's insistence that they knew nothing of the whereabouts of the couple wanted in Virginia for murder, the marshal had placed both men under arrest and had marched them off to Elizabethtown, where, said Father, they were probably, even as he himself spoke, being placed under lock and key, as if the two had been returned to the manacles of slavery.

"This shall not be allowed to stand!" Father bellowed.

Susan Epps was naturally alarmed as to her husband's fate, and Ruth and Mary rushed to console her, as did I. Father, however, seemed blinded by his rage, and ignoring the fears of the women and children, he stomped up and down in the room, counting weapons and imagining violent confrontations along the trail between North Elba and the Elizabethtown jail, which both he and I knew the marshal and his party would not reach until morning or even later, if on their way they stopped overnight in Keene at Mr. Partridge's house, as we ourselves had when first coming over here back in May.

"We can still catch the culprits, you and I," he said to me. "Lyman and Mister Fleete are surely afoot, made to walk in chains like captured animals while the white men ride. They must have passed by here this very afternoon while you were all at work in the fields," he suddenly realized. "Didn't you see them?" he demanded. "Good Lord, didn't a one of you children notice them on the road? Four white men astride horses and two black men treated like slaves before your very noses, and not a one of you saw it?"

I explained that we had all been hard at work bringing in the hay, that it was hot and we were way down at the lower end of the field by then, trying to beat the rain. It had not rained after all, but had merely threatened to do so all afternoon long and into the evening. Now we heard distant thunder rumbling in the west, and flashes of heat lightning crackled across the darkening sky.

"Bah!" he exclaimed, grabbing down our muskets and checking the powder and bullets. "What we need are swords," he muttered to himself. "Broadswords! So we can sweep down upon them like avenging angels!"

But as the evening wore on, the Old Man calmed somewhat and seemed to settle upon a slightly more rational strategy for obtaining the release of our friends, which relieved me. I had not liked much the idea of the two of us riding out alone in the dark and recklessly falling upon the marshal, his deputies, and Mr. Wilkinson, and probably Partridge, too, with nothing but two small-bore muskets and a pair of hand-axes between us. On reflection, Father now believed that he might obtain the legal and financial help of Mr. Gerrit Smith, whose influence in these parts was great, and to this end the Old Man commenced to write a set of letters and pleas. He also proposed to ride over to Elizabethtown tomorrow morning himself, armed, in case of emergency, and accompanied by me—there to speak with the local authorities and try to get our friends released on their own recognizance pending a trial, which he firmly believed would never take place anyhow.

"This whole thing is a dumbshow," he now insisted. "A charade. It's merely an attempt to intimidate the poor fellows," he growled. He believed that Marshal Saunders was only interested in putting a feather in his cap for capturing the Cannons and thus was trying to frighten our friends into betraying the poor couple and had no intention of trying them in court. Father was sure that Lyman and Mr. Fleete had no more knowledge of the Cannons' present whereabouts than we and were as ignorant as we of the Cannons' true reasons for fleeing their master and the state of Virginia—if indeed it was true that they slew the man in the first place. And if they did, so be it. How could we blame them? Father almost wished they *had* slain their master. "Only in an evil and inhuman land, Owen, is it a crime to slay the man who enslaves you. Remember that," he said.

When morning came and Father and I were preparing to leave for Elizabethtown, who should arrive at our doorstep but dear John and sweet Jason—my beloved brothers. It was a great reunion for us all. They arrived on horseback with the sun rising behind them, spotted first by Salmon, who gave the cry that brought us all streaming from the house to greet them.

They were gentle men, both alike in that way, and loving towards everyone in the family, especially towards our stepmother, Mary, and sister Ruth. With regard to Ruth they were probably no more devoted than I myself, but towards our stepmother they seemed as a pair to exhibit a greater affection and protectiveness than I could ever muster. This had always confused me somewhat, for their loss, when our mother died, had surely been as great as mine. Yet, apparently, it was not so, or at least for them the loss was not of a nature that restricted their ability to transfer deep affection and tenderness for our natural mother across to our stepmother. It sometimes seemed that the loss of our mother had actually enlarged my elder brothers' capacity to love her replacement, for they were more careful of Mary's feelings than were her natural sons even, Watson, Salmon, and Oliver. How strange it is, that brothers and sisters can share every important childhood experience and yet end up responding to those experiences in such dramatically different ways. What liberates and gives power to one child must often humiliate and weaken another, until it appears that our differences more than our sameness have come to bind us.

My elder brothers and I did not greatly resemble each other in physical ways, either, although it was clear to most people that we were blood kin. Even at that young age, in his late twenties, John was a large and thick-bodied fellow, strong and muscular and athletic-looking, but in the manner of a budding banker, perhaps, or a politician. He had a high and noble forehead, symmetrical features, long, soft, dark brown hair that he combed straight back over his collar, giving him the look of a scholar, which, in a manner of speaking, he was, for he had learned accounting and was at that time deeply engaged in the study of several of the newer sciences, such as phrenology and hypnotism. His voice was deep and authoritative, and he had a great, loose laugh, which I had imitated when I was a boy but now merely admired.

Jason was a shorter man than John, about the same height as Father, and more slender than I with my woodsman's build, but although he gave the appearance of delicacy, he was in fact extremely hardy and tough, a gristly man who moved in a slow, measured way that suggested deep thought, for his brow was characteristically as furrowed as a field in May, and his lips he kept pursed, like a man auditioning his words in silence before speaking them. In another age, or if he had been born to high estate and privilege, Jason might have been a philosopher or poet, a man like Mr. Emerson of Concord, perhaps, whose life, whose every act, was determined by the shape and substance of his thought. Jason was a man of sweet reasoning, his gentleness driven not by sentiment so much as by the innocence of logic. Unlike John, he was a man whom no one would follow into battle; but then, unlike John, he had no desire to lead. By the same token, he was equally disinclined to follow any man, even

Father. A poor soldier was Jason, he who would be neither private nor general.

Yet, fully as much as John and all our younger brothers, and as much as I at my best, Jason was loyal to Father and to the rest of the family. He was not in the slightest selfish; he was merely one who thought freely for himself. Contrary to how he has sometimes been portrayed in the various accounts of our family, Jason was a man of great courage, too, and until the end, he stood alongside us; and when, before we went into Virginia, he left our side, he did so out of deep conviction, not cowardice or self-interest. I always admired, rather than criticized, Jason for his willingness to resist Father's imperative.

Father had a power over us that seemed almost to emanate from his very body, as if he were more of a purely male person than we. While I have in my lifetime met a few other such men, who, like Father, seemed to be more masculine than the general run of men, as a rule they were brutal and stupid, which he surely was not. Like him, their beards were coarser, the hair on their hands, arms, and chests denser, their musculature and their bones tougher, heavier, more massy, than those of other men. They *smelled* more male-like than the rest of us. Even bathed and suited up for church, they, like Father, gave off the aroma of well-oiled saddle leather. None of those men, however, was as morally sensitive and intelligent as the Old Man, traits that made his masculinity so much more formidable than theirs. In ancient times, figures like Father, characterized in their appearance and manner by an excess of masculinity, were probably singled out in youth and made chieftain, clan leader, warlord. It was difficult not to bow before such a man.

Sometimes I thought this was how most women felt in the presence of men generally—like a small, hairless child, soft and vulnerable, before the large, hairy, tough, and impervious adult. It's what we mean, perhaps, by "womanish." Men like Father seem to evoke in all of us, male as well as female, long-abandoned, childlike responses which make us malleable to their wishes and will. Thus, when Father said, "Jump!" even though I was twenty-four, then thirty, then thirty-four years old, I jumped. I always jumped.

I am not ashamed of that, however. For, truth to tell, it was his gentleness, not his huge, male ferocity, that gathered us in and kept us there. We came to him willingly, not out of fear. His pervasive gentleness was like a sweet liquor to us, an intoxicant that left us narcotized, inducing in us a morbid susceptibility to his will. My most vivid memories of this most manly of men are of his face streaming with tears after he had struggled vainly for long days and nights to save his dying child. I think of his holding a freezing lamb against his naked chest under his shirt and coat, warming the creature with his own body, until the tiny lamb came slowly back to life and the Old Man could place it down beside its mother and step away and fairly laugh aloud with the pleasure of seeing it begin to nurse again. I remember Father tending to his wife and to each of his children when we were sick, hovering over us like a perfect physician, when he himself was ill and barely able to stand, tucking blankets around our shivering bodies, tending the fire, heating milk, manufacturing and administering remedies and medicinal specifics, long past exhaustion, until one or the other of us would begin at last to recover and was finally well enough to spell him, and then and only then would he allow himself to be treated. And though we often laughed and behind his back mocked Father for his long-windedness and certain other peculiarities of speech when he was trying to teach us a new skill—for he was one of those who teach as much by verbal instruction and repetition as example—withal, he was the most patient and tender teacher any of us ever had, who suffered our ignorance and ineptitude gladly, and never seemed to forget how mysterious and peculiar the world looked to a child and how even the simplest household or barnyard tasks seemed at first forbidding and complex.

No, it was the remarkable, perhaps unique, combination of his extreme masculinity and his unabashedly feminine tenderness that brought us willingly under his control and kept us there, so that, even when one or two or three of us seemed to wander off from his teachings and desires—as in the matter of religion, or, later, when he determined to go down into Virginia—none of us ever departed from him altogether. We merely on those occasions took a few cautious steps to his right or left side and tried to aid him in his work from that position, instead of from a position directly behind him. Even when John married Wealthy Hotchkiss and Jason married Ellen Sherbondy, and they moved out of the family household and set up on their own, they did it in ways that merely established new orbits that allowed them to function as satellites circling Father, like moons around a planet, and thus they were held as powerfully as before by his larger orbit, while he himself circled the sun. At an age when most men our age were running off to see the elephant, as we called it then—heading out to search for gold in California, staking out land in the further reaches of the Western Reserve, or following the crowds of bright, ambitious men and boys to New York and Washington—I and my brothers kept ourselves bound to our father's destiny.

With the sudden arrival at the farm of John and Jason, a day that turned out to be tumultuous and, ultimately, tragic began as a celebration of familial warmth and union. Over breakfast, Father apprised his elder sons of the ongoing situation with regard to the Underground Railroad, Marshal Saunders's pursuit of the Cannons, Mr. Wilkinson's betrayal of Lyman Epps and Mr. Fleete, and their recent arrest and removal to the Elizabethtown jail. And when he informed them of his intention to ride over to Elizabethtown with me for the purpose of arranging the release of the Negro men—"Even if it must be done at gunpoint," he said—John and Jason naturally chose to accompany and support us.

Once again, it fell to me to drive the wagon, while Father and my elder brothers rode on horseback. "We'll need the wagon to carry our friends back home," Father said, and, of course, I agreed, although Father or one of the others could have driven it as well as I. Mary and Ruth and Susan Epps packed two days' food for us, and the entire family stood by the door and waved cheerfully, as if we were setting out on a deer hunt, and we rode uphill back along the Cascade Road, east towards Keene and Elizabethtown.

We had not planned to stop in Keene, which we reached by noon, but as we passed by the rundown farm owned by Mr. Partridge, Father suddenly determined to pull up. "I believe I have some business with that man," he grimly announced, and pulled into the yard and dismounted. We followed, but did not get down from our horses, as he crossed the yard, strode across the porch, and rapped loudly on the door. There was a single, saddled horse at the porch rail, a bay that I thought I recognized but could not be sure until the door swung open and I saw Mr. Partridge's long, dark, gloomy face and behind him glimpsed the grizzled face of the slave-catcher Mr. Billingsly.

Billingsly darted out of our line of sight into the darkness of the room, but he surely knew that I and probably Father had spotted him when the door opened. This was a dangerous situation, and I jumped down from the wagon and signaled to John and Jason, who dismounted and joined me at the porch steps.

"What do you want here, Brown?" Mr. Partridge said, his voice a bit shaky with fear, as the three of us came to stand behind Father, each with a musket in hand. Father, too, had his gun with him, slung under his right arm.

"I've come to redeem my clock," Father announced. He reached down into his left pocket and drew out some coins, which he held in front of him, until Mr. Partridge unthinkingly extended his own palm. Father let the coins trickle into the other man's hand and said, "That, sir, is the cost of our food and lodging for one night, which you established back in May. You may count it, and then you will hand over my clock."

"You're crazy, Brown," he said, and he shoved the coins back at Father, groping at the Old Man's snuff-colored frock coat until he found a loosely open pocket and dropped them in, whereupon he moved to shut the door in Father's face. Father kicked the door back hard and shoved Mr. Partridge aside, and there stood revealed the slave-catcher Billingsly, who had drawn both his pistols.

Everything that followed happened in less than two seconds. I saw Mr. Partridge's dough-faced wife a ways behind Billingsly, her hands over her mouth, and beyond her was the old woman, her mother, calmly seated by the rear window, knitting, as if she were alone in the house. Mr. Partridge, his bearded face taut and drained white with fear, turned and grabbed Great-Grandfather's clock from the fireplace mantel and extended it towards Father, a last-chance peace offering. At that instant, Billingsly fired one of his pistols, missing Father, who stood directly before him, missing everyone, although we did not know it yet, and simultaneously several of us fired our rifles, a reckless, wild thing to do at such close range with so many innocent people close by, but we were lucky, for no one was struck—except for the one man who deserved it, Billingsly the slave-catcher. He howled in pain and went down, rolling on the floor and clutching at his thigh, where blood spurted crimson onto the rug.

I had fired my gun, I know that, and I later learned that John had fired his, but I do not know which of us shot Billingsly. Whichever, John or me, it was the first time one of us Browns had shot a man. I myself had meant not to hit anyone, intending merely to fire into the ceiling over everyone's head, hoping, I suppose, to control the situation by striking terror into Billingsly, not a bullet. John later said that he had definitely meant to shoot the man dead but had not a clear shot, so merely had tried not to hit anyone else, especially the women.

Who knew, then, which of us had shot him, and did it matter? One of John Brown's sons had done the bloody deed, and the day would continue that way, with John Brown and his sons wreaking havoc and spilling blood in the Adirondack mountain villages of New York. Whatever one of us did, we all did.

The man Billingsly was down, and his pistols were scattered across the floor. There was a loud battery of shouts, bellows, commands, and, from at least one of the women, high-pitched screams, and I do not know if I or my brothers or Mr. Partridge or even Billingsly was amongst the hounds who gave cry, although one of us Browns shouted, "He's down! He's down!" And another yelled at Partridge, "Don't make a move, mister, or I swear it, I'll kill you at once!" Several of us were calling to the rest, "Are you hit? Are you hit?" And, "No! Missed me! The coward missed me!" And, "Hold your fire! Hold your fire now!"

Only Father remained calm. He waited for silence, and when it came, the Old Man, as cool and unruffled as a frozen lake, took the clock out of Mr. Partridge's hands. Then he looked down at the bleeding slave-catcher, who squirmed and writhed on the floor in pain, and said in a clear, steady voice, "Mister Billingsly, this is the second time that you are lucky that we Browns have not killed you. I advise you, sir, to consider another line of business than hunting down escaped slaves."

He turned, closed the door behind him, and placed the clock into the front of the wagon, below the driver's bench. Then the Old Man and John and Jason mounted their horses. I jumped up into the wagon, and we rode quickly off, away from the valley, into the mountains and over the ridge to Elizabethtown, where, at around four o'clock in the afternoon, we drew up before the stately brick courthouse.

The jail was behind and belowstairs, and we walked directly there. I did not know Father's plan, or if he actually had one, beyond somehow convincing the Elizabethtown jailer to release Mr. Fleete and Lyman into our custody, which did not to me seem likely. But Father was adept at improvisation, so it was perhaps fortuitous, when we four Browns marched into the jail, armed and passably dangerous-looking, our faces flushed and hearts still beating rapidly from the shooting back in Keene, that we ran face-first into Mr. Wilkinson of Tahawus. He looked surprised and frightened to see us, naturally. He appeared to have just come in from a hard ride himself.

"Mister Wilkinson," Father said, "tell me your business here."

The man backed off and turned to the jailer, a small, mustachioed man seated behind a cluttered desk, putting papers away. "This here's John Brown!" Wilkinson exclaimed to the jailer, who did not appear to care. "He's come to break the niggers out of jail!"

At once, Father placed the mouth of the barrel of his musket next to the ear of Mr. Wilkinson. "You're right about that," he said. "Jailer, you can march back to the cells with my sons here and uncage the two colored men and bring them forward, if you will be so kind. Otherwise, I will blow this man's brains out."

Mr. Wilkinson whimpered and said that he had nothing to do with their being jailed, that it was all the fault of Marshal Saunders.

"Then what are you here for?"

"I came for my own business," he said.

"You lie, Wilkinson. Jailer," Father said, "tell me this man's business here. Now!" He cocked the hammer of his gun. Mr. Wilkinson shut his eyes tightly, as if he expected to hear the gun go off that instant.

Slowly, carefully, the jailer stood. John, Jason, and I all had our guns trained on him. "Wal, he come in to identify the niggers back there and sign some papers to it. Marshal said he was to do that. Hey, listen, Mister Brown," he said, "I don't know nothin' about these here niggers. You can do with them whatever the hell you want."

"Has Mister Wilkinson so sworn, that the men you have locked up for the marshal are indeed the fellows he says they are? Because I'm here to tell you they are not," Father said.

"Wal, no, not yet he ain't. They's just a couple of coloreds, far's I'm concerned, and I'm holdin' 'em for the marshal, like he asked, till he comes back from Port Kent."

"With no arrest warrant."

"Wal . . . yes, sir. Yes. That's so."

Grabbing Mr. Wilkinson by his shirt collar, Father drew him to the steel door that led to the cells and said to the jailer, "Come along, and bring your keys. Mister Wilkinson here is going to tell you that the men you have locked up are not the men the marshal is seeking."

"Wal, sir, y' know I can't release them without the marshal's say-so," the man said, although he was already unlocking the door to the jail.

"You will do as I say," said Father.

"Yes, sir, I b'lieve I will," he said, and he swung open the door, and we all walked into the cell block and went straightway back to where Mr. Fleete and Lyman awaited us. They both grinned broadly when they saw us and came to the front of their shared cell and grasped the bars, watching as the jailer unlocked the cell door and swung it wide.

"Mister Brown, we are mightily relieved to see you," said Mr. Fleete.

"That there fellow, he's the one told the marshal we run the Cannons off to Canada," said Lyman, pointing sternly at Mr. Wilkinson. "They come up on us over in Timbuctoo yesterday evening. Said we knew where the Cannons was hiding. Said they killed their master down in Virginia. We don't know nothing about that, now, do we, Mister Brown?"

"No, Lyman, we don't," said Father.

"This ain't legal, you know," the jailer said to Father, as we all marched back out to his office. Father still held Mr. Wilkinson by his shirt collar and had his gun tight against the man's ear.

"Just don't try to stop us," said Father, "and no harm will come to either of you. We'll all worry about what's legal and what isn't later on. Right now, however, these men have not been charged and therefore are free." He let go of Mr. Wilkinson and lowered his gun, and we did likewise with ours and, with Mr. Fleete and Lyman in the lead, made to leave the jailer's office. John was the last to depart from the building, and when he turned to draw the door closed behind him, as he told us later, he saw the jailer extract a handgun from his desk, and he shot the man. It happened so quickly and unexpectedly that we barely knew of it, except for the loud gunshot and the sulphurous smell of the powder, for we were already outside and crossing the grass towards the horses and wagon.

"Go!" John shouted, and we ran. "He pulled a gun!"

I leapt onto the wagon seat and grabbed the reins, and Mr. Fleete and Lyman, their faces filled with fear, jumped into the back. Father, Jason, and John mounted their horses, and we all broke for the road out of town. When the wagon passed the open door of the jail, with the others on horseback racing on ahead, I looked to my side and saw the jailer come to the door. He had been wounded in his left arm, but he held a revolver in his right, and he aimed carefully and fired once, and then we were gone, the horses pounding up the road, heading north out of town—towards the pass to Ausable Forks this time, instead of back the way we had come, through Keene, where we had shot Billingsly.

It was not until we had run nearly a mile that I took it into my head to check my passengers, and when I glanced back I saw with dismay that Mr. Fleete had been shot in the chest. Lyman sat ashen-faced and expressionless beside him, looking out at the passing scenery as if he were alone. Father and the others were still a ways ahead of us, too far to call, and so I drove on. Shortly, when we had gotten several miles out of town, I drew the wagon up under a tall spruce tree beside the road at the crest of a short hill. I turned in the seat and stepped into the back, where Mr. Fleete lay.

As if explaining a living man's absence, not a dead man's presence, Lyman said, "Ol' Elden Fleete, he's gone back to Africa."

"Oh, Lord!" I cried. "What have we done? What have we done, Lyman?"

"It ain't *we* that killed him, Owen."

Then Father and John and Jason appeared on horseback beside the wagon, and they looked down and saw what had happened and grew dark with anger and sorrow. Especially Father. "Bring him on back to Timbuctoo, where he can be dressed out for a proper burial. I only wish it were the slave-catcher who was dead," he said, "not the slave."

"Mister Fleete was not a slave, Father," I said.

"*We* know that, Owen. *We* know it. But those other fellows don't." He clucked to his horse, and we all fell into a somber line and made our slow way back down through Wilmington Notch to North Elba.

There was a terrible sadness amongst all the Negroes when we delivered Mr. Fleete's body over to them, but no indications of surprise. For them, I suppose, the astonishing thing was that one of them had managed to live so long without having run from the world and hid from it in a hole. That was something about Negroes which I found mystifying in those days—that they constantly expected death and yet did not anticipate it. Later, of course, I came to the same viewpoint myself.

But the consequences of our rash acts were not as dire as I, for one, expected, although they were, indeed, catastrophic for the Negro community in general. We had inflicted a serious wound on the slave-catcher (not a mortal one, it seemed), and that was probably a positive good. Although it seemed to me that there had been more than enough blood spilt. On the way back from Elizabethtown, John confided that he hoped Billingsly would come looking for revenge, so we could kill him properly. Two white men wounded for one black man dead: that was the trade-off. Not quite fair, I thought, but closer to even than most of these exchanges allowed. And we had surely scared our Keene neighbor Mr. Partridge straight back to his deer-hunting ways, stifling any rising ambitions he may have held for assisting slave-catchers and sharing in the rewards of that heinous activity. The unfortunate jailer in Elizabethtown, whose name I never learned, was one of those who, in Father's phrase, were merely doing their duty, and though he had paid dearly for it, he would have a scar to show and a tale to tell for the rest of his days. He would be able to say that he had been one of the first innocent victims of the Browns' nigger madness. Mr. Wilkinson, our one-time ally, had beat his retreat back to Tahawus, where he would continue to drive his Irish miners, but with no further pretensions to providing aid and succor to Negroes, and that was actually in the interests of Negroes and those of us who might have otherwise allied ourselves with him. It's always useful to know your enemy and to have him know you, as Father was fond of saying.

Despite their astonishment and sadness on learning of the death of Mr. Fleete, our family was overjoyed, of course, to see us return to the farm that night uninjured, and Susan wept with relief at the sight of her husband freed from jail. However, their anxiety, as we learned on our arrival home, had been greatly increased that afternoon by a piece of intelligence they had received in our absence from Captain Keifer. He had sent his eldest son down to North Elba on horseback to warn us of what we already knew, that Marshal Saunders had come looking for the Cannons in Port Kent, and to inform us of what we had not even guessed—that in truth, as the marshal had claimed, Captain Keifer had not transported the Negro couple to Canada after all. Further, the two had been surprised in the kitchen of the Quaker's home by the marshal and his deputies, and the man had promptly arrested the couple and was now transporting them south to Albany, whence they would be returned to Richmond, Virginia, there to stand trial for the brutal slaying of their master.

"What! How could that be?" Father demanded. "He deceived us, then! The Quaker lied! Good Lord, is there no one on this earth we can trust?"

Patiently, Mary related to him what the boy had told her. His father's boat had been forced back a few miles north of Plattsburgh by a sudden, dangerous turn in the weather, and by the time Captain Keifer made a second attempt to take them into Canada, his Underground Railroad operatives on the further side of the border had been notified by Canadian authorities that the couple was wanted in the United States, not for fleeing slavery, for which there were at that time no federal warrants, but for crossing state lines in flight from arrest for murder, and as a result they had refused to accept them. Not knowing what else to do with the couple, Captain Keifer had brought them into his own home in Port Kent and had attempted to hide and protect them there until such time as he could arrange to move them into Canada by some other means. Most of the villagers in Port Kent were soon aware of the presence of the Negro couple and did not object, and consequently Captain Keifer had grown careless as to their easy coming and going about the place. Thus it was not difficult for the marshal and his deputies to take them by surprise.

"Surely," Mary said, "the poor man is desolated by this turn of events. He asked his son to beg you for your understanding and forgiveness, Mister Brown," she said, addressing him as she always did—although in his absence she, like the rest of us, generally referred to him as Father or the Old Man. "The boy himself was mighty agitated and seemed burdened by guilt. Poor lad, all full of his thees and thous." She had comforted him as much as she could and sent him back with assurances to Captain Keifer that Father would bear him no ill will and would not judge him for this calamity. After all, Captain Keifer had more to fear now from the law than did any of us, she pointed out. "He has been harboring people who he knew were accused murderers, not just escaped slaves."

Father sat heavily down at the table and sighed. I sensed that he was giving something up. John and Jason and I glanced at one another nervously. What now? The ride from Father's peaks to his valleys was often a rough one, and we were still perched on the heights of our day's adventure, trying to sort out the meanings of our bloody encounters and the death of Mr. Fleete, hoping to be able to use them to energize us and entitle us to further brave acts. We were young men, after all, armed, freshly tested in battle, and puffed up with righteous wrath, and it did not take much in those days to set our hearts to pounding. Even Jason. We did not want Father to abandon us now and, as was his wont at times like this, to slump down into a slough of despond, where we would doubtless have to follow.

"Let me have one of my babies," Father said in a low voice. "Annie or Sarah. Let me have Sarah. Bring me little Sarie, will you, Ruth?" Suddenly, the Old Man looked very tired—bone-weary and aged.

Ruth went obediently to the sleeping loft to fetch the child. Father said, "Everything seems to have come undone, doesn't it, children? Our neighbors have abandoned us. Men have been shot. Blood spilt. And a beloved, courageous friend has been shot dead. And now those whom we would assist in their plight have been captured by the enemy and taken off south to be hung, or worse. Oh, I can barely think of it!"

No one answered. The younger boys, Watson, Salmon, and Oliver, lounged at the door to the further room, waiting eagerly for the bloody details, who shot whom and where, which they knew would come later, when we elder sons went upstairs to bed and were freed by the absence of our parents to brag to one another. Mary silently placed food down on the table, and Lyman, John, Jason, and I all drew up our stools and set to eating. In a moment, Ruth returned carrying the sleepy-eyed Sarah, and deposited the child on Father's lap. He smiled wanly down into her puffy face, and when she rose to wakefulness, recognized him, and grinned, he brightened somewhat and began to rock her slowly in his arms.

"John says I must return to Springfield," he said to us. In a calm, low voice, he explained that he was needed there to settle some painful arguments and tangled disputes between the woolen buyers and the sheep farmers in Ohio and our main support, Mr. Perkins—old claims and counter-claims that John thought would be more easily resolved if Father was there to face down these nettlesome people in person. It had seemed a bad idea to Father at first. "Now . . . now I don't know, maybe he's right. I had hoped to be needed more here, however, than in Springfield," he said, and he sighed heavily again. "I think our Negro friends across the valley in Timbuctoo, like our white friends here in North Elba, will no longer want to work with us. What think you, Lyman?"

Lyman looked up from his plate of ham and corn bread and baked beans, chewed silently for a moment, and finally said, "Mister Brown, I can't speak for them other folks. Just for me and my wife here. And we're going to do whatever you decide you need us for. You and your boys, you got me out of that jail today. And if it was me instead of poor ol' Elden that got killed, and he was the one sitting here tonight eating supper, I know he'd be telling you the same thing. But them other folks over at Timbuctoo, they're probably going to want to lay low for a spell. Sort of playing possum, you know. They got to, Mister Brown. You can understand that."

"Playing possum, eh? But not you and Susan?"

"No, no, we're colored folks, too, Mister Brown. For sure. But we're living here now in this house. We're not settled with them across the valley in Timbuctoo no more. That's why we've got to take more consideration of what you people do than they do over there. It's like we got this here debt that we owe to you and the family, Mister Brown. And we want to be paying it off." He looked across the room at his wife as if for confirmation, and she nodded, and he went back to eating.

"All right, then," Father said. "It's settled."

"What is?" said I, warm corn bread and butter like soft, crumbled gold in my mouth.

"We'll go down to Springfield with John and Jason."

"We?"

Father shot me a hard look. "You and I. Isn't that what, not so long ago, you were begging for, Owen? I need you there, for a month at least, while Jason returns to Ohio and sets things right for us out west and sees to his wife and poor Fred, who have been making do on their own these months. Taking care of Fred is no simple matter, as you know. The good woman probably did not bargain for that when she agreed to marry Jason."

"Ellen loves Fred, Father," Jason said. "Believe me, he's no burden to her. She has no fear of him, even when he goes off on one of his spells."

"Yes, well, even so, she needs you, son. And I need you there, too, to make what payments we can for the unsold fleeces and to explain our delay to the rest."

As fast as it could be said, then, it had been decided. Father, John, and I would return to Springfield, Jason would head back to Ohio, and Lyman and Susan Epps would stay on at the farm with the remainder of the family, tending to the harvest and setting the farm up properly for winter. Lyman had replaced me, as I had replaced Jason. And there was more. Father wished to travel to England, he said, where, according to John, the price for wool was now up to seventy dollars per hundred-weight, nearly twice what Brown & Perkins was getting for it in Springfield. He would go there and attempt to convince the British to buy American wool for the first time. By setting the British buyers off against the American, he might thereby break the monopoly that was crippling the producers and driving Father and Mr. Perkins deeper and deeper into debt as they purchased the wool and held it in the Springfield warehouse, waiting for the prices to rise.

But England? To travel across the sea and attempt to penetrate a market and deal with men we knew nothing about? That seemed fool-ish to me.

Not to Father. He would empty the warehouse and sail over with it. The tariffs were down. American fleeces could compete with the best in the world now, he insisted. John Bull had only to see it before his eyes and have a knowing man like Father explain to him the fine con-ditions under which those fleeces had been grown and make the nec-essary guarantees for future delivery, and the fellow would snap it up. Everyone knew that our free Ohio and Pennsylvania sheepmen could out-produce the poor, beaten-down Scots and Irish, once the market was opened to them. The only reason no one had done it before this was that the individual sheepman was incapable of delivering the required quantity of wool, and the devious American buyers had col-luded and done everything they could to discourage and sabotage cooperatives like ours. "This is the solution!" he exclaimed, happy now, excited again, sailing before a fresh breeze, well out of his doldrums of a few minutes earlier.

It was almost too much to keep up with, these switches and turns, descents and ascents of feeling and intention. Jason was happy enough, and looked it, pursing his lips in an anticipatory smile of returning to the arms of his bride and the comfort of their home in Ohio. And John was well-pleased, for he had come to feel like a proper businessman down there in Springfield and had moved into more or less permanent quarters with his wife, Wealthy. And Lyman could not have been in the slightest discouraged by the prospect of becoming foreman of the farm, with his wife, Susan, with Mary and Ruth and a hard-working brood of boys and girls to help him.

I wondered how Mary regarded the Old Man's decision: relief, I supposed, for his decision to call off the war against slavery for a spell— but dread and anxiety as well, for his forthcoming absence from her side as autumn and winter came on.

But the one, perhaps the only one, who felt deflated by these new plans, surely, was I, Owen Brown, he who barely three months before had wanted nothing so much as to return from the wilderness of these mountains to the bustling river town of Springfield. Something had altered my feelings in those intervening months. The work with Father and the others on the Underground Railroad, to be sure, those excitements and risks and the sense of being engaged wholly in a moral enterprise—they had changed me. But something more lasting than that had eliminated my earlier longing to leave this place, a thing that had grown out of our life as a family settled on a farm in these mountains.

For as long as I could remember, we had as a family been unified and empowered by the single great Idea. But despite that, or perhaps because of it, we had been fragmented and split off from one another—with Father charging about the countryside and traveling back and forth on his various missions; with strangers black and white coming into our household and departing as quickly as we became familiar with them; with half a household here and another half there; with plans and fantasies simultaneously multiplying and disintegrating, as circumstances shifted subtly or got dramatically altered by forces invisible and beyond our control; with the very shape and number of our family constantly changing from one season to the next, as a new child was born every year, year after year, 1834, '35, '36, '37, all the way to '48, and the terrible, sad deaths of children coming between those births, until we barely knew the names, birth dates, and death dates of our brothers and sisters. For every new child that arrived, there seemed to be one recently departed, due to the ague, to dysentery, to consumption, to calamitous accidental scalding, from the first Fred, back when I was but six years old, to the first Sarah, and Charles, Peter, and Austin, who all went in that horrific winter of '43, to little Amelia in '46, and most recently, in Springfield, the baby Ellen. Now, after all that, there had come a small but significant measure of stability here among these Negro and white farmers in these mountains, and for the first time in my life I felt I stood at the center of things.

I had not expected that. I had not in fact known that such a feeling was even possible or that, once experienced, it would seem, not merely desireable, but necessary. But it was here in North Elba and nowhere else that the whirl of the one great Idea seemed for me to slow and even to cease hurtling me from one place and set of feelings and loyalties to another. It was here that I felt like a normal son and brother in a normal family, farming our rough acres of northern land, tending our live-stock, and aiding our neighbors. I had even begun to imagine, on see-ing my sister Ruth grow attracted to Henry Thompson, my own possi-bilities for finding a wife here, building a house, raising my own herd of sheep, fathering my own children. And, alongside my Negro and white neighbors alike, continuing to do my bit of the Lord's and Father's work.

For the Old Man, of course, this was not enough. It was not nearly enough; it was in fact a sin, to be making a home and in addition doing merely our bit of the Lord's work. We had to be doing all of it; and all our work had to be the Lord's. Making a home had to be incidental. Or else we were doing Satan's work.

Thus we Browns were once again shifting our mode of contention against those who would oppose us, and shifting our base of operations as well. We would head south to Springfield and thence to London, England, from where, Father said, we might well briefly cross over to the Continent and there make an on-site study of Napoleon's military campaigns in the Lowlands. Upon the sale of our wool, we would return freed at last of debt, so as to devote ourselves completely, once and for all, to the proper business of waging war against slavery.

"Then shall all the world see the fruits of our discipline, of our prin-cipled savagery, and of our strategic intelligence," Father declared to us that last night in North Elba. Then might the war properly commence. This valley would be our base camp, our headquarters, as we moved down the Appalachians. Modeling our tactics and our principles on the tactics and principles that brought about the great achievements of Toussaint, Spartacus, and Nat Turner, we would liberate the South—plantation by plantation, town by town, county by county, state by state—until we had at last broken the back of the beast.

So, yes, he had his plan, even then. And little by little he had made it known to us. He had maps and texts to support his theories, and he would draw them out in the evenings to illustrate them to us and demonstrate their feasibility. Also, he was no doubt practicing for the time when he would have to place his plan before the gaze of more skeptical audiences than his wife and children and the Negro members of his household, audiences made up of people like Frederick Douglass and Gerrit Smith, men whose support he personally would depend upon and whose support his plan was in fact premised on.

To bed, then: the child Sarah, asleep on Father's lap, carried to her bed by sister Ruth; the lads Watson, Salmon, and Oliver grumpily climbing to the loft, to await the arrival of their elder brothers. And we did follow along shortly after, with Lyman Epps, who surely would have preferred to be sleeping in a private chamber in his own bed with his wife, but who must live like a Shaker now, celibate and communal. And Ruth and Susan Epps to the chamber where the females slept, where the little girls, Annie and Sarah, were slumbering already.

Leaving Father and Mary alone downstairs in their bed near the parlor fireplace, where the Old Man, I knew, in his enthusiasm for this new turn of events, and conscious of the oncoming prolonged absence from his wife and home, would be reaching towards her in the darkness, doing the Lord's work, being fruitful, multiplying. While Great-Grandfather Brown's clock ticked loudly from the fireplace mantel.

10

A sparkling blue day it was, in early September of that year, when the Old Man and I took passage for Liverpool aboard the side-wheeler *Cumbria*, a packet out of Boston. We had arrived in the city three days earlier, after nearly a fortnight's stay in Springfield, where Father had made his usual, tireless attempt to set things right with his and Mr. Perkins's creditors, succeeding only in extending his and Mr. Perkins's line of credit with the western sheepmen for the length of time it would take him to sell in England the wool he could not sell in America. Or *would* not sell in America. Not for the sixty-five cents per pound he was then being offered—some ten to twenty cents per pound less than he had agreed to pay the sheepmen in Ohio and Pennsylvania.

It was a simple problem. Father had taken shipment of vast quantities of wool from the west and had been storing it in the Springfield warehouse, after having promised, with Mr. Perkins's guarantees, to pay the western producers significantly more for it than the woolen merchants and cloth manufacturers in New England were then offering. And now, twelve and more months later, the producers were clamoring for their money, which Father, of course, did not have. To break a monopoly among the buyers, Father had tried to create a monopoly among the sellers. Basically, the problem had arisen because the buyers could afford to wait out the sellers.

In vain did I argue the wisdom of cutting all his losses off at once and returning quickly to the farm in North Elba, there to build a small tannery, such as he had established in New Richmond when I was a child, back before Mother died—a modest, local business adequate to our needs and in no way dependent upon his abilities to anticipate and resist the machinations of shrewd, calculating men of great wealth residing elsewhere.

To me, paper money, promissory notes, letters and lines of credit, market fluctuations, tariff laws, and so on were as abstract and metaphysical as German speculative philosophy. To Father, however, they were oddly concrete, as real as the food he ate, as the water he heated for his morning shave, as the tobacco-colored long-tailed wool suit he wore every day of his adult life. Consequently, he believed that he could move among the elements of finance with the same ease and control he employed in ordering up his supper in a hotel dining room or firing a kettle of cold water every morning or pressing out the wrinkles in his trousers by placing them beneath his mattress while he slept. He was like the unlucky gambler who can't believe in any luck but good and keeps on trying to cover his old losses by making new bets.

I never thought Father mad, as he was so often later portrayed, except now and again, and especially in these matters of finance. But it was a madness that in those days he shared with most men of ability and restless intelligence. It was like a plague, this dream of growing rich by speculation, and not to become infected with it was a sign of dullness and low intelligence. My argument against Father's scheme, then, carried very little weight. To him, it was the argument of a simple man or a man with no ambition.

Brother John, I believe, was on the Old Man's side in this and had caught the disease himself, although he had not as extreme a case as

Father's, and while Jason seemed as immune from the plague as I, he, unlike me, appeared little bothered by the Old Man's feverish schemes and delusions and, except when Father demanded his filial aid and comfort, tended quietly to his own affairs—his vineyards and orchards in Ohio. Jason maintained a benign independence of Father that I envied but barely understood. "Owen," he used to say to me, with that sweet, yet slightly ironic, smile playing across his lips, "you've got to let it alone. The Old Man's going to do what he wants, no matter how much you fret and fume over it. You might as well stand back, brother, and just try to enjoy the show."

It was never that easy for me. How was it possible not to go along with the Old Man and not fail him? I could not imagine myself doing it. I was tied to him like a wife, a child, a *slave*, it sometimes seemed—although, of course, I well knew that the chains that bound me to him were entirely of my own making. After all, from the end of my childhood, at about the age of sixteen, Father had not once forbade me from leading any sort of life that I wanted. That I was living *his* life, as it appeared, or one that was a mere appendage of his, was a measure not so much of his power as of my weakness.

In Boston for the few days before our departure on the *Cumbria*, I trailed after the Old Man like a puppy as he attended afternoon and evening public and private meetings. Abolitionism was everywhere in Boston then. Argued and articulated with all the zeal and refined intelligence of the old Puritans' debate over Free Will and Grace, it was, for all of that, mere talk, or so it seemed to Father and me—talk driven and framed by reckless passion, as if being right or wrong on the subject were more important to the debaters than saving people's lives, not to mention their souls.

We were staying at the home of an abolitionist colleague of Father's—a philanthropic friend of Mr. Gerrit Smith's, actually, from whom Father had obtained a general-purpose letter of introduction for use in England. The gentleman was the well-known Dr. Samuel Gridley Howe, and he and his pleasant, hospitable wife, the poet Julia Ward Howe, an heiress, had given us a room in their grand residence on Louisburg Square. It was a tall brick house with bow windows facing the street on every storey, so that you could stand and look down upon the busy street below, like a captain of industry surveying his shop. The city of Boston was like that then, a busy manufactory where everything, from bread and feathered hats to religious ideas and fine art, was manufactured, purveyed, distributed, consumed, and commented upon with remarkable efficiency and general alacrity, a humming machine in which every citizen was a part, from the humblest illiterate Irish newsboy or maid to the loftiest Harvard scholar or Beacon Hill theologian.

I loved the city at once and might well have run off from Father then and there and made it my permanent home, like the young Ben Franklin fleeing *his* home to seek his fortune in Philadelphia, had I, like Franklin, a proper trade or some other means of making my living than that of caring for sheep or homesteading northern wildernesses. If, in other words, I had not been my father's third son. It was strange, although I did not recognize it as such then, to be so young and to be filled already with regret. It was as if, at the age of twenty-six, I viewed my daily life with a nostalgia for a life that I had never led and never would lead. I knew other young men who felt as I did, but they were men who had married too quickly and woke every morning with the vain desire to start their lives over again, youths who, every day, by the time they dressed for work and came to the table for breakfast, had to accept yet again that they were stuck with a life they did not want. But no man of my acquaintance who was my age and was not unhappily married felt as sadly trapped as I. Nor would any one of them have understood it in me. They might well have wished to *be* me.

I remember that we arrived in Boston from Springfield by train in the late afternoon and had no sooner set down our bags and paid our respects to Dr. and Mrs. Howe than we were off, headed down the tilted brick sidewalks of Beacon Hill to the Charles Street Meeting House to see and hear the famous Mr. Ralph Waldo Emerson, who was to speak that very evening on the wonderful subject of heroism. Dr. Howe had put Father onto this event with the observation that the Concord sage would be addressing the issue of the proper response to slavery for the modern intellectual. It was apparently a talk the Doctor and his wife had already been privileged to hear at the Concord Atheneum, where it had been delivered to an audience of skeptics, a crew of Garrisonian, non-violent abolitionists, and had swept them all over to the radical side of the debate. An inflammatory gesture, then, was what Father expected, a call to arms, a prescriptive description of a new kind of American hero.

We arrived early and sat in the third row of seats, as close to the front as possible. Soon the large hall was filled, mostly with distinguished-looking men and women whose bearing and gazes were the epitome of benevolent intelligence and whose manners bespoke, not arrogance, but simple, if well-fed, self-confidence. A more civilized collection of human beings I had never seen, and I could not keep myself from turning in my seat and craning my neck to see and admire them as they entered from the darkening street and took their places.

Father sat stiffly with his hands on his knees, staring straight ahead, as if he were alone in the audience or were in an antechamber awaiting an interview with a prospective employer. There were several people who must be famous, I thought, if only because of the way other folks, when this one or that entered and took his seat, at once stared and whispered to their companions. But I recognized no one, of course. Could that handsome, eagle-eyed man be Charles Sumner? Could that small burl of a woman next to him be the famous agitator for female rights and abolition, Lydia Maria Child? Might the sublimely intelli-

gent Transcendentalist philosopher William Everett Channing be here amongst us?

I knew none of these illustrious people, of course, except by their marvelous reputations, and I believed that anyone who looked more distinguished than Father, as these people surely did, must be at least as distinguished as he and then some. Unlike Father, they had lived in Boston all their lives and came from wealthy old families and had been privileged by fine educations and social relations with one another: they were bound to be beacons on a height. So I believed. And Father's light, by comparison, was a flickering candle cupped in his hand against the wind. I was, therefore, not so much ashamed of Father in this context as sorry for him, especially sitting there stock-still and stiff in his seat, red-faced and tense, his large, workingman's hands and wrists sticking out from his sleeves, his mouth tight, his gray eyes staring straight up at the podium. In this impressive company of like-minded people, Father seemed, not enhanced, but sadly, surprisingly diminished.

And when a hush settled over the crowd and Mr. Emerson in utter simplicity and with no introduction came forward and began to speak, Father, poor Father, seemed even smaller than before, to the point of disappearing altogether from my ken, which almost never happened in a public place, for I was rarely able to ignore him or his reactions to a speech or sermon. Busily fashioning my own reaction around what I supposed was his, I seldom heard clearly the speech or sermon itself.

This occasion was different, however. To me, Mr. Emerson was every inch the ideal poet and sage, and if a man may be said to be beautiful, he was that. Slender, but strong and supple-looking, like a man used to outdoor exercise, of medium height with a noble carriage and easy, natural gestures, he stood before us and spoke in a voice that, while intimate and almost conversational in tone, carried to the furthest reaches of the hall, for his every word seemed raptly attended to, even by the last few fellows to squeeze in at the door in back. From his first sentence to his last, there was not a whisper or a rustle from the audience. He relied on none of the usual rhetorical flourishes of the arm and mighty brow that were then so popular with public speakers; none of the tricks of voice and variations of pace and volume to surprise the audience and gain its attention cheaply. Instead, he spoke simply, directly, in a way that made you feel that he was speaking to you alone and to no one else in the hall. His bright eyes were the color of bluebells and did not fix on any single person but fixed on the space just above one's own head, as if he were contemplating one's thoughts as they rose in the air. Now and again, he would glance down at the text before him, as if to take in a new paragraph or sometimes an entire page, and then his large, handsome head would lift, and he would go on, with no hesitation or break in the flow of his speech. He was at that time in his mid-forties, I suppose, in the prime of his manhood, although he seemed both younger—in the clarity and openness of his expression—and older—in the wise self-assurance of his delivery.

Awed and rapt as I was, especially at the start, I did not make out much of what he said, as he was at first speaking of figures and literary works I had never heard of—a playwright named Beaumont Fletcher was one, and various characters from the plays. But I did catch that he was indeed speaking of heroism and how it had been misunderstood in the past, as much misunderstood by poets and playwrights as by politicians. He intended here, he declared, to understand it freshly. And he seemed, as Dr. Howe and his wife had promised, to be applying that new understanding of heroism to our present dilemma with regard to the issue of slavery generally and the abolitionist movement in particular.

In the work of the elder British dramatists, he said, there was a constant, obsessive recognition of gentility, just as skin color is recognized in our society today. A marvelous and original reversal, I thought, of how we normally think of those two aspects of society—gentility, or the classes of men, and race. Opposites are made to seem apposite. Yes, this *was* a freshened way of looking at things.

Then, after a while, he began to isolate and examine the various manifestations of heroism, as if, on the surface, he were discussing merely the literary heros, but all the same, with hints and subtle asides, indicating that our present national crisis over slavery was the necessary field for such a person. He was calling for the arrival of a man out of Plutarch, one of Father's favorite authors also, I noted with pleasure, a man who could refute the despondency and cowardice of our religious and political theorists with "a wild courage, a stoicism not of the schools, but of the *blood!*" Mr. Emerson wanted a "tart cathartic virtue," he said, that could contend with the violations of the laws of nature committed by our predecessors and by our contemporaries. And here he lapsed into language—or I should say, he *rose* to language—that, although not once uttering the word itself, excoriated slavery horribly and with great originality. It is a lock-jaw, he said, that bends a man's head back to his heels. It is a hydrophobia that makes him bark at his wife and babes, an insanity that makes him eat grass.

A man must confront and confound all this external evil, he explained, with a military attitude of the soul. This is the beginnings of heroism, this attitude. The hero advances to his own music, and there is somewhat that is not philosophical in heroism, he noted, somewhat not holy in it. "Heroism seems not to know that other souls are of one texture with it. It has pride. It is the extreme of individual nature," he declared. These words struck fire with me, for, of course, they described my father perfectly, and I wondered if the Old Man himself realized it. Or was that, too, characteristic of heroism—that the hero does not recognize himself as heroic?

There was more, much more, that put me in mind of Father, as Mr. Emerson continued. Heroism, he told us, is almost ashamed of its body.

And this: that the stoical temperance of the hero is loved by him for its elegance, not for its austerity. "A great man scarcely knows how he dines, how he dresses; but without railing or precision, his living is natural and poetic."

Mr. Emerson spoke in an aphoristic style that, no matter how obscure or abstract his thought and language, made it easy for me to understand his ideas and remember his words and quote them afterwards to those who were not so lucky as to have heard them in person. I remember, years later, spouting, as if they were my own, Mr. Emerson's words that night in Boston. My companions were humble men, Negro and white men, huddled with me around a campfire in Kansas or holed up in a freezing cabin in Iowa or a farmhouse in Maryland, and I would try to inspire them by saying things like, "The characteristic of heroism is its persistency." And, "If you would serve your brother, because it is fit for you to serve him, do not take back your words when you find that prudent people do not commend you." And this, which became thereafter my personal motto: "Always do what you are most afraid to do."

High counsel was how I took Mr. Emerson's talk on heroism. High counsel, and prophecy, too. "Times of heroism," he explained, "are generally times of terror." And then he recalled for us the martyrdom of the brave Lovejoy who, in the name of the Bill of Rights and his right to shout against the sin of slavery, gave himself over to the rage of the mob. We now are living in a time of terror, was Mr. Emerson's point, and thus are we likewise about to see the arrival of our heroes. They are coming soon. And we must be prepared to recognize them when they appear in our midst, and Mr. Emerson was bending all his considerable, all his incomparable, talents and wisdom to that end. Who could not be grateful?

Well, Father, for one. Perhaps Father alone. In the midst of the applause at the end of Mr. Emerson's lecture, Father rose from his seat, to applaud the more enthusiastically, I first thought. But, no, it was to leave the hall, and with a glower on his face, he made his way past the laps of his neighbors and hurriedly, pointedly, stalked up the aisle to the exit at the rear. Shocked and more than slightly embarrassed by his rude departure, I followed, head down, and joined him on the street.

For a few moments, we walked in silence. "That man's truly a *boob!*" Father blurted. "For the life of me, I can't understand his fame. Unless the whole world is just as foolish as he is. Godless? He's not even *ratio-nal!* You'd think, given his godlessness, his sec-u-laahr-ity, he'd be at least *rational,*" he said, and gave a sardonic laugh.

"Yes, but didn't . . . didn't you admire his language?" Mr. Emerson had used language in an oblique and original way that, while it made his personality shine brilliantly, also had made the ostensible subject of his talk opaque, so that, to understand him, one had practically to invent for oneself what he was saying. I found this experience nearly wonderful, as if he were speaking poetry. But I knew not what to point to in Mr. Emerson's lecture that might have appealed to Father. If you did not swallow the whole of it, you could not accept a part. And if you accepted a part, you had to be nourished by the whole.

"His *language*? Come on, Owen. Airy nonsense, that's all it is. For substance, the man offers us clouds, fogs, mists of words. 'Times of ter-ror,' indeed! What does *he* know of terror? Ralph Waldo Emerson has neither the wit nor the soul to know terror. And he surely has no Christian *belief* in him! That's what *ought* to be terrifying him, the state of his own naked soul." He sputtered on as we walked back to Dr. Howe's residence, where the good Mrs. Howe had promised to leave us some cold supper.

I followed silently, pondering the meaning and import of his ful-mination, even as I nurtured an odd thought which had come to me towards the end of Mr. Emerson's peroration—that Father resembled no man so much as the Concord poet himself. The Old Man was a rough-cut, Puritan version of Ralph Waldo Emerson, it seemed to me that first night in Boston and for many years afterwards, and even unto the present time, when it matters probably not at all. But it was that night of some personal significance to me.

Even physically, the two looked enough alike to have been brothers—although Father would have been the cruder, more muscular version. They both wore old-fashioned, hawk-nosed, Yankee faces with pale, deep-set eyes that looked out at the world with such an unblinking gaze as to force you to avert your own gaze at once or give yourself over to the man's will. And just as easily and selflessly as Father believed in his God, Mr. Emerson believed in the power and everlasting truth of what he called Nature. For both men, God, or Nature, was beginning, cause, and end, and man was merely an agent for beginning, cause, and end.

As I walked, dropping further and further behind the Old Man in my reverie, I found myself amusing myself with the picture of Mr. Emerson coming off a meeting with Father and imagined him saying the same things to his son about the crazy man John Brown. "The man's truly a *boob*! For the life of me, I can't understand his fame!" For if there was a flaw in Mr. Emerson's argument, it is that he was probably incapable of seeing my father as the very hero he was calling for. And if there was a flaw in my father's heroism, it may be that he could not see himself in Mr. Emerson's portrait.

We turned off Charles Street to make our way uphill towards Louisburg Square, and I remember a young man striding downhill in our direction, well-dressed, fresh-faced, and whistling a tune—no tune I recognized; like a bird he was, whistling for the sheer pleasure of it. A purely happy fellow, undivided in himself, it seemed, as if he'd been successfully courting a lovely maiden and had been invited to return tomorrow evening to continue. He whistled past and continued down the street, to his bachelor rooms, no doubt. A happy man! I stopped in my tracks and watched him for a few seconds, wondering what it felt like, to be so uncomplicatedly happy as he, when Father called, "Hurry, Owen! Keep up, keep up! Don't stare after people like a bumpkin."

I quickly caught up to him, and when we had walked on in silence a ways, the Old Man, in a low voice that suggested he was having second thoughts, asked me what was my true opinion of Mr. Emerson's lecture. I saw that he was now somewhat embarrassed by his earlier outburst and that some of the poet's words may in fact have touched him. Perhaps he had been stung by their similarity to his own thoughts and beliefs and had never before heard them so handsomely expressed, and thus his anger had been directed not at Mr. Emerson but at himself.

"Truthfully?"

"Yes."

"Well, I have to say, I took his words as high counsel, Father. And prophecy."

He did not answer at first. Then he said, "High counsel, eh? You heard that? You heard that and nothing else, nothing that contradicted your beliefs?"

"No. What I heard only corroborated my beliefs and strengthened me in them. Not everything Mister Emerson said was altogether clear to me, of course, but all of it was very beautiful. All of it."

I thought that Father would then upbraid me, but instead he pursed his lips as he often did when thinking something through for the first time and said, "Very interesting. That's interesting to me, Owen. And prophecy? You heard that, too?"

"Well, yes. I believe so."

"Very interesting. High counsel and prophecy. Well, who knows? God speaks to us in unexpected ways. Even in the words of philosophers," he said, and smiled and reached up and put his arm over my shoulder.

We briskly walked that way, side by side, the remaining few blocks to Dr. Howe's home, and the entire distance, as I strode along, I whistled the same, nearly tuneless tune that I'd heard the happy young man whistle before. I believe that I felt for those few moments just as he had; and it was grand.

I was no more eager to depart with Father from Boston, even for a place as inviting as England, than I had been to leave Springfield for Timbuctoo, and for many of the same reasons. Here, in a city amongst a multitude of distractions and competing truths, it was easier not to succumb to the singular force of Father's truth. I was stronger here. Isolation—such as we had endured in Timbuctoo and even to a lesser degree back in Ohio and before that in New Richmond, and such as I knew I would endure with Father aboard a ship and in a foreign land— bound me, bound all us Browns, the more tightly to the Old Man's view of things.

Here in Boston, however, even more than in Springfield, I saw good men and women everywhere who despised slavery, who had thought deeply and long on matters of religion and moral philosophy, and who loved goodness and truth fully as much as did Father, and yet they seemed not so fierce and judgemental in their ways as he. Perhaps they were indeed soft and compromised by wealth and privilege, as Father claimed, made prideful by their fame and the admiration of their like-minded, high-minded compatriots. Perhaps Father was right, and they were, as he liked to say, "boobs." But I could not help but admire their easy tolerance of one another and their patient optimism. Father's way was lonely, painfully lonely to me, and I never felt it so much as when we were circulating in cities amongst the men and women who should normally have been our natural allies.

In the holy war against slavery, Father seemed more and more, and especially here in Boston, like a Separatist. I found myself growing cross and impatient with him for it and the next day nearly quarreled with him. He and I had gone down to the docks from Dr. Howe's to confirm our bookings aboard the *Cumbria* and to verify our Monday morning departure with the tide two days thence, and also just to look at the ship itself, to appraise her size and proportions, so as to anticipate better the degree of our physical discomfort for the duration of our journey. Neither of us had ever traveled so far before—our longest journey by boat may have been the ferry across Lake Champlain from Vermont to New York or a horse-drawn barge on the Erie Canal. And though, naturally, we did not speak of it to one another, we were both more than a little nervous and even somewhat fearful.

I had been noticing, as we walked along the thronged streets, printed advertisements for an address by Mr. William Lloyd Garrison that evening at the Park Street Church. They had been posted all over the city, many of them deliberately torn down and trampled underfoot, it seemed. Despite its reputation, Boston was no more undivided in those days over the issue of slavery than any other Northern city— which is to say that the white citizens who opposed the institution altogether, who were for abolition, complete and forever, in all the states, were a distinct minority—a tiny minority. And those who were *for* slavery, who thought it a positive good, which ought to be extended over all the western territories, they, too, were a tiny minority. The vast majority in between just wanted the problem to go away. And while the majority did not exactly approve of the enslavement of Negroes, they deeply resented their white neighbors who had chosen to make an issue of it.

In Boston, however, numbered among the people who did make an issue of it were some of the most respectable and admired citizens in the entire country. Thanks to the reputations of Theodore Parker and William Ellery Channing and Dr. and Mrs. Howe and dozens of other luminaries in the fields of education, the arts, public service, commerce, and religion, it was here, more than anywhere else in America, that civic virtue, high-mindedness, and theology had gotten associated with abolitionism. Overt opposition to it, therefore, got expressed mostly by ruffians and drunkards, while the respectable citizens stayed home, silently tolerated both sides, and felt smugly above the fray, as if the two minorities, in the eyes of God and the ongoing history of the Republic, neatly canceled each other out.

Stopped for a moment at a crowded intersection, I suggested to Father that it would be nice if we could hear Mr. William Lloyd Garrison speak tonight at the meeting of the Massachusetts Anti-Slavery Society. "We might not have another chance to hear him in person," I said brightly.

He shot me a puzzled, slightly irritated look and, without answering, darted into the cobbled street and strode on ahead of me.

I hurried to catch up, and when I was beside him again, I said in a loud voice, "Well, if not Ralph Waldo Emerson calling for a new heroism at the Charles Street Meeting House, then why not William Lloyd Garrison denouncing slavery at the Park Street Church?"

"What?"

"If not the radical Transcendentalist, then why not the radical Christian? Are we too pure for The Liberator, too?" Since my early childhood, Mr. Garrison's sheet had come to us on the front lines like a trusted messenger sent from the headquarters of the army waging war against slavery. Father had used that very figure himself. Numerous times, I reminded him.

"Yes, I have used the figure," he admitted. "But you mistook it. I meant it as a criticism of what's exactly the problem with these pacifistic 'society' men and women." We were by now down amongst the piers below the Custom House—a whole city of wharves and warehouses, a clattering tangle of crates, bales, tubs, and kegs and all manner of cartons and free-standing goods arriving, departing, and stopped at various stages in between; of shippers and trans-shippers and receivers of goods from all over the world. There was tea and silk from China, rum and molasses from the West Indies, carpets and ivory from India, and from the European nations everything from French lace to Lancaster steel, from Dresden paper to Portuguese wine.

"They think that we're the corporals and they're the generals," he went on. "And men like Garrison, all they're interested in is becoming commander-in-chief. So they waste their time and other people's money squabbling amongst themselves, while our Negro brethren languish in slavery. Action, action, action, Owen! *That's* what I want! Enough of this talk, talk, talk."

"Then you won't go with me," I said.

It was a noisy, chaotic scene down there amongst the stone wharves and warehouses, and difficult to carry on a normal conversation with wagons and carts rumbling past and stevedores, lumpers, and teamsters hollering and drunken seamen lurching through the throng. Although it was a September afternoon, it was as warm and humid as mid-summer, and most of the workmen were shirtless and sweating. Seagulls screamed and begged in brazen crowds or waddled along the edges of the piers or perched half-asleep on the stanchions and atop the hundreds of chimneys and masts of steamers and sailing ships and coastal packets reaching into the sky like a forest of pines. The smells of fish and rum were heavy in the air. In later years, I always associated those odors with the Boston waterfront: fish at the edge of turning, and the sweet, burnt-sugar smell of Jamaican rum—a dizzying, in no way unpleasant smell that touched my brain and staggered me like a drink of raw whiskey.

Father said, "Well, yes, I might be willing to hear Mister Garrison. Out of curiosity. But he's elected to speak on the Sabbath." He meant, of course, after sunset on a Saturday. "If it were to be a prayer meeting, fine. I'd attend. But otherwise, no. And it does seem otherwise, as he is a Quaker."

"May I attend, then, and report back to you?"

"As you wish. You're not bound by my religion, Owen."

"No."

"I will return to the Howes' and read awhile and pray."

"Why do I not feel released, Father?" I said.

He smiled back. "I dare not guess."

We did not speak of it again but went about our business at the office of the shipping agent for the *Cumbria*—which, to these landlubbers and viewed from the dock, appeared quite seaworthy—and returned to the Howes' in time for a pleasant early supper of stuffed grouse served on fancy China plates with genuine antique silverware from France. Later that evening, still secretly angry with Father, who remained closeted in our rooms at prayer, I headed out, by way of Beacon Street, to the Park Street Church, which was located not far from Louisburg Square on Beacon Hill. Beacon Street ran alongside the wide expanse of the famed Common, with a facing row opposite of large, old brick town houses, the patrician homes of many of Boston's elite. As I walked, I kept to that side of the street, close by the tall, elegant houses and as far from the darkened Common as possible, for there—lurking among the shrubs and trees and appearing suddenly out of the darkness to glare and howl at the decorous, well-dressed men and women walking peacefully towards the church—was the enemy.

They were boys, mostly, and young men, idlers and drunkards, brawlers, louts, whoremongers, and common thieves; there were numerous females among them, too, maps and doxies as wild and brutal looking as their brothers. It was not so much their unwashed physiognomies that made them appear brutal and coarse, as their rage. No matter how noble the human face in repose, how symmetrical, fresh, and clear it may appear, when the brow is bent and glowered down, the mouth misshapen by an obscene word, the nostrils flared in revulsion and the lips sneering, and when the fist gets doubled and held out like a weapon, one recoils as if from a sub-species, as if from a demonic, bestial version of one's self. How can we all be humans alike, when one of us has turned suddenly so ugly? And when a whole crowd turns ugly, turns itself into a mob, what species is it then?

I could fairly well smell the brandy and beer on the breath of the youths who stuck their whiskered faces out at me and brayed their Negro-hating sentiments at me and the other men and women who were silently, peacefully walking the sidewalk alongside me. The gang cackled and screeched and sometimes even tossed a rock and then ducked back into the bushes out of sight, to be replaced a few rods further on by another gang, whose drunken members would pick up the chant. "Nigger-lovers!" they hollered. "Yer nigger-lovers! Yer niggers yerself! Ugly black niggers! Ugly black niggers!" And so on, stupidly, even idiotically, they ranted—until we were walking a kind of gauntlet, it seemed, or proceeding through a maddened, howling mob to our own public hanging, headed not to a place of worship but to a scaffold. How courageous, I thought, were these men and women beside me, many of them elderly, who walked in silence along the sidewalk, being jeered and tormented by people with murder in their eyes. That our pale complexions protected us, keeping us from being physically attacked by them and possibly even killed, caused me to realize anew that white is as much a color as black. Our flag, our uniform, was our white skin, and while it provoked this attack from our fellow whites, it also shielded us from serious harm.

Nonetheless, once inside the large, clean, rationally proportioned sanctuary of the church, I breathed a great sigh of relief and realized that I had been seriously frightened by the harassment of the mob— although it was hard to distinguish fear from anger. My legs felt watery, and my heart was thumping. I wanted to strike out, to hit and hurt those foul mouths, and it had taken great restraint for me simply to appear to ignore them and walk serenely along to my meeting like the others, instead of picking up a loose brick or thrown rock and hurling it back at the coward who had thrown it, or chasing the fellows into the bushes and thrashing them there. I was a big, sturdy young man then and could easily have tossed three or four of them around like so much cordwood. Indeed, had one of them actually struck me with a rock, I believe I would have lost my serenity and rushed across Beacon Street after him. I was never a Quaker.

None of the others, however, as they entered the church, seemed in the slightest bothered by the caterwauling of the mob outside. They treated it like a disagreeable rain and seemed to brush it off their cloaks and shawls as they entered the foyer and greeted one another cheerfully and took their seats inside. Standing there in the foyer, shivering with rage—or fear—and tamping down fantasies of violent retribution, I, however, suddenly felt ashamed of myself. "Action, action, action!" was Father's call, but here, in this serene and pacifistic context, action seemed vile, easy, childish. Mr. Garrison's perspective, I knew, and that of the Anti-Slavery Society as a whole, was based on the Quaker philosophy of non-violence, and it was easy to criticize it from afar, while gnashing one's teeth over the ongoing injustice of slavery and its growing power in Washington during those years. But here, in the face of the mob, pacifism seemed downright courageous and almost beautiful.

I was suddenly glad that Father was not at my side, for although he, like me, probably would not have charged into the woods of the Common to thrash his tormentors, he surely would have entered the foyer of the church growling and snarling at the weakness of the Society members for not having created a stout and well-armed security force from amongst their membership and posting it all along Park Street to protect their meetings.

"If you behave as slaves, you will be treated as slaves," he often said. He said it to freed Negroes; he said it to sympathetic whites. "If you wish to do the Lord's work on earth, you must gird your loins and buckle on your armor and sword and march straightway against the enemy."

Ah, Father, how you shame me one minute and anger me the next. How your practical wisdom, which at times borders on a love of violence for its own sake, challenges my intermittent pacifism, which borders on cowardice. Your voice stops me cold, and then divides me. One day and in one context, I am a warrior for Christ. The next day, in a different context, I am one of His meekest lambs. If only in the beginning, when I was a child, I had been able, like so many of my white countrymen, to believe that the fight to end slavery was *not* my fight, that it was merely one more item in the long list of human failings and society's evils that we must endure, then I surely would have become a happy, undivided man.

With thoughts like these, then, and in a kind of dulled despondency, I took my seat in a pew at the rear of the sanctuary, for the church was nearly filled by now with proper Bostonians, all of them white people, well-dressed, with the benignly expectant faces of people gathered for the dedication of an equestrian statue. Indeed, the meeting itself, once it got under way, was not unlike just such a ceremony. Father would have been appalled, and even I was somewhat embarrassed for being there.

My mind wandered during the benediction and the welcome to new members and guests, and I did not rise like the other newcomers to introduce myself to the assembly—out of embarrassment, no doubt, but also because at the proper moment I was thinking of something else and was not sure, when I saw a scattering of folks in the audience stand and heard them, one by one, say their names, what the ceremony was all about. I was thinking about the packs of wild boys and men outside and their dark domain beyond.

Even before Mr. Garrison appeared, I rose from my seat and left. In a moment, I was back on the street. The howlers were gone, disappeared into the darkness of the Common, where I supposed they now lurked, waiting for their prey to emerge from the church, when they would resume barking and snarling at them.

I think back to that night from this vantage point a half-century later, and I cannot remember what, if anything, was in my mind when I crossed the street and stepped into the thicket there. I cannot imagine what my intentions were, as I stumbled down the unfamiliar slope in darkness and made my way towards the rough pasture in the middle, where in the distance I saw what appeared to be a scattering of small campfires and huts made of cast-off boards and old pieces of canvas sheeting. Now and again, the figure of a man or a pair of men passed near enough for me to see and be seen, and, once, a fellow said to me, "Evenin', mate," almost as if he'd recognized my face, and passed into the darkness close by. When I looked back over my shoulder to see where he had gone, I saw him stop and step forward from the shadows towards me, as if expecting me to follow. I said nothing and plunged ahead, in the direction of the distant firelight.

Giddy with an unidentifiable excitement and breathing heavily, as if after great exertion, I made my way slowly over the rough, cloddy ground, which gradually opened onto a broad, unmowed field. Oddly, I felt myself to be in no danger. I was not being pushed from behind, but rather was being drawn forward, as if by some powerful, magnetic force emanating from in front of me.

It was a clear, warm night. The sky was crossed with broad swaths of stars and a gibbous moon, which gave enough light for me gradually to gain a sense of the space I was in. Although it lay just beyond a ridge of elms blackly silhouetted in the moonlight, the city of Boston seemed miles from here. High-minded meetings and church services, elegantly appointed dining rooms and parlors and university lecture halls and counting houses, all the manufactories and dwelling places of proper

Boston, seemed far away—and when I pictured Father at that moment
seated in Dr. Howe's fine, paneled library in the house on Louisburg
Square, reading from the Doctor's leather-bound edition of Milton or
one of the old Puritan divines, it was as if the Old Man were located, not
a mere half-mile from me, but someplace halfway to California.

Suddenly, in a way that I had never experienced before, not even
when I went roaming through the nighttime streets and alleyways of
Springfield the previous spring, I felt free of Father. Free of the force of
his personality and the authority of his mind. Free of his *rightness*. Yes,
more than anything else, it was his rightness that so oppressed me in
those years. I could in no way honestly or openly oppose it. It
exhausted me, humiliated and punished me, and divided me against
my true self whenever I sought to liberate myself from his iron control
of my will. Inevitably, his moral correctness, which I could never deny,
brought me to heel. It was in my bones and blood to follow him wherever his God led him. For, although I did not believe in my father's God,
I believed in the principles that my father attributed to Him. And so
long as the Old Man did not waver in his loyalty to those principles, I
could not waver in my loyalty to the Old Man.

Yet tonight, in this strange sanctuary of darkness, I felt as if I were
afloat on stilled, black waters, drifting in a slow, aimless swirl whose
very aimlessness thrilled me. A slight shift in the breeze could fix my
direction or alter it, and thus I wandered left and right around boulders
and bushes, as the land sloped gradually away from the place where
moments earlier I had departed from the street. I slipped past a knot of
men gathered before a small fire and passing a clay jug and smoking
short pipes. One of them spoke to me in a friendly voice. "Out lookin'
for y' cat, lad?" he asked. I said no and passed on, and they laughed
lightly behind me. Ghostly figures stepped forward and silently withdrew, and every third or fourth of them hissed to me or beckoned for
me to follow.

Were these shadowy figures, these frail, gray wraiths and dark spirits, the same demonic figures I had seen earlier howling at the good Quaker abolitionists on their way to meeting? These people hardly seemed capable of raising their voices, much less shrieking obscenities and tossing rocks and other missiles. But then I saw a band of ruffians, seven or eight of them, boldly approaching me, swigging from a shared bottle and laughing boisterously. They marched straight towards me, as if we were on a path and their intent was to force me out of it. They were boys, fifteen or sixteen years old, amusing themselves by banding together and playing the bully to solitaries like me. As they neared me, one of them hollered, "Out of our way, ye damned bunter, or we'll slice off y' prick and make y' eat it!" and the others laughed.

Shabby Irish laddies they were, all puffed up with alcohol and the rough pleasure of each other's company, and I knew what they thought I was, out here in the night alone—a catamite, a molly-coddle, in search of another. Possibly, in a strange sense, they were right about who I was and what I was doing there, at least for this one night in my life. They had no way of knowing for sure, however, and neither did I. But regardless, I was not about to play the girl for them, or the nigger, and step aside so they could march past unimpeded. Instead, I waded straight into them, as if they were a low wave at a beach.

There is an anger that drives one, not to suicide or even to contemplate it, but to place oneself in a situation which has as its outcome only two logical conclusions—a miraculous triumph over one's enemies, or one's own death—so that the line between suicide and martyrdom is drawn so fine as not to exist. It was a contrivance of my own making, but I did not know it yet, when the first of the lads reached forward as if to grasp me by my placket, and I tore his hand away with my right hand and clubbed him in his grinning face with my left, sending him sprawling.

That was as close to miraculous triumph as I came, however. At once, the rest of the gang was upon me like a pack of wolves taking down an elk in deep snow. In pairs and from all sides, they darted in on me and struck me in the face and belly and groin, kicked at my knees, and although I did some damage to them, they soon had me crouched over, and in seconds, with several hard, well-placed kicks to my ankles, they had me on the ground face-down, curling in on myself to protect my head and nether parts from their continuing barrage of kicks and blows. They said not a word to me or to each other, and now that they had me down, businesslike, went straight to work, pounding at me as if they wished to murder me. The beating went on for many minutes, until I was beyond pain, or so encased by it that I could no longer distinguish the individual blows. Their boots and fists smacked loudly against my spine and ribs and the back of my head and the meat of my arms and legs, pitching my limp body this way and that, until finally the force of the blows tumbled me off the path into a shallow gully beside it, where there was enough bilge and foul-smelling trash that they did not want to pursue me there.

I lay still and kept my eyes shut and heard them spit at me but did not feel it. I heard them laugh and call me names that I did not understand, and then at last they either grew bored with the game or thought me unconscious or dead, for the spitting and derision ceased, and I heard their boots against the gravel as they strode off. And then silence.

For a long while I lay there in the wet filth. Every time I tried to raise myself, pain shot through my body and forced me back down. Then I believe I lost consciousness, for the next I remember is the broad red face of a white-whiskered police officer. I was lying on my back in the pathway, looking up at his worried expression. I remember his words to me. "Well, now, lad, I guess you're not dead after all," he said.

It took two policemen to bring me to Father at Dr. Howe's house, where I was laid out like a corpse on a pallet next to the fireplace in our chamber on the third floor. The Doctor and Mrs. Howe wished to attend to me personally, but Father, after examining me for broken bones and not finding any, other than several likely cracked ribs, would have none of it and insisted on cleaning and caring for me himself. To which I had no objection, for Father was a wonderful and knowledgeable nurse. I was not quite capable of making an objection anyhow, as I could barely speak through my bloodied and swollen mouth. Besides, I was deeply ashamed of my condition, of how I had gotten into it, and wanted as little fuss made over me as possible and as few witnesses. It was obvious that I had been set upon and beaten. The policeman, when he brought me through the door into the parlor, said only that he had found me like this in the middle of the Common, but, oddly, no one interrogated me further, not the police, not Dr. and Mrs. Howe, and not Father.

As soon as we were alone, Father stripped my torn clothing off and washed me down in placid silence, as if I were one of his lambs and had been attacked by a wild animal or a pack of feral dogs. Throughout, Father said not a word. Finally, when he had me wrapped in a warm blanket and I was drifting towards sleep, he peered down at my face as if examining it for further wounds and said, "Owen, tell me now what happened to you tonight."

"Is it necessary?"

He answered that he wished only to know how I came to be walking at night through the woods and fields of the Common, when the place was a well-known haunt of hooligans and prostitutes. "Your private business is your own business," he said, "but I pray that it's not what it looks like."

I almost wished that it were; it would have been somehow more natural; but I could not lie to him. I told him the story of my evening, just as I have related it now—of my having passed along the gauntlet of taunts and derision on my way to the meeting, and of the strange, yet seductive, passivity of the abolitionists as they walked through this assault and afterwards at the meeting, and of my slow-boiling, confused rage, how it eventually drove me from the meeting back to the street and thence into the Common.

Father drew a chair up to my bed, and with thread and needle in hand and my torn shirt, sat listening in grim, attentive silence as I spoke through broken lips. "I don't truly know why I went there, though. It was because of what happened earlier, I suppose. There were all kinds of strange, demented people in that place," I said. "It's as if the place has been specially set aside for them. I felt like I was inside a vast cage with packs of wild animals roaming, and that I was one of the animals." I told him that when a group of them wished me to step aside and defer to them, I had attacked them.

"You attacked *them*?" His eyes opened wide, and he ceased sewing.

"Yes."

He reached out and set his hand on my head. "You went in there and purposely attacked this gang of Negro-hating hooligans?"

"Yes. It looks that way. It felt that way, too."

"Didn't you realize, son, that they were capable of stabbing you, of killing you, of simply beating you to death, as they nearly succeeded in doing? Didn't you know that, or are you merely that naive?"

"No, I knew."

"Yet you went in there anyhow. You went after them."

"Yes."

Gently he stroked my hair. "I see you freshly, son." He sat back and looked steadily at me. "You have as much of the lion in you as the lamb. In my prayers tonight, I will be thanking God for that," he said, and smiled, and went peacefully back to his sewing, and I to sleep.

The next morning was a fine, bright day, still unseasonably warm. I woke feeling broken, however, in pieces and chunks, barely able to stand, pummeled by a hundred shooting pains from crown to foot, and feverish. It was Sunday, and I remember, when Father marched me off to church services, that I was fuzzy-headed and dizzy and only dimly aware of what we were up to. I did not recognize the streets we passed along, and if Father had told me that we were now in Liverpool and I had slept through the crossing to England, I would have believed him.

And before long I did indeed think that I was dreaming, for our reality that morning corresponded uncannily to a nighttime dream that I frequently had in those years. Father and I were the only white people in a crowd of well-dressed Negroes. As we moved through the large gathering of black, brown, and tan men, women, and children, they parted for us and nodded respectfully, some of the men touching the brims of their hats, the women politely averting their gazes, the children looking at us with surprised eyes—lovely people of all the many Negro shades, from pale butterscotch and ginger all the way to ebony and even a few of that most African hue of blue-black. It was as if every tribe of the continent of Africa, from Egypt to the southern-most tip, were represented there. Father walked cleanly through the crowd in his usual manner—back straight as a hoe handle, head pitched slightly forward and led by his out-thrust jaw, arms swinging loosely at his sides, like a man pacing out a field for a survey—and I struggled to keep up, my feet heavy and difficult to move, as if I were wading through mud or walking underwater.

Soon the crowd closed around him and filled in between us, and I found myself cut off from him, falling further and further back, and suddenly I became afraid, not so much of the Negroes who surrounded me as of being separated from Father. Like a small child, I cried out to him, "Father! Wait!" At that, the crowd seemed to part again and to open up a corridor between us. Father slowly turned and peered at me. Then, impatiently waving me on, he resumed walking up the broad steps of a small brick church and entered and disappeared from my view into the darkness of the sanctuary. The narrow corridor through the crowd remained open, however. Laboriously, I made my way along it, sweating from the effort and the heat of the day and the many aches and pains of my beating the night before, when I had walked another gauntlet, that one amongst white people. I was never so conscious as I was then, during those few moments that I spent traversing the short, paved space at the entrance to the Negro church of Boston, of the difference between the faces of the oppressors and the oppressed, or the faces of my white-skinned brethren and my black. And I was never so conscious of my own bewildering, sad difference from both. My face was invisible to me. Father! I nearly cried out. Wait for me! I cannot bear to be so alone! Without thee beside me, I seem not to exist at all! Without thee to look upon me, whether I am amongst white people or black, I am invisible!

I found him inside the church, of course, seated in a pew close to the front, and I took the empty seat next to him, fairly collapsing into it. He studied my face with sudden concern and felt my brow. "You're unwell, son," he said. "Perhaps you should have stayed at the Howes' today."

"No, no, I want to be here. I'm very happy here, Father," I said to him. And I was. Frightened of nameless things; and filled to overflowing with chaotic emotions; yet happy! I felt an inexplicable readiness, as if for a religious awakening, as if for an infusion of light and power. I sensed it coming, not from a truly divine source like Father's God, but from some other, up to now wholly unknown source of light and power, which lay outside myself and beyond all my previous experiences of awakening, beyond all my earlier resolves and oaths, all the sudden stages of my moral growth, all my old degrees and kinds of enlightenment and the pledges that had followed hard upon them. Filled with trembling expectation, then, I waited to become a new man. Or, perhaps, for the first time, a *man*.

And, indeed, it happened there, on that Sunday morning in

September, in the African American Meeting House on Belknap Street in Boston, Massachusetts. While the choir sang a familiar old Methodist hymn, I began to shake and shiver and then experienced a great seizure. I remember the beautiful Negro voices pealing like heavy, dark bells, like distant thunder rolling down the valleys and across the fields of North Elba, coming closer and closer to me:

> Come, O thou Traveler unknown,
> Whom still I hold but cannot see;
> My company before is gone,
> And I am left alone with thee.
> With thee all night I mean to stay
> And wrestle till the break of day!

The fingers of both my hands tingled and buzzed, and I believed that the power of movement had returned to my long-dead arm, and I looked down and saw it move unbid, saw it bend at the elbow for the first time since boyhood, saw it rise and fall as easily as my right arm, until I was clapping my hands together and swinging both arms like the rest of the congregation and like Father beside me. The choir sang, and the preacher, a large, white-haired, full-faced man the color of mahogany, joined in at the second verse, and the rest of the people sang, too, including Father, who knew the words well, for it was one of his favorites.

I could not sing, however. I knew the hymn by heart, but it was as if I had been struck dumb. I opened my mouth, and no sound came. In silence, I made the words:

> I need not tell thee who I am;
> My sin and mis'ry declare;
> Thyself has call'd me by my name;

Look on thy hands and read it there.
But who, I ask thee, who art thou?
Tell me thy name, and tell me now.

I did not believe in ghosts then, nor angels nor spirits of any kind, but it was as if I myself had become one, ghost, angel, or spirit, as if I had been lifted by the music and the clapping and swaying of the congregation and now hovered above them all, like a spot of reflected sunlight. Way down below, standing amongst the crowd of black and brown people, I saw clearly the two white men, my father and his large, red-haired son, swaying and clapping and singing with the others. For a few moments, I was split off from my body, entire and yet wholly invisible to the others, who sang with a mighty voice:

In vain thou strugglest to get free;
I never will unloose my hold;
Art thou the Man who died for me?
The secret of thy love unfold;
Wrestling, I will not let thee go,
Till I thy name, thy nature, know!

All the universe seemed contained for those moments in that room, and the room was filled with music. I watched as my body below began to quake, and I saw my head snap back and my eyes roll in their sockets. I saw Father stare at me with alarm, and when my body stiffened and jerked about as if in a death-dance, I saw him place his arms around my shoulders to calm and comfort me, for he could not know that I was insensible of him and as much at peace as I had ever been in my life. I wished that I could reassure him of that, but I could not. The standing crowd, intent on its singing and in perfect unison swinging their arms and clapping their hands, appeared not to notice the grimly anxious white man in the snuff-colored suit and his large, flailing son.

> What though my shrinking flesh complain
> And murmur to contend so long?
> I rise superior to my pain:
> When I am weak, then am I strong!
> And when my all of strength shall fail,
> I shall with the God-man prevail.

Slowly, I descended and re-entered my body, and it seemed to soften somewhat and then to resume its former comportment, and Father eased me back down into my seat. When I opened my eyes, there he was, looking earnestly into my face. I smiled up at him.

"Son? Truthfully, now. Have you been brushed by an angel of the Lord?" was his whispered question.

I said, "Yes."

He let a triumphant smile pass over his face and turned back to the front, where the members of the choir had now taken their seats and the preacher was moving towards the altar to begin his sermon. With a great barrel of a voice, large and round, he began. "My children. My brothers and sisters. Let me speak today on this question. Let me ask, let all of us ask, 'Why should the children of a King go mourning all their days?'"

He continued, but I heard almost none of the sermon and little of what followed, for I was still be-dazzled; and would remain so for many days and even weeks afterwards: bedazzled by my new solidity and strength, and by my wonderful clarity of purpose.

11

For Father, the long sea-voyage to England was a splendid occasion for his expectations of success to rise steadily. Leaps and bounds, in fact. Solitude, any kind of extended isolation from the everyday world of petty disappointments and frustrations, did that to him—released his fantasies from curtailment and got him feverish with mental dramas and schemes, which, with each new day's dreaming, he built upon freshly. Dream upon dream he went, quickly constructing an immense tower of expectation too fragile to stand against the first opposing breeze and too brittle to bend before the press of mundane reality. But there was no holding him back beforehand, no way of warning him or of forcing him to remember what happened last time. On a ship at sea for nearly a fortnight, with no one but the captain and crew and a handful of other passengers and me to correct him, the Old Man was free to sail, as it were, inside his own thrilled mind. And so he did.

The captain of the *Cumbria*, Captain Ebediah Roote out of New Bedford, a small, trim cube of a man with Quaker chin-whiskers, wanted only to make his passengers comfortable and then to forget them and attend to his crew, craft, and cargo, which were worth so much more to his employers than the comfort of the passengers. For this reason, he gave Father permission to conduct daily prayers and services in the main cabin, hoping no doubt that Father, with his evident fervor and tirelessness, would organize and sufficiently distract the rest of the passengers to keep them out from under foot. And, indeed, Father did just that, and perhaps as a consequence, at least from the captain's point of view, the crossing for the first eleven days went smoothly.

The *Cumbria* was a steam-assisted, two-masted packet of fifteen hundred tons, a small freighter built in the '30s and renovated periodically since. She provided few of the sumptuous diversions and accommodations of the more typical and modern passenger ships that crossed between England and the United States then. People who chose to travel aboard a freighter like ours were usually supercargoes—small-businessmen or their agents accompanying their own cargo—or poor students and artists traveling on the cheap, or people who did not want to be seen by members of their own society. We, I suppose, were passengers of both the first two types, businessmen, but, like poor students, without cargo, for our shipment of wool had gone before us. Nearly two hundred thousand pounds of borrowed Ohio and Pennsylvania wool, it lay ready for auction to the English cloth manufacturers—seven hundred bales of it stacked to the roof and surrounded by hundreds of tons of Irish, Scottish, and Yorkshire wool in a warehouse in Liverpool.

I remember cringing at the thought of it, almost with embarrassment, certainly with dread. Father, on the other hand, contemplated the image with pride and heady anticipation of a great, hard-earned triumph. "When old John Bull sees the quality of our stock, the price of his will drop like a stone, and ours will rise," he frequently declared, rubbing his hands together with glee. "And then, finally, our greedy New England merchants will find themselves competing instead of conspiring with one another. They'll be up against non-collaborationists! Real money-men! After this, they'll have to pay our price, or else we'll just sell it abroad!"

How, I asked him, could we be so sure that our wool was markedly superior to what the British grew?

"How? How? We've *seen* the shoddy goods they try to foist off on us poor colonials, pitching it to us at prices way above our own. Owen, that stuff's grown by *peasants!*" he pronounced. The Irish and Scottish shepherds were poor and demoralized, he explained. They were practically serfs, a conquered, abject population impoverished for generations by a feudal overlordship. They were farmers who couldn't even own the land they worked or the animals they raised, and thus they had no more pride in the products of their labor than did slaves in the American South. And off he'd go on an elaborate comparison between the products of slave labor and free, quite as if all the cotton being produced in the South by slave labor were not of sufficient quality to control the world market in cotton and make the slaveowners richer than Croesus and their senators and congressmen powerful all out of proportion to their numbers.

Dream on, Old Man, I thought, but said nothing. Scheme on, Father. But even if you're right, and the price of English wool drops like a stone because our product is so much more desireable in Liverpool than their own, the New England merchants will simply turn around and buy cheap English wool instead of ours, and the cotton kings of Washington, as soon as they discover it, will vote heavy tariffs on imports, until the prices are equalized again and the cost of trans-Atlantic shipping makes the difference, favoring the buyer at home again. A wasted enterprise.

None of that mattered to the Old Man, though. To him it was a self-evident truth: our wool was superior to the British wool; therefore, the British would pay more for it than for their own; and thus, despite the tariffs and the costs of shipping, we could beat the New England merchants at their own game. His anger—at the collaborationists, as he called them, and at English feudalism, as he saw it, and at slavery and the slave-powered cotton economy, which he viewed as the root cause of the sufferings of all Northern sheepmen—made him deaf and blind. Deaf to me, and blind to the winking smiles of the Boston merchants who traveled with us aboard the *Cumbria* and who were subjected to Father's constant explanations of his plans to crack the English woolen market.

Business was not his only subject, needless to say. Every day following breakfast, Father sermonized to our fellow passengers, leading his tiny congregation in long prayers and hymn-singing and Bible study. Later, he harangued them on the evils of slavery. His congregants were four Boston merchants, a young English journalist, Mr. Hugh Forbes, who said he was attached to the New York *Tribune* and was returning to England to visit his wife and children, and a middle-aged woman and her young female companion. These two were an aunt and her niece, going abroad for the senior woman's health, supposedly, although Father believed that the motives for their journey had more to do with the younger woman's likely pregnancy than the other's health. It was the journalist, Forbes, who most intrigued Father, for he claimed to have fought alongside Garibaldi in the recent, failed Italian revolution, was supposed to have written a two-volume manual on military tactics, and had once (or so he said) been a Viennese silk merchant. In Father's daily reports back to me in the cabin, the most frequently discussed passenger was Mr. Forbes.

Unfortunately, I was miserable and sick with nausea, with giddiness, headache, and vomiting, from the first hour of our crossing to nearly the end of it, from Boston Harbor to the Irish Sea. It was the first time at sea for me, and except for our return, it would be the last. According to several passengers and the crew, who had much experience in these matters, the crossing was a relatively calm one; yet I suffered as if we were aboard a small barque upon storm-tossed waters, as if we were at sea in a hurricane.

There was, of course, an element of convenience in this for me, for it kept me belowdecks in our tiny cabin day and night and thus well out of sight and sound of Father, except when he came to our cabin to report on his day's activities and conversations and then to read, pray alone, and sleep, all of which he did no more than necessary, as the cabin stank of vomit and my chamber pot, and my company was that of a man curled in his bunk like a cutworm, bloodless face to the wall, body wrapped in sweat-soaked sheets, conversation limited to moans and chattering teeth.

For a time, Father tried various remedies, some of them suggested by his fellow passengers and some by Captain Roote himself—drinking warm water, sassafras tea, herbal potions, eating bits of biscuit, loblolly, and so forth. But nothing cured me of my sea-sickness, and so, after a few days, I became a pathetic object of the other passengers' derisive, feigned concern, until gradually everyone, even Father, seemed to forget that I was aboard or else regarded me as if I were merely Father's cargo, out of sight and mind until we landed.

This did not displease me. I wanted no more than to be left alone with my thoughts and memories. For it seemed to me then, as it does even now, half a century later, that I was passing out of one life into another. I was like a snake shedding its skin. There was no single event or insight that had instigated this painful transition, nor was it the result of careful reasoning and analysis. Certainly, the three disturbing days and nights in Boston had played a crucial part, leading as they did to my seizure and apparent conversion at the Negro church, my "awakening." But the rapid collapse of our work back in Timbuctoo, its easy, deadly violence and our inability to stave it off—indeed, the relish with which we all, Father, John, Jason, and I, had taken it up, and then the tragic and, as it seemed to me, unnecessary death of poor Mr. Fleete—all this mattered greatly. And yet somehow, due mainly I suppose to Father's fervor and singleness of purpose, and due also to my ignorance of my own true nature, I could not fully acknowledge these experiences or absorb them with understanding. And so I welcomed the chance to re-read them, as it were, in my mind.

Meanwhile, Father preached to our fellow passengers and the ship's captain and crew. Much to their consternation, surely. It may have been the failure of his work in North Elba, combined with his fears of financial ruin, but he was possessed by a sort of mania during those weeks at sea, which must have frightened some of his listeners and surely amused others, for he would come back to our cabin in the evenings and condemn them all roundly for their mocking refusals to hear him out.

The merchants, he said, were more attentive and polite, more *religious* even, than the two Transcendental women, as he called them, and the English journalist, Mr. Forbes. Which was a puzzle to Father, because when it came to the question of slavery, it was the women and Mr. Forbes who sided with him, and the merchants who thought him foolish. "But regardless of their stance on slavery," he said, "they all split the Bible off from the Declaration and the Laws, and in that way they mis-read both. Consequently, every one of them gets away with feeling smug and above it all. I don't understand these people. It's the Holy Bible that impels us to action, and it's the Declaration and the Laws that show us precisely where to act. What's the problem with these people?"

My response was usually to groan in pain and queasiness and turn my back to him and stare at the wall next to my bunk, which seemed to calm him somewhat or at least to divert his attention and fix it onto the question of my cure. "Will you try to eat a biscuit, my boy? Just try a bite of biscuit."

"I can't keep it down. I can barely keep down warm water."

"Shall I sing to you, son?"

"If you wish. Quietly, though, please. My head pounds, and my joints ache."

"Quietly, then." And he would begin, in a low and tender voice, one of the sweet Methodist hymns. A verse or two into it, however, and his voice would begin to lift and grow in volume, and soon he was nearly shouting out the words.

"Father! My head! Too loud, Father."

"Of course, son. I'm sorry, I'm sorry, my boy," he would say, and he would begin the hymn a second time, quietly, almost whispering the words now, and of course it was not long before once again he was bellowing it out, obliging me to wrap my poor head in the pillow, which would cause him finally to cease his singing altogether and, not without a sigh to indicate the degree of his sacrifice, settle for silently reading from his Bible or in one of his accounts of Napoleon's campaigns, which he was then studying with an eye to making an on-site examination after we had completed our business in Liverpool.

With or without Father, daytimes I confined myself to our cabin. Prompted by necessity, however, it had become my habit after a few nights at sea to walk awhile abovedecks alone late, and I well remember one night in particular. Long after Father had come in, when finally he lay snoring in the upper bunk—from the first night out, he had made me sleep below, so as to ease my fits of sickness and not to wake him when I had to get down and use the chamber pot—I rose and pulled on trousers and shirt; and then, barefoot, my sloshing chamber pot held carefully in two hands and extended well before me, pitched my watery limbs and turbulent barrel of guts down the narrow, dimly lit passageway and made my way up to the main deck. At the stern, I tossed the contents of the pot into the sea and returned to midships, where I set the container down by the cabin passageway and took what had become my nightly stroll, such as it was—a circuit or three, depending on the tolerance of my roiling innards.

On this night the sea was calm and the breeze light. The

squeamishness of my stomach had somewhat abated, and I was able to look out over the glistening black waters without nausea and steady my gaze on the moonlit horizon without dizziness, and for the first time I actually enjoyed the slight roll and buoyancy of the ship below me and the tender flap of the vast sails above, the slosh and creak of the slowly turning sidewheel. I listened with affection to the groan of the masts and spars, the slap of the lines and whir of wooden pulleys, as the wind luffed and loafed overhead. The quiet, steady plash of the low waves as they met the bow seemed almost tropically soft, as if we were in the shallow, warm waters of the Caribbee, and for a long moment I quite forgot that I was cast upon the broad, fierce back of the old, cold North Atlantic.

Then, as I made my dreamy way around to the leeward side of the ship, I discerned the figure of a fellow passenger, a small, frail-looking woman wearing a heavy, dark woolen shawl over her head. She clung to the railing there and stared down into the inky depths as if lost in thought.

When I spoke to her, "Good evening, m'am," she turned abruptly from her reverie as if startled, and to reassure her I quickly introduced myself by name and said I was a fellow passenger, the son of John Brown, whom she had no doubt already met.

"Oh, yes," she said. Then, after a long silence, added, "The preacher."

We had not yet been properly introduced, due to my illness and persistent reclusion, but I already knew who she was, of course. I had glimpsed her when we first came aboard in Boston, and later Father had described her at length and had often speculated about her condition and reasons for travel.

She said her name, Miss Sarah Peabody, of Salem, Massachusetts, and held out her delicate, bare hand, which I grasped in mine for a second. Not knowing what then to say or do, I let go of it quickly, as if her hand were unnaturally hot, instead of alabaster cool. She seemed wraith-like, more apparition than mortal, the image of someone long dead or not yet born, this pale young woman—little more than a girl, I saw, when she opened her small, almond-eyed face to me. Not yet twenty, I thought. And in a dark, sharpened way, she was very pretty.

"Well, Father's not exactly a preacher," I finally said. "But, yes, I suppose he does tend to preach to folks. He's a man of religion, you might say."

She smiled lightly. "Mister Brown is an . . . *impressive* man," she said, with a hint of mockery in her tone. Her face was intelligent, and though she was clearly a genteel and refined person, she looked straight at me and, despite her fragility, spoke with mild self-assurance. She was a young woman who seemed sure of her gifts and their value. A new kind of female, to me.

I could not imagine her pregnant and abandoned, however—I could not imagine her *becoming* pregnant. Even so, there was something about her gaze and light smile that was not in the slightest virginal, that was bold and provocative, and I found myself defending Father to her, as if wanting her approval of him and, more to the point, of me as well. I told her that my father was a businessman, a wholesaler of wool. And that he was also a famous abolitionist.

"Really?" She arched her eyebrows and smiled more with pity than condescension. "A famous abolitionist? Strange that I've never heard of him. Although perhaps I should have." She began suddenly to speak with surprising animation. She had thought that she knew everyone of importance who was in the movement. She and her family, she said, the Peabodys, were all deeply involved in the struggle to bring an end to slavery and had been for many years. She and her family were also active in bringing about other reforms, she said, women's rights, education, and so on. Except for one aunt, she conceded. Not her Aunt Elizabeth, the woman with whom she was traveling to England, but another, her Aunt Sophia, who was married to an author.

"Poor Aunt Sophia, she follows the Democratic politics and principles of her husband. A fine and famous man," she said, "who ought to know better." She told me the author's name, Nathaniel Hawthorne. "You no doubt have heard of him and perhaps have read some of his tales," she said.

At that time, however, his name meant nothing to me. "I'm not much for tales," I said. When it came to literary matters, I told her, I was an ignorant country boy, a rough shepherd, whose reading was mostly still shaped by his father's tastes, which is to say, by religion and politics. Amongst the so-called moderns, John Bunyan was our tale-teller and John Milton our poet, and they were hardly moderns, were they? The rest, according to Father, was dross, or worse. Filth.

"Your father," she said. "The famous abolitionist."

"Well, yes," I said. "But perhaps he's better known amongst the abolitionists in Springfield and out west in Ohio, where we used to live." I thought for a moment to tell her of his association with Frederick Douglass and Gerrit Smith, but realized that I would be merely bragging, and besides, it would be as indiscreet as it was vain for me to invoke the names of those fine men merely to glamorize Father's name. Especially in the light of our recent escapades in the northcountry, adventures that neither Mr. Douglass nor Mr. Smith would care to be associated with.

"Actually, Father works pretty much alone, and with the Negroes themselves. Not so much with white people, excepting, of course, us family members. Which actually enhances his effectiveness, rather than hinders it," I added, and my voice and phrasing sounded in my ears precisely like Father's, as if he were speaking through me, as if, even in chatting casually with this attractive young woman, I had no voice or language of my own.

"Well, I'm sure your father is a hero," she said to me, and patted my hand, soothing a troubled child. "He does seem very much to have cast himself in the old-fashioned heroic mold. Like one of Cromwell's captains, the way he presents himself. Is he a man of action, as well as a man of religion?"

I could not determine if she was serious or making fun of me, and though I grew somewhat shy, I tried nonetheless to engage her bright spirit, which drew me irresistibly towards her. "Oh, yes, certainly. Action, action, action! That's Father's by-word."

"A man of action *and* a man of God! My goodness, what a rare combination. I don't believe I've ever met such a man, at least not until now. And you, Mister Owen Brown, in matters of war are you his lieutenant, and in matters of religion his acolyte?"

"You could say that. Regarding the war against slavery, I mean."

"Then you, too, are a man of action?"

"Well, less than he. No, not at all, in fact. I suppose I'm a follower."

"A man of God, then?"

"Less than he there, too. Not at all there, I fear. In religion, I'm not even a follower. Although I'd like to be."

She said to me then that she thought she and I were much alike, which surprised me, for at that moment, no one seemed less like me than this woman, and I told her so.

"But we're both attached to people of whom we are but diminished forms," she said, and at that point there began a most extraordinary conversation between us. Slowly, we walked the length of the ship and back again, opening ourselves to one another in a manner altogether new to me. And, as it appeared, new to her as well, for every few moments she would exclaim, "Heavens, I can't believe I'm talking this way to a perfect stranger!"

"I guess it's difficult to be strangers on a sea-voyage," I said.

"Yes, and I guess I'm even more lonely than I thought. You don't mind, do you?" she asked.

"No, no, of course not. I'm lonely, too."

I called her by her given name, Sarah, and she addressed me familiarly, too. She confessed that she had come out onto the deck tonight filled with despondency and hatred for her life. Everything so far had ended up disappointing her, she said. Everything. Despite that, or perhaps because of it, she spoke of her illustrious family, the Peabodys of Salem, Massachusetts, with an admiration that approached awe, even including her Aunt Sophia, the woman whose politics she had previously criticized. Now she described her aunt as beautiful and kind and endlessly loyal to her husband, a man who himself was a literary genius, she conceded, in spite of his being a Democrat and anti-abolitionist.

She contrasted herself with these brilliant and famous relatives: she was ordinary, she said, without their gifts of intellect or speech. And she was in no sense as virtuous as they. Her family members and their friends and associates were, for the most part, rigorous Unitarians and well-known Transcendentalists. But for all their liberalism in religion, in terms of their public and private behavior they were still old-fashioned, upright Puritans. "In other words, they are *good* people," she said. "Morally upright." Their generation had abandoned the Calvinist theology in their youth, but had kept the morality. She, on the other hand, having been encouraged by her elders since her nursery days to forsake the old Puritan forms of religion, had retained none of the Puritans' moral uprightness and rigor. She was a sinner, she said. A sinner without the comfort of prayer and with no possibility of redemption.

"I wonder, Owen Brown, do you think that this is what it means to be all modern and up-to-date?" She gave a short, metallic laugh, and, once again, I couldn't tell if she was serious. "Think about it," she went on. "In spite of the fact that our lies and weaknesses and our sensualities feel to us exactly like sins, we are no longer permitted to believe in sin. It's absurd!" she exclaimed. She went silent for a moment, when suddenly I realized that she was weeping.

"What's wrong? Can you tell me what's at the bottom of this, Miss Peabody?"

She didn't answer at first, and I regretted my question. Then she sighed and said, "The simple truth is that my life has no meaning to me. It's true, Owen Brown. None. I feel guilt, a great weight of guilt. But no shame!"

I touched her glistening cheek and said nothing. After a moment, I saw in the moonlight that she was smiling again. Though it was for me a struggle to follow the sudden twists and turns of her emotions and words, I had managed it nonetheless and believed that I understood her, at least momentarily, for I thought that I felt the same way as she—about life, about myself, about everything. Sarah Peabody's words and her tears and her abrupt and bitter laughter had given sudden, expressive shape to my own inarticulated despair. Although despair, like a miasma, had long influenced my mind and spirit—gray, noxious, slick, and spreading into every corner of my consciousness—until now it had remained wordless, unnamed. But here, thanks to this girl, I could name it. My life, like hers, had no meaning, except as a diminished form of other lives. Father's, in particular. And I, too, felt guilt and no shame.

"Then I'm as much a sinner as you, Sarah," I said. "More of a sinner," I declared, offering cold comfort, I knew. I told her that she wasn't alone, for I could no more believe in the God of our fathers than she. Despite Father's tireless wish for me to believe. Thanks to her family's apostasy, she was blameless for her fall from religion. But my fall, I pointed out, had been my own doing, not my family's. Then I told her of my "awakening" at the Negro church in Boston and how my lie had thrilled Father. "It wasn't wholly an act," I said to her. "I did feel *something*. But it certainly was a lie to let Father believe that I had been touched by the wing of an angel." I told her how my lie had sent the Old Man into a paroxysm of thanksgiving. I was guilty, of course, a sinner, but there was no God to punish me. So here I was, continuing with the charade and feeling guilty every moment, devouring my guilt as if it were delicious, nourishing food, but growing fat and sick with it, as if it were rancid. I told her that I felt like a man with a need for putrid meat.

She gently laid her small hand over mine. We were standing again by the rail where I had first seen her. "Oh, Owen Brown, be easy on yourself. Really. You don't know, maybe that *is* how it feels to be touched by the wing of an angel." Even so, she explained, I had only a little lie to live with, and besides, it was a lie that made someone I loved very happy. My father now believed that his son was a Christian. And that, therefore, he had himself a proper acolyte. "It's a good lie, Owen. There are such things, you know. Good lies. Even for us lapsed Calvinists. Don't abandon it. Keep it," she said. "For me, I'm afraid, it's different. Significantly different. My lie can't be kept, and there's no way for me to abandon it, or it me. And, worse, my lie makes no one happy."

Then, to my amazement, she told me the truth about her condition. "I'm unmarried, Owen, and I'm with child. I'm pregnant. As you may have already guessed," she said, but I denied it.

Another lie.

"What do you think of that?" she asked, looking into my face for the answer. "Really. Tell me the truth."

I could not speak at first. Finally, I managed to stammer, "Well . . . well, yes. That's . . . that isn't right. I mean . . . I'm sorry, really, I'm sorry . . . ," stammering not because of any shock or disapproval but because I had not the ready answer that shock and disapproval would have provided: the politely smiling lie. She saw that and seemed pleased.

For a moment, we stood there side by side at the rail, looking down at the black water in silence. Then I said, "Where I'm from, Sarah . . . actually, everywhere, a man is accountable to a woman and her family. But that . . . that seems not to be the case here."

"No, it certainly isn't. Seduced and abandoned. Is that how you describe it? I'm a young woman seduced by a cad and abandoned, Owen Brown. A fact soon to be visible to all." She gave one of her small, bitter laughs. "But nothing's that simple, of course. It never is. After all, I loved the man," she said. Then she confessed that she still loved him. She confessed that she had been willingly seduced. He was in no way a cad, and he didn't exactly abandon her. And in his own way, he was as trapped as she. Not by his body, of course, as she was, but by his circumstances. He couldn't marry her. Not even if he wanted to. He was married to someone else. Married to a fine, loving woman, in fact, whom she very much admired, and he had three beautiful children by her. And he had been as foolish and reckless and cruel to that woman and their children as she.

"But you're the one who has to pay the price."

"Yes, I must pay the price. At least publicly. There's your 'shame', Owen. My shame. Although it must also be my child's. But *he* pays another way. In secret. He knows everything that I know, naturally, but he can never say it, can never stand forth in public and accept responsibility for his sins. He can never be publically accountable, not without shaming his dear, innocent wife and children, which would only compound his sin. No, he will have to live with his guilt instead," Sarah said. And because it was a secret guilt, it would be compounded for the rest of his life. His sin was like the pearl of great price purchased with borrowed money, which he would never be able to pay back. Sarah's shame and her child's reflected shame might actually fade in time—her sin was public, or soon would be, but sometimes people forget and eventually forgive. "Especially if we aren't around to remind them with our physical presence," she said. "But his guilt will grow and grow. No one can ever forgive him, not even he himself, and he can never forget me. For as long as he lives, whether I live or die, I'll remain the emblem of his sin. I know him well, Owen Brown. He's a brilliantly sensitive man, and he makes all the finest moral distinctions. He's practically famous for it." She suddenly laughed.

"Is he a pastor?" I asked. I could not imagine any ordinary man capable of seducing this woman. He would have to have been a man of powerful intellect, a man possessed of a great gift of language, and certainly someone highly respected in her society.

"Is he a *pastor*? A *minister*?" She smiled evenly. "That's sweet. He might have been, I suppose. Born too late for that, though. But never mind who or what he is, Owen. Don't ask any further. I shan't tell, and it doesn't matter anyhow."

"I'm sorry," I said. "I didn't mean to pry. But I think you're way too kind to him. If I were your father or your brother, let me tell you, I'd deal with the fellow in a proper way. I'd make him ashamed, all right. A man like that."

"Owen, no. You don't understand. No one knows who he is, except me. No one. And the man himself. Oh, he knows! But I've told no one: not my family, not my aunt, no one. I've simply refused, and I never will reveal his name. Never. It's the only power I have over him." She laughed, then was serious again. "And remember, I love him, Owen. You must try to understand, I don't *want* to bring him down. He's a public man, and I don't want to ruin his life or scandalize his marriage or taint the lives of his innocent children. I've done enough damage as it is. And luckily, except for what I've brought upon my poor mother and father and my dear aunts, most of the damage I've done only to myself. And to my poor unborn child," she added, with immense sadness in her voice.

I said I supposed she was right. But I didn't understand.

She gazed into my face and abruptly laughed. "Really, sometimes I do wish I were a man. Look at you! You're in as much despair over your life as I, yet the most important question you have to deal with is how to be a man of action and a man of religion. How to be more like your beloved father. You feel like neither—you're not a man of action and not a man of religion—and so you pine away, like a poor seduced and abandoned girl."

"You make me feel foolish."

But so much of a man's life is merely a matter of choice, she declared—the right choice, the wrong choice. And even if a man makes the wrong choice, he can still change it. He simply has to change his mind. "You're a *man*, Owen, aren't you? And, really, when you have good health, you men *are* your minds. You can become a man of action, if you want. Or of religion. Or both. You may not end up famous for it, like your beloved father, but you can *be* it. Tell me, Owen, isn't that how it is?" She stared grimly down at the black waves and clenched the rail with both hands.

"Well, no," I said. "Or at least it never has seemed as easy as that. Not to me. But perhaps I should go in now," I said to her, for she seemed not to be listening anymore. I believed that I had been dismissed. "I must bid you good night," I said.

She looked straight out at the darkness and did not respond.

"Miss Peabody, I'm going in now. I hope . . . I hope that we can resume our conversation tomorrow."

"Yes," she said in a thin voice. "That would be nice."

"Good night, then, Miss Peabody."

"Yes, good night, Mister Brown."

I drew myself away and returned the long way around the bow towards the stairs that led belowdecks to our cabin, where Father lay snoring in sleep. She was right, I knew. My troubles were as nothing compared to hers. And much as I wanted to believe that my life, my fate, was sealed and that I was trapped as fully by my character as she was by her pregnant female body, in fact, my fate was not sealed, and I wasn't trapped. For I was, indeed, my mind. As were most men. And I could change it. I could simply change my mind, as she said.

I could believe the lie that I had told Father and become, like him, a man of religion. Perhaps belief could be willed into existence, just as unbelief could. It would not be entirely a lie anyhow, if, like Father, I was obliged to struggle against unbelief and sometimes, perhaps slightly more often than he, failed. Had he not, especially as a young man, now and then failed to sustain his faith in God?

And I could become a man of action as well. In the war against slavery, I had a wonderful cause, a wide field of worthy endeavor; and in Father I had a fearless and energetic model.

The wind had picked up slightly, and the ship had begun to slip and chop some, and the sails were snapping and the lines crackling overhead. My nausea was edging back. I grabbed up my empty chamber pot where I had left it and quickly descended to our cabin, and I went at once to my bunk and lay down to ponder these new and important matters.

I remember lying in my bunk the next morning, happily re-visiting the scene of the night before and making plans to see Sarah again that day, so that we could pursue the several strands of our conversation further. I was rehearsing sentences to say to her, repeating them to myself, as if memorizing a poem. It was a gray, blustery morning, and Father had earlier gone above for breakfast and to lead the daily prayer service, both of which I had begged off, due to my persistent nausea, which, because of the wind-roughened sea, had worsened somewhat.

He did not return to check on me at his accustomed time, and it was not until late in the afternoon that he finally hove into view at the door of the tiny cabin, holding to the jambs for support against the tossing of the ship. I was lonely and glad to see him, for we had not spoken when he left, and I wanted to tell him about my meeting with the remarkable Miss Peabody.

I had no intentions, of course, of telling him what of her private condition she had revealed to me, or of her beliefs and their profound effect on me, but I thought that he would be interested in hearing about her connections to the New England abolitionists. Actually, I simply wanted to talk about her, to put her into words—to think about her in a concrete way, so that I might be emboldened to seek out her company a second time and then pursue a true friendship with her.

Father sat heavily at the foot of my bunk and placed his Bible upon the narrow shelf beside him. "How goes it, son?" he asked.

"About the same. Worse since the weather turned," I said truthfully. I lay on my side with my knees pulled nearly to my chin.

He stared down at his hands on his lap and seemed oddly preoccupied. "Can I get you something to eat? Have you been drinking water? You must drink, son," he said in a low, disinterested way.

"I've taken my sips, what I can handle, at least. Nothing to eat, though, thanks."

He sat in silence for several moments, until I asked, "What's the matter, Father? Is something wrong?"

He sighed. "Ah, yes. There is. The girl I spoke of earlier. The one traveling with her aunt from Salem?"

"Yes? What of her?"

"Ah, the poor, distracted thing. She's gone and thrown herself into the sea."

I sat bolt upright and stared at him in disbelief. "What? Miss Peabody? No, that can't be true! Not Miss Peabody!" I cried. "How could she *do* such a thing?"

My first thought was that I had abandoned her. Then that she had gone off and left me behind, that she had abandoned *me*. All my thoughts were accompanied, as if prompted, by anger. And all were of myself. I should not have left her alone. I should have stayed with her the whole night long. I might have protected her against the darkness of her mind. I might have been able to keep her here in this world, for me. *I* and *me*.

"Yes, the same," Father said. "A sad and very disturbing act. I was obliged to preach a good while to the company this morning. I took my text from Jonah. It's a vexed and anxious company up there today. And the poor aunt, she's struck down with grief for her niece. I don't understand it. She must have been a bitter, angry child. I had to struggle just to make sense of it for the others. For her troubles, to shade her against the blazing sun of a woman's troubles, the Lord God had prepared her a gourd, and she sat beneath it and no doubt was glad of it. But when God prepared also a worm that smote the gourd and made it wither away, she was like Jonah, who wished more to die than to live. Angry as Jonah in Nineveh was that young woman. Even unto death. You know her name, Owen. How's that?"

"I believe . . . I believe that you told it to me," I said, and lay back down.

He slowly let his breath out. "Yes. Well, I really can't understand it. Suicide always escapes my understanding. Wherefore is light given to her who is in such abject misery, and wherefore is given life unto the bitter in soul? Wherefore, to one who longs for death and digs for it more than for hidden treasures, to one who rejoices exceedingly and is glad when she can find the grave? Wherefore, Owen, indeed? She was a pretty, smart young thing, Owen. I liked talking with her. A little too much educated by Transcendentalism, though. But despite that, I liked her. She talked right smart to me."

"Did anyone see her go? When did she do it?"

"Sometime in the night. No one saw. Her bed wasn't slept in, and when her aunt woke, she sent up the alarm, and the ship was searched stem to stern. But the girl was nowhere aboard. Her aunt has collapsed into grief. And regret. And shame, no doubt."

"Why? I mean, why regret and shame? She didn't drive the girl to suicide. A man did that. A coward."

"I know, I know, but her niece was in her care, and she seems to have loved the girl very much, and now she'll have to report the sad news back to her parents in Massachusetts. The man, well, whoever he is, he'll burn in hell. That's for certain."

"Maybe she's still somewhere aboard the ship. There must be places they haven't searched yet. No one came looking for her here, for instance."

"I vouchsafed this place, Owen. So you wouldn't be disturbed. No, she threw herself into the sea, poor child."

"Horrible."

"Yes. Horrible. She believed not, and she died in her sins."

Father went on like that for a while longer, as he often did after preaching or following a particularly upsetting event, muttering scraps and bits of Bible afterward, like sparks flaring in a dying fire. But I barely heard him. I drew into myself and tried to shut my eyes against the vision of the young woman dropping into the black sea, where she is cuffed and rolled and then embraced by the waves, until she is drawn down by the awful weight of her soaked clothing, her long, dark hair coming undone and fanning out above her head as she descends, her arms extended as if for balance, head thrown back for a last glimpse of the starry night above, and when she has no breath remaining, she opens her mouth, and the cold water that surrounds her rushes in and fills her, and her icy body plunges unresisting through the ocean like a shaft of light.

Again and again, I tried to wipe the vision from my eyes, to listen to Father, who was speaking of Deuteronomy now and the laws of treating with those who violate virgins, of the unknown man who had driven this young woman to such an extremity of despair that she would reject the light that God had given her. But his words flew past me like birds.

I hadn't loved the woman, of course. But I knew that I might have swiftly come to that, and thus her death struck me a blow all out of proportion to the length of our acquaintance. My pain was like an echo of a cry that I had made long years before. Again, I felt not that I had abandoned her but that she had abandoned me, and somehow, as the hours passed, it did not feel like vanity to think that. It felt like anger.

Now I had even more reason to keep to my quarters, and so for the few remaining days of the crossing I nursed my sickness with hurt and gloom and a curiously satisfying kind of mourning—satisfying in that I counted and contemplated all those whom I had lost so far in my short life, and in so doing was distracted from my nausea and general giddiness. Father came and went like a recurrent dream, and I barely knew whether it was night or day.

Until one morning when I woke, and my stomach for the first time seemed settled, and I was genuinely hungry. I sat up in my bunk and placed my feet down on the deck: the ship felt steady beneath me—although clearly we were still at sea and had not yet made land. The waters that carried us had changed, however, as if we had come in off the ocean and were traversing a lake instead.

Then Father appeared at the entrance to our cabin and in high spirits informed me that we had just passed the Scilly Islands off Cornwall and were coasting north in the Irish Sea, headed towards Liverpool. "We're in Cromwell's waters," he said with pleasure. "Imagine that, Owen! Come up and see the headlands off the starboard side. You'll imagine Cromwell's forces setting off to conquer and convert the Irish from paganism and papistry. Celts and Angles, Vikings and Romans, Picts and Normans—they've been sailing back and forth across these waters for centuries! Conquering and converting one another for a thousand years! It's wonderful, isn't it? The mad enthusiasm of these people!" He laughed.

He kept smiling happily and set about packing our two valises, our small luggage. "They're not like us Yankees, are they? We're a continental people, you know; they're island people. And what a difference that makes, eh? They're like the Fijis and the Hawaiians and those fierce, painted Caribs in their long, sea-going canoes, subduing their island neighbors and then a generation or two later being subdued right back. These days, of course, the Anglo-Saxons are on top and thinking it'll last for all time. But you wait: someday soon the rowdy Celts'll be back, and then the Picts. And who knows, maybe the Normans will make another run for it, eh? Napoleon nearly did it, and not too long ago."

"Could be," I said. "Could be." I gathered my gear and, after washing my face and neck and dressing in my one fresh shirt, went up on the main deck to enjoy the sight of land. There I saw from north to south a long row of white, low cliffs and beyond them a strip of cultivated fields, bright green, despite the lateness of the season, and overhead a pillowy bank of soft clouds breaking off to a blue sky. There seemed little more than small fishing villages along the shore; the ship was too far out for me to distinguish individual dwellings. No ports or large towns. It was hard to imagine, as Father had, the righteous armies of the faithful massing there.

The salty air was cool against my face. A fair wind blew out of the southwest, and the wheel churned steadily as a mill, and the sails bellied nicely and helped push the ship smartly north. Terns and gulls swooped low over the boat, and several of the passengers—bored merchantmen and supercargoes in shirtsleeves and a grim young man in a frock coat, whom I took to be the atheistic journalist, Mr. Forbes—idly tossed the raucous birds bits of biscuit. The merchants laughed to see the birds fighting amongst themselves and stealing crumbs from one another. The journalist, who watched the men instead of the birds, appeared to be sourly proving some other point.

But like the gulls, I was hungry, and I quickly made my way to the galley, where, although it was long after the hour when breakfast was normally served, I talked the cook into giving me several slices of hard bread and a portion of 'scouse, salt beef and potatoes and peppers mixed in gravy, and a mug of warm cider. Sitting myself down in the sunshine on a bulkhead, I ate and drank, and in short order I was a new man, ready to come ashore, eager to walk on solid ground again.

My melancholy preoccupations had begun to dissipate and scatter like yesterday's storm clouds in today's bright sun, when I saw standing portside, next to the rail near the bow, a woman whom I took at once to be Miss Peabody's aunt. She was situated exactly where I had last seen my friend, when I departed from her that fateful night.

The woman looked somewhat beyond middle-age and was large, unusually so, shaped like a bronze bell, and seemed the picture of solitude and loneliness. She wore a long, black dress with hat and gloves, and her face was covered with a black veil. I could not make out her expression, because of the veil, but she appeared to be looking back out to sea, gazing in the direction we had come, as if making her final goodbye to her poor, drowned niece.

I knew that there was nothing I could do or say that would comfort her. It was such a sad sight, and it so threatened to drop me back into my recent gloom, that I could not bear to watch her, so I picked myself up and strolled back to the stern of the ship, to make there my first casual conversations with the sailors and other men in the crew, conversations and inquiries that, had I not been stricken with seasickness, I would have undertaken at the very beginning of our journey. Now, as we neared our landing at Liverpool, despite the tragic death of Miss Sarah Peabody, and despite my lengthy illness, I found myself in excellent spirits, healthy and well-fed, newly befriended by cheerful, sturdy workingmen, and, concerning our business here, fast becoming as optimistic as the Old Man. I saw that there had been completed, almost without my intending or even hoping for it, a thorough-going transformation in my character and in my relation to my father. The process had commenced in earnest in Boston and had continued during the crossing and now, somehow, inexplicably, it seemed to have been completed by the sad, wasted death of the young woman Sarah Peabody—all accomplished, for the most part, without my awareness or understanding. Until it was over, that is, when—by remembering who and how I had been before, especially in relation to Father—I realized that I had become, in an important sense, a new man. No more the disgruntled, sulky boy who followed his Old Man around and waited for orders that he could resent. No more the pouting, conflicted ape. This new fellow, who had been a reluctant follower, was now an enthusiast, was a proper lieutenant, was a fellow believer! He might fail here and there—fail to act, fail to believe—but he would no longer question his aspirations or his commitment.

Thus I fairly bounced down the gangplank ahead of Father as we disembarked at the crowded quay on the Mersey River, where the *Cumbria* had docked and was already being unloaded by husky lumpers and stevedores and loaded onto carts and wagons by teamsters. It was a noisy, chaotic hub-bub of a scene: hawkers and higglers in tiny stalls, men in tall beaver hats on horseback and in carriages making their way through the crowd, ragged beggars on crutches with hands held out, a musician in a harlequin's suit with a monkey on his shoulder and a dancing dog on a string, and meandering gangs of urchins and skinny men in caps who looked like cutpurses; there were merchants, clerks, supercargoes, and shipping agents ticking off goods received and goods about to head out, and shirtless, orange-haired Irishmen lugging barrels and crates. Here and there, a distinguished-looking gentleman or lady arrived by carriage to greet a visitor or collect a parcel. People called and bawled to one another and sometimes grabbed my sleeve and tried to sell me food off their smoking carts: greasy, fried fish wrapped in paper, roasted potatoes, bits of meat on skewers; and old ladies carrying trays filled with jellied sweets accosted me at every turn; everyone was shouting at me, it seemed, but I understood barely a word I heard. Their pronunciation and the speed with which they spoke was all off. It was as if I were not in an English-speaking country at all, or as if I myself did not speak English. There were Negro men working alongside the whites, and Hindoos with turbans, and bearded men in black coats and hats whom I took to be Jews. There were tall, blond, white-skinned Swedes and florid Russians and even a few in the crowd whom I recognized as Americans, long-faced Yankees in black, and tanned Southerners with walking sticks and broad hats and pale suits. I felt that I had arrived in Phoenicia.

The buildings were high and looked ancient, mostly of gray stone, and the crooked alleyways and streets between them seemed narrower and smelled more of old food, beer, and human waste than Boston even. But there was a remarkable increase in human activity here, more noise, more color and variety among human types, than in Boston, which delighted me and seemed to please Father, too, for he had a small smile on his face as we pushed through the throng and made our way from the hurly-burly of the quay to the huge stone warehouse where he had arranged for our wool to be stored pending our arrival and now to be examined and graded and, presumably, sold.

While I stayed in the dimly lit warehouse and inventoried our nearly two hundred thousand pounds of wool and made sure that none of the bales that Father, John, and I had so carefully graded, labeled, and shipped from Springfield had been damaged or come undone in transit or storage, Father retreated to the office with the purveyors' agent, a Mr. Pickersgill, to set a time for the buyers to view Brown & Perkins's wonderful American wool. A pimpled teenaged apprentice watched over me suspiciously, as if he expected me to steal our own wool. All six hundred ninety bales of it, neatly packaged in burlap and tied with heavy cord, had been stacked in a bay near the rear of the huge, cool, cavernous building, and after I had examined and counted every one, I proudly signed the slip the boy had handed me—*Received in good order by Owen Brown, agent for Brown & Perkins, Springfield, Mass., U.S.A.*—and admired for a moment the tidiness of our bales, comparing them to the rough-looking stock that surrounded ours and rose in heaps nearly to the high, dark eaves, theirs, all of it, sloppily and irregularly packaged and tied. Then I picked up my valise and went straight out to the street, there to loll in the sun and admire the passing crowd.

It looks good for us, I thought. The Old Man was right. These British are no match for us.

Soon Father emerged from the warehouse, blinking in the bright light like a mole, but looking pleased with himself and eager to move to the next piece of business, which I assumed was finding lodgings. "Turns out we've arrived a day late for the weekly viewing and sales," he said. It would be six days before the buyers from Manchester, Leeds, and the other cloth-manufacturing towns returned to Liverpool to examine the wool that came in during the week and make their bids according to grade and quality. "So, my boy, we have a bit of a holiday in front of us," he said, and he rubbed his hands together in a show of pleasure. "What d' you say we take it?"

"What do you propose?"

"Well, let's just keep moving! Here we are, like Father Abraham sojourning in the land of promise, dwelling in tabernacles with Isaac and Jacob. We are strangers and sojourners here, as were all our fathers. Am I right?"

"Right! So where do you propose we go?"

"Why, to London! And to the very continent of Europe! We'll track Napoleon's hundred days' march, all the way from Elba to Waterloo!"

"We've only got six days for marching, Father," I pointed out. "Not one hundred. And we have to end back here, not Waterloo."

"And so we shall." He laughed and clapped me on the shoulder, and we stepped down to the cobbled street and joined the flow of the crowd heading into the heart of the city. He had learned from Mr. Pickersgill, the warehouse clerk, that if we hurried to Garston Street at Speke Hall, we could catch an overnight post-chaise to London. The train had already departed. "Let's go now!" he said. "It'll cost us less anyhow to sleep in a moving rattler than a bed in a boarding house that goes nowhere."

I had no money of my own, naturally, so wherever Father went, there close behind, of necessity, came I. As if I were in his employ, his apprentice boy. And in a sense, of course, I was. But I did not mind any longer thinking of myself that way, since our goals were now the same. After all, had I money of my own, I would have done just as he—I would have taken a holiday, ducked into a shop on the way for bread and cheese and a sack of shiny red apples, and made for the night coach or a rattler to London and beyond. Who knows, I might even have gone to Waterloo.

12

This was the first time that I had been out of my native land, and therefore the first time that I'd walked the streets of a country where slavery had been banished, and I felt cheerfully liberated by it. England was then, as now, of course, an antique monarchy, not a modern republic. Nevertheless, it was a freer country than ours, for no man could legally buy and sell another, and for that reason alone, as soon as we stepped ashore, the air we breathed seemed cleaner, fresher, more energizing, than ours at home. I think Father felt the same exhilaration as I. We did not speak of it to one another, however—it was as if we were superstitiously afraid to say the words "Negro" and "chattel" and "slavery," as if we both knew that merely to utter the words in passing would drop us back into the gloom and rage that we then associated with being citizens of the United States of America. We needed a holiday, a vacation from the obligation to be constantly conscious of our national shame, and when it came, we both took it with unaccustomed alacrity.

Our high spirits did not diminish, even when we discovered, to our surprise and my slight displeasure, that our fellow passengers in the post-chaise from Liverpool to London were Mr. Hugh Forbes, the English journalist, and Miss Elizabeth Peabody, from the *Cumbria*. But we did not raise the topic of Negro slavery with them, either; we did not say the hated words. Nor did they, probably because they had already heard enough on the topic from Father during the crossing and did not need or particularly want to hear more. Instead, all of Father's comments and observations were limited at first to remarking on the passing scenery and then to interrogating Mr. Forbes on the recently ended wars in Italy, on military tactics, and on the ideas and principles of the leader of the failed revolution, the famous Giuseppe Mazzini, whom Mr. Forbes, a man of numerous small pomposities, claimed to have known personally.

The vagueness with which he answered Father's questions made me suspicious of his claims, but Father seemed eager to believe them, and when in private, during a brief mail-stop outside Manchester, I whispered my suspicions to the Old Man, he just waved me off and explained that Mr. Forbes talked elusively and vaguely because he was British. "They all talk that way, Owen," he pronounced. "It's a national trait. They're a very circumspect people, y' know. Think of Shakespeare," he said. I did, and still did not agree, but said nothing more.

Miss Peabody, whom Father had described earlier as "a voluble woman with many sharp Transcendental edges," was quite obviously still stunned by the death of her niece and kept to herself, as was natural. I had mumbled my condolences, as soon as I realized who our veiled fellow passenger was, but otherwise we men deferred to her in silence and tried not to intrude upon her privacy and grief. Even Father left her alone, although I knew he would have enjoyed leading her in prayer for the salvation of her niece's unsaved soul. He believed, as the Bible showed, that God was sufficiently powerful and merciful to break His own rules from time to time and, if sufficiently prevailed upon with prayer, might be willing to admit a fallen suicide into paradise. But, for once, the Old Man politely restrained himself.

For me, it was exceedingly difficult not to speak to her of Sarah

Peabody, to tell the woman of my brief encounter with her niece on the very night of her death, for I was no doubt the last person to have seen her alive and to have spoken with her at length. Not that I could have told the aunt anything consoling. Still, I might have said that her niece had touched my heart with unusual force and had moved my mind in a significant way. I might have said that my brief meeting with her had unexpectedly clarified my thoughts and that I would remember her for the rest of my days, as indeed I have.

But our spirits, mine and Father's, were soaring, despite my distrust of Mr. Forbes and our constant awareness of the suffering of Miss Peabody. Not even the shocking sight at dusk of the sooty mills of Manchester and the blackened hovels of the thousands of laborers whose lives were given over to the mills dampened our enthusiasm and curiosity. The crimes evidenced by these monstrous, huge, prison-like factories were English crimes, not American; and the greed that drove the mighty engines of the mills and the owners' callous disregard for the lives devoured in their service were English greed and callousness, not American; and as we passed through the city, the raggedy, exhausted, vacant-eyed men and women and pathetic small children whom we saw wending their way along the narrow streets from the mills to their teeming tenements were English, Scottish, and Irish workers—not a one of them American. It was a luxurious detachment that we enjoyed as we crossed this benighted land, and though it was but a respite, I could only hope that we had earned it, Father and I, and that our inability when in America to disassociate ourselves from the sufferings of our Negro brethren, our constant anguish, shame, and rage when at home, had purchased this brief holiday honestly and fairly.

"This is a fine country, isn't it, Owen?" Father said, peering out his window at the passing villages and farms. He commented on the scenery as if we, his fellow passengers, could not see it, which was his habit anyhow, although it was somehow not so noticeable to me in America as here. "Their farming and stonemasonry are very good, Owen. But look, their cattle are generally only more than middling good, I would say. And on average their horses, at least those I've seen so far, bear no comparison with those of our Northern states, especially. The hogs look healthy and slick, though, wouldn't you say? And the mutton-sheep are almost as fat as their porkers."

Soon it began to rain, and then it grew dark, and our world was reduced to the cramped interior of the coach. While I tried intermittently to doze and Miss Peabody, as it appeared, gloomily meditated on the death of her young charge, Father drew Mr. Forbes forward into a discussion of military tactics, which rambled on into the night. Mr. Forbes did seem to know his subject, however, well enough at least to speak convincingly about the ways and means of training and maintaining a small, disciplined, easily deployed force of insurrectionists so that it could effectively oppose a much larger, slower-moving, national army.

This was, of course, the very subject the Old Man was most interested in hearing about, and he quickly warmed to it. I knew that he was transposing everything Mr. Forbes said, which mostly concerned the failed wars in Italy, into victory on an Appalachian landscape in the American South, and that, in Father's mind, Mazzini's ragtag army of republicans was a rapidly growing force of freed and escaped Negro slaves and a few courageous whites, a citizens' army broken into small bands operating from thickly forested mountains, fighting mostly with weapons seized from the enemy and living off the land and goods and foods donated by secret sympathizers, darting down from their mountain hideouts under the cover of darkness to make lightning-like raids against the lowland plantations, liberating the slaves there and steadily enlarging their forces with the able-bodied African men and women willing to join the fight, and sending the others north along the great

Subterranean Passway, as he called it, all the way up the chain of mountains from the Appalachians to the Alleghenies to the Adirondacks, on to the home base in Timbuctoo and thence to Canada.

Mr. Forbes was a slender, talkative man in his middle thirties, with a high, balding head and dark, wavy hair, which he kept long and combed across the top in a vain attempt to hide his baldness, although it shone through nonetheless. He had the chalky complexion of a man not used to outdoor work, dark, deep-set eyes, a long, aquiline nose, and he wore a drooping moustache. His teeth were not good, but, withal, he was a handsome man and intelligent-looking, if in a delicate, slightly effeminate way, as when now and again he winced at the rising volume of Father's voice and looked somehow pained, as if embarrassed, when the coach crunched over a stone or dropped into a narrow ditch and tossed him in his seat.

"I suppose some things seem obscure, Mister Brown, but really, they're quite obvious, aren't they?" said Mr. Forbes. "Once they've been pointed out, of course. Either by genius before the fact or, as is more often the case, after the fact by disaster. Don't you think so?" He had a habit of pausing in his statements and briefly admiring his fingernails, then going on. "For instance, Mister Brown, here's some after-the-fact wisdom, if you like. Taken from the Italian campaign. Taught by disaster." The smaller force, he said, had of necessity always to be made of men who, though they believed many things, *must* believe but two. Number one, each soldier must believe that he is engaged in a struggle in which he and his comrades are morally right and their opposition morally wrong. No middle way. No room to negotiate a compromise. It couldn't be a simple dispute over land. Basic principles, not mere borders, must be at stake. And number two, he must believe that he is fighting for his own life and for the lives of his loved ones. So that the only imaginable alternative to his participating in this dreadful war is death for him and his loved ones. No going home for a season to harvest the olives and the grapes. "Give me liberty or give me death," Mr. Forbes said, smiling. "That sort of thing. A bit like your American revolution, wouldn't you say? It helped, of course, that you were lucky. And had brilliant leadership, I must say. Brilliant. At a time when ours was inept. Lovely. For you, I mean."

Mr. Forbes did not seem particularly to *like* the brave Italian soldiers he was describing or even to admire the great Giuseppe Mazzini. Like many of the journalists whom I came to know later, during the Kansas War and afterwards, he seemed to feel himself superior to his subjects and affected a cynical and amused detachment towards them. This didn't bother Father, apparently, or else he simply didn't notice it, which worried me, as Father continued to interrogate the man and appeared at times to confide in him certain plans and intentions which I thought were better left secret. I would turn out much later to have been correct in my estimation of the character of Mr. Hugh Forbes, for, as is well known, he joined us as an ally late in the Kansas campaign and then at a crucial moment afterwards became one of our chief betrayers and nearly brought us down. For now, though, and even right up to the point of his betrayal, he was to Father a man possessing much valuable knowledge, and the Old Man meant to use him. I sat and watched and listened. And whenever I thought the Old Man was going too far, or coming too close, I interrupted him and led them to a different aspect of the topic, for I could not get him off the topic altogether.

The rain poured down, and the coach sloshed roughly forward towards London. The leather curtains flapped and slapped against the sides, and now and then a fine spray of water entered the dark interior, wetting us. Father asked Mr. Forbes, "I'm wondering, how, sir, would you be able to discipline and train such an insurrectionary force? You can't go out and conscript soldiers and drill them in public and instruct them and so on. You have to operate in secret and in small numbers. Especially in the beginning." No matter how much your soldiers shared those two essential beliefs—that in the face of outrageous wrong they were morally right, and that they were fighting for their and their loved ones' lives—they still were not professional soldiers, after all. Most of them would be unskilled laborers, he pointed out to Mr. Forbes. Our recruits, he explained, would be people who were likely to be illiterate, unused to military machinery and weapons, untrained in distinguishing between occasions that require independent action and those that require submission to authority. And they would be people who had been taught for generations to hold themselves beneath the very men they were now opposing.

"Is this theoretical, Mister Brown?" drawled Mr. Forbes. "Or are you planning a revolt?"

"Father," I said into the darkness, cutting him off. "Isn't it like Gideon and the Gileadites? In the war against the Midianites. Remember?"

"Ah! So it is! So it is! There's your answer, Mister Forbes. My son knows what you do not, sir. That the greatest military manual ever composed is the Holy Bible! Properly construed. And he's quite right, the answer to my question is in front of my eyes. For the Lord said unto Gideon, 'Whoever is fearful and afraid, let him depart early from Mount Gilead.' And twenty-two thousand men departed from the mountain, leaving behind ten thousand who were not cowards. And the Lord said, 'There are yet too many.' Too many! Imagine! Not too few. And the Lord conceived of a test for Gideon to put to the remaining people, such that all those who went down on their knees to drink were separated out, and there were then but three hundred remaining, only those who had put their hand to their mouth when drinking, the men too proud to go down on their knees even to drink from the river Jordan. And the Lord said unto Gideon, 'By these three hundred men will I save you and deliver the Midianites into thine hand.'

"And here, Mister Forbes, the Bible is very instructive in a most particular and interesting way," Father went on. "Gideon, who this time was instructed by his dream, divided his three hundred men into three companies of one hundred each, and according to the dream, he himself would lead one company only, and they would go to the camp of the Midianites at the beginning of the middle watch. Very useful instructions, when you think about it. The beginning of the middle watch. Smart, eh?"

"Considering that it came from a dream," Mr. Forbes said in a low voice.

Father ignored him. "And Gideon ordered each man to carry in one hand a trumpet and in the other a lamp lit inside a pitcher, and on hearing Gideon's own trumpet they were to break the pitcher and hold up the lamp and blow upon the trumpet and cry out, 'The sword of the Lord!' so as to look and sound like ten times ten thousand. 'The sword of the Lord!' And when they did that, Mister Forbes, all the hosts of the Midianites who were not slain at once by the sword of the Lord fled into the wilderness!"

I heard Mr. Forbes utter a loud yawn. "Amazing," he said.

"Yes. If your General Mazzini had looked more deeply into his Bible," the Old Man went on, "he might in the end have triumphed over his enemies." When Mazzini had wanted to know how to cut off his enemy's supplies, Father explained to Mr. Forbes, he should have read 2 Kings, chapter 19. And for setting ambushes, he might have consulted Judges 9, verse 34, where he would have been told to lie in wait against Sechem in four companies, or else divide into two companies, as did Joshua against Ai, and lead the enemy out of its fortress by having one company pretend to flee, and then the second company could enter the fortress and set it afire, and when the men of Ai saw that their citadel was in flames, they would turn and rush back to save it and would be caught in the open plain between the two companies of Joshua and cut to pieces. And to know how to slay an enemy chieftain

who is surrounded always by his guard, Father said to look into Judges
3, 19–25, and go to your enemy as Ehud went to Gilgal and say that you
have a secret errand to him from the Lord, and when Gilgal has sent
away his guard, thrust your dagger with your left hand into his belly to
the haft, so that the fat will close upon the blade and he cannot draw it
out and only the dirt will come. Then go forth and lock the doors upon
him and escape unto Seirath.

"Indeed," Mr. Forbes said. "With your left hand, eh?"

"Oh, yes! Facing him! Because of the placement of the internal
organs, the liver and the bowels and so forth," he explained. "So he'll die
at once and not cry out." For some time Father continued showing Mr.
Forbes the brilliance of the Bible as a military manual, citing chapter
and verse from a dozen different books, and I felt that his listener must
surely have fallen asleep, for he no longer spoke. I, of course, had heard
the Old Man employ the Bible this way hundreds of times before on
any number of topics, from the care of sheep to the management of
grief, and had myself fallen asleep in the middle of his citations, to
waken in time for the grand peroration at the end and nod agreement.
This was how the Old Man talked, how he communicated his thoughts
and beliefs, and it could be pretty impressive, because he knew his
Bible better than any man and could apply it with intelligence and
verve and sometimes, perhaps without intending it, even with humor.

This time, however, I heard him differently. For it was clear, as he
laid out one case after another, that he did indeed know more about
military tactics and strategy than Mr. Forbes, his presumed expert, and
probably knew more than General Mazzini, too. He was drawing on
the experience of a people who had conducted wars large and small for
thousands of years. Never mind that they claimed to have received *their*
instructions from the Lord, from dreams, or even from the entrails of
birds; Father's great knowledge of the Bible gave him direct access to
the experience of a thousand generations of military men and women,

providing him with the collective memory of an entire race of people. Father didn't read the Bible like a man who thought he was *like* the ancient Israelites; he read it as if he were an Israelite himself, as if he, too, were receiving instructions from the Lord. The man did not simply *remember* the Bible, as a person remembers the alphabet or even as he remembers old injuries or triumphs. No; for the Old Man, the Bible *was* his memory.

"Well, Mister Brown, that's all very interesting," said Mr. Forbes. "But I'm afraid the modern military mind requires a bit more than the Bible for its instruction. Times change, don't they?"

"Ah, but human beings don't!" Father exclaimed. "And, unfortunately, one of those things that do not change is the very belief, the delusion, if I may say so, which you have just now uttered, that human beings change. That, too, is constant, my friend. 'And God said, Let us make man in our image, after our likeness.' Times may change, sir, but the Lord does not, and therefore neither does he who was made in His image, for changelessness is in the nature of Him who hath made us. We are the same man as old Adam was."

"Indeed. Well, I'm afraid I'm not a religious man," said Mr. Forbes. He then announced his desire to sleep, promising to resume this most interesting conversation in the morning before reaching London.

Father said fine, fine, he too would like to sleep, and so would we all, Miss Peabody especially, he added, although she had said not a word in several hours and must indeed have been lost in her dark thoughts, quite unconscious of Father's and Mr. Forbes's conversation and unlikely to sleep, regardless of her fellow passengers' consideration or lack of it. She did not acknowledge Father's remark, nor did I, and so we all fell into silence.

Through the long night we made our bumpy, rain-chilled way, catching short naps as we could, stopping briefly for breakfast at an inn outside the village of Dunstable, a ways north of London, and made the vast capital city proper shortly before midday. Several times, the Old Man tried picking up his discussion with Mr. Forbes where they had left off, but the Englishman seemed reluctant to pursue it further and smiled condescendingly and put him off, as if he thought Father slightly cracked. I had seen that response in people many times before, hundreds of times, in fact, and I had almost always felt sympathy for them, even a little pity, with anger at Father mixed with embarrassment for myself. But this time I felt merely superior to Mr. Forbes and dismissive. He was too closed-minded, too conventionally educated, or perhaps simply too stupid, to appreciate the Old Man's originality and clarity, I thought.

You did not have to be a Christian to see that Father's insights into the nature of man were brilliant and that his principles were admirable; in fact, it probably helped if you were not a Christian, for many of Father's views significantly departed from those held by the modern churchmen. You did, however, have to look at things afresh, as if no one had ever asked your question before. How *does* one conduct an ambush? How *does* one assassinate an enemy chieftain? How *does* one oppose a large, well-trained professional army with a small, ragtag force of angry civilians?

In every case, the Old Man simply answered with another question: How is it done in the Bible? Unlike most Christians, Father did not go to the Bible merely to confirm what he wished to be the case, whether about man or God; he went there to inquire what was the case. And where better to look after all? Where else had the nature and doings of man and God been more closely observed over a longer period of time than in the Bible?

In London we did not tarry, and I barely had a glimpse of the city. Which I somewhat regretted, as it was the hugest conglomeration of people and buildings that I had ever seen or imagined, and I would have liked to take its measure, if nothing else. It consumed fully an hour for our coach to make its way from the edges of the city to the center. All those crowded, twisted, narrow streets and maze-like lanes lined with brick warrens and tiny, dark hutches—it was a literally dizzying sight, and I staggered when I stepped down from our coach to the street! The sky was but a thin, gray satin ribbon zig-zagging overhead, and a light mist drifted down from it upon us, making us shine like smooth, wet stone and giving everything a strange, heightened clarity. I wanted to walk off into the city, to leave the others behind and wander aimlessly, utterly anonymous and invisible in such a crowd.

But perhaps it was just as well that Father was so intent on getting to the continent of Europe, for it would have taken me months, even years, to gain sufficient perspective on the city and its thronged enormity to know where in it I stood at a given moment. I could see and wonder only at what was directly in front of me and had no way of knowing its relation to the rest. My viewpoint was all foreground, no background.

Father's was also, but this seemed not to bother him. From the instant that we stepped all stiff and damp from the coach to the cobbled street, he was busily arranging our departure for Belgium. Before bidding goodbye to our fellow passengers, however, he took Mr. Forbes aside and obtained from him both his London address and his address in New York, which he wrote into his pocket notebook. He then said that he would soon be contacting Mr. Forbes personally or would be sending one of his agents to speak with him in strictest confidence concerning a matter of grave importance and utmost secrecy. The agent would likely be one of his sons and would identify himself as such by recalling certain details of our voyage.

"You're quite serious, aren't you?" Mr. Forbes said. He stood, carpetbag in hand, his weight carefully balanced on one foot, the other nearly in the air, as if he were ready to run.

"I am, indeed, sir. I believe that I will want you for an ally in some business that I am planning. You have certain experiences and knowledge that I may have need to draw upon."

"I thought the Bible was all you needed."

The Old Man smiled slyly. "Perhaps the Bible has told me that I need a man like you at my side. Just as Abraham, to free his brother Lot from Sodom, needed the Canaanite chieftains."

"Ah, yes. Abraham. Very well, then," he said. "You are an interesting man, Mister Brown, and I believe you bear watching. And as I am a journalist, I shall do that. Shan't I?"

"Just so," Father said, and shook his hand firmly.

When Mr. Forbes had gone on his way, the Old Man turned to Miss Peabody, who stood beside a heap of suitcases, her own and, I assumed, her niece's. She appeared to be waiting for a carriage. Father said, "Is there any way I can help you, Miss Peabody?"

She politely answered no, that she had hired a porter and would be on her way directly to her hotel.

"My son and I would both once again like to express our sympathy to you."

She said, "Thank you, Mister Brown," and turned pointedly away from us, leaving Father's hand hanging in the air and mine just behind it.

"Goodbye, then," he called to her. "Goodbye! I will pray for your relief from sorrow!"

She did not answer, and we moved off from her. "I believe I offended her earlier," Father said in a low voice. "With my persistent sermonizing aboard the ship."

"Never mind. It's her niece who needs your prayers."

"Yes, yes, you're right. Of course. But I do go on sometimes. I forget myself."

I said to Father, "Speak to me about your conversation with Mister Forbes. Really, what do you need him for?"

He smiled, as if relieved not to think about the Peabody women and the sometimes ticklish business of his enthusiasm for prayer and sermonizing. "Wal, my boy," he drawled, "as the man himself said, he is a journalist. And though he is atheistic, he is sympathetic to our cause."

"But he's not an American. He's English."

"All the better. Americans are always readier to believe foreign reports on our affairs than they are the homegrown variety. Don't you think?" he said, mimicking the Englishman's accent. He laughed and grabbed up his valise and said, "Come on, m' boy, we've got to catch the very next train to Dover! Enough of these hard English coaches, eh? We can do it, if we hurry. We'll be on the other side of the English Channel by nightfall!"

We had disembarked at King Street near the Covent Garden Market Hall, and it was only a short walk to the station at Charing Cross, which was located on a wide boulevard called the Strand. Father strode along in his usual straight-legged fashion, led by his chin, and I scrambled to keep up, distracted by the passing crowd, by the elegantly coiffed and bustled women in their long dresses, the gentlemen with their canes and silk hats, the fine, high-wheeled carriages and tall chaises with liveried drivers and footmen and the handsome matched teams that drew them through the jammed streets.

The over-abundance of visible wealth, power, and suave self-assurance amazed me. This, I thought, is the other side of those smoking factories and the hovels we saw in Manchester and the other towns, where children collapse and die daily at their machines. And this is the visible profit produced by the terrible sugarcane plantations in Jamaica and Barbados, where slavery has been replaced by serfdom. The whole country seemed like a single, huge factory, whose raw materials and labor were fed into it from the barren hills of Ireland and Scotland and from distant tropical plantations. Liverpool was its shipping dock and London its counting house. I could not imagine myself as a member of the ruling class, one of these grand men and women passing me on the street; consequently, I thought that if I were an Englishman living in England, I would surely be one of those old Luddites, smashing machinery with hammers. And if I lived in one of the colonies, I would be like those old Maroons under Cudjo, escaped slaves living up in the mountains and slipping down to the plantations at night to set the cane fields on fire. In some countries, I said to myself, the only life you can properly desire is that of destroyer.

So on we went to Europe itself, hurrying east by train to Dover and by ferry boat to Flanders, and then by train again, click-clacking our way across green, marshy Walloon country to Brussels, and thence by foot, as the early morning mists rose from the meandering streams of Brabant, out the Charleroi road to the farm village of Waterloo, where a generation earlier the greatest armies and generals of Europe had hurled themselves against one another, settling in smoke and blood, once and for all, or so we believed back then, the fates of half the nations of the world. We knew nothing of what was coming after, of course; little enough of what had gone before. I was there that day merely because Father had led me there—Hurry, hurry, hurry!—and he had come to Waterloo because he wanted to see how, just when Napoleon was about to win it all, he had lost everything.

I was beginning to understand the Old Man's obsession with Napoleon and Waterloo. For a long while, it had seemed little more than another of his passing, erratic distractions, his characteristic way of not thinking about a thing that pained him, a practice that he was periodically inclined to indulge in, especially in times of stress, usually financial. Sometimes familial, of course. Sometimes political. But these wayward interests of his rarely lasted longer than the particular period of stressfulness, and as soon as the pressures on him eased a little, as they always did, he would return to his two great, permanent, ongoing obsessions—religion and the war against slavery.

This interest in Napoleon and Waterloo, however, had lasted longer than it should have. His expectations of financial success in the English wool market were now realistic, it seemed, and the pressures ought to have lifted. For the first time in years, he could think about wool and money without wincing in pain, which should have brought him straight back to slavery and religion. He did not have to think any longer about Napoleon—the greatest man of the century to most people, even to most Americans, but to John Brown, one would have thought, an evil genius, a small Corsican puffed up with delusions of imperial grandeur, a man whose vanity and shocking ambition had been responsible for the death and mutilation of hundreds of thousands of men at arms and the permanent impoverishment of millions of civilians. Father had no love for Caesar, and even less for those who, like Napoleon, wished to emulate him, no matter how brilliantly they waged war or how much adored they were by their followers.

That very morning, before leaving for the battlefield, I had asked him directly what was so wonderfully attractive about Napoleon. We were eating our breakfast, smoked fish and bread and cheese and rich, creamy milk—how clearly I remember that rough, fresh Flemish food! We were seated at a bench-like table in a roadside tavern a short ways outside the bustling, large market-town of Brussels, where, on our arrival late the night before, we had taken lodgings. We spoke no French, of course, nor any other European language, so Father had compensated by much pointing and by shouting in very slow English to the waiters, station attendants, and hotelkeepers, as if they themselves spoke English but did it badly and were hard of hearing. He managed to make himself understood, however, but only because our wants and needs were simple and obvious.

"I know that Napoleon's an *important* man," I said to him, "especially here, to the Europeans. But really, Father, what's he to us Americans, except a sort of cynical, power-hungry humbugger? In a democracy, a man like that would be successful only on the stage, or he'd be put in prison early."

Father laughed. "Or he'd run for senator from New York. And probably win it, too."

"I'm serious. Why do you admire him so?"

"*Admire* him, Owen? I loathe him! However brilliant a military man he was, he was nevertheless an atheistic monster, an egotistical dictator of the first rank. When he was finally declared dead on his little island of Saint Helena, while all over the world people wept, I cheered."

"Then why are we here?"

"Well, to put it simply, I want to understand why he lost. And this one battle made all the difference." It was Bonaparte's hundred days' march, Father explained, his final, mad plunge back into Europe from Elba, that intrigued him. Not that he was so successful, storming back from exile the way he did. Father said he would have expected that. It was a supremely intelligent move, with predictable results, once he made it. Except for his loss at Waterloo—that was not predictable. No, what intrigued and puzzled Father was that after such a success, which shocked and terrified all of Europe, in the end Napoleon failed. For future reference, Father explained, he wanted to know if Napoleon's defeat at Waterloo was due to a tactical blunder or to the superiority of Wellington and Blücher, the Prussian. Or did his own generals, the Frenchmen Ney and Grouchy, betray him? No evidence for that. Was it cowardice? Not likely. Too much caution? Highly unlikely. Too little? Perhaps. Regardless, it was important to know.

"You expect to learn that," I said, "here, now . . . what is it? Nearly forty years after the event?"

"Ah, my boy, sometimes you can only smell out these things in per-

son. When you walk the very ground of the history you're investigating, when you sniff the air, check the light, glance sideways and over
your shoulder, when you pick up a handful of the dirt and crumble it
between your fingers, you can learn things that no history book can
ever teach." Besides, he pointed out, the English historians all want to
celebrate Wellington, so they tell that version of the story, and the
Prussians are touting Blücher, and the French are intent on selling
everyone on either Napoleon's grandeur or the legitimacy of Louis
XVIII. The Old Man frankly didn't care who or what was won or lost
here. "I'm an American," he said. "I want only to know why he failed."

"Yes," I said, "but why do you need to know this? What's it got to do
with your plans?"

It was those one hundred days, he explained. One hundred days—
from Napoleon's unexpected departure with a half-dozen faithful lieutenants from the island of Elba, where he'd been exiled, to his arrival
here at Waterloo three months later with a quarter-million armed men
at his command. "That's what it's got to do with my plans," he said, smiling, and he got up from our table and made for the door. "Let's get going,
son!" he called. "We don't have a hundred days. As you said. We've only
got this one!"

The battlefield was a huge, rolling, hillocky expanse of low grass, like an
enormous cemetery without markers, criss-crossed by soft, overgrown
ditches and low ridges and bordered in the distance by a dark line of
yew trees, with squared-off, small fields beyond, where local farmers in
blue smocks and short spades made the fall turning of their soil by
hand. When we first arrived at the battlefield, the dew was barely off
the grass, and I followed the Old Man from site to site, while he
counted off steps, as if he were surveying the land and I were his assistant lugging the chain. Marking the advances and retreats, first of
Wellington's forces and the Flemish infantry, then those of his Prussian

counterpart, General Blücher, and the several French armies, Father seemed to have memorized the battlemaps, for he knew the exact positions of all the armies that had met here that June day in 1815, and he walked straight to them and paced off the distances between their lines.

"The ground all along here," he said, "where it slopes down to the plain, there, was soppy and wet. Yes, yes," he said, squinting down the field. On the night of the seventeenth, when Bonaparte arrived from Ligny, the Old Man explained, the ground was soft from two days and nights of rain, and then it stopped raining, and he waited until eleven the next morning. Up on the heights there, he said, pointing. Then, before marching against the Belgians and the Dutch, he waited for the ground to dry. That was important, the Old Man said—said to himself, actually, not to me. That was a crucial delay. It gave Wellington time to dig in on the opposite heights, Mont St. Jean they called it, barely a hill, but a good redoubt, if Wellington was given the time to fortify it.

Father strode abruptly down the long, grassy slope, to check the soil, I assumed, so as to determine how muddy it must have been at eleven A.M. on June 18, 1815, while I lagged behind and watched from the ridge. The sun had risen to above the hilltops behind us, and the day was growing hot, the air heavy with moisture. Making my way across the vast expanse of the battlefield, I came in a short while to a low grove of trees where a narrow stream wandered through. Here I took a seat in the shade beneath the trees, removed my hat, and leaned back against the friendly trunk of one and watched Father off in the distance, as he marched straight-legged uphill and down, counting out the paces, then stopped, peered around, touched the soil, scratched his chin, and, pondering for a moment, turned on his heels and marched off in a new direction, casting himself first as the entire army of one side and, a few minutes later, turning himself into the army of the other.

It was an amusing sight, and certainly he must have looked peculiar to the local farmers who were here and there working in the fields adjacent to the battleground—this lean, middle-aged man in a dark coat with flapping tails and a flat-brimmed hat set straight on his head, striding in geometrically precise lines beneath the hot, mid-morning sun over hill and dale, at meaningless points abruptly stopping and wheeling, pausing briefly with chin in hand, and suddenly putting himself on the march again. And while I myself was no more capable of actually seeing the things he saw out there than were those curious Flemish farmers who leaned on their spades and gazed after him, nonetheless I knew *what* he saw and heard and even smelled. I knew that he was deliberately, thoughtfully, with impressive, detailed knowledge, situating himself at the hundreds of points where the armies of six nations had met, and that he now walked in the midst of a thunderous battle, heard the angry shouts and pitiful cries of thousands of men falling face-first into the dirt and dying there straightway, saw the fire and smoke of long rows of cannon and the screaming horses going down and heard the crash of huge wagons and machines breaking apart, as wave upon wave of men marched suicidally against high walls of musketry, slashing sabers, blazing pistols, pikes, and daggers, until the lines broke and bloody hands reached out and grasped the throats of terrified, wild-eyed boys and men—farmers, artisans, and simple workmen fleeing for their lives, while all about the field human limbs were heaping up, arms and legs and heads severed brutally from the trunks, leaving howling, bloody mouths at the cut ends and the trunks cast down like so much meat, and the living, those who could still rise, staggering forward, covered with dirt, blood, feces, vomit, as behind them the corpses stiffened in the watery ditches and swelled and started to stink in the heat of the June day, and behind the corpses, up on the ridge, the generals plotted their next assault.

I sat on a hill in the shade of a tree, like one of the generals myself, and watched my father track and translate a series of elaborate, invisible runes in the distant fields. I watched a man controlled by a vision that I, his son, was too roughly finished to share, a vision that he would be obliged, therefore, to come back and report to me, just as he reported back to me his vision of the Lord. I believed in his visions, that they had occurred, and that they were of the truth—the truth of warfare, the truth of religion. This was what I had learned the night that I spoke with Miss Peabody aboard the *Cumbria*—her last night on earth and, in a sense, my first. I had changed my mind that night, as she had commanded, and forthwith had changed my self. In making my mind up, I had made my self up. And for the first time, the only necessary time, I had decided simply that my father's visions were worthy of my belief. The rest was like day coming out of night. I would remain, of course, a man made of ordinary stuff, and on my own had nothing else to work with. My great good fortune, however, was that my father was more of a poet than I, was a seer, and was perhaps a prophet. He was a man who saw things that I knew must be there but could not see myself, and because I loved him and trusted him, and because of the power of his language and the consistency of his behavior, my belief had swiftly become as powerful and controlling, as much a determinant of my mind and actions, as Father's belief was of his. In this refracted way— though I remained until the end his follower and continued to live with no clear plan of my own and no belief in God—I became during those days for the first time a man of action and a man of religion. The difference between us, between me and my father, is that I would inspire no one to follow me, either into battle or towards God, whereas he had me, and soon would have a dozen more, and finally whole legions and then half a nation, following him.

In the evening, after a supper of mutton that the Old Man much admired, we strolled until dark about the town of Brussels, and Father related to me his findings. We walked to the heart of the town and came out upon an ancient, cobblestoned market-square, where the town hall was located. There we admired for a while a large medieval statue of St. Michael trampling the devil under his feet. The statue had been placed on a spire atop the tall building, and to observe it we were obliged to stand at the furthest point in the square, our backs to a stone wall, peering up, as if watching an eclipse. Pronouncing the statue useful, Father declared it the sort of thing we ought to have more of in American towns.

"It's a Catholic statue, though," I pointed out.

"No, it's older than that. You don't have Catholics until you have Protestants. No, it's a Christian statue."

"And America is a Christian nation."

"It is, indeed," he said. "Or ought to be. It was surely meant to be."

We moved on then, and soon Father returned to the subject of Napoleon. All of Napoleon's reasons for being defeated at Waterloo, he stated, came down to his having lost the element of surprise. For three straight months, up to and including the time he arrived with his armies at Ligny and drove Blücher's Prussians from the field, Bonaparte had done the thing that was least expected of him. For that reason alone, all other things being equal or nearly so, he had come away victorious. But when he decamped at Ligny and moved on through the rain, he arrived at dawn at Waterloo, where he discovered that between his army and Wellington's somewhat exposed and approximately equal force, there lay a half-mile of marshy meadowland. Here, for the first time, he did the expected thing. He pulled up and waited for the sun to dry the field. That gave Wellington time to dig in and, as it turned out, time for Blücher's regrouped Prussians to arrive from Ligny. There was no way Napoleon could have defeated the Allies after that. For he had not done the *unexpected* thing. When Blücher arrived, it was nearly noon, and as the battle had just commenced, he was able to re-inforce

Wellington's army. That made all the difference. First, the element of surprise had been lost, and now things were no longer equal. Napoleon had to lose. Mathematics, simple numbers, had taken over. Certain victory was turned into a rout. For Napoleon, it was the end of his campaign, the end of his war, the end of his hundred days. There was nothing left for him now but retreat, eventual surrender, exile, the restoration of the monarchy in France, and a return to the *status quo* in the rest of Europe.

"What *should* he have done, then?"

"He should have done whatever Wellington least expected him to do. Which is, first of all, to attack. Attack at once." And not only should he have attacked at once, Father went on, for the mud would have hampered Wellington's army as much as his own, but he should have split his force into two equal-seeming parts. "Like Joab against the Syrians and the children of Ammon," he explained. "One part would be made the superior, however, the way Joab secretly placed the best men of Israel under his command and placed the rest, an inferior lot, under his brother, Abishai." Then Napoleon should have attacked from the two flanks, not to make a pincers, but to make two separate fronts, so as to force Wellington to divide his army into two parts also. Except that in Wellington's case, the two would not have merely *seemed* equal, like Napoleon's. They would in fact have been equal. Consequently, Napoleon's secretly superior half would have quickly overrun the British half opposing it. And his inferior portion over on the other flank would have triumphed also, because Wellington's side would have broken and run when they saw their opposite flank taken by a force apparently equal to the force facing them. "Just as the children of Ammon, when they saw the Syrians broken by Joab's army of the best men of Israel, fled from the inferior force under his brother, Abishai. Napoleon's greater false-half, in defeating Wellington's actual half, would be handing victory like a gift to his lesser half. Thus his army as a whole would have defeated Wellington's as a whole, and Blücher, arriving six hours later, would have been obliged to beat a hasty retreat back to Prussia. Napoleon would be emperor once again. He might still be emperor today."

We turned off the square onto a wide avenue and walked on, and while I pondered Father's findings and tried to apply them to his own planned campaign against the slaveholders of the American South, he whistled contentedly a favorite hymn and now and then paused to admire and comment upon the grand houses and impressive palaces of the town.

"It's a valuable lesson, then?" I said.

"What is?"

"Your discoveries concerning Napoleon's defeat."

"Yes, of course. We mustn't ever forget it. There will come a time, Owen, I promise you, when we will be cut down—unless we do the unexpected thing."

"When will that be? When's it coming?"

"Soon," he said. "Sooner than anyone thinks." He seemed then to drift off, as if observing future events with as much clarity as earlier today he had viewed the past. But a moment later, he abruptly returned and said, "First, however, we've got some business in Liverpool to attend to! We've got to sell some Yankee wool to our British cousins, my boy, and at a price that'll free us of debt, once and for all. I'm sick of living like a toad under a harrow!"

"Right!" I said, and laughed aloud. Not because of his figure of speech, but because it seemed so incongruous to be meditating one moment on warfare, ancient and modern, and the next to be planning strategy for the sale of wool. I could hardly wait for the day when we would no longer have to think about commerce and could bend all our energies and attention to war! War against the slavers! "I wish we could rush straight into battle now!" I exclaimed.

"Ah! So do I, son," he said, smiling. "So do I." And he walked on, hands clasped behind his back, head slightly bowed, as if it were the Sabbath and he were on his way to church.

Two days later, we arrived back in Liverpool and at once made ready to show our wool to the Englishmen. The morning before the auction was to take place, we came down bright and early from our lodgings to the warehouse, so as to be on the scene when the agents for the cloth manufacturers examined all the sheepmen's stock and set in their own minds how high they would bid later. This practice was a guard against being victimized by puffers, men who were sometimes secretly hired by the sheepmen to bid the prices up, and was, of course, when the prices for the various grades of wool were actually established and agreed upon among the buyers. It was no different here than in the United States, where there was a considerable amount of secret collusion between the buyers, most of whom had elaborate, long-term business dealings with one another, such as previous debts or deals, services owed or promised, goods with liens attached, and so on, often concerning some business quite other than that of purchasing wool and in some other city. Thus the auction itself was more or less a formality; there were seldom any surprises, and prices rarely moved up or down more than a fraction of a cent per pound.

In Springfield, for number 2 grade wool, before Father had withdrawn his entire stock from the marketplace to ship it abroad, Brown & Perkins had been offered, and had turned down, thirty-five cents a pound. Number 1 had been going for forty-one cents. The three higher grades, X, XX, and XXX, had been priced proportionally higher. Father's plan was to obtain in Liverpool a price of forty-five to fifty cents per pound for the number 2, low enough to undercut slightly the current English price, and to scale the other grades accordingly. After subtracting shipping costs and tariffs, he figured that he would still come out ahead by at least ten cents per pound, a net gain of twenty thousand dollars over what he would have gotten for the same wool in Springfield. Furthermore, as he had explained to me numerous times, by withdrawing Brown & Perkins's one hundred tons of wool from the domestic market, he had created an artificial shortage there, which would force the prices up for a time, and thus he would profit twice, here and now in England and next month in Springfield, when the fall fleeces arrived from the western sheepmen.

Father had me pull half-a-dozen bales of number 2 from different layers of our lot and haul them out onto the floor. This was normally a two-man job, but in those days, despite my crippled left arm, I was strong enough to handle a two-hundred-fifty-pound bale alone by grabbing it on top with my right hand and hooking the bale underneath with my left and slinging it up onto my right shoulder. If it was tied correctly and I had a strap, I could even lug it with one arm, like an enormous burlap-wrapped satchel. "Stack them over here, son," Father said, pointing to a place a short ways off from the others, so that our wool stood out from theirs.

I think that Father wished to make a bit of a show for the British gentlemen, who lounged about the cavernous space in several small groups, chattering idly amongst themselves, most of them in fine suits and silk cravats, affecting canes and wearing gloves and tall hats. We stood out anyway, due to our rough clothing and Yankee speech and manners, but the image of honest American yeomanry was perhaps what Father wanted to put on display, nearly as much as the wool from Brown & Perkins of Springfield, Massachusetts, and I wasn't displeased to play my role, the tall, strapping lad who tosses around two-hundred-fifty pound bales by himself.

Our counterparts, the British sheepmen, stood by their sample bales with caps in hand, silent, eyes cast down, as if they believed they were in the presence of lofty personages, feudal lords and squires, instead of scheming merchants. Father, by way of contrast, leaned against his stack of bales almost casually and whittled with his pocketknife on a stick he'd cut from the hedge by our boarding house and had brought along, I now realized, for precisely this somewhat theatrical purpose.

Soon a group of four or five buyers with slight smiles on their faces had gathered near us, examining our persons more than our bales of wool, all the while continuing to talk amongst themselves, in their drawling, nasal, English way, of their club dinner the previous evening. Then several more of the sanguinarians sauntered over, their walking sticks clicking across the warehouse floor, and soon there was a crowd surrounding us, looking bemused and a little bored. If they were impressed by who or what we were, they disguised it.

The clerk of the works, Mr. Pickersgill, a small man with a malmsey nose and Dutch spectacles, whose task it was to organize the sale and with whom Father had dealt on our arrival, came quickly out of his office and joined the group and nervously began to speak for us, as if we were Iroquois Indians and could not speak to these fine gentlemen for ourselves. "This 'ere's Mister John Brown from the firm of Brown and Perkins. It's a big lot 'e's got, sirs. Some seven 'undred bales at various grades. Hammericans," he declared, as if it were the name of our tribe.

"Indeed," said one. "From Pumpkinshire!"

"Extraordinary," said another.

"I like your cravat," said a third, a short, platter-faced fellow with an outsized head and a limp blond moustache. He removed one of his fawn-colored gloves and reached forward and tweaked the piece of soft leather that Father customarily wore at his throat, causing Father to cease his whittling at once and pull himself up straight and glare at the man, until he withdrew his hand and delicately wiped it with a handkerchief and replaced the glove.

There were several low har-hars from the group. Father resumed his whittling and said, "When you wish to examine my *wool*, gentle-men, please inform Mister Pickersgill, and I'll be glad to show it to you." He briefly stated that he had brought close to one hundred tons of clean, graded wool, all of it raised by expert sheepmen in the states of Ohio and Pennsylvania, and that his number 2 would prove superior to their X and equal to their XX, although he would price it to compete with their number 2.

There were a few snuffles of disbelief, and one of the Englishmen asked him who had graded his wool. "More to the point," he said, "who *cleaned* it?" and the company laughed, for it was unfortunately true that American wool was notorious in those days for not being clean, and a hundredweight of fleece might have as much as twenty pounds of dirt and feces stuck in it. This had been one of Father's ongoing concerns, making sure that Brown & Perkins wool was clean, even for the domestic market, where the practice of folding trash in with the fleeces was all too common. From the beginning of his and Mr. Perkins's Springfield enterprise, Father, although only a middleman, had made a great effort when purchasing the wool in the west to teach his shepherds how to wash their sheep thoroughly before shearing and how to pick the wool clean before shipping their clips to him in Springfield. His lectures on the subject at fairs and shows where he demonstrated his methods were famous among the sheepmen from New England to Ohio.

"Gentlemen, I have purchased every clip of this wool from shep-herds I've trained personally. It's been sheared from sheep whose stock I've improved with my own purebred merinos and Saxonys. And I myself am the man who has graded this wool. I've graded it, and my own sons and I have examined it before shipping for cleanliness." This was not exactly true, for it was impossible to examine closely two hun-dred thousand pounds of wool. One graded it by taking a single hand-ful of fleece from each shepherd's clip, and one sampled clips at random to check for dirt and hoped that the shepherds were as good as their promise to deliver clean wool. Which, for the most part, they were. Besides, Father could generally estimate two hundred fifty pounds of clean wool by casting his eye over its volume.

"An expert, then," said one of the Englishmen, a tub-bellied fellow with a yellow waistcoat stretched to its limits. "We have us an expert. He grades his own wool!" he said, turning to his fellows and smiling like a catfish.

"I *am* an expert, when it comes to grading wool. I've made it my business for nearly forty years, man and boy. Too many cunning shavers out there, gentlemen. Too many trimmers. Not enough honest men, like yourselves. But even so, a sheepman would be a fool not to know how to grade his own wool."

"And you're no fool, eh, Yank?" called one.

"Gentlemen," Father said, heating up, "I can grade wool in the dark."

"Indeed?"

"Aye. Blindfolded."

"Extraordinary!"

"I can read a clip blind, from a single tuft," Father declared, truthfully, for I had seen him do it hundreds of times.

The short man with the broad face and blond moustache then stepped forward and removed his own necktie, a blousy piece of fawn-colored silk that matched his gloves, and held it out to Father. "Perhaps you'd like to demonstrate, Mister . . . ?"

"Brown. Be glad to," he said, and he passed me his knife and stick, removed his hat, and tied the scarf around his head, blocking his sight.

"No help from you now, my fine golumpus," the man said to me, and he departed from the group and exited quickly from the warehouse, returning after a few seconds bearing a reddish tuft of hair in his gloved hand. "Now, Mister Brown, here's your sample," he said, and gave Father the tuft.

Father rubbed it between his fingers and dropped it at once to the floor. "Gentlemen," he pronounced, "if you have any machinery that will spin the hairs of a dog, one of those large, wire-haired red dogs, I believe, then I would advise you to put this into it," and with a flourish, he pulled off the blindfold.

After that, the Englishmen seemed more respectful of Father and more openly curious about our wool. We might be a couple of rustics from the republic of Pumpkinshire, but we were not fools.

Nor were they. After some pleasantries—during which the rotund man in the yellow waistcoat took a drink from a silver flask and extended it to Father, who naturally declined, suffering himself to be called, quite good-naturedly, a bloody parson—Father began once again to praise the quality of Brown & Perkins wool.

In the midst of his discourse, one of the more sober-visaged buyers, a man who up to now had been silent, interrupted him and said, "Mister Brown, I saw your son there setting out these bales. He's a stout lumper, I must say, especially with his dumb arm and all, my compliments, but really, sir, since it was so easy for him to heft these bales, perhaps you could have him replace them and pull from your stock a few that we ourselves might choose for appraisal. I'm sure you understand, sir." This man was tall and distinguished-looking, with a narrow gray beard. He was somewhat older than the others, and they seemed to defer to him—even Mr. Pickersgill, I noticed, whose interests were supposed to be the seller's, not the buyer's—for they all punctuated his statement with wise nods and pursed lips, as if for his approval.

Father wasn't pleased by the implications of the request, but he agreed to it, and I was obliged to haul the bales back, replacing them on the floor with three that the tall Englishman himself selected, all of them, like the first batch, marked number 2, the base-price grade.

"And now, my good man, if you would be so kind as to show us your fine American wool," said the Englishman, pointing with his cane at the center bale.

"My pleasure," Father said in a hard voice, and he cut the cord so as to expose a top corner of the bale.

"If you don't mind," said the Englishman, passing his cane to the man behind him, and he took the knife from Father's hand and swiftly cut away the rest of the cord, stripping the bale halfway down of its burlap wrapper. The snowy white fleeces, released to the open air, puffed up at once and grew to nearly twice their size, smelling sweetly of lanolin and freshly scythed grass, evoking a sudden, painful, unexpected memory of home, my first longing to return.

In silence then and in a strange sort of frenzy, five or six of the group rushed at the open bale and plunged their hands into it. They groped up to their elbows and pulled fleeces apart and grabbed great clumps of wool from the depths of the bale, sniffing it, rubbing tufts across their palms and between their fingers, passing snowy gouts back to their colleagues and reaching in for more. They were like a pack of ravening wolves. We had never seen this sort of behavior from buyers before and were stunned into silence.

Finally, Father recovered from his shock and called out, "Wait! Gentlemen, wait! You're ruining the bale! What on earth are you doing?"

They went on a few moments longer, until at last the tall man stopped and turned to Father and glared at him. "This, sir, is what you Americans call clean wool?" he said in a cold voice, and he reached back into the bale with both hands and drew from its depths a large quantity of wool, nearly a bushel of it, and dropped it at Father's feet. He retrieved his cane from one of his fellows and spread the wool out. It was filthy. Sticks, twigs, grass, and leaves and clots of dried fecal matter stuck to it.

Father's face reddened at once, as he realized what had happened. Bad luck, yes; but worse. Much worse.

"More dirty Yankee wool, eh?" one of the fellows in back called.

"Same old stuff."

"Filthy."

"Disgusting."

"So there's your Yankee parson, eh?"

Several men in the group broke away then and moved towards the English sheepmen further down. Mr. Pickersgill hesitated a moment, but quickly followed after them, as if eager not to be associated with us. The tall Englishman did not leave, however, and now he stared hard at Father, whose ears and neck were scarlet with embarrassment and anger. "Mister Brown," he said evenly, "I'm quite disappointed. Frankly, I took you to be an honest man."

"I am! I . . . this is a mistake, sir," he stammered. "A mistake. It's but a single bale. I . . . I myself have been cheated by this bale, sir."

"Indeed."

"No, really, sir. Why not examine another bale? Here, here, take a poke through this one," he said, indicating the next bale. "Owen, bring down some others for the gentleman to examine," he said.

"Never mind that. I think we've seen enough," said the Englishman. "Mister Brown, you'd have to open every bale and sort out all two hundred thousand pounds of your wool and separate the clean wool from the dirty and somehow wash and dry the rest, if you wished to sell it at the going rate now. You'd have to clean it the way it should've been cleaned in the beginning, and then repack it. All one hundred tons, Mister Brown. I rather doubt that you and your son have the time and money to manage that. And even then, Mister Brown, why should we trust you? Even then, no matter what you yourself claimed, we'd be buying the wool on faith, and there's a price for that, you know. It's not the going price, I'm afraid."

Father responded with silence and stared at the savaged bale with loathing.

"I'm sorry, Mister Brown. You seem like a decent fellow. I advise you to simply sell your wool here in Liverpool as it is. Get what you can for it, and return home happy to have sold it at all. There's enough of a shortage here this fall that you'll move it. It won't go untaken."

Father looked at him coldly. "You've got me in a vise, haven't you? You'll pay what you want for my wool, glut the market, and drive down the price of your homegrown stuff. Then you'll turn around and probably sell our wool back to the American clothmen, who'll pay dearly for it, due to shortages there." He was spluttering now, enraged, as his situation gradually became clear to him. The English buyers were about to make themselves a pretty profit twice over and in the bargain cheat the sheepmen on *both* sides of the Atlantic. They were probably arranging this very minute to provide short-term, high-interest loans to their New England colleagues for the purchase of Brown & Perkins wool in Liverpool at a lower price than it would go for at home.

"No one, except possibly you, is trying to cheat anyone, Mister Brown."

"I? I? I've been cheated more than anyone here!" Father shouted. "I can accept my personal share in this disgrace, sir, but I didn't know of it. I have been hurt here! Hurt worse than you can ever know. My partner, Mister Simon Perkins, has been damaged financially by this fiasco, as have I. But my honor has been damaged in this! My honor!"

"Yes. Well, I'm sorry for that, Mister Brown. Good day, sir," said the Englishman, and he walked away, leaving Father and me staring down at the wrecked bale of wool, its contents scattered over the floor at our feet. It was an ugly mess; it was also an indictment, and a trap. Father knew that he had been disgraced. And that it could only lead to further disgrace.

"Oh, Owen. What will I do? What will I do now?" His hard gray eyes suddenly softened and went wet, and his face fell and appeared to collapse into itself. I thought for a moment that he might sit down upon the floor and weep, and I reached forward and put my arm around his shoulders.

"Be the good shepherd, Father."

"Please, son. Don't talk nonsense."

"I mean it, be the good shepherd. Cease being the man who is the hireling and not the shepherd. Leave off being the man who doesn't own the sheep, and when he sees the wolf coming, abandons the sheep, so the sheep are scattered and slain."

"Yes. It's in the Book of John. Yes, I know."

"Be the good shepherd," I said again, for I wished him to understand that all these men were hirelings and wolves, and in this wool business we were but hirelings ourselves. And now, at the coming of the wolves, we appeared to have abandoned the sheep, who were our enslaved Negro brethren at home. "Be the good shepherd, the Bible says, and know thy sheep and be known of thine."

"Do I understand you, Owen?"

"I hope so. Yes."

"You're calling me back to myself. Aren't you, son?"

I told him that I was, and that we did not need to dwell so much either on victory or on defeat here amongst the hirelings and the wolves, so long as the outcome of our business with them was to depart from them at once and bring us back to our true selves. We should do here whatever we could and do it with equanimity and calm straightforwardness, I said, but then we should return at once to our true work, where our worth wasn't measured by our ability to obtain a few cents per pound of wool one way or the other. If we were doing our true work, our worth would be measured in links of broken chain, in manacles cast off, and in whips plucked from the hands of slavemasters and thrown upon the ground.

I was ashamed, I told him, to be as distracted as I had been lately by this business of selling wool, this business of being a hireling. I wanted to return to the real battle, to the only thing that mattered. I wanted to resume our war against the slavers and to wage war against them until they were dead, every single one of them, or until every Negro man and woman in America was as free as I was myself and our nation had become a holy sanctuary and was no longer a prison and a charnel house.

He smiled sweetly up into my face and embraced me. In a low, tremulous voice, he said, "You are fast becoming my greatest blessing, son. The Lord's greatest gift to me."

His old force quickly returned to him then, and he bade me pack up the strewn wool from around the floor and tie the bale back as before, while he went to Mr. Pickersgill and re-stated his desire to have our wool auctioned this afternoon as previously scheduled. "But I'll tell him not to accept less than twenty-seven cents per pound for number 2, thirty-five for number 1, and so on up the line." That would undercut the English prices enough to get it sold, he said, but not by so much that we'd be left with nothing to show for our troubles. It was less than what we would have got in Springfield last month, but it was the best we could do today here in England. "We'll just do what we can, and we'll move straight on from there. Right, son?"

"Right. Action, Father! Action, action, action!"

"Ah, that's the boy!" he said, his eyes gleaming with pleasure. "Owen, the Lord hath given thee an understanding heart. He hath given thee wisdom! Thou art my Solomon. I should have named thee Solomon!" he declared. "Should I do that, call thee Solomon?"

"No," I said, laughing. "Not unless you call yourself David."

His eyes widened comically, although he didn't intend to be funny, and he shook his head, as if to rid himself of the notion of being named David. Then off he hurried, to speak with Mr. Pickersgill, while I bent to the task of repairing the broken bale of dirty wool.

13

Our return from England to Springfield that autumn, hapless and empty-handed, the failed Yankee woolen entrepreneurs, was unre-markable—except for Father's renewed ferocity regarding the war against the slaveholders. We had, of course, heard the news, just before departing Liverpool, of the passage of the Fugitive Slave Act: it was in all the English newspapers. There were reports of disruptions and pub-lic demonstrations in Boston, New York City, and Philadelphia and widespread outrage, even among Northern whites who previously had been acquiescent, and calls for armed resistance for the first time from the Garrisonians (although Father did not count that for much). As a result of this cowardly piece of legislation, there was now no safe haven for escaped slaves anywhere in America. A Negro human being was like a wandering cow, identified by color and all too often by the owner's brand, returnable when and wherever found. And free Negroes, too, were terrified for their lives, for the new law turned every white citizen of every Northern state into an unpaid agent of Southern slaveowners and gave no legal protection to free Negro men, women, or children, any one of whom could be instantly transformed into an escaped slave merely by a bounty-hunter's say-so and hauled off to the South and sold as chattel.

Mostly, it was this Fugitive Slave Act that provided the Old Man with a new focus for his rage, which, since the debacle in Timbuctoo, had been somewhat deflected by the now-failed mission to England for Brown & Perkins and by our Flemish holiday, as I thought of it. Also, quietly, I had begun to encourage his rage, for I was now eager to test my own mettle in the fires of battle. This was a new role for me, heating up Father's blood, and it was strangely exhilarating to me. Who would have thought it: Owen Brown, the quiet son, encouraging the Old Man to march steadily against the enemy?

Despite our love and respect for him, I don't think we took his plan all that seriously, even when he rolled out his maps and described his strategies to people outside the family fold, as he had done with our friend Lyman Epps and poor Mr. Fleete, shot in the escape from Elizabethtown. Father had revealed his secret plan to a few white people, too, such as Mr. Thompson, our friend and neighbor in North Elba, before they broke over the matter of transporting the Negro couple from Richmond, and Mr. Gerrit Smith, back when he first made the arrangement to settle us in Timbuctoo. Whenever he did reveal his plan, the Old Man always swore his listener to absolute secrecy, naturally, but who would not eagerly guarantee silence? The plan seemed so crack-brained then that no one would have believed you if you told him what Old Brown was up to. We in the family certainly told no one, if for no other reason than that we were somewhat embarrassed by it. We wished to protect Father's reputation for probity, after all, and also our own. And who wants to be laughed at, especially on someone else's account?

Generally, then, until the autumn that Father and I returned from England, I had treated his plan for invading the South and liberating the slaves as another of his harmless diversions, an elaborate way for him to express the anger and frustration caused by his financial failures and by the pacifism and compromises of the other whites in the anti-slave movement and by the fearfulness and lack of unity among so many Negroes. It kept him from despair over his money-problems, and it stopped him from throwing up his hands in disgust and walking out on the abolitionists altogether. It was *his* fantasy, not mine.

There was one early occasion, however, when I actually, whole-heartedly, shared his dream of a war of liberation and terror. It occurred when he first revealed his plan to Frederick Douglass. I watched this distinguished, intelligent, worldly gentleman, a Southerner and an escaped slave himself, a man who knew the risks and stakes personally, a true warrior in the war against slavery—I watched Mr. Douglass take Father's military strategies seriously and felt ashamed of my skepticism and temporarily cast it off. Although it would be another two years before I rid myself of it for good, that night in '48 in Springfield, when Mr. Douglass first came to visit, was an important beginning of my life as a warrior, too.

I remember hurrying home on a dark, wintry night from the Brown & Perkins warehouse to our crowded little house on Franklin Street, hoping to be there in time for supper with the others. Walking slam-bang through the door into the front parlor, I saw Father seated at the table with a tall, broad-shouldered, dark brown man with a forceful jaw and a great leonine mass of hair. I recognized Mr. Douglass instantly, of course, for although I had not seen him in the flesh before this, engravings of his handsome, impressive face had appeared in any number of issues of The *Liberator* and other abolitionist periodicals. He was younger than I had thought him to be, still in his early thirties then, but with beginning streaks of gray in his hair. He had a massive face and a broad, high forehead, a wonderfully patrician look, but in an African way, as if he were a direct descendant of a long line of Ethiopian kings. Seated side by side at the old pine table where we normally took our meals, both men were gazing intently at a large sheet of paper—Father's map of Virginia and points south, I saw at once. His Subterranean Passway.

Back then, when we were newly located in Springfield and Brown & Perkins was briefly thought to be a thriving business, visitors to our home were often visibly surprised to see how modestly we lived. Mr. Douglass, in his fine woolen suit, sat stiffly at the table, his feet squarely under his chair, as if he were more accustomed to meeting white abolitionists in formal, velvet-covered parlors than in a workingman's dwelling-place. We owned very little furniture then, a continuing effect of the Ohio bankruptcy, which was actually of a benefit to us in that narrow, wood-frame row house—the rooms were tiny, like hutches, and we were a family of nine people and needed the space for our very bodies. We utilized the six small chambers in an unorthodox way, determined more by need than by convention, making the kitchen serve as a combination cookroom, washroom, and workshop and the front parlor as an office and for taking our meals. Father and Mary slept in the dining room proper, and we children, seven of us, were distributed by sex and age in the three sleeping rooms upstairs. It was a spartan home in a laborers' neighborhood but, withal, a cozy and cheerful place, where we had many guests and visitors, mostly unpretentious people, sheepmen from out west and Negroes connecting through Father to a line or way-station of the Underground Railroad, people who made themselves comfortable in such bare surroundings more easily, perhaps, than Mr. Douglass.

Father introduced me to the man. "This is my third son, Owen. He's been working late at the warehouse," he said, to explain the tufts of wool clinging to my clothing and hair and the dirt on my face and hands.

Mr. Douglass rose from his seat and extended his large hand and smiled gently. "A pleasure," he said, a simple statement made almost lordly by his powerful, deep voice and regal bearing. This was a man! I rubbed my hand on my coveralls and grasped his and shook it with enthusiasm, although I was too shy and awed by him to speak a single word.

"Mister Douglass is on his way to Rochester, from a speaking engagement in Boston. He learned of us from the Reverends Garnet and Loguen," Father said, obviously pleased by having been recommended by the two Negro radicals. "They said we were to be trusted. No small encomium for a white man, if I may say so, coming from those two," he said to Mr. Douglass with evident pride.

Mr. Douglass smiled generously at Father. "Yes, that's true, I'm afraid."

"When you've washed and changed your shirt, Owen, you may come and join us," Father then said.

I rushed through my ablutions back in the kitchen, where Mary and Ruth and the younger children were at work preparing supper. John was then still in Akron, finishing his business school studies, and Jason and Fred were situated in Hudson, minding Mr. Simon Perkins's flocks. Although I was the eldest son then in residence, I was still young enough to be surprised and honored by Father's invitation to join him and Mr. Douglass in the parlor.

When I arrived back at the table and took my seat next to Father, I saw that he was showing Mr. Douglass his sketches of the log block-houses that he intended to build at strategic points along the Passway, forts to serve both as supply depots for his army and as way-stations for passing the liberated slaves north—those who chose not to stay in the South and fight alongside him and his main force. Father had long ago designed these simple structures: easily defended, windowless cubes made of thick logs with firing slots and secret basements and long escape tunnels, they were to be tucked away in the narrow defiles and gorges of the Appalachians. He believed, against all conventional thinking on the matter, that a military force could better defend a low place than a high. In Deuteronomy, the Lord had warned the Israelites against settling in high places—and for good reason, according to Father. "First, because in a low place you'll have a well, and your water won't run out. And second, because if the defile is sufficiently narrow, you can't be surrounded. In order to lay a siege against you, the enemy will be obliged to divide his force and climb to the heights. At which point, you proceed at once to charge against the weakened force left below, and then you quickly surround the climbers on high, who will now be under siege by *you*, trapped without water and with no way down except by your leave."

"I see," said Mr. Douglass. "And you propose to man each of these blockhouses with a small force of . . . what? Twenty-five men at the most?"

"At most," Father said.

"Whilst your main army conducts forays into the flatlands below."

"Exactly."

"Fine, but how shall they be supplied? Your main forces can't do it. They'll be too busy eluding capture and hanging by the slaveowners."

"They'll be supplied from the North," Father explained. He would establish agents in Ohio and Pennsylvania, whose responsibility would be to gather and store supplies and arms purchased for them by radical abolitionist supporters and to ship them south along the Passway, even as freshly liberated slaves came north along the same route. No wagon would come south empty, just as no wagon would return empty, either: the Underground Railroad was to run two ways now, instead of one. Father's main army, he went on, would simply take its supplies, its food, fresh horses, and so forth, from the raided plantations. They would also have whatever food and supplies they were given by sympathetic Southern whites. For there would be some supporters among the whites, Father was sure, small farmers and the like, who, not owning any slaves, were bound to be profoundly disgusted by the ways that the system oppressed them, too, people who would therefore welcome the opportunity to aid and abet men come south to wage war against slavery.

Here Mr. Douglass shook his great head. "I think, Mister Brown, that you don't know those folks like I do. You're a white man and perhaps understand whites, but you're not a Southern white man. Go on, though. There's much to admire here anyhow," he said gently.

A sustained, guerilla war would swiftly drive the price of a slave worth one thousand dollars today to ten thousand dollars or even more, Father explained. The cotton could not be grown, harvested, ginned, shipped, and sold without a huge labor force, and there were not enough whites in the South to accomplish that great and economically necessary task alone. Father was convinced that if the fight lasted long enough and caused a sufficient number of slaves to escape, the costs of holding on to their slaves would so greatly outweigh the benefits that the Slavocracy would move to strike a deal that would free all slaves in exchange for their return home as paid workers. "Slaves run north for *freedom*," Father noted, "not work." If they had freedom, they would stay, and many of those now living in the North would likely return also. "I do not intend to *conquer* the South," Father declared. "I merely mean to make slavery prohibitively expensive. If a people cannot be made to do the right thing, Mister Douglass, then we must make them do the thing that is in their interest."

For this reason, he was convinced that his war of liberation must be undertaken now or very soon, before slavery was extended into the western territories. If we did not strike now, he said, when the Southern states, because of their dependence on cotton, were economically vulnerable and more or less evenly matched in Congress by the North, then we would be faced later with only two alternatives—division of the Union or a bloody civil war. Or perhaps both. The longer we delayed, the more successful the South would be in extending slavery into Texas and the other territories, and even into Cuba and Mexico. Expansion out of the South into the west and the Caribbean isles would diversify the slaveholding economy from cotton and soon make it powerful beyond belief, and as those territories became states, they would come to dominate the North in Congress. With a slaveowning Democrat President, Senate, and House of Representatives, the North would have no choice but to secede from the Union or, to avoid total absorption by the Slavocracy, go to war. There were already calls for secession-or-war from both sides.

"Yes, but let me be sure, Mister Brown, that you're not resurrecting that old idea of a black republic. Your plan could produce that. I would vehemently oppose that. A little land-locked Haiti, separate from and surrounded by a white United States," Mr. Douglass said. "I would not wish for that."

"No, no, no! Not at all. Well, temporarily, perhaps. But only as a way of keeping the venture from being mistakenly construed as a policy of the Northern states," Father insisted. He wished to do it more or less the same as the Texans had done against Mexico. He planned to publish assurances that as soon as slavery was abolished in every state and territory, his temporary Negro republic would be dissolved, at which time all conquered regions would be returned to the control of their original state governments.

Mr. Douglass sighed heavily, a melancholy exhalation, and peered down at the map before him. "The federal army will come after you, sir. It doesn't matter, North or South—they won't permit it."

It would take them too long to act, Father explained, and when they did, he would have moved his forces to another front. From the mountains of Virginia, we would slip down to the mountains of North Carolina and Tennessee and on into the hills of Georgia. We would be divided into small, highly mobile units, little more than bands, striking where least expected and then retreating to our mountain hideouts, disappearing into the upland forests like the Seminole Indians into the swamps of Florida. Also, as he pointed out, our campaign would have hundreds of thousands of civilian supporters, millions, North and

South, which would weaken to a crucial degree any federal army commissioned to stop us. "A federal army would have to cut down every
tree from Alabama to Ohio to defeat us!" Father said, wagging a finger.

"They well might. Perhaps—" Mr. Douglass began.

Father interrupted him. "Also, I believe that our job could be completed in a single year, too soon for them to muster the requisite force.
On the first day, right off, we'd issue a statement of our intentions and
show our willingness to negotiate a peace strictly in terms of the ending of slavery. We'd be absolutely clear that we have no other intention
but to end slavery. A war conducted without a precise goal can never be
won! Remember that, Mister Douglass. I learned it in Europe. By the
same token, the more precise the goal, the fewer soldiers needed to win
it. Learned that there, too. You must state your objective clearly and
then show that you're willing to die for it, and if you can demonstrate
that it's in your enemy's own interest to have you gain your objective, as
we'll do by making the market price of every slave in America insup-
portably high, victory will fall into your lap like an overripe fruit!"

While the two went back and forth, Father explaining and defending his ideas and Mr. Douglass questioning them, gently objecting here
and there, but gradually, as it seemed to me, going along, I looked
freshly at Father's map of his wonderful Subterranean Passway. It was
the central nervous system for his whole operation, a spinal cord that
ran from Timbuctoo south all the way to Alabama, with a thousand
nerve-like branches east and west along the way. I remembered, years
before, first tying into it from a western branch, riding down from
Ohio with Father and my brothers into the hills of Kentucky, where we
met slaves who had escaped from plantations far to the south in
Georgia and South Carolina, exhausted men, women, and children
who had been passed along for weeks, emerging blinking into the light
of freedom as if they had come up from a network of tunnels hundreds
of miles long. And I knew that Timbuctoo, where we would soon be liv-

ing, tapped into the Passway at its head in the Adirondacks, and lately we had come at it from the east here in Springfield, Massachusetts, where I had seen the great Harriet Tubman, she whom Father called The General, "a woman who is most of a man," he said, and heard her testify as to its existence. It was real, this Subterranean Passway. Father had not dreamed it up. The slaveholders had not been able to sever it or to block it permanently anywhere along its length. If they attacked it in one place, it appeared the next night in another. Father's plan for a guerilla war against the Slavocracy was, in fact, a logical extension of the ongoing work of the Underground Railroad, and he had focused his thinking on the one aspect of the Railroad that no other abolitionist had so far grasped—that its continued existence had slowly raised the dollar value of slaves. He was proposing simply to accelerate that process.

Mr. Douglass said to Father, "Well, I do admire your plan, Mister Brown. Or, rather, I should say that I admire portions of your plan. Naturally, you aren't the first man, white or Negro, to propose leading an armed rebellion among the slaves. It's a common enough dream. But, unlike most others, you've anticipated many of the difficulties. And you have the large picture in mind as well. One thing, however. A question. I have many questions, sir, but this one first. I assume that you yourself plan to be the general for this army. And also the president of this 'temporary' Negro republic in the mountains. Does this mean that you, sir, would be our Moses?" Mr. Douglass smiled, but his words belied the smile.

Father looked at him straight. "I'll tell you the truth. I'll tell you the reason I've revealed all this to you tonight, Mister Douglass. I would have *you* be the Moses of your people, sir. Not me, and not any other white man. No, Mister Douglass, I would be Aaron unto thee, anointed and consecrated by thee, and then I would go forth and make the blood sacrifice for both our peoples. The crime against one is the sin of the other, and to avenge the crime is to expunge the sin."

There was a long silence as the two looked directly into one another's eyes—dark, melancholy eyes and flashing gray eyes. On the Negro man's face was imprinted a great question, and on the white man's face a great statement, and the two, wordlessly, were struggling to make them match. I don't think that Mr. Douglass had ever heard a white man speak like this before, at least a white man whom he did not think crazy. And I don't believe that Father had ever spoken quite like this before.

In a low voice, Father said, "I have four grown sons who will follow me into the South."

Who was the fourth? I thought, and then remembered our poor Fred. But, yes, why not Fred, too? In this matter, what was true of John, Jason, and me was true of him also. Yes, we will follow you, all four of us.

Father then said, "I have raised every member of my family to take this war straight to the slavemasters. They and I are prepared to die for it."

Mr. Douglass slowly turned his great head to me. He looked me up and down and said, "Well, is this true, young man? That you're prepared to *die* in battle? To die for the benefit of Negro slaves? Are you ready to give up your young life so that another young man, whose skin is black, can live as a free man?"

I glanced again at Father's map of the Passway and saw that it was a good plan; it would work; he was right—victory would fall into our lap like overripe fruit. And I remember thinking then that I would not die; I could not: I was strong and intelligent, I could run very fast, I was a fine shot and a first-rate horseman and could live in the forest like an Indian: and so I said to Mr. Douglass, "Yes, sir, I'm prepared for that. Father has prepared me pretty well. He has anointed and consecrated me and prepared me for the blood sacrifice, like Moses did for Aaron."

I saw Father suppress a look of simple pride and perhaps surprise at the boldness of my speech. He said, "So you see, Mister Douglass. I may well be Moses, but only here, in my own house."

"Yes," he said. "I do see. And I confess, I'm mightily impressed by all this. My brothers Garnet and Loguen, when they told me that you're a very unusual white man, were not wrong." He admitted, however, that all talk of slave rebellion made him nervous, especially when it was generated by men who themselves, white or Negro, would remain safely at home in the North, while the poor slaves rose up and got cut to pieces. Very few men were willing to be a Nat Turner. "But no matter how it goes, win or lose, there'll be death and gore enough for any man, believe me, Mister Brown. No matter how ingenious your plan or how brave you and your sons are, there will be killing on both sides. And I'm not sure I want to be responsible for that. Not yet anyhow. These are mighty questions before us, sir."

Mary and Ruth had set the table and were now carrying our supper out from the kitchen in several steaming pots. Father cleared away his charts and papers, as the children came and joined us, and soon we were ten people gathered around the table. Father, as always, commenced to pray over the food. While he prayed, I stole a glance down the table at Mr. Douglass, who was watching the scene as if from a great height with an expression of sweet approval on his broad face.

I looked over the scene myself then, to view it from his mild perspective—and saw a deeply religious family of modest means, a family with great peace of mind, with total unity and strange clarity of purpose, the wife and the children, from the eldest to the infant, instructed and led in all things by the firm but kindly Puritan patriarch, this straight-backed, gray-eyed man with light in his face, praying over them all: and most amazing of all, they were a clan of white people who saw the world, inexplicably, the way Negroes did.

We did not, of course. Not back then, we didn't—except possibly for Father. As a family, we had not yet undergone our trial by fire, our harrowing in Kansas and Virginia. And I dare not believe that even Father saw the world back then in Springfield as Negroes did; it only seemed

so, because of the vast difference between him and other white abolitionists in their personal treatment of Negroes, and because of the quality of his rage.

Besides, I had lied to Mr. Douglass. I was not willing to die for the
freedom of the Negro, or for any other reason. But I did not know that
then—I had thought that I was telling the truth, when in fact I was
merely incapable of imagining my own death. Though I was twenty-
four years old, I was still a boy. It really wasn't until nearly two years
later, during my journey to England, that I came to a point where I was
truly willing to pay the price of being the man I wished to be and was
willing, therefore, to die in the war against slavery. Once I'd reached
that point, I was myself free and was no longer a boy. I had become a
warrior, and thenceforth began increasingly to be of good use to Father,
whose force and clarity of purpose, as happens to all warriors, sometimes weakened or grew confused.

Father had been right about the British cloth manufacturers. They had
purchased our wool at prices so low they could sell it at a considerable
profit straight back to their American counterparts, those same sly fellows whose monopolistic bids for Brown & Perkins wool had driven
the Old Man into the English market in the first place. Thus, by shipping his and Mr. Perkins's one hundred tons of wool off to England and
selling it at discount there, Father had succeeded only in increasing the
company's indebtedness to its western suppliers. He had nearly doubled it, in fact. And the sheepmen were furious. From their perspective,
their wool, a full year's work, had been practically given away.

For a few days, before leaving England, the Old Man had tried
blaming the sheepmen themselves, for trapping him with a few
unlucky bales of dirty wool, but that would not hold up. He'd trapped
himself, and knew it. In his rush to move all his stock to England, he
had abandoned his usual rigor in checking the wool, and he'd graded it

carelessly as well—a surprising amount of XXX and XX turned out to be number 1 and number 2. Thus, by the time we were aboard ship and headed home, he had ceased to blame anyone but himself, and for most of the crossing back, the Old Man beat his breast and spoke with thees and thous.

The truth was, again, that he had failed miserably, and there was no hiding it, not even from himself. The absurdity of his situation, the ridiculously tangled nature of his finances, had reached a point where he could no longer imagine ever getting free of it and would be forced to work now mainly to keep himself out of prison, for he knew that he was about to be deluged by a flood of lawsuits, large and small. Many of the sheepmen were convinced, unfairly but understandably, that Father had taken a bribe to ship their wool to England and sell it at such a devastating loss. They could not believe that a sane man would have done such a thing otherwise, and they were already serving notice to John in Springfield that they thought so. Fortunately, Mr. Perkins was still willing to stand by the Old Man, which would enable him to keep the family intact and sheltered in North Elba: if we had land, we could always feed and clothe ourselves. Father himself, however, would soon be racing from courthouse to courthouse, back and forth from New England out to the old Western Reserve, defending himself and Mr. Perkins against the myriad charges of fraud and deceit that were being raised by their creditors.

Knowing that this would become his main activity for a while had the unexpected benefit of taking Father's mind for the first time in decades completely off moneymaking. It would allow him, when he was not preparing his attorneys to defend him and Mr. Perkins in court, to concentrate on his anti-slave activities. The catastrophic losses in England were such that, at last, he would be able to forget about becoming a rich man. Released from that possibility, he went through a sort of sea-change and began to be instead the man who entered history.

And, of course, things had changed at home, too. The passage of the heinous Fugitive Slave Act at once lit up the Northern sky like sheets of lightning and electrified thousands of white men and women who up to now had regarded themselves as moderate abolitionists. And suddenly our anger, our consuming rage, did not seem so odd anymore. Which was strange to me, for I had grown used to our family's being both charged by its anger, as if it were our responsibility, and isolated by it, as if it were our curse. Now that rage was the norm, however, ours seemed to have been oddly premature and, in this new context, somehow inappropriate and useless. At least to me it did.

Father simply declared that it proved we had been right all along. But we had spent so much time and energy for so many years, all the years of my life, justifying in moral, legal, and Biblical terms the ferocity of our position, that we had not stepped away from it and considered its deeper and more personal sources. We had not even considered whether it had such sources. What was abnormal to others had long seemed normal to us—until, thanks to the Fugitive Law, everyone else turned out as alarmed and angry as we and as determined as we to commit acts of violence in order to deter the further extension of slavery. Earlier, our alarm and anger and commitment had seemed evidence of our election, as it were, proof of our moral superiority. Now, however, we were no longer positioned amongst our people like prophets, for every decent person in the North was finally awake to the emergency. Or so it briefly seemed. And during this period, instead of feeling at one with my neighbors and grateful for that, I began to wonder why had we seen so early the horrors of slavery, when practically everyone else was blind to it, and why we had been so ferocious, when nearly every other well-intended Northern white man and woman had merely been concerned or, at best, disgusted.

It is difficult for me now, a whole lifetime beyond those years, to cross over all the terrible intervening events and alterations in the sensibilities and values of ordinary folks and remember how we thought then. The Civil War changed everything for everybody, white and Negro, North and South, East and West; but it was the war before the War, in Kansas and then at Harpers Ferry, that changed us Browns. That's when we went from being angry activists and prophets in the wilderness to being cold-blooded warriors. We went from helping Negroes escape from slavery to killing those who would enslave them. Those were the years when John Brown and his sons—farmers, shepherds, tanners, hopeful businessmen—became famous killers.

Who else in our time went through this transition? No one, until later, when forced to by the War. By then, John Brown and his sons, most of them anyhow, were dead—slain in battle or executed on the scaffold. It was as if, when our white neighbors finally woke to the threat of slavery and grew angry, as angry as we had been all along, we moved at once to the next stage and in that way kept our old position towards them intact. It was as if our true nature, Father's nature, certainly, and mine, and to a lesser degree the nature of our family as a whole, arose from our insistence on maintaining a constant distance from others, on holding to our radical extremity. We would not allow ourselves to be like other white people. We would be angrier than they; we would risk and sacrifice more than they; we would be bloodier, more brutal, more consistently merciless and desperate than they.

We were becoming like Negroes, or wanted to become like them. Or, to be honest and exact, we were becoming the kind of men and women that we wanted Negroes themselves to be.

Can that have been true? For many years, I had sometimes thought that Father's obsession with the enslavement of the Negroes was an unnatural thing. No other white man or woman in my acquaintance was so singularly enraged by the fate of black people, not even the most radical abolitionists, not even Gerrit Smith, who had given so much of his huge personal fortune to the cause. There were heroes in the movement, of course, men and women like Theodore Weld and the Grimké sisters, even a few who had given their lives for it, like Lovejoy. And there were many unknown people, men and women in small towns, clergymen, teachers, even businessmen, who had risked fortune, reputation, and physical well-being in order to advance the war against slavery. And everywhere there were poor, humble, God-fearing white folks, ordinary men and women who daily made sacrifices and endangered themselves for the benefit of the Negro slaves.

But none of these, at least none that I ever met or even heard about, engaged the Negro on such a personal level as did Father. It was as if he secretly believed that at bottom he himself was a Negro. He seemed to believe that his white skin—and the skins of his children, too, and of his wife, and the skin of anyone who would cleave to him in his enterprise—was black underneath. As if his rust-colored hair, if he did not dye and forcibly straighten it, were black and crinkled. As if his old-fashioned, pointy, New England Yankee face, that long, narrow hooked nose, grim slash of a mouth, and large red ears, were a mask hiding an African nose, mouth, and ears.

In a racialist society like ours, such a belief might be seen as merely absurd or as self-contemptuous, especially by white people, and in any society, racialist or not, it might be viewed as morally reprehensible. He could be accused, after all, of appropriating another man's rewards for having endured great pain without having first been obliged to experience that pain himself. I have thought about this matter for most of my life, for I came to be very like my father in it, and I may well be dead wrong about it, but Father's love for Negroes was not a simple extension of his love of justice, of his belief in the essential equality of all mankind, or of his abhorrence of cruelty, which was the case for most abolitionists and which should have been sufficient unto the cause. And mostly was. For most white abolitionists it *was* sufficient, certainly, and for most Negroes. Negroes, after all, did not need white people to love them. They merely needed us to deal justly with them, to grant them legal rights equal to our own, and not to be cruel to them merely because their skins were darker than ours. They only wanted us to treat them as well as we treated each other. As they saw it, the word "colored" described all human beings. To Negroes, white was as much a color as black, red, or yellow—if not more so.

If the country had been made of one race of people, if everyone had been white, then Father would not have singled out white people for his love, obviously. But he would not have looked eastward across the Atlantic and loved African Negroes, either; or black-skinned people anywhere. No, he loved *American* blacks, and he loved them, I believe, because of their relation to the dominant race of American whites. He saw our nation as divided unfairly between light-colored people and dark, and he chose early and passionately to side with the dark. Something deep within his soul, regardless of his own skin color, something at the very bottom of his own sense of who he was, of who he was especially in relation to the dominant, lighter race, went out to the souls of American Negroes, so that he was able to ally himself with them in their struggle against slavery and American racialism, not merely because he believed they were in the right, but because he believed that somehow he himself was one of them.

Of course, he was *not* one of them. He was a white man, with all the inescapable powers, privileges, and prerogatives of his race and sex: he could vote, own property, move about the land and settle wherever he chose; he could belong to any institution or church or attend any school he could afford; he could borrow money and loan it; he could invest his money in land or livestock and grow rich or become a bankrupt; he could own firearms; he could go to sleep at night and not fear that he would be wakened by slave-catchers and bounty-hunters come to sell him down the river; he knew who his parents, grandparents, and great-grandparents were and where they were buried; his children and wife would never be taken from him by another man; he was a white man, and he knew it.

And yet are there not adult men and women, with all the powers, privileges, and prerogatives of adults, who secretly think of themselves as children? Is it not as if our large, hairy bodies are merely fortunate disguises, and some of us are children going about in the adult world like spies, our hearts breaking daily at the sight of what our fellow children must suffer solely as a consequence of their not being as cleverly disguised as we? In cautious silence, we observe the cruelties and indignities, the inequities and powerlessness they must endure, until at last their bodies, too, grow large and hairy like ours and they are able to pass into the general population of adults, where, like most people, they either forget that they were ever children themselves or else they, too, become spies. We dare not identify ourselves one to the other, for fear that we will lose the powers and privileges of adulthood, and so we remain silent, whilst other people's children are beaten instead of nurtured, whilst other people's children are humiliated and bullied instead of taught, whilst other people's children are treated as property, as objects of little value, instead of as human beings no less valuable in the eyes of the Lord than are we ourselves.

I believe that it was like this for Father, and became like this for me as well: that very early in his life, he came to feel towards white people generally as an unusually sensitive child feels towards brutal, unfeeling adults generally. He felt powerless, humiliated, and deprived, and felt it so strongly, so vividly, that he could not put it away when the circumstances which had brought about those feelings changed and no longer applied to him—that is to say, when he had become an adult himself and saw himself as white. Instead, he began dreaming himself as a Negro man, if he was anything like me—and I believe that he was—because his dream of himself as a child was too much a nightmare to endure and too powerful an experience for him to forget. This did not mean that he saw Negroes as children, and certainly not as child-like, any more than he saw himself as a child or child-like. He merely saw them, in their relation to white people, as his natural allies.

Once, I tried to bring this to him. I had been telling him of a dream I myself had had, in which I looked down at my arms and hands, and they were black. Where were we? I remember, it was the winter of '58, and we were in Kansas, crossing down into Vernon County, Missouri, the time that we brought out eleven slaves and made such a wondrous fuss, our first raid into a slave state, and Father and I drove the wagon. Jason and Watson were with us then, along with Jeremiah Anderson, Albert Hazlett, and John Kagi, several of the men who came out of the Kansas wars and made up the core of our little army later in Virginia.

In my dream, I was surprised to see that I was a black-skinned man, but the discovery had pleased me and even made me proud, although it made me realize that from now on, when amongst white people, I would have to hide my true self.

It was at that time a strange dream to me, and I asked Father as we rode along if he ever had such a dream. He said yes, certainly, he had often dreamed himself as a Negro man, and whenever he did, he took it to mean simply that the Lord was reminding him not to allow himself to feel separate from His Negro children. He had the dream mostly when Negroes were giving him a lot of trouble, he said. When they would not do what he wanted, or when he could not do what they wanted.

I asked him then, "When did you first know that Negroes were as human as you yourself?"

Father knew that I wasn't merely inquiring into the origins of his principles, for they had evolved naturally over years, as principles must. I was asking him about the sources of his understanding. He answered that he had been little more than a boy when, for the first time, he believed that Negro people were actually *people*, and he had never forgotten it. Many white people, including his own father, had taught it, of course, but Father had not until then truly understood it. Most white people don't ever get that understanding, he said. Just as most men don't believe, truly and deeply, that women are people. They think that, because they're different than we, they are another type of creature than we, as a beloved horse or dog is.

"I was twelve," he went on, "and my father sent me by myself with a herd of livestock—cattle, mostly, but a few wild steers, too, and pigs, a sizeable, troublesome herd—all the way to General Hull's headquarters at Detroit. It was a hundred-mile trek, west from our place in Hudson in Ohio along the long shore of Lake Erie through hostile Indian territory, because of the War and the British agitations, to where the American forces were holding off the British in the western campaign. No easy task for a boy of twelve," he said simply. Grandfather Brown was then supplying meat to the army, and Father had accompanied him on several previous journeys to the front, but this was the first time that he had done it alone. He had told this much of the story before, but mainly as an example of his youthful independence.

"Anyhow, I stayed up there for a spell with a very gentlemanly landlord, a man once a United States marshal, who held a slave boy very near my own age. The boy was a very active, congenial lad, intelligent and full of good feeling, and to whom I was under considerable obligation for numerous little acts of kindness. The master made a great pet of me," he said. The man had brought Father to table with his first company and friends and called their attention to every little smart thing he said or did and to the fact of his being more than a hundred miles from home alone with a herd of cattle.

"All the while, this fine Negro boy, who was fully my equal, if not more, was badly clothed, poorly fed and lodged in cold weather, and he was beaten before my very eyes with an iron shovel or any other thing that came to the master's hand. This terribly insulted my new-found pride in my accomplishments and my general smartness. It was as if I myself were being insulted and beaten. I'm ashamed to this day that I said nothing in protest," he declared. It brought him, however, to reflect in a way that was new to him on the wretched, hopeless condition of slave children. On their being without a father or mother to protect and provide for them. That lad was alone in the world, and it was hateful to Father, the way the boy was treated. "The boy was so alone, Owen, that later, in my bed, I wept bitterly for him." He said nothing for a few moments as we rode along the rough trail, and I thought that he was fighting off tears now at the memory of the Negro boy. After a while, he seemed to gather his emotions and said, "I was decidedly not a Christian at that age. But I remember wondering for the first time if perhaps only God was that slave boy's father."

"Who would have been his mother, then, if God was his father?" I asked.

"Well, he would have no mother, I guess. No earthly mother, for certain, and no heavenly mother, either. God alone would have to be sufficient. As He is sufficient for us all. And had he not been one of God's children, the boy would have been a truly lost soul. That was a thing I could not imagine in a child." He paused for a moment and added, "I understood that, I suppose, for I had lost my own mother by then."

"Like me."

"Yes. Like you."

Ordinarily, when such an exchange occurred between us, Father would have corrected me, pointing out that I had a mother, after all, my stepmother, Mary. But this time he must have been remembering with unusual vividness how it been for him when he, too, was only eight years old and had not yet found God when his mother died and left him with only his earthly father. When he had been a truly lost soul. So he did not correct me, and we rode on into Missouri in a brooding silence.

I had learned something important, though. For the first time, I had perceived, however dimly, that there existed a significant connection between the way Father felt towards the Negro and the terrible, desolating wound he had suffered in his heart when his mother died. Though no one knew of it, of course—probably not even Father himself—it was not his principles but the lifelong effects of his childhood wound that had made the American Negroes his natural ally and that, in their eyes, made him that rarest of things, a trustworthy American white man. They trusted his rage, which he had come to direct entirely against slavery. And they trusted his permanent suspicions of white people, especially when it came to the subject of race: he was always ready to be betrayed by whites and even often thought Negroes too easily duped by them. Also, Negroes trusted his inability to forget about race, his insistence on seeing it as a factor in every dealing, every relationship, every conflict, between any two Americans, whether they were of the same race or not. Father took race to be the central and inescapable fact of American life and character, and thus he did not apologize for its being the central fact of his own life and character. And to the degree that my nature resembled his, by virtue of my upbringing, of my own desolating wound, which was so like Father's, and of my having deliberately modeled myself on him, race was the central factor of my life and character, too. And by the time we returned from our English journey to Springfield and took up the fight anew, I had become sufficiently accepting of my nature that I, too, no longer apologized for it.

It did not take long for Father to throw himself into a plan for creating in Springfield an armed and trained militia among the Negroes there. And while it was perhaps my plan as much as his, for he had begun increasingly to consult with me, it was his forcefulness, his public voice, and his prestige among the Negro population that drove it to completion.

Ever since his first arrival in Springfield as a woolen merchant back in '47, he had attended the Zion Methodist Church, which was an abolitionist dissident church, half of whose parishioners were Negro, and he had preached there frequently and from time to time had taught a Bible class. Consequently, he was well-known and admired in the community he most wished to reach.

Within a day of our return from England, he secretly gave out to several of the most outspoken and respected Negro men of the town that he would be holding a series of late-night meetings at the Zion Methodist sanctuary, to which only Negro men and women were welcome. Further, they were to be Negroes who trusted in God and were willing to keep their powder dry. "I wish to speak with and listen to Negro Christians willing and able to give a white man a hard knock. No others. Prepare yourselves by reading and pondering the meaning of Judges, chapter 7, verse 3. Also Deuteronomy, chapter 20, verse 8," he instructed.

The meetings, he told them, would concern several proposals which he would be making solely to the people whose very lives were directly threatened by Mr. Webster's cowardly capitulation to the slavers—his "compromise." Father did not wish to address or hear from anyone else. He wanted no Garrisonians. No Anti-Slavery Socialites. No white people at all. "Let the whites make their own policy, as they always have. We must have our own."

In a thoroughly racialized society, it was a strange kind of loneliness, and perhaps a peculiarly American one, to feel cut off from your own race. But in those agonizing years before the War, for a small number of us, that's what it had come to. This matter of difference and sameness—the ways in which we were different from the Negroes and the same as the whites, and, vice versa, the ways in which we were the same as the Negroes and different from the whites—was a vexing one. If a white person persists, as we did, in delineating and defining these areas, soon he will find himself uncomfortable with people of *both* races—with the one, because of his unwanted knowledge of their deepest loyalties and prejudices, for, as a fellow white, privy to their private race conversations and an adept at decoding those closed, tribal communiqués, he understands their true motives and basic attitudes all too well; and uncomfortable with the other also, because, whenever he chooses to allow it, his pale skin will keep him safe from their predators.

If you yourself are not a victim, you cannot claim to see the world as the victim does. A man may have chosen deliberately to abandon one race—I will no longer adhere to white people merely because I happen to be one myself, says the good fellow—but if he is honest, he will quickly see that he is incapable of adhering to the other, too. Amongst Negroes, a white man is always white; they cannot forget it, and therefore neither can he. It's only amongst whites that he suddenly turns colorless, is privileged to forget his skin, is allowed to move inside it, as it were. But beware, because if he does forget his skin, he becomes like them—he becomes another, specially privileged white man, a man who thinks the word "colored" does not apply to him. No, in America, whites are as much stuck with their skin color and bannered by it as the Negroes, and the Indians and Orientals, too. We may be a society founded on racial differences, a society poisoned at the root, perhaps, but we also aspire to be a democracy. Thus, until we have truly become a democracy, every American, white as much as black, red, or yellow, lives not in his skin but on it. If one person is called "colored," let all be colored.

Paradoxically, then, it is when a white person *resists* the privilege of turning colorless that he frees himself, at least partially, from the sickness of racialism. It's the only way for a white man finally to clamber up and out of the pit of Negro slavery wherein this nation was unnaturally conceived and born in a bloody caul and raised into twisted, sick adulthood. He has to separate himself from the luxurious unconsciousness that characterizes his own race, without claiming as his own the historical experience of the other. There is a price, though. He pays with cold loneliness, an itching inner solitude, a permanent feeling of separation from his tribe. He has to be willing to lose his own history without gaining another. He will feel like a man waking at dawn in a village that was abandoned while he slept, all his kith and kin having departed during the night for another, better place in an unknown land far, far away. All the huts and houses are empty, the chimneys are cold, and the doors hang open.

If I had not known that Father felt as I did, if I had not daily seen his brow furrow with the pain of it, his shoulders slump with the fatigue of having constantly to defeat the cynicism it proposed, had not heard him reduced to a sputter, his words all run dry of meaning, then I do not think that I could have withstood that peculiar loneliness. Without Father's steady example and companionship, I would have capitulated to my own pain, fatigue, and frustration, and would either have given up and, lying to the whites, who sang one siren song of race, cleaved to them; or, lying to myself, cleaved to the blacks, who sang another.

At the start of the first meeting held in the sanctuary of the Zion Methodist Church, there were, to my surprise and pleasure, more than a hundred Negroes present, although by the end Father had driven away more than half. Like Gideon, he wished to separate the timid from the brave, and he did it with the fire of his rhetoric, the glare of his eye, and his insistence that if, in order to protect their homes and families from the bounty-hunters, they were not prepared to die, then they should depart forthwith.

They were, most of them, respectable freedmen, with even a few freed women in attendance and several deacons of the church and members of the choir. There were also numerous artisans and shop-keepers with whom we were well-acquainted—as Father made it a point to do business with Negroes whenever possible—and many young men whom I knew personally: roustabouts, stevedores, laborers, and factory hands with whom I had often spoken at abolition meetings. It was a crowd of earnest and intelligent people who understood perfectly the threat posed by this new slave-catching law, not only to the slaves who succeeded in escaping from their bonds but also to these free Negroes themselves, many of whose parents had been born in freedom in the North and had never been within two hundred miles of a slave state.

Well they knew that the color of their skin was now more than ever the mark of Cain. It was their brand, and with the passage of the Fugitive Law, they would have to prove that somehow the brand had been burned into their flesh by mistake. And who could prove this? Virginia courts had displaced Massachusetts courts. Any dark-skinned man, woman, or child, escaped slave or no, could be sworn a slave by a white man with forged papers and hauled back down South and sold off to the plantations there. At a single stroke of the pen, a free man or woman could be converted into valuable property. This was surely the evilest alchemy ever invented.

There was shock and anger amongst the whites of the North, cer-tainly. Daniel Webster's "compromise" may well have made more aboli-tionists of previously acquiescent whites than twenty years of steady preaching had done—which sometimes caused Father to say that the law must have been a significant part of God's secret design. But this gave lit-tle comfort to the Negroes, as the outrage felt by whites was mostly spent on stoking their own righteousness and warming themselves before its fire. "Words, words, words," Father said. "They won't act until they them-selves are physically or financially threatened," he insisted.

This night, for the first time, Father preached violence in public. Moreover, he preached it to Negroes. Defensive violence, however. An over-fine distinction, some might say, yet it was an important one to Father. He was still not ready to carry the war straight to the oppressor, although he had begun to insist that, by virtue of their support of slavery, white Southerners had established a condition of war against all Negroes and those whites who sided with them, and they had therefore forfeited their right to live. "Pro-slavers are fair game," Father had begun to say. His actions would not catch up to his words, however, until we got to Kansas. For now, a merely defensive action would have to suffice.

He began by asking his audience how they proposed to keep the slave-catchers from coming openly into the town and, with aid and comfort provided by the Springfield constabulary, taking off their sons and daughters to the cotton plantations of Mississippi and Alabama. How did they propose to prove that their child was not the same boy or girl who, according to the slave-catcher's sworn statement, had run off with Harriet Tubman to an uncle and aunt in Massachusetts? The slave-catcher would have papers to support his case. He would have depositions and warrants. How did they propose to support *their* case? Remember, Father said, the slave-catcher can look at your innocent, beautiful daughter and say, "That's not Ruth Johnson of Springfield, Massachusetts! That's Celia McNair of Tuscaloosa, Alabama, property of Mister Jubal McNair!" How did they propose to answer him, when the word of a Negro man could no longer stand in a court of law against the word of a white?

And how did they intend now to deal with the poor, starving escaped slave, wounded and bleeding from the rigors of his escape and half-frozen from the New England cold, when he came late in the night scratching at their door, begging to be let in and fed and warmed by their fire and hidden for a night from the hounds of hell bent on re-capturing him? That man, who might well turn out to be a brother or an elderly uncle, could be seized now and sent back without a Massachusetts trial. And they themselves could be arrested and jailed for having stolen a Southern white man's property—just as if his fine thoroughbred horse had been discovered blanketed and feeding inside their barn or his wife's pearls hidden in their flour tin. "How do you intend to deal with that?" Father asked.

Several of the younger men grew restless and angry at these words, as if they felt indicted by them, perhaps hearing Father's questions as accusations, and they stood up and began to edge towards the door. Others sat looking down at their hands as if ashamed, or crossed their arms over their chests and dropped their gaze, feigning deep thought, but mainly avoiding the eyes of their neighbors and of Father, especially.

His words surely caused them pain. He was saying nothing that they did not already know, but he was saying it in a way that must only have reminded them of their terrible helplessness. This made some angry, others ashamed, but it must have moved still others to some new and unexpected state of mind. The angry ones muttered and scowled and began to leave the church. Those who were ashamed averted their eyes. But the rest appeared to be waiting eagerly for Father to continue.

In the pew directly behind me sat brother John and his wife, Wealthy, the only other white people. I was seated in the front pew beside Father's friend Mr. Harrison Wheeler, the tailor, a brave man who had tried to escape from slavery three times before finally succeeding. Having taken the name of a dead cousin who had purchased his own freedom some years past, Mr. Wheeler now lived as a free man. I did not know his slave-name.

I heard the door opening and closing—people were departing from the church one by one. A general restlessness was sweeping over the crowd, as most of those who remained shifted in their seats and cleared their throats, coughed, and murmured to one another. Father stood at the front, silently facing us all, his eyes glaring out beneath his heavy brow, mouth tight as an axe and jaw set, his hands fisted on his hips and feet apart like a man challenging another to a fight. When several moments had passed and no one any longer rose from his seat either to leave or to speak out, Father resumed his challenge, this time not by asking what his audience intended to do but by speaking of himself instead and what he would *not* do.

He and his sons and daughter-in-law, he said—and here, as if amongst the crowd of black and brown faces ours needed identifying, he pointed straight at us, which made me hot with embarrassment—he and his family would not recruit and lead a militia of our fellow white citizens to drive off the slave-catchers. No, he would not go about the town arguing armed resistance with the Anti-Slavery Society folks, and he would not beg money from the gentry to purchase weapons, and he would not wheedle and whine with the Quakers and the Presbyterians and the Methodists to load their muskets and protect their free Negro neighbors and open their doors to escaped slaves and defend them with their sanctified lives. No, he had done plenty of that, and look at what it had got them. It had got them this cowardly Fugitive Law.

From now on, he said, he would leave the white people to their own devices, to their speeches and meetings, to their proud denouncements and announcements, their newspapers, their atheneums and churches, their poems and philosophical essays. Not for him, not for John Brown, to make soldiers of white poets, philosophers, clergymen, journalists, and clerks. Not for any man. He knew a useless thing when he saw it. He, John Brown, though a white man, would no longer speak to his fellow whites for the Negroes of Springfield or anywhere else. From now on, Negroes would have to speak for themselves.

For a long while, he went on in that manner, and it seemed to drive many of the older people from the room and the more prosperous among them as well, some of whom may have thought that there were, after all, quite a number of Negroes who had been speaking to whites for them for many long years now, speaking, testifying, arguing, and praying for help and understanding with extraordinary eloquence and power, and they did not need to hear this white man signing off on them. Did he think they would beg him to speak for them? Why should they? He was right: look at what it had got them.

There were now fewer than half a hundred remaining, somber-faced men of various ages and a few women here and there. Mr. Wheeler had not moved from my side, I was glad to see, nor had any of the people whom I knew from personal acquaintance to be brave and proud defenders of their few rights, people who would under no cir-cumstances shuffle and scrape before a white man. They leaned for-ward in their seats expectantly. There was in Father's words and man-ner something that they wanted badly to hear and see, and they wanted to hear and see it not only in a white man but in themselves. And, indeed, it was for us all now that he began to speak, substituting the word "we" for the "you" and "I" of his previous harangue.

We must take up arms, he said, and we must become united amongst ourselves, and we must be prepared to die in the defense of our homes, of our loved ones, and of our brethren who are in flight from the slave-catcher. We must go home and take down the old mus-ket or rabbit gun or the seldom-fired revolver that we bought at auc-tion, and we will clean and oil it and make sure that the powder is dry and that we have bullets a-plenty, and then we must go out and fire it in our yard and in the fields beyond town, to test our weapon and to improve our aim, but also so that the general public will hear reports of it and know that we are armed. And we will sharpen our knives and attach them to poles, and we will let ourselves be seen walking abroad in the bright of day and dark of night with gleaming pikes on our shoulders, so that the general public will know that we mean to engage the enemy in close quarters, if necessary. And we will let it out that, in our houses, in the windows above the doors, we have put large cauldrons ready to be filled with scalding hot water that can be poured down upon the slave-catcher when he comes with his writs and warrants and pounds on our door demanding entry. That way the general public will know that we will employ any means necessary to defend our homes and whoever happens to be inside them.

"We must form a cadre," he declared, "a rock-hard core at the center of our community. It shall be a League of Gileadites! And its members' names shall be known only to those of us who have taken an oath that, in the defense of our community and our enslaved brethren who have put themselves under our protection, in their names, we are prepared to die! Whenever the cry goes out from anyone in the Negro community for help against the slave-catcher, we will, like the old Concord Minutemen, drop our work or rise from our beds and grab up our weapons and come a-running!" No one who was himself not a Gileadite, he explained, would know which man among us had taken this vow, and thus no one would know which man among us was ready to die and was not afraid even of hanging for his actions. A single one of us standing invisible in a crowd of Negroes would make every person in the crowd more powerful, for all would be seen as potential Gileadites. We must let it out, therefore, without naming names, that some among the Gileadites were white men and some were Negro women, some were young and some were old, so that no single, small group could be separated from the population and persecuted generally. "In unity there is strength!" he stated. "And God will protect us only if we are willing to protect ourselves and each other."

There were a number of Amens and other shows of enthusiasm from the people, whereupon Father, without changing the stern expression of his face, extended his open hands, palms up, at his sides, as was his habit when particularly pleased with himself. Several men in the room, including Mr. Wheeler, had stood and, wishing to speak, were waiting, hats in hand, for Father to acknowledge and call on them. "Anyone who wants to be heard may come up here now and speak," Father said. "If there is a Gideon among us, let him come forward now, and let him forthwith divide the timid from the brave."

Mr. Wheeler and the others hitched a bit and sat back down, and when no one came forward, as Father knew they would not, for all those who would have opposed him or would have wished to wrest leadership from him had already departed from the group, he walked to the further end of one of the nearly empty pews and himself sat down.

A moment or two passed in silence, as if everyone were waiting for the arrival of an important visitor, and then Father rose again from his seat and returned to the front. "We will let the Lord separate us out," he declared in a low, calm voice. "Therefore, let us go to our homes now, and there shall each one of us pray alone for guidance in this matter. And whosoever returns to this place tomorrow night at this same hour, let him come prepared to swear the Oath of the Gileadites, which I myself shall be the first to take and then shall deliver to each of thee, one by one." At that, he marched down the center aisle of the sanctuary and passed out the door to the vestry beyond and into the cold autumn night, and the rest of us followed.

Father had inspired and moved us beyond measure, it appeared, and me he had moved beyond expectation. It was as if he had been speaking for me, and I had through him become wonderfully articulate and clear. It was as if my crippled arm had been magically healed and, full-faced, I had stood forward, bright and challenging, my two arms extended for the first time in public, and, speaking before an audience of hesitant, frightened, and angry people, an audience of suspicious Negroes, I had succeeded in transforming myself into an old-time, Biblical prophet capable of leading men into a holy war, a war in which, as a result of my words, men and women were prepared to sacrifice themselves for the lives of others and for the greater glory of God.

Father's thoughts and beliefs were mine. He had spoken for me, or, rather, I had spoken through him, and it seemed to me then to have occurred not because I had contrived for him to do it or had subtly managed him somehow—although in a certain light I suppose that my aid to him and reassurance could have been construed as such—but because now, for the first time, I was no longer resisting his will, no longer holding back from his calls for action, action, action. I had finally taken him at his word, the word which he had been laying in the porches of my ears since I'd drawn my first breath, and now his word was mine, his personal power mine, his ease with speech, his natural movement, his hard, gray eye, his intelligence and imagination, mine!

I remained, of course, still the hulking, crippled, red-headed country boy, the same shy, inarticulate bumpkin as before. But now all that was like a clever disguise designed to hide and shelter the real person inside—a man who, neither white nor Negro, was *dangerous*. A man who, whenever necessary, could step out of the shadows where in silence he silently labored his days away and suddenly stand revealed as a warrior for the Lord, a man of God who would inspire and lead God's chosen people out of Egypt into the promised land, and who would do it even as he denied he was doing it, who would be Moses while claiming merely to be Aaron. Whom or what we love, although it can never be our reason for loving them, we become. Without his love of God, my father, I saw, would have been a pitiful man. But in giving himself over to God, Father had become many times larger and more powerful a man than he could ever have been otherwise. Now I, too, having finally come to love my father as totally as he loved God—I, too, was no longer pitiful.

That same night, we adjourned to the rooms where John and Wealthy had been living—since the removal to North Elba, Father had not maintained living quarters in Springfield, and consequently he and I had been sleeping in the office of Brown & Perkins's empty warehouse. There Father instructed me to write up a statement of advice and principles which he could present to the Negroes tomorrow night and a draft of a pledge. He had arrived over the years at a high estimation of my literary abilities, although he had little more to go on than my letters and the help I gave him with his own. He also knew that I believed his style to be on the eccentric side of my own. Reluctantly, he had come to agree with me, and thus he frequently enjoyed employing me as a kind of village scribe, in which he was the village. He would say aloud what he meant or wished to mean, pacing back and forth, hands clasped behind him, brow furrowed in thought, while I scratched away with my pen, setting down his thoughts and intentions in language that I hoped would be readily understood by the man or woman to whom those thoughts and intentions were directed, a person who, with a transcription of Father's own words in hand, would very likely have been puzzled or merely annoyed.

With his composition "Sambo's Mistakes," Father had tried working alone, and I think that afterwards he was sorry he had done so and in time blamed its failure to be published on his inability to set down on the page the true nature of his thoughts. Since then, whenever he wished to make a written statement of any importance or delicacy, he'd taken to calling on me. Increasingly, this job of scribe had become a pleasure for me—it gave me, naturally, a certain degree of importance not otherwise available, and it provided me with the chance to voice some of my own thoughts and beliefs as well.

Father talked and tried out first one sentence and then another, rejecting, editing, retracing his words, struggling to make his statement to the Negroes. He paced the length and breadth of the sitting room and rumbled on into the cold autumn night, while John and Wealthy slept in the adjacent chamber, and I sat at the little table and by the dim, flickering light of a Nantucket lamp, wrote down much of what he said and most of what he meant or wanted to say.

It was nearly dawn before we had a preamble, which we entitled "Words of Advice," and a pledge, entitled "Agreement," whereupon we adjourned to the Brown & Perkins office and slept a few hours on our cots, before having to commence the day's work, which then consisted mostly of writing letters to attorneys and creditors and attempting to find a tenant for the warehouse who would take over Brown & Perkins's lease.

That evening, Father and I—this time without John and Wealthy, for she was newly pregnant, and they would soon be departing for their farm in Ohio and thus could not be a part of our work here—returned to the Zion Methodist Church, where we were joined by most of the Negroes who had remained until the end of the meeting the evening before. They numbered thirty-two men and nine women, the majority of them between thirty and forty years of age, with a sprinkling of very young and elderly men among them. Seen together like that, grim-visaged, muscular, and healthy, their dark brown and black faces stern and determined, they constituted a formidable-looking force. I felt proud to be associated with them.

More than half of the company were friends and acquaintances of ours, the best among the blacks of Springfield. I was glad to see Mr. Harrison Wheeler still there, and Deacon Samuels, also the apothecary Mr. Minahan and his teenaged son, and several of the fellows who at different times had worked alongside me in the warehouse sorting and baling wool, trustworthy young men with stout arms and strong backs and anger to spare. Most of the Negroes who were lucky enough to be properly employed or have a profession were engaged at a level below their natural or acquired abilities, and as a result a Negro apothecary often had the intelligence and many of the skills of a white physician, and a Negro laborer was frequently the equal of a white foreman. Thus Father's determination to do business with Negroes was based on no condescending desire to provide charity; it was, as he said, practical. And he was rarely disappointed by them—nowhere near as often as when he had to employ or deal financially with white people, who he believed were more likely than blacks to cheat or cut corners.

When everyone had been seated and the door closed and, at Father's instructions, bolted, we began with a singing of the hymn "Broad Is the Path That Leads to Death," a favorite of mine. Then Father announced that he would present to us a statement which he had drawn up. Holding the paper close to his eyes, like a court clerk reading a judge's sentence, he commenced to read.

> *Words of Advice! To the Springfield, Massachusetts, branch of the United States League of Gileadites. Adopted November 15, 1850, as written and recommended by John Brown.*
>
> *Union is Strength!*
>
> *Nothing so charms the American people as personal bravery. Witness the case of Cinque, he of everlasting memory, who seized the slave-ship Amistad, and the outpouring of sympathy and interest that followed hard upon it. The trial for life of one so bold and to some extent a successful man, for having defended his rights as a man in good earnest, aroused more sympathy amongst whites throughout the nation than the accumulated wrongs and sufferings of more than the three millions of our submissive Negro population.*
>
> *We need not mention our American white people's response to the Greeks who are now struggling valiantly against the oppressive Turks, their sympathy for the Poles against mighty Russia, and for the Hungarians against Austria and Russia combined, in order to prove this. The truth is, no jury can be found in the Northern states that would convict a man, whether black or white, for defending his legitimate*

rights to the last extremity. That this is well understood by Southern Congressmen, who now appear to govern us, we see by their insistence that the right of trial by jury should not be granted to the fugitive slave.

Then he recited several sentences which I had tried to excise but which Father had insisted on including, for he could not leave off giving advice of this sort, not just to Negroes, but to everyone. Although he assured me that it would be obvious to all that he was criticizing white people, not black, I knew how it would sound to his audience, for I had endured a form of the same hectoring lecture for my whole life. But giving unwanted advice was his characteristic tic, and there was no avoiding it, so I cringed and awaited its passing.

Colored people have ten times the number of fast friends among the whites as they suppose. But they would have ten times the number they have now, were blacks but half as much in earnest to secure their dearest rights as they are to ape the follies and extravagances of their white neighbors and to indulge in idle show, in ease, and in luxury. If Negroes in America were to demonstrate in their private and public behavior the virtues which whites claim to admire but seem for the most part unable to practice themselves, of temperance, modesty, and decorum in all things, thrift, and charity, then they would acquire for themselves the widespread admiration of many of those who today revile and scorn them for their frivolity and wastefulness.

Soon, happily, his scolding done, he was again delivering his charge to us.

Should one of our number be arrested, all the rest of us must collect together and sternly surround the officers and constables as quickly as possible, so as to outnumber and intimidate our adversaries, even those

who were not present and only afterwards heard rumor of our seriousness
of purpose and our surprising numbers. And no able-bodied man shall
appear on the ground unequipped and without his weapons, and thus his
intentions, clearly exposed to view. Your musket and your sword, you
may say, are to exterminate varmints. Let our adversary ponder whether
of two legs or four.

Let that much be understood beforehand by all who see us abroad in
the town, but our actual plans must be known only to ourselves, with the
understanding that all traitors, wherever caught and proven to be guilty,
must die. Yet we must not forget the admonition of the Lord to Gideon,
"Whosoever is fearful or afraid, let him return and part early from
Mount Gilead." That is, give all cowards an opportunity to show their
cowardice early, on condition of holding their peace and their tongues, for
while we do not want them among us when in battle, our victory must
be a victory for all.

Now this is most important to success. When the moment of
confrontation with the enemy arrives, do not delay for a moment once
you have made ready to strike him down! You will lose all resolution if
you do. And let the first blow be the signal for all to engage. And once
engaged, we shall not do our deadly work by halves. We will make clean
work of our enemies, as one would butcher a steer—and be sure you
meddle not with any others. Choose wisely who will be cut down, then
do it swiftly to him alone. By going about our bloody business quickly
and quietly, we will get the job done with efficiency, and the number that
an uproar would bring together cannot collect and stop us.

We will have the advantage anyhow of those who would come out
against us, for they will be wholly unprepared with either equipment or
matured plans. All with them will be confusion and terror. Then our
enemies will be slow to attack us after we have done up the work so
nicely. And if, after they have re-gathered their thoughts and the terror
has passed, should they still decide to attack us, they will have to

encounter our white friends as well, for we may safely calculate on a division appearing among the whites and by that means may get to an honorable parley.

Be firm, determined, and cool, but let it be understood that we are not to be driven to desperation without making it as awful a job to others as it is to us. Give them to know distinctly that those who live in wooden houses should not throw fire and that we are more able to suffer and make pay than are our white neighbors, for our very lives are at stake.

Also, after effecting a rescue, if you are assailed, we must not go to our own houses but make straight for the houses of our most prominent and influential white friends, carrying with us our wives and small children. This will fasten upon the whites the suspicion of being connected with the blacks and will compel them to make a common cause with us, whether they would otherwise live up to their previous professions of sympathy or not. They would have then no choice in the matter. Some of their own volition will doubtless prove themselves true, most others would flinch, but either way, we would be guilty only of taking them at their earlier words.

In the courtroom where a trial is going on which is more show than trial, we can disrupt the proceedings and effect a rescue if we make a tumult—by burning gunpowder freely in paper packages, if you cannot think of a better way to make a momentary alarm. And might not a lasso be applied to a slave-catcher for once with good effect? Well we might in the process give one or more of our enemies a proper hoist, but in such a case the prisoner will need to take the hint at once and bestir himself, and his friends in the dock should use the occasion to improve the opportunity of a general rush.

Hold onto your weapons and never be persuaded to leave them, part with them, or have them far away from you. Stand by one another and by your friends whilst a drop of blood remains in you or a breath of air. And, finally, be hanged on the scaffold or a gallows tree, if you must, but tell no tales out of school. Make no confession!

Remember and say it over and over, union is strength, union is strength! But regardless, without well-digested arrangements such as these, nothing to any good purpose is likely to be demanded, let the demand be never so great. Witness the hundreds of cases of capture and return to slavery, regardless of the protests raised afterwards, when there was no well-defined plan of operation or suitable preparations made and sworn to beforehand.

By these proposed means, the desired end may be effectually secured. Namely, the enjoyment of our inalienable rights.

To hear my written words spoken in his resonating, public-hall voice by Father to a sober-faced audience of people who, because of those words, were made ready to take up arms and slay the enemy was wonderfully thrilling to me, and I felt the blood course up and down my arms and could scarcely repress a smile from my lips. I trembled with joy, as much for the meaning of the words and the pictures they painted in my own mind of making quick and bloody work of my enemies, as for the occasion of hearing Father speak them; and when, in that small, dimly lit sanctuary, Father called out to the crowd of us, "Who will come forward and sign an agreement to adhere to my words of advice?" I was the first to stand and deliver. On either side of me, other men and women were standing and stepping to the front also, until in a moment nearly every person in the room had joined me there.

Father said, "Now, let me say it again. Whosoever is fearful or afraid, let him depart from us. But if ye depart from us, say nothing of what ye have heard here. For ye have also heard what shall be done by us with traitors." There were at that point a final few who made for the door, unbolted it, and disappeared into the night, leaving behind still more than thirty warriors to bind ourselves together and march behind Gideon against the Midianites.

"The Lord hath instructed us to reduce ourselves to this number," Father said, "so that when we have accomplished our task, we will not say, 'Mine own hand hath saved me.' We must thank only the Lord," he pronounced, and many in the group sang out, "Praise the Lord! Praise Him!"

Whereupon Father said, "This which I shall now read to thee is the Agreement, and when I have finished, come forward one by one and sign on this sheet of paper below it, so that we shall be bound together in this work as brothers and sisters, sworn to the death of every one of us." He told us then to place our right hands over our hearts, which we did, and in a loud, clear voice, he read the Agreement, which, though I had myself written the words for him in the late hours of the previous night, sounded to me as fresh and new as if I had never heard them before.

> As legitimate citizens of the United States of America, trusting in a just and merciful God, whose spirit and all-powerful aid we humbly implore, we pledge that we will ever be true to the flag of our beloved country, always acting under it. We, whose names are hereunto fixed, do constitute ourselves a branch of the United States League of Gileadites. We pledge that we will provide ourselves at once with suitable implements of war, and will aid those who do not possess the means, if any such are disposed to join us, to acquire and do the same. We further invite every colored person whose heart is engaged in the performance of our work, whether male or female, young or old, to join us in that work, which is the defense of our Negro brethren against the man-stealers and any of those cowards who would aid and abet them. All able-bodied men and women shall be prepared to die in this effort. The duty of the aged, infirm, and young members of the League shall be to give instant notice to all other members in case of an attack upon any of our people. Until some trial of courage and talent of able-bodied members shall enable us

to elect officers from those who have rendered the most important services,
we agree to have no officers, except a treasurer and secretary pro tem.
Nothing but wisdom and undaunted courage, efficiency, and general
good conduct shall in any way influence us in electing our officers.

Father laid the paper on the low table where normally flowers for Sabbath services were placed, flattened it with his left hand, and, saying, "So sworn, John Brown," wrote his name with a visible flourish. I then stepped to the table and took the pen from him, and saying the words "So sworn, Owen Brown," with trembling hand wrote my name below his. One by one, the rest came forward, following the procedure exactly. So sworn, Alexander Washington. So sworn, Harrison Wheeler. So sworn, Shadrach Benchforth. So sworn, Mary Benchforth. So sworn, Felicity Moone. So sworn, Ebidiah Smith. And on down the line, until all of us had sworn and signed.

Then, bearing the document in hand, Father walked from behind the table where he had stood throughout and came to stand beside us, facing the nave of the sanctuary, where a small cross was attached high on the white-washed wall, and he led us briefly in prayer, humbly beseeching the Lord to protect us in this mighty task. "Make us hard, Lord, hard, like a stone, so that we shall crush and make bleed the teeth of the slavers when they bite down upon us," he prayed.

When he had finished, we all said our amens, and the Gileadites somberly filed out to the vestry and into the night. Father and I lingered behind to put out the lamps and candles, and when everyone else was gone and we were alone in the darkness of the vestry, I said to him, "Who'll be the treasurer and secretary *pro tem*? And what will his duties be?" I couldn't see much use for there being a treasurer, as there were no dues or other monies involved with the League, and I was unsure of what a secretary would do, as it was difficult to imagine a secret society engaged in much correspondence or keeping minutes. But the night before, when composing the Agreement, I had been ordered by Father to allow for that one officer, and so, without understanding, I had written it in. Now it seemed important. Naturally, I myself wished to be that person but, because of the honor it implied, dared not hope that the job would fall to me.

"The treasurer and secretary will safeguard these documents," he answered, and he placed the Words of Advice and the Agreement with the signatures into my hand. "He will not deliver them to the enemy, Owen, even under pain of death. And when the time comes, as it surely will, that we receive monetary support for our work from our white friends, he will record such funds as we receive and will control their expenditure."

I said nothing, and when Father had closed the church doors behind us and we had stepped down to the dark, deserted street, I carefully rolled the documents so as not to crease them, and we began walking side by side towards the warehouse. Finally, I could stand it no longer, and I said to him, "So are you making *me* the sole officer for the Gileadites?"

"For now, yes. I'll speak of it first to the others, but I'm sure they'll agree to it. There's no one better qualified for the task. Do you mind?" he asked.

"No. No, I don't mind," I answered off-handedly.

But I remember thinking, At last! It has begun! At last, the *killing* has begun!

The wind outside my cabin has let up, and I hear mice skittering in the darkness across the warped, dried-out floors. Their bodies against the boards—though each weighs less than an ounce of fur and twigged bone, a mere thimbleful of flesh—seem nonetheless immeasurably realer than mine, weightier, as if the bit of stale, dusty air displaced by their tiny bodies and disrupted by their rapid movements alongside the crumbling walls exceeds in volume anything my body is capable of filling or disturbing. Yet I know that my presence, despite its frail ethereality, alarms them. The animals see and hear me the way they see and hear an ominous shift in the weather long before it occurs. I am like a ghost and in the course of this relation have traveled far and wide and back and forth in time, a dark spirit growing steadily darker, transported by memory and articulation and the compulsive direction of my thought. I can no longer say, Miss Mayo, whether I am in my cabin now in Altadena or our old house in '89 in North Elba. Darkness merges time and place.

Above me, in the bare attic room where Ruth and I and the younger children and Lyman Epps and his wife, Ellen, slept on our pallets, divided one from the other, males from females, like Shakers by a curtain on a string, I hear the dry rustle of squirrels, or perhaps it is a pair of raccoons—it's the shuffling gait of animals that have wintered inside, and now that spring has at last come to these northern Adirondack hills, they have mated, and the female has dropped a litter of cubs in her nest of sticks and leaves in the leeward corner, where since November she slumbered protected against the arctic snows and freezing winds. My sudden, unexpected presence here after years away has frightened the poor creatures. I hear the female trying to move her cubs to some place up there in the attic where she feels they will be safe, carrying them in her mouth one by one to the corner furthest from where she senses me. She senses the presence of an alien creature, possibly human, a *killer*, in one of the two rooms below.

Although I am still and it is dark and she can see and hear no one, can smell no sour human body, no tobacco smoke, no lamp, no guttering candle, nonetheless she knows that something like a human being, something like a killer, has entered this long-abandoned building and stands in silence now in the middle of the room below. She knows that there must be one of the killers, a human being, down here. The disturbance in the musty air can be nothing else, where for years there has been no human—no men with their dogs, no children even, with their small deadly weapons—except occasionally during the daylight hours, when a crowd of humans, male and female, smelling foully of death and making loud grinding and barking noises with their feet and mouths, come inside and stomp around for a while, as if contemplating taking up residence here, and then leave again.

Don't fret, little mother, I'll not hurt or hinder you. I may remain down here for a long while, perhaps for as many years as this otherwise abandoned old structure stands; perhaps longer; or maybe I'll stay only for this one night, I can't know; but don't you worry, you tiny, frightened mice and agitated raccoons and squirrels, and even you porcupines under the house gnawing on the rafters beneath my feet—all my killing is done now. The killing is finished. You needn't fear me, even you black bears whom I hear cough and growl outside in the yard, prowling the now-deserted site for refuse, quarreling over a few chicken bones and chunks of old bread tossed aside by the humans when they left this afternoon at the end of their ceremonies. Even the wolves slinking back down the valley from the ridge behind the house and the lion alone on the mountain need not fear my presence here. Every living creature is safe from me now.

But if they understood these words, no matter; they would take no comfort from them. They know us too well, our terrible propensity for killing. Of all the animals on this planet, we are surely the nastiest, the most deceitful, the most murderous and vile. Despite our God, or because of Him. Both. Our only virtue sometimes seems to be that we are as cruel and violent to one another as we are to the other species, whom we slay and devour, or slay for the pure pleasure of it and toss aside, or simply slay because it's expedient and heap up their corpses. I wish to warn them and to comfort them.

A pathetic wish; it serves no purpose. Sharp as their ears may be, they cannot hear these words, let alone understand them. I can warn and comfort no one, not even the dumb animals.

It's just as well not to try, for all I am now is a story being told for all practical purposes by a man whose only possibility for positioning himself to speak it rests with his imagining this old house, the overgrown yard that surrounds it, the huge, gray stone yonder, and the yellowing bones that lie in boxes buried in the hard ground beside it. I'm but one of the thousand stories of the mystery of being human, and all the other animals know that story already and know the nine hundred ninety-nine more; it's why they fear us: they know our nature, and don't require a ghost to tell it.

Since the day I left this house for Kansas and beyond, I have wanted to be back here again—but not for this. I never in my lifetime wanted it to be true that the mystery surrounding my father's life and death, the questions concerning his character and motives, even the question of his sanity, lay here in this house on this hallowed plot of ground. Though I better than anyone alive knew the answer to all those questions, which tormented so many good men and women, tormented everyone who loved him for himself and for what he did, I still during my lifetime did not say aloud what was the truth, not to myself and not to anyone else. I loved him, too, and loved what he did. So I kept silent and hoped that the questions would end, or that they needed no answers. I hoped that a mystery was sufficient.

After Harpers Ferry, I went away; I ran as far as the continent ran, to where there was nothing further than the endless, blue Pacific; and climbed a mountain there and built a cabin; and said nothing: nothing to the journalists, who found out from my brothers and sisters where I had hidden myself and came clambering up my mountain in Altadena to interview me; nothing to the historians, who mailed me long detailed lists of questions, which I tossed into the fire in my iron stove;

nothing to Father's old abolitionist friends and supporters, who came to my cabin seeking answers and left feeling pity for what the war against slavery and the deaths of my beloved father and brothers had done to me. I did not even speak of those matters with my brothers and sisters themselves, those who survived into old age with me, when in later years they arranged to gather together now and again in one of the houses they had scattered to, on a Fourth of July, sometimes on a Thanksgiving or Christmas holiday, and I would trundle down from my hermit's shack and travel the many hundreds of miles to their homes, where late in the evening they would share their memories of Kansas, of the work before Kansas, and of Harpers Ferry. At those gatherings they all thought me shy, inarticulate, perhaps not as intelligent as they, as they always had anyhow, and they were not wrong. But that did not mean that I did not know the truth about Father and why he did the great, good things and the bad, and why so much of what he did was, at bottom, horrendous, shocking, was wholly evil.

Within a few days of the swearing of the Gileadites in Springfield, our little army was dissolved. Or, more to the point, Father abruptly withdrew from its command and took me with him, leaving the Negro Gileadites to their own devices and stratagems, which, happily for them, turned out to be sufficient unto the day. But to be cast down from such a height of excitement and anticipation, as I was cast down by Father, was truly agonizing for me. In those days, my particular closeness to Father and the intensity and whole-heartedness with which I embraced his plans and dreams of carrying the battle straight to the slaveholders separated me from my brothers, and I could not pass it off the way John did when, within a few days of Father's and my somberly and ceremoniously pledging ourselves to defend with our life's blood the fugitive slaves, the Old Man, as was his wont, turned his attention suddenly elsewhere—to the sorry business of Brown & Perkins, as it happened. John simply shrugged his shoulders and set off on his own business, as he and Jason had so often done in the past. I, however, was crushed with disappointment and bitter frustration. And I was vexed with Father, more so than I had ever been before.

Looking back now, these many years later, I can see with some sympathy how Father was sorely conflicted then between what he saw as his obligations to his family and his creditors and to Mr. Perkins, who had stood by him for so long, and what he saw as his duty to oppose slavery. I was, of course, not so divided, but there was no place else I could go to wage war than with Father, no army in which to enlist but his, no one to follow into battle but him. When he decided once again to let the fight go, all I could do was gnash my teeth in rage and sharpen my long knife and clean my gun and dream of spilling blood.

I might have stayed on in Springfield, defying Father's order to return to North Elba and run the farm there, marching instead and on my own with the Gileadites—who, as it turned out, because of the fear they aroused simply by virtue of rumor and the sight of armed Negro men at the Springfield railroad station and on the streets, never did have the opportunity for an actual, bloody confrontation with the slave-catchers. Wisely, the man-stealers and their cohorts sought their prey elsewhere. But without Father at my side, I knew that I was not especially wanted by the Negroes anyhow. To them, I was merely one of the sons of Captain Brown, as they sometimes called him. I was the big, shy, red-headed fellow who ran errands for his illustrious sire. Any light on my face was reflected light.

Nights, as I lay in my cot and fumed over what I regarded as Father's dereliction, his defection even, I dreamed up bloody scenes to give vent to my wrath and my longing for battle. I aimed down the barrel of my gun and fired into the chest of the slave-catcher standing over the prostrate form of a fugitive. I sneaked up behind an auctioneer on his way to market with a bound gang of human chattel, and in full view of his victims reached around his neck and slashed his throat with my knife, retrieved his keys, and with my bloodied hands set the men and women loose from their fetters and led them into the woods and up into the hills. Visions of carnage and revenge filled my mind and strangely pleased me, easing me, calming my turbulent thoughts—so that I could eventually accede to Father's wishes and return to North Elba.

"I very much oppose having to go back there," I told him the night before I departed from Springfield. "I want to stay here and fight along-side the Gileadites." We were in the office of Brown & Perkins, and I had taken to my cot, prepared for sleep, while he worked on at the desk by lamplight, dashing off more letters that begged for time, for patience and understanding, for merciful delays of prosecution, that promised eventual, full payment, complete clarification and accounting, justice and restitution. This sort of letter he wrote himself, and he pointedly did not want me as his scribe.

He put down his pen and looked at me with irritation. "Owen, the Negroes don't need you here. They can protect themselves as well without you as with you. No one needs you here now. I don't. I need you to be with your mother and the rest of the family. We've gone over this. The winter is bearing down on them, and they're suffering because of the absence of a man who can run the place."

"What about Lyman? He's there, he's a man."

"It's not the same, Owen. I can't be there myself, because of these infernal court cases. You know that. The family needs one of us, and it's you, or it'll have to be me, to get them safely through the winter and put the place ready for spring. We don't want next year to go so hard. Think of your poor brothers and sisters, Owen. The babies. Think of your mother."

"She's not my mother," I shot back.

"We'll not go into that," he said curtly. "You're angry with me, I know, for having to go off like this, for my sending you north. But you should deliver it to me, who deserves it. Don't ship it to someone who doesn't deserve it." He turned abruptly back to his work. Then, after a few moments, he paused and without looking at me seemed to be reversing himself, for he offered to let me stay on in Springfield, if I wished.

I sat up in my cot, not quite believing him. But then he added that I could also go to Ohio with John and Wealthy, or join Fred and Jason at Mr. Perkins's place. I could go anyplace I chose. Accompany him to Boston to help prepare his lawyer. Follow him to Pittsburgh for more of the same. Even go off to California with all the other young fools and dig for gold, if I wanted. Follow the elephant. "It's your choice," he said. "But wherever you choose to go," he reminded me, still without lifting his eyes from the paper before him, "if you don't go to North Elba, you'll be abandoning your duty."

Besides, he pointed out, I had no money, no house, no land. Or had I some private wealth, and he somehow had not noticed? And I had no trade, other than farming and the keeping of sheep. Or had I been taking instruction by mail in business like John, or horticulture like Jason? If not, would I perhaps like to hire myself out as a day-laborer here in Springfield? And where would I sleep at night, once he closed down the business? Did I have friends who would put me up, people he had not heard about?

He knew the answers to all those questions, of course. He knew what I had to do. And so did I.

At dawn, I rose and packed my few possessions into a gunny sack, slung it over my right shoulder and took up my rifle, and said goodbye to Father. He placed around my neck a purse on a cord with fourteen dollars and some coppers inside to give over to Mary and to pay for supplies he had ordered in Westport for the farm, which I was to arrange to have transported on to North Elba when I got there. As always, he filled my head with last-minute instructions. Which of the merinos to breed this spring, which to sell, which to butcher for mutton; how much seed to set aside for a second planting if the first got hit by a late frost; which part of the acreage to clear next and which to leave for a woodlot; how much to pay in Westport for salt and flour, and who among the Negroes of Timbuctoo to hire and whether to pay them in goods or cash or crop shares. "Make work for them, if you can afford it, especially when the winter comes on. Even if you and Lyman and the boys are able to clear and cut on your own. They learn from your example, and it brings them a small cash payment as well, which they will surely need.

"Ah, Owen!" he declared. "I envy you, my boy. How I would love to be there now, clearing that mountain forest, working with my back and arms all day and gathering together with my precious family around the table at night," he said, smiling and inhaling deeply, as if he could smell the crisp, cold Adirondack air. "That's all the good Lord meant for a man to do. That, and to care for his neighbors. And you can do all of it up there. All of it. I envy you, son."

I thanked him for it, still sullen and resentful, and we embraced, or, rather, he embraced me, and I strode away from him, crossing through town to the main road north—headed home, for that is what it was now. There was no other place I could name as home than that tidy farmhouse on the edge of the wilderness. So there I went. Home.

I had five days of walking ahead of me. A few times I accepted a farmer's offer to put up in his barn, but otherwise I slept outdoors in a makeshift camp close to the road, huddled in my blanket before a small fire, like a tramp. I walked steadily from first light to last, up the long Connecticut Valley and across the Green Mountains of Vermont, then north again along the western shore of Lake George, past the ruins of old Ticonderoga to the glittering waters of Lake Champlain. There I stopped in Westport briefly on Father's business, and then headed upland into the Adirondacks. And the entire time, all five days and nights, I filled my mind with the conscious pretense that I was completely turned around, that my compass had reversed itself and I was walking south instead of north. I was moving down along the Subterranean Passway into Virginia and North Carolina. I was marching towards the slaves and their masters. The fugitive slaves followed their north star; I followed its southern twin.

It was like a dream, a beautiful, soothing dream of late autumn: low, gray skies, smell of woodsmoke, fallen leaves crackling beneath my feet, and somewhere out there, in the farmsteads and plantations ahead of me, swift retribution! Freedom! The bloody work of the Lord!

14

I arrived home in North Elba late in the afternoon just as it was growing dark, greeted by my brother Watson a half-mile east of the farm, out where the road from Keene crests the long rise through the notch. I saw him from a distance and did not at first recognize him. He was tall and lanky, all sticks and rope. He had turned onto the road, emerging from the woods there, leading the Morgan named Adelphi, hitched to a sledgeload of logs taken evidently from the back lot of the property, a forest of blue spruce that sloped towards Pitch-off Mountain.

Watson saw me and waved. Though he was barely sixteen then, he had added considerably to his height since I'd last seen him and walked like a grown man who'd done a hard day's work. In the months since my departure, Watson had managed to slip away from most of his boyhood, and when I drew near, I saw that his long, narrow face had the beginning haze of a reddish beard. It cheered me to see him so grown up. Nearly my height, he was well on his way to being taller than I, who up to now had been the tallest in the family.

For a few seconds, we grinned at one another with slight self-consciousness, and then I embraced him warmly and tugged his new whiskers. "What's this, Wat?" I laughed. "Growing yourself a beard, eh?"

He grabbed my beard and gave it an answering yank. "Everybody always says you're the handsome one. I thought I'd give it a try, see if it's the beard. It's just great to see you, Owen!" he exclaimed, and threw his ropey arm over my shoulder. He cocked his head and studied me and said that I looked different to him, that I'd changed somehow.

"Come on, I've not been gone that long."

"No, seriously, Owen. You're looking different. You didn't fall in love or something, now, did you?" he said, and shook my shoulder and grinned.

I confessed that it did feel weird to me, coming home this time, as if I had been away for years. My mind filled for an instant with the face of Sarah Peabody, but I swiftly put the image away, replacing her, as if for Watson's sake, with the sights and sounds of Liverpool, London, Waterloo.

"You're a famous world traveler now!" he said. "I want to hear about every single thing that you and the Old Man saw over there."

We walked along beside the horse and sledge, the broad valley opening out in front of us, with white-topped Tahawus and McIntyre in the distance and the burnished range beyond, and although it was a gray, overcast day threatening to snow, I saw again how lovely this place was. Of course, Father loved it here. How could he not? And how could he not have envied me for being free to return here? I thought, and regretted for a moment that I had been so disgruntled with him.

I was expected, Watson then told me. But expected sooner than this, he said, as they had received a letter from Father some days earlier, telling them I was on my way north. "Me and the boys thought you might've got distracted some over in Westport."

This surprised me. "When was his letter dated?"

He didn't know. The thirteenth, he thought. Yes, the thirteenth. "I copied it," he said proudly. "Like you used to."

How could that be? Two days prior to my signing the pledge with the Gileadites, Father had written to the family that I would soon be coming home? I grew angry again and freshly confused. He had already decided and had known, even as he was working up my spirits, that we would not fight alongside the Negroes of Springfield! He knew all along that I would be sent to North Elba. And had said nothing of it until afterwards, when he feebly claimed unexpected legal troubles.

What purpose could he have had—for the meetings, the sermonizing, the pledge? And appointing me secretary and treasurer—why? Was it all for show? And for whom? Not me, certainly. For the Negroes? Had he merely been putting on a play for the blacks of Springfield, working them up, organizing them for battle and steeling them to pledge and risk their lives, when he had no real intention of joining them himself, or even of allowing his son to join them?

I cursed aloud: "Damn him!"

"What's wrong?" Watson asked.

"Nothing," I said. "No, the Old Man, actually. It's just that he knew I was coming back here long before he told me. Even *you* knew before I did."

He laughed and punched me on the shoulder. "Ah, well, Owen, that's the Old Man, isn't it? You can forget about him now, though. He's there, and we're here. You've just been spending too much time with him and not enough with us. C'mon, Mother's going to be happy to see you," he declared. "And Ruth, too. Everybody!"

"Lyman, too?"

"Sure. Lyman, too," he said. "It's great you're home, though. Tell me everything. I want to hear everything. Especially about old John Bull. I want to hear all about England. And Flanders! What's *that* like?"

As we walked, I related some of the details of my journey, pleasing and exciting him to a surprising degree, as if I had been to the South Seas on a whaling ship. Down the long hill we went, and soon, although it was not yet four o'clock in the afternoon, we were walking in wintry darkness, as if dead of night had fallen. Then, in the distance,

I saw the glimmer of lamplight from the kitchen, and I made out the shape of the house. In this wide, dark, cold valley with the blackened mountains beyond, the house looked like a small ship bobbing at anchor in a safe harbor.

"You go in," Watson said. "I'll take care of Adelphi. We can unload these trees tomorrow in a twink."

I said fine and headed for the door, anxious suddenly and a little afraid, as if I were about to hear unwanted news.

But, no, everything was joy and thanksgiving, kisses and embraces and bright, shining faces. They all gathered around me, as if I were one of Ulysses' returning warriors, gone for long years instead of months, and put their faces next to mine and kept touching me with their hands even after we had hugged one another. My face nearly hurt from the smiling. They pulled my coat off me and bade me sit at the table, while the babies, Annie and Sarah, who, at seven and four years old, were no longer babies, unlaced and playfully drew off my boots.

Mary, sweetly calm in the center of the sun-shower, blessed me and thanked the Lord for my safe return. She looked healthier than when I had left, her round face reddened from the heat of the kitchen stove and the excitement, and I glimpsed her prettiness, saw her for a second as she must have looked to Father when he first met her some eighteen years earlier, a warm, soft, utterly benevolent presence in his unyielding, masculine world.

I held her hands in mine and said, "I'm truly glad to see you, Mary. Are you as well as you look?"

"Oh, my, yes!" she said, and laughed, and Ruth and the boys, Oliver and Salmon, laughed, too.

"What's the joke?"

"Oh, we'll tell you later," Ruth said, and ruffled my hair with her cool hand. "We've lots to tell. You and Father may not know it, Owen, but believe it or not, life goes on without you."

"Apparently," I said, and looked around the crowded room. There were Oliver and Salmon, lithe, tanned boys grinning like monkeys, and the little girls, Sarah and Annie, already back at work, the one churning and the other putting out plates. And then for the first time I saw Susan Epps, standing beside the stove in the further corner of the kitchen. Her hands were folded in her apron, and she was smiling gently at me, as if waiting for me to acknowledge her before she could greet me. At once I got up and crossed down the room to her and gave her a friendly embrace, realizing as I did so that she was pregnant, and well along with it, too.

"Yes, indeed," I said to her. "Life does go on!" and she gave a winning, shy laugh. I congratulated her and turned to look for Lyman. "Where's your excellent husband?"

There was a silence, and then Watson, who had come in from the barn and was shucking his coat by the door, said, "He'll be back soon."

"Soon?"

"Tonight. Or tomorrow night. He's moving a few folks north."

"Well, good," I said. "I was kind of afraid that the whole operation'd come to a halt. You know, after the business with Mister Fleete and our jailbreak."

In a low voice, Mary said, "It did stop things, Owen. At least amongst the whites."

"I'd expect some to cut and run."

"No, just about all have abandoned us."

"The Thompsons?" I asked.

"Yes," Mary said. "Pretty much."

"The cowards!" I said, and slapped the table with my hand.

"Not Henry, though," Ruth piped. "He's not abandoned us." I looked over and remembered the exchange that I had seen between her and young Henry Thompson at church.

"Yeah, but Owen's right," Watson said. "The rest are cowards. It's mostly just Lyman alone making all the runs now. I'd be there beside him, if the Old Man'd let me. It's this Fugitive Law; it's made cowards of our neighbors. People go over and harass the folks at Timbuctoo all the time, making like they're looking for escaped slaves. Even some folks we once counted as abolitionists."

I asked Susan, "Is this true?"

"Yes, mostly. But Lyman, him and a few others from there, are still taking people north. It worries me. But people get this close to freedom, you got to help them."

We talked then for a while of the increased difficulties and dangers of harboring escaped slaves and transporting them from Timbuctoo to Canada. Lyman had evidently grown fierce in the work, enraged by the death of Elden Fleete and his own brief imprisonment and made reckless rather than timid by it, joined only by a few of the more adventurous Negroes and by Henry Thompson, with no help coming from any of the whites in the northcountry, not even the Quakers in Port Kent. There were marshals and slave-catchers all over now, stopping off at the farm every few days and like plantation overseers checking the shacks and huts of Timbuctoo, intimidating the whites generally and the Negroes pointedly and employing Partridge and others like him to spy for them.

Shortly, we were enjoying a fine, ample supper of Brunswick stew made with squirrels shot that morning by Salmon and Oliver, and pickled beets and cucumbers, and a pile of Mary's famous Indian hoecakes—my welcome-home supper, Ruth called it. There was abundant good news, beyond Susan's pregnancy. Yes, it was true, Ruth and Henry Thompson had been courting, and as soon as he could arrange an interview with Father, Henry intended to ask for her hand in marriage. And the big, grinning secret concerning Mary was that she, too, was pregnant.

Startled, I put down my spoon and asked, "Well! That's something, isn't it? Does Father know yet?"

"Why, Owen, of course he does! I wrote to him right away. As soon as I knew myself, I told him. He was pleased as pie. Didn't he tell you?"

I said no, he didn't. "That is wonderful news, though," said I, weakly, thinking more of the difficulties promised by another child than the blessings. But now I understood why the Old Man had felt suddenly required to concentrate solely on work which would help support the family, and why he had put the Gileadites so abruptly aside, and why he had sent me back here. With his wife pregnant again, his sense of responsibility to his family would have been unexpectedly sharpened. He had not told me, no doubt, because it was still very early in her pregnancy, and after so many lost babies, Father had learned to protect himself by holding his excitement in abeyance: it had become characteristic of him to wait practically until the pregnancy was over before beginning to speak of it. Also, although he was a man who had helped a thousand sheep and hundreds of cows and horses to foal and had even helped deliver several of his own children, he was nonetheless peculiarly shy about talking of such matters when it came to humans.

I felt kindly towards Father again, and guilty for having been so quick to judge him. I upbraided myself and began to wonder whether I held some kind of permanent, unknown grudge against the man that kept me looking constantly for reasons to indict him, even while I went on believing that I loved and admired him beyond all other human beings. It was a strange, new question, and gave me pause.

The evening wore on, and as we talked and joked around the table and in the parlor afterwards, re-establishing our old, familiar roles and routines with one another, I was more or less forcibly integrated into the family, and gradually I began to understand some of the more subtle changes that had recently taken place at the farm, and mostly they disturbed me. The winter snows were about to blow down on us. But coming in, I'd noticed that a great deal of the autumn work on the place had not been done. The livestock had looked well-cared-for, but that, from long habit, was routine and to be expected. The boys had done a lot of hunting and fishing, I saw, with plenty of hides and pelts being dried in the barn—bear, wolf, the usual deer and beaver, a wildcat, even a pair of mountain lions—and an abundance of salted venison and trout and corned beef had been put up, but by the women, I assumed. Not half the wood in, and Lyman and the boys had cleared and burned less than five hundred square rods of the flatland that we'd need for spring planting and next year's hay. Blacksmith shop and butchering shed not closed in. Cold cellar not dug, and the soil already freezing hard. Barely half the fencing for the winter sheepfolds built. The barn had been closed in properly, but there were chicken coops and an extension for a winter pigsty that hadn't been started. They'd bred the dams for early lambing, Watson assured me, and had tanned the hides of eight deer, but hadn't gotten around yet to tanning the fleeces and pelts that Father had asked them to prepare for winter clothing. Fortunately, the women seemed to have done their autumn work—the smoking and salting of meats, putting up cheeses and lard, filling the root cellar with potatoes, squashes, and turnips—so we would at least have enough to eat.

But as I listened to the boys' excuses and explanations, mostly made by Watson, who as the eldest felt obliged to speak for them, I began to see that their failures had more to do with Lyman's continued and protracted absences from the farm, evidently caused by his work with the Underground Railroad, than by idleness or distraction on their part. They were, after all, only boys. Even Watson. They did not blame Lyman directly, but I saw that they wanted a proper foreman to organize the work every day and to provide instruction, oversight, and encouragement, and they needed a grown man's strong back to lift and heft alongside theirs.

Lyman's Railroad work had to be done, too, of course. Who could reproach him for it? Certainly not I, and in fact I intended to join him myself in his nighttime runs as soon as possible. But the farm had been allowed to slide. And unless we quickly pulled it back in line, we'd soon freeze, or our livestock would, and we'd starve, or we'd have to abandon the place altogether—and then no one would be able to work the Railroad.

I detected some small resentments against Lyman by the boys, evidenced by their clear reluctance to praise him or even to talk much about him, as if the subject held little or no interest for them. Mary and Ruth were voluble enough concerning the man, but I felt that they were not so much praising him as demonstrating to Susan their love and support of her, protecting her from embarrassment, and even at that, it was faint praise they were offering, more often excuses and explanations for his inability to run the place properly than proud descriptions of some specific accomplishment.

Also, without Father to generate and sustain the contacts with Timbuctoo, the family appeared to have fallen away from the Negro community without having built any compensatory alliances with the whites, except for Ruth's connection to the Thompsons, by virtue of her relationship with Henry. This was distressing. In this tough place, we all needed each other, white and Negro alike. But after the death of Elden Fleete, and with Father's and my departure following hard upon, the Negroes had been a little tetchy, Watson said. Understandably so. And there being no one left at the farm who could reassure them of our faithfulness to their cause, they had withdrawn almost all contact, despite Lyman's and Susan's continued loyalty to the family.

The Negroes were in bad shape, Watson said, and Susan confirmed: harried by the local whites, fearful of being carried off by slave-catchers and marshals, and not at all prepared for winter. Also, Watson explained, there was a growing number of whites, led by our old friend Mr. Partridge of Keene, who wished that both the Browns and the citizens of Timbuctoo would go back to wherever they came from. Some of these whites had previously been supporters of Father's efforts to help the Negroes, but now they, too, coveted the Negroes' and our land out on the flats—rich, silted land, rare in the Adirondacks, which they could see was not being farmed properly. By their lights, we were mis-using it, wasting our good fortune, and this angered them, for they were New England–style farmers, the type that likes to regard waste as a sin. Mr. Partridge, himself no great shakes as a farmer, was exploiting these resentments for his own purposes, which Watson said surely included gaining revenge for our having invaded his home in August, when we shot the slave-catcher and then freed Lyman and Mr. Fleete from the Elizabethtown jail.

Now, suddenly, where before I had thought of that episode with something approaching shame, I found myself regarding it almost with nostalgia, and I wished that we had done more damage than we did, wished that we had actually slain the slave-catcher and maybe Mr. Partridge, too, and wished that I had been the one to pull the trigger. There were tensions and conflicts everywhere breaking out, and I could not see how they could be quickly resolved, least of all by me. I could not step forward in church like Father and preach the Lord's work to the whites one week and then preach it to the Negroes the next, or walk into the midst of a crowd of white men at a cattle auction and scold them for their sloth and cowardice as only the Old Man could scold, and then ride over to Timbuctoo and do the same to a crowd of glowering, suspicious ex-slaves.

Even so, while there was little or nothing I could do to improve relations with the local people, white or black, I could nonetheless pull things together here on the farm. Eager to get an early start, and not a little tired from my journey, I begged off Watson's and Ruth's entreaties to tell them still more of the story of Father's and my travels abroad and climbed up to the loft well before the others. Lying in my cot there in the darkened chamber, I listened to the murmur of the voices of my family below: Mary and Ruth were carding wool and spinning, and the boys were coming and going between the house and barn, bedding down the animals, bringing in firewood, the last household chores of the day, while the little girls and Susan took turns reading from the primer, teaching one another to read and now and again appealing to Ruth or Mary to settle a dispute over a word's meaning or spelling. With those sweet sounds filling my ears, I drifted into peaceful sleep.

A while later, when the others came up to bed, I woke and listened in the darkness as, one by one, they, too, fell into slumber. But this time, however, I myself could not fall back to sleep. I lay wide-eyed in the silent darkness of the room for hours, my mind a-buzz with half-completed thoughts startling and interrupting one another. I could not figure what was keeping me so agitated—I almost never had any difficulty sleeping. Quite the opposite. Hours slipped by, and then I lost all track of how long I had been awake, and not until the first bleeding away of darkness signaled the near approach of dawn did I suddenly realize that I was waiting for Lyman to come home. And when I knew that, I thought only of it, and him. Until pale daylight began to filter into the room, when I rose and dressed and directly set about putting things right: like Father, the first one up and working.

I remember thinking on that first frosty morning home, as I walked the grounds and examined the outbuildings and livestock, that it would be a simple matter to make up for Father's and my lengthy absence and set the place straight. And, in a sense, it was simple, but not the way I expected. I calculated thirty days of steady work for the five of us—three boys, Watson, Salmon, and Oliver, and two grown men, Lyman Epps and me. I had learned early in life from Father how to organize a crew and lay out the day's work before breakfast, how to see each job through to the end before commencing another, how to make sure that each of us knew exactly what was expected of him for the entire day, and so on.

Father had never been easy with distributing authority of any kind anyhow, and he had failed to do it here also. Although, as usual, he had included in his letters long lists of things to do and when and how, he had simply left taking care of the farm to his family members and Lyman and Susan in a general way, without explicitly stating who was in charge of what and whom—so, in a way, it was more the Old Man's fault than anyone else's that the place had come undone. No family members were lazy or incapable. They had just needed a captain, or in this case, due to the captain's absence, a first mate. Without one, they had been working at sixes and sevens, each person responding only to his or her immediate needs, laboring more against each other than with each other, with no long view of things, no plan. Every man or boy for himself.

I will set everything right with ease, said I to myself. I had finished my inspection of the place with a circuit of the barn and a stop at the privy, where I noted the need to remove the season's night soil, and was about to return to the house and lay the kitchen fire for Mary before any of the others were out of bed. Between Mounts Tahawus and McIntyre the sun had already broken the horizon, and rosy streaks of new light spilled across the rippled, silvery sky. Over towards the village, the clouds were opening up, and in the dark blue western sky the morning star and a crescent moon were slipping towards the horizon. I stopped and took it in. It was dawn—first light, a marvelous, cold, half-illumined stillness—and made a comforting, reflective pause between night and day, between autumn and winter.

I could make out the village from the belfry of the church and a few threads of chimney-smoke rising from a black line of spruce trees by the river. There was a glaze of frost on the distant, yellowed fields and on the leafless branches and stalks of the chokecherry and alder bushes along the road from town and on the roofs of the house and barn and the unfinished outbuildings—a pale caul or a shroud, I could not say which, but it made everything look fresh and clean. I gazed around me and inhaled the cold mountain air with pleasure, the first pure pleasure I had felt in many days, since the night of the formation of the Gileadites.

My anger was gone. Soon everyone would admire me and be glad that I had come back.

As I neared the house to go in, I heard from the direction of the village the rumble of wagon wheels on the frozen road and the clop of a slow-moving horse. Around the curve in the road there came the second Morgan, Poke, the mare, pulling our old wagon at a plodding pace, and up on the box sat Lyman Epps, evidently asleep. Until the horse, smelling the barn, I suppose, accelerated somewhat and jolted him awake.

From the doorstoop, I watched him for a moment, without his having yet noticed me. He was exhausted, slump-shouldered, and barely able to hold his head up; his skin color was flat gray, like pewter, and his hair stuck out from under his cap in short, knotty clumps, and he seemed older, almost middle-aged: he looked more like an escaped slave himself, a man on the run, than a conductor on the Underground Railroad. How dangerously thin, especially now, I thought, was the line between an escaped slave and a freed slave, between the Negro man who was chattel and the one who was free. And how wide the gulf that lay between a Negro man, slave or free, and me.

He put up the wagon and unhitched Poke and led her into the barn to water and feed her and brush her down, still without having seen me. I was oddly hesitant about following him and speaking with him; yet we had much to say to one another. I felt shy as a girl with him, anxious and worried, even worried about my *appearance*!

Suddenly angry with myself, I strode across the yard to the barn determined to erase my self-consciousness and went in and greeted Lyman with false heartiness. "Hello, friend!" I loudly exclaimed. "Are you working late, or starting the day early?"

He smiled wanly and shook my hand. "Good to see you, Owen. When did you arrive?"

I told him of my return the previous day and jabbered on about my journey from Springfield. While I yacked and he listened, I helped him settle the horse and hang the harness, until finally I realized that he was standing at the barn door, politely waiting for me to finish so he could go into the house.

"I'm sorry," I said. "Here I'm keeping you from your wife. And you must be hungry and want to wash, while I'm going on about nothing."

"No, no, that's all right. I just needs to sleep some," he said, and yawned. "Pulled me a long ride last night, all the way back from Massena on them corduroy roads, you know. My backbone's sore."

"How many'd you take up?"

"A pair of 'em. Two men. From near Norfolk originally, off a Chesapeake Bay plantation. One a preacher. Preached my ear off the whole way up."

"You get them over all right? No trouble?"

"No trouble. No help, neither, but no trouble."

"Well, you'll have some help now," I said, adding that as soon as we had the farm readied for winter, I'd be working the Railroad with him. "That ought to shame a few other white folks back into action," I declared.

"I don't know, folks is pretty scared now," he said. "But good. I could use some help moving those as comes along from time to time. There ain't as many as before, you know. Not since the Fugitive Law."

"The Fugitive Law!" I said, and spat, like an actor in a melodramatic show.

"But I expect with winter coming," he went on, "we'll see a last batch making a run for it. So's they don't get stuck hiding out in people's attics down here till spring."

"Right, right, of course. But first we've got to—"

"In fact," he said, interrupting me, "Tom Grey over to Timbuctoo, you recall him? He told me of a family of five, maybe six, be coming through from Utica tonight or tomorrow. If they ain't already arrived. You didn't hear nothing 'bout that, did you? Tom said he'd send word over here soon's they arrived."

"No. No one told me anything. But first we've got to get this place in shape, Lyman."

"Yes. Yes, I know," he said, and turned to leave.

I reached out and grabbed him by the arm, more forcefully than I intended, causing him to stop and remove my hand as if insulted by it.

"I'm sorry," I said. "It's just I need to talk to you about the work, Lyman. Fact is, you and the boys have let things slide a little far, I think."

He turned to me, with his face cast to the side. I began nonetheless to list the various jobs and projects that lay before us and to put them in the order that we would follow, when I shortly realized that he wasn't hearing me, was merely waiting for me to finish so he could go inside the house. I grew impatient with him. In a sense, this was his farm, too, nearly as much as it was mine, and he had certain responsibilities towards it, which he clearly was not interested in accepting. "Lyman, you're not listening, are you?"

"Owen," he said, still without looking at me, "what I am is tired. My back feels broke from three days and nights up on that wagon out there. Maybe we can talk about these matters later, when I've got me some rest."

I don't know what came over me then, but my ears began to buzz, and a gauzy, blood-red screen dropped before my eyes. With no conscious intention or desire to do it, I grabbed Lyman by the shoulder with my right hand, clamped my left onto his belt, and lifted and flung him bodily across the room, banging him hard against the stall, causing the horses to roll their eyes in fear and stamp their feet. He slid to the floor, shaken and astonished, and looked up at me with fear in his eyes for the first time ever, which I took in happily almost, accepting his gaze with a strange relief. As if I had long wanted him to fear me.

He said in a steady, low voice, "There's something gone wrong in you."

My breathing came hard, although I had not exerted myself—I was very strong, and Lyman, not a large man, had not resisted me. "Maybe . . . maybe there is. No, nothing is wrong in me. But my priorities . . . I have to hold to my priorities. This farm, it's all so shaky. The winter's coming. You wouldn't listen."

Slowly, he got to his feet and brushed bits of hay off his coat and trousers and put his cap back on, restoring his dignity. "I'm listening now," was all he said.

"Well, we've got these priorities. The farm and all. And responsibilities, to the family. To your family, too. You and I, we've got to take care of them in the proper way. Then we can attend to the others, to the Railroad and all that. But it's not like we have Father here for that. Don't you understand?"

"I understand. Priorities. Responsibilities. I understand those things just fine."

He moved warily towards the open barn door, facing me all the while, as if he expected me to attack him again. And I was gladdened by his wariness. I knew that in an hour, perhaps in a moment or two, I would surely collapse inside myself with shame and would beg Lyman's forgiveness; but right then I was determined to keep myself open to these feelings of unexpected joy and to let them flow through me like a cold wind. By attacking Lyman physically, I had released in myself something dark and wonderfully satisfying. It was as if an ice-dam had let go, and huge chunks of ice, a flotilla of logs and fallen trees and frozen debris, were cascading over boulders and cliffs, making a great roar, and I was at this instant thrilled by the sheer power and noise of the flow.

I had done the forbidden thing. I had struck a black man.

I took a step towards him, and he jumped back, nearly out the door of the barn into the yard.

I reached for him, and he jumped again. "Why didn't you fight me, Lyman?"

He squinted up at me as if he had not heard right.

"I want to know. Why didn't you fight me, just now?"

"You think I'm a fool?"

"Is it because I'm white?"

He laughed coldly. "No, Owen, it ain't because you're white. I ain't afraid of your skin. I might be afraid of what you got inside your head, though. And I treat any man twice my size with a certain caution. That's all."

"Well, it's over," I said. I couldn't apologize, not yet, but I said, "I swear, I'll never do that again."

He hesitated a moment and stared at me, and I saw that the fear had dissipated somewhat, replaced by something harder, darker. "Maybe so. Maybe not. Time will tell that." He looked more sad than anything else. He said, "You tell me something, though."

"What?"

"When you grab onto me like that and toss me down, you doing it because you *can*. Is that because I'm a whole lot smaller than you? Or is it because I'm colored?"

I was silent for a few seconds but did not look away. "You know the answer to that."

"Say it, then."

"It's not because you're smaller than me."

"Right. It's my skin. You're afraid of my skin. But I ain't afraid of yours. Which is why I didn't fight you back. That's what we got here. Ain't it?"

"I can't lie to you."

"'Appreciate that," he said. "I'm going in now. We can discuss all those priorities and responsibilities of yours later on, if you want. But I got some of my own need tending first." He turned, straightened, and walked towards the house and went quickly inside.

I saw smoke curling from the chimney; Mary had set the fire, and I could see her through the window at the stove, smiling broadly at Lyman as he entered, and Susan crossing the room towards him with her arms out. The others were probably already up and about, too, and were greeting him, welcoming him home, relieved that he had gotten back from the border safe and unharmed. And I saw that I, who was going to lead them, would now have to follow.

We remained friends, Lyman and I, but only of a sort, for there was now between us a nearly tangible distance, as if we were condemned to carry a long stick together, which connected us one to the other and at the same time kept us strictly apart. Each man was at all times painfully conscious of the other's presence and, when it occurred, his absence as well. A difficult intimacy; but it was all we had now.

I made no further argument against his priorities or for mine, and whenever he took the horse and wagon and was gone from the farm for two or three days at a time, I barely acknowledged to him that I had noticed. When he returned and had rested, he would come directly to me, say nothing about where he had been, and politely ask where did I want him to work that day. I assigned him to whatever task was at hand, and he pitched himself whole-heartedly into it. But then a few days or a week would pass, and word would come that he had passengers waiting over at Timbuctoo, and he'd be gone again.

I forbade the boys to join him on these runs, causing at first some tension between me and Watson, particularly; he had grown stridently anti-slavery—as a way of asserting his new manhood, I supposed. But he was eventually mollified by my promise that, as soon as we had the place in shape for winter, he and I both would join Lyman carrying slaves to freedom. We'd go back to "the work."

By the time the snows were falling heavily and regularly and temperatures no longer went above zero and the winds from Canada had begun their scraping howl, there were no more escaped slaves coming our way, and we all, even Lyman, from then till spring, spent our days and nights pretty much inside. By mid-December, however, before the heavy snows and cold hit, we had managed to cut and stack close to fifty cords of firewood, most of which, to Lyman's and the boys' credit, came from hardwood trees that they had dropped and trimmed in the forest earlier in the autumn. We finished the cold cellar and the other outbuildings, fenced in the sheepfolds, bred the ewes, did all the fall butchering, ran a short sawdust barrier around the base of the house, and completed half-a-hundred other chores and jobs—all of it done before winter finally descended with its full strength.

After that, Lyman withdrew and spent his days mostly in his blacksmith's shop, manufacturing ironwork for the farm, everything from nails to fireplace dogs, and I worked alone, too, usually in the barn, where, among other useful things, I built a set of sled runners and affixed them to the wagon in place of the wheels, making a sleigh of it, which enabled us to get quickly and comfortably to church on the Sabbath and into the settlement, where we milled our grain and corn, sold fleeces, leather, and woolen cloth for a little cash money, and visited the few families we still felt comfortable with, such as the Nashes, the Brewsters, and the Thompsons; with the latter, through the connection between their son Henry and sister Ruth, we were becoming nicely linked.

I remember that winter, despite the tense stand-off between me and Lyman, as the most peaceful of all our winters in North Elba. Perhaps it was because we were free for once of "the work" and because Father was away. It put us more at ease with our neighbors, certainly, for it made us more like them—abolitionist in principle but not in action; devoted to our farm and livestock, but not at the cost of not socializing with our neighbors; religious to the point of regularly attending services on the Sabbath and otherwise honoring the day as we always had, but not preaching to everyone and thumping people with the Bible on every possible occasion.

Except for the fact that we had a Negro man and woman living with us in our house, we were no different from any other white family settled in that area. Like them, we holed up against the winter, did some hunting, ice-skated on Mirror Lake, repaired and built tools and furniture, spun wool and wove cloth, tanned hides and made new boots, harness, hats, and belts, and tended our flocks and cattle and horses. We ate our stores of salt pork, mutton, venison, and salt fish; we ate it roasted, boiled, baked, and in stews; with potatoes, squashes, beets, beans, pumpkins, carrots, and turnips from the cold cellar. We drank plenty of fresh milk, made cheese and butter in abundance, mashed our apples into cider, and warmed ourselves before the fire with sassafras tea. Like all good abolitionists, we eschewed sugar, but for sweets we had gallons of honey taken in the early autumn, and as we would not be able to tap our own trees till spring, we swapped hides with our neighbors for their extra maple syrup, using it to flavor meats, vegetables, and bread, and made maple sugar from it and sheets of hard maple candy. And we grew healthy and strong inside our warm house.

We said grace over every meal, prayed together in the evening, and sang the old hymns, and sometimes we even sang new songs, which we learned from our neighbors or from Susan or that Mary remembered from her childhood. We read The Liberator and Frederick Douglass's North Star and from Father's collection of books, and we older folks taught the little ones their ABCs and numbers, while Ruth worked with Susan and Lyman, teaching them with the primer to read adult books and periodicals.

And we read Father's letters. Every few weeks, a new, long letter arrived from one of the stops in his odyssey through the courts, letters from Springfield, Troy, Pittsburgh, Boston, and Hartford. Instructional and scolding, as always, but also warm and affectionate, they were. As had been the practice for many years, we read them aloud, and then I or Watson copied the letters; we left the originals out on his desk, for further perusal and to keep track of his instructions, and placed the copies in Father's steel box, protecting them against flood, fire, or theft. For posterity, as Father said, although up to that time preserving his letters had seemed mere vanity to me—especially after the Gileadites and our adventures in England, which had left me feeling somewhat disillusioned regarding posterity's interest in my father and his work.

But increasingly that winter, Father's letters spoke in unusual detail of his meetings with famous men and women, abolitionists all, some of them well-known white ministers and teachers, like Reverends Channing and Parker and the famous Horace Mann, some of them known as well for their support of female rights, like Dr. Howe and Miss Lydia Maria Child and Miss Abby Kelley, who was one of the best orators he had ever heard, said Father. There were famous Negroes, too: he met with Bishop Loguen in Syracuse and confided his plan, which, according to Father, "Bishop Loguen thinks noble and very possibly workable." At a meeting in Hartford, he heard Miss Harriet Tubman address a hundred white people very bravely. Personally introduced to her afterwards by Frederick Douglass, Father said he "spoke at considerable length with her and found her a great warrior." In Boston, he frequently found himself in the company of literary people and mentioned Thomas Wentworth Higginson and a young editor of The Atlantic Monthly, Franklin Sanborn, who took him to Concord to meet personally with Ralph Waldo Emerson, whom Father now admired, and his friend Henry Thoreau, "a firebrand on the subject of slavery," wrote Father, "but a strangely misanthropic fellow, due to his loss of religion, I believe. I know nothing of his writings, but Mr. Sanborn assures me they are very good." There were even some businessmen, he told us, who were becoming interested in aiding the movement generally and Father in particular: a fellow in the cloth-manufacturing business named George Stearns and "several rich men who want their money to go for something more substantial than speeches and newspapers and travel expenses for public speakers. I intend to satisfy them of this," he wrote.

For one as close to Father as I, it was difficult to see him as others did. But it could not be denied that when he held forth on the subjects of slavery and religion in a public forum, he had a commanding presence, despite his high-pitched voice and stiff, somewhat Puritanical manner, and the more people deferred to him, the more he seemed to warrant their deference, for the attention and respect of strangers made him appear to grow literally in size and stature, as well as in lucidity and brilliance of speech. And he was never so tall and straight, never so articulate and convincing in argument, never so unquestionably honest and sincere, as when holding forth on the inextricably entwined subjects of slavery and religion.

It was as if Father saw all Americans residing inside a cosmic allegory, like characters in a story by John Bunyan, and his personal force and intelligence were such that he could make even the most materialistic of men believe it with him. People had grown more desperate now, more pessimistic as to the inescapable, gradual ending of slavery in America, and many who in the past had been content to oppose slavery merely with words were now beginning to consider more drastic action. As one of the very few who had come forward with a specific plan of action, and as perhaps the only man who seemed capable of carrying it out, Father was therefore a considerably more interesting figure now than he had been a mere six months earlier.

Also, it was of no small matter, I'm sure, that Father was unique

among white abolitionists by virtue of his having captured the trust
and admiration of Negroes, given him not because of his political
power or wealth or social standing, for he had none, but because of the
pure force of his anger. What in Father frightened the whites pleased
the blacks. Frederick Douglass, Bishop Loguen, Reverend Highland
Garnet, Harriet Tubman—they all vouched for him, spoke of him as one
of them, and this surely must have impressed the whites sufficiently to
balance their fear of him.

He was, after all, quite unlike the rest of the better-known white
abolitionists. First off, he was a physically tough man, and it showed.
Although he had never fought in battle, he gave the impression of a
man who had. Tanned and lean as a braided leather quirt, straight as a
stick, he had the physical energy of a man half his age. His spartan reg-
imen of little sleep, basic food, no alcohol or tobacco, was impressive.
Also, he spoke knowledgeably of weapons and of the acquisition and
deployment of men, horses, and supplies; he understood principles of
attack and siege, strategic retreat, counter-attack, and ambush; he had
studied the memoirs of great generals and the histories of famous campaigns with sufficient diligence that he could sound like a man who
had been at Waterloo with Napoleon himself, who had fought alongside Garibaldi, who had ridden with Cortez against the invincible
Montezuma.

The winter in North Elba, even by our old Ohio and New England standards, was long and brutal. But our Adirondack neighbors deemed it
mild, and despite our secret suspicion that it would never end, spring
did eventually come trickling in, and with it came the time for the
birth of Susan's and Lyman's baby, an imminent arrival which was
regarded by all of us as a great event. We had come to know in varying
degrees how Susan had lost her previous children to slavery, and
though he never spoke of it, we believed that Lyman was eager to

become a father. This would be his and Susan's first child born in free-dom, and its birth would be a visible emblem of their great sacrifice and triumph.

Susan had taken to sleeping downstairs with Mary, whose own baby was not due till early June, the two pregnant women sharing Father's and Mary's large bed by the stove; Lyman, of course, had con-tinued to sleep up in the loft with me and the boys on one side of the curtain, Ruth and the girls on the other. It was not an uncomfortable arrangement, however unconventional, and it was practical, contriving as it did to make the hours we spent in bed a businesslike affair difficult to corrupt with indolence or socializing, for as soon as you woke, out of politeness and modesty, there was nothing to do but rise from your cot and dress in the dark and set about to work. Our sleeping arrange-ments, except when Father was at home, when they provided him and Mary with a small privacy, functioned strictly to enable us to sleep, nothing else. Which was, no doubt, as Father had intended.

The animals were restless, shedding their shaggy winter coats and eager to be let out of their pens and stalls after long confinement, and the lambing had begun in a promising way, and we were looking for-ward to a successful shearing. Also, we had two new calves and a large litter of pigs to add to our livestock. The mountains were still as shrouded by snow and bleak sheets of ice as in January, but down in the cleared valleys and flatlands surrounding North Elba, the snow had diminished to long, rounded peninsulas and smooth-shored islands melting into the yellowed, soppy fields and soft, two-feet-deep blankets that lingered in the woods and dales and on north-facing slopes. The Au Sable River was running freely again, and the lakes and ponds, although they had not begun yet to crack and boom and break up, were no longer safe to cross with a sleigh.

Suddenly, we were once again busy outdoors, clearing new ground, burning stumps and building fences, preparing the land for plowing as soon as it dried, tapping sugar maples and boiling down the sap in huge cauldrons. With each new day the sun rose earlier and set later, and every night we fell into bed exhausted from our work and rose in the morning eager to return to it. We had entered what our laconic neighbors called, not spring, but mud season. Where, for months, the frozen, rock-hard roads, lanes, paths, and farmyards had been buried under head-high drifts, they were now cleared of snow and ice and stood revealed as made entirely of soft, sticky mud—heavy, deep, corrugated rivers and ponds of it. The mud was everywhere, impossible to keep out of the house, off our tools and boots, wagons, animals, and machinery, and we slogged through it as if through molasses.

I hung the sleigh runners in the barn and put onto the wagon a new set of large, wide wheels, which I had built myself during the dark winter months, six-foot wheels with iron rims that had been crafted by Lyman in his smith's shop. It was hard going, but with the new wagon wheels and by using both horses instead of only one, we were able to travel nonetheless. And travel we did. For there was movement again on the Underground Railroad, and this time I meant to take Watson and join Lyman myself in conducting the fugitive slaves, who were beginning to emerge blinking and fearful from their wintry hiding places and make their way north once again, passed as before from hand to hand, cellar to cellar, and attic to attic, up along the route from Utica to Timbuctoo to Port Kent and on by cart or sleigh to French Canada; or sometimes, via Lyman's favorite route now, traveling northwest from Timbuctoo over the deepest Adirondack wilderness to Massena, thence to the St. Lawrence crossing at Cornwall and into Ontario there.

We Browns were going to be alongside him this time, armed and vigilant. I wished to make it clear to Lyman that he and I now shared the same priorities. I could not bear the thought that he might think me interested only in the farm, as had undeniably been the case in the

autumn. These fluctuations in policy, I knew, were a sign of my confusion then, but it felt not so much like a moral confusion as a temporary
and strictly personal conflict between loyalty to Lyman and loyalty to
Father. With the autumn and winter behind us, I believed that I was
able once again to be loyal to both.

Slave-catchers and their collaborators that spring were skulking
like hungry wolves in and around all the towns and cities that lay along
the usual routes north, especially in western New York and in the
Hudson and Champlain valleys from Albany to Plattsburgh, and as a
result, agents of the Underground Railroad in places like Utica,
Syracuse, and Schenectady were sending many more fugitives than
before over the considerably more arduous Adirondack mountain and
wilderness route that Lyman favored. This in spite of the harsh
weather, the bad roads, the long distances between stations, and the
threat of meeting wolves and other wild animals. Along about the middle of March, fugitives first began arriving late at night in Timbuctoo,
and the next morning one of our few allies from the settlement, a person known to us, would arrive at the farm to apprise us of the situation.
That same night, regardless of our obligations at the farm, Lyman and I
and Watson would hitch up the team and drive the wagon over to
Timbuctoo, where we would pick up our poor, frightened human cargo
and carry it north to Canada and freedom.

Happily, during this period Lyman and I came to be like brothers
again. We renewed our old joking manner with one another and even
began having serious talks on such subjects as religion and the relations between men and women. But not race. Prior to our confrontation in the fall, race had been the central subject of all our serious talks
with one another, and we rarely, if ever, discussed our true beliefs
regarding religion or men and women. Now, however, race was the sole
unspoken subject between us. We could talk truthfully and as equals
about the Lord, about His work, and about being men, like any two

friends of the same color, but we could no longer talk about one of us being black and the other white. I secretly grieved over this particular loss of intimacy, for I had never shared it with a Negro man before. But at the same time I was glad of it, too. Perched up on the box alongside Lyman, with Watson crouched at the rear of the wagon with his rifle at the ready, our precious cargo huddled out of sight underneath the tarpaulin, I felt somehow freed to pretend that Lyman, like me, was a white man, or that I, like him, was black, and we were merely two American men out doing the Lord's work together.

There were fifteen or twenty runs that spring, but I remember best the morning in mid-April when we came back to the farm from an especially arduous run to the Ontario border. We had been gone for three days and four nights, had almost lost the wagon in a muskeg south of Potsdam, had been forced to travel half a day off our route on an old lumbermen's trail to find a place where we could safely ford the Raquette River, and at the end had narrowly escaped a pair of slave-catchers encamped outside Massena, just south of the border. Watson had performed bravely, and though he claimed to have shot both of them when they pursued us in the gray, early morning light for several miles along the bank of the broad, still-frozen St. Lawrence, he certainly hit one, which discouraged the other, and thus we were able finally to deliver our cargo safely at the crossing to Cornwall.

The trip back to North Elba, though less risky—since now the only Negro aboard was Lyman, who always carried his old, tattered manu-mission papers in a wallet strapped to his leg like a knife—was not much easier, as the weather alternated between rain, sleet, and snow. We crossed marsh and muskeg, saw mists at dawn rising off the wilderness lakes where deer and moose came down to the edge to drink and look up and watch us as we passed along the opposite shore. We penetrated deep into the ancient blue spruce and balsam forests, passed through miles of beech woods and hickory, circled beaver ponds, saw the tracks of lion and heard the howl of wolves and the coughing bark of bears, were brought up short at fast-running, rock-bottomed streams choked with snowmelt and overflowing their banks and sending us back up into the woods on lumber trails in long complex loops until we could return again to the road, which was never a real road, only a lonely, wagon-wide path through the northwoods, a deer trail become an Indian trail widened by horses and sledges bringing out timber and by supply wagons going into the camps.

As on other such difficult, demanding treks, with little or no sleep, we had gone a whole day without food, without seeing a settlement or farm or even another human being, save for an occasional trapper crossing the trail into the deep woods to check his lines, furtive and solitary as a wild animal himself. What did the enslavement of three million Negroes mean to him? Or the Fugitive Slave Law? Did he know, much less care, who was President? Had he even heard of abolitionism? Sometimes when I saw one of these pelt-covered, bearded fellows with his backpack and steel-toothed traps and long-barreled rifle disappearing into the wilderness, I almost envied him. His ignorance and single-minded pursuit of the skins of animals was a kind of innocence that I would never know again, if I had ever known it at all.

It was dawn when we finally arrived at the farm. The overcast sky was soft as flannel and gray in the east above Tahawus and soot black in the west. It had rained most of the night, a raw, penetrating rain that had soaked straight through our cloaks and hats and made our bones feel brittle as iron. As we pulled into the yard, we saw lamplight inside the kitchen and smoke from the chimney, and Lyman remarked on it, for normally, with Father away, no one would be out of bed this early. I think that we both at the same instant realized what had wakened the family, for without saying a word to one another, as we passed the house, I handed the reins to Watson, and Lyman and I jumped down from the wagon and made for the door.

It was indeed as we had expected—Susan's baby had come. Susan's baby—Lyman's baby as well. Yet somehow I could not see it that way. Even then, long before I had come to any awareness of the true nature of my feelings for Susan, I seemed to be cutting Lyman out of his privileges and prerogatives, so that when I looked from face to face in the warm, dimly lit kitchen and saw only grief and exhaustion, saw none of the exhilaration and pride that I expected, I did not think once of Lyman's loss. Only of Susan's, and in some small, illegitimate way, my own.

Mary slumped at the table with her Bible open before her, but she was not reading from it; she merely gazed out the window opposite at the slowly brightening field and woods beyond. Ruth was seated on the bed next to Susan, wiping the woman's face with a damp cloth. Ruth's expression was grim, tight-lipped, frightened, but accepting, as if during the night and long hours into dawn she had learned some terrible thing about her own coming fate. The other children moved about slowly in their pantaloons and union suits; half-dressed, sad-faced waifs they seemed, trying to put together a bit of breakfast for themselves. The women looked drained and exhausted; they had clearly been up all night, struggling to bring a child into the world. Susan herself, mother of the child, lay back among the pillows with her eyes closed, her hands beneath the covers, all color drained from her face so that she was nearly as white as Ruth, and for an instant I thought that she had died and felt a moan begin to rise in my throat.

Then her eyes blinked open. She turned her head slowly on the pillow and, expressionless, looked at her husband and me at the door, the two of us huge and cold, noisy in our heavy boots and rain-soaked clothes, clumsy, obdurate, and male, all out of place in this silent, warm, sad company of women and children. I was thinking hard thoughts. So many babies are born dead, you dare not wish for them to be born at all.

And so many die right after they are born, you wonder why they were allowed to live in the first place. And if they live awhile, so many soon sicken and die, you wish they had died at the start and had not let you learn to love them. The women, they weaken and grow sadder with each loss, but the men, what do they do? I thought that they must gnash their teeth and pound the walls with their fists, as I did then. I balled my right hand into a fist and banged it hard against the wall, one, two, three times, each blow stronger than the last, until I thought I would bring down the wall like blinded Samson. Then, frightened by my own fury, I went to a far corner of the room and closed my eyes and wished for words of prayer, but found none.

In a strangely cold tone, Ruth said, "The baby was born dead. We have wrapped it for burial. You will need to dig a grave for it, Owen. Do it now," she said.

I cleared my throat and said, "And Susan? How is she?"

Mary spoke then. "She'll be fine, I'm sure. Do as Ruth said, Owen. Dig the grave. Susan will be fine. The midwife from Timbuctoo was over to tend her and left only a short while ago. She knows all the old remedies, and Susan has been treated by them. The baby has no name, but we need to bury it, so we can say our prayers for it. Lyman may want to make a marker, but there's no need. It never drew breath," she said, and added, almost as afterthought, "It was a baby boy."

Throughout, Lyman had not made a sound or a move from the door. He stood there now, immobile and as silent as when he had come in. I had tears running down my cheeks, yet his eyes were dry and cool, his face impassive. My body was hot with rage, and I could barely keep it still, but Lyman stood with his hands slack at his sides. He was more a carved block of ice in the dead of winter than a man. He held himself like that and regarded his wife with strange placidity, as if he had come upon her sleeping and did not want to waken her but merely wished to watch her awhile without her knowing.

Finally, Susan said in a voice that was almost a whisper, "I'm sorry, Lyman."

He twisted his lips as if to clear his mouth of an unpleasant taste, and when a few seconds of painful silence had passed, he said, "It was not meant to be." And then abruptly he turned and departed from the house.

I followed him out the door, still shaking with what I thought was rage and grief. Unable to say anything useful or comforting to Susan, still unable even to pray, I proceeded at once to follow my stepmother Mary's order to dig a grave for the infant. That would be my use. Then, before I had reached the barn, Lyman came riding out on Adelphi.

I reached up and grabbed the bridle and asked, "Where are you going?"

"Timbuctoo."

"Why?"

"I'm going to put my cabin straight."

"What? Why do that now? I don't understand."

He would not look at me. "I'll be back in a few days, and I'll be taking Susan then."

"What are you talking about?"

"I'm saying what I'm saying."

"But you can't leave," I said. "She needs to be here, and she needs to have you with her."

"No. She and I need to be amongst our own people. I don't want to have to explain it to you, Owen. But it ain't right for us to be living here anymore with you Browns. There's too much gone wrong for us since we moved over here, so we're going to go on back now, soon as Susan's ready to travel that far."

"No," I declared. "You can't do that."

He sighed and shook his head. "Don't know that you can stop me, Owen, since that's what I'm determined to do."

"This is Father's horse you're riding," I said, as if that would stop him. It seemed to me almost unthinkable, that he would remove Susan and himself from our house and return to their bare little cabin in Timbuctoo. Did he think that we had cursed him, had put a hex on him?

He looked down at me with irritation and something like pity on his face. "Fine," he said, and he swung down from the horse to the ground, handed me the reins, and walked away. I stood there holding the horse and watched in silence as he strode across the yard to the road, then down the road in the direction of the African settlement, until he was finally gone from sight.

When I returned the horse to its stall in the barn, Watson was there, brushing down the other Morgan. "I thought Lyman went off on Adelphi," he said. "What's the matter? He was weird."

"Yes, well, there's bad news," I said. "Susan's baby, it was born dead."

His bright face suddenly went slack and pale. He said nothing, simply stood there with the brush in his hand, open-mouthed and silent, as if he had been hit in the chest and had lost his breath.

"I need help digging the grave, Wat," I said. "Will you come with me?" I had picked up the spade and pick and stood by the door.

"Yes, sure. Oh, this is pretty terrible for them, isn't it?"

"Yes. It's terrible."

"Is Susan all right?"

"Yes. She'll be fine in a few days."

"What about Lyman?"

"Lyman's upset, but he'll be all right."

"Where was he off to on Adelphi?"

"Stop asking questions," I said, handing him the pick. "Just follow me; we'll dig the grave."

He shrugged his bony shoulders, grabbed up the pick, and traipsed along behind me, a pair of gravediggers on a cold, gray, drizzling dawn.

A hundred rods or so beyond the house, in a clearing near a stand of birches, my brother Watson and I dug a deep hole in the wet, rocky soil. Afterwards, I built a small pine box and into it placed the tiny body of the infant wrapped in a plain, earth-colored scrap of wool and nailed it shut. We never saw the infant itself, only its humble shroud. Then Watson and I lowered the box into the hole and filled it and covered the opening in the ground with sod. It would remain unmarked. And by the time we came seven weeks later to bury Mary's and Father's unnamed infant in its unmarked grave, the grass had grown tall over the first grave, and daisies were blooming there, and you could not see where it had been. Although I knew exactly where the first grave was located and saw it clearly, as if there were a tall, engraved marble stone at its head:

> Unnamed Baby, born to Susan & Lyman Epps
> "We shall not all sleep, but we shall all be changed"
> I Corinthians 15:51

It was a terrible time then, with the baby born dead and with Lyman and Susan gone off to live amongst the Negroes in Timbuctoo and with Mary's own birthing date fast approaching—in itself not upsetting, even to me, but it meant that Father would soon be coming to North Elba, which now, more than ever before, filled me with nameless dread. Why was his coming so dreadful? He was my father. I loved him. I believed that I had done nothing wrong.

I could only say to myself that it had to do with the disarray that I saw all around, and I knew he would see it the second he drew up before the house—the Old Man could smell disorder in the air—and in short order he would set everything right again. Humiliating me. Even so, I felt strangely paralyzed, and my anticipation of his coming only seemed to make it worse.

Spring planting went ahead, but it was more Watson's and Salmon's doing than mine, and it was done in a desultory fashion; and though we continued to clear back the forest at a fairly good rate, cutting and burning and pulling stumps off nearly a half-acre of ground a week, we did it sloppily—unscientifically, Father would say—like hired laborers without a foreman. And the house was falling into steady disrepair, as we could not seem to find the time or the energy or the wit to repair the damage done to the roof and chimneys by the winter winds and ice.

And we had no excuses this time; we could not tell ourselves, or report to Father when he arrived, that we had been too busy doing the Lord's work to do our own. We were no longer conductors on the Underground Railroad. Father's great Subterranean Passway, at least our small section of it, had gone dead. Without Lyman to act as liaison between us and the citizens of Timbuctoo, we were unable to carry fugitive slaves north. Without Lyman, no one came to us anymore for help, which disappointed me greatly and made me a failure, not only in my own eyes but in the eyes of Watson, and of Salmon, too, who had grown as passionate as Watson on the issue of slavery and as eager as he to oppose it.

They could not understand my reluctance to confront Lyman forthrightly and honestly. "Why'n't you just go over there and make it clear that we're ready to run folks north in our wagon as soon as they show up in Timbuctoo?" Salmon demanded. "Just put it to him, Owen. What's the big deal between you and Lyman anyhow? So what if he wants to go back and live on his own land in Timbuctoo? Seems only natural, don't it?"

"You don't understand."

"No, I don't."

"He doesn't want anything more to do with us Browns."

"Why? Because of Susan's baby? That can't be it. We didn't have anything to do with that. It was the Lord's will."

"I don't know, Salmon. You talk to him, if you want. You go over there, and you plead with him to provide us with passengers for our wagon and team so that we can feel better about ourselves. You tell him how much he needs us to help him help his Negro brethren, Salmon. You know what he'll say?"

"What?"

"I . . . I don't know. I don't know what he'll say. I just know that I can't go to him. Not now. Maybe not ever."

"Sounds crazy to me," he said, disgusted. And he did, indeed, that very day of our conversation, ride out to Timbuctoo all by himself, only to return in the evening clearly disappointed and not a little confused. He came in at supper and sat down sullenly at the table without taking off his hat and coat or wiping his muddy boots.

It was Ruth who asked him what Lyman had told him, for she, like everyone else in the family, had known why the boy had gone over there. Mary had even put up a basket of bread and preserves for Salmon to carry to them. I said nothing, and neither did Watson, who I think had guessed by then that there was something dark and personal between me and Lyman, something that could not yet be named by either of us, for neither Lyman nor I knew what it was ourselves. We merely felt its power and acted on it, as if we had no choice in the matter, as if it were a shared compulsion of some sort, the nature of which would become apparent to us and nameable only later, when it no longer controlled us.

"I never even saw him," Salmon said. "I tried talking to some others, Mister Grey and the other Mister Epps, the choirmaster. But they said there was no Underground Railroad in Timbuctoo. Like I was some kind of slave-catcher or something. Didn't know what I was talking about. Lyman, they told me, was gone off."

"They say where?" Watson asked.

"Nope. Just gone off. You know how they can get when they don't want you to know something. They smile and tell you something half-right and half-wrong, act like they don't know the truth any more than you do. 'Lyman, he gon' off somewheres, Mistah Brown.' I'm telling you, it was like I was the sheriff or a slave-catcher, the way they treated me."

"Did you go to his cabin?" Watson wanted to know.

I remained silent throughout, as if none of this concerned me.

"Yep. And it looked like he'd been doing some work on it. Has himself a pretty decent kitchen-garden under way, too. I even saw Susan," he said, and I put down my knife and spoon and looked up.

It had been just over a month since they had left, that long since I had seen her, and suddenly, upon hearing her name in my brother's mouth, imagining him in her presence, I realized that during those thirty-odd days and nights I had thought of almost no one else. Her face, her voice, her shape and movement, had constantly been in my mind. No matter what I was doing, no matter whom I was talking to, it was Susan I was thinking of, missing, pining for, longing to speak to. And to touch. Lyman, whenever I thought of him, as indeed I frequently did, came to my mind only as an obstacle to my reaching his wife. He was a curtain blocking my view, a rock rolled into my path, a palisado surrounding the object of my desire.

That I had not once, until this moment, stepped back from my thoughts and observed their peculiar nature shocked and alarmed me. But that's how powerful they were, how all-consuming. Once I knew my thoughts, however, I was first appalled and then instantly repelled. Of course! I reasoned. This was the source of the pain between me and Lyman. And he had known it long before I did, surely. He had seen that I was in love with his wife, and naturally, as soon as he could, he had withdrawn her from me.

My blood washed over me. I felt absurd, and then guilty, and wished only that I could somehow purge myself of my love for Susan and make amends to Lyman. It also occurred to me that this had been the source of my anxiety about Father's imminent arrival in North Elba: I was afraid that he would ask after Lyman and Susan, and when I replied that we had not seen them since their return to Timbuctoo, he would look me in the eye, and he would know at once what I myself had gone months without even guessing.

Abruptly, I stood up and left the house. It was nearly dark, the temperature dropping fast as the sun sank behind the mountains, with the smell of mud and melting snow mingling in the cold air. I went behind the barn and walked up to the grove of young birches there and cut off a switch and stripped it of its new, red buds. Back inside the barn, in the darkness, with the animals shifting their weight quietly in their stalls, I barred the door and stood in the middle of the large room. I pulled off my shirt and drew the top of my union suit to my waist, exposing my naked upper body to the chilled dark. Then I began to beat my chest and back with the switch—slowly and lightly at first, then faster and with greater force, and soon I was doing it with genuine fervor. But it was not enough. The switch was too light and broke off in my hand.

For a moment, I stood half-naked and foolish, out of breath, angry at myself, as if I were an iron object that I had stumbled against in the dark. I remembered Father's strip of cowhide, which he kept out here to discipline and chastize the younger children, although he rarely used it nowadays. I knew exactly where it was, hung on a nail by the door. It was short, not quite a yard long, but heavy and stiff and dry with disuse, with a sharp edge to it. I reached out in the dark and took it down. The strip of old leather felt in my hand like a weapon. I had not actually held it myself since childhood, since that time when Father had bade me beat him with it, when it had felt alive to me, like a serpent. Now the quirt was dead, heavy, an almost wooden extension of my arm, as if my right hand were grasping my crippled left, and I whisked it through the air and struck myself with it many times—perhaps a hundred strokes, perhaps more. The pain was very great. I thrashed myself around in the darkness, slamming myself against the walls and stalls, knocking over tools and sending buckets flying, thrashing like a man caught by a seizure, until at last I was faint from the pain and exhausted and fell to my knees and did not get up.

But the scourging did not work. Nothing would work to purge my thoughts of Susan or alleviate my guilt for having betrayed Lyman. Not prayer, certainly. I prayed so constantly and loudly in the days following that Ruth and the boys teased me and said that I was practicing for Father's return, and Mary told them to leave me be, I was only doing what was right in the eyes of the Lord; she wished the rest of the family were as devout as I. But in all my prayers I heard no voice except my own, and my own repulsed me, until eventually I could not bear to hear it anymore and gave off prayer altogether and did not join them in the evenings or when they went to church on the Sabbath. I went generally silent on all matters, not just religion, which was how people were used to me anyway.

I thought that I might cleanse myself with work, but that, too, was to no effect, for I was too distracted and anxious to complete any single task without rushing off to begin another, and all I accomplished was to create an even greater disarray and disorder on the place than had existed before. Trees half-cut or, if cut, left to lie and rot on the ground; chimneys pulled apart and not put back together again; fenceposts driven into the ground but left standing without rails to connect them; half-a-dozen rows plowed, but then the horse unhitched, taken off to haul stones from the river, with the plow abandoned in the middle of the field: it rained for most of those days, and I rushed about as if every day there were a bright sun overhead, a madman farmer, and my brothers and sisters and stepmother watched me with fear and bewilderment. My family kept the house running smoothly and the livestock fed and properly cared for, whilst I made a mess of the rest.

There was no way for me to tell them of the source of such turbulence; I was too ashamed. And besides, as the days went on, I myself had grown as fearful and bewildered as they, for I was no longer sure that my strong feelings for Susan were generated by love for her, so much as by a morbid, cruel desire to take away from Lyman his greatest treasure. I did not love her; I hated him. What perversity was *this*?

I needed Father to arrive home. Only he, I believed, could provide me with the order and structure of thought capable of leading me out of this wilderness of tangled desire and rage. Come home, Father! I began to say to myself, as I raced uphill and down. Come home and control me, Old Man. Bring me back to myself. Come and deliver me over to a thing larger than these strangely disordered longings. Tell me what it is I must do, and I will do it.

Then, suddenly one morning, there was the Old Man, appearing in our midst like the missing main character in a play, taking over the stage and putting everyone else at once into a supporting role. Which was how we wanted it, of course. Without Father, we had no hero for our play, and whenever he was absent, we undertook our parts without purpose or understanding. We forgot our lines, positioned ourselves wrongly on the stage, confused friend with foe, and lost all sight of our desired end and its opposition. Without the Old Man, tragedy quickly became farce.

Father seemed to know this and almost to welcome it, for when he returned home after a long while away, he always came with a fury, bearing down on us like a storm, crackling with noise and electrical energy, full of clear, irresistible purpose and making thunderous statement of it. He appraised the situation in a second, and before he was even off his horse, the man was barking out orders, schedules, and plans, was making announcements, establishing sequences, goals, standards, setting everyone at once diligently to work for the common good.

Accompanied this time by Mr. Clarke, the Yankee shipper from Westport, he brought supplies, seed, flour, salt, and nails. For the younger children, little gifts—a new Bible for Sarah, a box of paints for

Annie, a penknife for Oliver—and for Mary, a silk handkerchief: all presented first thing, unceremoniously, off-handedly, as a greeting. For Salmon, Watson, and me, he had firm handshakes and quick commands to help unload the supplies from the wagon, so Mr. Clarke could move on and make his other deliveries in the settlement before nightfall. He would be returning here in the morning to pick up our furs and as many fleeces as we were able to release to him: that would be Oliver's job, counting and tying for shipment and sale the spring fleeces and the winter's catch of pelts—beaver, lynx, marten, and fisher. That's what Mr. Clarke especially wanted. Father said to get going now, son, that's a big job, and something was telling him that some of those pelts still needed scraping before they were ready for market, and the other boys were going to be too busy to help him. Mr. Clarke drove a hard bargain and would not accept a bloody hide, Father warned.

Up on his wagon, Mr. Clarke laughed and recalled for Father how he had lost to him his best pair of Morgans, thanks to Father's nigger, which brought to Father's attention the absence of Lyman and Susan. He scanned our little group out there in the yard before the house—Mary hugely pregnant and beaming with pleasure at the sight of her husband; Ruth tall and slender and fairly bursting with the secret of Henry Thompson's promise to ask for her hand in marriage; Salmon, Watson, and I already lugging barrels from Mr. Clarke's wagon to the barn; the little girls, Sarah and Annie, as if honored by the task, together holding the bridle of Father's horse, a fine sorrel mare which I recognized as having once belonged to Mr. Gerrit Smith, and, indeed, it did later turn out to be a gift from him.

Father asked where were our friends, referring to them as Mr. and Mrs. Epps, a tacit correction to Mr. Clarke.

I paused at the rear of the wagon, a keg of nails on my shoulder, and Father caught my eye. "Owen?" he said, as if I were the sole reason for their absence.

Mary said, "I would have written about it to you, Mister Brown, but I thought you were coming sooner than this."

My silence probably told him as much as any words could have then. He nodded and said that we would discuss this later, meaning after Mr. Clarke had left us. I quickly went back to my work, and Father resumed issuing orders, even as he dismounted and embraced Mary and walked arm in arm with her towards the house. Over his shoulder, he instructed Salmon to kindly water the horse when he had finished unloading, and brush her down and set her out to pasture without feeding her grain, as she'd been fed this morning in Keene. Not at Mr. Partridge's, you can be sure of that, he added. Her name was Reliance, he said, and she was reliable. And then to Watson he said that he could see fencing half up, half lying on the ground, and he'd better set to work on that at once, boy, or we'll be chasing cattle day and night. And me he instructed to check Mr. Clarke's bill of lading against our goods received and sign it for him, then put myself to work on getting the south meadow turned under by nightfall, so we can harrow and plant tomorrow. He had observed coming down from the notch that the frost was well out of the ground there. "Come to the house at noon for dinner," he said to me, "and we'll lay out the rest of the planting then. We have lots of hard work to do, boys, so put yourselves to it! I'll examine the place and view the livestock in a while this morning and will travel over to Timbuctoo this afternoon. By this evening," he declared, "we will all know who we are and what we're doing here!"

And then he was gone into the house.

Silence. Watson, Salmon, and I looked somberly, gingerly, at one another. Then Watson shook his head and grinned. "Well, I guess the Old Man's back," he finally said. "Hoo-rah, hoo-rah."

"Yep," said Salmon. "Cap'n Brown's home for three minutes, and we already got our marching orders. He ain't gonna be very happy when he finds out about Lyman, though."

"I don't know," Watson said. "The Old Man'll set it right. He has a way with Negroes."

Mr. Clarke laughed. "Your old man has a way with white folks, too," he said, his spectacles glinting like mica in the morning sun. "Talked me into giving him more credit than I ever give a poor man nowadays."

"You'll get your money," I said. "Don't fret yourself."

"Yeah, well, we'll see, Red. We'll see how them pelts and fleeces add up," he said, and handed me a stub of a pencil and the bill of lading, which I signed with a surly flourish, *John Brown, by his son Owen Brown,* and as I wrote the date, I realized that tomorrow was Father's birthday.

I was twenty-seven that spring. When Father was my age, he had been married for nearly a decade and had fathered four children. His wife, my mother, had not yet died. When he was my age, he had already made himself a professional surveyor, had established a successful tannery that employed two grown men and four or five boys, had built a house, raised a herd of blooded sheep, cleared twenty acres of hardwood forest and carved a farm out of the wilderness of western Pennsylvania. He had founded a settlement school, and when he was my age, at a time when most respectable white people preferred that folks show slavery their blind eye, he had publically pledged his life to its overthrow. At twenty-seven, he knew what he stood for, what he could and could not do. At my age, Father had become in all visible ways a man.

And here was I, still a boy. How was that possible? In what crucial ways was my nature so different from his that our lives and works would diverge by this much?

John had once said to me, in a complaining tone, that Father had taught us to be afraid of no man except him. And it was true. Father always insisted that we think for ourselves in every way, except when we disagreed with him, and that we hold ourselves independent of every man's will, except his. He wanted us simultaneously to be independent and yet to serve him. Father was to be our Abraham; we were to be his little Isaacs. We were supposed to know ahead of time, however, the happy outcome of the story—we were supposed to know that it was a story, not about us and our willingness to lie on a rock on Mount Moriah and be sacrificed under his knife, but about our father and his willingness to obey his terrible God. That was the difference between us and our father. We had him for a father, and he had someone else.

His father, like ours, had taught his son John to be independent of all men, but Grandfather had included himself, the teacher, amongst them. He, too, like Father, had told the story of Abraham and Isaac to his eldest son, but he had told it in such a way that it was not about the nature of obedience or sacrifice; it was about the nature of God. Grandfather Brown was a gentle, rational man whose greatest difficulty was in accommodating his character to a cruel and inexplicable universe, and unlike his son, he was not bound by a lifelong struggle to overcome his own willfulness and vanity. It's their own secret struggles that shape the stories people tell their children. And had I been blessed with a son of my own, the story would have been told yet a third way. The central figure in it would have been neither Abraham nor God. It would have been Isaac, and the questions my story asked and answered would have been Isaac's alone.

I would have told my son that Isaac's father, Abraham, rose up early in the morning and led Isaac up into the mountain of Moriah, claiming that he had been directed to do this by God, in order there to make a sacrifice unto Him. And Isaac believed his father, for he loved him and had never known him to lie. And when they had reached the mountaintop and Isaac's father had clave the wood for the burnt offering and Isaac saw no lamb there, the boy spoke unto Abraham, his father, saying, "Behold the fire and the wood, but where is the lamb for the burnt offering?" And his father said unto Isaac, "God will provide a lamb." But when Isaac saw his father come forward with a rope and a knife in his hands to bind and slay him upon the altar they had built together, he understood that he himself was to be the lamb. He was afraid and asked himself, Did he love his father so greatly that he could not flee from Moriah back into Canaan, where lay his aged mother, Sarah, or that he could not follow his father's bondswoman Hagar and her son, Ishmael, who was his brother, into the wilderness of Beersheba? He said to his father, "I heard not this command from God. It comes to me only from thee, and thou art not the Lord, nor canst thou speak for Him. For thou hast taught me that, and I have believed it, and therefore now I must flee from this place, or else abandon all that thou hast taught me." Whereupon his father fell down upon the ground and said that an angel of the Lord was calling to him out of heaven, saying, "Abraham, Abraham, lay not thine hand upon the lad, for now I know that thou fearest God, seeing that thou hast not withheld thy son from me." And Isaac showed his father where behind him a ram had been caught in a thicket by his horns, and Abraham went and took the ram and offered him up for a burnt offering in the stead of Isaac, and father and son prayed together, giving thanks unto the Lord, and descended together from the mountain feeling wise and greatly blessed by the Lord. That is the story I would tell.

In the evening, after supper, Father bade me give him my views regarding Lyman's decision to live away from us. I knew that he had already spoken with Lyman himself that same afternoon in Timbuctoo and had heard his version, and that he had obtained Mary's view of the matter as well. The former I knew nothing about, for I had not spoken with Lyman myself since the day he departed from us; the latter I knew to be one of placid, unquestioning acceptance: as far as Mary was concerned, Lyman had decided that he and Susan could live more naturally on their own land among their own people, that was all. "And perfectly understandable, too," Mary said, when Father raised the subject. "Especially after the disappointment of the baby." We were all gathered in the parlor, where Father was preparing to lead us in prayer.

"Yes. The baby," he said, closing his eyes and looking down as if to pray for its soul. We stood in silence for a moment, and the soul of the infant born dead did seem to flit through the room and then swiftly disappear. That was how it was whenever Father was present—the entire spirit world was strangely enlivened. Then Father said, "I urged them today to come here and retrieve its body and re-bury it properly in the Negro burying ground over there. I assume they'll do it tomorrow. But before they do, I want to know how it goes between you, Owen, and Mister Epps in particular. And with all the Negroes, too, not just him. I perceive a point of strain, a serious weakness in our relations with them, son. And I believe that you are the fault," he said. "Give me simply your views on why they've separated from us and, a thing which distresses me much more, why the Underground Railroad no longer runs through this valley. The two are obviously connected."

Everyone in the family looked at me, except for Father, who had opened his Bible and appeared to be studying tonight's reading from the Scriptures. "Yes, probably they are connected," I said. "No other whites in the settlement are willing to carry fugitives north. They are as cowardly as ever. More so, of course, since the Fugitive Act. And the Negroes themselves dare not try it, either. Except for Lyman. But Lyman chooses not to enlist our aid anymore, and he has no wagon, not even a single horse or mule. So there it is. No one goes north anymore, unless on foot, and that apparently has discouraged the conductors below from sending fugitives on to North Elba. Instead, they take the greater risk of sending folks by way of the Lake Champlain route and the Rochester-to-Niagara route."

"Well, that's been taken care of," Father said. "I've today written to Mister Douglass and a person in Utica whom I cannot name. Service will resume shortly. But you still haven't told me your view of Mister Epps's departure from us."

"What did he tell you himself?"

"He would say nothing on the subject."

"Nothing?"

"No, nothing, Owen."

"Then I can say nothing, either."

He looked up and studied my face for a long moment. I remember the sound of Grandfather's clock ticking. Then he said, "Very well, Owen. It shall remain between you and Mister Epps. Let us pray, children." And in his usual manner, he began to pray.

It was only a matter of days before the Old Man had the farm up and running again—which pleased me, of course, but alloyed my pleasure at the same time with a measure of guilt. A few days more, and he had resumed service on the Underground Railroad between Timbuctoo and Canada, an activity which of necessity I joined. But sullenly at first, I confess, for its resumption was based on Father's having re-established his old close and trusting relations with Lyman and the other Negroes of the settlement. Within a few short weeks, it was as if the Old Man had never left. He returned to preaching every second or third Sabbath at the Congregational Church in North Elba, a church he nonetheless would not formally join, and he undertook once again to conduct his weekly class on the Bible, which was attended by sometimes as many as a dozen men and women of the village, white and black. He happily approved of young Henry Thompson's wish to marry Ruth and used it as an opportunity to bridge the distance that had marred relations between our two families, bringing the Thompsons into the abolitionist fold once again, and where the Thompsons went, many other local families went as well.

Father's physical presence could inspire people, could instill in them a quantity of courage even to the point of recklessness, which, when he was not himself physically present to argue, chide, and explain, seemed to dissipate as fast as it had arisen. It was not so much his oratory that did it, although to be sure he spoke well and preached with conviction and imagination on any number of subjects, from abolitionism to animal husbandry, from the Bible, which he knew better than any trained and ordained preacher I had ever met, to the United States Constitution, which he knew like a Washington lawyer. But it was not his oratory that swayed people. Quite the opposite, in fact.

Instead, folks were impressed and then, perhaps to their surprise, led by his stubborn refusal to rely on common oratorical devices and embellishments, by his evident disdain for the tricks of voice and gesture that most public speakers relied on in those days. As if he were a Channing or a Parker or a white Frederick Douglass, he made people feel empowered by having come in contact with him, so that they felt larger, stronger, more righteous, clearer of purpose and more sure of victory than they ever had before. But unlike those exemplary speakers, Channing, Parker, Douglass, and so on, Father never lifted his voice, never shouted, never pointed to the heavens, never quoted Ralph Waldo Emerson—he never quoted any writer, except for those who wrote the Bible, the Declaration of Independence, and the United States Constitution.

The effect of Father's speech and personal presence on otherwise rational and even skeptical men and women was uncanny and never failed to amaze me. No matter the audience—a hall filled with illustrious New England abolitionists or a convention of hundreds of distinguished Negroes, his country congregation at church on the Sabbath or a gathering of Negro farmers at a barn-raising in Timbuctoo, a meeting of his fallen-away white neighbors in North Elba or his own family gathered around the fire at home—Father always spoke simply and directly, his hands at his sides or merely clasped in front of him, an ordinary man in a plain brown suit who happened to possess the truth. Some of it was his sense of timing: he had an instinct for knowing when to remain silent so as to gather everyone's attention and when to speak so that it would sound most impressive; thus, when he was expected to speak up, he often held his peace and stood against the furthest wall, and when he was expected to go silent and withdraw, he suddenly came forward and gave sharp utterance to his thoughts.

His voice was in no way stentorian or authoritative: it was pitched at not quite the level of a tenor's. Most people who wrote about him afterwards regarded him as tall and well-built, a man of heroic proportions, but Father was of average height, tanned and sinewy, strong but not bulky or broad, and he walked like a soldier on parade, straight-backed and a little stiff-legged, with his arms swinging. His face was essentially that of a Yankee farmer: sharp-nosed, with tight lips and a jutting chin and a rough-hewn man's large ears sticking out beneath his coarse, reddish-gray hair, which he wore cropped short and spikey, like a stevedore's. The visible center of his face was in his eyes, pale gray and fierce and steady. When the Old Man locked his gaze onto yours, it was very difficult not to give way before it, as if he'd seen your secret shame. Like an owl or a hawk, a powerful bird of prey, he rarely blinked. He could hold your gaze with his as if with physical force, as if he had reached out and clamped onto your chin and cheeks with both hands and had drawn your face up to his so that he could stare directly into it; and look into it he did, deeply, with curiosity and undisguised self-interest, as if he were examining, not a human soul, but a complex, unfamiliar piece of machinery, which, if properly understood, might save him a lifetime's labor.

In early June, as Mary came close to her time, we were conducting to Canada an elderly couple whose sons had gone before them the previous year and a young boy accompanied by his gentle, bespectacled uncle. All four had escaped off the same Maryland plantation, which had become notorious along the Railroad, due to the cruelty of its master, a Dutchman named Hammlicher, and to the particular viciousness of his white overseer, a man named Camden, and due to the fact that Harriet Tubman herself had taken a special interest in facilitating the escape of the Hammlicher slaves. Mysterious, elusive, and yet seemingly everywhere at once, Miss Tubman was thought to have had a family connection among the Hammlicher slaves, through one of her own lost children, perhaps, and thus had lent it her special attention. Already at least fifteen of the several hundred human beings owned by this man had been spirited up along the Chesapeake Bay to Philadelphia and New York and thence on up the Hudson to Troy and freedom. But now, because of the increase in the number of slave-catchers in those cities along the old route, Miss Tubman had decided to send her charges north across the Adirondacks by way of Timbuctoo.

When Father had met her in Hartford that winter, he had convinced her of the good use to which she might put this previously obscure route, and his personal connection with her, when he revealed it to the Timbuctoo Negroes, had instantly won them back. Father's reputation for honesty was such that no one questioned his claim; it was sufficient unto itself. How could they have refused to ally themselves with John Brown, when he came to them with the endorsement of the famous Harriet Tubman? The great Harriet! The General! None of them had ever met her or even seen her at a distance—she was all legend to them, one of the great African women, like Sojourner Truth, who seemed less a modern American saboteur of slavery than an ancient spirit-leader, an invincible, sometimes invisible, female warrior protected by the old African gods. Father's having met and, at the instigation of Frederick Douglass, having spoken privately with Miss Tubman gave him an authority that at once renewed Lyman's commitment to running fugitives with us Browns and drew with him more of the others in the settlement than we would need. It made our Timbuctoo stop on the Underground Railroad suddenly important in the only world that mattered to the Negroes and to Father, and once again, increasingly as the summer wore on, the only one that mattered to me.

Slavery, slavery, slavery! I could not have a thought that was not somehow linked to it. It was an obsession. At times, it came to feel like a form of insanity, for I was incapable of a normal thought, a single private thought that began and ended with me and did not identify me as a white man. And this was all due to Father.

It was during our run with the four Hammlicher fugitives that Mary came to her time. And before we were able to get back from the Canadian border to North Elba, she gave birth to a son, her next-to-last child, born strangled and crushed by the terrible trial of his birth, leaving Mary herself nearly dead and Father frantic with fear that he would lose her.

The excitement of our run to Canada had made our blood race, and we were still thrilled by it when we returned home. It was almost as if we had Miss Tubman herself aboard, her long rifle at the ready, and for the first time in months there was no tension between me and Lyman, which put even Father into a jolly mood as we rode the wagon back down along the rough roads from Massena. We had passed a party of Indian hunters along the way, Abenakis, French-speaking Algonquins from Lower Canada, a remnant of a remnant people, and had engaged in deep speculation amongst ourselves as to their racial origins, Lyman arguing for ancient Africa, Father for Asia, and Watson for the Lost Tribes of Israel.

Then, when we arrived at the farm, we were met by the grim sight of a birthing gone bad, the sad familiarity of it, the desolation and dashed hopes and expectations, the terrible, bloody, failed work of it, and all our male heartiness and camaraderie, our blustery pride in our good and difficult work, went suddenly silent and cold. Men go numb at these times, I discovered. That's what they do. All feeling bleeds out of us. We suddenly realize that we know nothing of what it means to the woman who has carried this child inside her body for nine months and has suffered through the excruciating pain and work of bearing it and has had to see its tiny body emerge into the world lifeless, battered and bruised by the vain effort, a grotesque, sorrowful waste. We do *think* sorrow and grief and pity. But we *feel* nothing. Husbands, fathers, sons, and brothers, we all respond the same way. First we say to ourselves that we are to blame, then we say that we are unfairly deprived; we are the cause, we are not the agent; we are the custodian, we are a mere bystander: every feeling is cut down by its near opposite, so that in the end we come up numb, silent, too large, too rough, too coarse, too healthy and strong, to be in the same room with the poor, devastated women, our shattered, weary mothers, wives, daughters, and sisters.

Numb. Cold. This, I know, was how Father felt that June afternoon when we men, dirty, exhausted, full of our own importance and valor, entered the house and saw that Mary's baby had been born dead. We are there at the beginning and almost never at the end. Father, Watson, Salmon, Oliver, and I, and it was how Lyman felt, too, and how he had felt when his own baby was born dead, I now understood. There's no way to change this; we are men and must remain men. It was how my brothers felt, their young faces dark and worried with the fruitless search for an appropriate emotion. And it was how I felt. Numb. Cold.

But so different was it from when I had exploded with rage on the raw, gray morning seven weeks before, when Susan's baby was born dead, that I was forced to remember the earlier event anew and this time to regard it with dismay. My rage then made no sense to me now. Lyman's silence and withdrawal, which had seemed strange to me then, I now saw as having been the only sensible, normal response for a man.

I should have reacted as he had. From what hole in my unconscious mind had that rage of mine emerged? Why had I not reacted instead with this all-too-familiar, cold cancellation of feeling that surrounded me now?

I saw that my anger had been caused not by Susan's suffering and loss at all but by my guilt for wishing that I could have stood that morning in Lyman's place instead of mine, for believing somehow that I should have been Susan's husband and the father of her dead infant and should not have been this farmer standing at his side. I had felt guilt but could not show it, even to myself, and so I had pounded the walls with my fists and roared like a wounded lion. Lyman had instinctively understood the nature and source of my rage, and he had hastily withdrawn himself and his wife from my presence and had stayed away from us, until now, until Father had returned and displaced me and reshaped the family and its priorities. Until once again it was slavery, slavery, slavery. And—inescapably—race, race, race. Until once again, due to our obsession, we were, as it were, insane. Which to the Negroes, to Lyman, made us perfectly comprehensible and trustworthy—sane. Not just another dangerous batch of well-intentioned, Christian white folks.

Mary's recovery from her delivery was slow and erratic. It had, in fact, been many years since she had been able to return to her normal state of good health following a pregnancy; she was no longer young, after all, and this had been an especially difficult and painful birthing, leaving her physically devastated, without even the joy of a new infant to help her heal.

Father managed to obtain several postponements of trial downstate, where he had been scheduled to defend himself and Mr. Perkins against their creditors, and he by-passed the July convention of the American Anti-Slavery Society in Syracuse, so that he could stay at the side of his wife throughout this period of her recovery. Night and day, he prayed at her side and nursed her back to health in his inimitable, tireless fashion, leaving most of the work on the farm and the risk and work of running the Underground Railroad to his sons and Lyman and the other residents of Timbuctoo. But it was not clear, until nearly a month had passed, that Mary would recover at all. She waxed and waned, came forward and fell back, with the entire family growing increasingly fretful. Each day commenced with an announcement from Father as to our mother's condition, followed by appropriate family prayers, either for her continued good progress towards health or for a fresh resumption of that progress. Happily, the Lord blessed us all, and slowly the good woman began to come around, and from midsummer on, her progress was steady and in a straight line, until Father was freed once again to resume his normal activities at his usual, furious pace, exercising over us and everyone associated with those activities his characteristic authority and force.

The farm was flourishing, religion was properly established, and our white neighbors had begun again to join us in aiding our black neighbors and the fugitive slaves. Sister Ruth and Henry Thompson were set to marry in the fall, as soon as Henry and his brothers finished building the couple a proper cabin on a piece of land that his father had deeded over to them. Miss Tubman and associates of Mr. Douglass were steadily sending escaped slaves north to us from Utica, Syracuse, and Troy, two and sometimes three times a fortnight, and though ours was a difficult route, it was now the safest, as slave-catchers and their helpers no longer dared to come slinking around North Elba or Timbuctoo. The word was out: the mad abolitionist, John Brown, and his sons and neighbors and a pack of Gerrit Smith's niggers were holed up there in the mountains all armed and ready to drive off anyone who came looking for fugitives.

Emboldened by this change in the community, the residents of

Timbuctoo began to move about the settlement more freely and to mingle with the whites in a more regular fashion, showing up at barn-raisings, for instance, in considerable numbers and taking their ease down at the grist mill or joining the whites after church at a huckle-berry-picking prayer picnic up on the sunny slopes of Whiteface Mountain. On several of these occasions, I saw Susan, always at a distance from her, which distance I studiously kept, but each time I saw her—a glimpse of her coffee-brown face, half-hidden by her bonnet, or her shoulder and arm, visible for a second, until a crowd of Negroes surrounded her—my heart pounded like a hammer, and the blood rushed to my ears, and if I happened to be speaking with a person, I began to stammer and had to lapse into silence or else sound foolish as a moon-calf. I averted my gaze and then stole glances out from under it, until she disappeared from my sight.

She, of course, made no attempt to speak with me. Nor did Lyman, when he was with her. Any initiative would have to be mine, and I had neither the courage nor the clarity to take it.

I know now what was the cause and true nature of my fixation on the woman, how thwarted and misshapen it was, how far from its true object; but I did not understand it then in the least. I was ashamed of it, naturally; but ashamed for all the wrong reasons.

Often, at an hour close to dawn, I found myself, after a long night of prowling alone through the forests, lurking in the close vicinity of the cabins of Timbuctoo, peering through the mist and the languorous, sifting pines at the very cabin where she slept beside her husband. I would crouch in low bushes for hours, lost in a sort of reverie, my heart furiously pounding, my hands trembling, my legs weak and watery, as if I were a hunter who at last had sighted his long-sought prey. Then I would suddenly shudder and come back to myself and, horrified, would steal away home.

These prowls were not unlike my sordid, secret, nighttime walks

several years earlier in the streets and alleyways of Springfield, and my
family accepted them more or less as they had then, which is to say, as
evidence of a solitary young man's restless nature. And to a degree, they
were correct to think that. Also, I always carried my rifle and sometimes brought home the carcass of a raccoon or fisher or some other
nocturnal animal, as explanation for my having been out so late and
long. As long as they did not interfere with my work on the farm,
Father did not acknowledge my late night absences; perhaps he did not
even notice them, so preoccupied was he that summer, first with
Mary's long recovery, then with the planting and further clearing of
our woodlands, and with his local abolitionist activities and the
Railroad. Also, he was busily educating his neighbors as to the advantages and virtues of raising blooded stock by selling them some of his
Spanish merino ewes and carting his best ram around for stud and
showing off and now and then selling one of his red Devon cattle. After
lengthy negotiations by mail with a farmer in Litchfield, Connecticut,
whom he knew from his past dealings with Wadsworth & Wells, he
had succeeded in having a fine young Devon bull delivered as far north
as Westport for him. I do not know how he paid for it, as such an animal did not come cheaply; possibly with promises of eventual returns
from stud fees, possibly with a portion of the monies he accepted from
our neighbors to help feed and clothe the fugitives. It was not beneath
Father to mix ingredients like that; despite all, he was still unaccount-
ably optimistic when it came to financial matters. But in early July, he
sent Salmon and Oliver over the mountains to the lake to retrieve the
beast, and soon it had become a source of much pride and the occasion
for his traveling about the settlement in the attempt to improve the
stock of his friends and neighbors.

Thus, except for my brothers, who watched me go out late and
come back in the early pre-dawn hours, my nighttime prowls went
largely unnoticed by the family and, in a significant sense, unnoticed

by me as well. My brothers teased me some, privately, for they suspected that I was secretly courting one of the maidens in the settlement, but they did not otherwise speak of it.

Then in August, like most of the farm families of the region, we took ourselves, our best produce and manufactured items, and our finest livestock down to the Essex County Fair, in Westport. We loaded the wagon with jugs of maple syrup, Mary's and Ruth's quilts, blankets made from the wool of our sheep, willow reed baskets and fishing weirs, tanned hides, and various leather items the boys had made during the winter—wallets, purses, sheaths for knives, belts, harnesses, and, a specialty of Oliver's, plaited bullwhips. Father made up a small, hand-picked herd of merino sheep, together with his finest red Devon heifer and the widely admired new bull, and off we went—a triumphant return to Westport, as it were, proof that our spiritual errand into the wilderness, despite our reputation as non-farming, abolitionist troublemakers, had turned out an agricultural success, too.

Father rode at the front on his fine sorrel mare, which later carried him all through the Kansas wars with great strength and courage. He loved that animal as he had no other and trusted no one not a family member to care for her and trusted not even us to ride her. I drove the wagon, with Mary and Ruth beside me, the younger children all crammed in with our cargo, and the boys came along behind with Father's little herd of blooded stock, helped by our black collie dogs, the type Father preferred over all others, despite their diminutive size and their uselessness for hunting.

We arrived in mid-afternoon, in high excitement. There was a light off-shore breeze, and in the east, across the glittering waters of the lake, a towering white bank of clouds rose from the softly rounded hills of Vermont into the bright blue sky, where it broke apart and scudded off in pieces to the south, leaving us here on the western shore to bask in bright sunshine. It was the first agricultural fair ever held in the region, a visible sign that the northern wilderness of New York State had finally been settled and conquered by farmers. People came to it from all over the Adirondacks. They trekked in from their log and daub-and-wattle cabins in the furthest, most isolated valley and bog—squatters, grubstakers, miners, shag-bearded trappers and hunters dressed in the skins of their prey. Merchants and storekeepers, boatswains, blacksmiths, and coopers rode down in carriages from the prosperous shoreline towns to the north, like Port Kent and Plattsburgh, or rode up from Port Henry and Ticonderoga or sailed across from Shelburne and Charlotte in Vermont, readier to buy goods and livestock than to sell. The big dairy farmers and sheepmen rode in from their fifty-year-old farms on the broad, rolling meadows of the older villages inland, like Elizabethtown, Jay, and Keene, their wagons and carts stacked high with the fruits of the year's labor, touting their skills and bearing evidence of the generosity of the fertile Lake Champlain and Au Sable River floodplains. From the newer outlying settlements tucked up among the mountains, North Elba, Tupper Lake, and Wilmington, came the poorer, hardscrabble farmers, folks like us and the Thompsons and the Brewsters and the Nashes, recent settlers who were still chopping small fields out of the upland forests and had not much to show for it yet, although we Browns intended to give that the lie. Many of the citizens of Timbuctoo came over also, a two-day trek on foot, bearing on their backs and in wheelbarrows—for they had no wagons at that time and no draft animals—garden produce to sell and exhibit in the halls, hams and maple syrup and candy and cheeses, packs of furs and hides, caged fowl, and a variety of crafted objects: reed baskets, woven hats, and prettily dyed cloth. There was even a small number of Indians, Abenakis and Micmacs, who had paddled down along the lake shore in canoes from their last remaining encampments, north of Plattsburgh, coming more out of curiosity, it seemed, than to exhibit wares or to buy and sell livestock and farm goods, for they had none to sell and no money with which to buy. Their abject poverty and loneliness were apparent to all, and they seemed more like refugees in the land than its original masters, a people exiled without ever having left home. It was difficult to know how to feel towards them, and so we tended to watch them in silence and from a distance and not to speak of them at all, even to one another.

This was the largest gathering of people that Mary and the children had seen since leaving Springfield and the largest gathering of north-country people that any of us had ever seen. Young men and women strolled hand-in-hand openly, and gangs of boys roughed each other up and organized teams for ball games and other sports, and girls walked demurely in pairs in their vicinity. Old folks and distant family members renewed connections with one another, while men compared crops, animals, and prices and talked politics, and women set their smallest children free to run and turned to one another in friendship and cheerful confidentiality.

There was a quarter-mile race track without a hoofprint on it yet and a white, freshly painted grandstand ready to be filled that evening for the first time. Behind the grandstand were ten or twelve long, low barns for livestock, and beyond the barns was a pair of fenced circles with stoneboats, where ox- and horse-pulling contests were already under way. Beyond these were several large exhibition halls for showing and judging produce and crafts, and then rows of small, canvas-sided booths where shifty-eyed characters plied the crowd with games of chance and sold cheap novelties and gew-gaws. Nearby, clouds of fragrant smoke poured from pit-fires where flocks of chickens were grilled and whole hogs roasted on spits and potatoes and unshucked ears of corn cooked in the ashes.

We registered our livestock and installed them in the barns and pitched our camp alongside several other families from North Elba, in a grove of low pines directly behind the sheep barn, and in short order we all separated from one another, each to follow his or her particular interest. Father headed straight for the sheep barn and, of course, very soon found himself lecturing on the proper care of sheep and wool to anyone willing to listen, a sizeable number of farmers and sheepmen, in fact, who had on their own gathered around the box-stalls where he had installed his merinos, for the large, healthy, heavy-fleeced animals were an excellent advertisement of Father's skills and knowledge. Ruth went off in search of Henry Thompson, who was not at his family's camp; Mary and the girls, Annie and Sarah, disappeared in the direction of the exhibition halls; and the boys, Watson, Salmon, and Oliver, raced away with a gang of young fellows from North Elba, leaving me to wander the fairgrounds alone.

I saw her almost at once. I had lingered in the sheep barn, listening to the Old Man hold forth for a few moments, and then, when I caught myself saying his sentences silently ahead of him, had drifted away, and as I passed out of the low shed and made my way towards the booths on the midway—suddenly, there she was. She was a considerable distance away but glinting brightly in the crowd, like gold in gravel, outside one of the exhibition halls—she was the only Negro in a group of white women and girls that included my stepmother, Mary, and sisters Annie and Sarah. Susan's pale gray bonnet hid her face from my view, but I knew instantly, from her posture and the precise tilt of her head and the easy gestures of her hands, that it was she, and my heart leapt up.

She and Mary talked together for a few minutes longer, and then Mary embraced her and, with the other girls and women, drew away and strolled inside the hall, leaving her to stand alone outside with a characteristically bemused expression on her face. She was wearing a red and white plaid dress, which I recognized as one that Ruth had given her last winter, and carried a wicker basket, over which she had draped her shawl. For a moment, she seemed unsure of which direction to go, but finally she turned to her left and made her way towards the fairway.

I followed at a discreet distance, until she turned into a narrow, shaded space between the second and third exhibition halls. No one else was there, and I quickened my pace and came up behind her and said her name.

She turned abruptly, her dark eyes open wide, frightened to see a man suddenly this close to her, for I had come to within a few feet of her before speaking. Then she recognized me, and the fear left her face, replaced at once by a heaviness—a sadness, as I saw it, which produced in me a corresponding sadness and made me wish to embrace her, but I withheld myself and in a trembling voice said that I was happy to see her.

"It's been a long while, Mister Brown," she answered. "I was pleased to see your mother looking so strong again. And Annie and little Sarah."

"Yes. We all miss you, Susan."

"Well. That's nice, Mister Brown. Thank you."

We made light, nervous conversation for a few moments, asking after each other's health, speaking of the weather, the surprising size of the fairgrounds, the great number of people, and so on—until I suddenly heard myself blurt, "Susan, I must tell you, Susan, that in his heart my father has replaced me. He's replaced me with Lyman."

"What . . . what do you mean?"

"I bear Lyman no resentment for this, but it's hurt me, Susan."

She appeared shocked and said that it could not be true. "You shouldn't be envious of Lyman. He loves and admires your father over all other men," she said. "But you, you're your father's son, Mister Brown. And your father, he loves you for that, I know. More than he can ever love Lyman."

"No! You don't understand. You see, Lyman is more important to him than I am. And with good reason."

She sighed heavily. "What are you wanting me to say to you, Mister Brown?"

I was silent for a moment. Finally, I said, "Please, just tell me why you've moved away from us."

For the first time, she shifted her eyes away from mine. "Well, I explained it to your mother and your sister back then, back when we first decided. It was due to Lyman wanting to farm his own land and to live in his own house. That's all. We been with you all for a long time."

"No, not Lyman! I know why he left, and I know the *real* reason, too! I'm the cause of that. No, I want you to tell me why *you* left us."

"It's very simple, Mister Brown. I went where my husband said. That's the whole of it. And you're not the cause of anything Lyman done, Mister Brown," she declared. Then she lifted herself to her full height and said, "This is not a right conversation for us to be having."

"Yes, it is, because we need to talk. I need you to hear me. Even though you'll despise me, because it's . . . it's a sin for me to feel for you as I do, and I have no right to say anything about it to you, because—"

She placed her hand gently on my arm and stopped me. "Mister Brown, please, sir, I know you're a decent man. You are. But you are all mixed up," she declared, looking straight at me. "I'm saying this to you, Mister Brown, because I like you, I truly do, and I know you don't mean me no harm. But Lyman, he told me what happened last winter between you and him, when you come back from all your travels to England and you beat on him out there in the barn that day. So I know things, Mister Brown. Maybe more even than Lyman knows, since he is a man and is a little mixed up about these same things, too. But I've watched you, Mister Brown, and felt sorry for you, because I can see that you are all confused and mixed up and angered. Maybe due to your father. Who is a strong, good man doing good works, and he believes that he needs your help, so he won't send you off from him. Mainly that, I think. That, and us being coloreds and you wanting to help our people like you do. It's the two things. They make you think about Lyman too much, which is how you come now to be thinking about me too much."

"No," I said. "It's not that. None of it."

"Just stop that now! Stop. I'm not angry with you, Mister Brown, because I know you don't mean any harm. But I'm a colored woman, and my husband is a colored man. And we wouldn't be having this conversation, you know, not a word of it, if my husband and I was white people."

I stepped back from her. "Yes. You're right. Please, then, please tell me what should I do."

"Do? Not for me to say, Mister Brown," she said tenderly. "I know you want to be natural and peaceful and respectful with colored folks. But if you can't, well, maybe you should stick to your own kind. Lots of good folks, white and colored alike, that's what they do. Go away from your father and live amongst white people. Why not go out there to Ohio, Mister Brown, where your other brothers are, and find yourself a wife and settle down with her?"

"A white woman."

"Well, yes."

For a long time, I said nothing. Then I whispered, "I can't do that."

She smiled at me, but as if from a great height. "Well, Mister Brown, then I don't know what you can do," she said. And, abruptly, she turned her back and walked away.

15

"You ain't half the man your father is."

The words came without warning, and they chilled my blood. They do even now, more than a half-century later. They were true then; they are true now.

The first time I heard them, they were uttered by Lyman; but after that, from then on, they were said to me in my own voice, the sentence dripping into my ear like slow poison. You ain't half the man your father is. To silence them, I would, again and again, for years, be obliged to rouse myself into a fury, a literal blood-letting, making of my whole body a visible and tangible shout. For as long as my shout reverberated in the air, I would not hear them.

You ain't half the man your father is. And who *was* he? Twice the man I was, and twice the man he seemed. And yet not half himself, either. Before Kansas, the Old Man had always been larger than his reputation; after Kansas, he was smaller. Although, over time, he himself changed not a whit. I changed, certainly, and nearly everyone else changed. But not Father. Merely, his reputation caught up to the reality and then surpassed it, so that the man who, outside the family, had been known as a somewhat peculiar radical abolitionist with a violent temperament, a somber activist with a huge reservoir of religious enthusiasm, a wild fellow who, despite his vague, crack-brained plan for a slave insurrection, was nonetheless oddly trusted by influential and otherwise rational Negroes and was likewise understandably mistrusted by most whites—that man came over time to be known as a heroic guerilla leader, a courageous and brilliant military man who feared only God and had no other ambition than to bring slavery to an end. He came quickly to be known as a magnificent fighter on horseback, an inspiration and example to lesser men, which is to say, to all decent, anti-slavery white men: for none of them, no matter how thoroughly he loathed slavery and loved his Negro brethren, in his loathing and love was as pure as Captain John Brown, as clear-eyed as he, as unequivocal and uncompromised as he. So that when my father— Father, the Old Man, Mister Brown, Citizen John Brown—got himself turned into Captain John Brown, it was not merely a military rank that had been added to his name but an honorific, and the rank, as if he had been given it at birth, instantly became an integral part of his name, permanently attached to his identity, like that of Governor Bradford, Admiral Nelson, Chief Tecumseh.

In North Elba, though, and to Lyman Epps especially, Father was known entirely for what he was—known more clearly for that to Lyman than even to me. So when Lyman told me I was not half that, he downright shriveled me. He struck my manhood away and left me standing before him a child. Worse than a child: a failed adult.

Most men secretly know that there lies hidden inside them the boy they once were and believe they still are, and all the work a man does in his life is accompanied by various stratagems designed to keep that child hidden from view. From his own view, especially. But that night in late summer at Indian Pass, which lies yonder in the darkness seven miles to the south of our old farmhouse, when Lyman raised his lip and sneered and then declared that I was not half the man my father was, he made it impossible for me ever after to hide my true self from my false self. It was as if, that night in the cave, Lyman were the only man alive who could testify as to both my true character and the true character of my father: he was our sole shared character witness and, thus, was the only man capable of making the comparison between me and Father and making it stick.

I don't know why this was so. Lyman knew us both well, of course, intimately, domestically, out in the fields, and on the Railroad running slaves north; for several years, he had observed both Father and me more closely than had anyone else who was not a family member. But that was not it. The truth is, I made Lyman the authoritative witness myself; I myself validated his testimony.

As instructed by the Old Man, Lyman and I had been three days and nights down along Indian Pass, cutting a trail wide enough for a man on horseback to get through to North Elba from the old Tahawus mining camp. Father would be away that September, once again—this time, as usual, for the last time, he hoped—settling his besieged financial affairs with Mr. Perkins, and he had charged the two of us with this task before leaving. The Underground Railroad station at Timbuctoo, with its links south to Tahawus and north to Canada, was the one segment of Father's Subterranean Passway that he felt he could control, and he wished to make it a model and a beginning for the whole. He intended to make it off-limits at pain of death for slave-catchers, man-stealers, and bounty-hunters, so that once he had made this small segment of the Railroad secure, with armed men posted at the passes and gorges and up on strategic ridges, with fortified resting places and storehouses along the way, and with only the most trusted radical whites living in the farmlands below the Adirondacks allowed to provide arms, provisions, and safe houses, he would begin extending the Passway southward into the Appalachians, mile by mile into the mountainous forests of eastern Pennsylvania, until he came to western Maryland, where he would commence his invasion of the enemy's homeland itself. By this means we would bleed the South white, he declared. His fantasy for years; and then his dream; and finally his plan, too: now the three had at last coalesced, and he was beginning in this small way in our very neighborhood to put all three, fantasy, dream, and plan, into action.

At the Tahawus mining camp, called the Upper Village, there was a new manager, a man named Seybolt Johnson from Albany, replacing the previous supervisor, the infamous Mr. Wilkinson. Mr. Johnson was a genuine abolitionist, faithful and true, who had worked the Underground Railroad for years out of Albany and Troy. With the passage of the Fugitive Slave Law, he, like so many others, had sought alternative routes north for the escaping slaves, and as he was a longtime employee of the Adirondack Mining Company's main office, in Albany, he knew, even before he assumed the position of manager of the Tahawus mines, that he could play an important role in aiding the Underground Railroad out there in the wilderness. Which he had done, for on his arrival at the Upper Village, he at once contacted Father and quickly arranged to regularize the passage of escaped slaves from towns and cities south of Albany to the Upper Village mining camp and on through the northwoods to Timbuctoo, North Elba, Paul Smith's famous hunting lodge, Massena, and Canada.

Father trusted Mr. Johnson, mainly because Frederick Douglass and Harriet Tubman trusted him, but also because, immediately upon his arrival at Tahawus, Mr. Johnson had set about to improve the lot of his Irish workers, who had suffered so terribly under the iron hand of the hypocritical Mr. Wilkinson. Mr. Seybolt Johnson was that rarity, a white man of the managerial class who felt towards his workers and Negroes alike that there but for the grace of God went he. "The man is a true Christian," Father had pronounced after his first visit with him. "We can work with him."

Thus Lyman and I, with axes and crowbars, were sent out to bush the old footpath through Indian Pass and make it into a proper trail. Starting at Timbuctoo, we worked from north to south and in three days had gotten nearly to the halfway point, about seven miles in from North Elba, with Mount Colden on our right and, hovering above its shoulder, the huge, rocky chest and head of Mount McIntyre. Mount Marcy—or Tahawus, as we still called it, Cloudsplitter, the old Indian name for the giant—was on our left, its great shadow permanently cast across the rocky bottom where we labored day after day and camped in a sweet-smelling balsam lean-to at night. Indian Pass was dangerous, rough ground. A man or a horse could easily fall and break a leg or tumble from a ledge into a rocky pit. The long, narrow defile was shaded in the daytime, and down in the gorge between the mountains, the Northern Star was blocked out at night, and moonlight rarely fell, and a man had to be able to trust the feel of the trail under his feet in order to get through. It was all too easy to get lost there, even at midday, to wander inadvertently down a bear path or deer trail and soon become disoriented in the darkness and dense woods. People had been known to disappear into these woods and starve or freeze to death, their picked bones found years later by a lone hunter or trapper.

The pass itself was colder than the peaks and cliffs that towered above it, and in some places slubs of old, gray snow remained year-round. High, sheer walls of mossy rock rose up beside us and disappeared into the mists overhead, while below on the floor of the gorge we chopped, dug, and shoved, and when necessary laid down narrow log bridges to cross the gills and brooks and the peaty muskegs that abounded there. We would finish one arduous task of clearing and move on to the next bend in the path and instantly come to a new obstacle—a fallen, primeval spruce tree six feet in circumference, a head-high tangle of thick, twisted roots, a mudslide, a wall of enormous boulders—which we were obliged to cut or move aside when we could or, when we couldn't, carve a pathway through lesser trees or around smaller rocks. Our simple intent, our one thought and standard, was to make it possible for a horse or a string of horses, by day or night in any season, to carry frightened, exhausted fugitives from slavery through to freedom. That thought drove and organized us, and as we worked we talked of little else.

At night, though, lying back on our mattress of layered balsam boughs, with the fire guttering out, we spoke of other things, naturally. Lyman and I had not been together like this for a long time, a sad time, which I regarded with considerable regret. But out here alone in the wilderness, as of old, we soon found ourselves speaking our innermost thoughts to one another once again, talking of our respective childhoods and early days, our hopes for the future, and our beliefs regarding all first things. Our lives in every way were significantly different, but in a paradoxical way, this let us know all the better how we ourselves might have lived, had Lyman been born white and I black. Despite our differences, Lyman and I regarded ourselves, except for race, as remarkably similar, the way that lovers often do.

This is a complicated and painful recognition for a black and a white man to make. On both sides, envy and anger get confusedly mingled with love and trust. And so it was with us. Or at least with me. I now knew, for instance, that my thwarted love for Susan was my love for Lyman gone all wrong, fatally corrupted by guilt and envy. I did not want to love her—I did not love her at all—so much as I wanted to neutralize my powerful feelings for Lyman. For they had frightened me: they were unnatural; they were the unavoidable consequence of a manly love finding itself locked inside a white man's racialist guilt, of Abel's sweet, brotherly trust betrayed by Cain's murderous envy.

We were on that third night out seated before our fire, after having eaten a supper of trout pulled from a pool in the trickling beginnings of the Au Sable and potatoes carried in from home, and we were speculating on the nature of the earth before the arrival of the plants and animals—whether it had been a warm planet, as some scientists were then claiming, or cold and covered with ice, as others thought, or whether the Bible was to be believed in this matter in a literal way, when so many self-professed Christians nowadays, even including Father, regarded its description of God's creation of the earth as figurative and allegorical.

"Either way," Lyman said, "we know God created everything. The whole kit an' caboodle. Question is, first time around, was it ice or was it fire? Did things heat up to get to where they are now, or cool down? With all that business about the darkness and the firmaments between the firmaments, it must've been ice," he declared. "I'm holding out for a world of ice that God sets to slowly melting over the years, especially in the years since the birth of Jesus, as the Christian religion gets spread over the world. Starts way down in the Garden of Eden and moves out from there. Which is why the Bible comes from the desert anyhow. Egypt and all that. On account of it being close to Eden and it being already warm there first."

Lyman's accent had slipped to the South, as it usually did when we were at ease alone together and as I imagined it did when he was speaking only with black people. He slurred his vowels, dropped consonants, and let his grammar follow different, less logical rules and conventions than those that guided white people's grammar. When he talked this way, which was his natural speech, I was often inclined to let my own speech drift over in unconscious mimicry, for it was to me an attractive way to speak—smoother and slower, softer and more intimately expressive than my own habitual pronunciation and grammar permitted. I envied its intimacy especially and longed to escape from the formality of my accent and the impersonal logic of my sentences. But whenever I heard myself trying it, I grew severely embarrassed, as I could not speak Lyman's English without hearing myself in blackface. I felt like an inept imposter, an unskilled actor mouthing lines not his own.

Reluctantly, I would return at once to my accustomed manner of speaking, which had been influenced so profoundly by Father's that, in the context created by Lyman's fluency and ease, my words seemed to be coming from Father's mind and my voice from his lips. Consequently, instead of sounding like an untalented minstrel showman making a mockery of Southern Negro speech, I sounded to myself like a tinny, nervous imitation of my old-fashioned Yankee father.

I have no idea of how I sounded to Lyman's ears. If he envied the formality of my pronunciation and the rigorous, constricting logic of my grammar, he showed no signs of it. Merely, when amongst white people, he spoke in the manner of a poor, uneducated Southern farmer who was white also, and since he was, after all, a Southerner, it seemed authentic enough, at least to white people. Perhaps he was simply a better actor than I and could move from Negro to white speech without exposing the gap between his true and false selves. I, it seemed, could not, no matter how I spoke. Which is one reason why I so often chose to remain silent. Until now. When there is no one left to hear me but the dead, and you, Miss Mayo.

Lyman said, "There's still lots of places around here, even, where the old, original world ain't got warm yet. So you can still see how it was back in them olden days, if you wants to. Got 'em close by, even." He told me then of an ice-cave located not a hundred rods from where we sat. There were a number of ice-caves up here along Indian Pass, he said, which were known to the people of Timbuctoo and carefully avoided by them. "On account of them ol' African superstitions an' such. But they don't bother me none. It's older folks, mostly, who is scared to go inside. They warns you off 'em like the devil live there. Ain't nobody live there. Too cold, 'specially for the devil," he said with a short laugh. "You wants to see one?"

I said sure, and we each stuck a pitchy pine-branch into the fire and, torches in hand, marched single-file into the darkness beyond our camp, moving uphill along a rocky rivulet. Soon we approached the sheer, high walls of stone that mark the highest point of the pass, where the trickling waters split and half the trickles run south and grow in time into the mighty Hudson and half run north and become the Au Sable and empty finally into the St. Lawrence. Here Lyman turned off the narrow path to his right and began to scramble uphill over riprapped rocks and tangled roots. I followed close behind.

Suddenly, I felt a breath of cold air in my face, as if a huge, dead thing had exhaled. Lyman disappeared from my sight, and I thought the freezing breath of the dying monster had blown his torch out, for all I saw before me was a clutch of low balsams and behind them the perpendicular face of the rock wall. "Lyman! Where are you?" I cried.

His voice came back all hollowed out: he was inside the cave. "Cup your torch, and come forward," he said.

I did as instructed, and the balsams easily parted, and in a second I found myself gone from the familiar world of trees and mountain streams and purple-blue night sky. I was standing beside Lyman inside a high, rock-walled chamber—standing in the very mouth of the monster. Looking down its half-illuminated length in the flickering light and leaping shadows, I could see the throat and belly. It was as if we had been swallowed whole by Jonah's whale. The chamber was freezing cold and the air damp and still, and our warm breath blew pale clouds that lingered before our faces. There were long, white icicles hanging from the crackled sides and sharply angled top of the cave, and thick, yellowish tongues of ancient ice along the floor, dirtied and stained by the animals that over the years had wintered here—the old beasts: bears, catamounts, fisher cats. No human could have stayed here long; it was too cold, too dark, too cruel a habitation to visit, except briefly and only to escape blizzard, flood, or fire.

Then the ice-cave was suddenly like a tomb to me, a stone sepulchre, and we were locked inside it, as if a rockslide had sealed off the

entry from the world outside. I imagined this but also for a moment
believed it—that we two were actually trapped inside this cold, rock-
walled chamber together, and no one knew. No one would come and
dig us out. No one would ever find our bones or know what had happened here. We had been at last cut loose from everything in the world
outside that had long separated us one from the other—the color of our
skin, our war against slavery, Susan, Father. Even God! It was a vision
that promised the end of solitude. I glimpsed in this moment the possibility of escape at last from my terrible isolation. The loneliness that
had cursed me since childhood and that had surrounded me like a caul
seemed for the first time to stretch and extend itself like a pregnant
woman's belly to include another human being inside, who was a man
like me, who was my twin, myself doubled and beloved, and who was at
this instant looking back at me with love.

I reached down and shoved the unlit end of my torch into a notch
between two rocks beside me so that it continued to burn. Then I drew
out my knife and opened it and placed it into Lyman's right hand and
laid my right hand on his shoulder.

He looked at the knife and at me. "Why you givin' me this?"

"I have a confession to make."

"No," he said in a low voice. "You don't."

"Yes, I do. And I'm ready to die for it. But only at your hand."

He snorted, derisively almost. "I don't want no confession from
you, Owen Brown. Whatever you done, you already done it anyhow."

"No. Not yet. My confession will be the act."

"Yes, you has. Ain't nothin' you confess to me I don't already know.
Susan told me how you spoke to her. An' I seen you sneakin' 'round our
cabin nights. And now you wants me to forgive you for it? Or else to *kill*
you?" He laughed. "No. I ain't gonna give you that, not neither one. You
wants to kill yourself, now, that's different. Why not anyhow? Sneakin'
'round after a colored woman, a *married* black woman. Like she's not as

good as a white woman and deserving the same respect? Or like I'm not as good as a white man? When here you is, the son of John Brown." He curled his lip and stared me in the face. "You ain't half the man your father is," he said.

He handed the open knife back to me, turned, and left the cave for the world outside, while I dropped precipitously down a well of darkness, his words echoing in my ears as I tumbled and pitched and turned—descending into myself once again: no-man.

In time, my torch flickered and finally went out and fell over, hissing like a snake against the ice it had fallen on. I stood alone in the darkness and cold of the cave like that for a very long while, before I stirred and groped along the granite wall and found my way back out. By the time I stumbled back into our camp below, Lyman had wrapped himself in his blanket and was asleep at the further end of our lean-to, or appeared to be. I drew my blanket around me and curled up opposite him. But I did not sleep. Like a dead man, I lay with my eyes wide open, unblinking, staring at the night sky, with no words and no human voice in my ears but the words and voice of Lyman's terrible truth.

For the two days that followed, we worked in near silence, speaking to one another politely but only when necessary, as we chopped trees and roots and pried, rolled, and lugged stones off the path that led through the mountains to the Tahawus mining camp. What was there now to say? It had already all been said—and Lyman's final words to me in the ice-cave had permanently closed off any further conversational intimacies between us. I had not told him what by me still wanted telling, but he had made it clear that whatever I might say, it needed no hearing from him, and I could only accept that judgement.

Hard labor it was, then, made harder by the silent distance that stretched between us, and at night we fell back into our respective nests and dropped quickly into sleep. Days, it rained periodically and then cleared, and raggedy blue skies appeared overhead for a while, and then it rained again. For the most part, Lyman and I worked separately and as far from one another as possible. The nights were cool, and a steady wind blew out of the southwest up along the narrow defile, twitching the high pines and spruce trees into their raspy, long song.

We were now well beyond the crest of the pass, and as we worked our way further along it, the burble of south-flowing rills and brooks soon became the crash and thrum of a large stream—the Opalescent, which emptied into Lake Colden below and then became the headwaters of the mighty Hudson. At night, we heard the gruff cough of a bear, the distant howl of wolves, the dour call of the owl, and at dawn the song of the whip-poor-will and the wood thrush, and the raucous cries of ravens on the heights. But our human voices rarely joined the forest chorus, rarely intruded on our private thoughts or broke our self-imposed solitudes.

On the morning of the third day following our visit to the ice-cave, we came out of the long, forested gorge onto the northern shore of Lake Colden, which stretched before us black and glittering in the sun. From the marshy shore on our right where the Opalescent emptied into the lake, a pair of loons rose like scratches on the sky and crossed overhead, disappearing into the spruce forest. A broad grove of drowned trees spread along the further shore, standing like the gaunt pikes of a medieval army. For a while, we worked our way along the western shore of the oval lake, keeping to the high, dry ground amongst beeches and hickory trees, blazing the trees to mark the trail, and moving at a pretty good clip, for the ground was relatively smooth now and there was not much heavy cover—ferns, briars, and hackberry thatch, mostly, due to its having been scorched a few years back by fire.

By midday, we were nearly past the lake and were about to re-enter the deep forest that for a mile or so of short ridges and gullies led gradually downhill to the mining camp; we expected to finish our job and reach the camp by dark. It had become our habit to stop at noon to rest and eat dried venison and apples and corn bread, gone stale by now, and Lyman, who had been working a few rods ahead of me, leaned his axe and crowbar against a birch tree and headed on a line towards a narrow, flat rock that extended a ways into the lake. I put my tools and pack down and followed, not for companionship anymore, but because his pack held our small stock of food.

Although it was a seasonably cool day, the sun shone down brightly, and the sky was cloudless and stark blue, a taut blanket that stretched from horizon to horizon. In a moment, I had caught up to Lyman, who was pushing his way through a chest-high thicket of willows. We were in a low, wet place and could see but the tip of the rock just beyond the willows, and only now and then. I cut to his right, following what appeared to be an easier path to the rock, and when I came out of the thicket, Lyman was on my left and a few feet behind me. He was still struggling to get through the willows. But when I turned and extended my hand to help him, he had ceased moving altogether. On his sweating face was sheer terror—as if he had seen Satan or God.

I turned slowly around, moving just my head, and saw what terrified him, and it terrified me as well—a long, tawny-gray mountain lion backed up to the edge of the rock, with nothing but the glittering lake behind it and dark water on both sides and we two puny humans in front. The lion had been surprised by our sudden, upwind approach, and now it no doubt believed itself trapped by the water and by us. The animal was no more than ten feet from me, its great tail switching like a snake. Its shoulders were hunched low and its hindquarters lower, coiled to spring. Its small, feline head was nearly all mouth, as if it had been split in half by a hatchet, with black lips and tongue and enormous fangs.

I had never seen a mountain lion alive this close, although with Watson I had tracked and shot two the previous year up on McIntyre.

I was as fascinated and thrilled by its fierce beauty as frightened of it. I had no weapon, other than the pocketknife I had pathetically proffered to Lyman back in the ice-cave. But I knew that Lyman had his pistol in his rucksack. I stood squarely between him and the lion and had a much better shot at it than he. And I was the better marksman anyhow, and was even to some degree famous for it, while Lyman was equally famous for his inaccuracy.

I showed him my open hand, and with extreme delicacy and without taking his eyes off the beast, he drew the pistol out and extended it to me. Moving slowly and keeping my eyes fixed on the huge cat's yellow eyes, I took the butt of the gun into my right hand, squared my body, and laid the barrel across my left forearm, which due to the old injury was as steady as a window sill and accounted in no small degree for my good marksmanship. Lifting my forearm, I aimed at the lion's pale brow, at the top of the inverted V mid-point between its eyes. I thought I could smell the lion. I remember, as I drew back the hammer with my thumb, inhaling deeply—rotten apples—when, without warning, at the last possible second for it to flee, the lion sprang from the rock. It crossed through the air some eight or ten feet to our left and towards the shore, its forepaws reaching the gravelly bank with ease, its hind paws barely touching the water, and was gone into the brush. It crashed away in the distance for a few seconds more, and then silence. Not even birdsong.

Slowly, I exhaled and at once began to tremble. My legs went all watery. I was glad, truly glad, and relieved that it had escaped. Seen this close, the animal was too beautiful to wish dead. I was not altogether sure I could have killed it with the pistol anyhow, for I would have had but one shot, and the lion, a large male, appeared to weigh close to two hundred pounds and, wounded, would have been even more dangerous than when merely startled and inadvertently trapped on its peninsula. Still trembling, I stepped up onto the rock and sat down on the spot of bright sunshine where the lion had been taking its solitary leisure a few moments before and handed the pistol up to Lyman, who had followed me.

"That was the biggest lion I ever seen," he said in a low, amazed voice, to which I merely nodded. "Don't know who was more surprised, though, him or us. Never come up on one like that before," he said. He was holding the pistol at his side, and I looked at it and suddenly realized that I had neglected to let the hammer down—the pistol was still cocked. Hair-triggered. If he mishandled it, the pistol would fire.

I stared up into his narrow, dark, closed face: he was thinking not of the gun in his hand but of the lion, I saw—the beautiful, powerful, ferocious mountain lion, an animal from another world than ours, a beast controlled and driven, from its first breath to its last, by hungers and fears that Lyman and I had been privy to only in the most terrible moments of our lives. We could not forget those moments; the lion could not distinguish them from any other. The beast's sudden, long leap from the rock across water to land had been extraordinarily beautiful and at once familiar and strange, like the best, last line of a beloved hymn, a graceful arc from bright, certain death to the dark, impenetrable mystery of the forest. Why could I not make that same leap? From my place out there on the back of the rough, gray rock, I peered across the water to the thicket of willows at the shore and the trees beyond, up the beech- and hickory-covered slope to the spruces and the tangled heights and rocky parapets above, where I imagined the lion now, moving in solitude freely and safely all day and night, tracking down its prey and suddenly leaping upon it, pulling it to the ground with its great weight and the brutal fury of its attack, rolling it over in the soft, rust-colored pine needles, and burying its hungry mouth in the body.

I heard the explosion of the gun and was not startled by it. I looked up at Lyman. For a split second, he understood everything. Then his astonished, yet utterly comprehending gaze turned blank and flat as stone, and a huge, red blossom erupted in the center of his chest. His mouth filled with blood and spilled it, and he pitched forward head-first. His forehead, when it hit the rock, made an evil crack, like the snap of a dry stick.

He rolled over once onto his back, and the upper half of his body slipped off the rock into the water of the lake. A cloud of blood spread from the hole in his chest and grew large in the water and quickly surrounded him, enveloping his chest, shoulders, arms, and head entirely, like the billowing masses of a woman's silken, scarlet hair.

The human body is a sac filled with blood—puncture its skin, and the shape and color of the body are grotesquely re-arranged and changed. It's no longer human, its skin is no longer white or black. Half in the lake and bathed in the spreading swirls of his own blood, Lyman could have been a white man or a black—there was no way to tell which. Blood is red.

But I was the man who had never been able to forget that Lyman, while he lived, was black. Thus, until this moment, I had never truly loved him. He was a dead man now—finally, a man of no race. And as surely as if I had pulled the trigger myself, I was the man, the white man, who, because of Lyman's color and mine, had killed him. It was as if there had been no other way for me to love him.

There was nothing for love, now, but all-out war against the slavers. My nature was fully formed; and it was a killer's. And only by cleaving strictly to Father's path would I be kept from killing men who did not deserve to die. Father would be my North Star. Lyman Epps would be my memory of slavery.

When Lyman was slain by the accidental firing of his own pistol—reported as such by me and believed at once by all—I did not know that four months later his grieving widow would give birth to his son. I deprived Lyman of that, too. Susan would name the infant after his father, and he would grow up to become famous in later years as a singer of religious songs. At the time of his birth, however, I was long gone—following Father's instructions to gather up Fred in Ohio. The younger Lyman Epps, the man who, because of me, was born and raised fatherless, I saw and heard sing on the day of the interment ceremonies below Father's rock. His sweet voice rose into the cold May sky like the pealing of a bell as he sang "Blow, Ye Trumpets, Blow" over the box that contained the bones of eleven men and should have contained my bones, too.

A terrible irony that would have been, had my bones joined those others. His splendid voice honors my burial, without his knowing that, by my refusal that long-ago day at Lake Colden to save his father, I was his father's murderer. Although I told the truth then, when his father died, and I have told the truth now, these many years later, the one was a lie, this other a confession. For the one was told to the living by a man struggling to stay alive, a man still ignorant of his true motivations and weakness; and this other was told to the dead by a ghost wishing solely to join them.

The story of how his father died, when his mother finally conveyed it to him, surely must have cut the boy's heart, leaving him scarred and wary all the years of his life. It was necessarily the story that I myself told to Father and to the manager of the Tahawus mining camp and that they in turn told to others. Accompanied by a pair of fugitives—two strong young men led by Harriet Tubman herself off a North Carolina plantation and brought out from Albany by Father—they came up towards the pass searching for Lyman and me, after we had not turned up at the camp at the appointed time, for they needed us to convey these fugitives on to Canada. At the lake, they found Lyman's body where it had fallen, bled gray in the water, and me they found on the rocky heights above, howling like a wounded animal, with no memory of how I got there.

I had cut my crippled arm up and down its rigid length with my knife and had smeared my face with blood and had rolled in dirt and leaves. Father calmed me and, holding me in his arms, managed after a while to extract from me a description of what had occurred, and finally led me back down from the crag to the lakeside, where the others had constructed a litter to transport Lyman's body home to Timbuctoo.

Father explained that he was obliged to return that day to Albany for one of his court appearances, and Mr. Seybolt Johnson could not be away from the mining camp, so I and the two frightened young fugitives were pressed into carrying Lyman's body back along the trail we had just cut through the pass to Timbuctoo.

"When you're back there, let Watson deliver Lyman's body to his wife, and let him then carry these fellows on to Massena and the crossing to Canada," Father instructed, speaking to me as if I were a child and taking care also to write his orders on the back of an envelope, which I was to place in Watson's hand as soon as we arrived at the farm. I was then to leave at once for Ohio, he said, to retrieve Fred, who had been too long alone. It had been several months since John and Jason went off to Kansas with their wives and little sons and put up their homesteads there.

Father placed his hands on my shoulders and in a soft voice said that he thought I was too shaken to stay in North Elba now and needed some time away. He perceived the depths and power and the true nature of my feelings, if not their source, and I believe that for the first time he was afraid for my sanity, afraid that if I stayed in North Elba close to the Negroes and especially to Lyman's widow, I would try to take my own life. He was right.

The true story of Lyman's death, however, my confession, Lyman's son never heard, man or boy, and has not heard now and never will, unless, when he himself dies, he comes over to our old farmhouse and family burying ground and finds me still talking into the darkness—the mad ghost of Owen Brown, he who was the murderer of the elder Lyman Epps, he who was the secret villain of the massacre at Pottawatomie, the meticulous arranger of the martyrdom of John Brown, and the cause of the wasted deaths of all those others whose bodies lie now before me.

The younger Lyman Epps will not end up buried here; his bones will molder next to his father's and mother's, three miles yonder in the old Negro burial ground of Timbuctoo. And if he learns the truth of why his father died, he will hear it from his father, the only man who knows it as well as I.

But does my beloved, murdered friend Lyman speak on into the night over there, as I do here? Impossible. Unlike me, Lyman died with a clean conscience. Thus he surely went instantly silent.

IV

16

That was the year of the terrible Ohio drought, when the hay burned in the fields, and the soil crumbled into dust and was blown into dunes, and so many farmers, especially the younger ones, were pulling up stakes and heading for the western territories to start over again. From Pennsylvania to Michigan, crops failed before they blossomed, and the fields lay fallow, and the cattle and the swine were killed and butchered early to keep them from starving to death. Men and women looked out at their parched fields and up at the clear, blue sky and shook their heads and said, Enough! We'll go where there's rain falling. And my brothers John and Jason and their young wives were among them that year.

It was the year that the copperhead Franklin Pierce of New Hampshire, the drunken Yankee minion of the slaveholders, became President, putting an essentially Southern, pro-slave government finally in place and setting up passage of the Kansas-Nebraska Act, which would turn an old-fashioned land grab into a holy war. It overthrew the Missouri Compromise and transformed the old western frontier, making it for all practical purposes into a foreign land, which in that year began to be fought over by the people of two distinct, bordering nations, the slaveholding South and the free North.

By converting the western territories into an object of conquest, the Kansas-Nebraska Act split the country more effectively than any of the battles and wars that followed. The North and the South competing for Kansas in the 1850s were like France and England at war over Canada a century earlier. Except that in Kansas the stakes were higher. Every American knew that if the pro-slavers captured the territory, they would at once make it a slaveholding state in a democratic union that would be governed from Washington by a slaveholding majority of the states, and as a direct result, three million Americans and their descendants would remain permanently enslaved. The North, hopelessly a minority, would have no choice then but to secede from the Union or commence a war of liberation against the South.

And would white Americans go to war to liberate black Americans? Unthinkable. At that time, before Harpers Ferry, with no real blood yet spilt in the name of the cause, the North would have merely shrugged and turned its back on the slaves and the Southern states altogether, and in a businesslike manner would have looked northward for expansion and marched into Canada.

It was also the year of the birth of Father's last child, Ellen, named for the baby who had died in Springfield back in '48. With the birth of this child, the Old Man had fathered on two women a total of twenty children. Of the twenty, only eleven were to live beyond childhood; and of those, three more would die in their youth, cut down in the war against slavery; which left, from the eldest, John, born in 1821, to the youngest, Ellen, born thirty-two years later, only eight who survived into adulthood.

It was the year that Lyman Epps and I finished our elaborate dance, and I went howling into the wilderness, leaving wreckage and smoldering ruin all around behind me.

And it was the year that I followed Father's orders and went out to Ohio to put my brother Fred under my control and bring him back to the farm in North Elba, although in the end I did not bring him back. Instead, I disobeyed Father and took him with me to Kansas, following my brothers John and Jason into the battle there, and eventually by my actions forcing Father to do the same. It did not seem that way at the time, of course, but it does now.

It was autumn when I arrived in Ohio, and the drought had ended some months earlier, but the effects of its devastation were still all around, many empty, abandoned farms and storefronts and fields gone back to brush and weed—as if the landscape had recently been visited by a Biblical chastizement. It was like that for me, too. That warm October evening at Mr. Perkins's large, prosperous farm a few miles outside Akron, with all the turmoil and madness of North Elba only a few weeks behind me, I was still trembling and distracted by consider- ations of my own recent proximity to murder and perversion. Otherwise, I might have been more astute in my dealings with Fred, whose nervous condition was, in fact, far worse than mine. I would have put my mission to him in a gentler way.

Unlike me, however, he seemed on the surface to be at relative peace with himself—sitting out with Mr. Perkins's flocks of merino sheep all day long like an ancient shepherd with his crook and pipe, rounding them up at day's end with his little black collie dog, and returning them at nightfall to the fold. Evenings, he retired to a small hut that he had built of cast-off lumber, where he prepared his modest meals over a tin stove and read by candlelight from his Bible and slept on a reed mat on the floor. In my agitated state, I envied him for the monkish simplicity of his life and thus did not see the turbulence it hid and anticipated nothing of what was coming.

Though not a large man, Fred was sinewy and tough and very strong, like Father. His face also resembled Father's, with a hawk-beak nose and deep-set gray eyes under a heavy brow. His hair was stiff and straight, more brown than red, and he had grown a scruffy, wild beard. The last time I saw him, he'd been a boy—not a normal boy, to be sure, but more child than man. All that had changed considerably in the years between. I was not so much shocked or worried by the changes, because Father and my older brothers had prepared me, as I was intrigued by them. With his dark, leathered skin, he looked like a man of the desert, a bedouin or an ancient anchorite living on locusts and honey, an effect emphasized by his clothing—loose deerskin trousers held up by a length of rope, and a shearling vest with no blouse beneath it, and rough, Indian-style moccasins which he had evidently made himself. Artlessly, but all the more artful for that, Fred cut an impressive figure.

When I got to the Perkins place, it was nearly evening. A stable-hand pointed me to Fred's hut, adjacent to the sheepfolds out behind the large white farmhouse, and I went straight there, intending to visit with Mr. and Mrs. Perkins the next day and inform them of my intention to take my younger brother away with me. I wasn't especially eager to see them. Father was supposed to have written them of my mission, so I anticipated no trouble, but I did not particularly like Mr. Perkins and his wife. Despite his many years of generosity to Father, I somehow blamed Mr. Perkins for Father's financial troubles. I saw him, at little cost or risk to himself, as having offered the Old Man the opportunity to develop his wild financial notions unimpeded until he had been overthrown by them. In the normal course of events, Father never would have gotten his warehousing scheme off the ground. But Mr. Perkins was a very rich man, a banker who had made a fortune in the canal business and speculation in the early '40's land-boom, which had bankrupted Father, and for him, the sheep business was only a distraction of his old age, a game played with idle money that allowed him to feel like a country squire and attend to something other than his many physical ailments. And I think Father's skills as a breeder of merino sheep and his energy, earnestness, and honesty fascinated Mr. Perkins, who was in all these ways the opposite. Also, he knew that, however much of his money Father lost in the wool business, Old Brown would pay Mr. Perkins back, no matter how long it took. Meanwhile, he had the continuing benefit of having at least one of Brown's sons to tend his flocks, which gave him an indentured, highly skilled worker with no fixed term, a hostage, almost a slave. Insensitive to these distinctions and similarities, the man was also definitely not an abolitionist, and Mrs. Perkins even less so, and we had long ago been instructed by Father, of all people, not to discuss or preach abolitionism around them. From the Book of Proverbs, he counseled us, "Better a dry morsel and quietness therewith, than a house full of sacrifices with strife."

But, happily, his relationship with Mr. Perkins was at last drawing to a close, he explained, and he no longer felt obliged to keep one or more of his sons tending the man's flocks. More pointedly, however, the Old Man was alarmed. "Fred's been showing some wildness," he said, brought on, he assumed, by John's and Jason's leaving to go down into Kansas without him. So I was dispatched out to Ohio in order to "handle" Fred, as Father put it, and bring him home. With one remaining suit to be heard at trial, which would require him to go to Pittsburgh to defend himself and Mr. Perkins into the fall, Father, following the tragedy at Lake Colden, instructed me to depart from North Elba at once.

He wasn't inventing this errand out of whole cloth just to get me away from Timbuctoo for a spell, although that was a benefit. Simply, the Old Man couldn't leave Fred unattended in Ohio much longer, and he did not wish to have him placed as far from his personal supervision as Kansas. In Kansas at that time, the pro-slavery Border Ruffians were already pouring into the Territory from Missouri, with an equal number of Free-Soilers heading down from the North, and both sides were spoiling for a fight. But Father had no intentions of going out there himself, not even for cheap, abundant land and for an honorable fight. He had land in New York, and his warrior's mind was still on Virginia and the Subterranean Passway. If he was going to fight the slavers anywhere, he insisted, it would be there.

In July, he had written to John, No, *if you two boys and your wives and children must go, fine, do so. I'd go with you, if I could, but I can't. You'll just have to leave Fred temporarily alone at the Perkins place, until I can figure a way to get him home here in North Elba.* Father thought it too dangerous in Kansas for Fred, who turned twenty-four that year and, according to John and Jason, had grown increasingly morbid and subject to unmanageable bouts of melancholia, which were often followed by inexplicable rages. His melancholy, I remembered from when he was in his teens, was a kind of heavy affectlessness and lassitude, driven, it seemed, by delusory convictions of his own sinfulness, which, after a period, shifted into a state of wild intolerance of the presumed sins of others. He, the most innocent of boys, the most trusting and honest, the most childlike, could not reside inside his body without despising it, and when he could find nothing more in himself capable of sustaining this loathing, he turned it onto the real and imagined sins of others, becoming suspicious, mistrustful, and wary.

Up to now, in Akron, the dark effects of his seizures had been mostly overlooked by John and Jason and their wives, not without some difficulty, however. But tending the flocks of Brown & Perkins (of Mr. Perkins alone, actually, now that the company had been officially dissolved), with or without John and Jason to watch over him, Fred was nonetheless in familiar territory, surrounded by neighbors and relatives who had known and liked him since childhood and who would not exploit or abuse him or take particular offense from his delusions. That was just Fred, people said. Sometimes he was worse, sometimes he was better; either way, everyone who knew him knew also that he was basically harmless.

❏

When I first came up on him, he was drawing water from the well, and he heard me and turned and spoke to me in his old, slow way, as if we had never been apart and I had merely gone to the house for a moment and was now returned. "I believe it's time to wash," he said. "D' ye want a drink of water first, Owen? You look like you could use it, brother." He picked up a wooden ladle from the lip of the well and dipped it into the bucket and extended it to me.

I thanked him and drank. He was perfectly right, I was dry, and at that moment, although I had not known it, preferred a cool drink of water to just about anything else. Refreshed, I set down the ladle and grinned and laid my hands on his shoulders and said how good it was to see him, as indeed it was. I loved Fred—we had been boys together, and I had loved him and had felt protective and custodial towards him long before I was conscious of there being any basic difference between us. We shared the same mother, he and I, and had marched off to school together, and had played and then worked alongside one another for years. I knew the shape of his eye, his inner face, better than that of any other human being, except perhaps Father's, and what you have once known so well you must love always.

Together we lugged water back to his hut, where we washed off the day's sweat and dust, his from the fields and mine from the road, all the while talking in our old, laconic way. He was in adulthood like my childhood imaginary friend, his namesake, had been. It was only in Fred's company that I did not feel tongue-tied and conversationally inept and thus could speak in the manner that felt natural to me. Freed of my usual vanity and fears of sounding dull-witted, ill-educated, and rural, I could speak slowly and obliquely, and by indirection say and find true direction out. In speech, Fred and I were both oxen, but unlike me, he was an ox who never tried running with the horses. He drew his load of thought and feeling at the same steady, slow pace and direction, regardless of who accompanied him or whatever rocks, stumps, and gullies got in his path.

One by one, he asked after Mary and Ruth and the younger children in North Elba, and I reported on each, honestly, if obliquely, for the direct truth about each could not be said without making a narrative the length of a novel. Mary is nursing Ellen, the new baby girl, I said, at her age more worn out by the pregnancy than the birthing and glad that her other female children are now old enough to take her place in the kitchen. I told him that Ruth was living nearby but was pretty much taken up with meeting her new husband's needs, which I described as complex if inconstant. Watson was in love with a religious girl, a Methodist, had gotten religion himself, and was building a mill, which he hoped would make him rich. Salmon was improving the scruffy local apple trees with cuttings from trees from Connecticut, and Oliver, though barely fourteen years old, had gotten hot with anti-slavery fever and was running fugitives night and day, and when he was home he was usually asleep.

And so on down the line I went, until I had made small portraits of everyone, except, of course, for Lyman and Susan, whom I did not mention and of whom he did not ask. He knew about their presence in our life, naturally, but he had never met them. To Fred, they were like so many of the Negroes who had briefly resided with us at one time or another over the years, invited in by Father for asylum or merely to rest during their long, dangerous journey out of slavery. They were more the continuing context than the content of our lives, and since Fred could safely assume that our context was unchanged, he did not need to ask after it or be told.

He made the two of us a simple supper of cabbage soup and rivels, which was very good with biscuits, and while we ate, he reported to me about the sheep, which he referred to as *his* sheep. Afterwards, we were silent for a long time, until finally Fred pursed his lips thoughtfully and furrowed his brow and said, "Why'd you come all the way out from North Elba, Owen?"

"Well, the truth is, the Old Man's finished up his association with Mister Perkins," I said.

"Oh. That right?"

"Yes. And he wants me to bring you back up there."

"He wants me to leave my sheep and go with you?"

"Yep."

"Oh," he said, as if it mattered not in the slightest to him where he went or why. He lit a tallow candle and stretched out on his pallet and opened his Bible and began to read in it.

I sat by the stove on a three-legged stool, wondering how long it would take us to arrange properly for our departure from this place . . . if we would have to hang around until Mr. Perkins hired himself another shepherd . . . if it would be adviseable for me to go on down to Hudson for a few days to visit with Grandfather and our other relatives . . . if John and Jason had left any of their possessions with Fred, or did they take everything to Kansas with them, and how did one do that, transport so much so far . . . just letting my mind drift idly, when suddenly Fred shut his Bible and in a loud voice announced, "Owen, it'd be best if I didn't go with you."

"Why do you think that?"

"Well, the fact is, I carry within me a great many lusts. And so long as that is true, I do not care to place myself amongst other people," he explained in his slow, careful way. "Especially amongst girls and women. Here in my cabin and out there in the fields alone, I ain't so tempted as when I'm with other people. Particularly those of the feminine persuasion." He opened his Bible again and read aloud: *Every man is tempted when he is drawn away of his own lust and enticed. Then when lust hath conceived, it bringeth forth sin. And sin, when it is finished, bringeth forth death.* He leafed ahead to another passage, obviously much-read, and recited, *Whosoever is born of God doth not commit sin; for his seed remaineth in him: and he cannot sin, because he is born of God.* "Y' see, it's because of my lust, Owen, that my seed doth not remaineth in me. I can't keep it inside me. I am not yet born of God," he pronounced.

I did not know what to say then. We both remained silent awhile, until finally I asked him, "Do you pray, Fred? Doesn't that help some? You know, with keeping the seed inside and all."

"Yes, I pray a heap. But it don't do any good. It's been better since the others left, though. John and Jason and their families. Since then I've been able to move out here and be by myself and have mostly holy thoughts. No, I ought to stay right here where I am, Owen. It's for the best. I know that."

"Father won't permit it," I said firmly. "C'm'on, Fred, you know if I go back without you, the Old Man'll come hopping all the way out here to fetch you himself. And he'll be mad at us both then. Up there in the mountains, you'll be fine. The Adirondacks is still a wilderness. You can build yourself a hut there as well as here," I told him, and gave him to understand that he'd be even more alone in North Elba than he was here in Akron.

"No, Owen, that ain't true. All the whole family'd be around me. It's the way we are. Remember, 'Every man is tempted when he is drawn away of his lust and enticed. Then when lust hath conceived, it bringeth forth sin: and sin, when it is finished, bringeth forth death.'"

"Come on, Fred, you're sounding like the Old Man," I said. "Thumping yourself on the head with the Bible. Ease up on yourself, brother. You're the best of all of us." Then I repeated Father's charge to me and declared forcefully that we'd speak to Mr. Perkins in the morning and make our arrangements to leave here as quickly as possible. "They need us back at the farm," I said, lying a little. "Not out here tending Mister Perkins's flocks and arguing theology and sin all night."

I asked him if he had a blanket I could sleep in. Silently, he rummaged through his few possessions and drew out an old gray woolen blanket, and when I saw the thing, I recognized it at once from our childhood—one of the blankets spun and woven in the New Richmond house by our mother long years ago. He tossed it over to me, and I clutched it close to my face and inhaled deeply and grew dizzy with nostalgia. For a long moment, I kept it against my face, traveling back years in time, whole decades, to the long, cold winter nights in the house in the western Pennsylvania settlement, with me and my brothers and sister Ruth, all of us still innocent little children, huddled under our blankets in the big rope-bed in the loft, while below us, Mother tended the fire and cooked tomorrow's meals, and Father sat on his chair by the whale oil lamp and read from his books, and all the future was still as inviting to me as it was unknown.

Finally, I stirred from my reverie and asked Fred, "How'd you come still to own one of these blankets?"

He didn't answer. He just looked down at the packed dirt floor.

"I'd have thought they were all lost or worn out by now. Did John give it to you?"

In stony silence, he blew out the candle and lay down on his pallet, his back to me, as if gone to sleep.

"Shall we take it with us?" I asked him.

"You can keep it, if you want," he murmured.

I couldn't accept it from him; it was too precious a gift. But deciding it best now to leave him to his thoughts and, in fact, eager to be immersed in my own, I lay down on the packed dirt floor close to the stove, where I wrapped myself in the sweet-smelling blanket, and swooning with freshened memories of Mother and our childhood home, I was soon asleep.

While I slept, the terrible thing that Fred did to himself took place. Or, rather, he determined then to do it and had actually commenced, so that even though I was awake when it was done, I could not stop him. I thought it was the sound of an owl or a ground dove that had wakened me, a low, cooing noise coming from outside the hut, but when it persisted and brought me wholly out of sleep, I realized that it was something else, some night creature that I could not name. Lifting myself on my elbows, I saw that the door to the hut lay half-open, letting in long planks of moonlight. Fred's cot was empty.

The cooing sound, *Whoo-hoo, whoo-hoo,* I realized, was being made by Fred outside. But I couldn't imagine what it signified, so I unraveled myself from my mother's blanket and stood in stockinged feet and peered carefully out the door, as if afraid of what I would see there.

He had his back to me and stood some five or six paces from the hut, and from his head-down posture, legs spread, both hands in front of him, I thought at first that he was making water. His trousers were loosened and pulled down a ways. *Whoo-hoo, whoo-hoo,* he sang in a light voice, as if chanting a single pair of notes broken from a tune that he could not get out of his mind. Then I saw the knifeblade flash in the moonlight, a cold, silver glint that he held like an icicle in his right hand, saw it disappear and then re-appear streaked red, as he made a quick swipe across the front of him, as if he were facing the exposed belly of a ram lamb held from behind by a second shepherd, the way we had done so many hundreds of times for Father, who with that same swift, efficient stroke of a knife castrated the poor animal, severing the scrotum and releasing the testicles into his cupped hand.

I shouted Fred's name, but it was too late. As if to answer me, he made a chilling little bleat, his only cry, and he turned and showed me the terrible breach he had made in himself. Blood spilled from the grisly wound and flowed in a thin skein down his bare legs onto the wet grass.

He hurled his testicles away into the willow thicket with great force, as if violently casting out a demon. On his face he had an expression of wild pride, as if he had come to the end of a long, exhausting day and night of mortal combat and had triumphed over an ancient enemy and had castrated the corpse and now stood over it all bloodied. He seemed dazed, stunned by the totality of his victory. It was as if, for a few seconds at least, the terrible pain of his wound had been erased by its very extremity and by the significance of its meaning.

Then his wild, proud expression disappeared, and he was possessed by a sudden placidity—a great calm. I rushed forward and embraced him and bloodied myself in doing it. I never felt such a sadness as I felt then, for it was in both of us. He relaxed in my embrace, and all the force seemed suddenly to go out of him. The insidious little pocketknife, for that is all it was, fell to the ground, and his knees buckled, and he began to collapse. I lifted him in my arms as if he were a bale of wool and carried him back inside his hut, where I laid him down on his cot and at once set about washing and dressing his wound.

It was a single, neat cut straight across the sac. He had a practiced, shepherd's hand, which was lucky, for he had severed no big vein, and the bleeding, although bad, did not threaten his life and soon abated somewhat. This allowed me to wash his wound with water that I heated on his little iron stove and to dress it with strips of cloth torn from my shirt, wrapping him loosely about the groin in such a way that he would be protected from infection and accidental injury, and the healing could begin.

It would be several weeks before Fred could walk properly again and we could take our leave, finally, of the Perkins place. I wrote Father at once and told him of the incident—better for him to learn of it first from me than anyone else, I figured—although I feared that it might bring him hurrying out to Ohio, which I did not particularly want, nor, I thought, did Fred. In my letter, minimizing the degree of Fred's injury, but admitting nonetheless that he had effectively gelded himself, I reassured Father that I could nurse Fred back to health myself, and he evidently believed me, for he remained in Pittsburgh, while I stayed by Fred's side. During the weeks that followed, I tended him day and night, as Father himself would have done, and never left him alone, except for the few hours a day when I myself was obliged to watch Mr. Perkins's sheep. Luckily, the collie dog was clever and needed little supervision, so it was not an onerous task to double as shepherd and nurse. Besides, when I informed Mr. Perkins that, as soon as he was able to travel, I planned to take Fred away with me, he promptly found himself a new shepherd boy from a family in town.

Right up to the morning we departed from that place, Fred believed that we were returning to North Elba, and I myself thought so, too. But then came that misty, gray dawn when we slung our rifles and our small bundles of clothing, food, and trail blankets over our shoulders and walked down the long driveway to the road that passed by the Perkins place. I had kept Mother's blanket and viewed it now as mine from childhood and never spoke of it to Fred. It was my inheritance.

When we reached the road, without a glance or a thought one way or the other, I turned southwest, instead of northeast, and Fred followed.

For a few moments, we walked along in silence. "Where're we going?" Fred finally asked.

"Well, to Kansas, I guess."

A quarter of a mile further on, he spoke again. "Father wants us to go to the farm in North Elba. That's what you told me, Owen."

"Yes. But we're needed more in Kansas."

There was a long silence as he pondered this. Finally, "Why?"

"To fight slavery there."

More silence. Then, "Doing the Lord's work?"

"Right."

"Good. That's real good."

"Yep."

A little further down the road, he said, "But what about Father? He won't like this, Owen."

"Maybe not, at least at first. But don't worry, he'll come along soon to Kansas himself. He won't let you and me and the boys do the Lord's work, while he stays out east doing Mister Perkins's. Anyhow, John says there's going to be shooting in Kansas before long. That'll bring the Old Man on. He hates it when he can't give us the order to fire," I said, and laughed, and he laughed with me.

So on we went, walking and sometimes hitching rides on wagons, barges, canal boats, moving slowly west and south into the territory of Kansas—a one-armed man and a gelded man, two wounded, penniless, motherless brothers marching off to do the Lord's work in the war against slavery. In this wide world there was nothing better for us to do. There was nothing useful that anyone wanted us to do, except to stay home and take care of the place and the women, which neither of us wanted to do and neither could do properly, either. We had to be good for something, though: we were sons of John Brown, and we had learned early in our lives that we did not deserve to live otherwise. So we were going off to Kansas to be good at killing. Our specialty would be killing men who wished to own other men.

17

At first in Kansas was the waiting—waiting for the Old Man to bring us the new-style, breech-loading Sharps rifles and horses and winter gear for waging war against the Border Ruffians, waiting for Father to raise abundant funds and supplies in Syracuse and Akron and decide to come out to Kansas after all—the same as when, after Kansas, we waited out the winter in Iowa; and then, still later, as when we huddled together in the cold, unlit upstairs room of the Kennedy farmhouse outside Harpers Ferry and waited for Father to return empty-handed from his final, fateful meeting with Frederick Douglass, so that the assault on the Ferry could begin at last. We were always waiting for Father in those days; and it was every time in the same, humiliating way—quarrelsome, disgruntled, in confusion and disarray, incompetent, undisciplined, often physically ill, and all our best intentions and his careful instructions gone somehow weirdly awry, as if we secretly meant to sabotage him, we the loyal, dependent sons and followers of John Brown lying in our cots, cold and damp, scowling up at the ceiling or into the walls, filled with dread at the thought of the Old Man's arrival, and yet at the same time nearly giddy with impatience for him to come and darken the portal with his familiar shape and lower his head and walk into the tent, there to kneel down by one of us, the sickest, always the sickest, whom Father could identify at a glance, and which was John at that time when the Old Man first arrived out there in Kansas at the pathetic encampment we called Browns Station. My waiting, of course, was more colored by dread and impatience even than that of my brothers, for, in coming out here with Fred, I had disobeyed the Old Man and needed to know how he viewed me now.

John had gone down with the ague, but it had gotten worse, and soon he was taking short, shallow breaths, as if his lungs had gotten enflamed. Feverish and shivering, subject to visions and spurts of wild, incoherent speech, he had been sick for a month by the time Fred and I got there from Akron. We had taken the old river-route down the Ohio and up to St. Louis by the Missouri, and when we got to Browns Station, we found John unable to eat and barely able to sip water, despite the tireless, silent care of his wife, Wealthy. And it was not long before Fred and I, too, lay wrapped in all our clothes and blankets in the cots on either side of John, whom we followed close behind in the degree of our sickness, I, like him, with the ague, and Fred, weakened from our travels and still healing from his terrible wound, unable to act without being led by one of his brothers. Neither of us could provide leadership for him. Or perhaps, in our chilled despondency, neither of us wished to. So he had simply imitated me, as if I were imitating John. And perhaps I was.

It was not yet the dead of winter; it was, in fact and by the calendar, still autumn, and the snow was not so bad as it would have been by now in North Elba. Yet I had never felt so cold up there in the eastern mountains as out here on the western plain. It was as if in Kansas the sun had gone out permanently. The icy, relentless wind off the flat expanse of land blew day and night and froze our clothes and hair and the beards of the men and stiffened our faces and rubbed our hands raw and made our bones feel like iron and never ceased blowing against the tents, snapping them like sails in a hurricane, threatening all night and day to tear the canvas from the poles and rip the guy-lines and stakes from the hardened ground and expose our poor, blanketed bodies to the low, gray western sky, as if they had been put out there by the Indians for the coyotes and vultures to devour and for the old Indian gods to receive into paradise.

Was it true that I had not seen Jason and his wife, Ellen, for weeks? They seemed to have withdrawn permanently to their own tent, on their adjacent claim, not physically ill, as we were, but demoralized, withdrawn, selfish, and still stunned with seemingly endless grief over the death of their little boy, Austin, whose body they had been forced to bury and abandon back in Missouri. They had crossed the river en route from Ohio in late summer, and during the brief trespass upon a corner of the slaveholders' evil land, as if under a curse, they had lost their only child to cholera. The disease had slain half the passengers of the boat, and with the exception of poor Austin, all the victims were Missouri Border Ruffians and their families coming across to Kansas to claim the territory for slavery. Jason's and Ellen's beloved little boy had been snagged by that rough justice and died, a compensatory price too high for them yet to comprehend.

When John and Jason and their matched families decided to come out from Ohio, after their farms had been ruined by the terrible drought of the previous year, it was in search of new, cheap land, so as to start their lives over. But they also came to wage war against the slavers and to capture the Kansas Territory for the North. Thus it was both a rational, opportunistic thing to do—and there were thousands like them from all over the North, doing it for no other reason—and one that glowed with abolitionist righteousness as well. This was the sort of venture that had always appealed to John, but it had the added benefit of allowing him, by emphasizing the moral aspects of the venture, to advertise it effectively to Jason, who had not been as quick to leave the dried remnants of his Ohio orchards as was John to abandon his scorched, hardcake fields. So while Jason and Ellen had gone out willingly, they had not gone eagerly, and perhaps for that reason, the death of their son, Austin, and the need to abandon his body in a shallow grave on a bluff overlooking the river in slaveholding Missouri had made the couple quickly bitter. And there was the painful, ever-present fact that John and Wealthy had their little son, John, whom they called Tonny, still with them. John's and Wealthy's good luck, then, might have contributed, too, to the sourish relations that prevailed between the brothers and their wives when Fred and I first arrived at Browns Station, bedraggled, like a couple of tramps, many months later.

In a flurry of letters to Father in North Elba and then to him in Pittsburgh and to me in Ohio while I was watching over Fred, John had written that, to survive the surprisingly violent Kansas weather and the rapid influx of Border Ruffians from Missouri, he needed soldiers, cohorts, reinforcements; he wanted up-to-date weapons and cows and swine, blankets, grain, dried beef and salt fish: he was awaiting the arrival of the makings of an invading army. What he had got instead was a pair of scrawny, exhausted refugees carrying no more than their blanket-rolls and their twenty-year-old muzzle-loaders. We must have been a disappointing sight, Fred and I, that morning when we arrived at the camp, one of us blank-eyed and struck dumb by the enormity of his self-mutilation, still hitching himself along with a rough crutch, and the other, me, a nervy man with a crippled arm glancing back over his shoulder with the wariness and guilt of a criminal, our clothes shabby and dirty from our arduous journey, bringing to our brothers in their place of brave settlement, this desolate place where they had chosen to make their permanent homes and take their self-defining stand against slavery, nothing but our craven needs for comfort and love.

But if we were disappointing to them, they and their settlement were just as much a let-down to us, for we saw, not the neat log cabins and lean-tos amongst the cottonwood groves and broad, fresh streams and high, grassy meadows of Kansas that we expected and that John had described to us in his letters. We saw instead a pair of tattered, flapping tents, a single, broken-wheeled wagon, cold firestoves outside, four bony horses nibbling at the frozen turf. And over all, a pervasive gloom and lassitude—an atmosphere worsened by John's illness and by Jason's and Ellen's withdrawal to the privacy of their own tent, which they had pitched on their land claim several hundred yards down the draw from John's and Wealthy's towards the Osawatomie River.

On our arrival, Fred and I had visited and greeted them separately, as if they were John's jealous and unhappy neighbors, instead of his beloved younger brother and sister-in-law sharing a calamity; afterwards, we had encamped up on the ridge in John's second tent, and that made Jason and Ellen think that we had chosen John and Wealthy over them. And when, in a few days, I fell sick myself, it was simpler for me to move in with John, where Wealthy could the more easily tend us both, and then Fred followed, perhaps because he knew not what else to do and now hated being alone with his thoughts. He came into the tent and placed his bedroll on the other side of John, so that there were three of us lying there, crowded into a single small, dark space, whilst poor Wealthy tried to keep the fire going outside, despite the wind and the snow and the lack of good, dry firewood, caring for us as if we had been shot and wounded in battle instead of having declined spiritually into a muck of despondency and sloth and after a while had weakened and got physically sick as well.

Wealthy had her poor, confused son, Tonny, beside her at every step, clinging to the folds of her dress and whimpering all day and night about the cold and from constant hunger and showing even then the first signs of slowness that would later grow into retardation and cause her and John so much sadness and worry. But if she had not had him there, I believe that Wealthy would have walked on one of those long winter nights straight into the darkness that surrounded us then and disappeared, only to be found days later, frozen to death in some gully. For she was as angry then as any woman I have ever seen in my life. She was silent, and she fumed. And with every good reason. John, Jason, Fred, and I, we were all of us pitiful, shameful specimens of manhood. We were not worthy of her; nor of Jason's wife, either. Here we were, the four eldest sons of the great John Brown, four sickly, miserable fools, foundering in gloom, gone all weak and cowardly. I confess it, it was the women who were strong and they who, to all intents and purposes, kept us alive, until the winter morning when the Old Man finally arrived and began to set everything straight.

And it happened just as I imagined it would. Just as I hoped and dreaded it would. The tent flap was drawn suddenly away, and against a milk-white sky loomed the dark, familiar shape of Father in his broad-brimmed black hat and his greatcoat. He entered the tent, glanced quickly around in that expressionless way of his when he has come upon something complicated and unfamiliar, surveying the scene with as little emotion as possible, until he has acquired from it all the information necessary for a proper response, which in this case was to go straight to John, who in his delirium and fever had neither seen nor heard the Old Man enter, whereas both Fred and I, like startled rabbits, had sat up at once.

In silence, the Old Man felt John's forehead and then bent his head to his eldest son's chest and listened to his clotted lungs and his heart. Behind him I saw shades flitting beyond the thin canvas, rough profiles of other people moving about outside, and heard the creak and clank of saddles and harness and the low voices of my brothers Salmon and Oliver, which surprised me, for I had thought Father was coming out alone, and I heard a male voice that I did not at first recognize, then the voices of the women, Wealthy and Ellen, and Jason, too, as if a crowd had gathered out there.

In a somber voice, Father said his first words to us: "We've got to place a fire in here and set a kettle of water to steaming and clear his lungs. I don't suppose you boys have any stovepipe handy, or you'd have already done that."

I shook my head no, and Father stood up and passed by me without saying anything more. For a second, he paused over Fred and looked down at him with great sadness. In a thin, apologetic voice, almost a child's, Fred said, "It's John and Owen who are sick, Father. Not me so much."

"Yes, I know. And I know about your injury, son. Owen wrote me of it. We'll sit and have us a proper talk later," was his response, and he went directly out. He said nothing to me then of my having disobeyed him, nor did he speak of it afterwards. It was as if his silence on the subject were my punishment, for it did, indeed, feel like one.

Things changed quickly then. Father set everyone to work at once—even me and Fred. Even, in a sense, John, who was obliged, with Wealthy's help, to change out of his filthy, damp clothing, and after washing himself from a basin of water heated on the fire that Salmon had quickly got blazing outside, he put on some of Salmon's and Oliver's extra garments, which were his size and, more importantly, were dry and clean, and then Wealthy wrapped him in several of the fresh blankets that Father had brought and propped him up in his cot, so that his lungs could expand somewhat, Father said, and still following the Old Man's instructions, she shaved her husband's scruffy beard and combed out his matted hair.

Father gave few explanations; he merely gave orders, and then set to work himself. "Jason, you and Salmon pack in from yonder grove of cottonwoods as much deadwood as you can find in an hour. Then start a greenwood smokefire and cut and dry us a few of those old oaks.

"Ellen, you go on down to your stake there below and empty out your tent. Fumigate and scrub it clean, air out all your blankets, and tighten those slack ropes up a mite. And when you put your things back inside, leave the rear wall clear, as we'll be setting a campstove there.

"Wealthy, when you've finished shaving John, you do the same as Ellen with these two tents up here. And why'n't you put little Tonny to work right away at carrying out as much as he can lift by himself? The lad needs to know he's useful.

"Oliver, here's the money and a list of items to purchase in town. Start now and be back before midday, so we can have our stoves set up by nightfall. Unload the wagon first, my boy, we'll be needing some of those goods and tools right off."

He helped Oliver wrestle down a barrel of salt, another of corn meal, many new gray woolen blankets, a large supply of dried Adirondack venison mixed with berries, Indian-style, and axes, spades, half a dozen unmarked wooden crates, and a pine box, carefully fitted and sanded smooth, which I thought might contain rifles, for it was the right size and Father himself lifted it from the wagon and carried it with considerable delicacy to a knoll a short ways off, where he set it down on the ground and then for a short time stood motionless over it, as if in prayer, before returning to the encampment.

To my surprise and pleasure, besides having recruited Salmon and Oliver, Father had brought out from North Elba our neighbor and brother-in-law Henry Thompson. Henry was the most fervent aboli- tionist of all the sixteen Thompson sons, a tall, strapping, young fellow who idolized Father. The Old Man instructed him to begin at once building a proper corral for the horses, and he told me and Fred to take ourselves off with him and give him what help we could. "A little movement and fresh air will improve you," he said, and we instantly complied, and of course he was right—in a short while, quite as if we had been able-bodied all along but merely had not known it, both Fred and I were cutting and dragging poles from down by the river up to a narrow defile close to the camp where Father had determined was the best location for a corral. Later on, by midday, as ordered, Oliver returned from the town of Osawatomie with stovepipe and three tin campstoves, and Father promptly installed one in each tent, and when he and Oliver had them properly working, he sent Oliver off to commence digging a proper privy and then turned to educating Wealthy as to the best care and treatment of John, whose color, now that he was breathing more easily, had already begun returning to his face.

In half a day, Father had turned Browns Station from a place of desolation into a proper frontier settlement. The tents were tightened against the wind, and with sweet-smelling streams of woodsmoke flowing from their tin chimneys, they looked secure and warm, even cheerful, situated in the protective crook of a narrow, forested cut that switch-backed down a long, grassy decline to the meandering river below. Spade and crowbar scraped against dirt and stone, hammers pounded stakes and drove nails, and axes and handsaws bit into wood, sending blond chips and sawdust flying. The air was filled with the bright clatter of leafless trees falling, of brothers calling to one another through the cold afternoon as the light began to fade—the sound of men happily at work, eager to finish their tasks before dark. There were the startled neighs of horses suddenly released to pasture inside a temporary corral made with a rope strung between trees, the bang and scrape of pots and pans being washed, the snap of wet laundry hung to dry in the breeze, and someone down in the cottonwoods even began to sing—Salmon, I realized; of course, it would be Salmon, for he had the best-pitched, clearest voice of us all and the sharpest memory for the old hymns—and first Father joined in with him, and then one by one the others picked it up, even Fred, even me.

> Who are these, like stars appearing,
> These, before God's throne who stand?
> Each a golden crown is wearing;
> Who are all this glorious band?
> Alleluia! Hark, they sing,
> Praising loud their heavenly King!

Towards evening, Oliver came marching proudly into camp with his old Kentucky rifle in one hand and, in the other, four fat prairie chickens, low-flying ground birds somewhat like our partridges, which he delivered over to Wealthy and Ellen, two to each woman. After praising the lad in such a way as to goad the rest of us to go and do likewise every day from here on out—"For I have seen considerable game on our way here," the Old Man said—he then bade us all to cease our labors now and follow him out to the knoll, where he had earlier laid the mysterious pine box. Even John, with Salmon and Oliver half-carrying him, was obliged to come out to the windy hilltop.

Now, I thought, now each of us will be given his own Sharps rifle! I had come to despise my old muzzle-loader: it didn't suit my fantasies or my intentions in the least; it was a boy's smooth-bore gun, suitable mainly for shooting birds and raccoons; I wanted a weapon that would let me slay men. I wanted one of the famous new-style, breech-loading Sharps rifles that fired with deadly accuracy ten times a minute. Manufactured in the armory at Harpers Ferry, they were the so-called Beecher's Bibles which that winter had commenced appearing all over Kansas in the hands of the more radical Free-Soilers. First sent out in crates marked Bibles by the Reverend Henry Ward Beecher's congregation in Brooklyn, New York, they were being purchased and shipped to the Free-Soil settlers now by churches all over the East. I was sure Father would not have come out without at least one case of weapons from the Church of the Holy Rifles—he was not in Kansas, after all, to farm.

But when we had all gathered there on the knoll, I saw that, sometime during the day and without my having observed him, Father had dug a deep hole in the ground next to the box, and for the first time I began to see that it was perhaps not a crate of Sharps, but something else, for the box resembled nothing so much as a finely carpentered coffin. Father looked down the line of us and reached out and drew Jason and Ellen forward to the center, where he stood, so that the three of them were now standing before the box, and at that I understood finally what was inside the box and why we were gathered out here.

The sky was darkening down in the east and cream-colored in the west, and the chilled, late afternoon breeze blew into our faces. Without looking at any one of us, staring instead down at the box before him, Father said, "Children, when I rode out from the east I carried with me a whole set of maps. A whole passel of maps, and overlapping they were, and one of 'em, Jason, was sent to me by you, as you know. That was the very detailed map that led me to the grave that you dug in slaveholding territory, where you wrapped in a blanket the body of your poor little boy, Austin, and buried him whose soul has now gone on to God in heaven. But whose body lay buried in Missouri soil.

"Among my other maps, Jason and Ellen, and above all of them, the master map, as it were, is the one that guides them all—the map that is given to me by the Bible. It is God Almighty's plan of these United States, which I carry with me wherever I go, and on that map this Kansas Territory is still free and will remain free so long as I draw breath. Children, I mean to lay those two maps over one another, Jason's very detailed drawing of where his child lies buried, and God's equally detailed plan, and align them." He then looked straight at Jason and Ellen and said to them, "I know, my children, that you were surrounded by the enemy back there in Missouri and were afraid therefore and were maybe somewhat confused as to what was fitting and proper. I don't mean to scold or upbraid you, children, but I myself could not abandon that boy's body in slaveholding territory.

"I went there to my grandson's grave, to pray over it, as you asked me to do, but then, when I had completed my prayers for his soul, I realized that I could not tolerate the thought of anyone with my blood and name lying under a little wooden cross in a potter's field in a slave state. The very thought of it enraged me. So I retrieved Austin Brown's body from that tainted ground, and Henry and I built it a proper coffin and placed it inside and put it into my wagon, and now we have carried it here to Kansas, where men and women and children are not chattel, here to bury it properly, here to place and mark his gravesite on God's map of this land and not Satan's!"

Then, with the darkness coming slowly on, Father handed ropes to Henry Thompson and me, which we draped beneath the pine box, and holding to them, we lowered the coffin slowly into the earth. Jason and Ellen held each other and wept. Wept with grief, but I am afraid also with shame. For Father had shamed them terribly with what he had done.

When the box had gone down into the hole, we filled the hole with dirt and moved from the gravesite one by one in a kind of confused browse, as if we were both reluctant and eager to get away from it. Last to leave were Father and Jason and Ellen, and I heard him say to them, "Tomorrow you will make a cross with your boy's name and dates on it.

And you will set it at the head of the grave, *there*," he pronounced, and placed his foot firmly on the ground at the place beneath which he knew the boy's head lay. Directly, then, he departed from the knoll, leaving Jason and Ellen alone at the gravesite. Thus ended the harsh, sullen division between Jason and his Ellen and the rest of us. We were all one family again.

18

And yet I felt, in a new, peculiar, or maybe just unfamiliar way, alone again. Not an *isolato*, as I am now, or merely lonely, as I had been before Kansas, but solitary in the way of the devious Iago in the famous play about the Moor by William Shakespeare. Iago is the man who remains, no matter how crowded the stage, incommunicado, unknown, locked inside himself as if inside a dungeon. And while, certainly, in all matters I did as Father wished, I nonetheless became under him in Kansas, like Iago, my own man. Not Father's. Father was my white-skinned Othello.

We did not go straight to war against the Border Ruffians. We could not, due to John's lingering illness and the need to set our tattered, windblown camp straight and make rudimentary householding possible. Also, at that time the Border Ruffians were still holding their fire and were confronting us and our Free-Soil neighbors with little more than loud, drunken talk and empty threats. The Kansas War was something that was happening mostly in the newspapers of the Southern states and back East. And for a spell Father seemed more intent upon finding surveying work for himself than in leading us into battle against the slavers, and consequently he spent a considerable amount of time away from Browns Station, in Topeka and Lawrence and up on the Ottawa Reserve, surveying town sites and claims and marking the borders of the Indian territory.

It was a good place and time to be a surveyor. There was much confusion and controversy then concerning the settlers' claims and legal title to lands, thanks to the rapid influx of impoverished squatters and the large-scale purchases of land by outside speculators like the New England Emigrant Aid Society, whose shareholders, despite their stated ambitions to settle Kansas with Free-Soilers and keep the West from becoming part of the Slavocracy, were in it to make a profit and did not mind if they made it off Indian land, government land, or land claimed by some poor grubstaker from Illinois with a single, sorry ox and a wife and five hungry children, a man too illiterate to register his claim properly.

To the east and south of Browns Station, the Southerners for months had been pouring across the Mississippi and Missouri Rivers into the territory in ever greater numbers than the Free-Soilers. Not three miles from us there were slaves owned. With the encouragement and connivance of their dough-faced President, Franklin Pierce, the pro-slavers had already elected themselves a bogus legislature and governor situated in Leavenworth and had passed their disgusting "black laws," which made it a crime to read and write or even think and speak as we Browns did every day of our lives, laws which we now took special pleasure in breaking every chance we got, not only to express our contempt for them, but also to goad the Ruffians into trying to enforce their laws, which, so far, they had been reluctant to do. We, of course, had few dealings with them, anyhow, and did business mostly with folks who were allied with us, especially those who, like us, counted themselves radical abolitionists, at that time a distinct minority even amongst the Free-Soilers. Even so, most of our presumed allies, like most Northerners then, were as anti-Negro as they were anti-slavery: they wanted to keep Kansas soil free, all right, but free and white. To them, slavery was little more than an unfair labor practice imported from the South.

In his capacity as surveyor, despite his politics and principles and his usual inability to keep them to himself, the Old Man nonetheless passed unimpeded through the lands controlled by the pro-slavers, for they were as eager as the Free-Soilers to ascertain the limits and extensions of their land-claims, certain as they were then of outnumbering us and fearful, therefore, only of our encroaching on their lands illegitimately. Father was just the scrawny old Yankee surveyor with his wagonload of instruments and lines traveling across the plains of eastern Kansas looking for work.

Once again, as he had for a spell back in North Elba, the Old Man called himself Shubel Morgan. The name of John Brown was pretty famous by now and daily growing more so, especially out here, where he and his sons were known these days to be armed with Sharps rifles and Colt revolvers. He had indeed, as I'd hoped, lugged out from Ohio two unmarked crates that turned out to be packed with weaponry, and he had distributed a Sharps and a Colt revolver and a sharpened broadsword to each of us. All that winter into the spring, whenever we rode into Osawatomie or up to Lawrence for supplies or to send mail and messages east, we brandished our new weapons, like our politics and principles, with unabashed pride, and soon all around the region John Brown and his sons came to be regarded by both sides as potentially troublesome.

As the surveyor Shubel Morgan, however, and with his rifle and Colt and broadsword tucked out of sight in the wagon box, Father was able to put himself on friendly terms with most everyone he met. Thus did he quickly gain wonderful intelligence of the meandering rivers and sparkling creeks, the densely wooded gullies, washes, ravines, and gorges that criss-crossed the vast, grassy plains like the lines of a flattened hand. Also, he learned the names and locations of the cabins of every pro-slave settler in the region and in short order knew them as well as the names and locations of the Free-Soil settlers. He observed and tallied up the pro-slavers' weaponry, too, and the number of horses they had, and he discerned something of their general character, which he thought little of. "Cowards," he reported, "and drunkards. Illiterate, ignorant fools with no taste for a real fight, unless it's over a woman or a jug of corn liquor."

There was down on the Pottawatomie River, not far from Browns Station, a particularly nettlesome settlement of Border Ruffians that Father liked to complain of, the Shermans, the Doyles, and the Wilkinsons, our nearest neighbors, in a sense, although to call them neighbors was a gift, for they despised us as much as we them. They were landless farmers who'd drifted up from the Southern hillcoun-try and built tippy, dirt-floored cabins where they made their babies—angry, poor, ignorant people who took their greatest pleasure in puffing up their sense of their own worth by making drunken threats of violence against Northern abolitionists and against us Browns especially. So far, they had not delivered on any of their threats, and none of us thought they could stay sober long enough to carry it off.

There were not many Negro slaves in the region, half a hundred perhaps, rarely more than one or two attached to a single owner, as most of these pro-slavers, like our Pottawatomie neighbors, were failed, landless farmers come out from Tennessee and Missouri and parts of the deeper South, many of them without families, even, and with almost no livestock. And Father was right, there was amongst all of them a surprisingly high proportion of reprobates, whiskey-sellers, thieves, prostitutes, tramps, gamblers, scamps, and other parasites who had followed the Southern settlers as if they were a conquering army instead of a migrating mob of ignorant farmers desperate for cheap land.

In fact, the motives of the pro-slavers for coming out to Kansas were no less mixed than those of us Free-Soilers: like us, they had come for land, for pecuniary advancement, and to wage war over slavery, usually in that order. And, to be truthful, their wild, violent, racialist, and pro-slavery rhetoric was no more incendiary than ours. The difference between the two sides was that, whereas their rhetoric was Satan's, ours was the Lord's. They shrieked at us from Satan's camp, and we trumpeted back from the Lord's.

That is how Father saw it. We were not superior to the pro-slavers by virtue of our intrinsic morality or our intelligence or our farming and animal husbandry skills or our weapons or even our courage, he daily preached to us. No, we were made superior solely by virtue of Him whom we had chosen to follow. The stinking darkness of institutionalized slavery had made the Southerners into a foul and corrupt people. It had stolen their souls and had made them followers of Satan. For centuries, they had resided in a permanently darkened pit, and thus, to them, the world was a dimmed, low, pestilential place. We, however, when we gazed onto the world, we stood as if on a peak bathed in the bright light of freedom, which enabled us to see the true nature of man, and therefore, simply by following our own true nature, we were able to follow the Lord God Almighty. And after much scrupulous examination, having confidently discerned the Lord's will, we naturally had determined to make all men and women free. If, to accomplish that great task, we must put to death those who would oppose us, then so be it: it is the will of the Lord: and in this time and place, He hath no greater work to set before His children than that they stamp upon the neck of Satan and crack the jaw of his followers and liberate all the white and black children of the Lord from the obscene stink and corruption of slavery. Simply, if we would defeat Satan, we must first defeat his most heinous invention, which was American Negro slavery.

I believed this. All of us at Browns Station believed it, regardless of the differences amongst us regarding religion. In our little army of the Lord, John and Jason were positioned at one extreme, freethinkers, downright agnostical skeptics; and at the other were poor Fred, tormented by his visions of a punishing God who now spoke to him personally on a regular basis, and Father, who appeared to believe that he himself was sometimes allowed to speak for God; the rest of us fell in between the two extremes at various places, which felt temporary, like stops for rest on a long journey. Nevertheless, every one of us, even the women, Wealthy and Ellen, and our brother-in-law Henry Thompson, believed that we were now about to devote our lives to the very best work we could imagine, so that if God indeed existed, it was His work that we would be doing here. And if God did not exist, then it did not matter. For, regardless of our differences, all of us believed in a law higher than any passed by a bogus or even an authentic and legal legislative body of men, and belief in that higher law required us to dedicate our lives to the overthrow of chattel slavery and racialism. And perhaps it was only chance that had placed us here in Kansas, or maybe Father was right and it was in the end God's will, but either way, here we were, situated precisely where the battle could no longer be avoided, where the enemy had pitched his tent virtually in our very dooryard, and where we would be obliged to rise up at last and slay him.

My older brothers saw that and trembled with fear or sadly anticipated grief. Although he accepted its inevitability, Jason, especially, did not want war. The man was preternaturally sensitive to the suffering of others and could barely watch the slaughter of a hog, but even he no longer believed that there was a way to end slavery without killing people. He, more than any of the rest of us, had originally come out to Kansas strictly to farm. He had even brought along cuttings from his Ohio vines and eight sapling fruit trees, and while the rest of us sharpened our swords and ran bullets for our revolvers and Sharps repeaters and attached bayonets to long poles, Jason merely watched with a terrible sadness in his eyes, planted his vines and little trees in the newly thawed ground, and kept mostly to himself. His wife, Ellen, and John's wife, Wealthy, were naturally as reluctant for us to go to war as was Jason, but the women, too, knew that it could not be avoided now, unless the Lord Himself intervened, and there was no sign of that. They seemed to accept it as their fate, although Ellen was starting to talk about returning to Ohio in the autumn, with or without Jason, if fighting broke out.

Brother John had always been an anti-slavery firebrand, certainly, but he was also an ambitious, somewhat worldly man and still seemed to hold out hopes for a political victory, as we would soon have in the territory a sufficient number of Free-Soilers to establish a legitimate Free-Soil legislature and governor of our own and pass an anti-slavery territorial constitution that would get Kansas admitted to the Union as a free state. Well-spoken and more educated than the rest of us, John had it in his mind to get elected to the Free-Soil legislature in Topeka. There was a significant number of radical abolitionist settlers in and around Osawatomie and Lawrence who were eager to support him, and every day hundreds of Eastern radicals who honored the name of John Brown were coming down into the territory by way of the new Iowa–Nebraska trail, settlers who back home had regularly read The Liberator and The Atlantic Monthly and would be proud to vote out here for the son and namesake of Old John Brown, the famous abolitionist from New York State, friend and associate of the even more famous abolitionists Gerrit Smith, Frederick Douglass, William Lloyd Garrison, Dr. Samuel Howe, and Thomas Wentworth Higginson.

Salmon and Oliver both were hot-blooded boys eager to test their mettle in a good fight, and they had long ago grown used to following, if not Father himself, then me. They were wholly reliable, therefore.

That left to constitute our little army only Henry Thompson and brother Fred. Henry was newly married to Ruth, his wife back in North Elba residing during his absence with the Thompson clan, but despite that—because he believed in Father's wisdom and moral clarity even more than Father's natural sons did—if the Old Man let him, Henry would follow him straight into the jaws of hell. And then there was Fred, poor, wild Fred, whose dreams and visions seemed to have become so thoroughly intermingled with his daily reality that he thought we had already gone to war against Satan: with Fred, the main difficulty for us lay in holding him in check until such time as we needed him to start firing his Colt and laying about with one of the terrible, ancient, double-edged broadswords that Father had brought out with him from the East and which Fred wore strapped to his waist day and night.

Including myself, then, this was the core of John Brown's little army of the Lord. Before long, we would be joined at times by as many as fifty others, some of whom stayed on for the duration and followed the Old Man all the way to Harpers Ferry, some of whom weakened and fell away, especially after the news of what happened at Pottawatomie got around, and some of whom were slain in battle. Father was our general, our commanding officer, our guide and inspiration, the man whose words chided and corrected us and gave us courage and direction, and without whose example we would have foundered from the start.

Left to his own devices, however, the Old Man, once he had got our camp up and running again and had us properly armed and organized into a fighting force, would have fallen back into his lifelong patterns of wait and see, of delay and discuss, of research and reconnoiter, of organizing his followers and enticing them to war and then stepping away and leaving us to *our* devices—just as he had done in Springfield with the Gileadites, just as he had done all along: for while Father was a genius at inspiring and organizing men to wage war, when it came to leading them straight into battle, he needed someone else—he needed his son Owen—at his ear. *Action, action, action!* may have been his constant cry; but at crucial moments he needed someone else to whisper, *Now!* Until that spring in Kansas, he did not truly know this. Nor did I.

It began in a small way. While Father was off at the Ottawa Nation, making one of his interminable surveys, it happened that below us, down in Douglas County on the far side of Dutch Sherman's camp, a Free-Soil settler from Ohio named Charles Dow, a man whom John and Jason happened to have known back East, was cutting timber for his cabin and got into a row with his nearest neighbor, a pro-slaver from Virginia named Frank Coleman. The Virginian claimed that the trees were his, not Mr. Dow's, and shot and killed Mr. Dow in cold blood. A few days passed, and when the Virginian was not arrested, John, who was now up and about and had begun active politicking, contacted Mr. Dow's numerous Free-Soil friends and called for a protest meeting up in Lawrence. As Lawrence was by then fully a Free-Soil redoubt, John and I and Henry Thompson expected no trouble and rode up for the meeting unarmed. It was the last time we did that.

Just south of Lawrence, we were met at the Wakarusa bridge by a large troop of heavily armed Border Ruffians, deputized and led by the sheriff of Douglas County, a pro-slave appointee named Samuel Jones. Without ceremony or explanation, they put their guns on us and demanded to know our reasons for going into Lawrence. When John forthrightly said that we were going there to attend a meeting that he himself had called for the purpose of protesting the unpunished murder of Mr. Charles Dow, the sheriff promptly arrested him for disturbing the peace and took him off at gunpoint towards Leavenworth.

Henry and I galloped straight on to Lawrence, where we quickly rounded up a band of close to thirty men with Sharps rifles and rode out after the sheriff. We managed to throw down on him and his ragtag troop and their prisoner before they crossed the Kansas River into slave territory. Wisely, they did not resist, and we promptly took John away from them and rode in triumph back to town, where John and, to a lesser extent, Henry and I became instant celebrities.

Humiliated and enraged by this act, the sheriff had ridden back to Leavenworth, where he informed the bogus governor Shannon that there was under way in Lawrence an armed rebellion against the laws of the territory. At once, the governor mobilized the Kansas militia and put it under the command of the slaveholding senator from Missouri, Hon. David Atchison, a drunkard, who brought into his force the leaders of several other whiskeyed-up bands of Border Ruffians, and loudly vowing to exterminate that nest of abolitionists, the whole gang of them headed for Lawrence.

We learned this the day following our protest meeting, when we were riding peacefully back from Lawrence. Nearing Browns Station, we met up with a breathless rider come from the Shawnee Mission over near the Missouri border, a Free-Soil settler who had raced all the way to Douglas County to spread the alarm. He told us that more than two thousand Missourians and members of the Kansas militia were taking up positions on the Wakarusa south of Lawrence, and they intended to burn the town to the ground.

Angered and alarmed, we rushed on to Browns Station to round up Father, our brothers, and our weapons. When we arrived, we saw that Father had returned from the Ottawa Reserve and, unaware of what had transpired, was engaged in preparing to join us in Lawrence to protest the killing of the Ohioan Charles Dow. Quickly, John related what had happened, and the Old Man, I remember, reacted with what seemed like delight.

"It's come, then," he said, rubbing his hands together. "The time has come at last."

First, however, we needed to run off another hundred bullets, he declared. Dutifully, Salmon and Oliver set to work.

"Father," said I, "the Border Ruffians very likely have already placed Lawrence under siege. We must hurry."

"I know, I know. But our friends up there will need all the bullets we can carry," he replied, and instructed us to fasten our pikes with the bayonets attached to the sides of the wagon box, to affix them with the blades pointed to the sky, so that we would impress the enemy with our machinery. An old Roman military tactic, he explained.

"Come on, Father, let's just toss everything into the wagon and get on to Lawrence now. We can do all this up there."

No, he thought that we might have to fight our way into the town, since the Ruffians had probably taken their position on the Wakarusa bridge, which lay between us and Lawrence. We would have to make all our preparations for battle here and now, he declared.

Then there were provisions to pack. The siege might last a long time, he pointed out. And the broadswords wanted more sharpening. And then the wagon had to be loaded with exquisite care so as not to damage any of the weapons, and so on, until finally it was dark, and we still had not left Browns Station. Since there was no moon that night, it was too dangerous, Father thought, to travel up along the California Road to Lawrence with so many Missourians about, for we did not want our weapons and horses to fall into the hands of the enemy, did we? We had better wait till morning, he decided.

John slouched off towards his lean-to, frustrated and angry, although Wealthy was not, and Jason was not, nor Ellen. Henry agreed with Father, of course, for no other reason than that Father had said it. Fred did whatever he was told, and Salmon and Oliver, gnashing their teeth, did, too, and followed the Old Man's orders to empty the wagon once again and re-balance the load.

Finally, after having pondered the matter awhile, I moved in close to the Old Man and said to him, "Father, listen to me. If we do not go now, many good, slavery-hating men will die because of it. And the Lord needs those men alive, Father. Not dead."

Slowly, he turned and gazed into my eyes; I thought he was angry with me and would sharply condemn my words. But, instead, he settled both hands onto my shoulders and sighed heavily, as if relieved of a great burden. In a low voice, he said, "I thank thee, Owen. God bless thee. I'm not afraid of this enemy," he said. "But I am too much afraid of leaving things to chance. It's my old habit of procrastination. I'm merely weak and don't trust sufficiently in the Lord. Go and get the others, son. We'll load the wagon and leave for Lawrence at once."

Getting up to Lawrence on a moonless night was not easy. It was a fifteen-mile ride, and we were obliged to ford the Marais des Cygnes River and several lesser creeks and then make our way over rough, pitted and gouged ground as we crossed the southeast corner of the Ottawa Reserve, until we reached the darkened cabin of the Indian trader Ottawa Jones and his white wife, where the California Road joined the Santa Fe Trail. From there, the route lay over mostly high, flat prairie on a trail that was little more than a track beaten into the thick, high-grass sod by the hundreds of westering wagons that had passed this way in the last few years. The horses needed no guidance then, and we began to make good time. Father was in the lead, up on his fine sorrel mare, Reliance, and Oliver drove the heavily loaded wagon, our Roman war machine, which was drawn by our old North Elba Morgans. John and Jason each rode their horses, brought out with them from Ohio, but the rest of us, Salmon, Henry, Fred, and I, walked behind the wagon.

By the time we crested the last rise before the Wakarusa River, a few miles south of Lawrence, it was nearly dawn, and in the pale, pinking light we could see the encampment of the Border Ruffians spread out below—not thousands of armed men, as we had expected, but many hundreds, with dozens of fires burning. The entire force was in disarray, however, with no one on watch at the bridge or guarding their scattered horses. Large numbers of men appeared to be drinking whiskey and carousing, while others slept in makeshift bedrolls or lay in heaps where they had fallen sometime during the night. A general debauch was still going on, with discordant strains of fiddle music coming up the slope, accompanied by obscene shouts, bawdy songs, and occasional, random gunfire. We held up in the shadows of a copse of cottonwood trees on the ridge above and for a long while studied them on the floodplain below. They did indeed look to our eyes like Satan's own dispirited, disorganized army of volunteers.

I came up beside Father, and he said to me, "Well, Owen, as I feared, they lie between us and the bridge. What say you?"

"They look like a pack of drunken cowards to me."

John then moved his horse alongside Father's and proposed that one of us sneak down on foot and cross the river above the bridge and slip into Lawrence, to inform the leaders there that we had arrived this far and ask for further instructions. "It might turn out that it'd be better for them if we stayed hidden here," he said. "Outflank the Ruffians, you know?"

"Useless," said Father. "If we are to serve any purpose in this, we must get into Lawrence itself."

"The Missourians are rabble," I said. "Knockabouts. They haven't the right or the will to stop us, if we simply go down there and cross over. The Lord will protect us."

I leveled my rifle at my waist and commenced walking downhill, the same as when I'd walked in amongst the wild boys and men in

Boston. Immediately, the others followed, as I knew they would. Father rode to the front again and led our little band down the crumbly slope and straight into the rowdy encampment. We did not look to one side or the other but marched on a line across the broad, grassy floodplain that led to the river and the town of Lawrence beyond.

The Ruffians got up and parted as we passed, then came forward and stared at us, their mouths open, evidently astonished by us and unsure of what we meant to do, cowed by our wagon rattling its tall spears and our heavy broadswords and revolvers strapped to our waists, our Sharps rifles leveled and cocked. A few hollered at us and cursed, but weakly, and we did not acknowledge them. Not one man made a move to stop us. In moments, we had marched through the stumbling, drunken throng of disheveled men, had crossed the narrow bridge to the other side of the Wakarusa, and were moving straightway on to Lawrence, where, as we rode and walked into town and made our way around the rough earthworks they had thrown up, we were greeted by the frightened citizens with huzzahs and much jubilation. Only then did we look at one another and start to smile. Even Father.

The besieged townsmen gaped at our weapons—our broadswords and bayonets in particular, for they were formidable and implied on our part a desire for bloody close combat. And all the citizenry were mightily impressed by our having parted the army of Border Ruffians as if they had been the Red Sea and we the ancient Israelites coming out of Egypt. We were, at least for the moment, heroes. And we wanted to stay that way, especially the Old Man, who at once, before he had even dismounted, as if in a fever, began to harangue the leaders of the Committee for Public Safety who had come to welcome us, insisting that they brook no compromise with the enemy, make no peace treaty or agreement with them. "We should strike now," Father declared, "whilst they're still be-dazzled. Round up a hundred men, and I'll lead them!" he commanded.

No one obeyed. They merely kept telling him how pleased they were that we had joined them, giving little speeches, the way committees do.

"Let me speak to the man in charge," Father finally said, and he and John and I were immediately taken to address Messrs. Lane and Robinson, who were located in an upstairs room of the half-finished Free-State Hotel, a cavernous stone building on Massachusetts Street in the center of town, which the Committee for Public Safety had appropriated for its headquarters. Mr. Robinson, who had been a physician and was now the chief agent for the New England Emigration Aid Society and who eventually became the Free-Soil governor of the territory, shook Father's hand with unctuous pleasure and nervously passed him on to his evident superior, Mr. Lane, a lean, blade-faced man in rumpled clothing with a red kerchief around his neck, a well-known radical abolitionist who'd been leading settlers into Kansas by way of Iowa and Nebraska all year. He was a natural leader of men, comfortable with his authority and a shrewd exhorter. His voice had gone raspy and hoarse, evidently from making too many speeches to the crowd of defenders outside, and he appeared to be greatly fatigued. He seemed not to have slept in a week and spoke to us while lying down on a horsehair sofa.

John, whom Mr. Lane already knew from his politicking, introduced Father and me, and after greeting us, Mr. Lane explained that, as he was pretty far along in his negotiations with the pro-slave governor, Mr. Shannon, and the leader of the militia encamped beyond the Wakarusa, Mr. Atchison, he did not want to disrupt things. "It's all at a most delicate moment," he said. But even so, he was glad to have reinforcements from Father, whom he referred to as "the aged gentleman from the state of New York." He urged us to hold off from any violent action until or unless a peace treaty became impossible. "I don't want anyone killed," he said. "Least of all women and children. And that's no army out there by the river, as you surely saw. It's a mob, and their leaders have almost no control over them."

But there was no reasoning with Father. Nor with me, for that matter, although I stayed silent and let Father speak for me. He stormed up and down the lamp-lit room, declaring that we should launch an attack this very minute, time was wasting, we could achieve complete victory over these scalawags now and be done with it.

"Father, for heaven's sake," John finally said. He was himself plenty relieved to hear that a peace treaty might be at hand. "Hear Mister Lane out." But the Old Man's blood was up for battle now, and he did not want to hear any talk of compromise with men who would enslave other men. He stated that a condition of war existed between the Free-Soilers and the pro-slavery men, and we must give no quarter, especially now that John Brown and his sons had shown everyone what cowards the Ruffians were.

I was glad to hear the Old Man going on with such ferocity. I had never before felt as I did then, like a true warrior, invulnerable and powerful: a righteous killer. I felt, and evidently Father did also, a strange, new invincibility, which we must have obtained from having marched untouched through the ranks of the enemy. It was as if we were wearing invisible armor and could not be harmed by bullet or sword. I wanted to test that armor, to risk it against the guns and swords of the Border Ruffians, and Father's words spoke for my desires. So go on, Old Man, I thought, rouse these people to fight! Don't let them go maundering on about negotiations, treaties, and orderly retreats. We want to rout the slaveholders! We want to send them howling back to Missouri, leaving a trail of blood behind and a territory cleansed of the evil of slavery forever.

Taken aback by Father's furious declarations, Mr. Lane, a cynical man, evidently misunderstood the Old Man's motives. It was as if he believed that what Father wanted was glory only, and not necessarily the immediate death of his enemies. He interrupted Father, and as if to placate and thus to silence him, abruptly proposed to commission him a captain in the First Brigade of Kansas Volunteers. He would give him his own command, he said, a company to be called the Liberty Guards, which would consist of the Captain's own brave sons and other men, up to a total of fifteen, as were willing to volunteer to join the company under Captain Brown's personal command.

This seemed to surprise Father and to please him greatly, for he stopped his fulminations at once and thanked Mr. Lane and then begged to leave, so that he could quickly begin interviewing men who might wish to join him.

"Captain Brown," Mr. Lane said. "I salute you, sir, and I thank you for your willingness, even at your advanced age, to join in the defense of the people of this poor town." He lay back on his sofa, draped one arm across his chest, and closed his eyes, dismissing us.

"I should like to make my son Owen here my lieutenant, if you have no objection, sir."

"Excellent, Captain. Fine. Whatever you wish," he said, and Mr. Robinson officiously ushered us from the room.

As we descended the rough staircase to the large, open hall below, Father instructed John and me to circulate in the town and recruit the best Christian men we could find and bring them to him out on the barricades, by which time he would have a battleplan. "I did not bring those rifles and swords all the way out here for nothing," he pronounced.

John hung back noticeably, until Father asked him what was the matter.

He then stepped up to the Old Man and looked him straight in the face. "I want to know, Father, why didn't you ask Mister Lane to make

me a lieutenant, too? This is no criticism of Owen," he said. "I just want
to know your thinking on the matter."

Father smiled and said, "You're a good man to wonder that and to
want the same as Owen." He placed one hand on John's shoulder and
the other on mine and looked at us with evident pride. "You, John," he
said, "you will be my political officer. I can't limit you to a military role.
You have too great an ability for dealing with people for that, and
besides, we must keep the tasks separate. Owen will be my military
officer, which is why I've made him a lieutenant. Boys, I tell thee, there
will come a day when you will think back to these moments which
have just ended, and you will see them as having begun a mighty thing.
I promise thee. There is a plan behind all this. The Lord's plan. And He
has given me mine."

John shrugged, evidently still unsatisfied, but unwilling to pursue
his point further, and departed from us to do as Father had asked, while
I eagerly went a different way, also in search of recruits for Father's
company of Liberty Guards. To my surprise, I was immediately successful, as there were in Lawrence at that moment hundreds of men
who were eager to follow the newly commissioned Captain Brown, for
the nature of our arrival had thrilled the town and our reputation for
valor and righteousness had swiftly grown large. It took me barely an
hour of hurried conversations with men in the barber shops and stores
and in the hotel lobby before I found myself walking the main street
with forty or fifty of them trailing behind. When finally I thought I
had enough, I turned back to take them to Father, and along the muddy
street came John, leading an equal number.

Father was at the earthworks, which was a ditch and a head-high
bank of dirt heaped across the wide central street at the edge of town.
Most of the town's defenders had positioned themselves behind the
bank with their rifles and were watching the fires of the enemy camp
across the river with mild curiosity and not a little fear. Father was

engaged in heavy discussion with several men, militia captains like himself, urging them to join him in a frontal charge against the Ruffians. Red-faced, stamping angrily and flailing his arms, Father was arguing strenuously with the gentlemen. "Those who don't have guns can be armed with pitchforks!" he said. "If my company leads the charge, and the entire populace comes rushing out against them, the Ruffians will be terrified and will flee back to Missouri for their lives!"

The other militia leaders would have none of it, however. But then Father saw me and John approaching with our flock of volunteers, and abruptly he turned away from his colleagues and led our troop towards our Roman wagon, where the other boys were lounging around, chatting like old veterans with various townspeople.

The Old Man jumped up on the box and, placing his hands on his hips, surveyed the crowd of volunteers. "I can take no more than eight, for a total membership of fifteen," he declared. "And you must be as willing to die for the cause as my sons and I myself are." Quite a few drifted away at this. "We are here to slay the enemy of the Lord. I want bloodthirsty men at my side. No kittenish weaklings, no mild-mannered Garrisonians, no cowards who prefer peace with the slavers to war. And no men whose courage depends on whiskey. I want temperance men." Here a number of men turned and strolled away. "And ye must be Christians," he said. "True soldiers of the Lord is what I need! Ye must be armored by God, for we are going forth to smite His enemies down!" And now there were but a dozen remaining. "And ye must swear, as I and my sons have sworn, to wash chattel slavery off the map of this territory. Even if it be washed with thine own blood. Ye must swear to purge it from the nation as a whole. What we begin here will not end until the entire country is free!" Now there were only three men standing by the wagon, one of whom, it turned out, was the well-known journalist Mr. James

Redpath, from the New York *Tribune*, who would follow us through-out the Kansas wars and make us famous all over the East but would not join us in battle. The two others, as it happened, we already knew and did not want—Mr. Theodore Weiner, a big, brutal Dutchman who kept a store on the Pottawatomie Creek a few miles below our camp, and an older man, Mr. James Townley, a longtime settler in Osawatomie, originally from Illinois, who had acquired a reputation for quarrelsomeness.

From his perch, Father looked sadly down at them. "Well, if ye be all who remain . . . then I believe I have the men I need," he said, and he bade them raise their right hands and swore them into the Liberty Guards.

But there was to be no battle that day, although the episode, thanks to Mr. Redpath's lively, vivid dispatches back East, soon came to be known as the "Wakarusa War"—when the brave citizens of Lawrence, Kansas, under the courageous leadership of Captain John Brown, drove off a thousand Border Ruffians and afterwards forced the pro-slave leaders to accept conditions that amounted to total surrender. The real-ity was that, while Father railed in vain against the citizens of the town for their reluctance to follow him and charge the Missourians' camp, Messrs. Lane and Robinson slipped out the back of the hotel and rode down to the town of Franklin, a few miles south of Lawrence, where they secretly met with the pro-slavery governor of the territory, Mr. Shannon, along with Senator Atchison and several other leaders of the Ruffians. These men had grown alarmed at having lost control of their supporters and consequently agreed to take their ragtag army back to Leavenworth at once, if the case of the shooting of the Ohioan Mr. Charles Dow was dropped by John's protest committee of Free-Soilers. The committee, they insisted, had been an act of provocation. Its disso-lution would restore the peace. Messrs. Lane and Robinson thought that a perfect arrangement. They drew up a treaty, signed it, and returned to Lawrence to oversee the quick withdrawal of the Missourians and to enjoy the gratitude and adulation of the Free-Soilers.

Except for us, of course. We admired them not a whit and thought their treaty a surrender. Nonetheless, we stayed on in Lawrence for a few days longer. We were the only ones who had dared to confront the Ruffians directly and were much admired for it, especially by the younger men in town, and this puffed us up somewhat and took some of the sting out of Father's failure to enlist more than two sorry men in his Liberty Guards, and it justified his anger at Lane and Robinson for having bargained with the enemy. Finally, though, we grew restless, and John and Jason began to worry about their wives and John's son, Tonny, so Father, who had been spending much of his time giving interviews to Mr. Redpath and the many other journalists who were flocking into Lawrence, gave the order to depart for home.

Home was then still our tents at Browns Station, John's and Jason's land claims, and at one point on our way back there, I had with Father a small conversation that turned out later to have large consequences. It was late in the afternoon, and we were a few miles past the old California Road and the cabin of Ottawa Jones, traveling along a broad ridge that curved slowly above the floodplain of the Marais des Cygnes River. I was coming along at the rear of our little train, deep in thought of home at that moment, which meant memories of Lyman and Susan Epps and the calamity at Lake Colden, when I was brought suddenly out of my dark, cold cavern of thought by the clatter of hoofbeats. Father had turned his red horse back past the wagon to the rear, and when he drew abreast of me, he dismounted and walked along beside me in silence for a ways.

Finally, after a while, he said, "I had a most interesting word with Mister Lane before we left."

"You mean he granted you an audience." Still smoldering with anger for having been betrayed by Lane's cowardice and ambition, I could barely speak of him except with sarcasm and disdain. Popularity, that's all these men cared about, top to bottom, from the traitorous New Englanders Franklin Pierce and Daniel Webster down to the pullets who ran the Committee for Public Safety of Lawrence, Kansas—these men sold their souls for the adulation of a mob, while the bodies of millions of Americans continued to be sold on the auction block. That's how I reflected then: the second a subject was introduced to me, regardless of what it was, I would find my thoughts connected to a series of pulleys and belts, as if my mind were a factory, so that the mere mention of Mr. Lane's name brought me in seconds to the grisly specter of permanent Negro slavery.

Father said, "I informed him that I intended to resume the fight that had been so unfortunately interrupted by his willingness to negotiate with the slavers."

"What did he say to that?" It was raining lightly, and the ground was muddy and dark, even up here on the ridge—hard going for the horses. Our company now included Father's new recruits, one of whom, Mr. Weiner, had his own wagon, and the journalist Mr. Redpath, who seemed to think Father a moral and military genius, a view the Old Man did not discourage, for he knew that the man's communiqués were rapidly enlarging the reputation of John Brown back East and would encourage continued financial and logistical support for our venture, regardless of what the rest of the Free-Soilers wanted. Father now knew that here, as much as back in North Elba or Springfield, it was not enough merely to be against slavery. Too many Free-Soilers, in reality, only wanted peace. Thus, so long as we were allied with white people, we had enemies amongst our own ranks. Here, in the absence of free blacks, we were obliged to do the Lord's work alone.

"Mister Lane urged me to hold my fire but to keep my powder dry."

"That old saw."

"Yes. But he also revealed to me that he had met with Governor Shannon a second time, after the Ruffians had withdrawn back to Leavenworth. They got the governor so drunk that the man signed a document which authorizes the Free-Soilers to use force the next time the Missourians enter our territory."

"What does that mean to us?"

Father laughed. "Why, it's a legal license, son! A license to shoot Missourians. Or anyone else who would obstruct us in the work. We would do it anyway, I know, but this makes it legal."

"Well, good," I said grimly.

"I thought that would please you," he said, and slapped me on the shoulder. Then he mounted his horse and rode to the front of the line and led us home.

With the death of Lyman Epps, I had crossed a line that I would never cross back over again. I could not: Lyman's death at Lake Colden had made me permanently a different man. It froze me at the center of my heart, gathering ice in layers around it, so that, in a short time, I had become outwardly a hard man, a grim, silent warrior in my father's army, soon to be a killer more feared by the slavers for his cold, avenging spirit than any Free-Soil man in all of Kansas. More feared even than Father, Captain John Brown himself, Old Brown, who, at least until Pottawatomie, was viewed by the slavers and even by most of the abolitionists as dangerous mainly because of his peculiar, but not especially long-lasting, influence over the young, idealistic men coming out from the East and because of his refusal to work in concert with the regular Free-Soil militias, even the one led by his son John, and with the legally instituted authorities in Lawrence. Oh, Father stamped his feet and grew nearly apoplectic with rage against the regulars, as he did against the President of the United States, the Democrats, and even the Republicans, against the abolitionists back East who were now and then reluctant to send him money and arms, against the timidity of the Free-Soil authorities in Lawrence and Topeka, and, always, against the pro-slavers, the Missourians, the Border Ruffians, the drunken Southern Negro-hating squatters down along the Pottawatomie River who were threatening in their newspapers and meetings to wipe the Yankees, and especially us Browns, off the face of the earth. But in most people's minds, even in the minds of our enemies, the Old Man was, indeed, an old man, "the elderly gentleman from the state of New York," a man in his middle fifties. His rage and spluttering, given his radical abolitionist ideology and his old-fashioned, Puritanical form of Christian belief, were understandable, if not quite coherent.

No, the man that people on all sides worried about was me, the red-headed son, the one with the crippled arm. My brothers told me this with a mixture of pride and mild concern. They reported that of all the Browns, I was viewed, as much in Lawrence as among the pro-slavers in Atchison, as the most dangerous. They said it was because I spoke to no one, except Father and my brothers, and showed no human feeling, except for a single-minded desire to exterminate the man-sellers. They were right to fear me. I was an assassin with no principle or ideology and with no apparent religion, save one: death to slavery.

My brother John, widely admired for his probity and his physical courage, had succeeded in being elected to the Free-State legislature and had been commissioned a lieutenant and given command of a militia unit, the Osawatomie Rifles, a defensive force meant to include all able-bodied anti-slavery men in and around the town of Osawatomie and Browns Station, our home territory. Father, however, insisted on withholding himself from the Rifles—no one could imagine him taking orders from John anyhow, but it was a lifelong pattern for him to keep himself separate and distinct from another man's army. Except for Jason—who, by following John into the Rifles, had chosen the route least likely to lead to violence—the rest of us stuck with Father and viewed ourselves strictly as his men and subject to no other authority than his.

Counting Father, then, we were now a band of six: brothers Fred, Salmon, and Oliver, our brother-in-law Henry Thompson, and me. Watson was still back in North Elba, taking care of the farm and family—my old job. Here and there, at different times, we were joined by some of the more radical, quarrelsome, old-time settlers, like the Austrian Weiner and James Townley, and by the newcomers to Kansas who had heard of Captain Brown back East and wanted to fight slavery alongside him and his sons; they were mostly young hot-bloods who made their way to Lawrence and came down to Osawatomie and found our camp and rode with us awhile and then drifted over to one of the more regular militias or grew discouraged by the rigors of the life and took out a land claim and built a cabin on it and began to farm. A few stayed on with us, or came and went and came back again—those who could comply with Father's ban on whiskey-drinking, swearing, and tobacco, who were willing to honor the Sabbath with him by listening to him preach and pray all day, and, most importantly, men who were able to subject their wills entirely to his, for he brooked no correction or argument, and he consulted no one. No one except me—who had the Old Man's ear now and knew when to whisper into it and urge him on to action, who knew when and how to suggest retreat, who knew exactly the way to buck him up when his spirits flagged and how to calm him back to reason when his temper made him intolerant and his frustration with the peace-making cowardice and caution of others turned him into a sputtering dervish.

❑

There was that spring greatly increased, widespread provocation amongst the pro-slavers, and threatening noises from the clans of Border Ruffians down along the Pottawatomie, and at Browns Station, especially, we were increasingly agitated and kept ourselves in a constant state of alarm, if not readiness. All the Free-Soil militias were pledged to participate strictly in defensive action, but it was growing less clear by the day as to what that term meant. Particularly in the face of constant death-threats from the settlers on the Pottawatomie—the Dutch Sherman faction, as we thought of them. They had settled that narrow, eroded gorge several years back, well before the passage of the Kansas-Nebraska Act, and thus they were mainly concerned with land-grabbing, not politics. We knew that they were using the slavery issue only to justify burning and driving us out and capturing our claims up on the more fertile open floodplain of the Marais des Cygnes, which, in their ignorance, they had passed over when they first came out from Arkansas and Tennessee.

Then one day late in April, the pro-slavery Sheriff Jones rode over from Atchison to Lawrence with a small posse of U.S. troops and apprehended six Free-Soil citizens and charged them with contempt of court for refusing to identify the leader of the party that had rescued John the previous month, that brave adventure which had led to the first Lawrence siege and stand-off. That same night, an unknown person shot Sheriff Jones outside of Lawrence as he and his troop of federal soldiers were leading their six prisoners off to Atchison. The prisoners did not flee, however, and Jones did not die of his wound. In fact, to my and Father's astonishment, the entire town of Lawrence and its leadership were aggrieved by the shooting and publically apologized for it and condemned the unknown shooter outright.

The shooter, of course, was me. In company with the Old Man and my brothers. We had learned of the sheriff's mission and had ridden over towards Lawrence to help oppose it, and at nightfall, a mile north of Hickory Point, had come up on the posse and prisoners on their way back to Atchison, where the six were to stand trial. There were but four soldiers in the posse and the Sheriff. The Old Man was all for throwing down on them at once and seizing their prisoners in person and delivering them safely back to Lawrence, where he said we were sure to be acclaimed as heroes, recalling, perhaps, our previous miraculous intervention.

I said to him, "No, it's near dark. They'll hear us coming and will run. Or else they'll use the prisoners as hostages and put up a fight. The prisoners may be killed and the slavers escape."

"But Jones and his men are cowards at heart," the Old Man argued. "They're just conscripts. And the Lord will protect His children." We were perched unseen in the growing darkness on a rise, hidden in a stand of black walnut trees, and Sheriff Jones's party was heading slowly along a draw below, which led south to the crossroads of the Santa Fe Trail and the old California trail, thence north and east to Atchison. The sheriff was in the lead, and his prisoners were seated in a trap driven by one of the troopers, while the others rode along in a line behind.

"Look, it's almost too dark to do anything at all," I pointed out. "But I can bring down the sheriff with a single shot now. The soldier-boys will panic, and the children of the Lord can escape in the confusion. We'll pick them up later for return to Lawrence." I got down from the wagon box and took a position behind a tree and leveled my rifle.

In a second, Father was at my side. "Hold up, son. Maybe we should think on this a bit."

"If we think on it, the opportunity will be lost."

I did not say it, but we both knew that if I did not drop the sheriff now, Father would once again be jumping up and down in a foaming rage, crying that nothing had been done to oppose this outrageous illegality, and he'd be blaming the men in Lawrence for their failure of nerve, instead of himself for his. I was as weary of his complaints as I was of their inaction.

He nodded approval, and I turned back to my task, aimed, and fired. Done. Sheriff Jones toppled from his horse.

A simple act. But instantly, with that shot, much changed.

With that one shot from my Sharps rifle, we shucked our identity as defenders of freedom and became full-fledged guerilla fighters. I knew it beforehand and intended it and recognized it when it happened.

Having finally gone on the offensive this way, we could no longer claim to ourselves or to anyone else that we had come out here to Kansas to farm or even to make Kansas a free state. No, it was now inescapably clear to all, but especially and most importantly to the Southerners, that we Browns were here in Kansas solely to wage war against slavery. The Missourians and pro-slavers all over the South who had been screaming for abolitionist blood, who had cried in the headlines of their newspapers, *War to the knife, and knife to the hilt!* were justified now. Their very lives, as much as their foul institutions, were under attack. We were their enemy now, as much as they had been ours all along.

The sheriff had gone down. But then he crawled to the wagon, and to our surprise, the Free-Soil prisoners from Lawrence helped him aboard and laid him out and appeared to be tending to him, while the soldiers got off their horses and drew close around the wagon and waited to be fired upon. "Did you kill him?" Father asked in a tense whisper. "Did you kill the man?" He was at my ear and had a hand on each of my shoulders. The others, Fred and Salmon, had come forward and were crouched behind us.

"No."

"You bloodied him, though," Salmon said. "They're ripping off his shirt."

"But why are they helping him and not escaping?" Father asked. "All they've got to do is run, right?"

No one answered.

"I think we should go down there and I should address them," Father announced.

"No," I said. "Better they don't know who has shot at them or from where. Make them think we're everywhere. A single, well-aimed shot can be more terrifying than a fusillade."

The Old Man pondered that for a second, and then he smiled. "Yes. Good. That's good, Owen. Very good. Come on, boys," he said, suddenly in charge again, although I detected a new note of apprehension in his voice. Certainly, Father understood the implications of this act as well as I did. "Let's ride on to Lawrence. And we'll say nothing of this to anyone. Nothing. All either side needs to know is that there are some abolitionists who are not afraid to shoot, and that such men are everywhere—nowhere and anywhere. They don't need to know the names of the shooters. Not yet anyhow. You look down there, boys, look," he ordered, and pointed into the arroyo below at the sight of Free-Soil prisoners and federal troopers scrambling to protect and aid a fallen proslavery sheriff. "See how little we can trust even our own kind. Traitors," he pronounced them. "There below, children, there are the Israelites who betrayed Rehoboam, the son of Solomon, gone to worship the golden calves of Jeroboam. Look at them, boys. Let us, from here on out, keep completely to ourselves," he said. "Completely."

And so we did. There were, of course, immediate and serious consequences to my shooting the sheriff, but they were not by us particularly unwanted. Although we were widely suspected, by both sides, to have been the hotheads who wounded Sheriff Jones, Father neither admitted nor denied the charge and said only that he himself had not fired on the man but it was a shame he hadn't been killed. The pro-slavery newspapers went wild, and rumors of imminent war flew across the territory, exciting and frightening everyone on all sides. Missourians and other Southerners gathered together in packs along the border, as if ready to invade. Mobs in Atchison and Leavenworth captured a pair of prominent Free-State men there on business and tarred them and stuck tufts of cotton all over their bodies, tied the men to their horses, and sent them down the Santa Fe Trail, where they were found the next day a few miles north of Lawrence.

It was around this time that, with John and Jason spending so much time up in Lawrence with the Osawatomie Rifles and the Free-State legislature, Father decided that we had better send the women and Tonny over to Uncle Sam Adair's place in the village of Osawatomie. He also decided to abandon Browns Station and move to a temporary camp in the trackless brushland along the Mosquito Creek, a camp that every few days we could shift to a new location. We were free as the wind off the plains now, able to appear and disappear almost at will. Everything we owned we carried in one wagon, and most of what we owned was weaponry. We were all of us on horseback by now, thanks to stock we had liberated from the hands of the slavers, although we had not saddles for everyone, and Fred and Oliver, when he wasn't driving the wagon, rode bareback. Roaming the rolling, treeless hillcountry and slipping along the dark river-bottoms where black walnut, oak, and cottonwood trees grew in lush groves, we were more like a roving Indian band than a company of white guerillas. Our chieftain, who was Father, of course, always Father, set policy, but I decided day-to-day on how best to implement that policy.

Then, on the second of May, when we were encamped in the woods just south of the old French trading post on the Marais des Cygnes, a rich Missouri planter named Jefferson Buford, who had rounded up close to four hundred men from all over the South, led his mob straight across the border into the territory. Not ten miles from us, men were flying banners that cried, *The Supremacy of the White Race!* and *Alabama for Kansas!* A day later, we heard from a local Free-State settler that, out on the Peoria Indian lands, fifteen miles from our old camp at Browns Station, a company of some thirty or so Georgians loosely attached to Buford's force had pitched their tents and were carousing, working up their courage with whiskey and insults. It was country that we knew firsthand and well, so on a cold, overcast day, Father and I rode out there in the wagon to reconnoiter and see what we could learn of the character of Colonel Buford's force. We pretended to be government surveyors running a line that happened to lie in the middle of their squat. Calling ourselves Ruben Shiloh and his son Owen from Indiana and pretending to have no opinions on the struggle over Kansas, Father and I stopped for a while by the Georgians' cook wagon, where most of the men had assembled to drink corn whiskey and lounge idly by the fire, two of their favorite activities, it seemed. We secretly counted the number of their horses and weapons, sidearms mostly and old, single-shot hunting rifles, and we talked a little and listened a lot, as they loudly cursed the abolitionists and swore to kill every last one. They loved their leader, Jefferson Buford, and called him Colonel Buford, although, when Father asked, they could not say in which army or militia he had been commissioned.

They were a staggering, loutish bunch of poor, ignorant, landless Southerners, men who bragged that they had come over to Kansas to help themselves first, by seizing abolitionists' land-claims, and the South second, by killing as many Yankee nigger-lovers as they could find. "Especially those damned Browns," whom they'd been hearing about from the Shermans and Doyles down on the Pottawatomie. "Them Browns're goin' first!" they declared. We tipped our hats and rode on.

Later, in the wagon on the way back to our camp, for a long time Father and I were silent, each of us lost in his own thoughts. Finally, when we were four or five miles from the Georgians', Father turned to me and said, "You know, Owen, the real problem here isn't what it seems. It's not our differences from those fellows. The real problem is that those men truly don't understand us."

"How's that a problem?"

"It just came to me, so I'll have to say it as I think it. But the pro-slavers, all these Border Ruffians coming over from the South—fact is, they think we're just like them except that we're Northerners, that's all. They think that, like them, we've come out here at the behest and in the pay of a gang of rich men and politicians. In their minds, we're out here following some Yankee version of their Colonel Buford, and, like them, all we want out of this for ourselves is a piece of free land. Strange. But that is the problem."

"What's the solution, then?"

"I'm not sure. I think we have to show them somehow that they're wrong about us. We should figure out how to show these Southerners the true nature and extremity of our principles. We have to show them the difference between them and us. Mainly, they have to see that we are willing to die for this. For they are not. And more to the point, because they are not willing to *die* for their cause, they have to see that we are willing to *kill* for ours. There it is! That's our secret strength, Owen. All those poor, drunken fools and thieves, they really do believe that we are cowards, no different than they, and that Kansas, since they presently outnumber us, is easy pickings. And if they cry bloody murder and threaten to burn down our houses, it's only because they think that as soon as the battle starts, we'll pack up and run north and leave them our land."

"They'll see otherwise," I said.

"Now is the time, I believe. It's time, Owen, time to buckle on our swords and wade straight into their midst. It's time to wreak bloody havoc. We need to slay so many of them with a single, terrifying blow that the rest will start having sobering second thoughts."

"Fine by me. I'd kill every last one. Give them only enough Kansas soil to lie down dead in."

"You would, but maybe you won't have to. I know men like this. I've seen them everywhere, even in the North. It's a basic human type. These fellows are only the degraded, pathetic pawns of other men, who are much more evil than their pawns. Oh, sure, these poor, deluded fellows hate Negroes, all right, and they love slavery. But not because they themselves own Negro slaves or depend upon them to work their puny farms. You don't see any slave-traders amongst these fellows, do you? And no cotton planters, either. No, these are *poor* men, Owen. And like most people, North and South, but especially South, they're landless and slaveless and ignorant and illiterate. They're serfs, practically, but with no lord of the manor to protect them. And it's because they've been taught for centuries to love and envy the rich man who owns slaves that they hate the Negro, and now they have come out here to conquer Kansas for slavery. That's all. Poor, deluded fools. Because their skin's as white as the rich man's, they believe that they might someday be rich themselves. But without the Negro, Owen, these men would be forced to see that, in fact, they have no more chance of becoming rich than do the very slaves they despise and trample on. They'd see how close they are to being slaves themselves. Thus, to protect and nurture their dream of becoming someday, somehow, rich, they don't need actually to *own* slaves, so much as they need to keep the Negro from ever being free."

"Very nice," I said. "But how do you propose to show them this?" I asked, out of politeness more than interest. Father's endless, convoluted theories concerning slavery and Negroes frequently strengthened my brothers' resolve, and even from time to time charged up the Old Man himself, but they had long since ceased to motivate me. I had my own motivations, which needed no firming. Iron hardeneth iron. For me, the soft, warm days of pusillanimity were long gone.

"Well, there's only one way. We must strike pure terror into their hearts, Owen. Pure terror. Pure! We must become *terrible!*" he growled. We had to make the Border Ruffians understand that they had to be ready to die miserably for this. If we showed them that their bits of Kansas Territory would not come to them otherwise, they'd go galloping straight back to Alabama and Georgia, where they could lie and boast in the taverns and bawdyhouses all they wanted. All we cared was that Kansas be left a free state, so that we could go back to Father's old plan of breaking the rich slaveholder's back by drawing off the Negro labor force with the Subterranean Passway, his plan to turn the Underground Railroad into a north-flowing river of fugitives. Then, to get their sugar and cotton and corn and tobacco grown, the planters would be forced to turn to their fellow whites and would start enslaving *them*. And when they did that, poor white men would know their true enemies at last. They'd see that their true allies all along had been us abolitionists and the freed blacks living up North and the Southern Negroes who still remained in bondage. With its main supports gone, Satan's temple of slavery would come tumbling down, and then the Negro would no longer be despised in the land. The poor, landless black man and the poor white would fall into one another's arms.

"Sounds good, Father," I said. "Sounds real good." I cracked the reins and moved the wagon a little more smartly along, as it looked like rain in the west. The huge, milky-white Kansas sky had gone all yellow near the horizon and then had suddenly darkened overhead. Long grasses riffled and swirled in the wind like the soft surface of the sea, changing from pale blue to green to steel gray in the broody, late afternoon light. Our trail was an ancient buffalo road, a grass-covered depression through the high, flat, endless field, which we followed as if in the wake of a westering ship, and I half-expected to see eddies of foam and bubbles out there before us. Ragged sheets of lightning shook down from the southern sky, and a few seconds later, the rumble of thunder rolled across the plain like distant cannonfire.

"What say you to that, son?" Father shouted over the wind. He was holding on to the seat with both hands, as the wagon bucked and dipped across the rough, grassy plain towards the long, purple line of cottonwoods in the river-bottom ahead, where our camp was located.

"To what?"

"To my thoughts!"

"Oh, I like it!" I shouted back.

"Like what?"

"Becoming *terrible*! I like becoming terrible!"

He loosened one hand from the box and flung his sinewy arm around my shoulders. "Oh, thou hast lately become a true soldier of the Lord, Owen!" He pulled me to him and laughed. Then suddenly the sky opened up, and a cold rain poured down, silencing us for the rest of the way into camp.

Once there, when we had climbed down from the wagon and come into the flapping tent, Salmon, Fred, Oliver, and Henry greeted us with great excitement and gave us news that set us immediately to loading the wagon with our weapons, and with Oliver up on the box driving the team and Father and the rest of us on horseback, we six headed on through the downpour straight on to Lawrence.

In our absence, the boys had learned that the Missourian Colonel Buford and his four hundred Southerners and hundreds more in smaller gangs of Southerners were headed for Lawrence from several directions, and this time they were coming in determined to burn the town to the ground. To justify their attack, the pro-slavers now had a legal pretext, in that, a few days earlier, a grand jury in Atchison had indicted all the Free-State leaders for high treason and the editors of the *Herald of Freedom*, the Free-State newspaper, for sedition. This time, the Border Ruffians meant to stamp out the abolitionists once and for all. They meant to take our citadel and burn it and sow salt where it had stood and wipe all memory of Free-State resistance from Kansas forever.

The possibility of this occurring brought Father to a fever-pitch of excitement. As usual, it was the idea of battle more than the reality that made the Old Man's blood boil and his tongue wag. In some surprising ways and more than he thought, Father resembled the very Southerners he claimed to be at war with. Up to a point, it made him an effective leader of more conventional men than he, which was most men, of course, but that point was where the battle itself actually began.

He was not afraid exactly; Father was a courageous man. Simply, it was as if he could not cease controlling a situation, and whenever he reached that moment when he no longer was able to shape and determine things, he backed off. Which was why, I suppose, he needed me. I made no show of this and do not think that I tricked him into depending on me or moved him in any way contrary to his essential desires, even though he never quite said outright that, once he had properly positioned himself at the edge of battle, he needed me to bring him over it. Rather, it was our unstated agreement, our tacit understanding, that he was the one to lead us to the precipice, and I was the one to carry us across.

Out on the California Road, where it joined the Osawatomie Road down to our old, abandoned camp at Browns Station, we met up with two companies of volunteers, about thirty men, parts of John's Osawatomie Rifles, as it turned out, who were milling about and apparently going nowhere. The rain had let up, and the men were shaking off their clothes, drying their weapons, and scraping mud from their horses' shoes. They had built a huge fire, as if they meant to stay awhile or even overnight, for it was nearly dark by then.

They were more concerned, it seemed, with organizing themselves into a regular troop of soldiers than with riding straight on to defend Lawrence from the invaders. John explained to Father that they had lately received contradictory reports from Lawrence and wished to wait for further orders before leaving this part of the territory undefended against the numerous bands of Buford's Ruffians who had been roaming the region for weeks, threatening to shoot, hang, and burn Free-Staters. Their first responsibility, he said, was to protect the Osawatomie section of the territory, not Lawrence.

This infuriated Father. He had moved to the wagon, where, to address the group, he stood up on the seat, with Oliver at the reins beside him and the rest of us on horseback. Earlier, back at the camp, we had loaded the wagon with the usual sheaf of pikes and sharpened broadswords, and we were armed in addition with our Sharps rifles and our revolvers. Though we were but six men, or five men and a boy, we had the weaponry of a dozen. "The Missourians are all at Lawrence, burning it down!" the Old Man shouted at John and the others. "It's only you boys and your women and children who are left here!"

"We don't know that," John coolly answered.

"Well, then, you're welcome to stay put until you do!" the Old Man snapped, and he leapt to the ground and took the bridle of Reliance from me and signaled for us to depart. At once, Oliver drew the wagon back onto the muddy road, and we headed at a gallop northward across the darkening plain towards Lawrence.

□

I remember two more meetings out on the road that night, before we went to Pottawatomie and did the terrible things there. The first was a rider who had been sent down to Osawatomie from Lawrence by the Free-State authorities, Colonel Lane and Mr. Robinson. He was a screw-faced boy of sixteen or seventeen, his horse all lathered from the long ride, and he at first mistook us for the advance contingent of the Osawatomie Rifles and thought that Father was John himself, Lieutenant Brown.

"No, I am *Captain* Brown," Father said to the lad. "His superior officer and his father. What news have you?"

The Osawatomie Rifles, the boy said, were instructed by Colonel Lane to return to their homes and not to come on to Lawrence.

"And why is that?"

"Because it's all over, sir. No need to come in now, Cap'n Brown. And they ain't got any food, except barely enough for the folks as is already there. President Pierce's federal troops are running the entire town," he said. "They come in and parleyed awhile with the Missourians and sent 'em back peaceful." The Free-State leaders, he explained, had decided not to oppose Colonel Buford and his four hundred Border Ruffians when they first appeared at the edge of town, and the Southerners had then proceeded to ride into the town and sack it. They had broken up all the printing presses and had gotten drunk on as much whiskey as they could find and had burned several stores and even shot the Free-State Hotel full of holes with a cannon. "But they didn't kill nobody, Cap'n Brown. They just did whatever they wanted, and all the folks stood in the street and watched 'em like it was a circus, and then the Federals come down from Leavenworth and got 'em to agree to head back to Atchison."

The boy smiled, as if he had brought glad tidings, but his news made Father crazy, and when the Old Man drew out his revolver and started waving it around, I thought he might shoot the boy. Instead, he leapt down from his horse and seized the lad by his collar and dragged him off the road a short ways into the high grasses, where he shouted into his face that he would put a bullet in the boy's head here and now if he was not who he said he was and if what he had told us was a lie. "Because it sounds like a perfect lie!" he declared. "Designed to hold us out of the battle!"

The boy crumpled to his knees and began to cry, which seemed to soften the Old Man, or at least to convince him that the boy was not lying, for he holstered his gun and lifted the lad to his feet, brushed the mud from his trousers, and brought him back to us. Then he instructed him to ride on to where John and the Rifles were camped and give them his unfortunate news, which he was sure they, at least, would welcome. Glad to be released, the boy mounted his horse and left us at once.

We ourselves did not know what to do then. Go on to occupied Lawrence, or ride back to our camp on the Marais des Cygnes, southeast of Osawatomie? Neither route took us where we had hoped to go, which was straight into the noise and smoke of battle. Ride back and pitch our tent with John and his Rifles and our pacificist brother, Jason? That seemed somehow shameful, embarrassing, at the least, although none of us said it outright. Our blood was all heated up; we could feel it coursing down our arms to our hands and pounding in our necks and ears. Even Oliver, I realized, as I looked up at him on the wagon box, was caught up in it: his hands were locked in white-knuckled fists, his boyish jaw was clenched tight as a vise; and Henry and my brothers Salmon and Fred, they, too, were poised to ride straight into battle.

Father stood by the wagon alone and breathed heavily in and out, as if re-gathering his strength, like an ox after a long pull. Finally, I said to him, "I'm for riding into Lawrence and finding Colonel Lane and the others who are responsible for this betrayal. Then we should take them out and execute them for it. Put an end to this constant accommodation." I meant it and, if Father had agreed, would have done it. But he did not agree.

"No, no, this is not over yet," he said. "Keep in mind the story of Joab, who slew Absalom, causing King David such a lamentation and dividing the Israelites against themselves, which greatly weakened them against their enemies. No, boys, we must let the Lord decide this."

"Decide what? Our cause is lost, Father! Lost without even a whimper from those cowards in Lawrence, and now the whole territory, it looks like, is ruled by Franklin Pierce's soldiers. We're ruled by Washington turncoats in league with the Atchison pro-slavers and Buford's mob of Southerners."

"We might yet upset this neat arrangement. Something must be done, though. Something dramatic and terrible," Father said, and when he said that word, "terrible," I knew what he meant.

"Who shall we do it to?" I asked. The others—Salmon, Fred, Oliver, and Henry—were silent and wondering; they did not yet know what Father and I were speaking of.

"I guess it'll have to be the Shermans and the Doyles and so on, the men down on the Pottawatomie," he said.

"That's fine. But we better do it quickly, while the hornets are out of the nest. Do you think Dutch Sherman and the Doyle men are at home anyhow? They might have ridden with Buford's army."

Father thought not—they were pro-slave and anti-Negro, all right, and plenty loud about it, but they were family men and had their land claims already settled and had built cabins and weren't likely to be running with that crowd. "We will go down there tonight," he said. "And we shall treat with the men only, and make quick, bloody work of it, whilst the surrender and the sacking of Lawrence are still in the air, so that everyone in the territory on both sides will know why it was done."

My brother-in-law, Henry Thompson, then spoke up. "Mister

Brown, do you mean for us to *kill* the Shermans and the Doyles?"

"Yes, Henry, I do," Father replied. "Boys, Owen has seen it straight. After the debacle in Lawrence, if we *don't* do this, our cause here in Kansas is wholly lost, and lost without a fight."

"But do we have to kill these men? They don't own any slaves. They're just loudmouths."

Fred said, "Shut up, Henry! You have to do what Father says. He has spoken with the Lord all these years, and you haven't. It's what the Lord has told him to do."

"Are these men not our sworn enemies, boys?" Father asked. "Have they not hundreds of times sworn to kill *us*?"

They all four nodded agreement—slowly and reluctantly, however.

Henry said, "But we have never thought they would ever actually *do* it. I mean, kill us outright. You know, unless they were provoked or something."

"This will provoke them," I said. "Either you're with us on this, Henry, or you're against us."

"What about John and Jason?" Salmon asked.

"The choice hasn't been put to them," I said. "So they're neither for nor against."

Father added that, as officers in the Free-State Militia, John and Jason were obliged to follow the orders of their superiors, even if their superiors ordered them to capitulate to the enemy, which, in a sense, they had already done. As irregulars, we were not so bound. Besides, John was a member of the Free-State legislature and had sworn to uphold the laws of the territory. The only laws we had sworn to uphold were the Lord's.

"And the Lord wants us to do this thing?" Fred asked.

"He does," Father pronounced.

"Good," Fred replied, and the others nodded agreement again, this time with firmness.

❑

This may seem strange to one who was not there on that May night out on the plain—to us it was apposite and just, and not at all strange—but at that moment, when we had reached our decision to go to the cabins on the Pottawatomie and kill the men who lived there, a single rider came out of the darkness from the direction of Lawrence, bringing news which, although it was awful news, seemed nonetheless to have been sent by the Lord Himself, sent with no other purpose than to give us permission to do this thing and do it now.

Oddly, we did not hear him approach, perhaps because our attention was so taken up with our wrangle. He seemed to emerge from the darkness like a ghost—but it was only a man, a man in a long white duster, riding a pale gray stallion, and although we were startled by his sudden appearance, we were not frightened by it, as he seemed to bear us no enmity. We did not know him, had never seen him before, and he did not introduce himself or ask who we were. He was a tall, well-built man of early middle-age, blond-haired, with a full beard. I recall him exactly. He pulled up beside the wagon and touched the broad brim of his hat with a gloved finger.

With no further greeting, he said to Father straight out, in an even voice, "You may wish to know, sir, that early yesterday it was reported in Saint Louis that Senator Charles Sumner of Massachusetts was brutally assaulted in the Senate chamber. You may also wish to know the name of his assailant, Senator Preston Brooks of South Carolina. The senator from Massachusetts, a strong supporter of the abolitionist cause, which I take to be your cause as well, was beaten unmercifully by the Southerner. He was clubbed on the head with a stout cane, and it is very likely that he will not survive the attack."

I had never seen Father as wild as he was then. He pulled off his hat and threw it on the ground. His face reddened with rage, and his brow darkened down as if his brain were on fire. He lifted his arms into the air and cried, "How can this *be*! How can such a thing *happen*!"

I said nothing, but the others, too, cried out their shock and anger at this latest outrage by the slavemasters. Then the messenger, if that is, indeed, what he was, said to us, "I bid you good evening, sirs," and, touching his hat a second time, rode slowly off, disappearing into the darkness as silently and swiftly as he had come.

For a long while after that, Father and the boys acted crazy, as if trying to outdo one another in their ranting and their wild promises to avenge this heinous crime against one of our heroes. I waited until they began to calm somewhat, and when I thought they could hear me clearly, I said, "It's time now to go down along the Pottawatomie, where we can sharpen our swords and commence to use them."

That silenced everyone, even Father, who seemed to break out of a trance. He shook his head violently, as if ridding it of evil spirits or bad dreams, and suddenly he was scrambling up on Reliance and shouting for Oliver to get the wagon moving. He took his own reins in his hands and slapped them against the flanks of the Morgans. The horses leapt forward, and Oliver was obliged to run and grasp onto the rear of the box and clamber aboard whilst it was moving. We watched for a minute longer, saying nothing, and then the others, Salmon, Fred, and Henry, mounted their horses—I had never got down from mine—and we took off at a full gallop, chasing after Father and Oliver, the wagon rumbling in the darkness ahead of us and ahead even of Father, racing along the rough old buffalo-track, the California Road, that led down from the heights of the Ottawa lands to the winding, narrow cottonwood valley of the Pottawatomie.

Who can say which event is accidental and which is not? Or even if there exists such a thing as a true accident, a purely causeless event? When you take away belief in God's will, then every untoward event and every blessing is viewed as merely the result of history; or else its origin is said to be a mystery; or else we lamely and with extreme insecurity reason backwards from effect to cause—from consciousness of guilt, for instance, backwards to the sinful act. Thus, if my feelings of guilt were made a measure of my intention, I have to concede that, even though I was not aware of it at the time, I nonetheless fully intended to kill my beloved friend Lyman Epps and only arranged for it afterwards to resemble an accident, in my own eyes as much as in the eyes of others. And thus it would, indeed, be as I felt it (but did not believe it) afterwards—a crime. A murder. By the same token, by the weight of guilt, I fully intended to go down there along the Pottawatomie Creek that night with my father and brothers and haul five men who claimed to love slavery and hate Negroes out of their cabins and butcher them for the sheer, murderous pleasure of it. For afterwards that is how guilty I felt, as if I had done it for the pleasure of it.

But if events are driven not by a man's unconscious desires, and not by pure mystery, and not by some deep, unknown historical force—then what? After all, I was not obliged by circumstances or by any other man to go there with my sword and brandish it the way I did. No, I hold myself responsible for my own bloody acts. And I believe that I am further responsible, and to nearly the same degree, for the bloody acts that night of my father and brothers, too. For without my having instigated the attack and then goaded them when they grew timorous and frightened by the idea, they would not have done it.

Simply, I showed them at the time and afterwards that if we did not slay those five pro-slave settlers and did not do it in such a brutal fashion, the war in Kansas would have been over. Finished. In a matter of weeks, Kansas would have been admitted to the Union as a slave-state, and there would have been nothing for it then but the quick secession of all the Northern states, starting with New England, and the wholesale abandonment of three million Negro Americans to live and die in slavery, along with their children and grandchildren and however many generations it would take before slavery in the South was finally, if ever, overthrown. There would have been no raid on Harpers Ferry, certainly, and no Civil War, for the South would not have objected in the slightest to the break-up of the Union. Let them go. We will happily keep our slaves.

When we went down to the Pottawatomie, I believed all that. And in spite of my guilty feelings, I believe it still. No, I swear, I did not go down there for the pleasure of killing my enemies, nor did Father, nor my brothers, despite what the writers, North and South, puzzling over the causes of that event, have said in the intervening years. On that dark May night in '56, I truly thought that we were shaping history, that we were affecting the course of future events, making one set of events nearly impossible and another very likely, and I believed that the second set was morally superior to the first, so it was a good and necessary thing, what we were doing. We could slay a few men now, men who were guilty, perhaps, if only by association, and save millions of innocents later. That's how terror, in the hands of the righteous, works.

And we *were* right, after all. For it *did* work. The terror and the rage that we caused with those murders ignited the flames of war all across Kansas, to be sure, and all across the Southern states and in the North as well. We turned Kansas bloody. With a single night's work, we Browns made the whole territory bleed. The Missourians came flying back across the river determined anew to kill every abolitionist in Kansas, and the Northerners were forced to return blow for blow, until both sides lost sight of the possibilities of a short-term peace and were instead engaged in a fight to the death. Which was exactly as Father and I and, to a lesser degree, the rest of us Browns wanted.

If we had learned anything over the last decade, it was that there was no other way to defeat slavery, except with a willingness to die for it. We had learned what the Negroes long knew. And thus we merely did what the Negroes themselves had done over and over in the past—in Haiti, in the mountains of Jamaica, and in the swamps of Virginia—but could not do out there on the plains of Kansas. We did what we wanted the Negroes to do in Kansas. By slaying those five pro-slavers on the Pottawatomie that night, we placed hundreds, thousands, of other white men in the same position that we alone amongst the whites had held for years: for now every white man in Kansas, anti-slaver and pro-slaver alike, had to be ready to die for his cause.

If Father wanted to believe that it was the Lord's will we were enacting, fine. I had no argument with him on that, not anymore: out here, living our lives in public, what Father called the will of God I now called history. And if history, like the will of God, ruled us, then whatever moral dimension it possessed came not from itself or from above, but from our very acts, and that it would show us our true fates, for good or for evil.

That is why we killed those men.

I remember we drew the wagon into a narrow cleft in the steep, rutted ridge on the north side of the trail, with the rain-filled creek below us on the left, the land claim and cabin of James Doyle of Tennessee a quarter-mile or so dead ahead, and the others, Sherman's and Wilkinson's, a short ways beyond. It was pitch dark, but we lit no torches. I instructed the boys and Father to hitch our horses here and place our rifles in the wagon and leave them, explaining that, as the three cabins we meant to strike were all within a half-mile of one another, we could not risk a gunshot. Then I handed out the heavy, razor-sharp broadswords, one to each. No one else spoke a word, not even Father.

By the time we reached Doyle's cabin, it was close to midnight, and the clouds had broken open, floating across the satiny sky like soldered rags. There was now a quarter-moon in the southeast quadrant, casting a shifting, eerie light, glazing gray the low trees and scrub alongside the trail. We could see the rough, pale wooden shingles of the roof of the cabin below, when suddenly we heard a low growl, and out of the shadows a pair of huge mastiff dogs came charging towards us, all fangs and ferocious, yellow eyes. With a single swipe of my sword I sliced the first animal across its neck and shoulder, and it fell dead at my feet, nearly decapitated. Fred struck at the other, injuring it in the haunch, sending it howling into the woods behind us, away from the cabin.

Father, who had been next to me in the lead, stopped in his tracks. "Ah, we're done for! The Doyles'll be up and armed now."

"No," I said. "Just keep moving fast; don't hesitate. They'll likely think the dogs are chasing deer. Come on!" and I stepped in front of him and jogged down the scumbly trail to the front door of the cabin. The shutters were bolted, with no light visible inside and no sign of life, except for a thick rope of silver smoke rising from the fireplace chimney. When the others, panting more from excitement and fear than from exertion, had arrived at the stoop with me, I reached forward and banged roughly on the door with the handle of my sword.

A man's voice inside drawled, "Who's there? What d' yer want?"

I looked to Father, whose leathery face had gone white. His cheek twitched, and his lips were dry and trembling. I was afraid he would not speak to the man; and I could not. Finally, after a few seconds, the Old Man cleared his throat and asked in a thin voice the way to Mr. Wilkinson's cabin. *Friend* Wilkinson, he called him. Words were Father's saving grace. I would not have thought to say that.

I heard someone push back a chair and walk across to the door and lift the bolt away, and when he had opened the door a crack, I kicked it and swiftly put my shoulder into it, throwing the door open and tossing the man, James Doyle, for that is who it was, back across the tiny room, and we all burst into the cabin, filling it completely, sending the Doyles, a family of six people, back against the further wall, where they cowered in fright. They were a dry little old bald-headed man, his plump wife, and four children, two of them bearded men in their twenties, the others, a girl and a boy, very small, under fifteen.

They were frightened and astonished by our sudden, huge presence, and when Father shouted to Mr. Doyle that we were the Northern Army and had come to capture him and his sons, Mrs. Doyle at once commenced to weep, and she cried to her husband, "I *told* you what you were going to get! I *told* you!"

"Hush, Mother!" Mr. Doyle said. "Hush, for God's sake! This here's Mister Brown, ain't it? From over to Osawatomie. We can reason with him."

She wept profusely and for a moment dominated the scene, mainly by begging Father not to take her son John, who was only fourteen, she said, a mere boy with no notion of these things.

Father said to her, "The others, your elder sons, are they members of the Law and Order Party?"

"Never mind that!" bellowed Old Doyle. "What do you want with us? We ain't but farmers like you, Brown!"

"Thou art the enemies of the Lord," Father pronounced, and he ordered the two grown sons, named Drury and William, and Old Doyle, the father, to come out of the house with us, which they did, leaving wife and mother, son and daughter, and sister and brother weeping and wailing behind in the doorway, for they knew what was about to happen.

Quickly, we marched the three men, coatless and hatless, back up the narrow, curving pathway to the moonlit road. The two younger men were barefoot and walked gingerly over the stony trail. Oliver, Fred, and Henry were in front of the prisoners, Father, Salmon, and I coming along behind, and when we reached the level plain above the creek, a hundred yards or so from the cabin, where the dead dog lay, Father said to stop now.

One of the Doyles, William, saw the dog and cried, "Oh, Bonny!"

Father said, "The Law of Moses states that the fathers shall not be killed for the crimes of the sons, nor the sons for the crimes of the fathers. But here father and sons both are guilty."

"It's not necessary that they understand what's happening to them," I said. "Let's just get it done." I was suddenly afraid that we had come this far and now the Old Man would once again end it too soon with palaver and prayer. I remember raising the blade of my sword over my head with my good right hand, the moonlight glinting off its edge like cold fire, and then I brought it down and buried it in the skull of James Doyle, splashing the son next to him, Drury, with his father's blood. Fred and then Henry Thompson and Salmon joined in and began hacking away at the brothers, chopping them apart at the arms and slashing them in their chests and bellies, and even Oliver got in some blows with his sword. I heard several of us shriek during the slaughter, but I do not know which of us did that, except that it was not I who shrieked, and I remember that the Doyles themselves never uttered a single sound, not one cry, but fell silently to the ground like beeves being butchered in a stockyard. Sinew, muscle, bone, and blood flew before our eyes; the bodies of our enemies were slashed, cracked, and broken. Human beings were sliced open by our swords, and there the darkness entered in.

And Father? Where was Father? All the while, he stood away from us, and he alone did not use his sword. He watched. And when we were done with our murderous work, when the three Doyles were stilled at last and lying at our feet in bloody chunks and pieces, making huge puddles of blood on the ground, Father stepped forward and drew out his pistol. He leaned down and placed the barrel against the cloven head of Old Doyle and fired a bullet straight into the man's brain, as if into a rotted stump.

"The others will hear that," I said to him. Oliver was weeping, and

Henry, who suddenly, in the midst of the killing, had commenced to vomit, was now hiccoughing violently. The two of them staggered in small circles in the darkness, pounding their feet against the hard ground in a slow, furious dance, whilst Salmon and Fred stared down at the bodies of the slain men in silence, as if they had come upon them unexpectedly and did not know how they had died.

"Let them hear it," Father said. "It will make no difference. Come, boys," he said, and led us away from the place where we had slain the Doyles, down the trail towards the Wilkinson cabin, which was located on the claim adjacent to Doyle's, in a grove of old oak and cottonwood trees closer to the creek.

Here the Old Man for the first time took charge completely. He banged on the door, and before anyone inside had a chance to answer, he demanded to know the way to Dutch Henry's cabin, which was widely known as a meeting place for pro-slavery settlers. Someone, presumably Mr. Wilkinson, began to answer, but Father interrupted and told him to come out and show us the way.

When there was no reply, Father waited a moment and then said, "Are you of the Law and Order Party?" meaning, was he pro-slavery.

Wilkinson answered forthrightly, "I am, sir!"

"Then you are our prisoner! I order you to open your door to us at once, or we shall burn the house down around you!"

"Wait! Wait a minute. Let me get a light," Wilkinson said.

Father replied that he would give him thirty seconds and commenced counting, but before he had reached twenty, the door was opened, and we all marched inside the cabin. Here, again, there was a terrified wife and four children, all of the children small, however, little more than babies. Wilkinson was in his mid-thirties, a tall, gaunt Southerner with a great jaw, standing in his underwear and stockinged feet. His wife, also tall and thin, in a flannel nightgown and cap, stood by the fireplace, with the children huddled close around her.

"Who are you!" the woman screamed at Father. "Are you the devil? You look like the devil!"

"My wife is sick," Mr. Wilkinson said. "Let me stay here with her till morning. Post a man here, and you can come for me then, when we'll have someone to tend the babies for her. We got us a woman coming then."

Father ignored his drawling pleas. He set Oliver and Fred to search the house for weapons, and they quickly turned up a rabbit gun and a powder flask. "Bring them with us," the Old Man said. Salmon and Henry he told to pick up the pair of saddles that were lying on the floor next to the door and carry them up to the road. We were short two saddles, and I had spotted them myself when we entered the cabin. To Mr. Wilkinson, Father simply said, "Come along now," and he pointed the tip of his sword at the man, whose face went rigid at the sight of it. He made no answer and walked stiff-legged from the cabin, and Father followed.

The wife called after him, "Dad, you'll want your boots!"

"He won't be needing them," I said.

"What are you going to do to my husband?" Her deep-set eyes, her small, round mouth, her nose, her whole face, were all circles inside circles, a great, concentric, plaintive whorl that threatened to draw me out of myself and towards her, and I stepped backwards as if afraid of her.

"Nothing," I said. "We ain't gonna do nothing to him. Just make him our prisoner."

"Why? What's he done?"

"For exchange. We'll exchange him with the Missourians for one of ours," I said, and stumbled backwards from the cabin and turned and ran to catch up with the others, who had disappeared into the darkness ahead.

By the time I reached the place where the path joined the main trail, they had already killed Mr. Wilkinson, and he lay on the rough ground in a splash of moonlight with his throat slashed, a huge, tooth-less yawn from one side of his massive jaw to the other, and he had a great, raw wound on his skull, as if he had been scalped by Indians, and one arm had been nearly severed from the trunk.

"All right, now," Father said. "Let's get on to the Sherman cabin." He told us to hide the saddles and the rabbit gun in the brush so we could pick them up later.

But then Oliver began to cry. "I don't want to do any more of this!" he wailed. "I *can't!*"

As if reminding the Old Man of something he had forgotten, Fred leaned in close to Father and said, "He's not a grown man yet, you know."

I said, "Maybe Oliver should go back for the wagon and come down along the trail, pick up these here saddles and so on, and meet up later with us below."

"Yes, fine. Do that, Oliver. The rest of you follow me," Father said, and we went from there down to our final stop, the cabin owned by Dutch Sherman, the Missourian who, of all the pro-slavers settled along the Pottawatomie, was the most outspoken and threatening. It was he whom we had most particularly gone looking for that night, and as it turned out, he was the easiest to kill. Not because we hated him more than the others, but because he physically opposed us, fought us furiously until he was finally dead.

Evidently, he had heard the gunshot from up above, where Father had fired his revolver into Mr. Doyle's head, and had come out to inves-tigate, for we met him up on the road a short ways from his cabin. Father, Fred, and I were in front, with Henry and Salmon trailing behind, and we came upon him suddenly before he knew we were there. He was standing by the side of the road, urinating, and had not heard us approach. He was a muscular keg of a man, red-faced, with a bull neck and thick arms, a mustachioed Dutchman of about forty, famous for his temper. We threw down on him with our swords and Father's revolver, and Father said that we were capturing him for the Northern Army. "You are our prisoner, sir."

He buttoned himself up slowly, methodically, and glared at us, all the while muttering in his hard accent, "So it's you damned Bible-thumping Browns, is it? You are worse than the niggers. You are a bunch of god-damn Yankee trash come down here for stealing our niggers and our horses and then to go off feeling all good for it. You are a pack of god-damn hypocrites, coming around here in the dead of night like this for robbing a man and to terrorize him. Tell me what in the hell do you think you are doing!"

When Father answered, "The only thing we're robbing you of tonight is your life," Mr. Sherman understood the dire situation he was in, and he went wild. He exploded in fury, grabbing the barrel of Father's revolver with one hand and punching him repeatedly in the face with the other. He was very strong, and when Father could not get the weapon loose of his grip or protect himself from his pummeling fist, I was obliged to bring my sword into play and, with a single stroke, severed the man's hand at the wrist. Both hand and revolver fell to the ground. He howled in pain and rage and charged at me with his head lowered and butted me in the face, bloodying my nose and knocking me backwards onto the ground. With his remaining hand, he grabbed my dropped sword and swung it like a scimitar in a wide circle, clearing a space to stand in and hold us at bay. His severed hand lay on the ground, and his chopped wrist sprayed blood, draining him white, yet still he staggered in a circle, flailing the sword at us, causing us to leap back from him and look for an opening to take him down without being injured by him. I had scrambled back to my feet, my face covered with blood, and when I saw Father's revolver lying on the ground next to Mr. Sherman's hand, I darted over to it, grabbed the weapon, and, from a crouching position, looked up into the maddened face of Dutch

Sherman looming over me. His sword, my dropped sword, was about to come down on my head. At the same instant as I shot the man in the chest, Henry caught him from behind across the mid-section with his sword, and Fred sank his sword into the man's shoulder. He was dead before he hit the ground.

No one said a word for a long time after that. Void of feeling and thought, we stumbled down to the creek and washed our swords and our hands and faces in the cold water and waited there, seated on the rocks, for Oliver to arrive with the wagon. Each of us had withdrawn to a chamber deep inside his head and had locked himself in there alone. When, after about an hour, Oliver still had not come, Father abruptly got up and walked back along the road a ways to Dutch Sherman's cabin and soon returned, leading a pair of Mr. Sherman's horses, bridled and saddled. So we would be called horse-thieves, as well as murderers, assassins, cold-blooded executioners. He gave the reins to Salmon and Henry and in a somber, low voice instructed them to ride back along the ridge and see if anything had befallen Oliver.

But just then we heard the familiar sound of the wagon creaking down the road towards the creek, and a moment later it appeared, with Oliver looking terrified and aghast. He had passed all the sites of our killings, had observed the mangled corpses on the ground from his seat up on the wagon, and the bloody spectacle of it had changed him.

Father said to Oliver, "Are you all right, son?"

"I feel dead," he said in a flat, cold voice. "I feel like I'm dead."

"Then you are all right. You can't feel otherwise, son, after a thing like this. There will be no more of it, I promise thee," he said, and climbed up onto the wagon and took the reins. Fred and I climbed up behind Salmon and Henry on the stolen horses, and the six of us quickly rode out of that ghastly place, heading southeast from the Pottawatomie creek-bottom to where we had left our horses tied, and thence on to our camp on the Marais des Cygnes.

Before us, the darkness had faded from the night sky, and we traveled over the tall-grass plain beneath a pale blue canopy. The moon had set, and the last stars, like silver nails, had pinned the canopy overhead. Behind us in the east, the rising sun would soon crack the black, flat line of the horizon. There long, ragged strips of silver-blue clouds lay banked in tiers, tinged with red, as if the heavens were bleeding.

Let them bleed, I thought. Let the heavens rain down on us in gobbets and pour rivers of blood over the earth. Let the sky bleed all its color out, and let the earth be covered over with gore—I no longer care.

Let the soil here below stink and turn to a scarlet muck, and let us crawl through it until our mouths and nostrils fill with it and we drown in it with our hands on each other's throats—I no longer resist this war. I relish it.

19

Dear Miss Mayo, I have again, as it were, mislaid you: days, weeks, possibly whole months, have passed without my clocking them, whilst I've scribbled away at this, my long-withheld confession, page after page. And when I have finished covering yet another page or chapter of it, I reach for a fresh sheet of paper or an unused tablet, and finding none at hand, I write on the backs of old, filled sheets (which once again I realize that I have somehow neglected to send to you), and I go on setting down my tale in the margins and even between the lines of passages that, for all I know, I must have written to you sometime last spring or winter—passages, pages, entire tablets that, in my urgency to continue writing, I have elbowed to the edge of my little table and have let get lost amongst the pages and tablets previously heaped there and that now slowly tumble to the floor. They clutter there at my feet and pile like autumn leaves and scatter and drift across this dim room in the cold winds sifting through the cracks in the walls of my cabin and blowing beneath its flimsy door.

I have gotten lost inside my confession, as if it were my very self— my only remaining self. I am alive, oh, yes, but my life is long over, and thus I am no more now than these words, sentences, episodes, and chapters of my past. Yet from time to time, at moments such as this, I do rise, like an old, befuddled bear who wakes reluctantly from hibernation and breaks off his unbroken, winter-long dream, and I stumble blinking from the cave of my narration into blinding sunlight, where suddenly, forcibly, I recall the now long-past occasion and need that brought me in the first place a willingness to speak of these things. Which is to say, I remember thee, Miss Mayo, way out East in New York City, poring with steady perseverance over the hundreds of accounts of Father's life and the numerous interrogatories that you have no doubt taken from the still-living men and women who knew us back before the War and whose tattered memories, though rent and shot through with age, provide them, and now you and Professor Villard, with varying versions of the same events that I dreamed clearly in my cave, as clearly as if they actually occurred there, and that I have been setting down for, lo, these many, unnumbered months.

But I do remember thee, Miss Mayo, and my promise to compose for you my own account and place it safely into your hands, so that you in turn can aid and advise the distinguished Professor Villard in his composition of what you and he surely hope will become the final biography of John Brown. And if I have been too distracted and confused and enfeebled, if I have been too disembodied by the act of telling this tale, to sort and order these pages and arrange to have them placed into your hands somehow, if, in other words, I have been too much a garrulous ghost and too little a proper respondent, then I apologize, Miss Mayo, and ask your forgiveness and understanding, for there is no other way for me to have told what I have already told and to say what I have yet to say. For though a man trapped in purgatory, if he would escape it, may seem betimes to speak to the living, he speaks, in fact, only to the dead, to those who in hurt confusion surround him there, awaiting his confession to set them free.

These things which I alone know—of the death of Lyman Epps and of the brutal massacre down by the Pottawatomie and the turbulent, bloody events that followed, of the climactic raid on Harpers Ferry and the martyrdom of my father and the cold execution of my brothers and our comrades—these things, when I have finished telling them, will not alter history. They will not revise the received truth. That truth is shaped strictly by the needs of those who wish to receive it. No, when I have said them, the things that I alone know will release from purgatory the souls of all those men whom I so dearly loved and who went to their deaths believing that they held their fates in their own hands and that they had chosen in the fight against slavery to slay other men and to die for it.

When I *kept silence, my bones waxed old through my roaring all the day long.* But I am no longer silent. I am saying that those men did not so choose. I chose for them. Their fates were in my hands alone.

There is much, of course, that I am leaving out of my account, much that need not be told here by me. Most of what happened back then occurred in full public view, anyhow, and is known to the world; it needs no corrective from me: I'm not writing a history of those years or a biography of my father. I leave those high tasks to you and the professor. I have neither the mind nor the training for them, nor the inclination. As for the wider events across the nation and in Washington during those years, when the slaveholding South like a gigantic serpent slowly wrapped the rest of the Republic in its suffocating coils: I leave to others the obligation to set straight that record; and for the most part they have already done so, the journalists, the historians and biographers, the memoirists, and so on. The fact that nearly all of us then engaged in the war against slavery believed in the late '50s that the war was all but lost, that much today, if little noted by the world, is nonetheless collected and recorded there. I needn't recount these highly visible public events, although I do wish you to know how, over time, they made us believe that our entire government and even our nation's destiny itself had been stolen from us, as if we had been invaded and all but conquered by a foreign, tyrannical power.

We were enraged by this, to be sure, and howled at it, but when the slavery-loving, Negro-hating mobs gathered legitimacy in Washington and in the Southern press, when the Border Ruffians were portrayed as legitimate settlers and the overseers of human chattel as statesmen, when our leaders, like Senators Douglas and Webster, sold us out for a handful of silver coins and our heroes, like Senator Sumner, were clubbed down in the Capitol building itself, our rage turned suddenly to cold desperation. We who early on had been merely anti-slavery activists and who, slowly over the years in defense of our own rights of protest, had evolved, almost unbeknownst to ourselves, into guerilla fighters and militiamen—we now became terrorists. And having become terrorists, we found ourselves almost overnight made emblematic to those remaining white activists who mostly sat in their parlors or at their desks grieving over the loss of their nation. We inspired them, and they encouraged us. And so we waged their war for them. Unwilling to do more to regain their nation than write a poem or a cheque to help arm, clothe, and feed us, they were often objects of scorn and derision to us, although we were, of course, grateful for their poems and monies and used both to solicit still more monies and, with our purses thus fattened, purchased more Sharps rifles, more horses and supplies, more of the terrorizing broadswords and pikes.

Ah, but you know all this. You are an educated woman, who has sat for years at the foot of a wise and learned historian, a man whom I know also by reputation as the illustrious grandson of William Lloyd Garrison. The grandsire, of course, I was myself, through Father, personally acquainted with, and his nobility of purpose and great personal courage I hope I have not impugned in these pages. It's just that, in the heat of battle and in the face of imminent death, I habitually bore towards Mr. Garrison and most of the other white abolitionists my father's long-held resentment and impatience. And even today, these many years after, it still rankles that, whilst I and my family and our comrades were laying about in Kansas with our broadswords, bloodying ourselves and our enemies and putting at ultimate risk our lives and our immortal souls, Mr. Garrison, Mr. Emerson, Mr. Whittier, and all those other good men and women back in Boston and Concord and New York were adjusting their sleeves so as not to spot their starched cuffs.

I hear you protest, and I apologize; I concede: it was not the fault of those good men that we risked our lives and butchered the men and boys down on the Pottawatomie and in the ensuing several years raised homicidal havoc across the Kansas plain and even into Missouri itself, or that later we marched into martyrdom in Virginia; these things we did, not because others did not, but because we ourselves almost alone could not bear to see the war against slavery come to an end there. Out there on the old California trail, we understood what no one else in the country could have known, not in Boston or New York or Washington or even in the capitals of the South. We were on the battlefront, and that night in May of '56, with the news of the abject sack and surrender of the town of Lawrence to the Border Ruffians still drumming in our ears and barely hours later the sudden arrival of word of the near assassination of Senator Sumner in Washington, we believed that the war was all but over and done with. On that night, we saw Satan settle comfortably into his seat and commence to gather his slaveholding minions in to serve and honor him.

Though it's not my intention here to explain or excuse our acts, mine or Father's or those of any who followed us, I do want you to understand that we were desperate men. And of all of us, I suppose I was the most desperate. We were made so, me especially, by three inescapable realities: our position on the ground out there in Kansas; the clarity of Father's understanding of the true nature and scale of the war against slavery; and our principles. We could not be where we were, know what we knew, uphold what we honored—and do other than we did. And joining us were other men for whom these same three circumstances applied as well: not many, a dozen, twenty, usually one at a time and on occasion arriving in groups of three or four, but enough of them quickly came forward and joined our band, especially after Pottawatomie, that we were before long no longer a small, guerilla force made up only of Old Brown and his sons but an actual, insurrectionary army that was well-armed and was growing rapidly in size and fearsomeness.

Sometimes as many as fifty men, sometimes as few as ten, we stayed on horseback day and night almost continuously and, all that summer and into the next year, conducted swift, daring, terroristic raids against the Border Ruffians and their supporters amongst the settlers, moving our encampment every few days from one tree-shrouded river-bottom to another. We burnt down the cabins and barns of the enemy and liberated their property, their horses and cattle and supplies and weapons, and although some men, even amongst our allies, called it looting or simple horse-stealing, for us it was merely a necessary and legal continuation of our war policy, for it weakened our enemy on the field and frightened him everywhere, whilst us it strengthened and our allies it encouraged.

During this period, dozens of journalists came out from the East by way of St. Louis, Leavenworth, and Lawrence, or down from Iowa to Topeka, and entered thence into the war region of southeastern Kansas. The more intrepid among them, like Mr. Redpath and Mr. Hinton, would eventually make their way to the marshes and ravines and the cottonwood groves along the Marais des Cygnes and the Pottawatomie or out onto the high, grassy plains of the old Ottawa Reserve, where they would find and follow our band for a few days or a week until, exhausted by the pace of our steady marches and raiding and by Father's night-long monologues and preachments, they would head back to Lawrence or Topeka and dispatch back to the East vivid accounts of Old Brown's indefatigable and brilliant campaign against the pro-slavery forces. Soon they had made him a heroic figure out of some old romance, like a legendary Scottish Highlands chieftain lead-ing his doughty clansmen against the British invader, and by summer's end his name was on the lips of nearly every American, North and South. To all, he had become a figure perfectly expressive of the anti-slavery principle.

And naturally, as his fame spread across the nation, brave, reck-less, principled young men itching for battle began to join our ranks. You know the names and reputations of many of the best of them, I'm sure, for they were later with us at Harpers Ferry and entered history there: the fierce, intelligent, and well-spoken John Kagi; and the kindly, black-eyed giant, Aaron Stevens; and poor John Cook, who was a genial man but dangerously indiscreet; and Charlie Tidd from Maine, a man with a terrible temper but withal an almost feminine sweetness; and Jeremiah Anderson, the guilty grandson of Virginia slaveholders; and young Will Leeman, barely seventeen when he first showed up at our camp: these men and numerous others whose names and fates you know were with us, but also over time a hundred more, who were just as steadfast and brave and who remain nameless, they were with us, too, and sometimes fell in battle and ended in unmarked graves or beneath humble, forgotten, untended wooden plaques in an overgrown Kansas field or back yard—farmers, carpenters, and clerks, they all, in their churches and meeting houses in Ohio and New York and New England, heard about Old Brown and his men or they read about us in their newspapers, and they dropped their hoes and spades or put aside their pens and eye-shades and, like the Minutemen of their grandfathers' generation, picked up their rifles and made their way west and south to Kansas, where they got passed along, one to the other, by our growing number of supporters and allies, until they finally one morning walked through the trees into our camp and presented themselves to the lean, leathery old man seated by the fire going over his maps, the legendary John Brown himself.

There were, of course, some young men of a quarrelsome and wasting nature who joined us and stayed awhile as regulars in our Army of the North, as Father sometimes called his force, men who were taints and whose reckless, violent behavior caused many amongst the anti-slavery residents of Lawrence and Topeka and even back East privately to condemn our work, despite the continuous hosannas in the press. These were fellows who could not keep the pledge they made against the use of alcohol and tobacco or would not subject their wills to Father's and would have been more at home in the bands of marauding Border Ruffians or brawling with each other in the saloons and muddy alleyways of the shabby border towns along the Missouri River. They did not last long with us. If Father or I found one of them drunk or if, on his or my command, a man did not at once rise from his blankets and mount up with the others at midnight and ride out in the cold rain to make a dawn raid on a pro-slaver's farmstead twenty miles away on

Ottawa Creek, Father was fiercely adamant and had me drive the man from camp like a dog.

I spoke for Father in all matters, except when he chose to speak for himself, which occasions were rare and made all the more impressive by their rarity. Even my brothers Salmon and Fred and Oliver and my brother-in-law Henry Thompson addressed Father through me, and it was through me that he spoke back to them and to the other men. To the journalists, of course, he spoke for himself, for no one, certainly not I, was as articulate and clear and poetical as he when it came to defining and justifying his grand strategy. With his actions in Kansas, Father wished to inspire a similar set of actions by other men all along the thousand-mile border between the North and the South, from Maryland to Missouri: by his and our example, he wished to make warriors of abolitionists and freedmen, and insurrectionists of slaves.

Your researches must have made known to you by now that after the night of the Pottawatomie Massacre, as it quickly came to be called, my elder brothers, John and Jason, were no longer with us. They were not purged from our band by Father, however; they took themselves from it. And it was just as well for them and for us, for they were not cold enough.

When, on that morning in May, we had finally washed all the blood from our hands and faces and had cleaned our broadswords in the waters of the Pottawatomie, we then came somberly, silently away from Dutch Sherman's place, ascending from the dark, gloomy river-bottom in the wagon and on horseback along the winding, northerly trail to the grassy plateau above. Swaths of ground-fog hovered over the trees in the distance, where the Marais des Cygnes meandered eastward towards the town of Osawatomie, and the tall grasses glistened in the morning sunlight. We came over into the open, newly green meadows and leafy copses outside the settlement and after a while arrived at the crossroads where John and Jason and the Osawatomie Rifles still lay encamped, waiting for instructions from their superiors in Lawrence.

The men of John's outfit were mostly young fellows, husbands and sons, Osawatomie homesteaders mustered abruptly into a militia company to defend and protect their homes against the Missouri marauders. Thus they could not have joined us in our work anyhow and still retained their commission under Colonel Lane and Mr. Robinson. It was not that Father had mistrusted them, especially John and Jason; it was merely that he respected their charge and mission and knew its difference from ours.

Our arrival at their encampment that morning, however, was met with grim silence by them, which puzzled us. They were mostly standing together near their low, smoky breakfast fire, and as we drew near, they watched us and said nothing and did not even raise a hand in greeting. It was as if we were a painting of six travelers, three on horseback and three in a wagon, being hung on a wall in a museum, and they were a group of silent, thoughtful observers standing ready to examine it. I remember, as we neared the fire and dismounted, that it was Jason who first separated himself from the men and came forward, while John looked on woefully, and the others merely gazed coolly in our direction as if from a great distance.

Jason glanced over the horses and saddles we had taken from Mr. Wilkinson, then abruptly took Father's hand in his and led him a short ways off. I followed, while the other boys stayed in an isolated knot by the wagon.

Jason said to Father, "Did you have anything to do with that killing over to Dutch Henry's Crossing?"

Father looked surprised by the question. "What've you heard?"

"A few hours ago, just after sunup, one of the boys from over there rode through, all distraught and weeping in a panic," he said. "We got out of him that his father and two brothers and some other men had been savagely murdered. He said they'd all been chopped down by swords and cut horribly. It was an uncalled-for, wicked act!" he pronounced. Then he looked down at the broadsword I wore on my belt and was briefly silent. "The lad was pretty confused," he went on, turning back to Father. "But he claimed it was the Browns that did it. He was clear on that. Then he rode on to Osawatomie. To raise the alarm."

We were all three silent then. At last, Jason said, "Did you do it, Father?"

"I slew no one," Father declared. "But I do approve of it."

"I'll go the route for you, Father, if you're innocent. But if you did this, you know I can't defend you. It's a despicable act. I must know where you and the boys have been all night."

Father said simply, "No, Jason, you don't."

Jason looked at me then. "Do you know who did this?"

I hardened my face and showed him its side. "Yes, I do. But I shan't tell you."

His voice lowered almost to a whisper, Jason said, "This is mad." Then, harshly, he shouted towards the wagon, "Fred, come over here!"

Fred obeyed and came forward and stood beside me with his head hung low, and at once he said to Jason, "I didn't do it, but I can't tell you who did. When I came to see what manner of work it was, I couldn't do it, Jason!" Tears were streaming down his face.

"You realize that now we're all going to suffer!" Jason said to Father. "Do you realize that?"

"No, you're wrong," said Father. "Those men were the enemies of the Lord, and they deserved to die, no matter who did it. For without the shedding of blood, there is no remission of sins. I will tell you this much, son: I myself killed no one. But if the slavers *think* I killed their kith and kin, that's fine by me. All the better. Now they will know our extremity. Now they will know what they're up against," he said.

But Jason was no longer listening. He had stepped unsteadily away a few paces, and he turned and, nearly staggering, walked off from us and the men of the militia.

The sight of him, shocked and clearly appalled, pointedly separating himself from Father and me and Fred and making his way along a zig-zag path over the rise and down the ravine towards the river, told the others that the boy's dawn account had been true, and it seemed to release the men. At once, they busied themselves with breaking camp and bridling and saddling their horses. A few seconds later, John was left standing alone by the fire—a captain overthrown and abandoned.

He looked first at us and then at his men, then back at us again, as if torn and dismayed by the choice that had been forced upon him. Finally, he called out to his men, who were mostly already on horseback by now and were clearly prepared to depart: "Wait up! Hold up a minute! This business isn't settled yet. You fellows are still under my command."

Henry Williams, a storekeeper in Osawatomie, a big-shouldered man with a dark, rubbishy beard, said, "No, we're electing us a new captain, John. We ain't riding under no Brown." The others nodded and murmured agreement, and Mr. Williams turned in his saddle and said to them, "Who d' you boys want for a captain? Any nominations?"

One of them said, "You'd do fine, Henry."

Another man, a tall, rawboned man in a canvas duster, said, "My vote's for Williams. He's got sense. And he's got family and his store to protect. He ain't going to do anything so stupid as killing off folks at random," and he glared first at Father and me and then directly at John.

John said, "I've got family."

"Yes," the man said, "so you do," and he turned his horse and rode out from the camp, onto the crossing.

Mr. Williams said, "Listen, Browns, if I was one of you, I'd find me a hole and stay in it till winter. Then maybe I'd light on out of Kansas and go back to the states. All across the territory now there's going to be hell to pay. You damned Browns," he declared, "you're plain crazy. Even you, John. Jason, too. I like you and him well enough, but your name is Brown, and we can't be under you no more. Not now," he said, and clicked to his horse and went out from the camp to the crossing. There he took his place at the head of the gathering column of men, and when they were arranged in a military line, he led the troop down the road towards Osawatomie.

Soon they were gone from sight, and we could no longer hear their hoofbeats. A crow circled overhead and cawed. Seconds later, another crow appeared beside it, and the two carved wide loops against the cloudless sky. Shortly, Jason returned from the river-bottom, looking aghast and pale, as if he had been gazing at the corpses of the five men we had slain barely three hours and five miles away from here. Fred moved back towards the wagon. John had not spoken once yet to Father or stepped from his spot by the dying fire.

Father put a hand on my arm and said, "What d' you think's best now, son?"

"Attack."

"You think so, eh?"

"Worst thing we could do is what Mister Williams said, hide in a hole. We're instruments of the Lord, are we not? So let the Lord lead us. 'To teach when it is unclean and when it is clean: this is the law,'" I quoted to him.

He made a small smile. "'And if the plague be in the walls of the house,'" he came back, "'then the priest shall command that they take away the stones in which the plague is, and they shall cast them into an unclean place without the city.'"

"Should we be stones cast out? When we can be the priest's men, instead?"

Father nodded, and then he called to Salmon, Oliver, Fred, and Henry, who leaned by the wagon. "Mount up, boys. We're riding on over by Middle Creek a ways."

"What for?" Salmon asked.

"To find us a camp where we can rest in peace a day."

"What then?" Henry wanted to know.

"Then we'll see some action. From here on out, we're going to be on the attack, boys."

Jason sat down heavily on a nearby log and, placing his forehead against his knees, wrapped his head with his arms, as if hiding his father and brothers from his sight and hearing. John remained standing by the dwindled fire, all disconsolate and downcast.

I said to him, "You coming?"

He shook his head no.

"Suit yourself," I said. "Jason?"

He didn't answer.

"You boys maybe ought to think about moving your wives and Tonny permanently into town or down to Uncle's place," I told them. "It's going to start getting plenty hot around here now," I said, and climbed up on the wagon seat next to Oliver. Father had mounted Reliance and was out in front of the wagon. "Okay, Father," I said to him. "Let's move."

He nodded, and we rode off across a broad, high meadow northwest of the crossroad, away from our old settlement at Browns Station, away from the town of Osawatomie, away from poor John and Jason. I remember I turned in the wagon and peered back at them, and my elder brothers were standing with their arms around each other, as if both men were weeping and trying to console one another.

I did not think then that what later happened to John and Jason would occur, but when it did, I was not surprised. By then, Father, Old Brown, had become the feared and admired Captain John Brown of Kansas, had become Osawatomie Brown, the victor of the Battle of Black Jack, the one nationally known hero of the Kansas War, and he was back in Boston, working his way across the entire Northeast, raising funds and making speeches to thunderous applause. And through it all, from that May day forward, the cold, silent man at his side, the large, red-bearded fellow with the gray eyes who spoke to no one but to Captain Brown himself, was me. My two elder brothers had been all but removed from Father's life, and I had replaced them there.

20

I'm trying to recall it: how I came to be knocking at the rough plank door of Uncle Sam Adair's cabin in the nighttime; and when exactly it occurred, that same night or the next. Things happened so quickly back then that, although I can with ease summon them to my mind in sharp, vivid detail, sometimes their sequence blurs. But I do know that it was right after we had made our first secret campsite over on Middle Creek in amongst a clutch of black oak trees, and had slept awhile and rested our animals and prepared our weapons for battle, that I went to my uncle's cabin. I have no diary at hand, for none of us kept one, and of course I have no calendar from those days. But I do remember that, towards the end of our first night in camp, while the others were sleeping, on Father's orders I rode one of Dutch Sherman's liberated horses out to the Osawatomie Road, intending to slip into town under cover of darkness to be sure that Jason's wife, Ellen, and John's Wealthy and little Tonny were safely ensconced with friends there.

Yes, it was not until the second night that I made it over to the Adair cabin. For, when we had first got to Middle Creek, the boys, Oliver, Salmon, Fred, and Henry Thompson, were exhausted—oddly so, it seemed to me, despite the fact that we had all been awake for nearly forty hours straight, for Father and I were not in the slightest fatigued.

Quite the opposite: he and I were exhilarated and filled with new and growing plans and stratagems for raiding and terrorizing the Border Ruffians and pro-slave settlers. The boys, though, were all but useless, at least for a while, until they could begin to put the killings behind them. Fred wept, and he declared again and again that he could not stand to do any more work such as that, and Oliver wrapped himself in his blanket on the ground and would not speak to any one of us, while Salmon and Henry huddled together and read in their Bibles.

Father sat on the ground beside Fred and said to him, "God will forgive thee, son. I have prayed and listened with all my mind and heart to the Lord, and I know that we have done His will in this business. You can let your conscience rest, son," he said, and stroked poor Fred and comforted him tenderly, while I went to the other boys and made my rough attempt to do the same, although they were not inclined to be comforted by me or Father and in a listless way said for us to just leave them be, they were tired and wished only to sleep.

So while the others slept or sulked or read, Father and I busied ourselves throughout the afternoon into the evening, constructing a crude lean-to of brush and a corral for the horses; and after dark, when we dared finally to set a small fire, we made a little wicker weir and caught and cooked us some small fish from the creek and ate and talked in low voices until late. Father was worried, I remember, about the women and Tonny, his only grandson, and when I volunteered to go into town to be sure they were safe, he at first said no, it was too dangerous, but I persisted, and finally he relented and gave the order. He said he would write some letters and send them with me and that I should try to get them to Uncle Sam Adair, his brother-in-law, for posting. "I want to have my own say-so on this business," he said. "To get the truth out, before folks hear erroneous reports of it first. I don't want the family at home fearing for our lives. Or for our souls, either," he added.

I agreed and said that I would also try to speak with John and Jason, to see if they would now change their minds and come in with us, for we would be much stronger with them than we were without. "True. True enough," Father said. "But remember, son, it's we who have made the blood sacrifice. They haven't. This war's no longer the same for us as it is for them."

I asked if he thought they might betray us, for Jason was at bottom pacifistic and John a political man, but he assured me they would not: he had asked the Lord how he should treat with them, and the Lord had told him to trust all his sons equally. "The Lord saith, 'Those that thou gavest me I have kept, and none of them is lost but the son of perdition; that the scripture might be fulfilled.'" He often spoke of the Lord in this familiar way, for it was around this time that Father had begun his practice, later much commented upon, of withdrawing from camp to commune alone with God, more or less in the manner of Jesus, for long hours at a time, returning to us clear-eyed and energetic, full of intention and understanding. I can't say what that was like for him, whether he was during those hours an actual mystic or was merely deep in solitary prayer, but the practice brought him a piercing clarity and a regularly freshened sense of purpose, which suited my private desires ideally, so I did not question it.

"You may ask them if they wish to join us here under my command," he told me. "But don't press them on it, Owen. I don't want to force them into choosing *against* us. A time will come," he said, "when events and the cruelties of men will bring them over on their own, and when that happens, John and Jason will prove our strongest allies."

He drew out his writing kit and for an hour or so was absorbed in writing several letters, one to Mary and the children in North Elba, I later saw, and others to Frederick Douglass and Gerrit Smith, and hurried me out of camp then, instructing me to return quickly, for we would now be obliged to return to action at once, so that the other boys could get the Pottawatomie killings behind them, he explained.

"They'll need to stare some of these slavers in the face again and re-learn what sort of beast we're dealing with here."

It turned out that, for the moment, at least, all was calm in Osawatomie: Ellen and Wealthy and Tonny had on their own fled our decrepit tents and half-built cabins at Browns Station for the town, evidently on the advice of friends who had heard about the Pottawatomie killings. I spoke briefly there with Wealthy at the door of the little house owned by the Days, distant relatives of hers from Ohio. It was close to dawn, still dark, and I had come in stealthily on foot, with my mount left hidden in a grove of trees by the west ford of the river, and had knocked quietly at the door, waking the dog, which someone inside quickly shushed.

Then I heard Wealthy's voice on the other side of the door: "No one's here but women and children," she announced.

"It's me, Owen. Are you all right?"

"I can't let you in. The Days are very afraid."

"I understand. Father just wants to know that you're safe."

Opening the door a crack, she showed me in a slat of candlelight her worried, pale face and said, "We're safe, so long as we keep from you boys and Father Brown."

I asked her then if John and Jason were out with Uncle at his cabin, but she said that she could not tell me. I knew then that they were with Uncle. They were safe, she said, but in hiding. The Ruffians burned Browns Station to the ground this very night, she said, and stole all they could carry. Among the Free-State people, John's and Jason's innocence was well-known, she told me, but no one was eager to risk protecting them. "Please stay away from them, Owen, until this thing calms down," she pleaded.

I said that I understood her fears and that my report back to Father would comfort him, and, bidding her good night, slipped out of town and reached my horse without being seen. All that day, I hid in the tall grasses atop a rise out by the road to Lawrence, with my horse grazing well out of sight in a nearby ravine, and watched riders in the distance heading back and forth between Osawatomie and Lawrence—hectic armed men of both sides gathering in bands to search for us: one side, the Free-Staters, to capture us and no doubt turn us over at once to the federal authorities as a peace gesture; the others, pro-slave marauders, to shoot us on the spot. And I knew that there would soon be a third side: federal troops from Forts Leavenworth and Scott, sent on orders from the President himself to capture us and march us up to Lecompton for trial or else to turn a blind eye, as they had done so many times before, and hand us over to the Ruffians and let them avenge themselves on us.

When darkness had fallen, I rode down to the Lawrence Road and turned east towards town and sometime after midnight pulled up before the Adair cabin. I was frightened, certainly, but I was unattached and free, and all manner of men were trying to kill me: I was like a hawk or a lone wolf or a cougar. No one had a claim on me but Father, and though he did not know it, his claim had been given him by me, so that, in a crucial sense, the claim was reversed and was mine, not his at all.

The cabin, a two-room log structure that had been serving as Uncle's parsonage until he could get a proper house finished in town next to his church, was dark and appeared abandoned, for there was no smoke rising from the chimney. I knocked on the door, but no one answered, so I knocked again, but still no one answered. There were no horses about and no dog. Maybe the Adairs have fled, too, I thought, and knocked again, loudly, and called, "Uncle! It's Owen here! I'm alone, Uncle!"

"Get away!" my uncle shouted back from inside the cabin, startling me. "Get away as quick as you can!"

"I just want to talk some with John and Jason."

"No! You endanger our lives! They won't speak with you. You and your father have made them into madmen."

I told him then to unbar the door and let me see for myself how mad they were, but he said he would not and told me again to leave at once. "You are a vile murderer, Owen, a marked man!" he said.

"Good," said I. "Because I intend to *be* a marked man!" And stepping away from the door, I mounted my horse and headed off down the road again, west and then south to our camp on Middle Creek, where I knew Father and the others were impatiently awaiting my return. Father, at least, would be impatient, for I was sure that he would not commence raiding without me. The others I could not be so sure of. For we had all been changed.

John, as I later learned, went insensible and nearly mad and remained so for many months, even while a prisoner of the United States Army, his condition having been exacerbated greatly by the terrible cruelties inflicted upon him by the soldiers after they captured him, hiding nearly naked and babbling, in the gorse bushes several miles behind Uncle's cabin, where, following my brief visit, his delusions had chased him. Jason declined into a passive, self-accusing grief, which, though it later passed and he did indeed, finally, although only for a while, come over to our side in the war, drove him actually to seek out and surrender himself to the United States troops. His release was quickly arranged, unlike John's, which took until the following spring. I think Jason's personal safety and the safety of his wife, Ellen, were his main concerns and motives in all that he did from then on, for as soon as he was able, he sent Ellen back to Ohio, along with Wealthy and Tonny, and well before the end of the Kansas War followed them there himself.

Oliver and Salmon shortly came round to their normal senses, as did Henry Thompson, but they, too, were different people than before: they were warriors now, men who no longer questioned first principles or premises or Father, and consequently they fought like young lions, as if every new war-like act were an erasure, a justification, of the Pottawatomie killings. Thus it was for them no longer so much a matter of making Kansas a free state as it was of killing and terrorizing the pro-slavers, purely and simply. Strategy, long-range goals, overall plans—these were not their concern. For them, the war was merely a day-to-day killing business, work organized and laid out by Father and me, as if we were laying out farmwork in North Elba.

As for Fred, poor Fred: he was now even more wildly religious than before, and if Father was not an actual mystic and speaking privately with his God (which, as I said, he may well have been), Fred surely was. Happily, however, Fred's God merely confirmed what Father's was saying and released him to follow Father's orders with murderous enthusiasm.

Father was changed, too. It soon became clear, and surprised even me—perhaps especially me—that Pottawatomie had been a great gift to him: for it returned him to his purest and in many ways most admirable self, the old, fervent, anti-slavery ideologist, and added to it a new self, one that up to now had existed only in his imagination: the brilliant tactician and leader of men at war. All his years of studying the science of war suddenly came into play and of necessity were being put to good use out here on the rolling plains of southeastern Kansas. And with each new military success, from the Pottawatomie killings on, with Black Jack and the Battle of Osawatomie and all the lesser raids and ambushes and breathless escapes from our pursuers, his confidence swelled and his enthusiasm for the work increased, so that before long it was no longer required of me to goad or brace him in the least, and in fact I found myself barely able to keep pace with him. This was a most welcome development, for it restored to us our relationship of old. We were once again in proper balance. He was once again Abraham and I was Isaac.

Yet despite this, or perhaps because of it, I myself was not changed by the Pottawatomie killings. No, I remained the same man who had migrated out to Browns Station from Ohio with his self-mutilated brother, the man who had watched in silence and did not stop his beloved friend from killing himself that day in Indian Pass, and who loved his friend's wife in order not to love his friend. I was still very much he who had carved the farm in North Elba out of the wilderness while running escaped slaves north to Canada, the fellow who had sailed off to England and in the crossing found his heart and spirit uplifted and enlarged by a woman bearing a sorrow and a wound he did not wish to comprehend. I was still the man whose spirit one moment rose to the ceiling like a hymn in a Negro church and the next insinuated its way towards a perverse brawl in a nighttime park, the man who when still a boy humiliated himself and demeaned a poor Irish girl of the streets in the back alleys of Springfield: all the way back to the boy, the very boy, who stole his grandfather's watch and lied about it and for his lies was made to chastize his father's bare back with a switch: I remained him, too.

Yet was it not due solely to this strict, stubborn persistence of my character that, in point of fact, I, too, was now a different man than I had been before? For I now inhabited a world in which I was no longer seen as the outcast, the grunting, inarticulate, crippled Owen Brown whom everyone easily loved but no one feared: a man not half the man his father was. If instead I now found myself twice the man my father was, as indeed betimes I did, it was not because I had changed but because, after the Pottawatomie killings, whether they were with us that night or not, my father and everyone else had changed.

Over the following months our deeds drew to our side as many Free-State men as were repelled by them. Those who stayed on and endured our hardship and deprivation and the almost daily risk to our lives were of necessity physically hardy fellows, but they were also the most courageous men out there then and the most dedicated to the anti-slavery cause. Father would have said it was *because* they were dedicated to the anti-slavery cause. "It's a mistake," he told me, "to think that bullies make the best fighters, or that violent, cruel men would be fitter to oppose the Southerners than our mild, abolitionist Christians. Give me men of good principles, God-fearing men, men who respect themselves and each other, and with a dozen of them I'll oppose any hundred of such men as these Border Ruffians!" But this was a grinding, dangerous business after all, and those who undertook it had to be physically as well as mentally and spiritually tough: we were no regular army with a quartermaster and wagonloads of supplies, tents, and arms and plenty of fresh mounts following us around. We lived off the land, as they say, and *al fresco*, and were constantly on the move, armed, supplied, fed, and clothed strictly by what equipment and livestock we could liberate from our enemies.

We went barefoot in camp, to save boot leather, and when it rained stripped off our clothes and packed them to keep them dry. For weeks at a time, we subsisted solely on skillet bread made from Indian meal and washed it down with creek water mixed with a little ginger and molasses. By mid-summer the rivers were so low and the water so stagnant that we had to push aside the green scum on the surface before we dipped our cups to drink, and many of us were much of the time ill with the fever and ague.

Father said, "I would rather have the small-pox, yellow fever, and cholera all together in my camp than a man without principles." Throughout, he was cook, nurse, and teacher for his men, to set us a clear example, that we would in turn act as cook, nurse, and teacher for one another; and he instructed us constantly as to the purpose and eventual aims of our work, so that we would understand that we were enduring these privations and risking our mortal lives to further a truly noble cause. He never tired of exhorting us to treat as a heinous, soul-damning sin any temptation to submit to laws and institutions condemned by our conscience and reason. "You must not obey a majority, no matter how large, if it oppose your principles and opinions." He said this to each new volunteer and repeated it over and over to him, until it was engraved upon his mind. "The largest majority," he explained, "is often only an organized mob whose noise can no more change the false into the true than it can change black into white or night into day. And a minority, conscious of its rights, if those rights are based on moral principles, will sooner or later become a just majority. What we're building here is nothing less than the free commonwealth promised us by our Declaration of Independence and prophesied and ordained by God in the Bible."

He enjoyed making our camp into a philosophical and political classroom, and such were the power of his ideas and the force of his expressiveness that even though many of his men were either illiterate and unused to abstract disputation or else were agnostical, they were nonetheless, for the most part, eager students. He instructed the men as to the faults of both parties in Kansas, showing, of the pro-slavery side, how slavery besotted the enslavers of men and coarsened them and made them into brutal beasts. Of the Free-State side, he said that, while there were many who were noble, true men, unfortunately they were being led by broken-down, cynical politicians of the old order, timid men who would rather pass high-sounding resolutions than act against slavery with a force of arms. He insisted that a politician could never be trusted anyhow, for even if he held a decent conviction, he was ever ready to sacrifice it to advantage himself. Father argued that society as a whole must come to be organized on a different basis than greed, for while material interests gained somewhat by the institutionalized deification of pure selfishness, ordinary men and women lost everything by it. Despite his earlier attempts to acquire wealth, he believed that all great reforms in the past, such as the Christian religion, as well as the reform which we ourselves were now embarked upon, were based on broad, generous principles, and therefore he condemned the sale of land as a chattel, for instance, and thought that it should be held in common and in trust, as had been practiced by the Indians when the Europeans first arrived here. Slavery, however, was "the sum of all villainies," and its abolition was therefore the first essential work of all modern reformers. He was perfectly convinced that if the American people did not end it speedily, human freedom and republican liberty would pass forever from this nation and possibly from all mankind.

Father, as always, slept little, as did I myself now, and often it turned out that only he and I would be awake keeping late watch, he having early dismissed the grateful regularly scheduled watch, and as he was, like many surveyors, a thorough astronomer, he enjoyed pointing out the different constellations and their clock-like movements across the deep, velvety sky. "Now," he would say, "it is exactly one hour past midnight," and he would show me which stars to separate from the myriad of lighted pinpoints overhead and how to line them up so that they resembled the hands on Grandfather's old clock. He often turned rhapsodical at these times. "How admirable is the symmetry of the heavens! How grand and beautiful it is! Look how in the government of God everything moves in sublime harmony!" he declared. "Nothing like that down here with the government of man, eh?"

Father was pretty easily brought to heightened emotion in those days, even to the point of shedding tears and sometimes to loud laughter as well, which was uncharacteristic and probably due in part to the generally high level of tension and excitement that we habitually and necessarily lived with out there on the plains all that year and into the next. It made him seem physically larger than he was and gave his personality added volume, too, and because of his acts of violence against the enemy and his growing reputation as a warrior and successful leader of men, notwithstanding the fact that he always went about well-armed, with twin revolvers and his broadsword at his belt, a Sharps rifle close at hand, and a dirk in a scabbard above his boot, he was never, as sometimes of old, an object of derision: his manias were widely regarded now as passions, his stubbornness as belief in principles, his willfulness as self-assurance, and his Bible-based strategies as brilliant innovations in the science of warfare.

Even the enemy regarded him that way. They were not wrong to do so, of course, but it helped that, compared to us, our Free-State allies were timid and that our enemies were disorganized, ill-trained, often drunk, and inadequately armed. And as the Border Ruffians were mostly natives of Missouri rivertowns and did not live or work in Kansas, they did not know the countryside as well as we. The federal troops, though well led and equipped, were young, frightened conscripts and few in numbers, too few by far to patrol that vast a region effectively. And it was helpful, too, that Father, for the first time in his life, was lucky.

The famous Battle of Black Jack is an example. It has been written about often and described as a turning point in the war against slavery, but certain defining elements of the story always get left out. A bright, sunny Sunday morning in early June it was, and we had all gathered in a field out on the Santa Fe Trail near the tiny, mostly burned-out, Free-State settlement named Prairie City. Father had led us there to confer with a Captain Samuel Shore as to the possibility of combining our force with Captain Shore's so-called Prairie City Rifles, one of the few Free-State militias aggressive enough to merit Father's approval. We were also there to attend an outdoor service led by a popular itinerant preacher by the name of John Moore, two of whose sons had recently been captured and hauled off by a large band of marauding Border

Ruffians led by the Virginian Henry Clay Pate. Pate would in time become a well-known colonel of the Fifth Virginia Cavalry in the Civil War, but in Kansas, though at bottom a pro-slavery Ruffian, he was a deputy United States marshal and had assisted the federal forces in the recent capture near Paola of brother John and had helped take in Jason also and had been pushing on into Kansas with his pack of Ruffians in search of us remaining Browns.

We had close to a dozen men in our group at that time, not including the journalist Redpath, who afterwards wrote up the story for the Eastern newspapers. Having arrived late, we stood on horseback at the edge of the crowd close by the road, which was more a rutted wagon track there than a proper road, when Fred drew first my and then Father's attention to three riders approaching from the east, the direction of Black Jack Spring. As we had intelligence that Pate's band of Ruffians had recently been seen encamped out there at Black Jack, and as the riders were strangers to all, Father decided to grab them. "Owen, take five of the men and run those fellows down," he said, and returned his attention to Preacher Moore's ongoing peroration.

With Fred, I gathered together Oliver and three others (I think including August Bondi, who after Harpers Ferry was said, first by the Southern press and then by the Northern press as well, to have been a Jew, but who, as far as I knew, was merely agnostical and of Austrian parentage) and rode out to meet the strangers. As soon as they saw us coming, they broke and ran like rabbits across the plain in three different directions. Like rabbit hunters, we split into two parties of three, enabling us quickly to cut off and capture two of the men, whom we marched at gunpoint back to the service, which had by then ended, thus freeing Father to interrogate the terrified fellows.

"I am Captain John Brown," he announced to them, and needed little more to obtain their swift confession that they were from the camp at Black Jack. But not of the party of Henry Clay Pate, they insisted, which no one believed, so we bound them and turned them over to Captain Shore, who had one of his Prairie City volunteers march the two back to town, there to await negotiations with the Ruffians for an eventual exchange of prisoners—a useful, widespread practice among the warring parties that, for a while, until the Ruffians started executing their prisoners, helped keep the bloodshed down on both sides.

Immediately, most of the congregation called for a raid on Pate's camp, their ardor being somewhat heated, perhaps, by the reported presence in the camp of the two sons of Mr. Moore, a man whom they now loved, and by Pate's having aided in the capture of John and Jason, which was widely seen by Free-State people as unwarranted. Father, however, advised the excited crowd to wait till nightfall, so they could arrive in Black Jack at dawn, when least expected. This was wise, because the delay allowed those who had been merely carried along by the enthusiasm of the moment to separate themselves from men who, like the Gileadites, could be relied upon in a fight, which ended up being all of our group and most of Captain Shore's militia.

Around four o'clock the next morning, we arrived at the copse of black oak trees for which the spring had been named. We were situated on a long slope a half-mile north of the Ruffian encampment and could see in the gray dawn haze their line of covered wagons below, with the tents pitched behind them and, on the wooded slope to the rear, their picketed horses and mules. As there were no fires and no other activity evident in the camp, we assumed they were still sleeping, so we dismounted and, leaving Fred in charge of the horses, made our way stealthily downhill through the brush, where we split into two groups, Father's nine men and Captain Shore's fifteen. At this point, about sixty rods from the wagons, we were discovered by a sentinel who had been posted up by the picketed animals, and he fired his musket and shouted the alarm: "We're under attack!"

Like bees swarming from a hive, the half-dressed Ruffians ran from their tents and commenced firing on us. Instantly, Captain Shore and his men, who were in a somewhat more exposed position than we, laid down a barrage of return fire, while Father led us on the run off to the right a ways, ordering us as he ran not to fire yet. "Hold your fire, boys, and remember, when you do shoot, aim low!" That was always his advice: get to close quarters and aim low. And aim for the body, not the head. "Every one of us would be dead by now," he often said, "if our enemies had aimed low."

After a few moments, we had made our way to a protected position in a ravine to the right of the wagons. From there, we could get clear, covered shots on the Ruffians, so we laid down our own barrage, which drove them to the backside of their camp into a further ravine, where they kept up a steady fusillade against both Captain Shore's men in front of them and us on the flank.

As Captain Shore's men had commenced firing earlier than we and more recklessly, they were soon out of ammunition and could no longer return fire, and because they were the more exposed, they started taking on injuries, and several of his men cried out, "I'm hit! I'm hit! Someone help me, I'm a dead man!" One fellow over there was sobbing like a sorrowful woman. I saw three of Shore's men—one of them the preacher Moore—break and run back up the long slope towards the grove of black oaks. Then three more fled.

We were trapped, with no alternative to seeing it through to victory or death; and the men knew that now. Father prowled back and forth behind us, scolding us and bucking us up and pointing out targets as they appeared, making of himself a most obvious target in the process, but seeming not to care, as if daring the enemy to shoot him. Several times I shouted, "Father, stay down!" but he only scowled at me, as if I were being cowardly. There was shooting coming from all directions and from both sides: terrified men were firing their weapons randomly at targets made invisible and everywhere by simple human fear: our boys were firing as much at Shore's men as at Pate's, and both those bands were shooting in our direction also, and we all may even have fired sometimes at ourselves, so that when Henry Thompson took a bullet in the thigh and rolled away from me, slapping at his wound and hollering, "Damn! Damn! Damn!" as if he'd been stung by a red-hot coal, I didn't know if he'd been hit by a Ruffian's bullet or a Free-State militiaman's. I couldn't even be positive that I hadn't accidentally shot him myself. Father rushed to Henry's side and ripped a strip of cloth from his own shirttail, took out his dirk, and with it and the strip of cloth made a tourniquet for him.

Somewhere in here I remember Captain Shore appearing in our ravine with a small number of his men, those who had not cut and run: he was telling Father that they were out of ammunition and would have to retreat or else go for reinforcements. He had one man dead, five who were wounded, and six who had deserted. The Ruffians had dug in good, he said, and could wait us out, unless we got more men and ammunition quickly. He seemed much discouraged. Father was disgusted and told him to go on back for reinforcements, then, and take the dead man and the wounded with him, including Henry Thompson.

Then, when Shore and his men had left, Father told us to open fire on the Ruffians' horses and mules, which were picketed in a rope corral a short ways uphill from the tents. "It'll distract them so Captain Shore can get his men out, and maybe it'll even draw a few of them out of their hole to where we can pick them off," he said. He told us this time not to aim low but to shoot at the animals' heads, because he wanted them to die, not to suffer, and they were easier to hit than men anyhow.

We obeyed and shot into the wild-eyed herd of animals. The horses and mules neighed and brayed loudly when they were hit, and they tripped and trampled upon one another in the dust, as first one poor beast went down and then a second and a third. It was an awful sight, and I had trouble going along with it, but I said nothing and fired away with the others. I shot horses and mules and men that day and had very few thoughts of what I was doing or why, but at one point, in the midst of this carnage, I suddenly saw us all, almost as if I were not a part of it: bands of terrified white American boys and men killing each other and screaming bloody murder into one another's faces and shooting down poor, dumb animals, slaying one another and our livestock and terrorizing our mothers and wives and children and burning our houses and crops—all to settle the fate of Negro Americans living hundreds and even thousands of miles away from here, a people who were much unlike us and who were utterly unaware of what we were inflicting upon each other here on this hot June morning in amongst the black oak trees of Kansas. It was no longer clear to me: were we doing this for them, the Negroes; or were we simply using them as an excuse to commit vile crimes against one another? Was our true nature that of the man who sacrifices himself and others for his principles; or was it that of the criminal? You could not tell it from our acts.

Firing on the horses and mules evidently surprised and distracted the enemy sufficiently to cover Captain Shore's retreat from the battlefield, but it drew none of the Ruffians from their cover, and as soon as all the animals were down, they started in again on us. From their ravine behind the tents, they kept us huddled under a blanket of rifle-fire, and as we could get no good angle on them, we were obliged to lie low and prepare for their final charge, which we figured was coming next. Father instructed us to have our broadswords and revolvers at the ready. "Wait till they close on us, boys, and pick your targets carefully. If their leaders go down at the start, the rest might flee, even though they hugely outnumber us."

But then an astonishing thing happened. I was lying with my back to the ravine, facing uphill towards the grove by the spring, so I saw it all: Fred, alone on horseback, appeared at the edge of the trees and was surveying the scene below with mild surmise, when suddenly he raised his broadsword over his head and came galloping full speed down the long slope straight towards us and the enemy beyond, shouting loudly as he neared us, "We have them surrounded! We have them surrounded!" All firing ceased, as Fred rode across the cleared space that divided us from the Ruffians, still waving his cutlass and bellowing, "We have them surrounded!" Then he disappeared into the bushes off to our left, and we saw him no more.

We were silent for a moment and looked at one another in puzzlement.

"That was Fred," Salmon said. "Why do you suppose he did that?"

Father answered that he didn't know, but look, and sure enough, there came Captain Pate and one of his lieutenants, walking towards us and waving a white flag. What followed is well known: Pate wished to obtain a truce, he said. He declared that he was a deputy United States marshal sent out by the government to capture "certain persons for whom writs of arrest have been issued—"

Father cut him off and in his coldest voice said, "I've been told that before, sir. I know who you are and why you are here. You will surrender unconditionally, Captain Pate, or we will leave every one of you lying dead with your animals over there."

"Give me fifteen minutes—" Pate said, but Father again interrupted and drew his revolver on him and commanded him to have his men lay down their arms. We put our weapons out where they could be seen and aimed them straight at Pate and his lieutenant.

Father said, "You're surrounded, you realize."

"But we're here under a white flag," Pate said. "You can't throw down on us with a white flag showing. That violates the articles of war."

"Who drew up those articles?" Father asked. "Not I. Not thee, Captain Pate. No, you are my prisoner. And if you don't tell your men to lay down their arms, I'll shoot you dead."

You could hear it in his voice and see it in his eyes: Father was ready to kill the man and let himself be shot for it at once, as would surely happen, for he and Pate and Pate's man stood alone up on the lip of the ravine, fully exposed to the guns of the enemy. Luckily, Pate was no fool: he could read Father's intent and was himself not eager to die. He agreed to surrender and sent his lieutenant trotting back to his lines to instruct his men to lay down their arms and march out with their hands on their heads. Which, a few moments later, they did, surprising us, when they were all lined up before us, with their numbers, for there were twenty-six of them, uninjured and well-armed. Pate's men were, of course, even more surprised when they saw how few we were, and they were angry at their captain, who lost much face by the surrender and later complained bitterly of what he called Father's "deceptive, casual disregard for the rules of war."

Thus ended the famous Battle of Black Jack, which Father, in a letter to the New York *Tribune*, rightly named "the first regular battle fought between Free-State and Pro-Slavery forces in Kansas." We had killed four men and wounded nearly a dozen and captured more prisoners in one sweep than had so far been captured by all the Free-State forces in total. In the North and amongst the Free-Staters, John Brown came away with nearly heroic stature; to the Southerners, he was now the devil incarnate.

Had it not been for Fred's miraculous intervention, however, his mad, delusional charge onto the battlefield, the Battle of Black Jack would have ended much differently. His son's apparent madness was Father's good fortune: for Fred did, in fact, believe that we had the Ruffians surrounded, and he insisted for days afterwards that he had seen Free-State men on all sides firing on the Ruffians from the bushes and slaughtering them without mercy. He had acted, he said, to end the terrible slaughter of the Missourians.

We knew, of course, that he had only seen the horses and mules going down, that it was the slaughter of the animals that had maddened him, and I said as much to Father.

"The boy was not disobedient unto the heavenly vision," he answered. "That is all that matters."

I see that, almost inadvertently, I have been writing you much that concerns my brother Fred, and perhaps I should complete his story here. Towards the end of August, I walked out one morning from camp alone very early to observe the sun rise, an event I had not seen in several weeks, for we had been night-raiding for a long while at a hectic pace over in Linn County and during the daylight hours had mostly hidden out in the marshes and deep gullies, sleeping whenever we could, and thus we had had little opportunity or time for admiring God's orderly governance of the universe, as it were. Recently, however, we had succeeded in driving a herd of nearly one hundred fifty head of liberated Ruffian cattle into Osawatomie for distribution amongst the people there and, feeling protected by their gratitude, had encamped a few miles from town and, for the first night in a fortnight, been given a normal parcel of sleep. Thus we felt able to lighten our vigilance somewhat, causing Father to release me from my usual task of overseeing the watch, and I had been allowed to enjoy a full night wrapped in my blanket by the guttering fire.

When I first rolled out of my blanket that morning, Father was nowhere in sight—commiserating or consulting with his God in the bushes someplace nearby, I supposed. I was surprised, therefore, when, as I emerged from the tree cover and approached the grassy ridge above our campsite, I spotted him profiled against the sky there, gazing eastward towards the horizon, as if he, too, had come out to see the sun rise. It was a cool, dry morning, not quite dawn, with no breeze. The sky was enormous and loomed above us like a tautly drawn celestial tent, and the land swept darkly away beneath it like a vast, chilled desert. Back in camp in the gully, it was still dark as night, although up here the southeastern sky had faded to a soft, crumbly gray, making Father's figure a sharp, paper-thin silhouette against it. I silently took my place beside him on the ridge, and together we stared out across the rolling prairie in the direction of the settlement of Osawatomie, some five miles distant, down along the Marais des Cygnes.

A moment or two passed, when, out on the horizon, there appeared parallel to it a long string of silver light. Soon it had thickened into a metallic strap and broadened, and after a few moments, the lower edge of the silver strap took on a golden hue, while above the strap the fleecy clouds began to go from gray to yellow to red, as if a fire were being lit below them. It was strikingly beautiful and strange in its clarity and exactness. I said to Father, "It looks like it's a miniature scene and close to us. Like a painting, almost, instead of huge and far away and real."

The Old Man merely nodded and said nothing. Perhaps he was used to such visions. I lapsed back into silence and continued watching the eastern horizon slowly shift color and shape. Soon, when I knew that the scarlet disk of the sun was about to break the horizon and shatter the scene with its rays, I saw an extraordinary thing. It's something that occurs rarely, but nonetheless normally, at sea or on the desert, and also, on the rarest of occasions, happens out on the prairies of the West, where it appears in more nearly perfect detail and on a much grander scale. Commonly called a mirage, it's disdained for that, despite its beauty and rarity, as if it were merely an illusion. But it is in no way an illusion. It is real and is taking place in present time. What one sees is not a hallucinated or imagined scene: when, as on this morning, the atmospheric and geographic conditions are perfectly aligned, objects and entire scenes and events located far beyond one's normal range of vision are brought close and are made sharply, silently visible; or else the beholder himself is instantly transported from his former spot across the many miles of prairie, carried as if on a Mohammedan flying carpet and brought face-to-face with a scene that he could otherwise have only imagined or dreamed.

It is actually unclear which is moved, the scene in the distance or the observer here at hand. Perhaps it's that the visible aspect of a thing, of any thing, is like its smell, and when atmospheric conditions are right, its visible aspect can be carried away separately, like a spoor, to an observer who is situated many miles distant and who then is enabled to see the thing up close, the way one can sometimes wake to the smell of coffee being brewed over a fire far down the valley from one's bed and think it's being made in the next room.

This is what Father and I saw: at first, there was a misty, grayish scrim that rose from the horizon and became a semi-opaque sheet. Then, evolving out of a series of dark, vertical threads and strings, solid objects began to appear against it, and in a few seconds, a familiar bit of scenery had taken shape—the road that led past Uncle Sam Adair's cabin, on the near side of Osawatomie. There were the trees and the creek and the burnt-over stumps of his field and even the smoke curling from his chimney. In the further distance, I saw a man walking from the spring with a bucket in each hand.

The man was Fred! My brother Fred, barefoot and shirtless, was walking slowly towards the cabin, looking lost in thought or prayer. I was too astonished and pleased by the sight to speak of it. Three days before, Father had ordered him to Lawrence for supplies and mail from home and to ask for reinforcements for the defense of the town of Osawatomie, but Fred had felt indisposed from a recent onslaught of the ague and had begged to stay at Uncle's for a while, until he recovered, and Father had relented. I had not expected to see him again for a week or more, and now here he was, soundless as death, but very much alive and before my eyes making his slow way along the roadway from the spring to the cabin, as if he were alone and invisible to all eyes but his own.

At that instant, there came three riders over the crest of the hill a ways behind Fred, men whom I recognized at once as Ruffians, men who had been riding with John Reid, the Mexican War veteran from Missouri who had given himself the rank of general and headed up one of those bands that had been in particular hot pursuit of us Browns since Pottawatomie and Black Jack months earlier. Reid had threatened noisily on many occasions to burn down the entire town of Osawatomie, but this was late August, and we had begun not to take these blowhard threats too seriously, for we had most of these men well on the run all across the territory by now, and despite their numbers, all they were capable of were random raids on isolated cabins and farms. It was from some of Reid's people, in fact, that we had stolen the herd of cattle recently left off with the citizens of Osawatomie—stolen *back*, I should say—and the three I now saw riding up on Fred I had marked then as villains, and Father and I had even briefly spoken with them: coarse, brutal men whose main object was looting and pillaging the farms and lands of Free-State settlers.

"Fred!" I cried. "Look behind you!"

"He can't hear you, Owen," Father said in a low voice. "He may be done for."

Helplessly, as if bound to a stake, we watched from our spot miles from the scene, while the three riders approached Fred from behind. They had come over the rise from the direction of town, sent out, as I quickly surmised, to reconnoiter for General Reid, in preparation for his oft-threatened raid on the settlement. Their presence probably meant that Reid and his hundred-man force of Ruffians were close by. But Fred did not seem to recognize the men at all or to regard them as enemies. He turned and stopped in the road, and as they neared, he stood and watched, apparently unafraid, as if the men were merely local Free-Staters not known to him.

Father and I were close enough to the scene to see over his shoulder, as it were, and we stared in silence as Fred nodded good morning and the others touched the brims of their hats and made to pass, when one of the men, the large-bellied fellow in the center, gave Fred a hard stare. I would later learn that this was the Reverend Martin White, a notorious and malignant pro-slaver from Arkansas who back in '54 had come out to settle and preach to his fellow pro-slavers, one of those men who, after the Pottawatomie affair, had become fixated on avenging himself against us Browns.

Although I could not hear him, I saw him speak to Fred and found that I could read his lips somewhat: I *know you!* he seems to say. And Fred, who still has not recognized the danger, advances open-faced towards the men to greet them, his buckets still in his hands, his bare chest exposed to the riders, who draw out their revolvers and throw down on him. Fred stops in his tracks now and looks wonderingly, innocently, up at them, as once more the man in the middle, Reverend White, silently mouths some words: *You're one of John Brown's boys!*

By now, Fred's face has gone all dark and serious, for he has finally seen the dangerous fix he is in, and he shakes his head no, he's not one of John Brown's boys.

I *know you!* White declares.

Fred again shakes his head no. He mouths the words I *don't know John Brown.*

Where's he hiding?

I *don't know him.*

Yes, you are his son! says White, and he levels his revolver and fires straight into Fred's pale, bare chest.

The bullet killed him at once, and he fell like a stone in the middle of the road. For a few seconds, the riders stared down at his crumpled, lifeless body and the spilled water buckets. Then they spurred their horses into a gallop and rode off, heading away from town in the direction they had come, no doubt to bring Reid's force straight on.

Dark blood poured from the hole in Fred's chest and puddled over and around his body. A light breeze lifted and flattened the leaves of the nearby cottonwood trees and sifted the tall grasses alongside the road. And now, slowly, the scene began to fade from view, gathering itself back into the dark threads and strings from which it had emerged, until once again Father and I were gazing across the featureless prairie towards the eastern horizon, staring at nothing, and the sun was risen, blasting back at us, radiant and bright yellow and orange, driving the fleecy, gold-tinged clouds from the skies and bathing our faces in its light.

"Murderers!" I cried. Enraged and horrified was I—but I spoke also as if to verify the actuality of what I had just seen, for I could scarcely believe that it had truly happened.

"He denied me," Father said in a low voice.

"They shot him like a dog!"

"If he had not denied me, they wouldn't have shot him. They would have taken him prisoner is all, as they did John and Jason. I'm sure of it."

"No. Even if you're right, it's not *true*," I declared. Fred was gone, and gone from us forever—my wholly innocent brother, my childhood companion, the boy and man I had loved and envied more than all the others, the one I would have been myself, if I had been strong enough, clear enough, humble enough, if I had been a Christian: my best brother was dead.

Father turned to me and said, "What do you mean, it's not true?"

"Fred has been killed! And that's the simple fact of it! *That's* the truth of the matter. Why he was killed, or how he might have avoided it—those aren't important now, Father. He's dead. He's your son, my brother, and he's *dead!*"

I looked into Father's ice-gray eyes and saw a strange sort of puzzlement there, and for the first time realized that he could neither comprehend nor share my feelings at that moment, and thus he did not in the slightest understand me. He did not know who I was. Or who Fred had been. And consequently, in a crucial way, though he had seen it with his own eyes, he did not know what had just happened.

Suddenly, I felt pity for the Old Man. Despite his intelligence and his gifts of language and his mastery of stratagem, he possessed a rare and dangerous kind of stupidity—a stupidity of the heart. It was possibly the very thing that, combined with his intelligence, gifts, and mastery, had indeed made him into an irresistible leader of men, had made him a resourceful and courageous warrior and even a powerful, rigorous man of religion; but his stupid heart had also made him dangerous, fatally dangerous, to anyone who loved him and to anyone whom he loved back. More than the rest of us, Fred had loved the Old Man; and Father had loved him more than all his other children back. And now Fred was a dead man.

"He has made the blood remission. He is with the Lord," Father said, and he turned to go. "Come on, we have to rouse the boys. Reid's prepared to raid Osawatomie, and we have to warn the people and help defend them." He paused for a second and said, "I believe that the Lord has given us this vision for their sake, not Fred's."

Then he left me. I lingered a moment longer, watching the sun blot out the eastern horizon with its light, and saw Fred's open face float against the light, and his slow, thoughtful gestures and ways, and heard faintly in the breeze his gentle, abrupt voice—an illusion this time, no mirage, no vision given by the Lord, and it was already beginning to fade. Then slowly, reluctantly, so as to depart from it before it disappeared altogether, I turned away from this weak, diminishing apparition of my dead brother and followed Father's cold, dark form down the ridge into the camp.

On that day, the day that his son was killed, Father fought the battle that made him known as Osawatomie Brown. Until his own death and for many years after, even to today, it was his public name. Perhaps—despite my account and because of yours—it will be his name forever. Other men, most of whom had never seen him in the flesh—the journalists and hagiographers of the North, mainly—gave it to him, but he quickly embraced it himself and took to signing, with a vain flourish, his letters and the autograph books of his admirers with it: *Osawatomie Brown*. Or sometimes, more formally, *John Brown of Osawatomie*. On the day that he sacrificed his best son upon the stone altar of his belief, Father within hours was transformed from a mortal man—an extraordinary and famous man, to be sure, but, still, only a man—into a hero bathed in swirls of light. It mattered not whether they liked his ways or admired his courage or believed his words; the American people from then on viewed him as more and other than a man.

This transformation, before anyone else even knew that it had occurred, Father already understood and had begun using for his own secret purposes. In the mind of the South, he would be Baal and Anathema. And in the imagination of the North, he would make him-

660 Î RUSSELL BANKS

self a Greek or Roman hero, Achilles in his tent or Horatio at the bridge, or one of the old, impetuous, dragon-slaying heroes of Arthurian romance, each of whom in the beginning surely had been, like him, a flesh-and-blood man who, one day, when a sufficient number of stories about him had accumulated in the public mind, stepped across an invisible line and, as if by magic, became other than human: the son lay murdered in the dusty Kansas track, and the father would ride down that track into legend. So that, in the North, Osawatomie Brown soon reached the point of fame where he could lose a battle, and it would nonetheless be regarded as a victory—a triumph, if not for him or for the anti-slavery forces, then for the human spirit. In the South, his victories signaled the coming millennium, the impending war between the races, and his losses entered the accounts as proof, not of his military feebleness or personal failure, but of his enemies' courage and virtue in defense of slavery. All men now measured their stature and meaning against Osawatomie Brown's.

In mundane reality, however, the Battle of Osawatomie was neither loss nor victory: I was there. It had no political or military stature and no philosophical or religious meaning. I broke and ran with the others, abandoning the town to the Ruffians' scourging fire and pillage; I know what it was—merely a failed defense on our part, and a looting raid on theirs.

Neither Father nor I, without having agreed between ourselves, said anything to the others in our party of what we had witnessed from the ridge at dawn that morning, except that we had spotted General Reid's scouts returning from Osawatomie, riding away from the settlement east to west, towards the Lawrence Road, where, according to rumor, Reid's force had temporarily bivouacked. And when we rode down from our camp into town, passing Uncle's cabin, where Fred's body lay inside on a plank table, we did not stop to pray over it or to speak solemnly with its sad, frightened attendants of Fred's brief life and useless death; we rode straight on to warn the settlers of the imminent raid from General Reid's band of irregulars, which we knew numbered in the hundreds.

Reid had been moving across the countryside for weeks, gathering all the loose gangs of marauders into a cohesive force. Rumors, until then mostly discounted by us, had been flying from one Free-State redoubt to another: that he wished to make a final, defining attack on Lawrence and then on Topeka, the capitals of Kansas abolitionism—attacks that we knew would not be tolerated by the federal army, in spite of the unspoken, continued support of the pro-slavers' interests by the President and his Secretary of War; not wishing to get caught between the Ruffians and the federal troops, we had left the defense of both cities to their own citizens. And until we saw Reid's scouts returning that morning from Osawatomie, we had not thought that he would bother taking Osawatomie, in spite of its reputation as an abolitionist stronghold and, notwithstanding our long absence from the place, its reputation as the Kansas base of the Browns. By this time, Wealthy and little Tonny and Ellen had returned to Ohio; John and Jason were in Topeka; and our brother-in-law Henry, after suffering his leg wound at Black Jack, had gone home to sister Ruth and their little farm in North Elba. Most of the other inhabitants had fled the town by now as well, so that it was a cluster of barely twenty families—poor, stubborn folks who had refused to abandon their cabins and property to the pro-slave predators of the region but who, unlike the more organized and well-armed citizens of Lawrence and Topeka, posed no real threat to the Ruffians.

However, due to our having distributed amongst them the one hundred fifty head of cattle that we on nighttime raids had been liberating piecemeal from small bands of Ruffians over the previous weeks, we had unintentionally made the town an object of General Reid's especial attention, and it now appeared that he had stopped on his march towards Lawrence and was coming in unexpectedly from the west, moving south of the Marais des Cygnes River and north of the Pottawatomie, a narrowing wedge of territory that pointed at the heart of the town where the two rivers met.

At the low log blockhouse—actually, more a storehouse than a fort—we combined with Captain Parson's small homeguard of boys and old men and spread out amongst the trees at the edge of the settlement and dug in there to await the arrival of Reid's men, with the river, at the one place where it broadened and went shallow and was thus fordable, at our backs. "Never defend an unfordable river," went one of Father's maxims, "or the Lord may have to part the waters for you." At one point, before we had dispersed and taken our positions in the woods behind rocks and logs, Father and I had a moment alone. We were standing on a high, shrubby overlook, with the Marais des Cygnes passing below us. Father was seated on a stump, slowly sharpening his cutlass and every few seconds casting a wary eye up the trail, where we expected soon to see Reid and his men come riding in.

"Why not pack everyone up and safely abandon this place, Father?" I asked him. "Innocent lives will be lost defending it, and Reid's going to take it anyway."

"The apostle saith, 'Rebuke with all longsuffering,'" he answered without looking up from his work. "'For the time will come when the people will not endure sound doctrine, and they shall turn away their ears from the truth and shall all be turned into fables.'"

I sighed. "All right, fine. But tell me what you propose to accomplish here."

"Apotheosis, son. Apotheosis."

"You expect to *die* here?"

"Oh, no! Just the opposite. God does not want me to die yet. He has something further for me to do. Something much larger. I know this."

"You know God's mind?"

"Yes," he said, calm as a counting house clerk.

"How do you come by this knowledge, Father?"

"The Lord speaks to me. He shows me things. You know this, Owen," he added with some impatience.

A moment passed in silence, while I pondered his claim—for this was the first time that he had said it so bluntly—that not only did he see what the Lord wished him to see but he had God's very words in his ear. Finally, I asked, "And what does the Lord say to you? What does He say of me, for instance?"

He turned his face up to me and gently smiled. "The Lord says that I shall never weep for thee, as King David wept for his beloved son, Absalom. And as I must weep for Frederick. And that I shall never wish to have died for thee, as King David wished to die for Absalom. Today, Owen, the Lord hath delivered up the men who hath raised their hand against me, and all who hath raised themselves up against me to do me hurt shall someday be as that young man is. Frederick. My son." He paused for a few seconds, then went on. "I swear it, and the Lord hath promised it. For if I must, to smite these men I will carry this battle into Africa."

"Africa," I said.

"You kill a serpent by striking off its head."

Africa? Was my father, indeed and at last, mad? I was long used to his reliance on elaborate, obscure figures and his habit of displacing the immediate present with the Biblical past, and while usually I could follow his circumlocutious path to his meaning without much difficulty and often found his meaning original, profound, and insightful, this time he had me. Africa! Had the shock of Fred's murder begun to settle in and madden him? He had so far evidenced no grief or outrage over it, but deep feelings too much denied or suppressed can inexplicably erupt in fissures elsewhere.

"Look, they're here!" he suddenly said, sounding almost relieved, and he stood and pointed towards the western track, where there came the first of Reid's force over the horizon, and following close behind came a great troop of men on horseback, riding three abreast and at full gallop. Father slapped his sword into its scabbard and instantly began giving orders. "Hold your fire, men! Aim low, and wait till they're upon us!" he shouted, as he ran from one man to another, his dozen fighters and Captain Parson's twenty more, encouraging them and bucking up their courage in the face of this most formidable, terrifying force.

Straight on the riders came, as if expecting no one to oppose them, as if we had indeed done the rational, expected thing and abandoned the town to them. Soon they were only a quarter-mile off, well within range of our Sharps rifles, of which we had perhaps ten, and still Father said to hold fire, wait for his command, and then they were within range of our muskets, but he would not let us shoot yet, so we held back a few seconds longer, until they were fit targets even for our revolvers, when finally Father called, "Fire!" and thirty guns—thirty rifles, muskets, and revolvers—roared as one, and twenty or more of Reid's men cried out and fell like clods of dirt. Those who were not hit in the fusillade wheeled away from the trail and, firing wildly from horseback, fled into the woods in several directions at once, while we reloaded and went on shooting at the riders and killing those on the ground who had gone down not dead but merely wounded in the first volley.

Reid's force was like a huge wave rolling in upon a rock. And when the riders had fallen away before us and their ranks had broken on both our flanks, they at first swirled and scattered amongst the trees in confused eddies, then made their circuitous way to a height back up the road a ways, well beyond the range of our guns, where they re-gathered in military formation, as if preparing to roll in against the rock a second time. Meanwhile, Father strode back and forth among his hunkered men, making sure that no one had been shot and readying us for the renewed attack, assuring us that the Lord would protect us and walking about in full view of the enemy, as if he needed no such assurance himself.

I lay tucked in behind a low, brush-covered hummock, studying through the gaps in the brush the moves of the enemy on the distant rise, when I saw one of Reid's men dismount and get down on one knee and carefully aim his long rifle in our direction. There was a puff of white smoke, then the sound of a single gunshot, and when I turned to see where the bullet might have hit, Father was standing next to me, still recklessly exposed to the enemy.

He stepped close, turned, showed me his back, and said, "Can you see anything torn or bloody, Owen?"

I replied that I could not.

"Well, I believe I just took a terrible rap on the back from that fellow's long rifle."

"What! Then stay down!"

He grinned and said, "Don't fret yourself, son. The Lord doesn't intend for me to be shot in the back. He just wants me to keep facing His enemy, that's all. It's a little reminder."

I remember turning towards Reid's men then and seeing for the first time their cannon. This was no guerilla skirmish; this was warfare. They had rolled the weapon out and were loading it with grapeshot. A moment later, they fired the thing, and it made a terrible roar, snapping off whole trees and tearing down branches overhead. They quickly reloaded and fired a second time, with the same, frightening effect. It made a deep bellow and then a shriek as the grape whistled over our heads and crashed against the trees and hummocks, splintering and smashing everything it hit. While the cannoneers with each new firing brought their weapon closer and closer into deadly range, the rest of Reid's men, gathering courage from its destructive power, dismounted and formed large companies of shooters and commenced to advance on foot upon our position, stopping every ten or fifteen yards to aim and fire their muskets, driving us slowly back towards the river.

Father kept exhorting us to hold our ground and wait for close quarters and aim low and so on, but first Captain Parson's men and then Father's, too, even Salmon and Oliver, were now in full retreat, firing and running, ducking behind a tree or a rock and firing and running again. I stayed at the front beside Father and watched them fly past. Father and I looked at each other and said nothing. Here several of the men were shot and went down—older men: Mr. Partridge, as I recollect, and Mr. Holmes—and this terrified the rest even more and turned their more or less orderly retreat into a pandemonious rout, until finally even Father at this point gave up the fight and, showing the enemy his back, made for the river, with me close behind.

I remember stopping atop the bank, the last of the Osawatomie defenders to flee, and looking down at our men as they waded through the chest-high water, with Father coming after, as if he were not following them but was in hot pursuit—a revolver held high in each hand and his battered old palm-leaf hat set squarely on his head and the tails of his mustard-yellow linen duster floating out behind.

He cut a ludicrous figure. Except for those men—both ours and the enemy's—who lay dead on the rough ground behind me, they all did. It made no sense to me, none of it. I no longer knew what I was doing here or why. For a second, I thought of turning away from Father and the others and walking straight towards Reid's cannon and riflemen, offering myself up to them—as a prisoner, if they wanted, or as a sacrifice—just to end it, to finish this mad fight and give sense, if not to my life, then to my death. In a world where every man was trying for no apparent reason to kill the other, the only sensible man should have long since been slain. Like poor, murdered Fred.

Then I heard Father's hard voice call up to me: "Owen! God sees it, Owen! God sees it!" And with that, down the embankment I scrambled and into the river and on to the further bank—saved once again from myself by my father's call to come along, come and kill men another day.

We arrived late that evening, foot-sore, weary, and sullen, at Uncle's cabin, which Reid's marauders, having marked it already with Fred's cold-blooded murder, had passed over and left intact. Earlier, as we regathered on the far bank of the river, we had stood awhile and watched the smoke rise over the village of Osawatomie, where the Ruffians were gaily pillaging and burning. Now and then, the silence was broken by the whoops of the victors and the random sounds of their guns being fired exuberantly into the air. That there was still in effect, despite contradicting claims on both sides, an unwritten law against violating or otherwise injuring women and children was cold comfort to us: houses and barns filled with the long, arduous summer's harvest were going up in flames, and Free-State livestock was being herded together for travel east to feed hungry mouths in Missouri, and stores and the several public buildings were being looted and burned to the ground. All over the region, the grassy plains and pretty cottonwood dells were scarred by the blackened ruins of farmsteads and crossroads stores, and the trails and roads were increasingly haunted by the wagons of burned-out Free-Staters and pro-slavery families alike returning with their few remaining possessions and animals to their home states—ruined by this war, slump-shouldered, disillusioned, and broken.

Uncle was alone in his cabin when we arrived. Having determined to stay and minister to his tiny flock, he had long since sent his wife, Flora, Father's half-sister, on back to Ohio for the duration of the hostilities. In spite of his connection to us Browns and of having briefly harbored John and Jason after the Pottawatomie massacre, he had managed, by virtue of his simple decency and even-handedness in all his dealings, to escape persecution by the roving bands of Ruffians. There are all sorts of Christians, and Uncle Sam Adair was, to my mind, a simple Christian, for, although he hated slavery, he regarded all human beings as equally fallen from grace and equally capable of salvation. He was thus essentially pacifistic, like Jason, and did not believe that it was necessary to kill people in order to free others. From the beginning, this had separated Uncle from Father, although Uncle was not severe about it—except, of course, for a spell following the Pottawatomie killings. So while he did not exactly welcome us into his home that night, he nonetheless permitted us to enter and view Fred's body and make the necessary determinations for his burial.

The main room of the cabin was dimly lit by a single oil lantern and a low fire in the fireplace. We crowded in—Father, Salmon, Oliver, and I—and stood facing the long table where Uncle had laid out the body. He had put Fred's boots back on him and his shirt, buttoned to the throat, and had washed and shaved his face, so that Fred seemed almost to be sleeping. Fred in repose and in that flickering light had an angelic face, soft and pink and round, more like our mother's than Father's. There was something, not female, but decidedly feminine in Fred; in this he was not much like his father or brothers, we who seemed so wholly masculine, unyielding, and crude. Even when a stoical, solitary shepherd in Ohio, where he had resembled no man so much as John the Baptist in the wilderness, Fred had had about him a delicacy and finesse, a physical sweetness, that had set him apart from other men in a way that, after his self-mutilation, became even more pronounced than before: somehow, that most violent and most masculine act of self-reproach, in Fred's hand, had looked nearly gentle, and it had neither frightened nor embarrassed any of us. We had been saddened by it, of course, but not intimidated, as we would have been if one of our other brothers had done it.

I cannot say what Father thought or felt that night as he looked down on Fred's body. He did not weep, nor for a long while did he say anything. Always, as regards his children, Father's thoughts and feelings were strong, but they were also at times somewhat gnarled and stunted, as if our very existence were a chastizement to him. When a decent amount of time had passed in silence, Uncle cleared his throat and coughed nervously and said, "Would you like me to say the prayers for the lad, John?"

At first, Father did not respond; then he slowly shook his head no. I looked at his face and saw again that there was something newly broken in him: a piece of his mind that hitherto had been intact was now cast off from it, and he was no longer merely suppressing his emotions, his rage and grief, saving them for a later, more appropriate hour and place: his mind now was less a finely calibrated engine than a monument: it had become like chiseled stone, cut and carved in a permanent way, and I saw that what Father did not express he did not feel.

He stepped away from Fred's body and, passing between us, went to the door and said for Uncle to bury Fred here on the property and to mark it properly with his name and dates. "And say upon it the words of the apostle, 'For whom the Lord loveth he chasteneth, and scourgeth every son whom he receiveth.'" Then, abruptly, he asked Uncle how many horses he had.

"A pair," Uncle told him. "And I still have a mule."

"I will need them, along with your wagon. I'll replace them in a few days. The boys and I have an appointment with some Ruffians, and I don't want to disappoint them by arriving late." It was his intention, he said, to nip awhile at the flanks and heels of Reid's army, until we had ourselves fresh mounts and supplies, and then he would come back around, before heading into Africa.

Uncle looked at him with the same bewildered amazement as I had earlier. "*Africa*, John? What are you saying?"

"You will know it when I've done it," Father said. And at that I suddenly remembered his old plan, his Subterranean Passway into the South, and I finally understood his meaning and knew that for him, and for us, this dismal, murderous war in Kansas was nearly finished.

"Come on, boys," he said. "Your brother is with the Lord. You'll see him again soon enough." Then he stepped from the cabin into the night, and we trooped silently after.

V

21

There commenced then a lengthy period which in hindsight could be called the calm before the storm, although we did not know then that the storm was truly coming, even though Father increasingly predicted it. He never said the name of the place, Harpers Ferry, Virginia, the town down in the very heart of the Slavocracy where the federal government manufactured its famed Sharps rifles. He called it Africa. But we knew roughly the place he meant and that a new, more dangerous, and more consequential work on a different front was about to begin.

And having come to this point in my account, dear Miss Mayo, where begin the more publically known and recorded events in Father's life, let me declare that I wish only to tell you here what you cannot more easily and reliably learn elsewhere from the now hundreds of published histories and memoirs of those days half a century gone. My memory for facts, dates, names, and so on is not sharp; it never was: you don't need me for those anyhow. But my feelings and emotions, my whole sensibility, are today, as I scribble here in my cabin, the same as they were back then. I fear that is all I have now to offer you. It is as if I have throughout these intervening years been insensible to everything that has since then occurred or passed before me, and I am today in my brain and heart the very same man I was a half-century ago, a man suffering incoherently through each new day, whether in North Elba or Kansas or Virginia, with no sure knowledge of what the next day will bring. I am still a man stuck in that same, old killing game, a man who—having contrived to set his father in motion and having shaped matters in such a way as to set the Old Man onto a bloody track straight to perdition, or at least to purgatory—is condemned to follow him there and, if possible, with these words, with the truthfulness of this account, with this confession of my intentions, my desires, and my secret acts, finally to release him. I want Father's soul to be free of me at last, and mine to be free of him, regardless of where from this purgatory we each afterwards must go.

I wonder sometimes if you can understand this. And if you can accept and make use of it. Oh, I know that there is a public reality and a private reality and that my best use—for you, for me, and for all those lingering ghosts as well—has been to keep to the private and ignore the rest. But even so, I do want my story, if possible, to impinge upon the public reality, on history, and I mean here and there to tell it accordingly. For instance, it has become almost a commonplace in recent years to say that Father, like many Christians of his generation, began as a principled, religious-minded young Northern man agitated by Negro slavery in the South and racialism everywhere, and that, like many such men, he understandably became in middle-age an actively engaged opponent of slavery and racialism, but that in his old age he changed, suddenly and inexplicably, into a free-booting guerilla, whence he moved swiftly on to become a terrorist and finally, astonishingly, a martyr. Thus, looking back through a glass colored by the Civil War, most Americans nowadays find his actions incomprehensible, and they call him mad, or wish to. So while I'm here to tell you certain things that you cannot otherwise know, I also wish to remind you that Father's progression from activist to martyr, his slow march to willed disaster, can be viewed, not as a descent into madness, but as a reasonable progression—especially if one consider the political strength of those who in those days meant to keep chattel slavery the law of the land. Remember, all-out war between the North and the South was unthinkable to us: due to an ancient, deeply ingrained racialism, any war undertaken by the citizens of the North for the purpose of freeing an enslaved people whose skins were black seemed a pure impossibility. We believed instead that the Northerners—when it finally came clear to them what we already knew, that the South now wholly owned the government of the nation—would simply secede from the Union, leaving behind a nation in which a huge number of our fellow Americans and all their unborn progeny were chattel slaves: literal, unrepatriated prisoners-of-war. Before that could happen, we meant to liberate as many of them as possible. And failing that, failing to free our prisoners-of-war prior to the eventual and, as it seemed to us, inevitable cessation of hostilities between the Northern and Southern states, the one side cowardly and the other evil, we meant to slay every slaveholder we could lay our hands on. And those whose throats we could not reach directly or whose heads we could not find in the sights of our guns, we would terrorize from afar, hoping thereby to rouse them to bloody acts of reprisal, which might in turn straighten the spines of our Northern citizenry and bring a few of them over to our side.

We did not want the North to secede from the Union and make its own slave-free republic or join with Canada in some new, colonized relation to Olde England or even make with Canada an independent, slave-free nation of the north. And it never once occurred to us that the Southerners would leave the Union. They didn't have to. They already owned the entire machinery of government in Washington and in those years, the late '50s, were merely solidifying and making permanent their control of it by carrying slavery into the western territories. In our own way, with no knowledge of the coming Civil War, we were fighting to preserve the American Republic.

But I was speaking of my father's gradual progression from anti-slavery agitator all the way to terrorist, guerilla captain, and martyr, how it seemed—not in hindsight, but at the time of its occurrence—a reasonable and moral response to the times and to the deep, continuous frustration they created. Father may have been the first to resort to pure terrorism for political and military purposes, but the wisdom and necessity of it were early on as plain to the other side as to us: they never needed our example to inspire them to butcher innocent civilians. And without Father, that's what I would have been, merely an innocent civilian, wifeless, childless, and alone, a Northern bachelor tending his flock of merinos out on the rolling, grassy shoulder of the Marais des Cygnes a few miles from the abolitionist enclave of Osawatomie—easy pickings for one of the roving, drunken bands of Ruffians, who would have treated me as they treated so many other isolated Free-State farmers and herdsmen: they'd have shot me dead, burned my cabin, stolen off my sheep and horse, and ridden on to the next farmstead.

Sometimes I think it would have been better for me, for Father, for our entire family, for *everyone*, if it had happened that way. Better for everyone, perhaps, if, back in Springfield, when Father gave me leave to go my own way and not return to North Elba, I had gone. "Just go, Owen, follow your elder brothers to Ohio and beyond, if that's what you prefer, or follow the elephant and go to Californ-i-ay in search of gold, if that interests you!" If I had taken him at his word and, with his permission, had forsaken what he called my *duty*, so many terrible things would never have happened: the death of Lyman Epps; Fred's self-mutilation and migration with me to Kansas; and Father's, and Salmon's, Oliver's, and Henry Thompson's, migration there, too, for without me and Fred in tow, John and Jason and their families surely would have given up that first cruel winter and come home to Ohio; and then there would have been no Pottawatomie killings and possibly no war at all in the Kansas Territory, which in '58 would have come into the Union as a slave state instead of a free, an event surely to be followed by the secession of most of the northern states and their probable, eventual union with Canada. There would have been no debacle at Harpers Ferry. No Civil War.

Think of it! Father would have ended his days peacefully in the manner he so often wished, as a farmer and preacher in North Elba, aiding and instructing his white and Negro neighbors, dying in old age in his bed, surrounded by his beloved family, and buried in the shade of his favorite mountain, Tahawus, the Cloudsplitter.

Is it ridiculous and grandiose to speculate this way? To think that so much depends upon so little? Miss Mayo, I think it's no more ridiculous or grandiose than to believe that our trivial lives here on earth are watched over and fated by an all-seeing, all-knowing God. But cannot the law of cause-and-effect be rationally thought to operate from the ground up, as well as from the top down? And if there is an order to the universe, then all our affairs here on earth are, surely, inextricably linked one to the other. I believe that the universe is like a desert, and each of our lives is a grain of sand that touches three or four adjacent to it, and when one grain turns in the wind or is moved or adjusted even slightly, those next to it will move also, and they in turn will shift the others next to each of them, and so on, all across the vast, uncountable billions of grains in the desert, until over time a great storm arises and alters the face of the planet. So why should I forbid myself from believing that my single action, or even my inaction, one day in my youth in my father's warehouse in Springfield, Massachusetts, altered history? And that it was instrumental in shaping, not only my destiny, but Father's, too, and my entire family's, and even, if I may be forgiven this vision, the destiny of an entire people?

Which is why I did what I did—why I returned that fall from Springfield to the farm in North Elba, why I went there to do my *duty*.

For even if we cannot know the ultimate consequences of our actions or inactions, we must nonetheless behave as if they do have ultimate consequences. No little thing in our lives is without meaning; never mind that we can never know it ourselves. I did what I did, my duty, in order to free the slaves. I did it to change history. It is finally that simple. My immediate motives, of course, at every step of the way were like everyone else's, even Father's—mixed, often confused and selfish, and frequently unknown even to me until many years later. But so long as I was doing my duty, so long as I was acting on the principles that I had learned when a child, then I was bending my life to free the slaves: I was shaping and curving it like a barrel stave that would someday fit with other lives similarly bent, so as to construct a vessel capable of measuring out and transporting into the future the history of our time and place. It would be a history capable of establishing forever the true nature and meaning of the nineteenth century in the United States of America, and thus would my tiny life raise a storm that would alter the face of the planet. Father's God-fearing, typological vision of the events that surrounded us then was not so different from mine. My vision may have been secular and his Biblical, but neither was materialistic. They were both, perhaps, versions of Mr. Emerson's grand, over-arching, transcendental vision, just not so clearly or poetically expressed. At least in my case. In Father's, I'm not so sure, for the Bible is nothing if not clear and poetical.

In a sense, I suppose that what I am inscribing on these pages is the Secret History of John Brown. You may, of course, do with it what you wish, or do nothing with it, if it seems worthless to you and Professor Villard. As I have said, we each will have very different uses for it anyhow, uses shaped by those to whom we each imagine we are telling our respective tales. For you and the professor, it is told to present and future generations of students of the history of nineteenth-century

America; for me, it is being told to the dead, the long dead and buried companions of my past. And told especially to my dead father.

Your history of John Brown, however, will be of no use to the dead. It is for the living and the unborn: you are in the business of creating received knowledge. I am in the business of coming along behind and correcting it. I remind you of this for several reasons, but mostly so that you will understand that what I leave out of my account is all that I see no reason to correct or to enlarge upon. Simply put, I accept the truth of whatever is absent from these pages.

And for that reason, you will not find here any further description of the war in Kansas, even though it continued to burn beyond the so-called Battle of Osawatomie for fully another year and a half, before finally flickering down to a charred pile of ash in the winter of '58, with the Free-State forces arrived at last in exhausted ascendancy. By then, Father's and my attentions were elsewhere. His attention was on the Eastern sources of funding for his African Campaign, as he had come to call it; mine was on the recruitment and training, in our secret encampment at Tabor, Iowa, of the young men who would follow Father into Africa, and the long, broody wait for him to signal that the moment to attack had at last arrived. Also not here: Father's lengthy visits and planning sessions during the spring and summer of '57 and all throughout '58 with Frederick Douglass in Rochester, New York, and Gerrit Smith in Peterboro; and, over in Massachusetts, his fiery speeches at Springfield, Worcester, Medford, Concord, and Boston; and his stay in Concord with the distinguished authors Messrs. Emerson, Thoreau, Higginson, and Sanborn, all of whom have since published what I assume to be truthful accounts of Father's appearance, words, and deportment there. By then, his apotheosis was nearly completed anyhow, and he was to everyone he met a grand, Cromwellian figure transfigured in the glow of their lofty, optimistic thought. But I was not myself present at any of those meetings so cannot know how, in fact, he behaved.

I do not include here anything that I myself know nothing of or know only through hearsay. For instance, Father's journey to Canada in April and May of '58, where, at the famous Chatham Convention of Negro leaders, he first presented to the public, as it were, his plan for the Subterranean Passway and obtained from the most prominent Negroes, Frederick Douglass and the Reverends Loguen and Garnet and Harriet Tubman and others of that radical ilk, the same sort of trust and financial support that he had earlier secured in private from the radical whites in New York and New England. It was at Chatham that he recruited into our little army its first Negro member, Osborn Anderson. Later, of course, as you may know by now, there were four other Negroes who went the full route with us, courageous, doomed men—the mulatto Lewis Leary and his nephew John Copeland, who had been a student at Oberlin College in Ohio; and the splendid Dangerfield Newby; and Frederick Douglass's friend and valet, Shields Green, of whom, despite his willingness to abandon Mr. Douglass and follow Father, I had no particularly high opinion, and of that I may later write. I have at this moment no desire to puncture Shields's somewhat inflated reputation, for he was young and ignorant and surely did not realize what he had let himself in for, when he left his protector and went down with Father into "the steel trap," as Mr. Douglass called it. He died horribly. One must, as long as one remains alive, forgive the dead everything.

There is, of course, the well-known story of Father's seeking out and recruiting in New York City Mr. Hugh Forbes, the conceited British journalist who had accompanied us on shipboard from Boston to Liverpool and by carriage to London during our ill-fated voyage abroad. That sordid story has been told often elsewhere, told more by Father's enemies than by his friends, probably because of its tendency to portray Father as a deluded old man or, at best, as disastrously naive. I'm reluctant to enter it here, however, because Forbes, too, like Shields

Green, may be dead by now, and I had few dealings with him myself and from the start viewed him as a callow, cynical, pompous man and a dissembler. But then, I was never so innocent as Father, especially when it came to a certain type of man, of which Forbes was a prime example—the carefully reticent, smooth-talking fellow with a casual claim to experiences and knowledge that, to Father, were cosmopolitan, which is to say, European. And because he did not boast in the usual loud American way of having fought alongside Mazzini and Garibaldi in Italy and of composing a military handbook for the Austrian army and reporting on the cataclysmic events in Europe in '48 for the New York Herald and his own periodical, The European, but instead implied and insinuated them into conversation in the educated British way, the Old Man, the rough-cut Yankee auto-didact, believed him and hired him on as our only salaried recruit. He even commissioned the velvety fellow with the rank of colonel and sent him west to Tabor to drill and train his troop of young, ragtag volunteers, all of whom by then were hardened veterans of the Kansas campaign and needed, not drilling exercises, but weaponry, supplies, and more fighting men. We certainly did not need a man like Forbes, Colonel Forbes, telling us what to do.

Little matter, for he did not turn up in Iowa for months anyhow, and when he finally arrived, he was mainly taken up with the composition of his military handbook for the coming American anti-slavery revolution, which, thanks to Father, he was convinced was imminent, a volume that, as soon as it was properly published, he expected to see purchased and eagerly read by all Americans, north and south, and by Europeans, too. He expected this book to make his personal fortune.

Though Forbes was the first, he was the most transparent of the many men who tried to exploit Father for personal, financial gain. There was also the growing number of journalists who wrote for the Eastern newspapers and periodicals and now followed Father everywhere and sent back to their editors lavishly embellished accounts of the Old Man's adventures in Kansas and his public appearances in New York and New England. Father had taken to traveling under the name of Shubel Morgan again, ostensibly to conceal his identity from federal officers still seeking to arrest him for his actions in Kansas, and wore the long white beard with which after his death he was so famously portrayed; but under any name and in whatever disguise, the comings and goings of Osawatomie Brown were by now well-known to the press, for he had become a colorful character, one whom all Americans enjoyed reading about, regardless of their views on slavery. With these journalists I have little quarrel, however, for quite as effectively as they exploited him, Father exploited them back by using their vivid, exaggerated stories of his military exploits and his spiritual and moral clarity to advertise and confirm his own accounts of his bravery, personal sacrifice, and character.

Most of the other profiteers—at least until later, after Harpers Ferry, when the sale of Father's personal letters and effects and the odd, cast-off article of clothing or weapon became as lucrative as the sale of portions of the True Cross—were small fellows, merchants, mainly, and tradesmen out to extract from Father's purse as much as the market would bear for guns and bullets, sabers and saddles and other war supplies. Exploiting a market inflated by the Old Man's needs for secrecy and speed of delivery, they picked Father's pocket, which had been filled and re-filled again and again by his now-loyal cadre of Eastern gentlemen of means, men who had finally decided that Father was right, that the war against slavery would have to be carried into Africa, and Osawatomie Brown was the only man to do it. They were Mr. Gerrit Smith, as always, and Dr. Howe and Messrs. Lawrence, Stearns, Sanborn, and Higginson. Good men, all, if not personally courageous. And I do not fault them for denying Father in the weeks and months immediately following the uproar at Harpers Ferry, any more than one can fault Peter for denying Christ. Later, in the aftermath of the Civil War, they did return to his side and glorified his memory with more than appropriate praise.

Forbes, though, was a cat with a different coat. And I'm reminded by that figure that he wore a green velvet jacket and fringed doeskin boots and affected a cane with a silver knob. He even sported an ostrich feather in his hatband. All of which made him look ridiculous out there in Iowa, especially when he pulled a face and moaned about the fate of his poor wife and babes, who were supposedly living in abject poverty back in Paris, France. He claimed that their sacrifice was made so that he could continue with his noble mission of assisting and guiding Osawatomie Brown in the great attempt to liberate the American slaves. He declared that he was personally re-writing American history.

He actually said this to me himself. It was out in Tabor, in April of '59, when we were holed up at the farm of a Quaker supporter of Father's, a man originally from Indiana who believed that we were preparing, not for war, but for a massive flight of Negro refugees out of the South—which was essentially true, although our intended means to foment that flight were unlikely to have met with any Quaker's approval. Perhaps, like so many self-proclaimed pacifists gone bone-weary of battling the pro-slavers' endless stratagems and violence, he had intuited our true plans and welcomed them, but did not wish to be told of them in any detail. Regardless, all that winter and into the spring, he had allowed our shabby troop of sometimes twenty, sometimes fewer than ten, to ensconce itself secretly in his barn by night and train in his fields by day. There Forbes had us marching up and down like toy soldiers, mainly it seemed for the pleasure he got from hearing his own British gentleman's voice bark orders at American country-boys.

I remember the April afternoon when, all sweaty and covered with dirt and seeds and thistles from the fields and gullies that we had spent the day conquering for our colonel, I left the other men and, approaching Forbes, asked if I could speak with him privately. He was seated in the shade of a cottonwood tree on a stool he had borrowed from the Quaker's kitchen and, without looking up from the papers on his lap, said to me, "It's appropriate, Lieutenant, when requesting permission to speak, to salute your superior officer and address him by rank."

He had been with us only a week by then, but already I was sick of him, and the other men downright despised him and were starting to blame Father for his presence among us. John Kagi had declared the night before that he was ready to shoot the fellow dead, and only my loyalty to Father had kept me from running him straight off the place myself. That and my fear that, if he were overtly resisted by us, he would at once turn on us and reveal Father's plans to the federal authorities—which, as is now well-known, he eventually did. It is true: months before it took place, Forbes came close to ending the raid on Harpers Ferry. Luckily—or, as it turned out, perhaps unluckily—no one in the government or the press believed then that any man, not even the notorious terrorist Osawatomie Brown, would contemplate mounting a privately financed armed raid on a federal weapons manufactory and depot in the fortified heart of the South. Thus, after Forbes turned on us and until the raid itself finally occurred, his words bore no credence with anyone on either side, which is what saved us for another day. By then, of course, he was seen as a fellow conspirator himself and was pursued by the government and fled into England, where he may indeed be living today, an old dandy in doeskin boots, dining out on stories of his early involvement with the famous American anti-slavery guerilla leader and martyr, Osawatomie Brown. I suppose it's on that possibility that I criticize him now.

Out there in Iowa, despite his constant admonitions, I neither saluted Forbes nor addressed him by rank. I said straight out that the men and I were faithful to Father and to our common cause, but I could no longer assure him that one or more of the men would not shoot him. I emphasized, so as to make my own position clear, that his murder would be a betrayal of Father's wishes and detrimental to our common cause. His murder by one of us could undo us altogether. I wanted him to know who and what were keeping him alive.

"You're quite serious, Brown."

"Quite, Forbes."

He still had not looked up at me. "You know what I'm writing here, Brown?"

I knew very well: he had held forth on the virtues of his tract numerous times. "A military manual," I said.

"Yes. But more than that, Brown. It's a manual, all right, but one composed specifically for the use of men fighting to end slavery in America. And like all such manuals, it's a history of the time and place of its own composition. D' you understand that, Brown?"

"You mean it's about us. And about you."

"Precisely. And the chapter I'm presently engaged in writing is called 'The American Garibaldi,' which is concerned with nothing less than the necessity and means of transforming ordinary citizens into soldiers. Of transforming peasants—ignorant farmers, laborers, woodcutters, and the like—into disciplined soldiers. Now, what do you suppose General Garibaldi would have done if one of his Italian lieutenants had come up and spoken to him as you have just spoken to me?"

"Well, Forbes, I don't rightly know."

"No. No, you don't. That's the point. Y'see, I know things that you don't. Which is precisely why your father hired me on and commissioned me with the rank of colonel." Here he digressed awhile to complain of Father's not having paid him as he had promised, along with some sorrowful reminders of poor Mrs. Forbes and his hungry babes in Paris, France, until at last he returned to the subject at hand—mutiny.

"General Garibaldi," he said, "would have instructed his lieutenant, as I am you, that it was the *lieutenant's* responsibility, not the general's, to put down any potential mutiny. And if the lieutenant could not do it, then the lieutenant himself would be regarded as mutinous and would be peremptorily shot by firing squad."

I looked back at the boys lounging in the field behind me and could scarcely keep a straight face at the thought of Forbes ordering them to stand in formation for my execution. "He'd have said that, eh? The general."

"Yes, Brown. And then, just as I myself am about to do, he would have stood and left his lieutenant to ponder that statement, and he would have brooked no further discussion on the subject of mutiny." Forbes closed his writing book and, as predicted by himself, stood and walked off towards the barn, leaving me, like General Garibaldi's lieutenant, to ponder his statement.

Forbes surprised me, though, for that was the last I ever saw of him. I said nothing to the men of my strange conversation with our colonel, and after a while we all wandered back to the barn and washed and, as usual, prepared our frugal evening meal of hoecakes and stew, until finally someone noticed that Forbes was nowhere about. His horse was gone, and all his gear. "Good riddance," Kagi muttered, and all concurred. Without meaning to, I had scared the fellow off. He took himself so seriously that I had taken him a bit seriously myself, or perhaps I might have humored and endured him longer and spared us much risk afterwards.

Later, I learned where he had gone—east to New York City, thence to Washington, where he had commenced his vain campaign to betray Father to our enemies. In time, Father learned of Forbes's failed attempts to convince the Secretary of War and the various newspapers of our plan—thanks to a flurry of frightened letters from friendly abolitionists in the War Department and the journalist Mr. Redpath, who at once told Messrs. Smith and Higginson and Dr. Howe. Typically, they panicked, but to the Old Man, Forbes's attempted betrayal was a positive development, as it had created amongst our supporters a greater urgency for the battle to begin at once. And, further, the peculiarly deaf ears of the War Secretary and the others to whom Forbes had spoken only confirmed in Father's mind that God was still his protector, and by winnowing Forbes out, the Lord had merely been correcting Father's error in having judged the man useful years earlier when they first met.

In his letter to me, summoning me and the rest of the troop to disperse to our respective homes and await his marching orders, he told me all this. He ended his long letter by writing, *I believe that the Lord was merely testing my acumen, as well as my faith, back then, as He always does. And in the unpleasant matter of Mr. Forbes, the Lord hath found me sadly wanting. But now, thanks to the steady increase in my faith and trust in Him, the Almighty hath again protected me from my own folly. Now, come directly home to North Elba, son,* he wrote. *The Lord is making it so that we must act quickly!*

And so, once again, this time for the last time, I came through the Cascade Notch from the wilderness village of Keene into North Elba and, out there on the freshly greening Plains of Abraham, set up on the rise just beyond the bulky shadow of Father's beloved Mount Tahawus, sighted our family farm. So sweetly self-contained and four-square it seemed in the pale June light that I dared not recall to my mind my gloomy reasons for having returned here—for it was merely to say goodbye, perhaps forever, to my beloved brothers, those who would not accompany Father and me south, and to my dear sisters and stepmother, who had already endured so much for us and would soon endure unimaginably more, and to the place itself, where, to all intents and purposes, I had grown in my cumbersome way into manhood.

I think back to those olden days now as I thought back to them then and approach the doorway of the house as I approached it then, with fear and literal trembling, for so much has changed in the intervening years, the years since the death of Lyman Epps and my flight into the West and my return today, so much has changed in the world at large, and yet I myself have not been altered—I am still that same, half-cracked man, Owen Brown, lurching forward into history on the heels of his father, resolving all his private, warring emotions and conflicted passions in the larger, public war against slavery, making the miserable, inescapable violence of his temperament appear useful and principled by aiming it, not at himself, where perhaps it properly belonged, but at his father's demonized opponents. For otherwise, how would I have turned out but as a suicide?

And having admitted that, I suddenly understand what must follow upon the completion of my confession! For then I will, at last, have no longer a reason to live. I will be ready to become a ghost myself, so as to replace in purgatory the long-suffering ghosts this confession has been designed expressly to release.

Dear Miss Mayo, since I wrote the lines above, I have been briefly away from my table, searching through the rubble of my cabin for my old revolver, my sidearm in Kansas and at Harpers Ferry and the long, furtive years of flight afterwards. I located it at last in a cache of Father's letters from '55 and '56 (which I had previously overlooked and promise now to send to you when I finally gather and send on all the scattered pages of this sorry, disheveled account), and when I came upon it there in a corner beneath my cot—along with some two dozen rounds of ammunition—I confess that I felt a strange, new kind of glee. I know not what else to call it than glee: it is a peculiar, altogether unfamiliar emotion to me.

I have placed the revolver, my old Colt .45, now cleaned and loaded, upon the writing table, and every time I come to the end of a sentence, I look up from the page and see the weapon there, waiting patiently as an old friend set to take me on a journey, and I feel again that exotic, anticipatory glee.

It is late summer—here and everywhere that my mind goes—and the mowing has evidently been interrupted by this morning's rain, and the deserted fields glisten silvery in the sun as I pass along between them, on horseback then, in my mind and memory now, making my slow way through the notch and over the Plains towards the farm. The storm clouds have broken and blown away to the east, leaving great, spreading shreds and swaths of deep blue sky. Off to my left and behind me looms the craggy granite peak whose very name I cannot let enter my mind without Father's dark face also entering there, for I have come over the years so to associate the two, as if each, mountain and man, were a portrait of the other and the two, reduced to their simplest outlines, were a single, runic inscription which I must, before I die, decipher, or I will not know the meaning of my own existence or its worth.

There is no one in the fields and no other person on the narrow dirt track coming my way towards the farm or from it towards me, and no cattle or kine or horses grazing in the pastures and pens. No dogs and none of the fine, blooded, merino sheep whose dams and sires Father brought up from Springfield in the spring of '50, when we first settled here. No smoke rises from the chimneys of the house or from the tanning shed or from Lyman's old forge, and except for the thin rattle of the frigid waters of the Au Sable over rock in the wooded valley below and the shudder of the breeze amongst the topmost branches of the ancient pines towering on the slopes above me, there is no sound—no one is cutting wood or hammering nails anywhere in earshot, no one digs a well or a pit or ditch, no one opens or closes a door or a window. Even the birds—silent as ghosts!

Father wrote that he would meet me at the farm, that we would all meet in North Elba—we in the family who will go down into Africa together: my brother Watson, only twenty-four years old, who returned here to the farm after his turn in Kansas and Iowa ahead of me and who will die miserably in Father's arms of gunshot wounds in less than four months' time; and our youngest brother, Oliver, a boy of twenty-one and already battle-hardened from the Kansas campaign, but bookish withal and about to marry a daughter of the Brewster family nearby, a girl who will be a widow before turning twenty; and two of my brothers-in-law from the Thompson clan, William and Dauphin, whose elder brother Henry sacrificed all he dared in Kansas and returned to North Elba over a year ago to recover from his wound at Black Jack and live again as a farmer and husband to our sister Ruth and thus will not die in Virginia with his brothers. The others, sixteen of them—although Father thought there would be thirty or forty or even more—will join us when we ride south, or they have already been sent there by the Old Man to reconnoiter and await our arrival: John Kagi, who even now is in Virginia, ascertaining the number and quality of the forces that will oppose us; and John Cook, disguised as an itinerant schoolteacher, obtaining and fitting out for our *rendez-vous* the soon-to-be-famous Kennedy farmhouse on the heights north of Harpers Ferry, the place where we will make our headquarters during the weeks leading up to our assault on the armory and town below. Brothers John and Jason, with their families in Ohio, will not join us in battle, Jason on principle and John, against his principles, out of fear. Brother Salmon, at Father's orders and despite his loud protestations, has been stationed here at the farm to care for Mary and our sisters and to manage the affairs of the family, which the Old Man knows will become exceedingly complex after the raid, regardless of its outcome.

But on the day of my arrival at the farm, no one is there to greet me; no one reaches out to embrace me and welcome me home. Shadows flash across the ground at my feet, as the broken, silver-edged clouds pass over the house and break and merge and break again—the earth keeps spinning on its spine and rolling around the sun, whilst here on the ground all is still, fixed in time and place like a lacquered insect impaled upon a pin: the lane off the roadway; the barn and outbuildings; the house itself. And there, yonder in the center of the yard, is Father's rock, head-high and the size of a room. The chunk of dark gray granite sits settled upon the ground as if placed there for no other purpose than to mark the eventual gravesite of Father himself and of my brothers Watson and Oliver, of the Thompson boys, William and Dauphin; and to memorialize the impetuous John Kagi, the noble Aaron Stevens, who will take four shots in the body before he falls, and John Cook, who will be captured in the Pennsylvania woods a few miles north of Harpers Ferry and dragged back to Virginia to be hung alongside Father and the rest; of the quick-tempered boy from Maine Charlie Tidd, and Jeremiah Anderson, avenging himself upon his grandfather, a Virginia slaveholder, and Albert Hazlett, who followed the Old Man to victory in Kansas and will follow him to the scaffold in Virginia; and of the stoical Edwin Coppoc of Ohio and his younger brother, Barclay, and the free Negro John Copeland, as intelligent and articulate as a Brown; and of the Canadian spiritualist Stewart Taylor, and Will Leeman, the youngest of the raiders in our band, a Maine boy who went to work at fourteen in a shoe factory and at seventeen came out to Kansas for no other reason than to fight alongside the great Osawatomie Brown; and of Osborn Anderson, the Negro printer who joined Father in Canada, and Frank Meriam of Massachusetts, and Lewis Leary, the mulatto man who said he was descended from the Lost Colonists of Roanoke Isle, and the tall, handsome Dangerfield Newby, an escaped slave whose abiding hope for the raid was to free his wife and children, but who will die of a six-inch spike shot into his throat by a pro-slaver's musket; and of Frederick Douglass's man

Shields Green, whom we called Emperor, a man born a slave, who freed his body and gave it over to the cause, but never quite freed his mind. . . . There sits the huge, rough Adirondack boulder, a chunk of the mountain Tahawus, ready to memorialize the short lives and violent deaths of the men whom I will ride into battle with and then betray. It will be their ghostly watchtower, the place where they will gather together afterwards and wait in silence through the long years, as winter snows blow down from Canada and sweep across the Plains of Abraham and as spring rains wash and thaw the land and soften it for the grasses and flowers of summer and as the autumn leaves catch and collect in low, moldering piles. Great-Grandfather John Brown's Yankee slate marker leans against the rock, brought north from Connecticut, as Father long intended, to remind all men and women of the unmarked graves of the old Revolutionary War hero and of brother Fred, whose dates have been freshly cut into it and whose body lies beneath Kansas soil, forever lost to us: both those accusatory souls will linger with the others here as well, for it matters not where lie today the bits of bone and the shreds of cloth they once wore: their spirits have all returned to this one spot, this cold, gray altar, here to be stared and wondered at by casual passers-by, to be prayed over by those who would come out and pay homage to John Brown and his brave men, and to haunt and chastize me for all the remaining years of my life, even to today, this long, ongoing day of my inevitable return. It is here, before this stone altar, that I must make my final confession and my sacrifice.

Cold stove, aprons drooped across chair-backs, muddy boots stacked in the rack by the back entry: I stand in the dead center of the room and cock my head like a hunted animal listening for the hunter; no, more like the hunter poised for the sound of his prey. But I hear nothing, not even a mouse in the wall or a squirrel skittering across the cedar-shake roof. No brother or sister turns in sleep in a narrow cot in the loft overhead; no one sighs and peers from the small, square window up there. There is not a breath, human or otherwise, to ripple the still, funereal air of this house.

Perhaps I have unknowingly arrived home on the Sabbath, the Lord's one day of rest, when, after six days of tending to our puny needs, He commands us to tend His. Perhaps everyone has departed for the small white church in the settlement below, there to pray for strength now and divine grace at the moment of death and salvation and eternal life thereafter.

Everlasting life—what a horrid thought! Although sometimes I have believed that it would not be a terrible thing to be *killed* eternally. To be slain again and again, until I no longer feared death. Then life would be the illusion, and dying and being born again to die again the only reality: the world, which has no experience anyhow at being me, would simply go on being itself. I might become good, finally: a perfect man, like a Hindoo saint, with no stern, bearded God lording it over me, enticing me with guilt and shame and principles and duty, and making goodness an irresistible obligation, impossible to meet, and not simply man's natural condition.

Ah, but I was born and raised a Christian, not a Hindoo! I can only glimpse these things but now and then and cannot sustain such a perverse, foreign view of life and death for longer than it takes to write it down here. Worse, I am a Christian without a God, a fallen man without a Saviour. I am a believer without belief.

I'm unable to say how long I have stood here in the house thinking these strange thoughts, but the shadows have grown long, and the room has nearly fallen into darkness, when finally, for the first time since my arrival home, I hear the sound of another living creature: the slow hoofbeats of a horse, then of several horses approaching the farm at a walk, and the sharp bark of a dog—from the high, thin sound of it, a collie dog—and the laughter and easy talk of human beings! From the window I see, coming through the dusk, my family: there at the front is Father, white-bearded and looking ancient in the face, though still as straight-gaited as ever; and my stepmother, Mary, and my sisters seated up in the wagon; and my younger brothers and brothers-in-law and sisters-in-law, and with them, afoot and on horseback and riding in a trap, half a dozen more, white people and Negroes both, our longtime north-country neighbors and friends coming gaily along the lane from the settlement as if from a holiday outing.

Suddenly, the empty vessel has been filled, and out of invisibility and silence, I have been made visible to myself, and audible! I call out to them, joyous and grateful for the simple fact of their existence elsewhere than in my mind and memory, and rush pell-mell from the house to the yard and greet them there. These beautiful, utterly familiar faces and bodies are real, are tangible! And here, at last, clasped to the bosom of family and friends, I am one with others again! As when I was a child and my mother had not died yet. As when Father had not begun to block out the sun and replace it with his own cold disk, as when he had not cast me in his permanent shadow. They all touch me, and they even embrace me, and they say how glad they are to have me with them again. Though nothing is forgotten, all is forgiven! Even Susan Epps is here amongst them, and she has beside her, holding tightly to her skirt, a small boy—her son, Lyman's son, emblem of her love for him and his forgiveness of me, for that is how she presents the little boy to me, saying simply, proudly, "I have a son to make your acquaintance, Owen Brown," and that is how I receive him, and he me.

Sister Ruth declares that she, too, will soon have a child to make my acquaintance, a nephew or niece, and there will be others coming along before long, for here are Oliver and his pretty young bride, Miss Martha Brewster, who have this very afternoon become husband and wife! A wedding, one I could have attended myself, Ruth tells me, had

I arrived in time or had they known of the imminence of my return so as to have held off the wedding for a few hours. But no one knew when Owen would appear, except Father, she says, and nods approvingly at the Old Man, who kept insisting that Owen would get home in time for Oliver's and Lizzie's wedding, and as usual Father was not altogether wrong, she adds, and not altogether right, and everyone laughs at that, for we are delighted when Ruth teases the Old Man, the only one of us who can do it and make him blush with pleasure from it and not scowl.

Mary, my dear stepmother, I first hold close to my face and then at arms' length, so that I can peer into her large brown eyes and see my own face reflected back and know that, even though I can never love her as she wishes and Father asks, she nonetheless loves me as powerfully as any mother can love her natural son and feels no loss for herself or imbalance in the exchange, only sorrow for me. My brothers and brothers-in-law and my old friends from Timbuctoo and the village of North Elba, all in the shy way of northcountry farmers, shake my hand and clap me on the shoulder and ask me to say by what route, by what roads and ferries and canals, came I home all the way from I-o-way; and how were the other boys, asks Salmon, when I passed through Ohio; and their families, asks Watson, and our uncles and aunts and cousins in Ohio; and did I visit and pray over Grandfather Brown's grave in Akron, asks sister Annie, the sweetest and most pious of Father's daughters and of Grandfather Brown's granddaughters. And to all I say yes and yes and yes: I have done everything that you would have me do, been everywhere you wanted me to go, said what you wished to have said yourselves, and now here I am standing amongst you, your beloved son, brother, uncle, dear friend, and I want nothing of life now but never again to leave this place and these people. I see the newly married and the recently familied and the several generations rising and all this beautiful, high meadowland and forest that surrounds us, and I permit myself the glimmering thought that someday soon I will ask to marry Susan Epps and raise her son and make for us a farm here on the Plains of Abraham. I will make of this joyful moment a starting point for a long, happy, and fruitful life, instead of making it the mocking, ironic end of a life that was short and bitter and barren.

Would that not be a wonderful way to end this story? With one wedding just finished and another soon to come—the third son of John Brown to marry the Negro widow of his dearest friend, to raise together his friend's, her late husband's, namesake into manhood here in the Adirondack wilderness, the three of them, one small family free of all the cruel symbolism of race and the ancient curse of slavery, a white man and a Negro woman and child held dear by a family and community that see them and deal with them solely as family and friends and fellow citizens?

Fantasy, delusion, dream! A guilty white man's chimera, that's all. It lasts but a second. It lasts until Father comes forward now and places his heavy hands onto my shoulders, and I am suddenly ashamed of my hope and can no longer look at Susan or her son or at anyone else. Only at Father: at his cold eyes, gray as granite. I feel him press his hands down with great force, as if he has settled a yoke upon my shoulders and wishes me to kneel under its weight. And so I do, I bend and kneel, and in Jesus' name he prays over me, thanking the Almighty for bringing me safely home, so that I can keep and fulfill my covenant with the Lord and can now go out from this blessed place and commence the great and terrible work that He hath ordained for us.

Amen, he says; and Amen says everyone else; and Amen say I, too.

22

We wake in darkness and long for light, and when the light comes, we wait for darkness to return, so that we can descend the rickety ladder from our crowded, windowless attic and warm our hands at the kitchen fire and walk about the yard awhile. We go out of the house either in pairs or alone, so as not to draw the attention of some errant nighttime traveler unexpectedly making his late way past the old Kennedy farm, someone who from the road would surely note, even in darkness, the presence of a crowd of ten or more men milling about the stone-and-white-clapboard house and wonder why they were there. The house is surrounded by woods, however, and is fairly remote, with the public road in front leading only and indirectly to the country village of Boonesborough, so that a pair of men or a man alone, if he remain silent, can walk back and forth before the house unseen for a spell, can stretch his cramped limbs and breathe the cool, fresh air of outdoors for the first time in twenty-four hours, and from the road no one not warned of a stranger's presence would see him. Even if by accident the traveler did catch a glimpse of a stranger or two standing in the yard, he would think nothing amiss, for Dr. Kennedy's family, now removed to Baltimore, has often rented its old, abandoned family farm to landless seasonal farmers, which was how John Kagi, when he contracted to rent the place for us, represented Father and his several sons—a Mr. Isaac Smith and his boys, from up near Chambersburg, Pennsylvania, looking for good Virginia farmland to buy and perhaps at the same time to graze and fatten a few head of livestock to butcher and sell in the fall to the citizens and armory workers of Harpers Ferry. Kagi, who seems almost to believe his lies himself, has a gift for story-telling.

The town of Harpers Ferry and the rifle and musket manufactories and the federal arsenal are situated in a deep, narrow gorge three miles south of here, on a spit of terraced, flat-rock land, where the Shenandoah cuts between two high, wooded ridges and empties into the Potomac. At first sight, it seems an unlikely place to make and store an army's weapons, vulnerable to attack and siege from the high bluffs on both sides of both rivers. But Father has explained that none of our nation's enemies could attack the town, so far from sea, without first having captured Washington, fifty miles downriver, or Richmond and Baltimore. The last place from which the federal government would expect Harpers Ferry to be attacked is by land, he says, smiling, and only our fellow Americans could manage that. Which is, of course, precisely where and who we are: ensconced northwest of the town up here in the Kennedy farmhouse, fellow Americans coming in under cover of darkness one by one from all over the continent—well-armed young men with anti-slavery principles in their minds and bloody murder in their hearts.

We have said our somber final goodbyes to our families and homes in the North and have joined the Old Man here—fifteen white men and five Negro, when we have all assembled—to wait out the days and weeks and, if necessary, months until he tells us finally that the moment we have been waiting for, some of us for a lifetime, has come. The plan, his meticulously detailed schedule and breakdown of operations, he has rehearsed for us over and over again, night after night, in the chilled, candlelit room above the one big room of the house, our prison, as we have come jokingly to call it. On the basement level, there is a kitchen, where sister Annie and Oliver's new wife, Martha, have settled in to cook and launder for us—they arrived back in mid-July, after Father, having determined that our disguise as land speculators and provenders of meat required the presence of womenfolk, summoned them down from North Elba. A short ways from the house is a locked shed, where we have stored our weapons, which we periodically clean and maintain to break the monotony of our confinement— some two hundred Sharps rifles and that many more pistols and a thousand sharpened steel-tipped pikes, all paid for by Father's secret supporters and shipped to Isaac Smith & Sons piecemeal over the summer months from Ohio and Hartford by way of Chambersburg, Pennsylvania, in wooden cases marked "Hardware and Castings." John Kagi, who once taught school in the area and knows it well, has functioned as our main advance agent here and has facilitated these delicate operations. Also, John Cook has been here for nearly a year already, sent down from Iowa by Father as a spy, because of his intelligence and Yale education and his much-admired social skills, and he has managed without arousing suspicion to gain employment as a canal-lock tender and last spring even married a local girl, whom he had got with child, which naturally did not particularly please Father, but it helped Cook settle into the daily life of the town, and that has proved useful.

We ourselves have arrived in a trickle, a few at a time. First, on July 3, Father and I and our old Kansas cohort Jeremiah Anderson came in by wagon from North Elba, and then soon after came Oliver and Watson and the Thompson boys, William, who earlier wished to be in Kansas with us and his brother Henry but never made it off the Thompson farm, and his younger brother Dauphin, only twenty years old, by nature a sweet and gentle boy, but who over the years has come practically to worship Father. From Maine comes Charlie Tidd and

with him Aaron Stevens, both hardened veterans of the Kansas campaign, and shortly after them, Albert Hazlett rides a wagon in, followed
by the Canadian Stewart Taylor, the spiritualist, who is convinced that
he alone will die at Harpers Ferry and seems almost to welcome it, as if
his death is a small price to pay for the survival of the rest of us. A week
later, the Coppoc brothers, Edwin and Barclay, will arrive at the farmhouse, lapsed Quakers who trained with us in Iowa. Then, late in the
summer, Willie Leeman will walk all the way in from Maine, and
shortly after him come the first of the Negroes, Osborn Anderson and
Dangerfield Newby, which pleases Father immensely, for he has begun
to grow fearful that his army will be made up only of white men. In the
end, there will be four more men to join us at the Kennedy farm: the
Bostonian Francis Meriam, unstable and inspired to join us by his
recent visit with the journalist Redpath to the black republic of Haiti;
and John Copeland, Lewis Leary, and Shields Green, the last three of
them Ohio Negroes, which, not counting our commander-in-chief,
rounds out our number at twenty.

But do not fear, this number will be sufficient unto our present
needs, Father has declared. We have pared away from our side all those
men who would defeat us through their cowardice and faithlessness.
We now have only the enemy to fight. July has turned into August and
is moving rapidly towards autumn, and as each new recruit joins us,
Father begins his narrative anew, an old jeremiad against slavery that
lapses into fresh prophecy of its demise, as weekly he adjusts his plan
for the taking of Harpers Ferry, so that it reflects the skills and personalities of the new arrivals, his increased belief in his recruits' commitment to the raid, and his growing awareness that in the end there will
be far fewer of us than he anticipated. The arrival of Mr. Douglass will,
of course, alter things considerably, even if he comes alone, but it's
mainly afterwards that his presence will revise our circumstances and
operations, Father points out, after we have seized the town and the cry

has gone out across the Virginia countryside that Osawatomie Brown and Frederick Douglass have begun their long-awaited war to liberate the slaves. That's when our sharpened pikes, with their six-foot ash handles and eight-inch knife blades bolted to the top, will go into action. Father believes that most of the slaves who join up with us will not be much experienced in the use of firearms, but until they can be trained and properly armed, these weapons will do them fine. Besides, the very sight of razor-sharp spears in the hands of vengeful liberated Negroes will help terrorize the slaveholders. Terror is one of our weapons, he says. Perhaps our strongest weapon. Until then, however, and for now, this is the plan.

From our blanket rolls scattered over the rough plank floor, we prop our heads in our hands and listen to our commander-in-chief, and each of us sees himself playing his role flawlessly, not missing a cue or a line, as if he were an actor in a perfectly executed play. Father sits on a stool in the center of the attic, and as usual, he first hectors and inspires us with his rhetoric and then runs through his plan yet again. He is the author of the play and its stage-manager and master of costumes and scenery and all our properties, and he is the lead actor as well—along with Mr. Douglass, of course, we mustn't forget him, for without Frederick Douglass, no matter how successful the first act is played, the second and third will surely fail. There may not even be a second or third. Everyone knows that. Father will reveal more about those acts later, he says, but for now we need be mindful only that it is overall a work, a performance, whose second and continuing acts will require not one hero but two.

The rest of us are important players, too, we know, but compared to the Old Man and Mr. Douglass, minor. Father insists that no, each one of us is as crucial to the success of this operation as every other: from top to bottom, we are a chain, and if one link breaks, the entire chain comes undone. But still, we know better. And so does he. Each of us twenty is replaceable, and until Mr. Douglass arrives, this will be the Old Man's show, and then it will belong to the two of them. It will never belong to us. Meanwhile, however, we listen to the Old Man's directions and memorize our lines and positions, so that when at last Osawatomie Brown steps onto the stage and begins the action, we will be able to follow his lead and efficiently prepare the way for the entry of the famous Frederick Douglass and his thousands of Negro actors, all of whom are as yet unrehearsed and have been cast as players only in our imaginations.

Even so, the time to act is fast approaching, Father tells us. Already there have appeared numerous signs from the Lord—such as the sudden recent arrival of the pikes from Chambersburg, where they had been oddly delayed for weeks, despite Kagi's best attempts to get them released and sent on to us. And soon from the Lord there will come additional signs, emblems and omens dressed as incidental events and information, to encourage us and make us the more eager to risk our lives in battle rather than continue with this suffocating waiting game at the farm on the Maryland Heights. For instance, Father will dispatch Cook down along the Charles Town Turnpike to determine the numbers and disposition of the slaves there, his only attempt to reconnoiter the region beyond the town of Harpers Ferry itself, and Cook will return aflame with news that the moon is right for insurrection, for it is nearly a dog-tooth moon, the type that makes Africans particularly discontented, he has learned. This, too, is a sign from the Lord, Father tells us. Cook has also been told of a young male slave at a farm nearby who just yesterday hung himself because his owner sold the man's wife down South. A shipment of spears suddenly released, a dog-tooth moon, and a hanging man: on the strength of these and other similarly propitious portents, Father has sent sister Annie and Martha back home to North Elba. We are now awaiting only the arrival of Mr. Douglass, who we hope will bring with him a phalanx of well-armed

Negro fighters from the North, although Father warns us that lately let-ters from his black cohorts back there are suggesting otherwise.

Finally, one night Father climbs up to our attic with his lamp in one hand and a fat packet of papers and maps in the other, and taking his customary seat at the center of the group, he spreads the contents of his packet at his feet. As he begins to speak, he raises one of the maps from the pile—we see at once that it is the now-familiar drawing of the streets and buildings of Harpers Ferry, made by Cook—and, as usual, he shows it to us and allows it to be passed amongst us, so that, while Father sets out the plan, each man can better visualize what he is to do and where he shall stand when he does it. This time, however, when he has gone through, once again, step by step, the taking of Harpers Ferry, he retrieves and sets aside Cook's map and is silent and looks somberly at his clasped hands, as if in prayer. After a long moment, without looking up, he abruptly declares that tonight he has decided to reveal to us that we will not be conducting the sort of raid that most of us still believe we have come here for. This is not to be merely a larger, more dangerous and dramatic, slave-running expe-dition than any of us has ever undertaken before. There is instead a much larger task before us, a greater thing than we have yet dared imagine.

Kagi has long known of this grand, about-to-be-revealed scheme, as have I, of course, and a few of the others, Cook, Stevens, and Anderson, and we have argued privately amongst ourselves as to its feasibility and have agreed, after much disputation, that it can be done and must be attempted; but my brothers Watson and Oliver have not heard it before, nor my brothers-in-law Will and Dauphin Thompson, nor has Father until now trusted any of the recent arrivals with this vision, for it is truly a vision and not so much a plan, and to see it as he does, we must first for a long time not have seen or heard much else. Our long confinement together and our isolation from the world outside have finally made us all visionaries, capable at last of seeing what Father sees and of believing his words as if they were true prophecy.

Here, men, I want you to examine *these* maps, he says, and he picks up and flaps at us a set of cambric-cloth squares onto which he has pasted the states of Virginia, Maryland, Tennessee, Alabama, Mississippi, Georgia, and the Carolinas—eight squares, and one state to a square. In the margin of each map, he has written numerals: 491,000, for the number of slaves in Virginia, he explains, 87,000 in Maryland, and so on, which comes to a total of 1,996,366 slaves, he pronounces, looking up at us. But he does not see us, his twenty followers, unshaven, unwashed, gaunt, and sober-faced, all of us young men and a few of us mere boys: instead, his gray eyes gleam with excitement at the sight of a spreading black wave of mutinous slaves, nearly two million strong, as all across the South they flee their cabins and shops and barns and rise from the cotton and tobacco and sugarcane fields and take up pitchforks, axes, machetes, and the thousands of Sharps rifles that will come flowing down the Alleghenies from the North; he sees them, first hundreds, then thousands, and finally hundreds of thousands of black men, women, and children, flowing down the country roads and highways, meeting in town squares and on city streets and merging into the largest army ever seen in this land, an army with but one purpose, and that is to take back from the slaveholders what for a quarter of a millennium has been stolen from them—their freedom, their American birthrights, their very lives. This raid will establish no Underground Railroad operation, he tells us, for regardless of scale, it is no mere slave raid. This will be an act of an entirely different order. Yes, after we have taken Harpers Ferry, we will make our appointed *rendez-vous* with Mr. Douglass in the Allegheny foothills west of here, as planned, but then we will not, as some of us believed, hole up in small forts and siphon escaped slaves into the North. Instead, we shall divide our forces into two portions, the Defenders, under Mr. Douglass's command, and the Liberators, under Father's, and whilst the Defenders protect and hurry into the North those women, children, elderly, and infirm slaves who wish to resettle there, the Liberators will commence to march rapidly southward along the densely wooded north-south mountain passes, making lightning-like strikes against the plantations on the plains lower down, seizing armories and arsenals and supplies as they go, building a cavalry, like Toussaint L'Ouverture, and even seizing artillery, like the Maroons of Jamaica, destroying railroads and fortifications. When the Shenandoah Valley goes, the plantations along the James River will quickly fall, and then the Tidewater tobacco farms, and when Virginia goes, the rest of the Southern states will nearly conquer themselves, there being down there, as in Haiti and Jamaica, such a disproportionate number of Negroes to whites. And there will be thousands of non-slaveholding whites, too, God-fearing, decent Southerners, who will come running to our side, once they understand that our true intentions are not to slay white men and women in their beds or to overthrow their state or federal government or to dissolve the Union, but merely to end American slavery. To end it *now, here, in these years*. Look, look! he says, excitedly showing us the map of Alabama, where with X's he has marked, county by county, the heaviest concentrations of slaves. When we emerge from the Tennessee hills here in Augusta County, the slaves will rise up spontaneously in adjacent Montgomery County, and in a week or perhaps two, when the news has arrived there, the same will occur in Macon and Russell Counties, and the flames of rebellion will leap like a wildfire from one district to the next, straight across into Georgia, whence the fire will roar all the way east to the Sea Isles, causing it to curl back north into the Carolinas, until we have ignited a great, encircling conflagration, which cannot be extinguished until it has burnt the ancient sin and scourge of slavery entirely away, from one end of the South to the other, from Maryland to Louisiana, until at last nothing remains of the Slavocracy but a smoldering pile of char!

The Old Man's peroration ends and is met with soft silence. At first, Kagi, Cook, Stevens, and Anderson look slowly around the dim, shadowy room, as if searching the faces of the others for a sign that their collective silence indicates collective skepticism, which was Kagi's early reaction to Father's vision, or dismay, Cook's and Stevens's first response, or simple awe, Anderson's. I myself look to my brothers' eyes, Watson and Oliver, seeking there a clarifying version of my own thoughts and feelings, for in my earlier disputations with Kagi, Cook, and Stevens, I defended the logic of Father's grand plan with no other desire than to defeat their objections to it, my old role, and in winning them over have not made my own private position strong to myself or even clear. But it is too late. Watson and Oliver and the Thompsons, my brothers and brothers-in-law, all of the men, wear on their faces a single expression, the expression worn also by Kagi, Cook, Stevens, and Anderson, and no doubt by me, too: it is the hungry look of a follower, of a true believer. There is no Thomas the Doubter in this room, no sober skeptic, no ironist, no dark materialist. We have all been confined here in this isolated place for too many weeks and months to have any mentality left that is not a piece of a single mind, and that mind is shaped and filled by Father alone.

But, yes, much of what you have expected will be met, he continues, calmer now, comforted by our silence. He again holds out Cook's large, detailed map of the streets and buildings of Harpers Ferry and says that we shall indeed, as we have intended all along, soon attack and seize the town. That has not changed. It will be our first formally declared act of war against the slaveholders, the first act of our mighty drama. And when we have seized the town, we shall, as planned, take control of the arms stored in three buildings there—the government armory, where the muskets are made, the Hall rifle works, and the arsenal. As we all know, there are no federal troops presently posted in the town and only a few private guards protecting these stores of weapons and munitions, so we will not be much opposed, and if we strike quickly and under cover of night, it will be done before we are even noticed by the townspeople. We shall nevertheless take hostages and hold them, probably in the armory yard, to protect us against the local militias, should they be roused, whilst we await the first reinforcing arrival of mutinous slaves from the surrounding countryside, and then, in a matter of hours, we shall have flown back up into the mountain fastness south and west of the town, whence shall come our Republic's salvation.

Shortly after nightfall on a Sabbath, it will begin with a fervent prayer offered up to God, that we may be assisted by Him in the total, final liberation of all the slaves on this continent. We shall not ask the Lord to spare or even to protect our own lives in this venture: our lives have been pledged strictly to our duty; that is all. We must not ask the Lord to release us of our duty. Then, with everyone gathered in the room below, so that we may be mentally clear as to our legal rights and obligations and our principles, Aaron Stevens, who has the most impressive voice of us all, will read aloud Father's *Provisional Constitution and Ordinances for the People of the United States*, which so nobly begins: *Whereas slavery is a most barbarous, unprovoked, and unjustifiable war of one portion of its citizens upon another portion in utter disregard and violation of those eternal and self-evident truths set forth in our Declaration of Independence: therefore, we, citizens of the United States, and the oppressed people who, by a recent decision of the Supreme Court, are declared to have no rights which the white man is bound to respect, together with all other people degraded by the laws thereof, do, for the time being, ordain and establish for ourselves the following Provisional Constitution and Ordinances.* He will read all forty-five articles, ending thusly, with the carefully worded reassurance that *The foregoing articles shall not be construed so as in any way to encourage the overthrow of any State government, or of the general government of the United States, and look to no dissolution of the*

*Union, but simply to amendment and repeal. And our flag shall be the same
that our fathers fought under in the Revolution.*

Following this somber recitation, our commander-in-chief will
administer anew to us as a group the same oath of secrecy that, individ-
ually, upon our first arrival at the farm, each of us has already been
sworn to. Father then will say simply, "Men, get on your arms. We now
proceed to the Ferry."

I am to stay behind with Francis Meriam and Barclay Coppoc, the
two men Father and I have come to view as the weakest links in our
chain, the one because of his physical frailty and tendency to hysteria,
the other because of his youth and his residual Quaker timidity. I
would prefer to be at the front with Father and the others, but I know
better than to object to this assignment, for no one else in the group can
be trusted with it, he says, and besides, it places me in a position of
authority as second-in-command and at Father's flank, so that if something goes dreadfully wrong, my duty will be to rescue them. My
immediate charge, however, is to transfer all the arms from the house
and storage shed, except for those taken by the advance party, to a
small, unused schoolhouse situated in the woods overlooking the
Potomac and directly across the river from Harpers Ferry, there to
await the first arrival of liberated slaves, to arm them and lead them
into the mountains, where a few days later we will *rendez-vous* with
Father and the others. On his map of Virginia, Father shows us our
Allegheny meeting place in Frederick County, which he himself
scouted years ago, while on a surveying expedition of lands owned by
Oberlin College. Mr. Douglass should have joined us by then, Father
assures us, and will take overall command of my unit. I am to remain as
captain of the new recruits, however, and as executive officer of the
operation, until Father himself has joined us. After that, I am to ride at
Father's side with the Liberators. I have also been charged with the
obligation to remove or destroy any incriminating evidence that we

might have left here at the farmhouse, such as letters, maps, journals, and other personal effects.

We have in our possession two wagons, one for my use and the other for Father's advance party. It must be on a night with no moon shining, no stars, a night overcast and drear, and when Father's men have loaded their wagon with the half a hundred pikes and twenty rifles they require for the taking of Harpers Ferry, immediately and without ceremony, at a simple command from Father, they will set off down the public road, Father perched on the wagon seat with his head uncharacteristically bent forward, stooped as if in deep thought or prayer, and our old North Elba farmhorse, the bay Morgan mare, between the shafts, and the sixteen men marching silently in the cold drizzle alongside the wagon and behind. I will stand by the door of the house with Meriam and young Barclay Coppoc and watch them disappear into the darkness as if being swallowed by it. I do not know yet what I will feel when that moment comes, but it will not be fear or dread. It is too late for that.

After a few moments, when we can no longer hear the tramp of their boots on the wet ground or the creak and chop of their wagon and horse, my two men and I will turn quickly to our tasks—Meriam and Coppoc to load our wagon with the remaining weapons from the shed, whilst I gather all our scattered papers from the house. By candlelight, I will prowl carefully through the entire house, from basement kitchen to our attic hideout, collecting every shred of paper I can find and stuffing all of it loosely into a cloth valise. To my slight surprise, I will be obliged to fill the bag several times over, emptying it each time in the basement next to the woodstove on the flagstone floor of the kitchen. Soon I will have made a large, disordered pile, at first glance much of it rubbish, which I plan to separate from the rest and burn. But when I commence to sort the papers, I will discover with a little shock that most of the remaining papers, a whole heap of them, are Father's, and amongst them are dozens of letters, many from family members in North Elba and Ohio, and numerous others, only slightly coded, written by his secret Northern supporters, Dr. Howe, Gerrit Smith, Franklin Sanborn, and so on, and even several letters from Frederick Douglass, and receipts for Father's purchases of arms back in Iowa and Ohio and for the pikes in Hartford, Connecticut, and here are all of Father's maps, the very maps with which he showed us his grand plan, and Cook's drawing of Harpers Ferry, and Father's pocket notebooks, where he has listed, county by county, as on his maps, slave population figures taken from the 1850 national census, and the names of many towns and cities of the South and their marching distance from one another, such as *Montgomery to Memphis, 3 da.*, and *Charleston to Savannah, 2 1/2 da.* I have known this would happen, for I have seen most of these papers, maps, and notebooks lying carelessly about for weeks, as if, having shown them to us, Father no longer wished to order or hide them, and I have felt a twinge of fear that, in the rush of last-minute preparations, he would neglect to take them up. But I would not reflect upon it until later, until after Father and I had ridden up for our final, secret meeting with Mr. Douglass in Chambersburg.

While I clear the house and my men stack the arms into our wagon, Father and his men will be nearing the covered bridge that crosses the Potomac from Maryland into the state of Virginia and the town of Harpers Ferry. This is how it will go. Around nine o'clock, the drizzle shifts over to a straight rain. At ten-thirty, they reach the Maryland Heights, a steep, wooded thousand-foot-high cliff above the cut of the Potomac through the Blue Ridge. Although from up here it is too dark to make out the shapes of the brick-front buildings and cobbled streets below, the men can see through the rain a few dim, last lights from the slumbering town. Passing by the abandoned log schoolhouse, where I am to store our weapons and later arm the escaping slaves, Father and his men descend on the narrow, winding lane to the grassy riverbank and march for a while alongside the wide, swift-flowing, steel-colored river to the covered bridge, which crosses to Harpers Ferry a short ways upstream from the place where the east-running Potomac River is joined from the south by the Shendandoah. Well in sight of the bridge now, its wide, black entrance beckoning like the mouth of a gigantic serpent, they leave the road and cross the C & O Canal at lock 23 and make their way in the cold rain along the tow path to the Baltimore & Ohio Railroad tracks running in from the east. Here the tracks turn, cross the canal, and pass through the covered bridge alongside the narrow roadway, passing over the wide, gray river in pitch darkness to the station and loading platforms in the town center, where they turn again and lead out of town on the further side of the Potomac into western Virginia and on to Ohio.

Father and his men are well down in the gorge now, as if they have entered the den of the monstrous snake. Behind them and before them on their left, like thick, black curtains hanging from the blacker sky, loom high walls, where clusters of scrub oak and thickets of thorn bushes cling to wet, rocky escarpments all the way to the tops, and tall, windblown chestnut and walnut trees rise from the bluffs above. There can be no return now: Father and his men have reached the bridge over the Potomac and must enter it and go on, straight into the town at the further end. Father halts the wagon at the entrance for a moment and stations Watson and Stewart Taylor as a rear guard on the Maryland side. Then, at the Old Man's command, Kagi and Stevens march straight into the mouth of the bridge. Fifty yards back, Father follows in the rumbling wagon, and the rest of the men, rifles at the ready and cartridge boxes clipped to the outside of their clothing for quick access, march wordlessly along behind, walking stiffly on the loose planks, as if on ice, and taking shallow, tight breaths, as if afraid to fill their chests with the blackness that surrounds them.

A few moments later, Kagi and Stevens emerge from the long

throat of the bridge. They are the first of the raiders to enter the town, and as soon as they have set their boots onto the rain-slicked cobbles of Potomac Street, a watchman hears their step and calls, Who goes there! Kagi answers, Hallo, Billy Williams! It's a friend! The watchman draws close to the two and lifts his lantern and says, Oh, it's Mister Kagi who's out so late, and they instantly throw down on him and take him prisoner and douse his lamp.

The raid has begun. Osawatomie Brown and his men are inside Harpers Ferry and have taken their first hostage. The raiders are able to breathe and walk normally now, and they move rapidly and efficiently from one place and situation to the next, exactly as planned and rehearsed. Turning right on Potomac Street at the B & O train depot, they pass the deserted porch and darkened windows of the Wager Hotel, where the last guests have finally gone upstairs to their rooms, and head straight towards the armory, a long double row of brick buildings situated between the railroad siding and the canal. On the left, adjacent to the gate of the armory grounds, there is a square brick building, a single-storey, two-room structure that serves as a fire-engine house for the town and a guardhouse for the armory. When Father has drawn the wagon close to the iron gate, the armory watchman, whose name is Daniel Whelan, cracks open the timbered door of the firehouse, pauses, squints into the darkness, and then reluctantly steps outside into the rain. In a sleepy voice, he says, That you, Williams?

Open the gate, Mister Whelan, Father says.

You're not Williams, says the watchman, more confused than frightened. At once, Oliver and Newby step forward with their rifles leveled and take him prisoner. Aaron Stevens grabs the crowbar from the wagon bed and twists it into the chain holding the gate. When the lock snaps, he and Kagi swing open the gate, and Father drives the wagon straight into the yard. The other men, including the two captured watchmen, follow at gunpoint, and Kagi swings the gate closed again.

Now Father climbs down from the wagon and, turning to his dumbfounded prisoners, declares that he has come here from Kansas, for this is a slave state, and he has come to free all its Negro slaves.

Williams and Whelan look wide-eyed in disbelief at the old man. The rain drips from the tattered brim of his hat and from his white beard. Barely hearing his words, they stare at him, this bony, sharp-eyed old fellow in the frock coat, who, except for his rifle and the two pistols at his waist, resembles more a poor, hardscrabble farmer from the hills than a Yankee liberator of slaves, and they look around at the small, shabbily dressed, heavily armed group of white and Negro young men who stand near him, and finally at each other, and say nothing. What is happening here? For Williams and Whelan, this is a strange, waking dream, a shared hallucination.

I have taken possession of the United States armory, the old man calmly continues. And if the citizens of the town interfere with me and my men, we must burn the town and have blood.

Father now proceeds to dispatch his men so as to take control of the remaining arms supplies and defenses of the town. Under guard by Dauphin Thompson and Lewis Leary, the two hostages are shut into the firehouse, while Oliver and Will Thompson are sent three blocks south on Shenandoah Street to take command of the bridge that crosses the Shenandoah River into town. The tollbooth proves to be empty and the bridge unguarded. Hazlett and Edwin Coppoc take over the arsenal, also unguarded, just off the main square and in sight of the hotel, where they will wait for further orders and a wagon to empty it. Stevens, Kagi, and Copeland are ordered to the rifle factory, which is located a short ways further down Shenandoah Street at Lower Hall's Island, a long, narrow rise of land in the Shendandoah River that is separated from the shore by a canal. Once more, a single watchman is surprised by the raiders and, when captured, is marched by Stevens back to the firehouse, leaving Kagi and Copeland behind to hold the rifle works. On his return to the firehouse, Stevens comes upon three half-drunk, unarmed young men, carousers straggling home late from the Wager Hotel, and he swiftly puts them under his gun and brings them in with the watchman.

It is not yet midnight, and both bridges into town, the armory, the arsenal, and the rifle factory have been brought under the control of the raiders. Six men have been taken hostage and locked into the firehouse. Unknown to the rest of its citizens, unknown to the world, Harpers Ferry, Virginia, belongs to Osawatomie Brown. Around this time, the rain lets up, and the clouds slowly pull away and open the starry sky to view. Soon the dog-tooth moon breaks the dark horizon above the Maryland Heights north of town, where, just before one A.M., as Father expected, a fourth watchman, Patrick Higgins, comes down the moonlit footpath from his home in Sandy Hook to relieve Williams at the Maryland side of the Potomac bridge. As he enters the covered bridge, Watson and Stewart Taylor, Father's rear guard, step from the shadows and capture the man. In silence, dutifully following the plan, they direct their prisoner to the bridge and commence marching him over to the firehouse, when suddenly Higgins turns and swats Watson on the forehead and races ahead of them into the darkness. Before Watson can stay his hand, Taylor raises his rifle and fires, his bullet slightly grazing the forehead of the escaping man, who is able nonetheless to get safely to the end of the bridge and into the Wager Hotel, where he is the first to raise the alarm, although he cannot say who has shot at him or why.

This is an eventuality that Father has anticipated, a part of his overall plan, and so long as it happens after the bridges and the arms stores have been captured and hostages have been taken, it does not much concern him that sometime in the night a shot or two will be fired, alerting the citizens that a violent action is under way. By daylight, they will know of it, anyhow, and will be told by him then of its purpose, and soon the whole country will begin to apprehend its scale. After all, this raid is meant to be a public act, not a private one, he has reminded us, and if our aims are to be met, we must actually *invite* a certain hue-and-cry and, so long as we are in control of events and not they us, welcome it. Still, the echoing sound of the first shot shocks the men, and Watson's and Taylor's breathless report that their prisoner has escaped into the hotel frightens them. Father, however, is calm as ice.

At this moment, he is mainly concerned with Aaron Stevens's mission into the countryside. He has sent Stevens with Tidd and Cook and three of the Negro men, Anderson, Leary, and Green, five miles west of Harpers Ferry to Halltown, where resides the wealthy planter Colonel Lewis Washington, a man who is a direct descendant of General George Washington and, for that, something of a local celebrity and politician, an aide to Virginia's Governor Wise. Further, he is known to have inherited from his incomparable ancestor an elaborately engraved pistol presented to the General after the Revolution by the Marquis de Lafayette and a ceremonial sword given him by King Frederick the Great of Prussia. The Old Man wants Colonel Lewis Washington as a hostage, and he wants to free the Colonel's half-dozen slaves, but most of all, to help place his own acts into their proper context, he wants General George Washington's pistol and his sword.

With a rail pulled from the fence by the meadow in front of the house, Stevens and his men batter down the Colonel's door and roust him and his terrified family from their beds. When the Colonel has dressed and has delivered over to the raiders his ancestor's famous weapons, Stevens formally places him under arrest and, leaving the man's wife and young children behind, seats him next to Tidd in a two-horse carriage appropriated from the barn. Behind them, Anderson, Leary, and Green have hitched the Colonel's four remaining horses to a farm wagon and have placed into it three liberated slaves, two men and a young woman—all they could find in the house and barn, or maybe they're the only Negroes on the place not too frightened to show themselves, Anderson explains to Stevens, for these poor people can't know for sure yet that we are who we say we are. Stevens agrees, and they start back along the Charles Town Turnpike towards Harpers Ferry.

A mile west of Bolivar Heights, still following Father's orders, they draw the wagons up before a large farm owned by John Allstadt, after Colonel Washington the wealthiest planter in the region and, like him, a slaveholder—the owner, in fact, of the young woman who was sold off into the Deep South and her young husband who a week ago hung himself because of it. A second time, Stevens and his men break down a front door and enter a stranger's home unopposed. They quickly make hostages of the man of the house, Mr. Allstadt, and his eighteen-year-old son, and unceremoniously liberate Allstadt's four remaining slaves, who are added to the group in the farm wagon. As instructed, Stevens and the other raiders are scrupulously polite to their prisoners and to the women and children, just as they were at Colonel Washington's, and they try not to frighten them overmuch and take pains to cause no unnecessary damage to the house or personal property, other than that of converting the slaves into free men and women. They state clearly to the whites their sole reason for breaking into their homes in the middle of the night and making prisoners of the husbands and sons—which is strictly to end slavery. If we are not opposed, Stevens says, no blood will be spilt. The husbands and sons, like the wagons and horses, will eventually be returned to them, but their slaves are no longer owned by them, he says. The slaves of Virginia are owned henceforth by themselves and cannot be returned to any man.

In the meantime, back at Harpers Ferry, at 1:25 A.M., precisely as scheduled, the Baltimore-bound B & O passenger train rolls in, and when it has hissed to a noisy stop at the station, the night clerk from the hotel next door skitters low from the door of the railroad station, and before the conductor can step down from the train to the platform, the man has leapt aboard, bearing the startling news that gunmen are out on the Potomac bridge and have shot a watchman, who lies bleeding inside the hotel! Worse, the other three town watchmen are nowhere about and may even have been murdered! And here's something else: when the clerk slipped unseen into the station by a rear window adjacent to the hotel, he tried to telegraph the stationmaster in Charles Town and discovered that the wires had been cut. There is something very strange, something *dangerous*, happening, and until now, with no idea of how many gunmen might be out there or where they may be hiding, no one but the night clerk has dared to leave the hotel or been able to raise a general alarm.

The conductor, A. J. Phelps, takes immediate charge and directs the engineer and the baggagemaster, who carries a pistol, to step from the train and investigate the bridge, for it may have been sabotaged. Who knows but what these gunmen are train robbers and have blocked the bridge somehow? If the tracks appear clear, he says, they straightway will pass across the river and, at the station in Monococy in Maryland, will telegraph the news of these startling events over to Charles Town, the county seat, where there is a federal marshal's office and a regiment of town militia available for help.

Sleepy passengers peer out their windows, wondering why the delay, as the engineer and the baggagemaster, his pistol at the ready, walk slowly along the station platform, step down to the railbed, and crunch over the cinders and gravel towards the dark mouth of the covered bridge. When the pair are about fifteen feet from the entrance, Watson speaks to them from the darkness ahead. Drop your pistol, sir, and both of you walk slowly towards us. Keep your hands in full view. You're under a hundred guns, gentlemen, and are now our prisoners. You won't be harmed, if you do as we say.

The baggagemaster lets his pistol fall to the railbed, and the two men, as instructed, extend their hands as if ready to be manacled and walk forward. Meanwhile, behind them, up on the platform, a Negro man named Hayward Shepherd, a freedman employed at the station as the night baggageman, has stepped from the office to the platform to see what is going on, and Phelps, the conductor—too far from the bridge for him or the clerk or anyone on the train to see in the darkness that the engineer and the baggagemaster have been all but taken prisoner—orders him to go and assist them in their investigation. Shepherd jumps to the ground and hurries to join the two, who have disappeared inside the bridge. When he, too, has neared the entrance and is now beyond earshot of the men on the platform, he hears a calm, low voice from the darkness, Watson Brown's, ordering him to stop and listen. Shepherd, a middle-aged bachelor affectionately called "Uncle Hay" by the white citizens of the town, stops and listens. In a conversational tone, Watson tells him what Father has instructed all of us to say to the Virginia freedmen. We have come from Kansas to free the slaves. You may join us in this enterprise or not. But if you refuse to join us, we will treat with you as with any white man who refuses to join us. We will be forced to consider you our enemy.

For a second, Shepherd hesitates, as if not quite getting Watson's meaning, and then abruptly he turns and runs. Watson—or perhaps it is Stewart Taylor, or maybe some other raider, standing in the shadows of the storefronts nearby; any one of us could have done it—fires his rifle, and Shepherd falls, mortally wounded by a single bullet in the spine, running through to the chest. With everyone watching him and no one daring to move to help—not Watson or Stewart inside the covered bridge, not their two prisoners, not the several raiders hiding in the shadows along the street or Father standing unseen at the gate of the armory, not the men up on the platform by the station or the passengers staring in horror from the windows of the train: no one who sees it can make himself come forward to help the fallen man—as Shepherd lifts his bloody chest from the cinders and with his arms slowly drags his numbed, dying body away from the bridge towards the station. After what seems like a long while, he succeeds in getting to a protected place below the platform that is close enough for Phelps and the hotel clerk safely to reach down and draw him up to it, where they quickly pull his body inside the station as if he were already a dead man.

Prepare yourselves for sad ironies, Father forewarned us, often enough for us to have expected it. But it has come nonetheless as a dismaying shock. Men, the cruel perversity of slavery will snap back betimes and will try to bite us in our face, he told us. We have to be hard, hard. This surely is what he meant: that in the liberation of the slaves, the first to die may well be neither a white man nor a slave, but a free Negro.

This sad event has the immediate good effect, however, of closing down the train and trapping its passengers inside it, with Conductor Phelps and the hotel clerk retreating to the station, and the guests, those few wakened by this, the second gunshot of the night, holing up inside the hotel. For the time being, the town is still ours. A little after four A.M., Aaron Stevens's party comes clattering down Potomac Street, the trap driven by Tidd, with Colonel Washington and Mr. Allstadt and his son in it, and the farm wagon driven by Cook, with the seven liberated slaves huddled in back. Stevens, who carries General Washington's pistol and sword wrapped in a blanket, and the other raiders, Anderson, Leary, and Green, are on horseback, their mounts taken from Allstadt's farm.

As soon as they have arrived at the armory yard, Father tells the newly freed slaves who he is, Osawatomie Brown of Kansas, which, as he expected, evokes in them a certain fearfulness, until he reveals that his principal ally is the famous Negro Frederick Douglass, an escaped slave himself, and this seems to impress and calm them somewhat, for these are Virginia ex-slaves and rebellious types, surely, or they would not have come in with Stevens and his men, and being from a border town, they no doubt have had secret access to abolitionist information and literature. He places pikes into their hands and stations them inside the firehouse to guard the growing number of hostages. For now, these white men are your prisoners, he says. Treat them honestly, for they are hostages, whom we will deploy if we need to bargain for our continued safety, and as we will be freeing them later, we want them to tell other white people the truth about us, that we want not revenge but liberty.

The seven Negroes, a woman and six men, several of them barefoot in the cold night, take up their pikes and hesitantly, as if they have no choice in the matter, follow their former masters into the firehouse, while Father straps on George Washington's scabbard and sword and adds to his pair of old service revolvers the General's engraved pistol and tooled leather holster. In all his armament, he is a formidable sight, a warrior chieftain, and with his Old Testament beard and fierce gray eyes and his battered straw hat and Yankee farmer's woolen frock coat and his—to the Negroes, to all people, in fact—peculiar way of speaking, he is a paradoxical one as well: a man out of time, without a shred of vanity or the slightest regard for convention, and though an old man, he is as overflowing as a boy with single-minded purpose and high principles, armed and clothed for no other task in life than this night's bloody work. The rest of the men, if they put their rifles down, and the ex-slaves, if they put away their pikes, could easily fold back into the general populace and disappear from sight, here or anywhere in America; but not Father: he is Osawatomie Brown of Kansas, and no

American, white or black, Northern or Southern, would mistake him for anybody else.

Although they are far fewer than he expected by now and seem somewhat confused and fearful, the arrival of these, the first of the freed slaves, has excited Father, and he orders Cook to drive one of the wagons over to the Maryland side, to the schoolhouse where I and my two men, Barclay Coppoc and Frank Meriam, will have cached the remainder of our arms, one hundred fifty rifles and another hundred pistols and most of the thousand sharpened pikes. Cook is to bring one-third of the pikes back into town, for, surely, by morning there will be mutinous slaves thronging to the armory yard. The remainder of the weapons are for me and my men to distribute first amongst the insurrectionary slaves who come in from Maryland, and then we are to carry the remainder up into the mountains for eventual dispersal there. By daylight, on both sides of the river, we will have hundreds of escaped slaves to arm, Father says, and must be ready for them in both places, or they will not believe that we are serious.

For now, until further orders, the raiders who are inside the town are merely to hold their positions—Kagi and his men, Copeland and now Leary, over at the rifle factory on Hall's Island, Oliver and Will Thompson posted at the Shenandoah bridge, Watson and Taylor still holding the bridge across the Potomac, and Hazlett and Edwin Coppoc guarding the arsenal; the rest of the men stand at the ready here at the center of town, in and around the armory grounds and the firehouse.

It is close to six A.M. The rain has ceased, and the heavy storm clouds have moved off, and as dawn approaches, the sky turns slowly to a fluttery, gray, silken sheet, with the high, wooded ridges in the east and north silhouetted against it. The brick storefronts and houses and offices of the town and the narrow, cobbled streets glisten wetly from the night's rain, and when the first light of the rising sun spreads across the eastern horizon, the faces of the buildings here below turn pink and seem almost to bloom, as if in the darkness of the night they existed only in a nascent form, not quite real.

Before long, the first of the armory workers, all unsuspecting, come drifting into the center of town in twos and threes from their small wood-frame houses above the cliffs on Clay Street, and as they walk through the iron gate into the yard, Father and the others grab them and make them hostages in the firehouse, until he has close to forty men crowded into the two large rooms and has to station several of his raiders inside with the freed slaves to help guard them. Then, by daylight, just as Father said it would, word of the raid gets out. Dr. John Starry, a local physician, is the first to raise the alarm. Summoned to the hotel hours earlier to care for the wounded watchman and the dying Hayward Shepherd by a courageous Negro barman who, at risk of his life, slipped out a side door of the hotel and down dark alleyways to the physician's house, Dr. Starry bandages the watchman's forehead and is at Shepherd's side when the poor man dies, after which, accompanied by the barman who brought him there, he succeeds in returning to his home undetected, where at once he rouses his family and neighbors. Then he rides to the home of the Superintendent of the Armory, A. M. Kitzmiller, bringing the scarcely-to-be-believed news. The armory, arsenal, and rifle works and a large group of hostages, including Colonel Lewis Washington, are all in the hands of an army of abolitionist murderers that is led by none other than Osawatomie Brown and aided by a wild gang of escaped, spear-carrying slaves! There is a full-scale insurrection under way! Brown has trained cannon on the square, the doctor reports, and is moving all the arms from the town into the interior!

Soon the bell of the Lutheran church atop the hill starts to clang, summoning the citizens to an emergency meeting, and a rider has been sent to Shepherdstown to call out the local militia, and a second has been dispatched to Charles Town for the Jefferson Guards, formed for the express purpose of meeting precisely this circumstance after the Turner rebellion back in '31.

Father and his men, when they hear the church bell ringing on and on for ten, fifteen, twenty minutes, know what is happening. Don't be frightened, boys, don't panic. There's still plenty of time, he assures the men. The hostages and practically every rifle in the town are in our hands. And the Lord is watching over us. We won't go down, boys, but if the Lord requires it of us, then it will be as Samson went. These people know that, and they don't want it, so we're still safe enough here.

It is full daylight, around seven A.M., when Father strides through the gate of the armory yard and approaches the railroad station and calls out for Mr. Phelps, the conductor. Come here, sir! I wish to parley with you! Phelps pokes his head out the door but refuses to come forward. I have decided to let you move the train on to Baltimore, Father declares. But tell your employer, and tell all the civil and military authorities, that this is the last train I will permit in or out of Harpers Ferry, at the extreme peril of those men we have taken prisoner, until we have finished with our business here.

Phelps nods, and he and the engineer and the baggagemaster return to the train, fire it up, and take it slowly towards the covered bridge and across the Potomac into Maryland. From the schoolhouse on the heights opposite, I watch the train far below snake its way out of the bridge and wind along the north bank of the river towards Baltimore and Washington beyond, and I know that within minutes, as soon as the train has reached the station at Monocacy, news of the raid will reach the main offices of the B & O. An hour later, in Richmond, an aide to Governor Henry Wise will disturb the Governor's breakfast with astonishing news, and shortly afterwards, in Washington, D.C., an adjutant general will burst into the office of the Secretary of War, who will read the wire from Governor Wise requesting federal troops and will at once ask for an emergency meeting with President Buchanan. More in line with Father's purposes—and I know this, too—by evening, every newspaper in the land will be shouting the news of our raid:

FEARFUL AND EXCITING INTELLIGENCE! NEGRO INSURRECTION IN HARPERS FERRY, VIRGINIA, LED BY JOHN BROWN OF KANSAS!! MANY SLAIN, HUNDREDS TAKEN HOSTAGE, FEDERAL ARMS SEIZED!!!

In morning light, a few personal weapons, mostly antiquated muskets and squirrel guns, have been located by the townspeople, and five or six of the more adventurous men among them have taken up firing positions on the hillside above the armory yard. It is not long, however, before they are spotted by the raiders, most of them Kansas veterans and much more experienced than the locals at this sort of action and possessing weapons of surpassing accuracy, so that the townsmen are barely able to open fire, when one of them, a grocer named Boerly, is shot dead by a bullet from a raider rifle, which causes a quick retreat amongst the others. It is mid-morning. The militias from Shepherdstown and Charles Town have not yet arrived, and in Washington, fifty miles to the east, federal troops are only now being mustered for railroad transport to Harpers Ferry. Here in town, their feeble efforts at defense effectively curtailed by the raiders' deadly accurate Sharps rifles, by their fear of endangering the hostages, and by their growing certainty that there are many more than Father's seventeen raiders occupying the town and hundreds more escaped slaves than seven, the citizens are limited to taking occasional, erratic potshots in the general direction of the armory, causing more danger and havoc to themselves than to the raiders.

Even so, over at the rifle works on Hall's Island, Kagi has grown increasingly anxious about the passage of so much time, for he and his two men, Copeland and Leary, though they have so far held the factory uncontested, are situated far from the hostages in the firehouse, and thus, of Father's force, they are the most vulnerable to attack from the townsmen. Kagi dispatches Leary to town on foot to request Father to send back a wagon and additional men, so that they can quickly load the seized weapons from the factory and begin their escape into the mountains. It is time. None of the raiders has been killed or even wounded. According to the plan, they should all be departing from Harpers Ferry by now.

And I, up on the Maryland Heights, should also have left by now. That is the plan, Father's plan, his vision of how it would go at Harpers Ferry on the night of October 16 and the morning of October 17, and everything up to now has gone accordingly. Except for the one thing: that the hundreds of escaping slaves whom we expected to come rushing to our side have not yet appeared, and the few who have are turning fearful and hesitant and may themselves have to be put under guard and made into hostages.

But that does not matter, I decide, as I watch from my perch above the town. Father's plan can accommodate that, too. We have seized at least three wagonloads of weapons, we have terrorized the entire South into believing that an insurrection has begun, and in the North we have raised fresh huzzahs and enthusiastic promises of material support and a coming flood of volunteer fighters—we have, indeed, begun an insurrection, which surely, thanks to the presence of Frederick Douglass, will catch and burst into flame in a matter of mere days, and if Father leads his men out of Harpers Ferry now and makes his appointed *rendez-vous* in the Alleghenies with Mr. Douglass, we will still be able to feed those flames and follow them into the deeper South, just as Father wished. It is not too late.

The slaves will come in, Father insists. They will soon start to arrive. We must give them every moment up to the last possible moment to learn of our raid and our intentions and to overcome their natural fears and flee their masters' farms and plantations for the town, which is still under our control. The second we abandon the town, the escaping slaves will have no place to go where they are not in terrible danger. For their sake, we shall continue to hold the town, he declares. Even as the Jefferson Guards ride in on the Charles Town Pike from the west and the Shepherdstown militia comes in along the Potomac road from the north and the troop train from Washington slowly approaches from the east.

23

But surely, Miss Mayo, surely you, of all people, must already know the part of my account that I am leaving out, and that it turns all I have been relating to you these many months into a fantasy, an old man's wishful dream, and makes of Father's exquisitely detailed plan a deadly chimera. For you, like the rest of America, have read and believed Frederick Douglass's eloquent narrative of his life and are familiar with his version of his final meeting with Father and me in Chambersburg. I have no quarrel with it—what Mr. Douglass says there is true: that for an entire day he and Father wrestled like angels, as the one struggled to keep the other from martyrdom, and the other fought to convince the one to save him from martyrdom by joining him there. And that both men lost the fight.

It was a curious, paradoxical situation, for the two loved and admired one another past all reasoning, and each, to complete his work, needed the other alive and at his side. Thanks to the peculiarities of the disease of racialism and that all Americans, although differently, suffer from it, Negro as much as white, the War Against Slavery could never be won by white or Negro people alone. More thoroughly than almost anyone else in the movement, Father and Mr. Douglass knew this, which caused them both frequently to be criticized by their racial brethren, the whites disdainful of Father's close, ongoing alliances with Negroes and the blacks suspicious of Mr. Douglass's apparent, privileged ease of movement amongst white gentility. Then, as much as now, men like Father and Frederick Douglass made people of both races, regardless of their politics and principles regarding racial matters, anxious and mistrustful. They were, therefore, each other's main comfort.

I cannot be exact as to the date, for while the details of everything that happened in those days are as vivid and sharply outlined in my memory as in a stained-glass window, more so than what transpired here in my cabin this very morning, the abstractions of duration and chronology are somewhat vague to me and are often lost altogether from my mind. But one Saturday morning a few weeks before the raid, Father came to me at breakfast and, taking me aside, said to hitch the wagon and come up to Chambersburg with him. "I have arranged for a meeting there tomorrow morning with Mister Douglass," he explained.

"Wonderful news," I answered, genuinely excited at the prospect, although my habitual laconic manner probably did not show it. I was often thought in those days to be sarcastic or sour, when I was instead merely frightened by the intensity of my feeling and wished no more than to protect myself and others from it.

"Oh, just do as I say, Owen. He has come all the way from Rochester for this. He writes that he wants to hear the details of my plan, but I can only reveal them to him in person. And so he has come."

Shortly, we were making our way in late summer sunshine through the rolling, blond, recently mown pastures and the peaceful farm villages of western Maryland into Pennsylvania, arriving by evening at our Quaker safe house, where we spent the night talking abolition and religion with the good, pacificistic, prayerful keepers of the house, friends and strong supporters of abolitionism generally and of Father in particular, people who believed that their friendship and support were being used by us to help establish a more formidable and effective Underground Railroad, a belief which Father took care not to disabuse them of or threaten.

Mostly, I listened, eventually stretching myself out on my blanket by the fire and finally falling asleep to the sound of Father's voice droning on into the night, as he explicated the true meaning in the Book of Matthew of Christ's ninth-hour cry on the cross, *Eli, Eli, lama sabachthani? My God, my God, why hast thou forsaken me?* "You must remember, friends, that since the sixth hour there had been darkness all over the land," he explained. "And the priests had reviled and mocked Him, saying, If thou be the son of God, then come down from the cross; and with the scribes and elders, they had all declared, Jesus saved others, but himself he cannot save. And then they said to Him, If you be the king of Israel, the true Son of God, then come down from the cross, and we will believe you. Whereupon Christ cried out, My God, My God, why hast thou forsaken me? and yielded up the ghost, so as to provide for all those who had mocked and reviled Him, even those who had crucified Him, both the question and the answer. For when He had yielded up the ghost, as all men must, the veil of the temple was rent, and the earth quaked and split, and the graves were opened, and many bodies of the saints that slept therein arose, and when the people saw that, all of them, even the Roman centurions who stood amongst the priests and scribes and elders, were struck with fear, and they said, Truly, this was the Son of God! *Eli, Eli, lama sabachthani!* Out of the pitch darkness came that most human cry of Him who believes in God, of Him who knows that He is the most beloved of God, of Him who is yet subject utterly to God's will. And thus, in asking His final question—which is not a self-serving plea such as we ourselves, like the priests and the scribes and the elders, might make, but a question that is asked by a child of its parent, by a son of his father, by one who does not doubt the existence of the other and does not question the power of the other—in asking that question, Why hast Thou forsaken me? Christ in His final act amongst men is truly exemplary. Which is exactly and most particularly how the Lord intended Him to be for us, as a gift, His greatest gift, a gift exceeding even life itself, a gift that defines for us the possibility of eternal life, and in the way that it is revealed to us, we are shown the sole means for obtaining it. Belief in the Lord, not special pleading, but belief, simple belief, as the child believes in the parent . . ."

Thus, as so often, was my descent into sleep contaminated and controlled by my father's words and my dreams shaped by them, so that, to the degree that one's waking mind is sculpted by the artistry of one's dreams, I was, the following day, when we rode out to the quarry where Father had arranged to meet with Mr. Douglass, locked into considerations, not of the question of the efficacy of martyrdom, but of its ultimate meaning, of its use as proof of belief. For I had come to see that it need have no practical purpose, that it required no particular objective or goal in this world, to be justified or desired. Its purpose was to strengthen belief, the martyr's belief in God the Father, in the Hereafter, in eternal life, in resurrection—in *something, anything*, other than the meaning and purpose here and now of the mortal life of the martyr himself.

By mid-morning, after much careful reconnoitering, we had taken up our position like watchful ravens at the quarry where Mr. Douglass in his narrative says that he finally found us—upon a cut-stone platform walled in and set high amongst slabs of gray rock from which we could obtain a good view of anyone approaching us without being seen ourselves. Father was still a fugitive then, with a federal price on his head, and I imagine that I was, too, although, so far from Kansas and with no one any longer actively pursuing us, it was easy to forget. But it was also true that, this early in the game and this late, it would be reckless for the Old Man to be seen meeting with Frederick Douglass so close to

the border of a slave state. And, of course, Father enjoyed the accouter-
ments of clandestinity for their own sake. Thus we hid ourselves up
amongst the rocks from Mr. Douglass and made him find us.

And eventually, after considerable trouble, which we watched from
above, he did. He came clambering over sharp-edged layers of granite
with a companion, a balding, large-eyed Negro man of early middle
years and athletic build. Mr. Douglass, as always, was dressed in a fine
woolen suit and wore a black cravat and brimmed hat; his companion
was in a workingman's blouse and pants and boots, with a tattered old
straw on his head; and the two were puffing and wet with sweat when
they suddenly came around a granite pylon and encountered us—no
doubt unexpectedly, for they had by then probably begun to believe
that we had been delayed or that they had misunderstood Father's
directions to the quarry or perhaps had gone to the wrong place in it.

"Ah, Brown, *here* you are!" Mr. Douglass exclaimed, much relieved.
He smiled, and the two men shook hands warmly and embraced.

Father began at once to speak of the purpose of the meeting, but
Mr. Douglass interrupted him and elaborately introduced his friend
Shields Green, who he said was very interested in meeting the famous
Osawatomie Brown and possibly in "joining him down here in the
fray," as he put it. Then he greeted me with a smile and handshake and
gave Father to understand that he and Mr. Green needed to catch their
breath for a moment or two. He was sorry, he said, that he had not
brought water or refreshment with him.

It was impossible not to honor Frederick Douglass. His handsome
presence was commanding without ever seeming pompous or condescending, and he was gregarious and gracious without a taint of servil-
ity. He made you feel that you and he were equals on a very high plane.
And he was the only man I ever saw silence Father good-naturedly.

He leaned against the rock wall of our aerie and fanned his dark,
bearded face with his hat-brim, while Shields Green sat and rested

upon a table-sized stone nearby and wiped down his neck and face with a large blue handkerchief. Finally, Mr. Douglass said to Father, "All right, Old John, let me hear it. There are some wild rumors circulating up North about you and your boys, and I need to know the truth of the matter. I'll tell you, friend, some of your strongest supporters and allies are afraid that you're about to commence some wild, foolhardy action down here, and I'd like to go home and tell them otherwise."

"There's nothing wild or foolhardy about my plans, except to men who lack courage and principles," Father began, and here he commenced the recitation with which I and the others hidden back at the attic of the Kennedy farmhouse had become so familiar that we could recite it word by word ourselves. He told Mr. Douglass how the old plan had been modified to such a degree that it amounted now to a new plan, and, just as with us, he brought out and unrolled his maps and went over each step of the raid, until he had got to the end of the raid and our *rendez-vous* in the wilderness with Frederick Douglass and the hundreds, perhaps thousands, of newly liberated slaves.

Mr. Douglass was silent for a few moments and studied the maps with pursed lips and furrowed brow. At last, he sighed and said, "I love you, John Brown. I do. You've been a true hero, and I don't want you killed. You and those brave young men with you."

"We may suffer losses," Father said, interrupting. "It's inevitable in war. But we will triumph over our enemies in the end. We will. I know it, Frederick. The Lord will protect us."

"The Lord can't protect you from the nature of that place, Harpers Ferry. It's a steel trap, John. You'll get in and not be able to get out. Please, forget this."

"Our hostages will shield us while we're down there, and the wilderness and the mountains will preserve us when we've left."

"No, no, no, no! Impossible! Remember, I know these white Southerners; you don't. These men will cut down every tree from here to Tennessee but one, and when they have caught you, they'll hang you from it. And along the way, they'll butcher any slave who even dreams of rebellion in his sleep."

"We'll be too many too soon for them to go against us, and we'll be everywhere across the South, so they'll never be able to unite against us in any one place. This is no conventional war I'm fomenting here, Frederick."

"The federal army, John. Remember that."

"Yes, and remember the Seminoles. The Alleghenies will be my Everglades."

"And our Negroes, are they to be your Indian warriors?"

"If you will lead them with me. If you are at my side, they will rise up and follow me into battle against their white masters." Then for a long while Father explained how their army of escaped slaves would be divided into two parts, one to conduct raids on the plantations and towns of the South, the other to provide logistical support for the raiders and safe transportation out of the South for those escaping slaves who, because of age or infirmity or temperament, were unable to join the battle or merely wished to flee into the North. It all seemed so logical and so likely to succeed that Mr. Douglass's persistent objections and skepticism began to look, to me, like a reflection of his character more than his mind, as if a fearful heart had shut down his brain.

Back and forth they went, first one arguing his case, then the other, like attorneys pleading before a stern, inscrutable judge. Who was right, Father or Frederick Douglass? Not in hindsight, but at the moment of their argument. In hindsight, Mr. Douglass obviously seems to have been right. But back then, before the raid, was not Father right to believe that if Mr. Douglass made the raid on Harpers Ferry the opening act of a slave rebellion led by him and Old John Brown together, then it almost had to be a successful rebellion?

"With you at my side, this enterprise will be larger than any previous event in American history. It will be a true revolution, the revolution we *should* have fought back in '76!"

"No, Brown, it won't. It'll be suicidal. Worse than Nat Turner. With or without me, it's destined to fail. We are too few, too poorly armed, too ill-equipped, and too untrained as soldiers to accomplish what you have imagined."

Father stepped away and stared down at the large, open pit of the quarry below. In a low, sulky voice, he said, "I'm glad you weren't around to advise our Revolutionary forebears, Frederick. We'd all still be British subjects."

Mr. Douglass smiled. "Yes, well, given the fact that the British have outlawed slavery for close to a quarter-century now, it might not be a bad thing to be a British subject."

For many hours, long into the afternoon, the two men went back and forth, first one making his argument, citing precedent and pointing to principle for support, and then the other. Shields Green and I listened first to one, then to the other, and said nothing: we were like children listening to their parents argue over a matter that, for good or evil, would shape all their lives to come and wishing that both parents could be right. Mr. Douglass would speak for a while, marshaling his arguments with care and generosity towards Father, with sympathetic understanding of the Old Man's objectives and firm disapproval of his means, not on principle but for practical reasons only; and Shields and I would nod, as if thinking, yes, Harpers Ferry *is* a steel trap, we will get in and never be able to get out, and if by some miracle we do fight our way through the outraged townspeople and avoid being cut to pieces by the local militiamen as we flee the Shenandoah Valley into the wilderness, then, yes, the federal army will be arrayed against us and will in a short while cut us off in our mountain retreat and will lay down a siege from which our only escape will be death by starvation or a bullet, and, yes, our raid and the mere threat of the slave rebellion it poses will bring down upon the head of every Negro in the South untold suffering, lynchings, mutilations, chains, for the worst sort of oppression imaginable would be the inevitable consequence of raising fear of a slave revolt in the hearts of white Southerners, and, yes, the Northern whites will not come to our aid, for they will never go to war against their white brethren in the defense of black people and a handful of white radical abolitionists: it is an absurd plan, absurd, and cruel beyond belief.

Then, as the sun passed overhead and moved towards the western Pennsylvania hills, and the shadows of the rock that surrounded us grew long, Father would commence to answer, and now Shields and I nodded in support of his reasoning, too, saying to ourselves, yes, we *can* take the town by surprise and hold it by means of hostages long enough to capture sufficient weaponry to arm the hundreds, perhaps thousands, of slaves who will surely seize the opportunity to rise against their masters, once they know they are being led by men they trust as warriors and as men of principle, and, yes, we can flee to safety in the densely forested mountains of the South, and with a hundred bands of disciplined, well-armed, guerilla fighters we can hold off any army for months, even years, during which time our ranks will swell to such numbers that the Southern states, just to restore their economy, will make peace with their workers, for is that not, after all, who has gone to war against them, their workers?

"In the end, Frederick, it's right principles and simple economics that will settle this thing in our favor," Father said, and I could not disagree.

Until Mr. Douglass, in his low, melodious, melancholy voice, answered, "No, John. It's *race* that will settle it. And it will settle it against us. Race and simple arithmetic. Not principles and not economics. Simply put, there are more of you in this country than of us.

This is not Haiti or Jamaica, and the northern United States are not a separate nation than the southern United States. It's race, John. Skin color and hair and physiognomy. You say *us*, John, and you mean *all Americans willing to go to war to end slavery*. But every other American who says *us* means race, means *us white people*, or *us Negroes*. You are a noble, good man. But you are nearly alone in this country. Even me, when I say *us*, I mean *we Negroes*."

"Then you will not join me."

"John, I cannot. My practical judgement forbids it. My conscience forbids it. My love of my people forbids it."

"You are making my task all the more difficult. Without you beside me . . . my boys, my men . . ." He stopped and could not speak for a moment. "Without you," he continued, "the slaves won't rise up and follow me in such numbers. . . ."

Mr. Douglass placed his heavy hands onto Father's narrow shoulders and looked into the Old Man's eyes, and I thought that both men would weep, for their eyes were full. "Please, come away from this. Come back with me, John. Let your son here return to Virginia by himself and send your men home. Fight this war on another front."

"This is the only front left to me."

Mr. Douglass turned away and said to Shields Green, "I shall return home to Rochester. If you wish, you may go back with me, or you may stay. You've heard all the arguments as well as I."

Shields looked at the ground and said nothing.

Father reached out and touched Mr. Douglass's sleeve and, in a soft, plaintive voice, almost a whisper, said, "When I strike, the bees will begin to swarm, and I will need you to help hive them." It was a trope that he had used many times, and he spoke it mechanically, as if his thoughts, as if he himself, were elsewhere now.

Mr. Douglass did not answer. He looked again at Shields Green and said, "What have you decided to do?"

Shields turned his face, not to Mr. Douglass, but to Father, and he replied, "I believe I'll go with the Old Man."

Mr. Douglass nodded and slowly shook hands with us one by one, and when he had finished, he embraced us each in a heartfelt way one by one, as if it were he who was going to war and not we, and then he departed from us straightway for his home in Rochester. That same night, Father, Shields Green, and I returned in the wagon to Virginia.

24

This morning I woke in the dark, and my cabin was cold as a grave, and my heart leapt up when I thought again that I had died in the night and had joined Father and the others in purgatory. But then the chalky light of dawn drifted through the window like a fog and erased the comforting clarity of darkness, and I saw where I was, crumpled under my filthy blanket in a corner—a scrawny old man with matted beard and hair lying in his dirty underclothes in an unheated, bare room, my shelves, cot, chair, and tabletop covered with paper spilling onto the floor. I saw that I am nothing but paper. My life has finally come to only this: a tiny bubble of consciousness surrounded by thousands of sheets and scraps of paper—these dozens of tablets filled with disordered scribblings and all the letters and notebooks and documents and yellowed newspaper clippings and tattered old books and periodicals that I so long ago promised to deliver over to you, a great, disheveled heap of words, an incoherent jumble and snarl of truths, lies, memories, fantasies, and even recipes and lists, some of the words as mundane as a description of the several grades of wool in 1848, others as lofty as philosophical speculations on the nature of true religion and heroism, words taken from the floor of the marketplace to Emerson's brain, but all of it, all these words, adding up to . . . what? To nothing worth anything to anyone but me, I suppose, and worth nothing to me; so why have I collected and saved it all these years?

I'm struggling to think clearly. Why did I pack and carry Father's letters sent and received and his pocket notes and the many ledgers and books, an entire wooden crate of them, away out here to my California mountaintop and keep them here beside me these many years? I added to them over the years, as books, articles, and memoirs were published, and now, in feeble old age, I have been adding to the pile still *more* paper, *more* useless truths and speculation. Why have I done this?

I know that I began with the belief that I would compose a relation of my memories and knowledge of my father and that I would send it to you and Professor Villard, along with all the documents that I collected and kept over the years—for your purposes, for the composition of what you properly hope will be the defining biography of John Brown, a great book, no doubt, scheduled to make its public appearance in auspicious conjunction with the fiftieth-anniversary celebration of the raid on Harpers Ferry and my father's capture by the federal army and his execution by the government of Virginia. But, surely, this long after I first began, that memorial year has come and passed us by. And yet here I sit, still scribbling, writing now in the margins of my long-filled tablets and on the backs of Father's letters and in his notebooks, even in the margins and blank end-pages of his broken-backed personal books, his *Flint's Survey*, his Jonathan Edwards, Milton, and Franklin, his own published writings, too, "Sambo's Mistakes" and the Provisional Constitution, old copies of *The Liberator*, scrolled maps of the Subterranean Passway, newspaper accounts of the raid and of Father's final words on the scaffold, and Redpath's and Higginson's and Hinton's and Sanborn's biographies and memoirs—each day that passes, I write a few new sentences, sometimes only one, and sometimes, when my heart beats fast with feeling and my vision of the past is sharp and bright, as many as a hundred.

But I have long since given up any hope of ordering these pages and sending them to you. I write now only so that I can someday cease to write. I speak in order to go silent. And I listen to my voice so that I will soon no longer be obliged to hear it.

That fateful October night at the Kennedy farmhouse, after Father and the others had departed for the town, I spent a good while gathering and heaping everything together on the floor in front of the stove, and when I stood and stared down at the mass of incrimination, it was like listening to a thousand low, choked confessions all at once, as if the voices, mingling and merging with one another, were the sad, accumulated results of a long, unforgiving Inquisition into the heresy and betrayal of their Puritan fathers by an entire generation of sons. I burned none of it. My heretical refusal to play Isaac to my father's Abraham seemed not mine alone: it felt emblematic to me—as if an Age of Heroism had acceded to an Age of Cowardice. As if, in the context of those last days at Harpers Ferry and the one great moral issue of our time, I had become a man of another time: a man of the future, I suppose. A modern man.

Stepping back from the cold stove, I set my candle on the table and blew it out, dropping the house into darkness. Then I went into the rain and crossed the stubbled field to the shed, where Barclay Coppoc and Frank Meriam had finished loading the weapons onto the wagon. Coppoc was seated up on the box with the reins in his hands, scowling impatiently at me, while Meriam sat ashen-faced behind him.

"You finally done in there?" Coppoc said.

"Yes."

"Well, then, let's get a move on. The Old Man must already be across the bridge. Me and Frank heard gunfire a minute ago."

"Fine," I said, and climbed onto the wagon, taking a place on the wooden cases next to Meriam. Coppoc clucked to the horse, Adelphi, the second of our old North Elba pair of Morgans, and we moved slowly away from the Kennedy farm onto the wet, rumpled road and headed gradually downhill towards the abandoned schoolhouse overlooking the river and the town below. By the time we reached our destination, we could hear guns firing below, intermittently and from several different places—from near the armory, we thought, then from the Maryland side of the bridge, and a little later from the factory at the further edge of town. As instructed by Father, we quickly unloaded the weapons from the wagon and stacked the unopened cases along the walls inside the one room of the schoolhouse.

About an hour before daylight, when the rain let up, we went outside and walked through the woods a short ways to the edge of a cliff high above the Potomac, and stood together there, looking down in the hazy, pre-dawn light. Behind us, still hitched to the empty wagon, the horse browsed peacefully on a blond patch of grass. The sky was smeared gray beyond the far, dark bluffs, and in the town below, a few lights dully shone from the windows of the hotel and firehouse. We could see the train where it had stopped on the siding next to the railroad station and a few dark figures standing on the platform. Coppoc said he could make out some of our boys and a couple of Negroes posted inside the armory walls by the firehouse, where the hostages were supposed to be kept, but I couldn't distinguish them from this distance.

Suddenly, Meriam, who had been strangely silent, blurted in his nervous, high-pitched voice, "Owen, where are the *slaves*? There should be hundreds of escaped slaves coming to us by now, right? Isn't that right, Owen? We've got all these damned pikes and guns and no one to give them to!" He laughed edgily.

"Shut up, Frank," Coppoc said. "They'll come in. And it's all right if they don't. Or if only a few make it here tonight. They'll catch up with us later in the mountains. We'll arm them then."

"No, Barclay," I said. "They won't."

"How's that?"

"They're not coming. Not now. Not ever."

The two looked at me angrily. " 'Course they're coming in," Coppoc said. "Good Lord, Owen, this is way beyond arguing now. We've got options anyhow."

"Yes, and we got ol' Fred Douglass a-waiting in the wings," said Meriam.

"No, we don't."

"Now, come on, Owen, what're you *talking* about?" Meriam demanded, his voice rising. "We got options. Plenty of 'em. You heard the Old Man, same as us."

"Say it, Owen."

And so I said it. "Boys, Frederick Douglass is in Rochester, New York, tonight, asleep in his bed. I know that, and Shields Green knows it, and Father knows it. We lied to you," I said. "At least, I did. Father and Shields, I think, lied to themselves and each other and believed their lies, and so they told you only what they thought was the truth." Then in a few sentences I revealed to Meriam and Coppoc what had happened at the quarry in Chambersburg and how later, riding back down to Virginia, Father had insisted that, once Mr. Douglass realized we were deadly serious, he would change his mind. Maybe he would wait until the raid had actually begun, but in the end Mr. Douglass would fly to our side, for he was a man of deep principle and great personal courage. Father was sure of it. And Shields had agreed, in a way that made it seem that his friend Mr. Douglass had given him some private assurances.

Father instructed us not to report to the other men what had been said at the quarry. "It will only make them unnecessarily fearful and will sow disunity amongst them," he said.

And we obeyed—Shields because he believed that my father knew things that no other man knew, and I because I was his son. "Shields thinks Osawatomie Brown is a prophet," I said.

"And I take it you don't," Coppoc said, disgusted.

"No."

"For God's sake, none of that *matters* now! What're we going to *do*?" Meriam cried.

"My brother Ed's down there," said Coppoc.

"And two of mine. And two brothers-in-law. And a father."

"Owen Brown, what kind of man *are* you?" Coppoc said, and turned away from me.

We heard more gunshots then, rifle shots, coming from the vicinity of the church a short ways above the armory and overlooking it. Some townspeople were running and ducking behind walls, and it looked like they were taking potshots at our men in the armory yard below. Then our men returned fire, and one of the townspeople went down. The others quickly grabbed up his body and pulled it behind a shed, and the guns went silent for a while.

Meriam was frantic by now, confused by the war between his mortal fear, which made him want to flee, and his long-held desire to become the man whose sacrificial death would save the others, and he careened amongst the trees like a blind man, while Coppoc stared coldly from the cliff to the town. "You should have kept them from going in," he said finally. "You should have told us the truth."

"That wouldn't have kept Father out. Nothing would. He'd have gone alone, if necessary. You know that. And there'd always have been some of the men to follow him. Maybe not Kagi, maybe not Cook or you. But your brother would. And mine, Watson and Oliver, and the Thompsons, some of the others. Those boys would follow the Old Man straight through the gates of hell. You know it as well as I. No, it's better they all went in together, not just five or six of them. Even me, if Father had not posted me on this side of the river, I'd have gone in, too. Twenty men have a better chance of getting out than five or six."

"Maybe. But only if they leave that place now," Coppoc replied, and then he declared that he was going over. He would tell them the truth of the matter himself. "To let them know their real situation," he said. He called Meriam to him, calmed him somewhat, and asked him to go down into the town with him. Coppoc explained that they could get across the bridge all right, as it was still evidently under Father's control, and if they hurried and got across before full daylight, they could sneak unseen into the armory yard and help the Old Man and the boys fight their way out.

Meriam agreed at once. Coppoc had resolved his dilemma. "It's how I knew it would happen," he said. "I foresaw it, and now it's the Lord's will running things, not mine. It's how it has to be. So I must go with you, Barclay."

"What about you, Owen?"

"Father said to wait here for the Negroes. You two ought to do the same. He ordered us to arm the slaves when they came here and to meet up with him and the others later in Cumberland."

"Well, now, that's done with, isn't it? Countermand the Old Man's order, for heaven's sake! You got the right. You're in command up here."

"My father does not want me to save him," I said.

"Seems to me that's the *only* order you're following. Back at the house there, when we loaded the wagon, I never smelled chimney smoke. You didn't burn those papers like he said to, did you, Owen?"

"I needed more time. There was more material than I thought, books and so on. I'll go back and destroy them later. Or carry them away," I added.

"So, Owen Brown, it's over. And you've single-handedly done the whole thing in. Amazing." Coppoc shook his head in weary resignation. "Well, what about it, are you coming with me and Frank?"

"No."

"You don't intend to try stopping us, do you?" he said, and he leveled his rifle at me.

"My orders are to stand fast, unless he sends for us. And if you go down there with what I've told you, Barclay, all you'll do is sow disunity amongst the men," I said. "Father was right about that much. One by one, they'll sneak off and run, and not a one will come out of that place alive unless every one of them believes he's fighting for more than just to save his own life. Those are brave men, Barclay, and they still have a chance, but this news will make cowards of them all."

"You sound like the Old Man. All theory. You ready, Frank?"

Meriam nodded solemnly, and they slowly backed away from me, with Coppoc still keeping me under his gun, although I had no intentions of trying to force them to stay. It was too late. They were already doing exactly what I feared the others would do, cutting away from Father and running for their lives. I knew that Coppoc and Meriam would never make it into town, that before they reached the bridge they would realize the extremity of their situation and would disappear into the Virginia woods, and that eventually they would be hunted down out there and shot dead or else hog-tied and brought in to be hung.

The dawn wind blew through the leaves overhead. Then I heard the train locomotive hissing and blowing steam below and turned my gaze back to the town. Slowly, the train pulled out of the station and entered the bridge. A minute later, it reappeared on the other, the near, bank of the river, where it bore away to the east, curling along the broadening valley of the Potomac, carrying to the nation the fearful and exciting intelligence of the Negro insurrection raised this October night by Old John Brown and his men at Harpers Ferry.

It was nearly full daylight, and the tall oaks stood around me like sentries. For a long while, as if I could not, I did not move. I was alone, as alone as I had ever been in my life. But strangely—all unexpectedly—free. As if, after a lifetime bound to my father's fierce will and companionship by heavy steel manacles and chains, I had watched them come suddenly unlocked, and I had simply, almost casually, pitched them aside.

But were my actions from then on those of a free man? I cannot say. To be sure, I followed no impulses but my own. It sounds ridiculous now as I write it, but when Coppoc and Meriam had been gone awhile, I climbed the branches of the tallest oak tree up there on the cliff, climbed to the topmost branch that would safely support my weight, and, with my Sharps rifle in my lap, made for myself a sort of crow's-nest from which I could see clearly the streets and buildings of Harpers Ferry—from the rifle factory at the further, southern end of town, where Kagi, Leary, and Copeland were pinned down by local riflemen, to the Maryland side of the B & O bridge, where Oliver, Will Thompson, and Dangerfield Newby were posted. I could also see along the remaining length of the high ridge of Bolivar Heights, down to where the road from the Kennedy farmhouse emerged from the woods and crossed the canal to the tow path. And I could look directly into the armory yard itself, where Father and most of his raiders had positioned themselves behind the high, iron-rail walls and cut-stone pylons and inside the firehouse with the hostages.

All was still and silent down there, until, from my watchtower, I saw Father walk out of the firehouse with a man I did not recognize and appear to send him from the armory across the open square to the hotel. After a time, the man returned, carrying a large, open carton of what must have been food—breakfast for the hostages and the raiders both, I assumed. Again, all was calm for a while, until around mid-morning, when movement and the sound of men and horses below me and to my right drew my attention away from the town. A large party of armed white civilians under the flag of the notorious Jefferson Guards was riding in from the west along the tow path.

At a point very close to the Maryland end of the B & O bridge, they spotted Oliver and Will Thompson and Dangerfield Newby, dismounted, and at once began firing at them. The three raiders took shelter behind the toll house and returned fire, but the fusillade from the militiamen drove them steadily backwards towards the bridge, where I saw Newby at the entrance suddenly fall down dead, slain by what appeared to be a long spike or a bolt shot from a smooth-bore musket that tore through him ear-to-ear at the throat. Dangerfield Newby—the mulatto slave-son of a Scotchman from Fairfax County, Virginia—was forty-four and the oldest, after Father, of the raiders. He had joined us early on, with the main intention of freeing his wife and children, who were slaves of a man in Warrenton, Virginia. A tall man of light color, well over six feet, and a splendid physical specimen, he was a melancholy man, a good man, and my friend. And now he lay dead—the first of the raiders to go down—while Oliver and Will Thompson fled to safety in the firehouse.

Soon after this, another detachment of armed civilians led by a man in uniform, a second militia force, I supposed, came riding into town from the southwest along Shendandoah Street, where they swiftly secured the Shenandoah bridge and took up positions behind the arsenal, thus commanding the town square and the front of the armory yard. Their position, combined with that of the Jefferson Guards at the B & O bridge, effectively shut off the only escape routes left to Father and his men. They also made it impossible for Barclay Coppoc and Frank Meriam or anyone else to slip in from the Maryland side and help rescue them. Except for Kagi and his men out at the rifle works, Father and his Provisional Army were now trapped with their hostages in the armory yard and firehouse.

In about an hour, a pair of men—one of whom I did not know and figured was a hostage, the other being Will Thompson, my brother-in-law—emerged from the firehouse bearing a white flag, the signal to parley. There was by now an emboldened crowd of armed townspeople in the square and on the porch of the hotel and the platform of the railroad station, and when they saw the two men come forward from the firehouse, the crowd rushed them and seized and beat Will, dragging him into the hotel. The other man they made much of and slapped him on the shoulders and offered him pulls from their bottles, for many of them were by now freely drinking.

A few moments later, my brother Watson and the dark-browed Aaron Stevens and a third man, another hostage, I assumed, came out of the firehouse and walked into the cobbled square with a white flag. Suddenly, there was a barrage of gunfire from the crowd, and Watson fell, and Stevens fell, both bleeding from the face and torso. The hostage ran towards the crowd, but Watson pulled himself to his knees and dragged his gut-shot body back inside the armory grounds to the safety of the firehouse. Stevens lay writhing in pain, shot four or more times and unable to lift himself from the pavement, when, strange to see, one of the hostages came out of the firehouse, picked him up, and lugged him across the square and into the hotel. Shortly afterwards, the same man walked from the hotel and returned to the firehouse, a hostage again, but choosing it this time, which made me think that Father must be close to surrendering, if for no other reason than to get medical attention for Watson, who had looked to be seriously wounded.

More time passed, while the crowd at the hotel and railroad station and in the town square grew larger by the minute and more courageous and raucous with drink and rage, when I spotted a man climbing from the rear window of the firehouse into the armory yard. It was not a hostage escaping, I suddenly realized, it was young Willie Leeman, our wild and pretty boy from Maine, skittering across the yard away from the front gate to the rear. A slender lad, barely twenty years old, he slipped between the bars of the wall, dashed across the railroad tracks, and made for the Potomac. I was not surprised to see him abandon the others. He had come up the hard way—Poor Willie, we called him. Sent to work in a Haverhill shoe factory at fourteen, he had run off at seventeen to join Father's volunteers in Kansas, where he had been difficult for us to control, a lonely, uneducated boy who liked his drink and when drunk shouted his principles to anyone who would listen.

Just as he reached the river, which ran fairly shallow there, and waded in, someone in the crowd spotted him, and a batch of men up on the railroad station platform commenced firing at him, while he swam frantically for the Maryland side. With bullets splashing all around, he managed to get no more than fifty feet from shore before he was hit. Unable to swim any further, he turned back and hauled himself onto a tiny mudflat and collapsed. Several men ran along the tracks and down to the shore, and one of them waded out to the islet where Willie lay bleeding, put his revolver to the boy's head, and shot him dead. The man returned to his comrades and they raced back to the station platform and joined the crowd, making from there a target of Willie's body, shooting into it over and over, as if it were a sack of wet grain.

By midday, the youngest of the raiders, Will Leeman, was dead; and the oldest, Dangerfield Newby. Inside the firehouse, and inside the hotel across the way, my brother Watson and Aaron Stevens lay wounded, perhaps mortally, and my brother-in-law Will Thompson, brutally beaten, sat in the hotel under armed guard. I was sure that Barclay Coppoc and Frank Meriam had by now fled into the woods, and there may well have been others among the raiders who, to save themselves, had abandoned Father—John Cook, who was clever and knew the streets and alleys of the town better than any of us and had friends and even family amongst the townspeople, he was one; and Charlie Tidd was another. I had seen neither of them all morning; nor Albert Hazlett and Osborn Anderson, who had been stationed alone at the arsenal. The small brick building on Shenandoah Street was close to the town square, and the militiamen, with guards posted at the doors, were now treating it as if they had taken it back.

At one point, I noticed a fellow walking exposed on the railroad loading-trestle that bordered the armory buildings, and when he neared the firehouse, he dropped to one knee and peered around the water tower from an angle that would have given him an easy rifle-shot into the firehouse, except that he did not appear to be armed. Even so, when the door to the firehouse opened, and I saw Edwin Coppoc and my brother Oliver standing there, I feared that the man on the trestle would shoot them, for they were exposed and unsuspecting. But, no, Coppoc spotted the fellow, raised his rifle, and fired, dropping him like a stone, at which point a second man, who had been following a few yards behind the first, shot straight down into the engine house and caught Oliver full-bore in the chest, knocking him backwards inside.

Coppoc's having killed an apparently unarmed man seemed to fuel the crowd's drunken rage. In minutes, they were dragging their prisoner Will Thompson from the hotel, pummeling and screaming wildly at him. They set him out on the edge of the B & O bridge, stepped a few feet away, and shot him many times, after which they tossed his body into the river, where the current carried it against a thicket of driftwood. It caught there, and as they had with Willie Leeman, the townsmen made a target of my brother-in-law and shot into his dead body for a long while.

About mid-afternoon, I noticed a significant number of gun-toting townsmen separate themselves from the mob and in an organized way move up Shenandoah Street in the direction of the rifle works, where it appeared that Kagi, Lewis Leary, and John Copeland were still successfully holding off the militia—thanks to the deep, fast-running, twenty-foot-wide channel that cut between the mainland and the island on which the factory was situated. A footbridge led from the shore to the

CLOUDSPLITTER 751

island, but the walls of the factory came right to the water's edge, as if to a moat, and up to now the militiamen had been hesitant about rushing it and had contented themselves with keeping the three raiders inside under siege. Now, however, encouraged by the arrival of a crowd of heavily armed townsmen, they put up a protective shield of steady gunfire at the factory windows, whilst a gang of men ran against the timbered gate with a battering-ram and smashed it in. Then the entire combined force of militiamen and townspeople charged into the factory.

A hundred yards downriver, from my treetop aerie high above the further shore, I watched three figures—a white man, whom I knew to be Kagi, and two Negro men, Leary and Copeland—climb out one of the large windows that faced the river. The three men hung from the sill above the churning water for a second and then dropped. In seconds, fifty riflemen were firing down at them from the upper-storey windows, killing John Kagi, who sank beneath the water almost at once, and hitting Lewis Leary numerous times but not killing him outright, for he managed to struggle back to shore downstream a ways, where a contingent of militiamen pulled him limp and bleeding up the embankment into custody. Copeland made it to a large, flat rock in mid-river, where he was immediately spotted by some Jefferson Guards posted on the further shore, who began shooting at him. Caught hopelessly in a cross-fire, he raised his hands in the air, and a few minutes later, a pair of fellows rowed out, made him their prisoner, and saved him from Willie Leeman's and Will Thompson's fate for another.

There was a lull until about three P.M., when a B & O train pulled in from the west and stopped on a siding at the upper end of the armory, a safe distance from the firehouse. Several dozen civilian riflemen stepped down from the passenger cars and quickly arranged themselves in assault formation and began marching on the firehouse from the rear. They had scaling ladders and got over the fence back there with ease and were halfway across the armory grounds before Father and the boys spotted them and began firing out the windows and the partly opened door of the firehouse. The raid might have ended there and then, but neither of the other two militia companies present in town thought to charge the undefended front gate and storm the firehouse, and consequently, in about ten minutes, despite taking some serious casualties, Father and his remaining men managed to drive the first company back out of the armory grounds and over the fence.

Towards dusk and starting around four P.M., more men rode into town, uniformed soldiers and officers this time—five companies I counted of the Maryland Volunteers, and several additional civilian militias from nearby towns like Hamtramck and Shepherdstown: hundreds of angry, frightened, armed white Southerners coming in on horseback and by train and on foot, until the town square and many of the main streets were filled with federal soldiers, top-hatted riflemen and sharpshooters in buckskins, excitable slope-shouldered boys with pistols, vagrants and drunkards, men, and women, too, carousing and firing their guns into the air and scuffling amongst themselves, and the occasional mounted U.S. Army officer waving his saber and trying vainly to restore order and bivouac his men.

Except for the pall of death that hung over the small, blockaded building at the center, it was a carnival scene down there—chaotic and sensual and violent, with torches and a bonfire, and there was even a fiddler, and drunken dancers lurched up and down the hotel porch. Hawkers were selling food and whiskey, caissons and wagons clogged the streets and gouged deep tracks across front yards, and a riderless, terrified horse galloped down a side street, scattering people in all directions, and down by the river, boys were still potshooting at the bodies of my comrades.

Overhead, the stippled ridges in the white October sky were plated with gold, and in the east, red and cold, zinc-colored streaks had appeared, as the rain clouds rippled and broke, and the autumn sun slipped quickly towards the darkly shadowed, wooded horizon behind me. It had grown suddenly cold, but there was still plenty of bright daylight up on the rocky escarpment, where I remained clinging to the topmost branches of the highest oak tree. Down in the gorge, however, where the two broad, slate-gray rivers converged, the town was falling into darkness. It had grown nearly impossible for me to make out what this morning I had climbed up into the tree to view and could not bring myself, these many hours later, to leave, despite the horror of it— my brothers and my friends making their last stand against slavery; and, of course, my father, Father Abraham, making his terrible, final sacrifice to his God.

In the end, I could see only the lights—lamps starting to flicker from the windows of the houses and public buildings, dancing torches and bonfires casting dark, erratic shadows onto the cobbled streets and against the red-brick sides of the buildings. Occasionally, there was the rattle of gunfire, but it seemed random and almost celebratory, not the sustained noise of combat. An excited waiting had begun down there, a tense, almost hysterical pause, as before the public execution of a famous criminal. I shifted my position in my roost amongst the spindly limbs of the tree, and at that instant from the darkness below heard a rifle shot ring out, and a bullet tore through the leaves close beside my cheek. Then a second gun barked, a muzzle-loader this time. I heard the ball crack against a branch a few feet above me, and a flurry of yellow leaves fluttered across my head and floated past to the ground. I was awash in the last remaining light of day up here, and the soldiers and townspeople below, standing in darkness, had finally seen me. A third shot went wide of the mark, but I heard it tick through the leaves of a nearby tree and saw the leaves fall. A fourth shot slammed into the trunk just below my foot, and I began frantically to climb down, which was difficult, for I had my rifle, useless to me now, and my crippled arm. I must get out of the light, was my one thought. Just a little ways further down, and I, too, will be in darkness and invisible. I let go of my rifle, heard it clatter to the ground, and felt my way to the next-lower branch. A whole crowd of shooters was firing at me now. Bullets zipped through the foliage and crackled against the tree, shattering limbs and tossing splinters, twigs, and leaves into the air: I saw that I was game, a treed bear, pathetically large and cumbersome, all unable to hide, unable to flee, but still alive and struggling to stay alive, still a pleasure to kill. Like the bear, I had fled to the topmost branches of the tallest tree in the forest, not, as I had thought, so that I could better view my enemy, but in terror and delirium and in the crazed hope that I could not be seen there.

With my left arm, I clamped myself to a slender branch close to my head and reached down with my right hand to grasp a sturdier limb below. I let my weight go and groped in the air for a footing, and for a few seconds my body was suspended entirely on my poor arm—that childhood curse: never had it so enraged and humiliated me as now! Suddenly, there was an extended barrage of gunfire from the town, a booming fusillade, and bullets and balls exploded through the tree all around me, snapping off limbs and showering me with torn leaves, and I thought, Surely, now, I am a dead man, they will kill me this instant, when the limb I clung to with my hooked arm let go. Shot through, it floated away from the tree still clamped in the crook of my arm, and I fell, slamming against the branches, tearing foliage away with my free hand—a long, clattering drop into the darkness and safety and silence of the forest.

Here in my cabin, I have fallen. A sympathetic act, no doubt, caused by my account of falling, and I watch myself now from outside myself and above, as astonished and detached as I was that October night on

Bolivar Heights, and as I was so many years before in the Negro church in Boston, and long, long ago, when I followed my brothers out along the steeply pitched roof and, in falling against the stone steps of the dry-cellar below, betrayed their Sabbath-day flight and permanently smashed my arm. It is as if a huge, invisible hand above me has pushed me down, or as if since childhood I have been carrying an insupportable weight and have finally been borne down by it.

I write these words with painful slowness now. I know that I am coming to the end of my ability to set down my story, which has proved to be not just my story, after all, but Father's as well. His is the one that I had hoped to tell you; the other, mine, which lies beneath it, I wished only to tell to Father himself and my brothers and comrades, those ghosts standing in the shadow of the mountain Cloudsplitter, the men whose bodies lie buried beneath the great, gray stone in North Elba.

I tell you this so that if you someday read these pages, you will know that I have finally gone where I always wanted to go, for this morning, after I fell, I managed in the fading dark to crawl across the cluttered floor to the table and locate there my old revolver: it lay cold and heavy as an iron skillet beneath a sheaf of loose papers, where I had placed it—how long ago? Weeks? Months? A year? It doesn't matter: there is no more time for me, no more chronology. I'm becoming my own ghost at last.

Father believed that the universe was a gigantic clockworks, brilliantly lit. But it's not. It's an endless sea of darkness moving beneath a dark sky, between which, isolate bits of light, we constantly rise and fall. We pass between sea and sky with unaccountable, humiliating ease, as if there were no firmament between the firmaments, no above or below, here or there, now or then, with only the feeble conventions of language, our contrived principles, and our love of one another's light to keep our own light from going out: abandon any one of them, and we dissolve in darkness like salt in water. For most of my life, surely since that day in October when I fled the field at Harpers Ferry, I have been a steadily diminishing light—until the day when I began to set down this long account, and my light flared up as it never had before. It has continued to burn brightly against the night ever since.

But now there is little left to tell, almost nothing, and soon I will learn if this has been all for naught, if this passage between the firmaments has been no more than the dying fall of a cinder into the dark waters of the swirling deep. When I have told the little that is left to tell, if I have not died by then and still have the bodily strength, I will simply put down my pencil and pick up my revolver, and I will use it to place me at my father's side, where I have always properly belonged. If I cannot lie there next to him and my ghost cannot reside alongside his, then it will mean only that my light went out forever on that night those many long years ago at Harpers Ferry, and this account has been but a meaningless, phosphorescent flare, the memory of light, instead of the thing itself, and it will not matter.

Here, Miss Mayo, is all that I have left to tell.

I took the horse and wagon and returned from the schoolhouse to the Kennedy farm. Once there, I pulled the wagon in behind the house, well out of sight from the road, and went straight to the storage shed, where in the darkness I groped over the half-dozen wooden crates that Father and the boys had emptied before setting out, when they loaded their wagon with weapons for the slaves. They had broken most of the crates apart in the process, and it took several minutes before I found one that was intact and had its topside boards. It was a crate that had contained the long pikes, those poles with knives attached that Father had imagined would terrorize the slaveholders. The box was stoutly constructed of pine and plenty large enough for my purposes, so I carried it to the kitchen and set it by the stove. Then I commenced filling it from the huge heap of papers and books that lay untouched on the floor where I had placed them the night before.

While I was in the midst of this task, I heard a group of horsemen approach from the direction of Harpers Ferry and stop before the house. "Hello, the house!" one of them shouted. "Anyone there?"

I quickly placed the lid onto the half-filled case. Then I lifted it and carried it out the rear door of the kitchen, where, silently, carefully, as if it were a child's coffin, I set it into the wagon bed. I climbed up on the driver's box and sat there, waiting.

For several minutes, all was quiet. Then I heard the clump of boots on the porch at the front of the house, and someone rapped on the door. "It appears there ain't anyone home, Cap'n!" he called back.

"No matter," came the response. "We got most of what we come for back at the schoolhouse anyhow." A moment later, I heard them leave.

I sat motionless for a long while, until the horse abruptly shifted her weight, signaling me to give her direction. But I had no plan. I barely had thoughts. I had spent my entire life following Father's plans, thinking his thoughts. And at that moment, as I sat up on the wagon with the reins in my hands and my horse impatient to move on, I did not know what to do or think.

I was in considerable physical pain, for I had cut and bruised myself badly in my fall, and my clothes were torn. I was lightly armed— I had my revolver but no rifle, which I had lost in the darkness after dropping it from my treetop lookout. And I had no food or supplies or money. But I was alone. Alone, and free. The entire continent lay out there. I was a man, a white man, and could go to any place on it where no one knew me, and I could become new. I could become an American without a history and with no story to tell. I believed that then and for many years to come.

So if I had a plan, that was it. If I had a thought, that was the thought.

I clucked to Adelphi and at the road turned her left, away from Harpers Ferry, westward. Before me, the narrow country road ran between low, split-rail fences towards the forest, and I remember, as the wheels clattered over the rough road, the sound of the long pine case thumping heavily against the wagon bed behind me. The sky had cleared, and a belt of stars shone directly overhead, and a bright quarter-moon had risen in the east. The trees were blue-black and flattened in the moonlight, and the fields seemed to be covered with a skin of powdery snow.